McFarland Classics

1997

1. Michael R. Pitts. *Western Movies*
2. William C. Cline. *In the Nick of Time*
3. Bill Warren. *Keep Watching the Skies!*
4. Mark McGee. *Roger Corman*
5. R. M. Hayes. *Trick Cinematography*
6. David J. Hogan. *Dark Romance*
7. Spencer Selby. *Dark City: The Film Noir*
8. David K. Frasier. *Russ Meyer—The Life and Films*
9. Ted Holland. *B Western Actors Encyclopedia*
10. Franklin Jarlett. *Robert Ryan*

1998

11. Ted Okuda *with* Edward Watz. *The Columbia Comedy Shorts*
12. R. M. Hayes. *3-D Movies*
13. Steve Archer. *Willis O'Brien: Special Effects Genius*
14. Richard West. *Television Westerns*

1999

15. Jon Tuska. *The Vanishing Legion: A History of Mascot Pictures*
16. Ted Okuda. *The Monogram Checklist*
17. Roy Kinnard. *Horror in Silent Films*
18. Richard D. McGhee. *John Wayne: Actor, Artist, Hero*
19. William Darby *and* Jack Du Bois. *American Film Music*
20. Martin Tropp. *Images of Fear*
21. Tom Weaver. *Return of the B Science Fiction and Horror Heroes*
22. Tom Weaver. *Poverty Row HORRORS!*
23. Ona L. Hill. *Raymond Burr*

RETURN OF THE B SCIENCE FICTION AND HORROR HEROES

The Mutant Melding of Two Volumes of Classic Interviews

BY TOM WEAVER

McFarland & Company, Inc., Publishers
Jefferson, North Carolina, and London

Front cover: From a still of *Invasion of the Saucer Men* (Photofest).
Back cover: "What seems to be the problem, officer?" Robert Clarke in partial costume for *The Hideous Sun Demon*.
Title page: Paul Blaisdell and Marla English, *Voodoo Woman*; and Herbert L. Strock (getting head scratched), *How to Make a Monster*.

The present work is a reprint, under one cover, of the library bound editions of Interviews with B Science Fiction and Horror Movie Makers: Writers, Producers, Directors, Actors, Moguls and Makeup, *and* Science Fiction Stars and Horror Heroes: Interviews with Actors, Directors, Producers and Writers of the 1940s through 1960s, *first published in 1988 and 1991 respectively.* **McFarland Classics** *is an imprint of McFarland & Company, Inc., Publishers, Jefferson, North Carolina, who also published the original editions.*

Library of Congress Cataloguing-in-Publication Data

Weaver, Tom, 1958–
   Return of the B science fiction and horror heroes : the mutant melding of two volumes of classic interviews / by Tom Weaver
   First work originally published: Interviews with B science fiction and horror movie makers. 1988. 2nd work originally published: Science fiction stars and horror heroes. 1991. With new pref.
   Includes filmographies and indexes.
   1. Science fiction films — History and criticism.   2. Horror films — History and criticism.   3. Motion pictures — Interviews.
   I. Title.   II. Title: Interviews with B science fiction and horror movie makers.   III. Title: Science fiction stars and horror heroes.
PN1995.9.S26W456   2000   791.43/615 21   99-48762
ISBN 0-7864-0755-7 (paperback : 50# alkaline paper) ∞

British Library Cataloguing-in-Publication data are available

©1988, 1991, 2000 Tom Weaver. All rights reserved

No part of this book may be reproduced or transmitted in any form or by any means, electronic or mechanical, including photocopying or recording, or by any information storage and retrieval system, without permission in writing from the publisher.

Manufactured in the United States of America

McFarland & Company, Inc., Publishers
   Box 611, Jefferson, North Carolina 28640
       www.mcfarlandpub.com

Preface to the Combined Edition

In the tradition of the immortal movie monsters who bounce back in sequel after sequel and remake after remake, the interviews featured herein were first seen in monster magazines of the 1980s, and then in two McFarland books. They've now been joined in an unholy union and once again endowed with the spark of life, this time by the alchemists in the shadowy recesses of McFarland's Classics division.

These interviews appear exactly as they did in my books *Interview with B Science Fiction and Horror Moviemakers* (1988) and *Science Fiction Stars and Horror Heroes* (1991); I get just this one page to make a few 1999 comments and to try to update you the gentle reader on the more recent activities of a few of these interview subjects. Sad to say, several of them — in fact, nearly a quarter of them — have passed on: John Ashley, Susan Cabot, Harry J. Essex, Gene Fowler, Jr., Albert Glasser, Herk Harvey, John Howard, Robert Hutton, Reginald LeBorg, Robert Shayne, Harry Thomas, Virgil W. Vogel, Jerry Warren, Robb White.

All the others are still hanging in there, and several (Richard Gordon, Howard W. Koch, Arthur Gardner, Anna Lee, Richard Matheson, for instance) are still plugging away at their noble professions. Most, however, are retired, which in a way is good, as the two books here bound as one are being directly reprinted in their original form. Updates to the filmographies that appear at the ends of many chapters were therefore not possible. I fretted about this ... until I realized that it didn't matter, since most of these people haven't *worked* since they talked to me! (Future interviewees be warned!) A few of these wonderful folks can be regularly seen at SF-themed movie conventions and autograph shows, fun offshoots of the sustained interest in their horror and sci-fi output.

Eleven years ago, after my first book of interviews (29 of 'em) appeared, several people asked me, "Well, who can you interview *now*? Who's *left*?" It's now 1999 and I've got several *hundred* additional interviews under my belt, and the end is not yet in sight, not even to *my* failing eyes. It's been a hell of a lot of fun — everything except the transcribing, that is — and I've come away with a lot of never-to-be-forgotten experiences, from riding a Florida rollercoaster with Anne Francis, to watching Greg Mank bust Robert Clarke's swimming pool sliding board. (Another Top Ten moment: Sitting with Samuel Z. Arkoff in a car that made a wrong turn onto a Manhattan one-way avenue, heading straight toward four lanes of fast-moving oncoming traffic. Without turning a hair or losing the ash from the end of his cigar, Sam glanced in the direction of our driver and muttered softly, "Ya better turn around..."). Many of these adventures were embarked upon in the marvelous company of Mike and John Brunas, my "Research Consultants" (and favorite friends), who pooh-pooh me every time I thank them.

One small admonition: Keep in mind as you enter this wacky world of B movie memories that these books contain many of my first-ever interviews, dating back to the early '80s when I was not too many years out of my teens. So please excuse the occasional dumber-than-usual question and my near-total concentration on the interviewees' SF-horror output. Take my word for it, I've gotten better at these things — I think. I *hope!*   — *Tom Weaver,* Fall 1999

Interviews with
B Science Fiction and Horror Movie Makers
Writers, Producers, Directors, Actors, Moguls and Makeup

by Tom Weaver

RESEARCH ASSOCIATES:
JOHN BRUNAS
MICHAEL BRUNAS

McFarland & Company, Inc., Publishers
Jefferson, North Carolina, and London

Dedicated to
Mark Martucci
He never believes me when I tell him this,
but I couldn't have done this book without him.

Library of Congress Cataloguing-in-Publication Data

Weaver, Tom, 1958–
  Interviews with B science fiction and horror movie makers.
  Includes index.
  1. Science fiction films — United States — History.
  2. Horror films — United States — History. 3. Motion picture actors and actresses — Interviews. 4. Motion picture producers and directors — Interviews.
  5. Screenwriters — Interviews. I. Title.
PN1995.9.S26W44   1988   791.43'09'09356   88-42641
ISBN 0-7864-0755-7 (paperback : 50# alkaline paper) ∞

British Library Cataloguing-in-Publication data are available

©1988 Tom Weaver. All rights reserved

No part of this book may be reproduced or transmitted in any form or by any means, electronic or mechanical, including photocopying or recording, or by any information storage and retrieval system, without permission in writing from the publisher.

Manufactured in the United States of America

McFarland & Company, Inc., Publishers
   Box 611, Jefferson, North Carolina 28640
      www.mcfarlandpub.com

Table of Contents

Introduction ix

John Agar 1
Samuel Z. Arkoff 17
John Ashley 37
Edward Bernds 47
Susan Cabot 65
Robert Clarke 75
Gene Corman 93
Richard E. Cunha *and* Arthur A. Jacobs 105
David Duncan 119
Anthony Eisley 129
Harry J. Essex 143
Beverly Garland 153
Richard Gordon 169
Jack H. Harris 195
Howard W. Koch 209
Bernard L. Kowalski 221
Reginald LeBorg 231
Paul Marco 249
Ib J. Melchior 261
Jack Pollexfen 273
Lee Sholem 285
Curt Siodmak 297
Herbert L. Strock 311
Gloria Talbott 331
Del Tenney 343
Harry Thomas 355
Jerry Warren 369
Mel Welles 381

Index 397

Introduction

The late 1940s were the dog days for the horror and science fiction film. The Universal monster rallies had come to an inevitable end, the Val Lewton B-picture unit at RKO had lamentably ceased production, and even bush-league Poverty Row studios like PRC and Monogram realized that audiences had finally succumbed to horror movie burnout. Occasionally one of the cheaper indies turned out a third-rate film like *Scared to Death* or *The Creeper*, but by and large the genre was in a state of limbo.

Then came the '50s.

With public consciousness now preoccupied with the A-bomb and UFOs, a fresh new wave of science fiction films began in 1950. Major releases like *The Day the Earth Stood Still, Destination Moon, When Worlds Collide* and *The Thing from Another World* rubbed elbows with creative little B's *(The Man from Planet X, Five)* and desultory Z's *(Untamed Women, Mesa of Lost Women)*. The floodgates burst. Important studios like MGM, Paramount and Warner Bros. acquiesced to audience demands and created well-mounted, respectable science fiction efforts. Universal, never quite able to shake off the tag of Hollywood's least prestigious "major," rejoiced in the comeback of the kind of film that helped build its fortunes twenty years before, and embarked on its own popular series of horror-accented sci-fi thrillers.

A good deal of the really interesting and innovative work, however, came from the low-budget independent studios like Allied Artists and the newly conceived American International Pictures. From 1955 to well into the 1960s, these distributors and others like them turned out an incredible number of pictures, surpassing even the horror heydays of the early 1930s and the early-to-mid-1940s. Despite their wildly varying quality (from gems like *Not of This Earth* and *I Was a Teenage Werewolf* to genuine dogs like *Teenage Monster* and *From Hell It Came*), these films developed a following whose loyalty stands undiminished after three decades.

This book pays homage to the many people that have contributed toward producing a body of work whose entertainment (if not always artistic) values have only increased through the years. Assembled herein is a cross-section of talents: writers, producers, directors, actors, actresses, even a movie mogul and a makeup man. We've kept our questions and interjected comments as terse and to-the-point as possible, our goal being to present a book in which the filmmakers and performers do nearly all the talking.

Fans of Hollywood gloss, be warned: This may not be the sort of interview book you're used to. There are no tales of multimillion dollar productions or of pampered glitterati, no elegant Tinseltown soirées, big premieres or jet-set ostentation. Most of the films discussed in this book are medium- to low-budget productions, some of them made by people who are at best footnotes in the big book of Hollywood history. Perhaps it *does* require something of an open and tolerant mind to see the good in pictures about Styrofoam crab monsters, Martian Jell-O, hubcaps, sparklers and bathospheres from outer space, thirtyish teenagers and bald midgets armed with vacuum cleaners. But this is not meant as any sort of apology. It takes far more talent and imagination to make a good film on a low budget than to make one with all the materials and means of a major studio at one's disposal.

The twenty-eight question-and-answer sessions in this book were conducted over a period of nearly five years, many in person and the rest via long-distance telephone. Prior to every interview, we researched and reviewed every fantastic film of each individual, and prepared lists of relevant questions. Although our emphasis is squarely on the 1950s era, many of our interviewees worked in the science fiction or horror genres long before and/or long after the '50s, and all of these additional films are fully discussed as well. The majority of these interviews originally appeared in such magazines as *Fangoria, Starlog, Fantastic Films, Filmfax* and others over that same five-year period. In compiling these articles for this book we have gone back to nearly all of our interviewees to pose additional questions and to bring the interviews up to date. Some of the interviews are now more than double the length of what initially appeared in the abovementioned publications.

It's been a fun and rewarding five years hunting down cult actors and actresses, favorite writers and directors and all the rest. Many are still active on the Hollywood scene, making them relatively easy to find, but others, long retired, led us on merry chases which ended in places like avocado farms, video stores and the Pacific Northwest. Of course there were disappointments along the way, from the polite and pleasant (and perhaps understandable!) refusals of people like Peter Graves and Ed Nelson, to the angry slamming-down-of-the-phone on the part of a certain male star of *The Atomic Submarine*. But these little letdowns are all part of the game, and we remain pleased and proud of the group we have gathered.

Certainly a tremendous amount of work remains to be done, and we hope to continue our tracking-down and interrogating for other interviews. Part of our inclusion criteria this time around was that each of the interviewees should have something of an identification with the horror or science fiction genres, or at least a sufficient number of credits to guarantee a multi-page write-up. But we also recognize that there are some very colorful and interesting one-shot sci-fi filmmakers and performers lurking in those Hollywood hills, and we hope

Introduction

to begin documenting their B movie experiences for the sake of posterity. None of these people is getting any younger (nor, come to think of it, are we); and we've already come "this-close" to missing out on a few of the people we *have* talked to. The enthusiastic response to our past work has made us feel that it's important as well as entertaining to gather these reminiscences for future fantasy film historians and fans.

No book of this type could possibly be written without the help of a veritable army of fellow fans, Hollywood contacts, well-wishers, glad-handers, film and tape sources and so on. Our sincere thanks are extended to Acquanetta, Bill and Roberta Amazzini, Ron and Loraine Ashcroft, Mr. and Mrs. Ewing Brown, Roger Corman, Edward and Mildred Dein, Carl and Debbie Del Vecchio, Richard Devon, David Everitt, Tim Ferrante, Mike Fitzgerald, Robert Franklin, Karin Garrity, Alex Gordon, Coleen Gray, Jonathan Haze, Scot Holton, Tom Johnson, Little Joe the Honey Bear, Bill Littman, Arthur Lubin, Greg Luce, Alex Lugones, Dave McDonnell, Mark McGee, Scott MacQueen, Greg Mank, Jacques Marquette, **our moms**, Cody Morgan, Jeff Morrow, Lori Nelson, Paul Parla, Gil Perkins, Rex Reason, Mary Runser, Sam Sherman, John Skillin, Michael Stein, George Stover, Maurice Terenzio, Tony Timpone, Katherine Victor, Virgil Vogel, Bill Warren, Ed Watz, Jon Weaver and Wade Williams. Some individuals deserve *extra* special thanks, like Robert Skotak, who loaned us rare and valuable behind-the-scenes photos, and Mark Martucci, who gave us unlimited access to his incredible video collection. James LaBarre guided us through the ins and outs of using a word processor and printer, and never seemed to mind that we were less interested in learning the system than in having everything done *for* us, time after time. Many thanks, James.

And of course we are grateful to our twenty-nine interviewees, who made all of this possible. This book is our thank-you to these highly creative and resourceful people (both before and behind the cameras) who prevailed over low budgets and abbreviated shooting schedules and produced films whose fan followings endure to this day.

Tom Weaver
John Brunas
Michael Brunas

I always kind of had the feeling that when people looked at some of these science fiction things, we were going to get a big laugh.

John Agar

ONE OF THE BEST-KNOWN stars of 1950s fantasy films, John Agar's science fiction credits range in quality from the top-of-the-line productions of Jack Arnold *(Revenge of the Creature, Tarantula)* to the bottom-of-the-barrel efforts of schlocksters like Bert I. Gordon and Larry Buchanan. While Agar has never appeared in a sci-fi classic, few of his acting contemporaries are as closely identified with the genre, and none can equal his output—a long list of memorable titles that also includes *The Mole People, Daughter of Dr. Jekyll, The Brain from Planet Arous, Invisible Invaders, Hand of Death* and more. With Richard Carlson, Beverly Garland and Kenneth Tobey, John Agar is one of the icons of '50s horror.

Agar was born in Chicago, the eldest of four children of a local meat packer. His 1945 marriage to "America's Sweetheart," Shirley Temple, brought him into the public eye for the first time, and a movie contract with independent producer David O. Selznick quickly ensued. Agar debuted opposite John Wayne, Henry Fonda and Temple in John Ford's *Fort Apache* (1948), initial film in the famed director's Cavalry Trilogy. Other early Agar roles included *She Wore a Yellow Ribbon* and *Sands of Iwo Jima* (both starring "the Duke") and the film noir *I Married a Communist*. His marriage to Shirley Temple ended in 1949, while his movie career continued. Agar made his fantastic film debut in the eight-day Sam Katzman quickie *The Magic Carpet* (1951), an Arabian Nights adventure, and other minor fantasy films *(Bait, The Golden Mistress* and the sci-fi/comedy *The Rocket Man)* followed. His science fiction career was in full swing by June, 1954, when production began on Jack Arnold's *Revenge of the Creature*.

Jack Arnold is considered one of science fiction's top talents in certain circles. How did you enjoy working with him?

I've always had nothing but great respect for Jack Arnold. I did *Revenge of the Creature* for him and then the next year we did *Tarantula*, and we got along very well. So far as I was concerned, he was a very knowledgeable director and he gave his all trying to make 'em the best that he could. Jack is a great guy; I don't think Universal was too kind to Jack, I think he should have been given a lot more opportunities. I went over and saw him at Universal a few years ago; he was going to do a remake of *The Lost World,* then all of a sudden the powers that be cancelled the thing on him. Of course you know that Jack lost a limb [to cancer]. The people behind *The Lost World* were going to go over to England and shoot it and Jack really *wanted* to direct it, but they didn't feel that he could physically do it. Then they changed their minds about doing the picture at all.

Did you enjoy the location trip to Florida for Revenge of the Creature?

I had never been to Marineland, and that was a lot of fun. We all got kind of carried away on that picture—we started having water gun fights and, gosh, it got to the point where one guy got up on top of a cottage with a bucket of water and poured it all over a bunch of people!

Previous page: John Agar and Mara Corday react to the off-screen terror of *Tarantula*.

Lori Nelson told us that that was the most fun she'd ever had making a movie.

We just had a heck of a good time. My wife Loretta joined me down there, and as a matter of fact she had a little part in the picture. Remember the scene at the lobster house when the Creature abducts Lori, and I dive off the pier after them? After that there's a shot of a guy and a girl in a boat; the girl's my wife Loretta.

Did you have to learn to use an aqualung for the underwater scenes in Revenge?

I learned to use an aqualung before that. Shortly before I did *Revenge of the Creature*, I went down to the Caribbean and did a picture called *The Golden Mistress* [1954], and I had to learn to use an aqualung for the underwater scenes in that picture. Nobody down there seemed to know anything about them, so I just went into the swimming pool at the hotel we were staying at, and I learned to utilize it. It's not all that difficult, but the one thing I didn't know about using an aqualung is that you can get an air embolism mighty easy—if you surface too quickly and you're holding the air in, you can be in a lot of trouble. I got into a ticklish situation: The underwater cameraman and I were swimming around this sunken ship, about forty feet down. There were some breaks in the deck and shafts of sunlight were shining down into the hold, and the cameraman thought it would be interesting to get a shot in there. So I swam in there, clear to the bow of the ship; I went to take a breath, to get air—and I couldn't get it! So I had to swim about twenty feet to the hole, just to get out of the ship, and then I had to swim forty feet up before I could surface. And in coming up I could *feel* the pressure on my body easing, releasing. Luckily somebody was watching over me, and I guess He showed me what to do. I had the sense *not* to hold my breath, to let it out, as I came up. I could have gotten into some real problems there.

Wasn't it dangerous swimming in the Marineland tank with all those sharks?

I was told by the people who ran Marineland that those sharks were really not dangerous; I had a tiger shark, an eight-footer, swim right over my head and it didn't pay any attention to me. I know Ricou Browning, who did the underwater work as the Creature, was being pestered more by the big sea turtles than by anything else—they'd come up and nip at him! But I did have one experience that could have been a little disastrous—there's one part of the main tank that had a kind of rock formation just below the surface. During the scene where the Creature escapes—grabs Johnny Bromfield, throws him in the water and kills him—I was standing at the far end of the tank. *Why* I did this I will never know *[laughs]*, but I dove back into the tank at that point, not realizing how close to the surface of the water those rocks were. If I hadn't flattened my dive at the last second, I would've hit it flush. This is just speculation, but if I had hit there hard and maybe gotten a bloody nose or something,

John Agar in a publicity pose for *Revenge of the Creature*. (Photo courtesy Steve Jochsberger.)

it might have been a different kind of story, according to what I've heard about sharks and the way they smell blood out in water.

What can you tell us about working with Ricou Browning?

Ricou was one of the most fascinating people insofar as his swimming was concerned—he had lung capacity that was just incredible. They would drop an oxygen hose into that tank and he would breathe through it; the oxygen was coming out of there with pressure and it would fill up the Gill-Man suit. So after he'd gotten the amount of oxygen he wanted, he then had to press the suit and get all the bubbles out. Then he would go and do the scene. I could stay underwater for over two minutes if I wasn't doing anything, but this guy was swimming and using a lot of energy. How he did that was just really amazing and marvelous to watch.

Richard Carlson, who starred in the original Creature from the Black Lagoon, *once admitted that the Gill-Man suit seemed so real that he got spooked shooting scenes in the studio tank.*

Well, when you see something that unusual, even though you *know* it's all make-believe, it *is* kind of a strange experience. If this *were* a real creature, what it could do to you wouldn't be pretty. So I can understand Richard Carlson saying that, especially in an underwater situation.

Recent Hollywood rumor has it that Clint Eastwood, who has a bit in Revenge, *also played the Creature in the on-land scenes.*

I don't remember Clint ever putting the suit on, but he may very well have; I do know that Ricou Browning never played the monster on land. Clint didn't go to Florida with us, so when the Creature broke away from Marineland Clint wasn't in the suit then. Now, he may have put the suit on for the scenes we shot back here; I don't remember him doing that, but that's not to say he didn't.

Would you agree that Tarantula *is your best science fiction film?*

Yeah, I guess that would be the one; *[laughs]* I really don't know. I am the *worst* judge of what I've done; I look back on all my pictures and insofar as I'm concerned I can see where I could have been so much better, could've done such a better job than what I did. I can *always* see that.

I had never planned to be an actor, and it was thrust upon me at a very early age. It was something I really wasn't ready for. Now I know exactly what George Bernard Shaw meant when he said that youth is wasted on the young.

William Alland, who produced Revenge, Tarantula *and other Jack Arnold films, once said that he feels slighted because Arnold seems to get all the credit for them nowadays. Was Alland a creative force as well?*

I agree wholeheartedly that William Alland was a force. He was the one that came up with some of the ideas and he produced the films, and he shouldn't be slighted at all. Those pictures, whether Universal wants to admit it or not, were moneymakers. There were three Creature pictures made, and I was told by a producer at Universal, Aaron Rosenberg, that *Revenge of the Creature* was the biggest grosser of all of 'em. I also heard that *Tarantula* was one of the top grossers of 1955; what they probably meant was that it was a top moneymaker in terms of what it *cost* and what it brought *in*, but I had heard that it was Number 5 in 1955.

The Mole People *is by far the least of your three sci-fi Universals. Would you put the blame on first-time director Virgil Vogel?*

Oh, no—Virgil Vogel is a nice guy and I don't blame that on Virg, *heck*, no. But to me, *The Mole People* was like some of those Larry Buchanan things

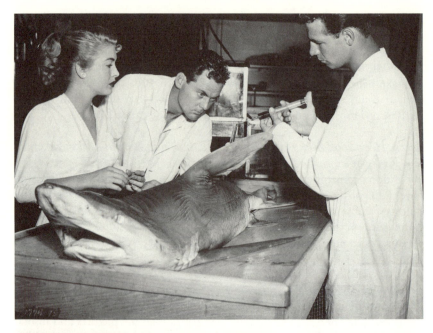

Top: Lori Nelson and John Agar in a serious moment from *Revenge of the Creature*. The lab technician (right) is Ricou Browning, who also played the Gill-Man. *Bottom:* Agar clowns with Mara Corday between takes on Universal's *Tarantula*. (Photo courtesy Steve Jochsberger.)

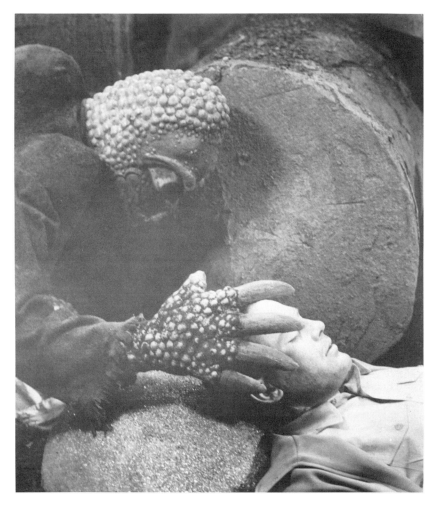

Agar is menaced by one of the humpbacked slave creatures in Universal-International's *The Mole People*.

I did down in Texas for money. In fact, it was right after *The Mole People* that I left Universal. I was there at the same time that they were grooming Tony Curtis, Rock Hudson, Jeff Chandler, George Nader — and *I* always kept gettin' the science fiction pictures. While I was under contract, the only Universal picture I did that wasn't sci-fi was a Western called *Star in the Dust* [1956]; that worked out well, and I felt that I didn't want to be just science fiction all the time. Bill Alland, for some reason, wanted me in all of his science fiction pictures, and when they came up with *this* one ... well *[laughs]*, the story just didn't gel with me at all. People coming up out of the ground looking like moles, and an underground civilization....

Too far out?

Yeah. I remember, too, that there was some silly dialogue in *The Mole People,* and I went to Bill Alland and told him, "Bill, people don't *say* things like this." He said something to the effect that he paid a guy a lot of money to write that dialogue, and I said, "Well, you got cheated!" And I think my nose got out of joint one time when I was on the set and Rock Hudson came over. He looked around at the production that was going on and he said, "How'd you get into *this* thing?" It was the kind of derogatory way that he said it—I don't know whether he meant it or not, but *[laughs]* that frosted me a little bit. I just never thought that *The Mole People* was as good a picture as *Revenge of the Creature* or *Tarantula*.

As a Universal contract player, were you in a position to turn down an assignment?

When you're under contract to a studio or to a producer and they assign you a project, if you don't do it they can put you on suspension and for the duration of that film you go without pay. I never turned anything down. They were paying me, and I figured that they were doing what was best for everybody concerned—not only for the studio but for me as well, because I was a member of their team, so to speak. Maybe I was naive, but I trusted them to guide my career.

Did you feel that the mole monsters in The Mole People *were effective?*

They were all right for the time; they didn't have the technology we have today. But at that time I thought that Universal had some of the best technicians in the business, as far as science fiction was concerned.

How was the special effect of men being dragged down under the earth achieved?

They put a rubber mat down over a hole in the floor; the mat had an X-shaped slit in it. Then they covered it with some kind of light material—it could have been Styrofoam—that was supposed to be earth or gravel. Even when someone was being pulled down through from below, the earth was held up—a lot of it could not fall through at once. The remaining earth would then cover up where they went through.

Why did you leave Universal after The Mole People?

I talked with Jim Pratt, who was the vice president over there, and I told him, "You know, I understand that you-all are grooming particular people, but I just don't want to *do* all these science fiction pictures." So when my option time came up, I said that I'd just as soon not stay on, and I didn't. I don't know, maybe I made a mistake, maybe they might've turned around and given me other things to do. I've made a lot of mistakes in my life *[laughs],* and maybe that was one of 'em.

Agar lent his talents to a number of B-grade sci-fi films of the late 1950s, including director Bert I. Gordon's *Attack of the Puppet People*.

One of your first pictures after leaving Universal was Daughter of Dr. Jekyll. *Were you disappointed to still be in that sci-fi/horror rut?*
  Well—yeah. I really didn't want to do any more of those pictures, but *[laughs]* at least I made more money on *Daughter of Dr. Jekyll* than Universal was paying me!

What do you remember about your co-star, Gloria Talbott?
  I really thought she was going to go on to do better things, but then what I guess happened was that she got married and got smart, and got out of the business. She was a very nice gal and we tried to do the best we could with *Daughter of Dr. Jekyll*. Some of those things work and some of 'em don't.

Did Daughter of Dr. Jekyll *work?*
  Not really. I did that picture strictly for the bread. I didn't *fluff* it—I did the best I could with what I had to work with—but it wasn't my cup of tea. I just didn't believe it.

When you weren't appearing in a science fiction film, it was usually a Western or a war picture. Were you more comfortable in those genres?
  To me, it's a lot easier to play in something that's real—a natural situation—than it is to deal with abstracts and things of the unknown. It's sort of difficult to make them come to life *[laughs]!* I always kind of had the feeling that when people looked at some of these science fiction things, we were going to get a big laugh. On a couple of occasions, some of the things that were supposed to frighten people really looked rather ludicrous—funny, rather than scary. I feel it's more natural to deal in something that people understand, rather than something that human beings don't come in contact with. It's a touchy situation to be in.

Did you enjoy playing a villainous Jekyll and Hyde–style role in The Brain from Planet Arous?
  Yes, and I wish I had gotten more opportunities to play *against* type. I'll tell you one thing, that picture was a very painful experience for me. When that alien being took over my body, they inserted these full contact lenses in my eyes. They'd painted 'em silver and they forgot that that doggone paint would chip off. Every time I blinked, some of that silver would come off the lens and it was like having sand in my eyes. But it was the best they could do; that was 1957, and they didn't know that much about contact lenses. It was very, *very* painful.

What did you think of that film's floating brain prop?
  Oh, I thought it was terrible—just *awful!* They really could have done a heck of a lot better than that—it looked like a balloon with a face painted on it. And that's probably about what it was, too *[laughs]!* I can't really remember exactly what it was, I just know it was ludicrous.

How did you get along with Bert I. Gordon on Attack of the Puppet People?

I don't know whether Bert Gordon liked me very much; we got into a little difficulty one night because he had promised me that I was only going to have to work until a certain hour. I was on a bowling team then and I was supposed to meet my wife and the team at such-and-such a time. Well, they carried me over past the time; Bert kept putting it off and putting it off, and I told him, "Look, you promised me I could be out of here by now, and you're foulin' me up!" I don't think Bert ever forgave me for that. I stayed and finished the work, but I don't think he thought I was giving one hundred percent. *Puppet People* was half of a two-picture deal I had with American International; the other one was called *Jet Attack* [1958], with Audrey Totter. That *Puppet People* was kind of a nonsense picture.

Was it difficult working with Puppet People's *oversized props?*

No, but that question reminds me of another time that Bert Gordon passed some kind of a comment. I had to climb a rope and pull myself up onto this giant table, and they were betting I couldn't do it. Bert Gordon was saying, "He'll never pull himself up there," and I said, "The hell I won't!" Don't tell me I can't do something, 'cause that's just when I'm going to go break my neck to prove I *can* do it. And I did it!

How much real guidance would an actor get from a director like Invisible Invaders' *Edward L. Cahn?*

Edward Cahn was Mr. Speed-O; he'd jump up and almost get in the shot before he'd yell "cut"! But in all fairness I have to say that directors like Eddie Cahn didn't really have a chance. They had a schedule to contend with, and they wanted those films finished *ka-boom.* I think he did the best he could with the time he had, but in something like *Invisible Invaders* it's pretty much, "Learn the lines and get 'em out." They just didn't have the money to stay there and work on it.

Did you go to see all of your movies when they were first released?

A lot of the pictures I made were not released — they *escaped [laughs]!* I didn't *avoid* looking at them, but there were some where I knew full well what they were going to be like before they were ever released.

You've been directed by a lot of actors in your time — Abner Biberman, Edmond O'Brien, Hugo Haas and, on Hand of Death, *Gene Nelson. Did you ever think about directing a picture yourself?*

Well, I had a thought about doing it back then, and then I decided that I preferred to be in front of the camera rather than behind it. But the temptation was there for a time. Speaking of Gene Nelson, *Hand of Death* was his first shot at directing, and I thought he did a very good job for his first go at it.

A monstrous Agar rebels against rising taxi fares in Fox's *Hand of Death*. (Photo courtesy Steve Jochsberger.)

Tell us a little about playing the monster in that film.

First they got some long johns and padded 'em to make me look like I weighed about four hundred pounds. Then they had this grotesque mask—a complete hood—and very large hands, to make me look burned. Our oldest boy, Martin, was maybe two or three years old at the time, and he came on the set with his mother and heard his dad's voice coming out of this monster get-up—and it scared him half to death! I had a tough time explaining it to him.

Was that an enjoyable change of pace, or was it too uncomfortable an experience?
Oh, no, it wasn't that bad—except at the very end, when I finally died. We went out to Malibu for a scene where I run into the ocean trying to get away from the police, and they shoot me. When I fell, the waves started knocking me around, and with that mask over my face I didn't know *where* I was! My eyes were set way back and the mask was sticking way out in front, and the only thing I could see was just directly straight out. I couldn't see the waves coming—that water was crashin' on me, and I was floppin' around, supposed to be dead *[laughs]*—! That was quite an experience.

How did you get involved on Journey to the Seventh Planet?
A guy named Sidney Pink had made some kind of a deal to make that picture over in Denmark, and he contacted me about going over there and starring in it. He had already done one over there, a thing called *Reptilicus*—they showed it to me over in Denmark, and *[laughs]* I didn't think too much of it. Anyway, my wife and our son Martin went with me and enjoyed the trip very much. Something that I'll never forget is that when we flew from L.A., we went the Polar route and I got to see the Northern Lights—the Aurora Borealis. I think that was the most incredible thing I've ever seen. When we came back here, we went over to American International and we looped a great deal of that picture—almost all of it. I don't know what the trouble was, but American International wanted it all redubbed, so that's what we did.

Compared to The Brain from Planet Arous, *what did you think of* Seventh Planet*'s giant brain prop?*
Actually, I believe that giant brain was done here, not in Denmark. The one in Denmark was worse than the one they did here *[laughs]*! They thought they could improve on it here, but as I remember it wasn't too good, either. So we did shoot some new shots for *Journey to the Seventh Planet* over here and they slipped a couple of 'em in.

Can you give us some background on the Larry Buchanan pictures you did in Texas?
What happened on those was that American International gave Larry Buchanan a budget to work with and scripts of pictures that they had already done. Larry, God bless him, is a nice guy but he really was not a director. He did the best he could, but he didn't even know enough not to "cross the line," which is one of the simplest things there is in directing. In the beginning, he didn't understand *that [laughs]*! The first picture I did for Larry was *Zontar,*

the Thing from Venus; Curse of the Swamp Creature came next; then we did a war film called *Hell Raiders* [1968]. Of course I never thought those things would ever see the light of day—that was the only reason I did 'em!

You were working on actual locations most of the time, weren't you?
We did work mostly on location, although there were a couple of sets. We went out to Gordon McLendon's ranch on *Hell Raiders;* for *Zontar,* they used a park in Dallas, and we did work on a couple of stages in that. A lot of *Swamp Creature* was done in a little town called Uncertain, Texas—it was called that because the people that founded it weren't sure whether they were in Texas or Louisiana.

What about an obscure film called Night Fright, *made by many of the same people but not by Buchanan?*
I don't recall too much about that movie. It was produced by an attorney down there and directed by Jim Sullivan, who was an assistant director for Larry Buchanan.

How did you land your role in Dino De Laurentiis' King Kong?
I went out to Metro-Goldwyn-Mayer, read for it along with fifty other actors, and the director, John Guillermin, said he wanted me to do the part. But to this day I simply cannot understand why they wrote my scenes the way they did. Toward the end of the movie, Jeff Bridges and the others are running around New York wondering where Kong has gone, and then they realize that he'll think of the twin peaks and go to the World Trade Center. So Jeff Bridges calls me from out of the blue, but the audience doesn't know who in the heck I am. When King Kong was brought in and showed off, I was not in any of those scenes, and I never made contact with Jeff Bridges—but he calls *me* and puts all that trust in *me*. I never could understand that! My character was supposed to be a Jimmy Walker type of guy. Then at the very end, after Kong's been killed, they tried to show that I was really not concerned about the girl [Jessica Lange] or what she'd gone through, I was just trying to get publicity because I was a politician. But that scene didn't come off, either, and I knew it wouldn't. I just believe that, insofar as that character was concerned, they really weren't thinking. But, hey, I took the money and ran.

To most of us who enjoy the B-grade science fiction films of the '50s and '60s, your name seems synonymous with that type of film. Do you appreciate or resent the association?
No, I don't resent being identified with them at all—why should I? Even though they were not considered top-of-the-line, for those people that like sci-fi I guess they were fun. My whole feeling about working as an actor is, if I give anybody any enjoyment, I'm doing my job, and that's what counts.

Considering the fact that you started out in first-rate pictures with people like John Ford and John Wayne, are you at all happy with the direction your career took?

Well, I think a lot of success was thrown at me too quickly and I wasn't ready to receive it. It was my fault if it didn't work out better; I can't blame anybody but myself.

How do you keep busy today?

I've been working with Brunswick Recreation Centers, with their Club 55 program, for the last few years. I travel around, kind of like a public relations guy, and try to get prime-timers — senior citizens — involved with the sport of bowling.

When you were making these sci-fi pictures twenty and thirty years ago, did you have any idea that they'd still be seen and appreciated in the 1980s?

[Laughs.] Well, I don't know; you didn't think about those kinds of things at that time. They're making a lot of science fiction pictures nowadays that they don't call me about — maybe the fans appreciated me in these films, but the people in the business today certainly haven't said anything about me doing any work for 'em. I think I have much more to offer as an actor now than I ever did as a young man; now would be a time for me to be a character actor. It hasn't worked out that way, but you never know what's going to happen. As long as there's breath in the body, I am still hopeful.

*Satisfaction is a matter of what your needs are,
and what you're accustomed to.... When I was kicked out
of college and went bumming for a year, riding freights and so on,
it didn't take a hell of a lot to satisfy me—just a full meal!
Now, later on, when I was eating very well ...
it would take a hell-of-a-lot* better *meal...!
So since the background keeps shifting,
you cannot establish an absolute.*

Samuel Z. Arkoff

IF THERE WAS EVER a movie mogul who needed no introduction to fans of exploitation films, it is Samuel Z. Arkoff. A prime purveyor of exploitation pictures for nearly a third of a century, the Iowa-born Arkoff co-founded American International Pictures with his partner, the late James H. Nicholson, in 1954. Under the aegis of Arkoff and Nicholson, the company survived in a constricting industry by catering to the whims of the teenage trade. AIP's long (350-plus) roster of kitsch classics, running the gamut from horror to rock'n'roll, from juvenile delinquency to Italian musclemen, and from Edgar Allan Poe to Annette Funicello, have already forged their own unique niche in film history.

After Nicholson's 1971 resignation, Arkoff assumed full control of the company and remained in charge until the 1979 merger with Filmways prompted his own departure. He is now the head of Arkoff International Pictures, where upcoming projects (with titles like *Phobia, Buried Alive* and *They're Here*) offer solid evidence that Arkoff has no intention of straying from his time-tested formula for movie success.

As someone who's always made movies for the youth market, what were your favorite types of films when you were growing up in Fort Dodge?

I'm a picture buff—I didn't have any favorites. I liked pictures if they were well done at all. But you have to remember that that was a whole different era. I mean, I can remember the advent of sound! I went through all the experimentation with sound, when they had it on disks; in fact, I can recall going to a picture starring Richard Barthelmess—it might have been *Weary River* [1929]—and I remember a scene with Barthelmess and his leading lady in a boat. And because it got a little out of sync, the love speeches he was making were coming out of *her* mouth, and vice versa *[laughs]*! Now *those* were interesting days!

When you and Alex Gordon were planning to make a movie around Mother Riley Meets the Vampire *footage, did you get to meet Bela Lugosi?*

I had a number of conversations with Lugosi, who was a very interesting man; by this time, of course, he was "playing the role" of Lugosi—you know what I mean. In fact, I was the lawyer on *Bride of the Monster,* which was one of the last pictures that Lugosi did before he died. The director on that was Ed Wood, who has since come to prominence. Ed was quite a character, a very interesting fellow, and now, through pictures like *Glen or Glenda* and the like, he has sort of a reputation—although in his own era he never made very much dough.

When you started American Releasing Corporation in 1954, it was clearly a bad time in Hollywood for independents.

When we started in '54, there were virtually no independents at all! The

Previous page: Movie mogul Samuel Z. Arkoff (seen here minus his trademark cigar) proclaims that "everything in our whole American economy is exploitation!"

only independents had been Bob Lippert, who was an exhibitor, and Sam Goldwyn; David Selznick had lost his patron, John Hay Whitney, and was just going through the motions. Other than those, the only independents in those days were the one-lung producers who used to go to Griffith Park or one of the movie ranches, and for twenty-five or thirty thousand bucks each make two Westerns, back-to-back, with the same cast, the same horses and virtually the same story. Maybe they'd change a villain or something, and sometimes they didn't change a damned thing.

We started at a time when everybody said it was crazy to start a picture company. Thousands of theaters were going out of business. Young adults were getting married and moving out into new housing in the suburbs. They were sitting out in their millions of new homes, having babies and watching TV. The only real constant audience which Jim Nicholson and I recognized— one which the majors didn't—was the youth, who *didn't* want to stay home, who had to get *out*. Drive-ins were opening up all over but of course at the beginning they bought pictures at the end of their run for flat prices. They were known as "passion pits," and they didn't give a damn about the pictures they showed—a picture was a way to attract the kids who had wheels.

And it was this youth market that you and Mr. Nicholson zeroed in on.

That's right. In the old days, all the way up to the late '50s, there *were* no youth pictures as we understand them. Fundamentally, there were Disney types of pictures for the small kids and there were regular "family" pictures for everybody else. A typical youth picture would have been an Andy Hardy film. Look at it this way: Andy's father was played by Lewis Stone, an impressive fatherly figure who also happened to be a judge. *Think* about that. Andy says to his father, "I'm going to do such-and-such a thing." The father says, "You'd better not, you'll get into trouble." Andy and his friends go off, get into trouble and can't get out, and now Andy comes back to his father and says, "Dad, you told us not to do this, but we did it. Now we're in trouble, and I hope you can get us out." And so the judge says, in a severe but sympathetic tone, "Okay, I'll get you out of trouble," which he does. "Dad," says Andy, looking up at his father, "I'll never do that again." And the whole adult audience creams in its pants.

That is what the youth picture essentially was—a moral lesson, a lecture. But by the late '50s the kids were beyond lecturings. And this led up to the '60s, which of course was a decade like no other decade in American life. When we made the *Beach Party* pictures, those pictures were not basically about the beach. They were set at the beach, but basically they were about kids who didn't have parents. Why? Because these were youth pictures made for youth. Not the youth of Disney, not the youth that all these moralists, these *spinsters* wanted "family" pictures for. Fundamentally what we were doing, starting in the '50s when we did *Hot Rod Girl, Dragstrip Girl* and all of those, was making pictures for teenagers who didn't want to have a lecture crammed down their

Youth-slanted double-bills like *Teenage Werewolf* and *Teenage Frankenstein* helped AIP to flourish while other Hollywood studios floundered.

throats. This is not only true of our pictures, it was true in real life, because it was in the late '50s and the '60s that you began to have youth going out on their own.

Tell us a little about your early dealings with Roger Corman.
   We had a four-picture deal with Roger, and he had a certain amount of money—something less than $100,000 a picture—as a budget for the total four. When he got to the fourth picture, *The Beast with a Million Eyes,* there was only about $29,000 or $30,000 left. So he did the whole picture, non-union, in Palm Springs, running away from the Screen Actors Guild and the IATSE. But when we got to the end there was no more money left and there was no monster. What we ended up using was a *teakettle,* with a lot of holes in it. Not a million holes, of course *[laughs],* but a lot, and the thing was obscured by the steam that was coming out of all the holes. That's ingenuity. Joe Levine, who was our franchise holder up in Boston and a great exploitation man in his own right, really got enthused about the piece of artwork we had made up for that picture. He and another big New England exhibitor had worked out this big campaign, and they were going to have a special promotion up there in that circuit. Joe brought the exhibitor out to see the picture. And when he saw it, he was somewhat crestfallen *[laughs]!* But the picture did very well, considering; it was a hell of an idea.

A lot of the basic concepts of your '50s films are still being used today.
   You're right about that. Other than the sci-fi films, which of course have progressed because we've learned a great deal about other planets and so on . . . you name me one horror or science fiction concept that wasn't used in the '50s—that wasn't either started or used in the '50s. Pretty hard to do, huh?
   Most of the ideas in many of these films today are really not ideas that were advanced by Spielberg or Lucas—although I won't take anything away from 'em. But the fact is that most of those ideas came out of the '50s. For example, in *It Conquered the World,* we had another odd monster—it looked like a pumpkin head—that enslaved people through little arrows that pierced the backs of their necks. That was one of the first times that was ever used—but it's been used in a lot of much bigger pictures since. So the *idea* was the thing in those days. Also, the state of the art in the '50s was not what it is today. Even if we had had more money, we could never have come up to what they're doing now.

The bigger sci-fi pictures in those days were the George Pal pictures.
   Which, in their own way, were pretty good. Much better, in a sense, than ours, I'm not arguing the point, but they also had probably ten, fifteen times as much money going into them. But George was a good man and a friend of mine—in fact, just before he died we were talking about doing a picture together. But my whole point was that it was the *idea* that was important in

those days. Now, along come these new state-of-the-art special effects—you might say that *Star Wars* was probably the pinnacle. I can remember everybody's awe at the special effects in that picture—and they *should* have been in awe, because that was an integral part of the story. It was one of the most judicious meldings of basic story and special effects that I think we've had.

Except that now it's gotten to the point where it's special effects for special effects' sake.

And that's bullshit! And I'll tell you why: because the public gets tired of special effects. I thought we came to the zenith in the summer of '85, when they came out with those three special effects youth pictures all in one week—*Weird Science, Real Genius* and *My Science Project*. Three in one week! In the first place, it's too many—the same market, all aiming at the same youth sci-fi audience. Now, all youth doesn't go for sci-fi. And also you have to be careful when you meld genres. You can do it—we've done it, too—but you have to be cautious because if you go a little overboard, you're going to lose the "other" audience, you may even lose both of 'em, as far as getting the big numbers is concerned. So now what we have is that we're getting pictures where the special effects outweigh and out-proportion the rest of the piece. *Young Sherlock Holmes* [1985] is another example—if you're going to make a Sherlock Holmes picture, then *make* one! What that really was is another of those so-called adventure pictures masquerading under a Sherlock Holmes title. For the Holmes people it was completely unsatisfactory, and for the people who wanted a special effects, adventure type of piece, it was not satisfactory either, because it was harboring under Sherlock Holmes, who means nothing to the big bases of teenagers today. What does the average eighteen-year-old kid know about Sherlock Holmes? It's completely outside of their ken.

Also, when they do all of these mechanical things, they're losing something that's very important: the interest of the audience in the movie's characters and their identification with people in trouble. It's very thin, very superficial. In the *Sherlock Holmes* piece, were you really *with* anybody? Nobody went to enough care to get you interested in the people, so you never really gave a shit. You've got to *care* about people, you have to be *concerned* when they have a problem. Oddly enough, it's almost like going back to the very origins of the business when you had superficial comics doing these chases and brawls. Today, you're supposed to be awed—or overawed—by the special effects. Well, I'm telling you that there's a limit beyond which the special effects just aren't going to take anybody. And I think that most young people today have seen just about all the special effects they care to.

Getting back to American Releasing and the mid–'50s, how exactly did you go about pretesting your movie concepts?

We started with a title, and then we'd make up some kind of a slick drawing. And then we'd send it around to half a dozen exhibitors that we thought were more than just real estate men and concession operators, and a few other people on the other side of the business, too, and we asked them whether they thought this had a *look*. It's always surprised me that so many of the pictures in our business are made without the sales department or the merchandising department being consulted. We didn't take a script and shoot it, and then, when the picture was done, send it to the advertising department and say, "Now, figure out how the hell you're gonna sell it." That's putting the cart before the horse, but a lot of companies still do that today.

I'm a great believer in "If you can't sell it, don't make it." American industry has used that kind of concept for years—they go out, test the market, talk to people and so on. But nobody in the picture business seems to want to test anything anymore. Now they want to go out with one thousand or two thousand prints and a big national campaign, *boom*. We tested. People think you can make a little picture and send it out, and then *[majestically]* the public *responds,* and word-of-mouth spreads. That's true, within reason. But if you go out with a little picture and go into a theater and spend a little money—as befits a little picture—how's the public going to come? What's going to bring 'em? A picture with no handle? That's why you have an exploitation picture—because if you don't have a big star or a pre-sold book and all of that, you *have* to have that handle.

What do you say to people who think that exploitation is a bad word?

Everything in our whole fucking American economy is exploitation! It simply means to exploit what you have; you have to have something to sell, you have to have a handle. We knew that stars weren't necessarily a handle, but the presence of a star or two helps make the picture look bigger, so the public will give it a chance. Then at least you have a chance, with enough advertising, to bring people into the theater, and then get word-of-mouth going. What happens with a little picture is, nobody comes the first week, the theater doesn't do much business, gets rid of that picture and gets another one in the second week. There's that old saw, "If there's no one to hear, there is no sound." If there's nobody to see it, where's the word-of-mouth going to come from? There's no blowhole somewhere that keeps telling what a wonderful picture it is. The whole point about it is, you need a gimmick. We didn't have stars—we created stars, but we didn't have 'em. So that was really how we sold those pictures.

Was ARC the first production company to try that approach?

Oh, no, I don't think so—but I think we brought it to a polish *[laughs]!* There was Barnum and Bailey, there was Mike Todd, there were all kinds of people throughout history who beat the drums—exploitation is not a new word. For me to say that we started the concept of exploring the worth of an idea based on a title and some rough artwork would not be fair; I can only say that maybe we added a little more gilt to the process.

For all of this business savvy, American Releasing got off to a pretty shaky start.

The exhibitors wanted to play all of our pictures as second features. Well, a second feature gets a flat price—$100, $200, maybe even $500, but it isn't going to get the percentage. We could never have made a go of it with second features; after a few early pictures like *The Fast & the Furious* [1954], *Apache Woman* [1955] and maybe a couple more, we realized that with second features we were going to go under. So we sat down and said that what we were going to do was to make exploitation pictures, put two of 'em together and then hold firm—we would play the two pictures for a percentage. Basically, we would be giving them two pictures for the same percentage they used to pay for one, which meant that they didn't have to pay for the second feature, we were *giving* it to them. And what's more, we told them, we were going to make it like a combination. What the majors used to do was to take one picture, which was (let's say) a Western, and then make the second feature completely different than a Western hoping to get a more diversified audience that way. That was really bullshit. The way to do it, particularly if you're appealing to youth, was to make two pictures on the same subject. So our first combination was *Day the World Ended* and *The Phantom from 10,000 Leagues*. Those two cost about a hundred thousand bucks apiece.

How did this new strategy work?

In the beginning, we couldn't even book 'em! The exhibitors said, "No, we don't want to play them together as a combination, we'll book them as second features." We just resisted and resisted, and I want to tell you, it got to be pretty tense. We were just sitting there and not getting any action from the exhibitors, who after all were very powerful. Finally we got a date in Detroit in the first week of December, which is *not* the best playing time in the world in Detroit. And there was a newspaper strike to boot! So we got up a promotion through the streets of Detroit—we had some kind of a horror caravan, with a monster and all that kind of stuff, and we had flyers that we dropped everywhere. And we did very well. With that one run we broke the barrier, the exhibitors booked them together, and we were off and running.

Wasn't The Phantom from 10,000 Leagues *a pick-up?*

There were a couple of guys, the Milner Brothers, editors who wanted to make a picture, and so we went to them. We made a deal for them to make this other picture and we put it together with ours, and we divided sixty-forty—we got the sixty because ours, *Day the World Ended,* was a little more expensive than theirs. So actually it was made to order—they made the picture but we had a hand in it. Lou Rusoff was the writer on *Phantom;* he was my

Three-eyed mutant Paul Blaisdell absconds with an unconscious Lori Nelson in the climax of *Day the World Ended*.

brother-in-law, and he wrote a lot of those pictures for us. He died just after he made *Beach Party*, around 1963.

Why did you change your company name from American Releasing to American International?
   We tried to get the AIP label in the beginning, but there was an American Pictures so we couldn't get it. We took the title we could get, which was ARC, and then the other company apparently went out of business and we got the other title.

Was AIP a reasonable success from then on, or were those early years still lean ones for all of you?
   They were lean years, for a lot of reasons. We didn't start with any money—we put bits and pieces of things together. For example, I'd go to the franchise holders in the U.S. and I'd get maybe $40,000 in advance for a picture to be delivered. And then I would go and get maybe $14,000 for the U.K., half of it in advance. And then I'd get a little money out of foreign—not much. Then I'd get about $25,000 from the laboratory in cash, plus a deferment, and then I'd get actors and others to defer their salaries for a time. And we'd put together fifty, sixty, seventy thousand dollars toward a $100,000 picture—

that's how we made our pictures. And we kept expanding, so even if we *had* been successful, we wouldn't have had any money. Probably the best thing that ever happened to us was the fact that we never had any room to breathe. We kept fighting and going ahead, we didn't spend much dough on anything — we certainly didn't spend it on ourselves! — and we just put every dollar back into the business.

Several of the people we've talked with about Roger Corman have resented his attitude and his methods.

Well, in the first place, let me tell you something. Roger's been a good friend of mine for a long time now — I met him when he was twenty-eight and I was thirty-five, so I've known Roger for thirty-three years. And Roger's a hell of a guy. Roger and I have had a lot of successes together; he made maybe forty pictures for us, give or take. I assure you of one thing — Roger's doing what he wants to do, for whatever reasons he has, because he's fully capable of doing anything he wants to do.

What sort of arrangement did you have after the initial four pictures?

Our relationship was just a working arrangement that was never really in writing. In fact, he formed a distribution company before New World called Filmgroup. During those days when he was making pictures for Filmgroup, he would make cheaper ones for himself and Filmgroup, but the minute he went above a certain amount he would come to us and we would do it. And then when he decided to get out of Filmgroup, he brought us over those pictures, and we released those for a time. We had a very informal arrangement and it was a wonderful relationship — still is a wonderful relationship, although we haven't done any pictures together recently. I think the last picture we did together was *Boxcar Bertha* [1972].

After what happened on Gas-s-s *[1970], he said he'd never do a movie for AIP again.*

I don't even think Roger was too fond of *Gas-s-s;* I thought that the title was about what the picture was. But, look — I'm very fond of Roger, I'm not going to pillory him for the press or for anybody else. We had our differences from time to time — very few differences, considering how easy it is to have them on something as highly charged as making a picture. We did a lot of pictures together, we had a great relationship, we have a great relationship now. He's a terrific guy and I'm proud to call him a longtime friend.

Were you impressed with his ability to grind out product quickly and inexpensively?

Of course — there was nobody better than Roger. He produced and directed four and five pictures a year, he was a hard worker, he always brought them in on budget — which is more than I can say for practically anybody else.

To tell the truth, there were times when he could've spent a little *more* money—and, boy, you don't hear anybody ever say that about pictures, especially me! But I thought there were a couple of pictures where he could have used a few more people in 'em—you know, to sort of fill up the scene *[laughs]*!

Would you agree that some of his early films have stood the test of time better than many of the other older AIPs?
That's not necessarily true. I like Roger's, but what about *I Was a Teenage Werewolf?* Herman Cohen did some very nice pictures—*Teenage Werewolf, Teenage Frankenstein, Horrors of the Black Museum* and so on. Those stand up very well. But Roger did more of the black-and-whites than any other single director did. I'm not taking anything away from Roger, but we did have other directors as well.

Tell us about your brief appearance in Corman's Hawaiian-made Naked Paradise *[1957].*
We went over to Hawaii—me, my two kids and my wife, Jim with his wife and three kids. Roger told me one day to come over to where he was shooting, and he gave me this one line to read to Richard Denning: "It's been a good harvest, and the money is in the safe." Now *that's* a key line *[laughs]!* That was my first and last role; I've never been asked back into any of 'em since!

Did you enjoy visiting the sets or meeting the stars of these early films?
What stars?—what kind of shit is that *[laughs]?* Look, I have nothing against actors—although I wouldn't say that some of my best friends are actors—but we'd meet 'em in the normal course of business. Actors are people—I'm not awed by them, certainly not overawed or anything like that. That's for fans—I'm not a fan.

Alex Gordon tells the story that AIP really didn't care to have veteran actors in their early films.
Well, for Christ's sake, Alex loved old actors—he used to drag these old actors around, and I sometimes thought he went out to the graveyards to find 'em *[laughs]!* He idolized old actors, he really did—that was Alex's bag. I wasn't against them, I just was against building a picture around 'em. Let me give you an example: When he brought around Anna Sten and used her in a movie called *Runaway Daughters* [1956], he thought that was a great coup. I thought it was a *coup de grâce!* She meant nothing *[laughs]*—nobody in the fornicating audience had the slightest idea of who Anna Sten was! She was never successful—Sam Goldwyn tried to build her up, brought her over from Europe, used her in three or four pictures, spent a lot of money on her. None of her pictures ever crashed through—and she'd played opposite some very good stars. She was a nice lady and I had nothing against her, but when Alex

wanted to give her top billing and all...! He also used to bring Raymond Hatton around a lot. Well, I remembered Raymond Hatton, he used to play in pictures with Wallace Beery. But at that point the young audience didn't even know who Wallace Beery was, and *he* was the *big* star!

I had nothing against oldtime actors; if Alex wanted to put an older actor into a role, fine, but don't try to base your pictures on them, particularly when you're trying to go for a young audience. I am not ashamed to say that I didn't want to play to empty theaters. And therefore you had to cast people who would bring audiences in; we didn't have stars but we created them, and they had a market. Like Annette Funicello: Annette did the Mouseketeer bit for Disney, and we turned her into a completely different kind of personality — Mouseketeer was little kiddie-time. But fundamentally I appreciate what Alex was doing; he just happened to love old actors.

What prompted his decision to leave AIP?

It was a completely voluntary act on Alex's part — he wanted to be bigger himself. We considered him a part of an organization, that he had certain functions and that he did them well. He really wanted, I think, to be kind of a sole star. So when he asked to get out, I told him, "Don't do it — you're making a mistake." But he wanted to do it, and so we bought him out. I still see Alex every now and then, I *like* Alex — but I don't think he should have left.

Because there was a sequel to The Amazing Colossal Man, *people assume that that was one of your biggest early moneymakers. Was it?*

Let me tell you our theory. The majors today make sequels, but they never *plan* for sequels, as a rule. A picture goes out and does very well — they make a sequel. Basically, they're looking for a follow-up to a successful picture. *We* were looking to establish a vein of ore that we could mine. A sequel didn't necessarily mean that the first picture was particularly successful; just as long as it was successful *enough,* then we'd make a second one. While *The Amazing Colossal Man* made money, it wasn't that it made so much money we *had* to do it — we were trying to open up a vein.

So then what were some of your better-grossing early double bills?

You have to remember that satisfaction is a matter of what your needs are, and what you're accustomed to. I can remember when I was kicked out of college and went bumming for a year, riding freights and so on, it didn't take a hell of a lot to satisfy me — just a full meal! Now, later on, when I was eating very well — and showing the evidences of it! *[laughs]* — it would take a hell-of-a-lot *better* meal to make me think it was a good meal! So since the background keeps shifting, you cannot establish an absolute. Take the gross on a picture: As pictures began to cost more, you had to gross more. So some of the earlier pictures which were kind of a breakthrough, like *Day the World Ended,* you

One of AIP's most memorable '50s productions was Bert I. Gordon's *The Amazing Colossal Man* with Glenn Langan.

always remembered as being very important to you. Now we surpassed the gross of *Day the World Ended* relatively soon after that—but even in that short amount of time our pictures had already started costing more.

We were told that the double bill I Was a Teenage Frankenstein *and* Blood of Dracula *had an interesting story behind it.*
There was a famous exhibitor in the Southwest by the name of Bob O'Donnell—he was the head of Interstate, which was *the* big company at the time. He was having an argument with some major companies about film rentals, and so he told us—on Labor Day—that if we could make a couple of pictures by Thanksgiving, he would play us in his Flagship Theater. We had never played that Flagship Theater, so we made those two pictures for him by Thanksgiving!

Made them from scratch?
Oh, no—the scripts for those two were already in the works before he asked. Look, we made *I Was a Teenage Werewolf*, which was successful—were we *not* going to do *Teenage Frankenstein?*

Why did Herman Cohen make a number of his pictures in England?
Well, because England was a good place to make 'em. That was a market that liked horror films, so you worked with them on these as co-productions, each party bearing half the cost. It made economic sense to make pictures in England.

AIP's formula for success seems so straightforward and so common-sensible; why weren't the other studios able to fully duplicate your success with exploitation films?
Because a lot of producers like to be dignified. They're basically narcissistic, a great many of them—they want to be considered cultured people, like so many other people in the United States. Fundamentally, a lot of them didn't want to do exploitation pictures. In fact, for years one of the great problems was that, even after the television era came in and it was known that it was primarily the youth who were going to the theaters, they were still doing remakes of pictures like *The Barretts of Wimpole Street* and all that kind of bullshit. That's what people want to make—it gives them a dignity.

But a lot of the smaller studios, Allied Artists in particular, were *churning out their own horror/sci-fi films at that same time.*
That's right, and by the spring of 1959 we knew we were in trouble. We had been making these combinations and being successful with them, but all of a sudden the market was inundated with copies of them. And a lot of these other pictures didn't have any originality—they were more or less copies of ours. What we did then was one of the most important things we ever did: We

said, "Look, the combinations aren't working any more. This is the way to go broke." So at that time we made two steps. First we said goodbye to the combinations. Then we decided that we were going to put the money that we used to put into *two* pictures into just *one* picture, and then we'd go out with it plus an older picture as the second feature. In other words, in June we'd come out with a new picture, and March's top-of-the-bill would become June's second. And then June's top-of-the-bill would later become September's bottom-of-the-bill.

That was also about the time AIP started picking up a number of foreign-made films.

Oh, sure. For instance, Joe Levine had picked up a Hercules picture and did well with it. There were a lot of Hercules pictures being made, so we also got a Steve Reeves Hercules picture. But we didn't want to make ours Hercules, so in the dubbing we changed it to Goliath, and the picture became *Goliath & the Barbarians* [1960]. We also picked up a picture called *The Sign of Rome* [1959], which had no gladiator, but in the dubbing we had the guy in it talk about the days when he *was* a gladiator, and we called the picture *Sign of the Gladiator [laughs]!*

Was Black Sunday *a pick-up, or was AIP in on that one from the start?*

That was a pick-up. I remember seeing that picture on a deadly cold morning in Rome. At that time, the Italians couldn't have both air conditioning and heat; when they'd turn off the heat in the spring, they'd never put it on again until late fall. So what happened was, they turned off the heat, and there was a cold spell. I can remember sitting in this damned screening room at eight o'clock in the morning — shivering, our overcoats on and everything else — and then this picture, *Black Sunday,* came on. And I'll tell you, it was really one hell of a picture. Mario Bava was really a master; if he had been an American or British director, I think he would have made it big. He had a real feel for this stuff.

How did you enjoy working with Vincent Price on Roger Corman's Poe films?

He was really quite a bright man — very educated, very cultured. We had a long relationship with Vincent, and I really thought he was a spectacular man in every respect. The same goes for a lot of the other horror people, but Vincent is in sort of a class by himself.

You know, it's very interesting that some of our best horror stars have really been very good actors in another milieu. Vincent started out doing serious stuff — he played on Broadway opposite Helen Hayes, playing Prince Albert to her Victoria in *Victoria Regina.* Lugosi had been a serious dramatic actor in Europe, and Basil Rathbone had been a stage actor. Rathbone had no humor; he was in a couple of our pictures. Vincent had a lot of humor, and

Pit and the Pendulum with Vincent Price and Barbara Steele ranks as one of Arkoff's favorites among his three hundred-plus American International Pictures.

so did Peter Lorre—he was really my favorite. We brought back almost all the great horror stars: Vincent, Boris Karloff, Lon Chaney, Jr., Peter Lorre and so on. The only one alive today is Vincent, and the odd part is that all the others died after making our pictures *[laughs]!* I don't know whether there's any direct connection....

Can you tell us a little more about Karloff?

A very dignified, very warm man. Naturally, I didn't know him at the start of his career; I met him for the first time in the late 1950s, when he was already up in years. But he had a wife who took good care of him—a very sweet lady. And, again, like Vincent, he was a cultured man. You know, it's really amazing about the horror stars, that so many of them were miles above the average actor. Vincent certainly is, and I thought Boris was. They were dignified men, they really were, and you treated them like dignified men. Those were good relationships, and I have very fond memories of working with them.

So no trouble with any of them?

Peter Lorre gave us a little bit of trouble; I think he would have liked to have gotten some more standard, "non-horror" roles toward the end — although as you know his first big hit was as the child murderer in *M* [1931].

And although I knew Basil Rathbone less than I knew the others, I felt that he was still playing other kinds of roles a little bit. My guess is that he was doing horror more for the money than because he really loved it; I always had the feeling about Basil that he would just as soon have been in a different type of picture. I think Vincent genuinely relishes it, and that Boris sort of did, too.

Critics complain that Vincent Price camped it up in the Poe films. Do you agree?

Well, I think that became a little truer as the years went by — and I think that's a natural kind of thing. I think if you do anything for a long time, that ultimately you have to satirize or spoof yourself. As the world gets more involved and intricate, I think that's a natural tendency. You see, if an actor is really a good actor, he doesn't really want to play everything the same way the second time.

I know that there's a funny story you tell about Conqueror Worm.

A very bright young director, Michael Reeves, wrote a script which he sent to us. It was based on a best-selling book in the U.K., *Witchfinder General,* a story about a witch-burner in Cromwell's era. Reeves sent it to us with the intent of getting some financing. The book had never been published in this country, and I just didn't think anybody in the U.S. gave a damn about Cromwell and such. By this time Jim Nicholson and I were fairly expert on Poe, so we looked at the poems and found one called *Conqueror Worm,* which fit pretty well in a way — although I guess a title like that could've fit a hell of a lot of things *[laughs]!* So we went in on it, and it was released in the U.K. and such as *Witchfinder General*—the book had a substantial audience over there — and in the United States as *Conqueror Worm.*

The funny part you're talking about was that Nat Cohen, with whom we'd made a number of pictures, had distribution rights in the U.K. and in various military installations. The picture played on bases and ships as *Witchfinder General.* So this whole group of sailors saw this piece under that title. And then a few weeks later they're in Hong Kong and they go into a theater to see a picture called *Conqueror Worm* — the same picture — and they damn near tore the theater up *[laughs]!*

Which were the bigger grossers, the Poe films or the beach films?

I think the beach pictures domestically and the Poe pictures internationally.

In what way did Sidney Pink's Reptilicus *initially fail to meet AIP's standards?*

Because it was shot in *Danish* English. Scandinavians have a particular kind of accent when they speak English — like a singsong. Sidney Pink made this picture in Copenhagen, and on one of my trips to Europe I made a stop there and Sidney, very proud of *Reptilicus,* ran the picture for me. And I said, "*Sidney*—we'll never get by with this!" He had been over there—where everybody talked like that—and he didn't realize that any American audience would have broken up immediately, particularly in that kind of picture. Sid didn't want to change it, and he sued us for not taking the picture. I told him, "Sidney, I'm not going to accept it—it says right in your contract that this English has to be English. This isn't English!" He was so clearly wrong, but he sued us—he was really bound and determined, so help me God! But on the courthouse steps—or almost—he decided in favor of the better part of valor *[laughs]*!

Did it bother you when people used to say you made irresponsible and inflammatory pictures?

That was ridiculous. You want to know something? It used to irk the *shit* out of me that we actually had at one time spinster types who used to picket the theaters where they played our monster pictures. These damned pictures now play on Saturday morning TV and afternoon matinees, and are even thought of as camp by the *kids,* for Christ's sake *[laughs]*! What the spinsters would do is, they would read the SEE's—SEE! this and SEE! that. They used to be kind of lurid, and these spinsters would believe that shit. Do you know that there were hundreds of papers in this country during the *Beach Party* days, which were the early-to-middle '60s, that brushed the navels out of the ads? Is it believable today? There must have been a whole generation of kids who thought that navels were dispensable, not realizing that without them their birth would have been somewhat questionable!

Why did Jim Nicholson leave AIP, and how did the company change for you after he left?

Basically I believe Jim left because it was getting bigger than he really wanted. He wanted to go off and do some pictures himself, and he did make a few successful pictures for Fox before he died. Of course the company did change for me after he left because he and I were practically interchangeable in some ways—although there were certain things that we did by ourselves. Jim certainly was without peer when it came to devising titles and that kind of stuff, and also for heading up the merchandising, artwork and so on. He didn't do the actual artwork—most of it was done by a fellow named Al Kaylis, who was very good—but Jim was really the key behind that. Do you remember the *Beach Blanket Bingo* campaign—"Ten thousand kids meet on five thousand beach blankets" *[laughs]*? Well, that was terrific, and that was Jim. At the beginning I did the legal work, but by this time we had our own legal department. I was really in charge of all of those areas, and of course I handled the problems, which were daily. That was not Jim's forte, he didn't like to be involved in problems.

So we had our respective divisions, but basically I would say we spent two, three, four hours a day every day together and made joint decisions. In fact, we were the only company I know that had joint chief executive officers. We continued on being very friendly after he left; in fact, I delivered the eulogy at Jim's funeral, which unfortunately came much too early.

Why did you resign from AIP after the merger with Filmways?

Because I couldn't get along with one of the asses who was heading Filmways. Being an independent to the end, I resigned.

What percentage of AIP pictures have you personally seen?

Oh, I've seen 'em all. Every one of them, sure. Now, I can't say that I necessarily always enjoyed them *[laughs]*...!

Which were your favorite AIP pictures?

I don't look at pictures from the standpoint of favorites. It was when we would hit upon a new genre, *that's* what gave me the big thrill—like when we did *Beach Party* and it worked. Our objective was to be able to open up a vein so we could mine the ore until the vein ran out. So when we hit a new genre—when we made our first motorcycle picture or beach picture or Poe picture, as examples, and those things clicked so you could make a whole string *more*—those were my favorite moments.

I don't mean to harp on this question, but there must have been some pictures that you especially liked.

Well, I had a few favorites—I thought *Pit & the Pendulum* was really very good, the best of the Poes. I thought *Dressed to Kill* was a hell of a picture, and so was *The Amityville Horror,* which was the biggest picture we ever had—in fact, the largest picture any independently produced, independently distributed company ever had in this country. One that really gave me a kick—because we didn't expect it to be that good or that successful—was *Love at First Bite* with George Hamilton as Dracula. A lot of people tried to ape that afterwards. It's tough to mix genres; lots of people have tried to meld horror with comedy, and it doesn't work very often. A horror picture really should have moments where you kind of rest up and laugh—even if it's a nervous laugh—and then go on to another horror. Some of these pictures which have been made in the last decade or so are simply one blood-drenched corpse after another. That's not really suspense, that's just plain bloody gore. They're unleavened—they need a little yeast. *Friday the 13th* started a whole inundation of that kind of piece, and there's still a market for it, although the market isn't as big as it was. But I think that basically those are over the hill.

Your own The Comedy of Terrors *did a good job of mixing genres.*

You've got to make them larger than life, but not preposterous. One of the great problems with young writers is that they have a tendency to think that they can spoof everything to a fare-thee-well. Well, you can't do that. Spoofs are very difficult; they used to say, "Satire is what closes on Saturday night." Since *Love at First Bite* there've been half a dozen pictures out where they've tried to do the same thing, and not a single one really worked. One of the reasons that they haven't is because they get too wild. Your piece has to be anchored in realism—then it's funny. But if it gets too far off that foundation, it becomes unbelievable.

What can you tell us about Arkoff International Pictures' initial production Night Crawlers?

We're doing that film for Cannon, a company that Golan and Globus say was based on American International. I'm willing to take the credit as long as they're doing well; if they don't *[laughs]*, I'm going to deny any resemblance! By the way, before he ever made a picture in Israel, I put Menahem Golan on a picture called *The Young Racers* [1963]. That film was directed by Roger Corman; first assistant was Francis Coppola; and Menahem was in there, really, as kind of a water boy—gradually, I think, he got a little more dignified status. His wife was also script girl. And the lead was Mark Damon, who now heads up P.S.O. Can you top that cast?

Is it a tough game today for independent producers?

It always goes up and down for the independent. But there's room for him, in one sense, that there isn't in American industry. Now, you take big American industry—take the automobile business. There's no room for the little guy. The thing about the independent in the movie business is that there's no way that a major can cut him off. An independent may have trouble, but there's always an independent picture coming down the pike that can get into the theaters, or into home video, or what have you. So no matter how difficult it is, there's room in a game like this because there's no way that anybody can spread-eagle the whole field. There's always a place for an independent, because there's always somebody who's going to come out of the woods with a picture that's a little different. Sure, it's a tough game; the amount of money that you put into these things, plus the prints and ads, is really ridiculous. If we had any sense, we could make more money with parking lots! It's just that there's something about this picture game that we like.

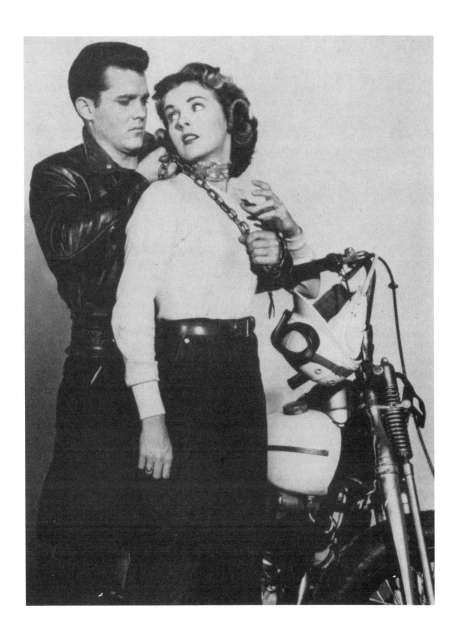

This is a terrible thing to admit, but maybe the key to my success with exploitation films is that I always liked those movies, and I never had any real reason to turn them down. I just enjoyed doing them.

John Ashley

AS AN AIP TEEN STAR, John Ashley appeared in such '50s kids-in-trouble pictures as *Motorcycle Gang, Hot Rod Gang* and, for Filmgroup, *High School Caesar*. In 1958 he was introduced to horror movies in *How to Make a Monster* and continued to thrive in the genre until the early '70s. In between the occasional A-picture assignment like *Hud* (1963) and his regular appearances in AIP's beach pictures, Ashley worked with such zero-budget luminaries as Richard Cunha *(Frankenstein's Daughter)* and Larry Buchanan *(The Eye Creatures),* and went on to carve a lucrative niche for himself in the Philippines as both a star and producer in a unique series of horror pictures that included *Mad Doctor of Blood Island* and *The Beast of the Yellow Night*.

Oklahoma-bred Ashley got his start in the movie business while on a vacation in California. A friend from Oklahoma State University got him onto the set of the John Wayne movie *The Conqueror* (1956), and Wayne in turn steered him toward a job on television in the William Castle series *Men of Annapolis*. One day, Ashley went over to the AIP offices to pick up his girlfriend, who was auditioning for a part in *Dragstrip Girl* (1957). AIP house writer Lou Rusoff saw Ashley waiting in the hall, decided the young man was the type the studio was looking for to play the *Dragstrip* male lead, and teen-pix history was made.

How did you enjoy working at American International?

It was a lot of fun, because it was a new company. Sam Arkoff, Jim Nicholson, Leon Blender and Milt Moritz were basically the cadre there. They made movies very quickly; they would come up with a great title, draw up an advertising concept, and then make the picture. Everything was *fast* — we shot them in ten days, black-and-white — but it was a great learning experience.

When I first went to work for American International, there were three little outfits working under the AIP banner: Alex Gordon and Lou Rusoff, who was Sam Arkoff's brother-in-law, had a little entity; Herman Cohen had another; and then there was Roger Corman, who had his little company. Roger and I became friends. I never worked for Roger as an actor, but then later on, when I got into producing, we did several projects together over in the Philippines. A couple of 'em were horror films, a couple of 'em were just exploitation.

How did you land your "special guest appearance" in How to Make a Monster?

How to Make a Monster was Herman Cohen's picture, and at the time I was under contract to AIP and had done two or three films for them. Herman came to me and asked if I would do this role — a musical number — and just play myself. That was casting more or less against type at that point, because I had been playing delinquents and heavies. I was beginning to do a little singing — I had a deal with Dot Records — and I think maybe that triggered it

Previous page: A publicity photo taken during Ashley's days as a movie juvenile delinquent at AIP. The gal is Jean Moorhead.

a little bit. Also, I had been down to the wire and lost the title role to Michael Landon in *I Was a Teenage Werewolf*, and Herman had kept saying, "Don't worry, we're going to work together." So, *How to Make a Monster* was the result.

Did you take an interest in behind-the-scenes goings-on at AIP, with an eye toward getting into the production end of the business someday?
No, I really didn't; basically, I was just having fun doing it. The first time I really began looking behind the scenes was when I started making the films in the Philippines. Most of those pictures I *was* financially involved with; I normally came up with half of the money, and then Corman, or Larry Woolner at Dimension, or AIP came in with the other half. That was when I really began to get involved in the production end.

How did production values on Astor's Frankenstein's Daughter *compare to those at AIP?*
AIP was low-budget — one hundred grand made a movie — but at least they shot on sound stages, and the size of the crew was bigger. *Frankenstein's Daughter* was *really* rock bottom. But the people involved were very nice, especially Dick Cunha, the director. You know, it's strange — I don't have a lot of memories about that picture, except that Harold Lloyd, Jr., was in it, and Richard Dix's son Robert, and Sandra Knight, who was quite nice. But it *was* quick, a little more down-and-dirty than AIP.

Did you get to know any of the classic horror stars who made cameo appearances in your beach pictures?
No, nothing other than meeting them on the set. Boris Karloff *[Bikini Beach]* I had met several times because he had done pictures for Corman. Vincent Price *[Beach Party]*, the same. I was a big fan of Peter Lorre *[Muscle Beach Party]*, but I only met him when we did the show. They were all very nice and friendly, talked to the young people and offered them advice on how to do a scene.

What was it like to be in your early thirties, yet still playing a teenager on-screen?
Strange. At the time I was never really consciously thinking, "Okay, I'm gonna try to play twenty." Maybe in my mind I felt I *was* ten years younger than my actual age! It never really hit me until we were doing the beach pictures. We were doing, I think, the third one, and I was thirty years old.

We shot the beach pictures in the wintertime, so they'd be available for release in the summer. So it was always colder than hell. They'd slap body makeup on Frankie Avalon and me, 'cause it was winter and nobody had a tan. I remember we were doing a scene one day when it was *really* cold, and the director, Bill Asher, told me and Frankie to do the dialogue and then just walk right on down the beach and into the water. So we did the dialogue and headed for the water, waiting for Asher to yell "cut." Our backs were to the camera so we were walking and talking, and Frankie said, "Man, can you believe us? Two thirty-year-old guys out here in body makeup and red trunks, and Asher's waiting for us to walk in that water!" Asher didn't yell "cut," we kept getting closer and closer, right down to where that fifty-degree water was starting to lap at our toes. Frankie and I just shoved our surfboards into the sand, turned around to look at Asher, shook our heads and walked out of the shot.

How did The Eye Creatures *come about?*
There was a guy named Larry Buchanan that came up with a formula of taking some of the early movies that AIP had done, *Invasion of the Saucer-Men* in this instance, and remaking them, shooting them in 16mm, with essentially just one supposedly recognizable name. I went down and did *The Eye Creatures,* which probably ranks right up with some of the all-time worst horror films ever made. Steven Terrell had originally played the lead in *Saucer-Men,* and here I was doing it again. We shot at the ranch of Gordon McLendon, a very wealthy fellow who had a beautiful ranch called Cielo, just outside of Dallas. We shot the entire film right there on his ranch, and it was a great treat for me because I was his guest there and I had this incredible bungalow suite—it was like staying at a very opulent hotel and having room service whenever you wanted it. Everybody else in the film was local, all from Dallas little theater and Dallas stage. The picture was made for an extremely low price—I mean, we shot it in sixteen, and I think the cost was *less* than $50,000, including the answer print. The monster looked like something out of the Michelin Tire ad!

What kind of shooting schedule was involved?
It was two weeks. Buchanan was a nice guy, and it was a real "at ease" pace; I mean, we just kind of worked until we felt like, "Okay, that's enough," then we'd break. It was very small crew, and quite well organized—Buchanan had it together.

How did you begin your involvement in the Filipino horror films?
The first picture I did there, *Brides of Blood,* was for a company called Hemisphere. I was going through my first divorce when a casting director called me and said, "Listen, would you like to go to the Philippines and do this horror film?" I said, "Yeah, why not?" I wanted to get out of town anyway.
The original deal was for four weeks, I think. So I went over there and started doing the film. They ran into some financial problems in the course of

Now a highly successful TV producer, former actor John Ashley has supervised such small-screen series as *The Quest, The A-Team* and *Werewolf.*

making the movie. We got about halfway into the picture when all of a sudden my agent called me and said, "We didn't get your check for last week, so don't go to the set." I had gotten to know Eddie Romero, who was the producer/co-director on it, very well, and I liked the Filipino people a *lot*—it was like a second home to me. I explained it to Eddie and he said he didn't blame me. So basically I would sit around—we wouldn't shoot until my agent would call me and say, "Okay, I just got another week's pay, go ahead and work another week." Four weeks wound up to be like ten, eleven weeks.

I finished the picture, came back and was living in Oklahoma, running some motion picture theaters. I had really forgotten about *Brides of Blood;* I thought it would probably never get released. Some time later, a distributor friend of mine called me from Kansas City and said, "I've got a picture opening here in town that you did in the Philippines. Would you come up and make some appearances at the drive-in?" This guy was a friend of mine, so I said sure. We went out and did all that, then he said, "Have you ever seen the movie?" I hadn't. So we sat in his car after one of the autograph sessions and watched it. He said, "Jeez, what'd this movie cost?" I had no idea, but I told him it couldn't have been that much. *Brides of Blood* wound up doing some business; they had some kind of gimmick with plastic wedding rings and stuff like that. My distributor friend called me again and said, "Listen, if I can come up with a group of investors and make a deal with you, would you go back to the Philippines and do another one?" I said yeah; if the money was there and he could get it together, I'd be interested. So that's really how it started. We then did *Mad Doctor of Blood Island* and *Beast of Blood*, both for Hemisphere.

How many pictures did you eventually make there?

In the Philippines? I think I did about twelve or thirteen over there. They're a little confusing, because the original titles have since been changed for television.

What were the budgets on the last two Blood Island *pictures?*

Certainly not in excess of $120,000–$125,000. I remember the most expensive Filipino production I was involved in was *Savage Sisters* [1974], which cost $230,000–$250,000.

Did you have cooperation from the government on these pictures?

Yes, we always did. They were very good, particularly in the early days, because the scripts were so generic. Later on, when we started doing *Savage Sisters* and others which involved a military posture within the film, we had some minor problems there, but normally we had great cooperation. Several times when we were down there shooting, martial law was in effect and they had curfews. We were able to make arrangements with the government to allow us to work after hours.

But at this point, you still had no financial involvement?

Not until *The Beast of the Yellow Night*. The fellow who owned Hemisphere in New York was rather ill, and Eddie Romero just said to me, "Look, why don't *we* do these together? I'll furnish the below-the-line costs, you guys come up with the above-the-line." So I did. Corman had just started New World, and *Beast of the Yellow Night* was one of the first releases that they had out.

Did you enjoy playing the monster in Yellow Night?

It was a lot of fun to do. I used a double in a lot of the long shots, but

John Ashley takes on all comers in the Filipino-made *Mad Doctor of Blood Island*.

in the scenes where the beast was talking, obviously that was me. But I didn't make the transformation until near the end of the film, which was about a guy who made a deal with the devil for his soul. As he gets worse and worse, finally there's this transformation.

Beast of the Yellow Night *is remembered as being one of your better-written vehicles.*

I agree with you. It was a screenplay that Eddie Romero had written, and it certainly was the most cerebral, if you can call any of these pictures that.

Didn't Roger Corman visit you down in the Philippines while you were shooting Yellow Night?

Yeah, he called me and told me about this picture [*The Big Doll House*, 1971] that they were going to do in Puerto Rico. I told him, "You ought to come down and take a look at the Philippines. I mean, it's all right here"— 'cause the picture was set in a jungle, and in a women's prison. So he flew to the Philippines, took one look and asked me, "Would you stay around and exec-produce the show?" So two of my partners and I put up the above-the-line, Roger put up all the rest of it, and I stayed and supervised that one. Then I went ahead and did *Black Mama, White Mama* [1972] for AIP; then, back to Roger for *The Womanhunt* [1972]. That was originally a screenplay called *Women for Sale,* and it was very much in the *Big Doll House/Big Bird Cage* syndrome: white women being kidnapped and sold into the white slave trade.

Then *The Twilight People*. When Larry Woolner, who had been working for Corman, split, part of their split was, he got *The Twilight People*. He distributed it, and it did well.

Isn't The Twilight People *one of your personal favorites among the Filipino horrors?*
   I think so. I just remember it was a lot of fun to do, and there weren't a lot of problems on it. And we did it so quickly! We were sitting around one day at lunch, Larry Woolner and Corman and I, in an Italian restaurant up near Corman's old offices on Sunset. We had walked down from his office, and were having salad. One of us said, "Well, what can we do now?" And somebody said, "What about *The Island of Dr. Moreau?*" And, "We can't do that, but what about half-beast, half-human?" And we just sat over lunch and made the deal. We wrote the script and, like a month later, we went over and shot it. It went very smoothly. It came back and did real well, real quick.

Tell us a little about your dealings with Corman.
   The thing that's fun about Corman is, Roger's a tough deal-maker—a very fair deal-maker, but he's tough—but once you make your deal, he leaves you alone and doesn't bother you. He lets you go off and make your movie. And I think that's why so many people have started with him, because he does let you go off and do it your way.

Eddie Romero had directed Terror Is a Man, *a picture very similar to* Twilight People, *back in 1959.*
   Conceptually, it was Roger, Larry and I who said, "Let's do *Dr. Moreau*," but I do remember Eddie saying that he had directed a picture called *Terror Is a Man*, and that there were some similarities.

Probably only because he ripped off Dr. Moreau, *too.*
   Exactly. Everybody rips off somebody.

Was makeup a major expense on The Twilight People?
   No, as a matter of fact, it wasn't. There was a local makeup man in the Philippines named Tony Arteida, a very, very creative fellow. All that stuff he did right there for us, with molds and appliances. The guy that we hired to play the Ape Man, he had that Neanderthal look to begin with *[laughs]*! And, strangely, it was not time-consuming—I mean, we never seemed to be waiting for the makeup to be put on. And I remember when I first saw the film, I thought, jeez, it worked better than I thought it would when we were doing it.

What were your budgets on some of these later pictures?
   The Twilight People was like $150,000. We got up to around $200,000

on *Beyond Atlantis,* because we had a lot of underwater stuff. And then *Savage Sisters* was the biggest of the bunch.

Censorship problems in the Philippines made that one of the places where your films could not be shown without major cuts.
True, we did have some censorship problems in the latter stages. In the beginning, we didn't; it was pretty open. Later on, after the Philippine government began to crack down on the local films, they determined that our films were *imports* to their market and they could not set double standards.

Weren't you originally scheduled to direct Beyond Atlantis?
There was some talk about that, yeah, 'cause I really liked the script and I thought maybe I would direct it. Then the production end of it got so spread out that I felt that for me to attempt to produce, direct *and* appear in it would really be difficult. So I changed my mind.

Did a better-than-average cast help that picture at the box office?
Interestingly enough, *Beyond Atlantis* was *not* a success, because we attempted to break the mold. Our original concept was to find these people underwater, and for the most part they were going to be at least topless. We got into the script—which was really a rip-off of *The Treasure of the Sierra Madre* [1948]—and Larry Woolner all of a sudden said, "I think maybe we've got something here that's a little bigger than what we've been doing." And then we got Pat Wayne involved; one of the provisos of Pat doing it was that it had to be PG-rated. We had to make a decision: If we wanted Pat, who was very right for the role, then we couldn't go with an R rating. So we went ahead and got Pat, and George Nader, and did it as a PG. I still believe that, had we done it a little *harder,* it probably would have done better. At least we'd have had a picture that was a little more exploitable.

One of the things that trapped us, I think, was that underwater footage is very tough to get, but when you do get it, it's *gorgeous.* But watching it is like watching slow motion. You spend all this money and time, so you feel like, "I don't want to take it out of the picture." I think that slowed the film down a lot. We also had a lot of problems with getting apparatus that these people could wear that wouldn't fall apart underneath the water, and the eyes on the fish people were very hard to do on the budget that we had. It wound up slipping a little bit from the original concept, but we just decided, "Let's try it." It was a bad call. I think that's the only picture that I had money in that didn't make it.

A few years later, you wrapped up your Filipino production sideline.
The last thing I did in the Philippines was my involvement in *Apocalypse Now* [1979]; Coppola and his people used my Philippine company as a kind of base of operations, so that they could deal through me. While I was killing

some time waiting for that to start, I did a local Filipino film that has never been released over here. It is a *wild* film—we did some things in there that you can't *do* anymore. For example, I played a doctor—I always seem to wind up playing doctors!—and we had a scene in which we got a human body, did an examination and then literally took the body apart. We did it with an actual human corpse—we made a deal, arranged to get a dead body from one of the prisons, and exhumed it. It was very graphic, very gory. A local guy released the film in the Philippines, then went to Hong Kong to redub it and do some work on it. He ran short of money, I think, and never could put it together.

So what brought you back to the States permanently?

I had maintained a residence in the Philippines and I would be there three, four months a year, then back to Oklahoma where I had my theaters. The theater business changed radically, I needed more time to devote to the theater end of it, and so I just couldn't afford the luxury of being able to take three or four months off.

What is the key to your success in the exploitation field?

That's an interesting question—I really don't know. This is a terrible thing to admit, but maybe it's that I always *liked* those movies, and I never had any real reason to turn them down. I just enjoyed doing them.

*[Zsa Zsa Gabor] was very difficult all through the picture
[Queen of Outer Space]. The producer, Ben Schwalb,
went to the hospital with ulcers halfway through the picture,
I was left to cope with her alone, and she damn near gave me ulcers!
It always bothered me that here on this planet Venus,
she was the only one who spoke with a foreign accent.*

Edward Bernds

48   B Movie Makers

ONE OF THE MORE PROLIFIC WRITER/DIRECTORS of the 1940s and 1950s, Edward Bernds is best remembered for his work in comedy: two-reelers starring the Three Stooges, *Blondie* and *Bowery Boys* features and many other shorts and features starring prominent funnymen (and women) of the period. It is curious that such a filmmaker should also be fondly remembered by fans of horror and science fiction films. Bernds' first fantastic production, *World Without End*, was a well-done "end-of-the-world" melodrama that stands with some of the better sci-fi efforts of the mid-'50s. Bernds later reinforced his reputation in the genre by directing the effective—although seldom revived—*Space Master X-7*, and by writing and directing *Return of the Fly*, a straightforward *Fly* sequel preferred by some to the original.

Bernds was born in 1905 in Chicago, Illinois. While in his junior year in Lake View High School, he and several friends formed a small radio clique and obtained amateur licenses. In the early '20s there was a considerable prestige for amateur operators ("hams") to have commercial radio licenses, and Bernds was in a good position to get into broadcasting when he graduated in 1923, a year when radio stations began popping up all over Chicago. He found employment—at age twenty—as chief operator at Chicago's WENR. When talking pictures burst onto the scene in the late '20s, Bernds and broadcast operators like him relocated to Hollywood to work as sound technicians for the movies. After a brief stint at United Artists, Bernds quit and went to work for Columbia, where he worked as sound man on prestige pictures like *It Happened One Night* (1934), *Mr. Deeds Goes to Town* (1936), *Lost Horizon* (1937), *Mr. Smith Goes to Washington* (1939)—and on less-celebrated pictures like Boris Karloff's *The Black Room* (1935) and other B horror films. Bernds later graduated to directing two-reel shorts and then to features, and helmed his first science fiction film, *World Without End*, in 1955.

How did World Without End *come about?*

A producer at Allied Artists, Richard Heermance, invited me to write and direct a science fiction picture. Heermance's starting point on the project had been some stock film from a Monogram science fiction picture of a few years before, *Flight to Mars*. It's strange how some producers, at least at that time, got hooked on the idea of saving money by using stock film. This stock wasn't that great, just a few miniatures of a rocketship in flight, and a crash landing. You could duplicate those stock shots for a few thousand dollars; are you going to make a $400,000 picture on the basis of saving a few bucks? I'm grateful that it was the starting point and gave me an assignment that I made a little money on, but the logic of it escapes me.

I had no directive on story, that was *my* starting point: astronauts encountering a strange planet. It was awfully tough to do anything new; the name of drama is conflict, and when the only conflict is with monsters, it isn't entirely satisfying. I was reading a nonfiction paperback book about science for the layman by Arthur C. Clarke, and there I came across the Einstein theory

Previous page: Director Edward Bernds (right) mingles with players Eric Fleming, Zsa Zsa Gabor and Paul Birch on the set of *Queen of Outer Space*.

that if you move fast enough, time slows down, and if you approach the speed of light, time stands still. And it hit me instantly that the place for our astronauts to land was back on Earth, only far in the future. So help me, it may have been done many times since—certainly that was used in *Planet of the Apes,* and Rod Serling used it many times in his series *The Twilight Zone*—but it was utterly new to me at that time, and it opened the door to the whole thing. The entire picture took on sharpness and meaning. I was glad to get the assignment, the money was satisfactory, and although the budget and schedule were more "B" than "A," it was to be made in Technicolor CinemaScope—A-picture mounting for a B-budgeted picture.

Your script was reminiscent of H.G. Wells' The Time Machine—*later made into a movie starring, coincidentally,* World Without End's *Rod Taylor. Did you derive any inspiration from the Wells story?*

I had read Wells' *Time Machine,* but it never occurred to me that there were any similarities. Wells' *Time Machine* was purely a fantasy about a magical bicycle-like device that could transport one backward and forward in time. I wanted my picture to have an arguably scientific basis.

The estate of the late H.G. Wells took Allied Artists to court over similarities between his Time Machine *and* World Without End.

I didn't know anything about that. There's no resemblance at all between Wells' book and *World Without End.* The idea of time travel is certainly not copyrighted. If anybody could sue anybody, I could sue Rod Serling for *Planet of the Apes,* because they definitely used my ideas about space travel and time travel in making that picture.

What about the production end of World Without End?

Not enough time, not enough money—the eternal complaint of the director. Heermance wasn't the ideal producer—to my mind, Ben Schwalb, the man who produced most of my Allied Artists pictures, was. Ben and I worked as a team, and he wanted quality just as badly as I did. Heermance wasn't interfering or destructive, it's simply that he seemed to be more interested in cost than quality—which is kind of strange, because *World Without End* may have been one of his first producer credits, and you'd think that he'd want it to be very good. If it was, he could take the bows, and if it went over budget, he could always blame the director. That was standard Hollywood procedure. But I did need more time on the film.

What would you have done differently with more time or money?

There are two things I remember especially: first, the closing sequence, which we shot out at the historic Iverson's Ranch. The closing scenes of a picture are the ones that people walk out of the theater with, the ones they remember. Ben Schwalb agreed with me. But on *World Without End,* with

CinemaScope hurls you into the year 2508!

WORLD Without END

a much greater potential for the picture to be a big moneymaker, Heermance cut down on the set for the final scene and the time I had to shoot it. I had wanted to *show* the world being rebuilt: trenches dug, buildings started, workmen swarming over them. I wanted to take a lot of care with those closing scenes. But there was no consultation, no give and take, no weighing of cost versus quality—just cut the sets and extras down, shoot it in half a day.

The second thing was the special effects. I wanted the operation of the spaceship to be as authentic and exciting as it could possibly be. My script detailed an elaborate and impressive series of special effects. What I got was a man who contracted with Heermance to supply all the special effects in the spaceship at a rather low price. They were disappointing. I did persuade Heermance to give this special effects man a couple of days to prepare, and then they gave me a day to shoot inserts—close shots—of radar scopes, speed indicators, oscilloscopes and so on, without actors. A day like that costs just a few thousand dollars instead of the cost of a full production, which might be ten times as much. The contractor wasn't even ready *then*. I did the best I could with what he did provide.

The scenes of the spacemen battling the mutates were well mounted and exciting.

We did get a pretty good crowd there; those were all stuntmen and they all took falls, and that cost money even in those days. We did have pretty good production there. It was strange—on some things Heermance splurged, and other things he clamped down on. He was not consistent.

Was it time-consuming having to make up all those mutates?

It required three or four makeup people to take care of those guys, but of course these stuntmen were cooperative. They'd help themselves—put the masks on, smeared the dark makeup on their bodies and so on.

You know, I invented the name "mutates" for *World Without End*. Now, of course, the accepted term is *mutants,* and it's kind of embarrassing to find myself out of step with accepted usage. I made up the word, and perhaps I made it up wrong. But *is* it wrong? True, there are supplicants, mendicants and applicants; but there are also advocates, associates and delegates. But I guess I'm outnumbered.

What about the giant spiders, which you later used in Queen of Outer Space *and* Valley of the Dragons?

Their legs were supposed to be operated by selsyn motors. The mandibles—the jaws of the big spiders—were spring-loaded, and snapped shut by magnets. The jaws worked all right, but the motor-driven legs ... sometimes

Opposite: Bernds' first and best science fiction film was Allied Artists' *World Without End* with Hugh Marlowe and Nancy Gates.

Edward Bernds (right) confers with executive producer Walter Mirisch during the production of *World Without End* (1956). Mirisch rose from humble beginnings at Monogram and Allied Artists, and later produced such films as *The Magnificent Seven, West Side Story* and *In the Heat of the Night*.

worked, sometimes didn't. The actors had to provide most of the struggle; they put most of the energy into the fights with the spiders. But they were good for a tremendous scream. What a gratifying thing that is, when you're watching one of your own "scare" pictures in a theater and you get a spontaneous scream from the audience. That is *great*.

My dialogue director was Sam Peckinpah, who later became a big-shot director noted as a kind of a stormy petrel. I found that he was a very mild, self-effacing kind of a guy when he worked with me. Sam worked on several of my pictures as dialogue director, and I helped him get what I think was his first job as a director. Years later, when I was at Columbia, I think in connection with *The Three Stooges Meet Hercules,* I got in an elevator with him; he had grown a beard, but I recognized him, and I said, "Hello, Sam." And he looked at me, didn't say a word, and walked out. I don't know what the hell was eating him. He had developed a reputation as an intransigent "angry young man" director. He could not possibly have *not* recognized me, so it kind of amused me—if he wanted to be a Hollywood character, well, that was all right with me.

Were you happy with your World Without End *cast?*

I wanted Sterling Hayden for the lead. The producer thought Hugh Marlowe was a bargain, and Hayden would have cost about four times as much. Hayden at that time was a splendid figure of a man and to my mind he gave an aura of strength, intelligence, integrity. I think he would have been great in it. I also preferred Frank Lovejoy for the part of Borden. He wasn't a star or a name actor, but I considered him a fine performer who'd provide the strength and believability the part demanded. But Lovejoy's agent demanded four times as much as we paid Hugh Marlowe—a bargain that I feel hurt the picture.

Why were you so disappointed in Marlowe's work?

Heermance and his boss Walter Mirisch thought Marlowe was a bargain because he had been in a very, very fine picture for Joe Mankiewicz, *All About Eve* [1950]. I had seen *All About Eve,* too, and I thought Marlowe's performance in it was very good, but there's a hell of a lot of difference between playing a Broadway writer in a picture where you can take infinite pains and time to get a performance, and what we had to do, where he had to play a virile, gutsy spaceship commander. I was disappointed in him, for a great many things. He was not prepared, he didn't know his lines, and that's unforgivable. He was lazy. We spent a lot of time out on location—hot, dusty, disagreeable old Iverson's Ranch—and, as you remember the picture, when they came down from the spaceship, they were loaded down with packs and weapons and things like that. Between takes Marlowe would shuck the pack, put his weapon down, find shade somewhere. Eventually we'd have to go send for him, find him. Then it took time to get the pack on again. This was unpardonable—the minutes that you lose are precious. Then when he'd get on the set he frequently didn't know his lines, he'd blow scenes. And most of all he didn't generate the strength that I wanted. The first time he opened his mouth, my heart sank. Believe it or not, some of that rankles to this day because, after all, the film exists to this day.

When an actor behaves like that, he tends to infect others. Chris Dark was like a spoiled kid: If Hugh Marlowe could goof off and sit in the shade and forget where he put his pack so the prop man had to find it, why, he tended to do the same thing. Rod Taylor was all right, he was very new to the business and anxious to please. Nelson Leigh was an old pro who, despite the discomfort, did his work, knew his lines, was ready when we needed him even on that hot, uncomfortable set.

How did World Without End *do at the box office?*

World Without End made a lot of money for Allied Artists, it got good reviews, and I'm grateful that discerning critics like it—but I still have the feeling it could have been better. I just needed more time—I *know* more time would have resulted in a better picture. Would it have grossed more? I don't know. Heermance's attitude was that a picture of this kind would gross a certain

amount and that any extra production cost would cut into profits. He may have been right, I don't know, but to this day I wish I had made *World Without End* with a producer like Ben Schwalb, who always wanted a picture to be as good as he and I could possibly make it.

How did you become involved on Queen of Outer Space?

As you probably know, [Hollywood producer] Walter Wanger thought that his wife, Joan Bennett, might be having an affair with her agent, so he shot the agent in the crotch—aiming at the seat of the difficulties, so to speak. Hollywood agents being what they are, a lot of people probably thought that he should get a medal, but instead he was sent to jail. I guess the man wasn't wounded too badly, and Wanger was out in a year or so. He needed a job, but the studios where he had been such a big man didn't want to give him a break. The president of Allied Artists finally did hire him, though, and Walter Wanger came to AA as a producer. He brought with him a ten-page outline by Ben Hecht called *Queen of the Universe*. I don't know how Ben Schwalb came to produce the picture instead of Wanger, but that's what happened. Charles Beaumont wrote the screenplay. I guess I had been working somewhere else and I came to the picture after the script was written. Ben and I agreed that it needed work—that, as a straight science fiction melodrama, it wasn't very good. By the way, I read the screenplay *before* I read Ben Hecht's original.

What kind of story was it that Ben Hecht wrote?

Hecht's original wasn't a motion picture story at all. It was just a satirical look at a planet ruled ineptly by women. There wasn't anything there for Charlie Beaumont to use except the idea of a planet ruled by women, so the screenplay was pretty much an original. But Ben Schwalb decided that it would have a better chance if we lightened it up—spoofed it—and we did. My friend Elwood Ullman and I did some rewriting—I wish we had done more. I think the light parts of it worked, but the melodramatic parts were ... a little heavy for my taste.

There may be a reason that Charlie Beaumont's version was, in my opinion, and in Elwood's, and in Ben Schwalb's, dead serious and dead dull. I met Charlie a couple of times just after he finished the script, and he looked terribly unwell. He was about twenty-eight years old when he wrote *Queen of Outer Space,* and at the age of twenty-eight he should have been in the absolute prime of life. Charlie died, much too young, in 1967.

How did you enjoy working with your stars Laurie Mitchell, Eric Fleming and Zsa Zsa Gabor?

Opposite: A Ben Hecht outline entitled *Queen of the Universe* furnished the basis for Bernds' *Queen of Outer Space* with Zsa Zsa Gabor. Allied Artists dispensed with Hecht's title because they felt it denoted a beauty pageant.

Dave Willock and Eric Fleming struggle to wrest a ray-gun away from burn-faced *Queen of Outer Space* Laurie Mitchell. (Photo courtesy Steve Jochsberger.)

Ben Schwalb had cast Laurie Mitchell in some of his previous films and liked her work. I interviewed her, I liked the way she read the part, I agreed to cast her and I wasn't disappointed. She did pretty well in what was pretty much of a thankless role as Queen Yllana. Eric Fleming was the male lead opposite Zsa Zsa Gabor—I believe it was one of his first movie roles—and he was a model of professionalism: always prepared, dialogue solidly memorized, all business despite Zsa Zsa's flightiness. Later, when he was the lead in the TV series *Rawhide*, I learned that he had become arrogant, hard-to-handle— undirectable, to quote Gene Fowler, Jr., who had directed a couple of *Rawhide* episodes. That's typical of actors who work in successful TV series.

You mentioned Zsa Zsa's flightiness...?

She's a beautiful woman, no doubt about that, but she was not very young even in 1958. We had some of the most beautiful women we could find, any number of beauty queens, and I think the competition was a little steep for her. She was not thoroughly professional, she didn't have her lines well prepared, she had a kind of a giddy attitude toward things.

We cast members of Queen Yllana's "posse" for size and good looks. We wanted beautiful Amazons. One that I remember very well was Tania Velia— Miss Belgium—who didn't have a particularly pretty face, but who had one of the most spectacular figures known to man. As they say in New York City, "What a built!" And, as I said, Zsa Zsa didn't exactly like the competition. I can tell you that when Tania Velia came into view, no male, cast or crew, had eyes for anything but Tania and her gorgeous superstructure.

Prior to production, I was seeing Zsa Zsa through wardrobe at Western Costume Company, and she began to make demands: Her clothes had to be made for her, she would not wear stuff from stock and so on. While she was trying something on or discussing something, I got to a phone and told Ben Schwalb that she was threatening to quit the picture if we didn't do everything she wanted. I told Ben, "This is our chance to dump her. If she wants to walk, let her walk." Ben said, "No, we need a star—without a star we haven't got a picture. Look, stars are that way—humor her." Well, she was very difficult all through the picture. Ben went to the hospital with ulcers halfway through the picture, I was left to cope with her alone, and she damn near gave *me* ulcers! It always bothered me that here on this planet Venus, she was the only one who spoke with a foreign accent.

I don't claim by any means that *Queen of Outer Space* is a good picture. Trying to paste satirical material onto a creaky melodramatic structure just didn't work very well. If the picture's shown on TV I won't watch it, because Zsa Zsa Gabor still gives me a swift pain. And, secondly, the film was shot in CinemaScope, and TV murders the composition. The better I staged and composed the shots, the worse the TV proportions butcher them. I was also disappointed with that big set at the end. Although the art director, Dave Milton, did the best he could with a whole stage, what we needed was a set like one that they would have in a James Bond picture. But we didn't have James Bond money!

What's the story on Space Master X-7?

Space Master X-7 was made for Robert L. Lippert's Regal Films, I think on a budget of about $90,000 which was low even then. Twentieth Century–Fox financed and released Regal Films but had nothing to do with the films until Lippert turned them over as a finished product. To my knowledge, Fox didn't even have veto power over cast, and I don't think they even looked at the final cut of the pictures!

Really!

The Twentieth Century–Fox executives, even the lower-echelon ones, never looked at the final cuts. There may have been several reasons for that; maybe even the lower echelon producers were too snobbish to get involved with Lippert's low-budget process, or perhaps they felt they were not equal to making decisions at that level of filmmaking. But most likely Bob Lippert—a rough, tough customer—just didn't want any kibbitzing on his films, and his autonomy may have been part of his deal. If there were any such thing as reincarnation, that man would have been a pirate in an early incarnation.

My producer, Bernard Glasser, bought the script for *Space Master*. It was written by my old friend Dan Mainwaring, in collaboration with a man named

George Worthing Yates. Their title for it was *Doomsday* something-or-other. They had written it on "spec" — that is, they had not done it on assignment, but to be sold on the open market. It hadn't been sold, and my guess is that Glasser didn't pay much for it. He *couldn't* have, with only $90,000 to make the whole picture! I guess I was working cheaply, too. I did an extensive rewrite job — no extra money for that, just my fee as a director. Mainwaring and Yates had written it without regard for expense, they wrote it as a big-budget production. I had to make it fit our budget and a shorter running time.

Again, as with Queen of Outer Space, *you didn't take any screen credit for working on the script.*

There were and still are credit-grabbers in the business who seize every opportunity to take credit that they may or may not deserve. I always prided myself on *not* grabbing credits — I considered it part of my job to make the script work the way I wanted it to. Strangely enough, Dan Mainwaring, who had been a good friend of mine, was kind of touchy about the whole thing — I think he thought that *he* should have rewritten it. But he was probably at least a $750-a-week writer, which we definitely couldn't afford. Dan was kind of a neurotic person, and he was furious. I guess he was realistic enough to know there wasn't enough money for him, but just the idea that anybody would touch his *gem*...!

What kind of revisions did you make?

I don't remember many details — it was a long time ago. I think I eliminated a train sequence; perhaps I substituted a plane for it. I recall using a four-engine propellor plane, probably a DC6, at Long Beach Airport. I was working under terrific pressure, making production decisions about casting, wardrobe, sets, special effects — our assistant director was trying to make up a schedule and a budget without a script to work from! I had to give him much of the information he needed verbally.

Was Space Master's *documentary style your idea, or was it spelled out that way in the screenplay?*

I think the script was mostly my creation — that is, the style, if any, and the viewpoint were mine. We couldn't afford to be anything *but* documentary — we were all over L.A.! *Space Master* was a prime example of what could be done with very little money.

Despite the low budget and the pressure you spoke of, Space Master *turned out quite well.*

Space Master was an example of independent moviemaking at its best. At Lippert, you had freedom to do it as you saw it. True, you only had $90,000 to spend *[laughs]*, but Glasser and I could do anything we pleased with it! All we had to do was bring back a good product for the ninety G's. *Space Master* was made with near hundred-percent efficiency and near hundred-percent freedom. Bob Lippert and his story editor, Harry Spalding, looked at the rushes, made occasional suggestions, but in the main Glasser and I made the picture our way, Glasser attending mostly to money matters and I mainly to the creative aspects. Of course, these functions overlapped at $90,000 — sometimes creativity had to make concessions to the hard economic facts of life, and sometimes creativity won out over dollars and cents. But Glasser and I were a pretty good team: He knew that if we were to get more assignments, our pictures had to be as good as they could possibly be on a quickie budget, and he contrived to squeeze every bit of production value possible out of every dollar. This squeeze was assisted to quite an extent by our hiring of Norman Maurer as a production assistant. His presence on the picture requires some explanation: Maurer was the son-in-law of Moe Howard of the Three Stooges.

And Moe Howard has a small part in Space Master.

Right. Moe did that part not because he needed the money, but because he loved acting — he really did. The thing he missed most about the Three Stooges two-reelers being terminated at Columbia was that he couldn't work any more. We'd been friends ever since I began directing the Stooges, so I was glad to cast him in the part of the cab driver. I had met his son-in-law, Norman Maurer, and knew him as a professional artist of considerable talent. Moe told us that Norman wanted to get a foothold in the production end of motion pictures and asked us to take him on as a production assistant. An artist can be a great asset to a motion picture, so we were glad to do it. Norman was a hard worker and made a big contribution to *Space Master X-7;* he gave the special effects men sketches of the Blood Rust, sketches that we could agree on before any money was spent on experimental presentations. Later, thanks to the start that *Space Master* gave him, he was associate producer on *The Angry Red Planet,* and was the producer of *The Three Stooges Meet Hercules, The Three Stooges in Orbit* and *The Mad Room.*

I guess that's about all for *Space Master* except that, for a picture made so many years ago, the script seems to be reasonably accurate, scientifically. In writing science fiction scripts I always tried to be true to the scientific facts and procedures as I knew them at the time. Another reaction that I had when I reread it was, how in the world did we ever do this in eight days?

Was Kurt Neumann, director of the original The Fly, *assigned to direct* Return of the Fly *before his untimely death?*

I don't think so. He died in 1958 and we made *Return of the Fly* in 1959. Kurt was only about fifty years old when he died, an untimely death, as you said. I made two other pictures for Robert Lippert in 1958, and I spent a good part of the year with Lippert's organization. I was working there when Kurt died, and attended his funeral. I think I would have known if I was, in effect, replacing him — I just don't think so.

Did you screen the original Fly *in preparing* Return of the Fly?

Although I know I've seen *The Fly,* I honestly don't recall whether I screened it for that purpose. The way I wrote *Return of the Fly* originally, we were going to use some of the film from *The Fly* as a lead-in, but for some reason we weren't permitted to do that.

Vincent Price liked my script for *Return of the Fly*—he wouldn't sign to do the film until he read a script, so as soon as I had a first draft I sent it to him. Then, after he'd read it, I visited him in his *palatial* home—that's a fancy word, but believe me, his place *was* palatial—and he said he liked the script. We discussed it at considerable length, he said he'd sign and he did. Some time later a problem came up: What Vincent read was a first draft, and like many first drafts it was a little overlong, and some cuts were made to trim it down and some changes made to bring about budget economies. Vincent liked some of the scenes we had cut, and he objected. If I recall correctly, they were mostly scenes with Danielle De Metz—scenes of warmth and charm, but, when you're pressed for footage, not truly essential to the progression of the story. But I conferred with Vincent from time to time, and I made changes that satisfied him.

What was Price like to work with?

A delight, no less. Thoroughly professional, always prepared, giving his best to every scene. His wasn't even the biggest part in *Return of the Fly,* but his star status and the strength he brought to his performance lifted it out of the B category it might have fallen into. The whole cast was good to work with—Brett Halsey was excellent, as always. I guess the number of times Brett and I worked together attests to the fact that I liked his work. David Frankham, who played the villainous Alan, was new to me, but he was everything I wanted as the charming, plausible, good-looking young Englishman who turns out to be a despicable double-crosser and killer. I wanted the contrast between the charming, pleasant Alan and the killer Alan to be a startling one, and David was everything I hoped for when I wrote his scenes. Danielle De Metz was very young, very pretty; practically no experience, but her youth and beauty were a plus. Maybe the fact that she wasn't an experienced actress made her performance seem more innocent and more real. I liked her looks and her acting, and I liked *her.* That's why I later cast her in *Valley of the Dragons.* I saw her just recently on TV in a British-made Richard Burton movie, *Raid on Rommel* [1971]—I hardly recognized her.

I've still got a copy of the script I used to shoot *Return of the Fly,* and glancing at it reminds me that we tried to cast Herbert Marshall to repeat his role as Inspector Charas from the original. I *must* have written with Marshall in mind because the role in my script is referred to as Charas throughout—but in the dialogue the character played by John Sutton was named Inspector Beacham. I'm not sure why we didn't get Marshall—John Sutton was very good but Marshall would have added stature to the part, and another link to the first

Fly would have been a definite plus. I was given to understand that Marshall was not well enough to take the part, but he made a half a dozen more pictures before his death in 1966, so I suspect that maybe his price was a factor in not hiring him. I wasn't told that; I'd have fought to have him, even if we had to strain the budget, if I'd known it was a matter of money.

What do you remember about the stuntman that played the Fly, Ed Wolff?

He was a circus giant, and he had very low endurance. With that head on and that heavy costume, we had to be very careful with him — we were afraid he'd have a heart attack and die! When we required him to run or anything, we'd have to give him several minutes to rest up. Like many giants, he was very weak.

Did Robert Lippert have any creative input at all on these Regal Films?

No. Our dealings were with the story editor, Harry Spalding, who was an excellent man to work with. A lot of story editors try to prove they're smarter than the people they're dealing with, but Harry was anxious to cooperate, and his suggestions were generally helpful. I was told that Lippert never read a script, that he depended on Harry to read the scripts and then tell him what they were about.

Wasn't Return of the Fly *shot on the Twentieth Century–Fox lot?*

Yes. We who worked for Robert Lippert were kind of "second-class citizens" as far as Fox was concerned — pariahs, so to speak. Fox didn't want us on the deluxe Westwood lot, but when the time came to do *Return of the Fly* they wanted us there. I believe this was a tough period for Twentieth and they wanted us to absorb some of their overhead. I'm sure Lippert made some kind of a deal where we weren't stuck with the full Twentieth Century–Fox overhead — he probably got some kind of concession. *Return of the Fly* was made at the Fox Westwood lot, with Fox personnel all the way through, even a cameraman. Fox just simply couldn't do things in any way except top-notch, and so our sets for *Return of the Fly* were as good as an A picture's would be.

It seems to me the Twentieth Century lot was a rather dismal place when we shot *Return of the Fly* there. Not much production, and many of the crew worried about their jobs. Buddy Adler was the ostensible boss — I knew him from Columbia, and as a matter of fact I directed a couple of second units for him there — and I considered him an all-American no-talent. In shooting second units I simply could not get a decision from him. He was so afraid of Harry Cohn that he was afraid if he made a decision and something went wrong, that Harry Cohn would rip his hide off — which Cohn was quite capable of doing.

The Fly *being the big moneymaker that it was, why did Twentieth Century–Fox entrust the sequel to Lippert's organization?*

Why we got *Return of the Fly* I don't know; maybe Fox thought that it was going to be a slough-off, just something to cash in on the popularity of the first one. But I also think it was kind of a bad time for Fox and they thought that they could capitalize on us, at a reasonable cost, and get a reasonable product. I think they *did*—the sequel, in spite of being in black-and-white, made them a lot of money.

Did you ever see the second Fly *sequel,* The Curse of the Fly?
I thought it was very bad. Everything about it was bad—it was so dull that I found it hard to stay with. It went nowhere—there was no storyline established—and I can't for the life of me see how Harry Spalding could have written it. Harry was so perceptive as a story editor, I can't see how he couldn't be perceptive about his own work.

Did you enjoy working in the science fiction genre?
Oh, sure. I think I was pretty well qualified—in radio from the days of crystal detectors; I was the chief engineer of a radio station in Chicago at the age of twenty; sound technician from the end of the silent era in 1928 until 1944. I believe that what the science fiction writer needs most is a sense of story and enough science to make the story work. Of course a critic might well ask, "How scientific is the basis for *Valley of the Dragons?*" The answer is, of course, that the basis of *Valley of the Dragons* is utterly unscientific and—*ridiculous* is probably not too strong a word for that. Science really takes a beating in that picture *[laughs]!* But it entertains people, and still makes money for Columbia.

Valley of the Dragons *uses so much stock footage from* One Million B.C. *that I assume it was the available stock which shaped your screenplay.*
Yes, *Valley of the Dragons* was built around the *One Million B.C.* stock footage. The story is this: Producers Al Zimbalist and Byron Roberts had formed a partnership to make an independent picture, preferably for a major studio. I knew Al Zimbalist, I was on the Allied Artists lot when he produced and Don Siegel directed *Baby Face Nelson* [1957], a highly successful low-budget picture. Byron Roberts had served as a production manager on some of my Lippert pictures, so I knew them both. Al Zimbalist's son Donald was a college student at that time, on vacation in England. He found an obscure book stall in London and picked up an old copy, possibly a first edition, of a Jules Verne book called *Hector Servadac, Or, Career of a Comet.* It was never published in the United States, probably because it was violently, *viciously* anti-Semitic. I'd never heard that about Jules Verne, so this was shocking; I suppose that's the kind of thing that prevailed in the France of his day. Well, Donald Zimbalist bought the book and Al, who was a born promoter, had two things to work with: First, the Jules Verne name meant box-office at that time, the title was unused, unknown, and the work was in the public domain.

Second, Al had an option to use any or all of the *One Million B.C.* film. Al and Byron needed somebody to put the two elements together to make a package, to present to a studio. So you're absolutely right, the stock did shape the story.

If all Donald Zimbalist did was bring home a book, why does he get story credit on Valley of the Dragons?

His dad asked for it. Al wanted Donald to have a screen credit, he pleaded with me to let Donald have story credit, and he finally talked me into it. Donald had nothing to do with it except finding the book. I was always a chump for a request like that, I guess. The thing I didn't anticipate was that the residuals went to him. I think of Donald Zimbalist every time I get a residual check on *Valley of the Dragons*. That film has tremendous vitality on TV—I get checks that *surprise* me. I also get residuals on the Elvis Presley picture *Tickle Me* [1965] that Elwood Ullman and I wrote, and it seems to me that *Valley of the Dragons* makes me more money in residuals than *Tickle Me* does! But every time I get a residual check, say for a hundred dollars, it kind of gripes me to know that Donald Zimbalist, wherever he is, is getting twenty-five. I may have got, through the years, a couple thousand dollars in residuals, and I guess Donald's got around five hundred. Well, maybe he needs it...!

Anyway, I used the Jules Verne premise of the comet scooping up the men and taking them into outer space—a pretty wild premise, but it worked all right for us. The story was then shaped around the stock stuff. I wrote a ten-page outline, and Al Zimbalist took it to Columbia in New York—to *New York,* not to Columbia in Hollywood—sold the deal and signed a contract to make the picture as an independent production. The Columbia executives here in Hollywood were not pleased at all: Al had gone over their heads to make the deal, and their noses were somewhat out of joint. I think they'd have been glad to see us fall on our faces, figuratively speaking. To get the deal, Al had agreed to a ridiculously low budget—I believe it was $125,000—and agreed that any over-budget sum would come out of his fee and Byron Roberts' fee as producer and associate producer, respectively. They couldn't touch my money for writing and directing because the Writers Guild and Directors Guild contracts with the studios wouldn't permit that. I couldn't work as "spec," as it were; I *had* to be paid.

You made Space Master X-7 *for $35,000 less than that.*

$125,000 under major studio conditions was, as I said, ridiculously low. That much money at Columbia wouldn't buy as much production as $90,000 did under the Lippert-type independent operation. We had all those expensive, inefficient departments to pay for. The bigger the studio, the bigger the overhead. Columbia was by no means the biggest studio, but it was big enough to really make the overhead rough. Al had made one smart move: He had bargained with New York to limit the charge for studio overhead. I never knew just what that limit was, but it was a life-saver. The Columbia executives expected us to go over budget, but we fooled 'em. The big lucky break we had was that we were able to use a half-million dollar mountainside set standing at Columbia that had been built for *The Devil at Four O'Clock* [1961]. That meant we didn't have to go a single day out on location; we shot all of our exteriors on this magnificent half-million dollar set. It was a tremendous money-saver. The cast was good, we had a reasonably fast cameraman, and we did the impossible: We brought the picture in on budget, Al and Byron didn't get pried away from any of their fees, and I had the satisfaction of thwarting the Columbia brass who were waiting for us to go over budget.

Among your five sci-fi films, which is your favorite?

World Without End. I had high hopes for it, and I took great pains in writing it. Of course there are disappointments in *World Without End;* I've already told you of most of them. It occurs to me that some of it may sound like the plaintive wail of a chronic complainer. It's true as I said that the everlasting complaint of the director, at almost every level, is, "not enough time, not enough money." But I directed forty-odd films and I was up against that kind of pressure on most of them; I coped as best I could and I don't think I complained unduly. Only on *World Without End* did I feel so strongly that with a little more time, a little more money and most of all with a little more support and belief in the project on the part of Dick Heermance, we could have had a better picture.

If I were active as a director today, I would revel and delight in the chance to use the great special effects available to the director of today. What a lift really great special effects might have given to *World Without End*—as a matter of fact, they would have helped most of the science fiction pictures I did. Oh, but why dream? *All* of my sci-fi films, even *World Without End* and *Return of the Fly,* were comparatively low-budget productions. The $90,000 it cost to make all of *Space Master X-7*—*all* of it—wouldn't buy a four-minute sequence of *Star Wars* or *Raiders of the Lost Ark.* And here's a sobering thought—sobering to me, anyway: unless I could crack that A-picture barrier now—*today*—I wouldn't have access to those great special effects, would I? And I didn't crack that barrier when I was active, so what the hell, there's no use crying over spilled milk, bygone years, bygone opportunities and films that might have been better.

*[Roger Corman] gave me a lot of freedom,
and also a chance to play parts that Universal
would never have given me. Oddball, wacko parts,
like the very disturbed girl in* Sorority Girl
*and things like that. I had a chance to do
moments and scenes that I didn't get before.*

Susan Cabot

THE LATE SUSAN CABOT was born in Boston and raised in a series of eight foster homes. She attended high school in Manhattan, where she took an interest in dramatics and joined the school dramatic club. Later, while trying to decide between a career in music or art, she illustrated children's books during the day and sang at Manhattan's Village Barn at night. It was at this same time that she made her film debut as an extra in Fox's New York–made *Kiss of Death* (1947) and worked in New York–based television. Max Arnow, a casting director for Columbia Pictures, spotted Cabot at the Village Barn, and a co-starring role in Columbia's B-level South Seas drama *On the Isle of Samoa* (1950) resulted. While in Hollywood, Cabot was also signed for the role of an Indian maiden in Universal's *Tomahawk* (1951) with Van Heflin. Studio executives viewing *Tomahawk* dailies were impressed with her screen possibilities and signed her to an exclusive contract.

At Universal Cabot co-starred in a series of films opposite leading men like John Lund *(The Battle at Apache Pass)*, Tony Curtis *(Son of Ali Baba)* and Audie Murphy *(The Duel at Silver Creek, Gunsmoke, Ride Clear of Diablo)*. Inevitably she became fed up with the succession of Western and Arabian Nights roles, asked for a release from her Universal pact, and accepted an offer from Harold Robbins to star in his play *A Stone for Danny Fisher* in New York. Taking advantage of being in New York again, she resumed her musical studies and entered acting classes with Sanford Meisner at the Neighborhood Playhouse. Roger Corman lured her back to Hollywood for the lead in the melodramatic rock-and-roller *Carnival Rock* (1957), and she stayed on to star in five more films for the enterprising young producer-director. Cabot's three fantasy films — *War of the Satellites, The Wasp Woman* and the cumbersomely titled *The Saga of the Viking Women and Their Voyage to the Waters of the Great Sea Serpent* — were made by Corman at this time.

After a highly publicized 1959 fling with Jordan's King Hussein, Cabot divided her time between TV work and roles in stage plays and musicals. During the last three years of her life she raised $500,000 for the American Film Institute's educational, training and preservation programs. Susan Cabot died on December 10, 1986, at age fifty-nine.

How did working in these Roger Corman films compare to working at Universal?

Totally *mad*. It was like a European movie — I mean, we'd have some sort of a script, but there was a lot of, "Who's going to say what?" and "How 'bout I do this?" — plenty of ad-libbing and improvising. But Roger was really great in a way; he was very loose. If something didn't work out, he changed it *[snap of the fingers]*, right away. He gave me a lot of freedom, and also a chance to play parts that Universal would never have given me. Oddball, wacko parts, like the very disturbed girl in *Sorority Girl* [1957] and things like that. I had a chance to do moments and scenes that I didn't get before.

Although Roger was — I suppose, still *is* — some kind of maverick, he's very

Previous page: During her Universal-International heyday, Susan Cabot played co-starring roles in Westerns like *The Duel at Silver Creek, Ride Clear of Diablo* and *Gunsmoke* (pictured).

bright and fast-thinking. He treated a lot of us shabbily in ways, and I'm sure we were asked to do things above and beyond what a major studio might have asked. But we all wanted the pictures to work, so we just pressed on.

How did you approach the role of the evil high priestess in Saga of the Viking Women?

I felt she was a misfit in that society; she had powers and a higher intuition, and a psychic sense of direction that the others couldn't pick up but she did. I especially liked the scene where I pleaded for the rain, and the rain came — I really tried to make that like a prayer. That kind of worked.

Did you enjoy playing villainous roles in Saga, Sorority Girl *and* Machine-Gun Kelly [1958]?

I loved it from the standpoint of their being a challenge, but it was very hard for me to play an unfeeling character — to do or say something cruel to another person, not feeling it in my bones or in my heart, and know that that other person is suffering. I've been victimized by people like that, and it hurts.

Any special recollections about Saga?

I remember the scene where the Viking women set out to sea in search of their men. There were, I believe, eleven girls in a Viking-type ship, and we were pulled out to sea, tugged by a rope attached to another boat. And the man who was towing us fell asleep! We started screaming at him, but the sound of the ocean drowned us out. Before we knew it, the bottom of our boat started to fill up with water, and we had nothing to bail it out with! I had boots on — I pulled them off and used them to get some of the water out — but all the other girls had sandals. We looked back to the shore, but the crew had already become minutely small in the distance.

We spotted two surfers not too far off, and Abby Dalton and I started screaming and waving our arms wildly. No response. Meanwhile, we had lost sight of the crew — we had sailed completely out of the cove and around, in front of a mountain.

How many of the girls knew how to swim?

Two — Abby Dalton and me! The surfers finally heard us and came over. They took a couple of girls and headed toward shore, and Abby and I took Betsy Jones-Moreland. By the time we finally got to land — the base of a mountain jutting out into the ocean — the tide was beginning to rise, fast, and the tiny strip of sand that was left began disappearing under the water. We couldn't just sit there, waiting for a miracle; we had to start climbing up the face of the cliff. And this was a high, hard climb — I mean, once you were halfway, and you were tired, you couldn't go back down again, you had to keep going up. It was very scary.

When we finally got to the top, we heard the sound of buses approaching, people running, trying to find us. I think I just yelled my head off at Roger—I just *blasted* away—because Roger had a habit of doing things like that. Tiny little things—like the time Abby and I almost went over a cliff on horses! They didn't show this in the film: The bunch of us girls had to ride through a mountain cave on horses, heading for an opening in the back. Roger was on an adjoining mountain filming the cave opening. *Nobody* told us there was a drop. Abby and I rode to the edge and stopped—but all the other girls were coming up on us, pushing in together! Abby and I had to try and hold everybody back, otherwise we'd have all gone over.

How about the scene where you're killed by the hunting dogs?

In order to make the two Great Danes run after me, the trainer wanted me to carry chopped liver in both hands—which is really yucky—to the spot where they were going to kill me. We rehearsed it a few times, but when the cameras were rolling the dogs wouldn't jump on me—they kept licking my face! I'm an animal lover, and I guess they knew it *[laughs]*! I made believe I was struggling, but it didn't work because the dogs didn't look the least bit ravenous, they looked like they were smiling. Finally I had to suggest to the crew, "Look, why don't you have two guys *throw* the dogs up at me?" So that's what we did—two guys came forward from the crew, each one took a dog and they threw them at me. I caught the paws of one dog, and started wrestling and screaming—but the dogs were still *[pausing to pant and lick at the air]* acting like puppies, having a ball! That was the only way we could get the scene on film.

When you finally got to see the finished film, what did you think of the special effects?

What special effects? The *sea serpent?* Oh, really *[laughs]*! Although, when we were in the boat, in front of the process screen, and that monster came up behind us, there *was* a start—we *were* scared for a moment. We were in the boat, on a sound stage, and people were shaking it, throwing water at us, blowing the wind fans. And when the monster came up, all of us shrieked—it was startling, even though it was on a flat piece of paper. Even though it might be a lousy film, or not well directed, or whatever the faults are—when you're involved in a situation and in a character, and in the period of the piece, that *can* happen.

How did you enjoy working with the Corman stock company?

I enjoyed our group—I think we had a super bunch, good talents. Barboura Morris was a lovely actress, a very sweet lady and a nice friend—but she always seemed very sad to me. I'm so sorry she's gone. Dick Miller was a nice guy, very cooperative; Richard Devon, an excellent actor; I loved Ed Nelson. Everybody worked hard, we worked spontaneously, we interplayed with each other—we had a real good group.

Hustled into production to capitalize on interest in the new space program, *War of the Satellites* pitted Cabot and hero Dick Miller (center) against alien *Doppelgänger* Richard Devon.

Any memories at all about War of the Satellites?
 I was fascinated with the spacesuits that we wore; that was kind of nice. And I liked the way the special effects people did the splitting, when Richard Devon divided himself into two characters.
 I'm sorry Roger didn't enlarge upon that plot; I think he had a little seed of something that could've been really good in that film. I remember the scene where I made a speech at the United Nations, and it posed an interesting question: If you have the ability to do something incredibly fantastic — and nobody else has it — how do you handle the responsibility, and not abuse the power? I liked some of the things Roger was trying to say with that.

Gene Corman had bit parts in Machine-Gun Kelly *and* The Wasp Woman. *Did you get to know him as well?*
 Gene was a lovely person and a fine man, and I respect his work. I liked Gene very much; he seemed the antithesis of Roger. Gene was a very low-key, gentle man; Roger seemed a driven man. Roger wanted to accomplish a lot, he had to have a lot of drive to do it, and he pushed through. He not only pushed through, he *punched* through! With a lot of energy — and a lot of disregard, at times.

Did you and Roger date?
 We had a few dinners, yes. And argued about the treatment of our fellow

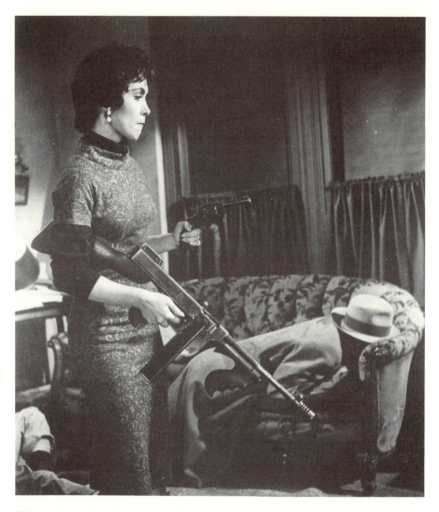

The late Susan Cabot gave one of her best performances as the scheming gun moll in Roger Corman's *Machine-Gun Kelly*.

actors. Having a social conscience — me, that is, I don't know about Roger — and being, I think, the only one he had signed under personal contract, I felt like a mother hen, and thought perhaps I could influence him to take it easy on the actors. Everybody wanted to please him, to make the pictures a success — but when he'd disregard somebody's safety I'd get real mad. And so we would argue a lot about that.

What would his comeback be?

"Oh, don't be so sensitive"; "we're just making a movie, don't take it so seriously." Things like that. But I have to say one thing about Roger: When

Hideously transformed by wasp enzymes, Cabot moves in for the kill on helpless Lani Mars in *The Wasp Woman*.

Sandy Meisner, who is a very respected acting teacher, came out here, many years ago, Roger began to go to his classes to learn how actors act and think and how they work things out. So I had to hand it to him — he was really trying to improve himself and develop, and see things from the actor's point of view. When a director does that, he becomes a better director.

Tell us about working with Charles Bronson on Machine-Gun Kelly.

He was very nice and very interesting — we shared a lot of feelings about certain things going on in the world. He spoke somewhat of his past; I came from a rough past also, so there was a kind of bond or camaraderie there. I was raised in eight foster homes — I don't talk about this very much — and we shared a lot of pain about some of that.

What can you tell us about The Wasp Woman?

That was a lot of fun and a real challenge. In that film I played Janice Starlin, a character who, through injections of wasp enzymes, goes from a woman of forty to a woman of twenty-two. I had to play the two roles differently. Older people usually move and speak more slowly, and I just used a slower pace, a more considered way of thinking for the "old" Janice. Acting spontaneously, full of life, doing things off-the-top — that was how I played the "young" Janice. Since I'm small — I'm 5'2" — another challenge was figuring out a way to attack 6'4" men and make it look credible. The only way I felt I could

Susan Cabot in 1985.

convincingly down a bigger person was through swiftness — by coming at them so fast, like a bolt of lightning, and staying right on target. It worked.

So you did do all your own stunts in the film?
Every bit of running, jumping, tackling, fighting and falling you see in that film, I did myself. One thing I remember in particular was that, as I attacked each character, I was supposed to bite their necks and draw blood. As I pierced the neck, to get the drama of the moment Roger wanted to *see* the blood. And so as I attacked everybody, I had Hershey's chocolate in my mouth — which I proceeded to *blurp,* right on people's necks *[laughs]!* What we did for Roger Corman — I mean, things that you could never do in a real studio but you did for this guy! Everything seemed unreal with him.

Your best scene as the Wasp Woman came at the very end of the film.
Well, after I'd done all those ghastly things I had to get my lumps at the end, right? That's a story in itself: The whole finale was going to be done in one shot — one shot! — and if anybody goofed, it *stayed* goofed. The hero would burst into the lab where I was lurking, and the fight would begin. We'd battle with a stool, back and forth, then somebody would throw a bottle of "acid" at me. After the bottle hit, I was supposed to duck out of camera range for just a few seconds while a prop man put liquid smoke on my antennae — the smoke showed the effects of the "acid." Then I had to go out through a window, backwards.

We started shooting the scene — Anthony Eisley discovers me in the lab, the fight begins, the stool, everything. Then they threw the bottle — which was supposed to be a breakaway bottle. Well, things started happening at that moment. Somebody had filled the bloody thing with water, and it hit like a rock! I thought my lower teeth came up through my nose, and I was sure I was bleeding under the mask. When you saw me holding my face in that shot, it was because I was hurt very badly. But I continued to go through the scene! Out of camera range, the prop man put the liquid smoke on my antennae—too much liquid smoke! I went crashing backwards out the window, and two men caught me on the other side. I started choking on the liquid smoke, but I couldn't tell them! The mask did not have a mouth—it only had two little nostrils and two globular eyes, and it was glued very tightly all around my neck. The smoke was going in the nostrils, and there was no place for it to go out! I was clawing and scratching, but I couldn't talk! At last somebody got the message and they poured water on me. I had to tear part of the mask off in order to breathe, and when I did I tore away some of my own skin. That left a big purple bruise on my neck for a very long time.

Did *Roger* do anything? Did *Roger* send me flowers? What year is it now *[laughs]*?

What made you decide to quit Hollywood after 1959?
I felt that I had more within me to explore, as a music and art major and as a person. And the way my film career was headed, I didn't feel that that was going to offer me a way to develop any more, except on a very superficial level. I mean, how many *Wasp Woman*s can you do *[laughs]*? I wanted to get back to New York—the Museum of Modern Art—my art studies. I began to study music again. I just went back to the things I really loved. I also traveled, and toured with a lot of musicals.

Do you ever consider getting back into the picture business?
I'd like to reenter the film industry, and work again. But any kind of work I do has to have dignity in the environment of that work. That's very important to me, because there's been such an abuse of actors in the history of Hollywood. But if the right part came along—colorful, fun, good people—then, yes. Sure.

Among the six films you did for Roger Corman, which ones are your personal favorites?
Machine Gun Kelly, Carnival Rock, Sorority Girl and *The Wasp Woman. Machine-Gun Kelly,* as a whole, was the most satisfactory. There was kind of a fun thing going on between the characters of Kelly and Flo—Bronson and myself—and there was a fondness there. I think that came out of the fondness that Bronson and I had for each other—we had an affection at that time. It was fun singing in *Carnival Rock,* and I had some really good scenes with David Stewart. *The Wasp Woman* was totally isolated from a normal kind of feeling, and that was a wonderful growth experience for me; I think that was the most

fun part I've ever had. To be able to go from a forty-year-old character to a twenty-two-year-old one was a challenge. Then, to be a monster—one of the very few female beasties in movies—was great fun. *The Wasp Woman* is very special.

... The Astounding She-Monster?
*I remember that the director, Ron Ashcroft,
planned to make that feature in a week's time
and I think we ended up making it in five days.
That was the astounding part of that picture!*

Robert Clarke

WAGING WAR with *Planet X*-men, *Captive Women* and *She-Monsters* in settings that ranged from *The Incredible Petrified World* to *Beyond the Time Barrier* has earned actor Robert Clarke an honored place in the pantheon of '50s monster fighters.

The Oklahoma-born Clarke abandoned his plans for a career in engineering when he caught the proverbial acting bug in college. Beginning in Hollywood as a $100-a-week stock player at RKO, he racked up early acting credits in such mid-'40s genre fare as *A Game of Death*, *Zombies on Broadway* and *Genius at Work*, as well as in Val Lewton's *The Body Snatcher* and *Bedlam*. Clarke graduated to lead player via strong co-starring roles in *Outrage* (1950) and *Hard, Fast and Beautiful* (1951), well-made dramas for Ida Lupino's Filmmakers production unit, and then starring roles in shoestring swashbucklers such as *Tales of Robin Hood* (1951) and *Sword of Venus* (1952).

In 1951, Clarke began his starring science fiction career with *The Man from Planet X*, and immediately followed up on this impressive start with the top role in the same producers' *Captive Women*. In the low-budget arena, he later toplined *The Astounding She-Monster*, *The Incredible Petrified World* and his own productions of *The Hideous Sun Demon* and *Beyond the Time Barrier*. Those were years of memorable experiences with the greats (and not-so-greats) of the genre.

How did you enjoy working with the Val Lewton unit at RKO?

Very, very much. Val Lewton was such a thoughtful type of individual, and he had a great capacity for kindness. He had very high ideals, and of course his artistic endeavors were far above those of most horror film producers.

Can you tell us a little about working with Boris Karloff on The Body Snatcher *and* Bedlam?

He was just delightful. At the end of one of the pictures, I think it was *The Body Snatcher,* they had a wrap party and Karloff was autographing pictures. I asked for one, and on it he wrote, "To Bob Clarke—Be as lucky as I am. Boris Karloff." Karloff was such the antithesis of what he portrayed on the screen: He had a very gentlemanly attitude, and in working in a scene with him he never tried to upstage you or to get the best of the scene. He was awfully kind, and his dressing room door was always open to anyone who wanted to say hello or chat with him. I never worked with any man that I had more admiration for.

Do you have a favorite Karloff anecdote?

Yes, I do. Karloff told me about the time that he went back East to do *Arsenic and Old Lace*. He hadn't been on the stage in so many, many years that he was literally suffering from stage fright. In fact, they let him sit in the audience the first few days of rehearsal. He told me, "I walked the streets of

Previous page: Robert Clarke and Marilyn Harvey flank the fallen body of alien Shirley Kilpatrick in a pensive scene from the micro-budgeted *The Astounding She-Monster*.

Among Clarke's first horror credits were supporting roles in Val Lewton productions like *Bedlam*. In this classic shot, Clarke (right), Jason Robards, Sr. (far left), and an unidentified player gang up on sadistic Boris Karloff.

New York all night long—I couldn't get up my nerve. Opening night, someone *pushed* me on the stage and I don't remember a thing—except that I had diarrhea for three weeks!"

How about Bela Lugosi on The Body Snatcher?
 Karloff used to call him "Poor Bela." And "Poor Bela" had *such* terrible problems with his back, and he was on drugs because of it. During the time that I was involved on *The Body Snatcher,* he hardly came out of his dressing room unless the assistant director called him. They had a daybed in there, and he was flat on his back on that couch nearly all the time. He talked very little to anyone, and obviously he wasn't well at all. It was very difficult for him to perform.

Most of your Body Snatcher *scenes were with Henry Daniell.*
 He was a smooth, accomplished and very professional actor. I was a bit overwhelmed, as were the other young stock players, Bill Williams and Carl Kent, by his extreme professionalism because he was a bit condescending in his attitude. The scene that we were involved with was mostly his scene—he was showing us how to perform the operation on the little girl. I had one line—"Bravo!"—and when I missed my cue, he went right by my line in his dialogue. But Bob Wise, the director, spoke up and stopped him, and said,

"Wait a minute—Bobby Clarke has a line there. Now, let's go back and start again, and let Bob get his line in." Unlike Karloff, Daniell was not the type to have empathy for young actors; "aloof," I guess, would be the best word to describe him. It was *his* scene, we were just window-dressing, and he couldn't care less whether we were there or not.

You had a more substantial role in Bedlam.

We were out at the RKO-Pathé Studios in Culver City, where *Gone with the Wind* [1939] was shot, and we were on one sound stage for over a month. Mark Robson, the director, was a marvelous man, he worked so carefully with us as actors. Today, directors don't have the time to do that. I remember a scene where we were playing a card game called paroli and, being demented, instead of betting money I was betting dogs—whippets and bassets and such. Robson made practically every little move for me—"When you place a card here, you do *this,* and then *that,"* and so forth. It's been over forty years, but I'll never forget how careful and meticulous he was. Robson, and Val Lewton, too, were both caring people, and they treated actors with respect, which is wonderful. I've had a couple of occasions in my career where the director would sit back near the camera and holler at you. I must give credit to Mark Robson for making my role in *Bedlam* more than it could have been; Robson gave me the kind of direction that brought out the best in me.

Was Val Lewton a hands-on, on-the-set producer?

I don't recall that he was so much that, no. He appeared on the set occasionally, but he wasn't looking over Mark Robson's shoulder; he had confidence in Mark and gave him full rein as director. And of course every day at the rushes, Lewton had a good opportunity to get a first-hand look at Robson's work, which was marvelous.

How did you get involved in The Man from Planet X?

Malvin Wald, a screenwriter and a partner in Filmmakers, told me that the writer-producer team of Jack Pollexfen and Aubrey Wisberg were looking for both male and female leads for that picture. Not too long ago, Jack Pollexfen said that Margaret Field—Sally's mother—and I were two of over a hundred actors and actresses that they interviewed. Margaret and I had recently done a picture together called *A Modern Marriage* [1950], she and I were both interviewed—I think together, as a matter of fact—and we were hired for the job.

Can you tell us a little about Pollexfen and Wisberg?

Jack was kind of a shy and diffident individual—erudite in his background, someone who you could imagine would plow through volumes and volumes of research material to get correct detail into his scripts. Wisberg was the more outgoing of the two; he was a bit more of the spokesman, it seemed to me. Nice men both, but very different from each other.

How did you enjoy working with director Edgar Ulmer?

Edgar and I worked very, very well together. He was never given the kind of opportunities he really deserved because he could make pictures so inexpensively that that's about all he ever got to do! He was so talented, in so many different areas. For example, on *Planet X* he painted the glass shots of the brock [a castle on the moors] — he did that as well as direct. The script originally was very, very talky — *long* speeches — and I'm sure he had a hand in the rewrite, too.

The one major flaw in Planet X *is that the dialogue is so overwritten. Do you remember that?*

I do, because it was hard to learn. The style was too literary, too wordy. Edgar Ulmer did his best to trim it, but I'm sure he was fighting with writers who thought every word was a pearl.

Where was Planet X *shot?*

Again, on a sound stage at RKO-Pathé. Except for maybe two or three shots outside, that's where we were for the six days it took to make the picture — they had it smoke-filled all day long, making it look like the moors. The inside of the brock were sets from the Ingrid Bergman *Joan of Arc* [1948]. Remember the village seen in the film? That was a painted backdrop! Talk about inexpensive — they really cut corners! And I got paid only $175 for the *whole picture*. The S.A.G. minimum then was $175 a week; today it's $375 a day. We got scale — and we worked from 6:30 in the morning till eight or nine at night every day, six days straight. *With* overtime, I think my check was for $210, and no residuals, ever.

Do you recall anything about the actor who played X?

Only that he complained — constantly — about how little money he was making. He had to be earning less than we were, and he didn't get billing, which I thought was unfair. People have asked me what his name was, and I've since forgotten — he was about the size of a jockey. He didn't like wearing that suit, and the mask was hot and very uncomfortable. He had a right to complain, and he did — a lot! A nice fellow, very cooperative, and he did his job well, but as far as I can tell he went on to great oblivion [*laughs*]!

Was it an enjoyable experience working on Planet X?

Oh, yeah. It was very, very hard work, but it was exciting because to us — to Margaret and me, especially — it was an opportunity that we thought might be the first step on the road to stardom. *The Man from Planet X* has certainly found a place in the annals of the science fiction genre, and I think it's one of the best films that I was in, especially when you take into consideration the budget and so on.

Clarke battles the vanguard of an interplanetary invasion in the cult classic *The Man from Planet X*.

Captive Women *cost twice as much as* Planet X, *but wasn't half as good.*

    I'd agree with that. Part of the fault was the fact that the director, Stuart Gilmore, was being given one of his first directing opportunities. Howard Hughes was the owner of RKO then, Gilmore had been a film editor for Hughes on *The Outlaw* [1943], this was one of Gilmore's first pictures and he was *lost*. Completely. The poor man had tremendous problems; there were too many people in the cast, too many actors with no dialogue in the scenes, and then the fact that they had over-extended themselves for special effects.

The trouble with that picture is that is blends science fiction with religion — a curious combination.

    Yeah, the whole film was ineffectual. Pollexfen and Wisberg were trying to make a better picture — sometimes Hollywood thinks that if you spend more money, you make a better picture. Well, this was one instance where that didn't happen. Gilmore was in over his head — he didn't know directing, and

I don't think he did too many pictures after that because he got a bad taste in his mouth from this one.

Wasn't there some rewriting while the picture was in progress?
Seemed to be, yeah. They would see the rushes and then we'd get new dialogue, new scenes. Part of it was that Bill Schallert's role was expanded—in some of the dailies that they saw he was coming across so well that they made the part bigger. He certainly deserved that kind of treatment; he'd also been in *The Man from Planet X,* and did an excellent job in both.

Tell us about working with Lon Chaney, Jr., on The Black Pirates *[1954].*
It was fun. He referred to himself as "the son of the *good* actor"—and then proceeded to have a big belt of booze *[laughs]!* But Lon was a fun-type man. One very unusual thing I learned about him was that he had a strange fear of going hungry. I had a friend who used to go fishing and hunting with Chaney, and this fellow told me that between L.A. and his ranch in San Diego Lon had several freezer-lockers *full* of frozen food—fish and meat and game— that he had either caught or he'd had butchered and stored, because of this inherent fear of going hungry.

What do you remember about The Astounding She-Monster?
I remember that the director, Ron Ashcroft, planned to make that feature in a week's time and I think we ended up making it in five days. *That* was the astounding part of that picture!

What kind of crew were you working with on films like She-Monster?
On *She-Monster,* we had a very minimal crew—one gaffer, a helper for him, one cameraman and one sound man. Just like with Jerry Warren, there was practically no crew at all. But Ronnie was resourceful—my gosh, was he ever! One of the things that he had envisioned was that the She-Monster would crash through a large window into the mountain cabin. They made the glass out of sugar and water and all, and as they were putting it in place they dropped the thing! If it had been me, I would have said, "Oh, hell, forget it," but Ronnie managed to put the few little fragments that were left back into the frame of the window and had her jump through. And then he edited it so that it looked pretty good.

Wasn't there a problem with the She-Monster costume?
The gal playing the She-Monster, Shirley Kilpatrick—a very well-endowed, buxom, beautiful girl, as I recall—had to wear a silvery, metallic-looking suit so that she would appear to be a monstrous yet appealing type of alien. It fit very tightly, and the first time she moved the doggone thing split, right up the back. She was so generously endowed that they couldn't do anything but put safety pins to hold it together in the back. So you'll notice that

the She-Monster always backs away from the camera—you never see her retreat from the scene other than she *backs* away—and the reason she was backing away was because, otherwise, she'd be showing her backside!

Those few little anecdotes are what I remember best about *Astounding She-Monster*—those, and the fact that the damn picture made so much money! I guess it was partially because of the title; it certainly was not a good horror film, but it sure made the bucks. Ashcroft paid me $500 a week, which I thought was a good salary for this type of picture, and he promised me 4 percent of his producer's share. Thanks to his honesty and integrity, over the period of the next eighteen months or so I made a couple thousand bucks!

Wasn't that what prompted you to produce The Hideous Sun Demon?

That percentage prompted me to do a couple of pictures on my own, *Sun Demon* and *Beyond the Time Barrier,* because I felt that Ronnie did pretty well with a picture made on a low budget and that I could do something as well or better. Ronnie liked to make films fast, and he did make them acceptable enough so that they would play, but I wanted to make something with a little more quality, which I believe I did with *Sun Demon.* I think Ronnie would agree that mine had more substance to it, story-wise and so on.

Who originally came up with the idea for Sun Demon?

I did. Actually, it isn't all that original in a sense because the basis is really *Dr. Jekyll and Mr. Hyde.* I had the idea for the plot, and then I had a writer, Phil Hiner, help me. I had known him in Chicago, when I was in the Signal Corps there in 1941–42. We just did a flipflop of the Robert Louis Stevenson plot—instead of the Jekyll and Hyde thing, where a man drinks the potion, we made it a scientist working with fissionable materials who has an accident with radioactive isotopes. That upsets his chromosome balance so that he reverts, in the sun's rays, to a reptilian type of monster. Phil and I wrote a treatment and he did a first draft screenplay called *Saurus,* which in Latin means reptile.

What were your first steps toward getting into production?

As a result of the friendship that I made with Malvin Wald, I went down to the University of Southern California and took a class under him in screenplay writing. As a result of *that,* I met several of the young fellows who were going to school there in the cinema department—Tom Boutross became my film editor and co-director, Robin Kirkman was associate producer and Vilis Lapenieks the photographer. They were all students there; in fact, they all lived in an apartment complex called Cinemanor.

I told them about the idea that I had of wanting to do a feature picture. Robin Kirkman, very, very fortuitously, said that he would like to invest. The two of us formed a partnership and the company was called Clarke-King Enterprises. Though he took credit as associate producer, Robin Kirkman really

Actors Robert Clarke and Robert Bice with unidentified woman in wardrobe for *Captive Women*. **(Photo courtesy Robert Skotak.)**

functioned more as a co-producer, and was a great help toward finishing the picture. As many pictures do, we ran out of money, and he was able to fund the finishing of the picture.

The fellow who got screenplay credit, a U.S.C. student named E.S. Seeley, was a friend of Robin Kirkman's. Very erratic and quite a difficult fellow — a real character. He did the final draft, and then we had it rewritten *again* by Doane Hoag, a man who worked in industrial films quite a bit. He did a good job polishing up the dialogue.

The tarnished character you play in Sun Demon *seems more true-to-life than the usual sci-fi protagonist. Who brought that to the script?*

Well, if I may take personal credit, I think that was my own input. I wanted to make it a more realistic, multi-dimensional character, with some bad qualities as well as some good.

How long did shooting take?
We shot on weekends. We'd have a spot picked for our shooting that weekend, we rented our camera, lighting and sound equipment on a Friday afternoon and we actually got two days of shooting for one day's rental. We thought that was pretty clever. We shot twelve consecutive weekends—we didn't shoot during the week because runaway production, or nonunion production, was not as prevalent then as it is now. We were nonunion—these kids from U.S.C. were all students, and they were paid something like twenty-five dollars a day and were delighted to be doing it. We were one of the first to use practical locations—when we needed a scene in a bar, we went to Santa Monica and asked a guy how much he would charge to let us come in and shoot the scenes in his bar.

Why did you feel you needed a co-director?
Mainly because, when I was in the monster outfit, it was extremely difficult to be doing that and also laying out the shots and so on. And it was also kind of an accommodation for Tom Boutross—he was the editor, and he thought a co-director credit would be a nice gesture. But Tom did a *lot* in the editor's room to make that picture work.

Where were some of your other locations—the Sun Demon's house, the beaches, the oil fields where he hides out and the gas storage tanks where he's killed?
The Sun Demon's house was located in the old part of Los Angeles, on a street called Lafayette Boulevard; the house is no longer standing. It was one of those big old mansion-type houses with four stories; then it was a rooming house. I remember telling a lady that I had been there shooting a TV series, *I Led Three Lives,* and I said I was interested in renting the house for a movie. She said, "Will you pay me as much as they did?" and I said, "Well, perhaps—how much is that?" And she said, "Twenty-five dollars a day." So *[laughs],* we wrote some extra scenes to have played right there in the house, because the price was so right! We worked there five or six different weekends! The exteriors, however, were an old mansion, once owned by Antonio Moreno, up in the Los Angeles–Glendale Hill area; it was a Catholic school then. We went out to Bass Rock, which is where we shot a lot of the exteriors where I'm walking along, looking over the cliffs. The beach scene with the girl was not far up the beach, near Trancas—a very fashionable area now. The oil fields were in the Long Beach area of what had been Signal Hill in the early 1900s. Many of those old wooden derricks still stand and still pump oil. The gas storage tank, which was located near the Union Station train depot, was made

After years as an actor, Clarke tried his hand at producing and directing on 1959's *The Hideous Sun Demon*.

available to us through the Southern California Gas Company. The height of that gas tank was something over three hundred feet, and when I took the dummy of the Sun Demon up to throw it off, my voice, as big and loud as it is, could not be heard by the camera crew down below. We had a very difficult time communicating.

And your budget?

Believe it or not, we started with $10,000 cash. Robin Kirkman and I each put in $5,000. That must seem ridiculous, but Roger Corman made *Attack of the Crab Monsters* for, I think, around $15,000, cash. Eventually our overall cost came to a little under $50,000. I even borrowed several thousand dollars from my brother and sister. Our lab bill came to around $8,500, and they were very lenient and allowed us to pay that off over a period of a couple of years.

Where did you get your largely unknown supporting cast?

We got them through members of the crew that knew of aspiring actors and actresses around U.S.C. We told them that this was a nonunion picture and we had them come out and read. We selected Nan Peterson because of her voluptuous figure; Patricia Manning was quite good. I don't know if they've done anything much since. Peter Similuk, who played the gangster, hadn't done much and he didn't come off all that well. Another fellow that didn't come off awfully well was Robert Garry, who played the scientist explaining my problem at the very beginning. The little girl, Xandra Conkling, is my niece; she's a grown young lady now and has four children. Her mother, in the film and in real life, is Donna King, my wife's sister. She was one of the original King Sisters during the big band days with Alvino Rey. My wife's mother, Pearl Driggs, was the elderly lady sitting out on the hospital roof when I get the first attack from the sun. The King Sisters' real name was Driggs, which they changed for obvious reasons—who'd go to see the Driggs Sisters?

Another King Sister, Marilyn, is credited with writing the song Strange Pursuit, *heard three times in the film.*

Marilyn is the youngest King Sister. She wrote it, and did her accompaniment. When they came out with *It Came from Hollywood* [1982] she was able to get a few hundred bucks out of them for the use of the song.

Did you play the Sun Demon throughout the film, or did a stuntman take your place?

All the stunts—all of the running, jumping and fighting—I did myself. No other actor played the Sun Demon. The suit was made on the base of a skin-diving wetsuit, and it was hotter than blue blazes! It was so hot that my perspiration ran down my body and *[laughs]* into my trunk area, shall we say, and during the fight we got so much energy going that one of the still shots shows me standing up there with this wet appearance—it looks like I couldn't make it to the men's room, but actually it was perspiration.

Was the construction of the Sun Demon suit a major expense?

For us it was a major expense—five hundred bucks was what it cost. I went to see Jack Kevan, the fellow who did *Creature from the Black Lagoon,* and he said, "To make what you want, I would charge you at least $2,000." He was not overpricing it, but luckily I found this fellow Richard Cassarino, who was a film buff and a sometimes-actor.

Do you mean Gianbattista *Cassarino, who is listed in the film's credits as art director and assistant to the producers?*

Gianbattista Cassarino was his *nom de screen*. A very happy Italian guy. He made a plaster mold of my head and then fashioned the mask on that. He was an artistic guy who contributed a lot to the picture—he was a set designer to some degree, and he also played the policeman that I fought on top of the gas tank. "Ben Sarino" [makeup man listed in the film's opening credits] was probably another *nom de screen* for him because we didn't want it to appear that one person was doing so many different jobs!

Makeup man Richard Cassarino puts last-minute touches on Clarke in *The Hideous Sun Demon*. (Photo courtesy Robert Skotak.)

Why did the film require three cinematographers?

Because some of them were not available weekend after weekend. When we'd say, "We're going to shoot next weekend," some of these fellows would say they weren't available, so we'd get somebody else. We didn't actually start with Vilis Lapenieks, but we found that his was the best work. John Morrill did at least half of it. Stan Follis worked with us throughout the picture as assistant cameraman and did some first unit work.

Did working with a largely inexperienced crew create problems?

We shot on the beach, live and with a sound recording, but the sound of the ocean drowned us out and we had to loop every line. One sequence in the oil derrick housing was shot silent and we had to loop it. That was a mistake; it was so late in the evening we let the sound crew go home, then realized we had this yet to do.

Missing from most prints of Hideous Sun Demon *is the scene where you pick up a rat and squeeze it so that its blood oozes through your fingers.*

It happened on the spur of the moment. We were trying to make a macabre type of sequence out of it. Similarly, when as the monster I killed the dog, that was somebody's idea of showing the violence of the monster, that the man had changed into a real malevolent type of creature. We didn't hurt the rat — we put some ketchup or something on it and squeezed it so that the ketchup would come out between the fingers. Actually, we probably shouldn't have used it; it was not in good taste and I'm glad that it has been cut. I don't even recall how we got the rat in the first place! But it *was* allowed to go free.

And how did Beyond the Time Barrier *come about?*

After we finished *The Hideous Sun Demon,* I was looking for a distributor. I went to Sam Arkoff and Jim Nicholson, and I made an arrangement for Nicholson to take the print and show it at his home. His daughters liked the picture very much, so Nicholson said, "Take it in and let Sam Arkoff see it." Afterwards, Sam asked, "Well, what do you want to do with it?" and I told him I wanted to use it as a door-opener, to produce other pictures. He wasn't interested at all; he said they had about all the producers they could use. But he still said he would like to distribute the picture.

I told him I'd think about it, but in the meantime I was put in touch with a company called Pacific International. John Miller and Mike Miller were trying to be another Arkoff and Nicholson, but as it later turned out they just didn't have the moxie or the know-how to do it. They were preparing a picture called *A Date with Death* [1959] starring Gerald Mohr and Liz Renay, who was Mickey Cohen's girlfriend, and they told me they were going to need a companion feature. I indicated that I might be interested if they'd make me the right kind of deal; I told them I'd like a three-picture contract, and they said, "Well, fine—if you don't require any money up front for your *Sun Demon,* we'll release that with our picture as a double bill." So we went on location to Roswell, New Mexico, to shoot *A Date with Death,* in which I had a supporting role, and then the picture I got to make for that company was *Beyond the Time Barrier.*

No temptation for you to direct, as you did on Sun Demon?

No, no—directing *and* acting is a tremendous chore. We got Edgar Ulmer, who had directed *Planet X,* as director and a friend of mine, Les Guthrie, as production manager. Working with Ulmer again was a lift because he was an extremely imaginative, creative director who got the most out of whatever was available and gave his all to the pictures. His wife, Shirley, was our script supervisor and his daughter, Arianne Arden, played in the film, as the femme fatale Markova.

Where did your Time Barrier *script come from?*

That was an Arthur C. Pierce script which I had read and liked; I optioned it and submitted it to the Millers. They had five other scripts under consideration, but this was better than any they had and they selected it. In addition to providing the script, Arthur Pierce came down to Dallas, was involved in some of the production and worked as an assistant editor later, in postproduction. He also did a brief cameo appearance as one of the mutants.

What prompted the decision to make the film in Dallas?
　The money was coming from Texas and they wanted to make the picture there. I think the budget was $125,000 and the schedule was about nine or ten days. We shot at the old 1936 Centennial Fairgrounds. The big, convention-type structures there were big enough to simulate sound stages, but the problem was that the sound in those large, empty buildings was like something out of a deep well—"echoey" and booming. The production crew had to hang a lot of old Air Force surplus parachutes all around to absorb some of the sound.

Where did you shoot your air base scenes?
　Those were done at Fort Worth's Carswell Field, an actual Air Force base for B52's; it was secured for us by Les Guthrie's father, "Pop" Guthrie, who'd been the location manager at Warners. The wrecked air base of the "future" scenes was nearby; Les Guthrie had gone on a location scouting trip and found this old World War II airstrip, with the remnants of the buildings and all, just as if it had been made for us! It fitted in beautifully with our story.

Who designed your futuristic Time Barrier *sets?*
　As I remember, it was our production designer, Ernst Fegté, who conceived the whole thing. He had been under contract to Paramount as a set designer, and he brought in these sketches, with the motif of the inverted triangles and all. Edgar Ulmer, being an artist and a former set designer as well, immediately loved his ideas.

Shortly after Time Barrier, *you announced another film,* The Frozen Continent, *which was never made.*
　That was a story treatment that Arthur Pierce had; I got an option on it and provided the financing for him to do a fifty- or sixty-page treatment. It was about an advanced civilization in a city beneath the sea in the Arctic. I was interested in raising money to do it or doing it through Pacific International as another feature, but that company's success was short-lived. Pacific International got into a bankruptcy situation because of lack of business ability in the area of distribution, and in a matter of eighteen months or so they went bankrupt. Once they went under, I didn't receive anything except my actor's salary, $1000 a week for two weeks, for *Time Barrier,* and I lost quite an amount of money, about $50,000, on *Sun Demon.* American International released *Beyond the Time Barrier* along with another Pacific International picture, *The Amazing Transparent Man,* because they bought them, at auction almost, for whatever lab costs were involved. They made out like bandits.

The way things turned out, do you ever regret having broken into production with The Hideous Sun Demon?
　Oh, no. I would never say I was sorry because if I had not done it, I think

I would have been sorry and would be saying that I wish that I had tried it. It was an interesting experience. I wish, of course, that it had turned out more profitably and that it had led to other things that would have been more mainstream. With Roger Corman, pictures like these were stepping stones to bigger productions. But I took such a terrible bath with the bankruptcy on both *Sun Demon* and *Time Barrier* that I just felt there was no way to make another one and come out with anything.

How did you get involved on The Incredible Petrified World?

That was a picture I made for Jerry Warren. Jerry was a guy who made a dozen or so pictures which earned money for him in the days when little pictures would play at drive-ins. He put so little money into them, and they were made with such terrible limitations. But he did put a lot of effort into them — I'll credit Jerry for having a great deal of drive, and for working as hard or harder than anybody else. Jerry came out to see me, brought a script of *Incredible Petrified World* and told me that if I'd defer, he'd pay me after we got through the picture, which he did.

Petrified World was shot in Colossal Cave in New Mexico. We drove over there in cars and stayed in some sleazy little motel, and it was hard — *very* hard — work. Jerry would feed us hamburgers for dinner and hamburgers for lunch — and maybe for breakfast, too! And I remember when we got over there I was astonished that the crew consisted of *a* cameraman, who did his own lighting, and *a* sound man. When one of us wasn't in the scene, *we* would hold the boom *[laughs]!* So that was it — a cameraman, a sound man and Jerry, who was a screaming director.

Katherine Victor describes him the same way.

I've always kidded him about that; I've told him, "You turn into a real Mr. Hyde when you get that camera switched on — suddenly you go crazy!" — which he does, he gets so emotional. When he'd holler at me, I'd holler back at him; there's no need for that, except that Jerry gets excited. But it would get me upset, internally, for him to be so obstreperous.

What about working with John Carradine?

What I remember best about Carradine is how strong his concentration was. Carradine was in the scenes we shot here in L.A., and I remember one night, in front of a garage, he had to do a long speech, almost a soliloquy, explaining some plot point. And he was so into that — right out there, practically in the street, without any setting of any kind or any actor to work with. He was just a marvelous actor.

How about on a personal level?

I enjoyed working with him very much. He was a true professional, and he gave every bit as much working for Jerry Warren as he would working for

Cecil DeMille or John Ford. He did not stint in the slightest in his performance. He was cooperative, easy to work with and he was not condescending — he was something of a star and we weren't, but he treated us as equals and fellow actors. I have great respect for him.

Would Jerry Warren holler at Carradine, too?
I can't recall him hollering at John; in fact, I question that he would.

Do you have fond memories of making films like The Astounding She-Monster, Secret File: Hollywood *[1962] and the Jerry Warrens, or were they all so rushed and so poverty-stricken that all the fun goes out of them?*
I did these quickies because I was raising two boys and trying to help support my wife; the money was there, and it seemed to be the thing to do at the time. I wouldn't say they were fun; you don't get to feel that you're doing something that might lead to better things, as I did on the Ida Lupino pictures. I got more enjoyment and gratification out of *The Man from Planet X* and *Beyond the Time Barrier* than I got out of these quickies that we did.

In the mid–'70s you planned a return to producing with The Sorceress. *Can you tell us about that?*
There's not a lot to tell. I again got Arthur Pierce to write a treatment of a story idea that I had come up with: it was about a young woman who had these powers of sorcery. We tried to modernize it for the day; this was about the time of Sissy Spacek's *Carrie* and pictures like that. We thought a film about sorcery and magic powers, things that could be achieved through special effects work, would have a good commercial reception. But I wasn't very successful at getting the necessary backing for it.

Your last sci-fi role was in Jerry Warren's comeback film Frankenstein Island. *What memories do you have of that film?*
Well, again, of Jerry's obstreperous ways as a director. He would get so involved that he would forget to use a certain amount of control in his direction to *anyone*—actors, camera, etc. He would get quite carried away. But there were good people on that particular film—Andrew Duggan, Cameron Mitchell, Steve Brodie and John Carradine. We went down to Escondido every weekend; [actor] Robert Christopher and I would drive down together. Bob Christopher also put in a lot of money and helped Jerry bail the thing out and get it finished. I'm sure that Bob wishes now that he hadn't; I talked to Jerry not too long ago, and he said that as far as any theatrical release is concerned he may as well forget it in today's market. They did make a sale to video cassette, but he said all that did was get him out of hock with the lab, and on the deal that they made with television, they got it in a good package but now they can't collect the money from the packager.

Frankenstein Island *was your first starring feature since* Terror of the Bloodhunters, *almost twenty years. Was it good to be back in the lead, or did the low-budget trappings detract from the experience?*

I think you just answered your own question *[laughs]!* The quality of a film has a lot to do with whether you can feel good about it. I had hopes for *Frankenstein Island* because one great thing about Jerry is that he has a lot of enthusiasm and he can get a lot on the screen for the kind of money he spends. But it soon became pretty apparent that this wasn't going to get much beyond what any of his others had achieved, and it wouldn't reach *Planet X* or *Time Barrier* or even *Sun Demon* as far as quality. It's slow, it's stodgy, it just plods along; Jerry cut and cut it, but it's still very ponderous.

Can we look forward to seeing you in any new horror/sci-fi films?

About two years ago I went to Kansas City to star with Ann Robinson in a film for Wade Williams called *Space Patrol.* For various reasons the producers were not very happy with the results, so now it's going to be seen as a movie-within-a-movie — they wrote a new script and shot forty-five minutes of footage, and the film is now called *Midnight Movie Massacre.* It now takes place in 1956, and it's about twelve people who go to a midnight show where the film Ann Robinson and I did, *Space Patrol,* is playing. Essentially *Midnight Movie Massacre* is a black comedy about a monster that lands behind the movie house and eats the people, one at a time, as they leave the theater. Wade says he still used quite a bit of the footage that we're in, and we still have the major lead billings. It should be out some time in 1988.

*A lot of the talent that Roger and I sponsored
was really germinated and brought about because
we didn't have the financing that other companies had.
Instead of the ability to write that check, we had to
go out with the ability to recognize that* talent.
And it worked out well for all of us.

Gene Corman

WHILE ALL SORTS of media attention has been lavished on Roger Corman, relatively little has been written about his producer-brother Gene. Not only has Gene been an active moviemaker in his own right, he actually preceded his older brother Roger in the film business and played a key role in getting his famous brother's first horror/sci-fi picture released. Both in the area of exploitation and mainstream films, Gene has been producing movies for over thirty years.

Gene Corman first brought the family name into the film industry as a motion picture agent. Beginning in 1956, he and his brother joined forces as producers to make such films as *Hot Car Girl, Night of the Blood Beast, Attack of the Giant Leeches, Beast from Haunted Cave* and *The Premature Burial* for distributors like Allied Artists, AIP and Filmgroup. Gene returned to the exploitation field in the early '70s at MGM when he produced several blaxploitation features such as *Hit Man* (1972) and *The Slams* (1973), as well as Paul Bartel's kinky thriller *Private Parts* (1973).

In the meantime, Gene Corman's more mainstream career was getting underway and has since come to dominate his filmmaking activities. *Tobruk* (1967) was an early success, followed later by such pictures as *F.I.S.T.* (1978) and *The Big Red One* (1980). Presently he is vice-president of Twentieth Century–Fox Television, but he doesn't let that mainstream success make him shy away from talking about his early days shooting monsters on a shoestring in Bronson Canyon.

As youngsters, did you and Roger share any interest in movies and filmmaking?

No, neither of us really was involved or even thought about filmmaking. We were born in and, for the first ten or twelve years of our lives, grew up in Detroit, Michigan. Our dad was a civil engineer, so you can see that there was no way, in Detroit, and with his background, that we would even have considered motion pictures.

If Roger hadn't gotten into the movie industry, do you think you would have?

I was in the motion picture industry *before* Roger was. I had become a motion picture agent and Roger, I think, was working for a steel company or an electrical company. He had graduated an engineer, but then had really no interest in pursuing it. So I preceded him into the business.

I remember when Roger made his first film, *Monster from the Ocean Floor*. He had done it independently, for very little money, without distribution. Obviously, the next order of business was to sell or to make a distribution deal. Being an agent, I negotiated the very first distribution sale for Roger and that film. Herbert Yates, the president of Republic, had an interest in it, but I sold it to Bob Lippert, who in the '40s and '50s had a company that was, in a larger way, an AIP-type outfit. Bob was one of very first who had franchised offices and/or states' righters working with him. As a matter of fact, it was funny—when I made the deal with Bob for *Monster from the Ocean Floor,* we

Previous page: **Gene Corman.**

made it for something like $110,000 as a pick-up. He was very pleased with that price. Then, when he got back to me with the contracts, he had changed the deal on the basis that we had not *spent* $100,000 on the film. I said, "Well, that was not the question! After looking at the film you were delighted to put up $110,000 as a pick-up." He said, "But now I've found out that you spent less than that—you spent probably seventy or eighty thousand dollars. I'm going to readjust it." To tell the truth *[laughs]*, I think Roger had spent like $35,000 on it, so everybody did well anyway.

What kind of response did Roger get from family and friends when he broke into filmmaking?
Everybody was somewhat in awe—they didn't quite understand. But since I had preceded him into it by a year or two, and seemed to be doing nicely, they were supportive. To all loving parents, the most important thing is that their children find a lifestyle that is compatible and that is meaningful for them. Even though our father had been an engineer and Roger had studied to be one, once Roger was out in the real world he decided that that wasn't for him.

How did you first become involved in the production of Roger's films?
I was vice-president of MCA for about seven years. Early on, it seemed to be an area that excited me, and I had a very responsible position. I represented Joan Crawford, Fred MacMurray, Ray Milland, Harry Belafonte, Richard Conte—I had a very strong list of stars at that point. But it wasn't really anything that I saw as terribly creative. And I found, as an agent, that I was functioning as a producer. For instance, with Joan Crawford, who had more careers than probably any other major star that I know of. Joan went through a quiet period after she left Warner Bros., and there was a question of how to place her, what to do with her. There was a Western book I had read, *Johnny Guitar* by Roy Chanslor, that was really suitable as a film vehicle for, say, Clark Gable and two women. I gave it to Joan to read, with the idea that maybe we would move it in a different direction: Maybe *she* would be the lead—*she* would be Clark Gable—and we'd put two other *men* in! I was representing Nicholas Ray at that point, too, so I put the whole project together. And I found I was doing the same with Fred MacMurray, and with Ray Milland when he left Paramount. I was, then, a producer! So I then moved, with Roger, into making the teenage protest films. It was a natural adjunct; having represented Nick Ray through *Rebel Without a Cause* (1955) and several of his other pictures, I knew through first-hand experience what the sum and substance was about. True, the first picture that we made together, *Hot Car Girl* (1958), had a very modest budget, so we were not able to do anything on the same scale as what Nick had done, but it served us well.

Actor Leo Gordon, who wrote Hot Car Girl, The Giant Leeches, Tower of London *and many of your other films, had to be one of the burliest, most brutal-*

looking movie tough guys in the business. It's almost impossible to picture him sitting down writing a screenplay.

Leo was a very burly, tough fellow, but — his background belied his looks. He was an avid reader, and he would read on many levels. And he was a very witty, interesting conversationalist. In many ways, his appearance in those tough-guy roles probably worked to his disadvantage, because to have Leo walk into a story conference was somewhat intimidating! I remember on *Tobruk*, having Arthur Hiller, who is really a very fey, gentle soul, taken aback when he met Leo — it took maybe two or three story conferences before he could come to grips with the size and bulk of Leo! The way he presented himself was intimidating.

When writing the original story for Night of the Blood Beast, *were you at all influenced by* The Thing?

How could you not be? We had to be, if only indirectly or subconsciously. That was a classic film then, a classic film today. The only disappointment is, when they remade it, they failed to understand what Howard Hawks was trying to convey. We shot *Blood Beast* in Bronson Canyon, and we also went up into the Hollywood Hills and used a radio station, right above the HOLLYWOOD sign, for the film's tracking station. Since we had a great deal of day-for-night to shoot, we were always chasing the shadows up there, trying to block out the sun *[laughs]*! That was one of the more mobile units I've ever been involved with. Normally, everybody chases the sun; *we* were chasing the shadows!

Why did you settle for a leftover monster costume in Blood Beast, *rather than an entirely new creation that might have served the picture better?*

Money. We found through experience that if you exceeded a certain figure, you were not going to get that additional money back. You must remember that most or all of these films were handled by states' righters or franchise holders, so you knew pretty well going in what your cost had to be. I think all our early films were in the area of thirty or thirty-five thousand dollars, plus the lab deferment. So for each picture we had a cost of approximately $50,000. The cost of trailers and advertising would then bring it up some more.

Were you present on the sets of your various pictures?

Always. I was a hands-on producer, and to this day I am still a hands-on producer. In my opinion, you cannot be an absentee producer.

One of your most accomplished films of this era was I, Mobster *[1958].*

I made the deal for Roger and myself to do that picture for Twentieth Century-Fox and Eddie Alperson, who had a budget unit independently financed by Fox.

For *Night of the Blood Beast*, Gene and Roger Corman got some extra mileage out of a monster costume made for the earlier *Teenage Caveman*. The uncomfortable-looking victim is Michael Emmet.

Would you have liked to continue making films for mainstream studios like Fox?

Yes. With a major studio comes major financing. And with major financing you have security — you can hire a better writer, possibly go for a book. All along the line you can strive for a greater degree of excellence and professionalism. For the most part, a lot of the talent that Roger and I sponsored was really germinated and brought about because we *didn't* have the financing that other companies had. Instead of the ability to write that check, we had to go out with the ability to recognize that *talent*. And it worked out well for all of us.

So I, Mobster *did whet your appetite to do more ambitious films?*

Yes. As a matter of fact I did do two or three other films for Fox, including one that [production chief] Buddy Adler particularly liked, *Valley of the Redwoods* (1960). That was a film I shot in Eureka, California, in CinemaScope, for something like seventy or eighty thousand dollars. It was so well received that Buddy wanted to make an overall deal with me, with the idea of doing more important films. Unfortunately he was stricken shortly after that and died within a year. I'd also made *Secret of the Purple Reef* (1960), a 'Scope, Technicolor film for Fox, shot in Puerto Rico.

You went back to science fiction again for Attack of the Giant Leeches *and* Beast from Haunted Cave.

At that particular period, the science fiction pictures were a very salable commodity. We had enjoyed a series of successes with them, we found them easy—*fun*—to make, and more readily marketable than most other types of films. If you got away from that kind of horror or science fiction, you found yourself truly competing with the major studios, and in that arena it was impossible. One, you didn't have the production values, and two, you could not afford the stories or the actors. For some reason the other studios had laid back and let science fiction alone for a great deal of the time.

Didn't you originally plan to star Ed Nelson in Giant Leeches?

It seems to me that Ed was going to star in it, but something came along that paid money *[laughs]*! And I think all of us might have gone with him had we been able to get paid as well!

Much of Giant Leeches' *running time is squandered on a white trash love triangle, but there are a number of grisly highpoints.*

It just seemed that in that kind of film you had to have two or three memorable moments—scenes that the audience would go away thinking about, talking about. Somehow, when you place people in jeopardy with leeches—with things that are distasteful—and then combine that with water, you somehow touch a very Freudian-ly responsive chord in people.

Can you tell us a little about how and why you and Roger formed Filmgroup?

Roger and I had made so many films, and the distributors were legion. If they stayed in business, there was always a question of "creative bookkeeping." If they didn't stay in business, there was the problem of trying to find out where the bank accounts were. Necessity was the mother of invention. We decided, if we were that unhappy with distributors, that it was a logical thing—if we had the product, why not have the distribution? Then we would know where the money was, because we would be the bookkeepers. So we did this. At that time, I knew a lot of the heads of the theater chains, so I could pick up a telephone and book. I became less enchanted than Roger did because I found myself suddenly involved more in that end of the business, and it wasn't something that appealed to me. If that had appealed to me — that kind of ... less-than-creative part of the business — I would have stayed an agent! That brought Roger and me to see that our goals were not necessarily always going to be the same. So then I went off and made films for Fox.

Did you or Roger work on any of the Filmgroup releases that did not bear a Corman name — pictures like The Wild Ride, The Girl in Lovers Lane, T-Bird Gang *and others?*

We kind of supervised 'em, helped put the crews together and offered a little bit of input, that sort of thing. But not much other than that.

What was the rationale behind taking Beast from Haunted Cave *on location to South Dakota?*

We were looking to find a different background. I mean *[laughs]*, we had used Bronson Canyon and all of the caves to such a point that even *I* was getting tired of that backdrop. I don't think I've returned to Griffith Park since! Bronson Canyon, the Arboretum — we'd outgrown those, because we'd done pictures there so many times. It just seemed that we had to do something different.

We had gotten some information from the Chamber of Commerce in South Dakota, and I think it had to do with the Black Hills, around Rapid City. Once we got there, we found that the Black Hills were such that, visually, you couldn't *hold* them. They're wonderful if you're standing five miles away, but once you're down there, close, you're always in shade, and it just didn't seem to work as well as I had hoped.

Then we found out there was a gold mine in Lead, South Dakota, so obviously that intrigued me and I wanted to use that mine. But there was no way I could get the permission. One of the officers of the mine told me of an old mine in Deadwood, twenty miles away. So we used the interior of *that* mine, and the mountain and snow around it. This was the first time I had tried to shoot in snow, and it was very difficult. But the picture had a whole new look.

Were you happy with Chris Robinson's spider-monster costume?

Yes, we were very, very satisfied. Chris at that time hadn't come to us as an actor, he'd come to us as a model maker. He approached me because he had seen or heard of the other sci-fi/horror films that I had made with monster costumes, and told me they could have been done better — which was true. I said I would have welcomed that, but with the constraints of a budget we had always come up with less than what was designed or sketched. With that in mind, he came forward with the monster costume for *Beast from Haunted Cave* — he did the costume, *and* played the monster in the film.

The exasperating thing about Beast *is that its climax is so frantic and the film ends so abruptly that it's not even clear who lives or dies.*

I think we tried to do that purposely, on the basis that we might have come back for a sequel. That would have been the only reason we might have done it that way.

With very few exceptions you seemed to shy away from availing yourself of Roger's stock company of actors. Why was this?

I think we were trying to expand the look of our pictures. So each one of us looked to see whether we could add to that covey of so-called stock players. I was not intentionally avoiding using them; we were trying to expand our coterie of players because we were distributing through insular companies. You can't always offer the same players to the public.

Why do you and Roger play small parts in many of your own pictures?

Generally it would happen when an actor didn't show up, but also it did save a few dollars. I mean, we were there all the time on these films, so why not? I played small roles in *Machine-Gun Kelly* (1958), *The Wasp Woman*, *The Secret Invasion* (1964) and so on. And I must tell you, it also was fun!

Why did you and Roger feel you had to get away from AIP to do The Premature Burial?

I don't think we felt we *had* to do that, it just seemed that we were able to structure a better deal with Pathé American. Pathé had wanted to go into distribution, and had in fact distributed a few films.

One of the first "legitimate" old-time Hollywood stars to lend his name to exploitation films was Ray Milland.

I had represented him as his agent for many years, so it was a good experience. I thought he was very good in that film; his very presence gave it a different look, and it had a truer feeling of the period with Ray in the role. I think this was one of the first pictures of that type he had done.

Why did AIP wrest The Premature Burial *away from Pathé American in mid-production?*

I think they didn't want to lose their identification with what at that time was the upscale, more sophisticated type of horror film. As I remember, Pathé did the lab work for AIP—AIP was one of their biggest suppliers of raw stock to be developed and printed. And I think at that point they leaned on Pathé and said, "Look, you're in competition with us, especially with this kind of a film. There are a lot of other labs out there who are really courting us, and would like our business."

How did you feel when Jim Nicholson and Sam Arkoff showed up on the Premature Burial *set and told you that they had managed to take over?*

Left to right: Brendan Dillon, Alan Napier, Hazel Court and unidentified players look on as Roger Corman positions the casket in the Corman brothers' production of *The Premature Burial.*

[Laughs.] I guess we kind of chuckled, and went along with it. We knew that they weren't joking — but also, Roger and I had had a long relationship with them. Like lovers — you have a spat, but you always find a need for each other.

How did Tower of London *come about?*

Leo Gordon and I were trying to come up with a variation on that genre — *not* to do Edgar Allan Poe, because it seemed to me that Vincent Price had done enough of those. We were looking to find another venue; we talked about Nathaniel Hawthorne, and three or four other ideas. Then I said to Leo, "Why don't we go to Shakespeare, and see where that takes us?" *Macbeth* didn't serve us, but the story of *Richard III* did. So that was how that came about — we were exploring the same genre, but a different author.

What was your budget on Tower of London?

Under $200,000, that I know. Building those sets was our major cost. It seems to me we shot that at the old Producer's Studio. Roger directed, with probably a shooting schedule of fifteen days.

Presuming that audiences might be tiring of Vincent Price/Poe films, Corman turned to Shakespeare and *Richard III* as the basis for *Tower of London* (also featuring Price, *above*).

Why, so late in the game, was Tower *made in black-and-white?*

That was not our decision, that was Eddie Small's—Eddie was an independent financier for United Artists. The cost of a color print was considerable in those days, and he took the hard line. That came as a surprise to us—none of us had anticipated shooting in black-and-white. This all happened probably two or three days before we rolled the cameras, when we were ordering the raw stock. Roger and I had some very strong discussions with Eddie, but it was a case of, "This is the way it's going to be," and he wasn't going to change his mind. What Eddie obviously decided was that Vincent Price had a built-in audience, and that they would not realize up front that they were buying a black-and-white Price film. They'd be taking for granted that this was in color.

How would you rate Price's performance in the film?

I thought Vincent was very good in *Tower of London*. It seemed that he had a real feeling for that period, and for that character. I kind of liked that film, and I know Vincent was always pleased with that performance.

How did the picture do at the box office?

We opened big — for that kind of film — but the down-the-line play was not what it should have been, because at that point the distributor knew he didn't have a color film. That was one of the things that aggravated us to a further degree — the fact that we were *right*, and it turned out to be "a Hollywood rip-off." The picture opened the way all Price pictures did, but did not have that solid, down-the-line play. *Tower of London* didn't do it — and, following that, it didn't do it in television — because it didn't have color.

One of your most intriguing films from that period seems to be The Intruder *[1961].*

The Intruder was a film that Roger and I always wanted to make, and it violated some of our basic precepts. We got ourselves so caught up in *The Intruder* that it was the only film that he and I personally financed that lost money.

Was Roger exaggerating when he told an interviewer, "We all risked our lives on this one"?

[*Laughs.*] We were run out of Sikeston, Missouri, the Klan came after us, they threatened us — Christ, I'd never gone through such an experience before in my life! And wearing glasses was no protection!

You had a curious supporting cast that included writers Charles Beaumont, George Clayton Johnson and William Nolan.

They were all as dedicated to this project as we were, and we were all friends. Also, Roger and I truly had no money to make this picture. So we called upon as many friends as possible. Each one felt strongly about the film, and they could play specific roles because those roles mirrored, in fact, their own personalities. And if their performances might not be up to what Mervyn LeRoy might have called for, they gave that picture a gritty reality. I think that in many ways the lack of professionalism helped that film.

What inspired you to make a career of the business end of motion pictures, rather than the more creative facets of writing, directing and so on?

That was where I first started—I would be producing and Roger directing—and so it seemed the logical road to continue down. Now that I look at it in retrospect, I probably should have directed, and I have had two or three different opportunities. Specifically when? When I had my own unit at MGM, in the early '70s. I was very autonomous there, and I could have done anything that I wanted as long as the budgets didn't exceed $500,000. So I guess it was just a case of where I found myself, plus the fact that I've been fortunate enough not to have any real problems getting films that I wanted made, made.

Which of your many films is your favorite?

My personal favorite is *Private Parts.* Among the older, "monster"-type things, I think *Attack of the Giant Leeches* is my favorite—although, maybe if I *saw* it again, I wouldn't *[laughs]!* We just had fun—we had such little money, and I remember the director, Bernie Kowalski, shaming me into getting into my bathing trunks and pushing a camera barge with a cameraman and crew on it through the water so they could film.

Roger's remained a sort of maverick while you've moved on to more mainstream projects. Are you happier where you are now?

Probably. I've had some nice experiences, and some of the films have been well-received—I think of *A Woman Called Golda,* in which I was fortunate enough to work with Ingrid Bergman, and we both won Emmys that year [1982]; and I did *The Big Red One,* which was America's entry at the Cannes Film Festival. It's been very comfortable and enjoyable, and I've met a lot of interesting people.

Do you think the day will come when you'll work with Roger again?

You know, we have not made a film together since *I Escaped from Devil's Island* [1973]. And, whether I've been at the Cannes Film Festival or just talking to the students at U.S.C., everybody keeps asking, "Isn't it time?" And Roger and I keep thinking, "It's *time!*"

So you do think it'll happen again soon?

I would think so, but I'm not at all sure when. We do talk, now and then, about trying something, doing something, and I think it would be kind of fun to do it all again.

There was X number of dollars, and you don't run over on these low-budget films—you shoot the opening scenes and the end scenes, and then fill in the picture in between. And so if you run out of days, somehow they'll dissolve between what you missed and the next scene in there. Fortunately we didn't miss anything, or if we did, it wouldn't have been missed. Believe me. —Richard E. Cunha

Richard E. Cunha
and Arthur A. Jacobs

GIANT FROM THE UNKNOWN, She Demons, Frankenstein's Daughter and *Missile to the Moon*—four horror pictures that any fan of '50s exploitation is sure to remember fondly. Unfortunately, little has been written in horror retrospectives about the director of these movies, Richard E. Cunha. A notable exception to this lack of Cunha exposure was a passage in a recent book on exploitation films which reported that "the late" Richard Cunha was "amazed, shocked and hurt over the bad reviews his horror films garnered. Despondent over the turn of events, he traveled to the Peruvian jungle and has never been seen since." Well, it seems fair to assume that Cunha *has* been seen by a number of people, such as those connected with the television commercials he made for twenty years after completing his last feature in 1961, as well as those people who now patronize his Video Depot shop in Oceanside, California. All in all, we are happy to report that Richard E. Cunha has managed to escape the exile and death designated for him by an imaginative "nonfiction" author, and has lived to tell the tale of his film exploits.

The Hawaiian-born Cunha received his film training in the newsreel and motion picture units of the United States Air Corps during World War II. He made his first step into the civilian film business by making industrial films and commercials, and then moved on to shoot, write and direct such early TV shows as *The Adventures of Marshal O'Dell* and *Captain Bob Steele and the Border Patrol* for Toby Anguish Productions. Cunha and his friend Arthur Jacobs then plunged into the adventurous arena of shoestring '50s exploitation by forming Screencraft Enterprises. Jacobs, who produced Cunha's first two pictures, joins the director for our discussion of *Giant from the Unknown* and *She Demons,* while Cunha, by himself and apparently still living, tackles *Frankenstein's Daughter* and *Missile to the Moon.*

How did you come to form Screencraft Enterprises?

Arthur A. Jacobs: Toby Anguish was getting ready to retire from the business, and Dick and I decided that we would like to take over his studio. I had had a small editorial service, and we decided to join forces, Richard and I, and take over the complete operation that Toby had, which included the stage, the dubbing facilities, the editing rooms and everything else.

Richard E. Cunha: We had a nice stage, it was two thousand square feet—forty by fifty—and it was great for all the kinds of things that we did back in there. We took over the studio and we used it as a production service—we rented out the stage, and we also did editing and dubbing for people.

Jacobs: Right. And we did the editorial on the last thirty-nine *Lone Rangers,* remember? Just prior to making *Giant from the Unknown.*

Cunha: So that's how Screencraft got formed—it was left over from Toby Anguish Productions, and so we inherited a great deal of studio facilities, and—

Jacobs: *Inherited,* Richard?! We hocked our souls for them *[laughs]!*

Cunha: It was all sitting, and so we got into film production. We made

Previous page: The first Cunha-Jacobs collaboration, made in the hope that "maybe we could make a dollar-and-a-quarter out of it."

some television commercials; I remember we did some Texaco commercials with Harry Von Zell....

Jacobs: Cheerios . . . Wheaties . . . we did quite a few now that I think of it.

What prompted you to make a full-length feature film, Giant from the Unknown?

Cunha: We had a friend, Ralph Brooke, who was interested in movies and things, and he kept egging us on and saying, "Why are you guys messin' around here, wouldn't it be better just to make a movie, or do *something?*" He finally convinced us that it would be kind of fun to do, and that maybe we could make a dollar and a quarter out of it. And that's when we decided to make *Giant from the Unknown*—what did we first call it?

Jacobs: *The Giant from Devil's Crag.* We were all sitting in the office one day—let's see, there was you and I, and Ralph, and [screenwriter] Frank Taussig—and we wondered, "What kind of a picture do we want to make?" And then we said, "Well, we should make a monster movie." Then, "What *kind* of a monster?" At first we tried to get a script already written; we had about a hundred scripts come in, and not one of them could we use.

Cunha: One had a giant lizard, and we couldn't afford the lizard *[laughs],* or *any* of those giant whatevers! About that time Bert I. Gordon was making films with giant spiders and animals and things. We figured we didn't have the talent for special effects, so we needed some kind of an inexpensive monster. And we thought, just a *giant*—we had seen a fellow, I think he was 7'7", that rolled around Hollywood for a while—and we decided that a monster that'd be inexpensive would be a big, tall guy. We interviewed quite a few people and ended up with Buddy Baer.

What was your budget on Giant from the Unknown?

Jacobs: I think it was budgeted around $55,000. And we had $30,000 cash. If I remember correctly, the final cost was $54,000 on that picture, and so we had about $24,000 that we owed when we finished—but we had deferments at the lab and so forth.

And your shooting schedule?

Cunha: We had six days of shooting—however, we had prepared the picture for at least a month ahead of time, and we tried to figure the schedule so that it would work out regardless of what happened. We shot at Big Bear, about one hundred miles or so from Los Angeles proper, up in the mountains, and we also shot a great deal in Fawnskin. The snows were a little late that year, and I know the resort areas were all anxiously awaiting the snow so that the skiers would come up. They were glad to have us at that time because it was just dried up, between seasons, so we were able to get a good deal on the motel that we stayed at. That helped a great deal.

We sent the word out on our first day of location that we were going to shoot at Paradise Cove, on the beach there. That was strictly to confuse the union representatives and the agents and so forth. And everyone was so surprised when we got on the bus and headed in the opposite direction from Paradise Cove! That gave us a two-day start on all of the unions before they really did find out where we were hidden, off in the mountains—and, by God, they found us!

Jacobs: They did find us!

Cunha: They finally located us, and we had to hide most of our equipment...

Jacobs: We had the trucks hidden in the woods, and, fortunately, we had used the five-dollar extras the first day.

Cunha: Yeah, we got them out of the way, because that was all very illegal...

Jacobs: All of our pictures looked like union representative conventions *[laughs]!*

Cunha: Okay, so we shot the film in six days; we averaged about twenty-one pages a day.

Jacobs: Except for that Wednesday when you shot twenty minutes of film—which I'll never forget as long as I live!

Cunha: Well, that was a very big day and we had to do that to get out in time.

Jacobs: From the time we decided to do the picture until the time we finished the answer print was sixty days—two months altogether.

Mr. Cunha, why did you photograph as well as direct Giant?

Cunha: I *was* the cinematographer on *Giant* and I *became* the director on *Giant!*

Jacobs: It was cheaper!

Why does Bob Steele, who played the sheriff, wear such a horrible white makeup in the film?

Cunha *[laughs]:* I remember the makeup man coming over to me after working on Bob and saying, "It's not my fault—he told me to do it!" When they get to be a certain age, a lot of people think white makeup makes them look younger. Bob just had this compulsion to put that on, and we kind of had to live with it!

What can you remember about your other stars—Ed Kemmer, Sally Fraser and Morris Ankrum?

Cunha: Ed Kemmer was fantastic—he was eager and Johnny-on-the-spot. And Sally Fraser was neat, too—she hadn't done a great deal prior to that but you wouldn't know it from the way she worked and her very professional attitude. Morrie Ankrum was actually recuperating from an operation when he did *Giant,* and he was just a real trouper. We were in kind of a rugged area there, but outside of the fact that he mentioned it to us once and his agent said to try and take it easy on him, he wouldn't let anybody know that he was in any pain or anything. He was just great.

Jacobs: And Buddy Baer was actually too sweet to be a monster. He was such a nice guy.

Cunha: He was a gem. He really pitched in and did everything.

Jacobs: What was the name of the fellow who made all the fiberglass stuff that we used? He did all the shields and the helmets and everything else.

Cunha: Harold Banks. He did all the armor, the hat, the swords, the extra pieces, the skull. It was our first experience with fiberglass—that was brand new at the time, they weren't making props out of fiberglass.

Jacobs: We couldn't afford the real ones, and he said he could make them out of the fiberglass. And I remember it stunk up the whole studio *[laughs]!* But he sure did a good job on it.

Cunha: He did a fantastic job. We saved a lot of money there.

Had you ever used makeup artist Jack P. Pierce prior to Giant?

Cunha: No, we never used Jack before. He was available, so we got in touch with him and he was very excited about it and was glad to get involved in it.

Jacobs: A *marvelous* man.

Was the Giant's makeup a Jack Pierce original, or was his appearance spelled out in the screenplay?

Cunha: No, we had no idea what the monster should look like, it was all determined by who we cast. And so when Buddy worked out so great, we said to Jack, "Okay, we'll go out and get the locations and set up and do some filming, and you bring out a monster." And he did, and it worked out great. I'm not even sure if we did any tests on that—did we ever do an experiment with him to see what he would look like?

Jacobs: No, Jack Pierce took Buddy aside, put him in the chair, and started working on him. I think it took about two, three hours.

Much of Giant *is photographed outdoors, to great effect, but several brief scenes are ruined by the use of obvious, painted backdrops. Why were these necessary?*

Cunha: We had to buy an inexpensive set and we had a few pickup shots that we had to do in there—when the Giant was shot, and some of the chases. To be able to pull it in on this kind of money it was necessary to use a painted backdrop and, again, a very fast schedule to get on there. Art and I ran the film just last night to remind ourselves what it was all about, and we were reminded of the big fight scene inside of the mill, which was a mill built for...

Top: When Astor Pictures insisted on a *Giant from the Unknown* co-feature, Cunha and Jacobs responded with *She Demons*. *Bottom:* Nazi diehard Gene Roth gets his just deserts at the fangs and claws of the *She Demons*.

Jacobs: *The Trail of the Lonesome Pine* [1936].

Cunha: It was originally built for that and it was left over there, and we worked till midnight shooting the fight sequence and discovered at the end of the night that the shutter in the camera was closed, and we had absolutely nothing that night. We had to come back and we had an abbreviated session the next night and the fight was cut down considerably from what it was before.

That was one of the picture's most atmospheric scenes, filmed in what certainly looks like an actual snowstorm.

Cunha: When we finally did get the snowstorm, it worked in great with the film; we were fortunate enough that it lasted for the sequence. I think we just barely got it all in before the snow left us. I don't recall having to make any phony snow.

Jacobs: We had a couple scenes that we had shot that didn't have snow in 'em, so we had to add snow optically, otherwise it wouldn't match. Richard, you sound like we were *anticipating* a snowstorm. If you remember, when we woke up that morning and there was snow on the ground, you lost ten pounds and turned gray *[laughs]*! We were halfway through the filming and there was no snow at the beginning! That worked out fine, though.

How did your second feature, She Demons, *come about?*

Cunha: We made *Giant from the Unknown* strictly on speculation. We said, "Okay, we're gonna make a picture"—which we were told was *not* the thing to do—and then we were going to put it under our arm, and Art took it back to New York.

Jacobs: It took longer to sell it than to make it *[laughs]*!

Cunha: Yeah, right! But we had a lot of confidence in it, and with the $54,000 budget we thought sure that we'd be able to come out of it okay. When Art got to New York—I think you ran it for various distributors, but Astor Pictures....

Jacobs: I had worked for Astor once, a long time ago—that's how I was aware of them.

Cunha: And so Astor came up and said, "Yeah, fine and dandy, we'll accept *this* picture only if you'll make some more for us," because they wanted to put 'em out in twosomes. And that's how the second picture, *She Demons,* came about.

What was your budget on this one?

Jacobs: They gave us $80,000 for *She Demons,* I think we spent $65,000.

Cunha: But that included our salaries for producer, director, and all that. By that time we figured that I was busy enough directing, and Meredith Nicholson, a very good friend of mine, did the cinematography on *She Demons.*

But this time you co-wrote the screenplay.
>   **Cunha:** I think at that time I did it because it was necessary.
>   **Jacobs:** Who else was gonna do it *[laughs]*? Somebody had to!
>   **Cunha:** I did it because we needed a script, and ... I was there.

She Demons *contains much more humor than any of your other films. Was this part of your contribution?*
>   **Cunha:** I think those are my private little jokes. I was trying to get even with the world at the time and just having a good time. These were really tongue-in-cheek films, and we enjoyed doing them a great deal and had as much fun as possible.

What was Irish McCalla like to work with?
>   **Jacobs:** *Sheena, Queen of the Jungle [laughs]!*
>   **Cunha:** I guess of all the people that we used in the first few films, she was ... well, she wasn't *difficult*....
>   **Jacobs:** No, she really wasn't, Dick, when I think back on it—not compared to some of the kids today. She had already had some notoriety, so, really, it wasn't too bad. You have to remember that actors and actresses are strange people anyhow, aren't they, Richard? They're all difficult, at best.
>   **Cunha:** She had always been a great pinup girl, and she had great boobs and stuff, but then she had this child and she lost everything up top. And we had the worst time trying to get this silly sequence of her nude back. We just had a *terrible* time! It was like she was doing a porno or something! Everybody had to hide, we had to get the guys off the set—we had pasties on her and everything else. It was just the fact that she had lost her bustline and she wanted everybody to remember her like she looked when she was a pinup girl.

What were some of your locations on She Demons?
>   **Cunha:** Paradise Cove was our primary beach location. The jungle sequences we did in Griffith Park, in Ferndale—the regular public trails there. One thing we had to do that they reprimanded us for was putting the dry ice into the stream there. They had already told us not to monkey with the water but of course as soon as we were alone we threw that stuff in—but they caught us.

Probably the best-remembered scene in She Demons *comes when Leni Tana tears off the bandages across her eyes.*
>   **Jacobs** *[to Cunha]: Who* was Leni Tana?
>   **Cunha** *[laughs]:* She was the lady that wore the bandages through the whole picture.
>   **Jacobs:** Oh? I always thought that was your *wife!*
>   **Cunha:** Leni Tana didn't want to wear all that terrible makeup under-

neath the bandages, and so my wife *was* the face for the "reveal" scene! However, Leni Tana walked around with the bandages the rest of the film.

Did the Diana Nellis Dancers, who did the dance routine in the picture, also play the disfigured She Demons?
   Cunha: Yes, they did. That was all part of the same group; we had our little company, if you please, and—
   Jacobs: And one bongo player! That was our whole rhythm section, one bongo player!

Why did you two separate after this first pair of pictures?
   Cunha: As we had mentioned, we had been doing a good deal of postproduction for Jack Wrather and the *Lone Ranger* company. And so, after we had finished these two pictures, Art had the opportunity to go with Mr. Wrather.
   Jacobs: I spent nine and a half years with the Wrather Corporation, ending up as vice-president in charge of production and distribution. I set up domestic and foreign distribution of their television company, and I was involved in the production of *Lassie* for many years. After I left them, I went to work for Danny Thomas, Sheldon Leonard, and Aaron Spelling, at Paramount. I was there for several years. And at that time I decided that I'd really like to see what happens to a picture when it's finished. I got into independent theatrical distribution in the U.S. In 1975 my wife and I moved to London, where I was an independent producer's representative. Right now I'm back in the States, I'm selling independent productions, and for fifteen years I've been trying to get Dick Cunha to make another picture with me *[laughs]!*
   Cunha: That brings us into the metamorphosis into Layton Film Productions. At that time, when Art had the opportunity to go with Jack Wrather, we dissolved Screencraft, and Marc Frederic, who was an investor, then formed Layton Film Productions.
   Jacobs: Which was the name of the street he lived on, if I remember correctly.
   Cunha: Yes, that's right—Layton Drive. He and I formed Layton Productions, and I made another three pictures *[Frankenstein's Daughter, Missile to the Moon* and the detective picture *The Girl in Room 13]* with him.

What were your budgets and shooting schedules on Frankenstein's Daughter *and* Missile to the Moon?
   Cunha: All of our budgets were under $80,000, and we tried very hard to bring them in for approximately $65,000 or less. I think we were successful in most cases. When we turned the negative over to Astor after the picture was accepted, we were paid $80,000. Our shooting schedules were always six days. I believe on *Missile to the Moon* they gave us an extra day of preproduction

where we did some of the monster scenes out at Red Rock Canyon, about eighty miles from Los Angeles.

What were some of your locations for Frankenstein's Daughter?
  Cunha: The exterior scenes were done at Marc Frederic's home. The interiors were a set. Our art director, Don Ament, was a super guy; I worked with him subsequently at E.U.E. Columbia for many, many years. Don was just a fabulous guy — he would go around and see what sets were available cheap, and then redesign 'em so they'd work out for us. He was great at that.

Can you tell us a little about your cast?
  Cunha: They were all keen. John Ashley ... Sandra Knight ... Sally Todd ... Donald Murphy was absolutely great. I don't recall what happened to any of these people; it always seems whenever I make a picture, that's the person's last picture *[laughs]!* It must be something I do...

Where did you get the props for your laboratory scene?
  Cunha: We got a character that was furnishing those to the studios, and we took what the studios wouldn't take — for a price, you know. We'd say, "We can't afford your real prices, so give us the junk from your backyard," and he'd say, "Okay, if you guys clean 'em up, make 'em look pretty good, you can have 'em." So we did it, and returned them to him in twice-better shape than he gave them to us.

Probably the best-remembered scene from this picture is when Donald Murphy gets the acid thrown in his face. Was that really Murphy under the makeup?
  Cunha: Yes, it was. And as I recall — *vividly* — the makeup man on that, who by the way was Paul Stanhope, created that remarkable effect with torn Kleenex tissue. I was quite pleased with that, that worked out very well. We did want Jack Pierce to do the makeup on that, but he was not available for the picture.

Paul Stanhope was your makeup man? The credits list Harry Thomas.
  Cunha: Stanhope was just not ready for us; he was used to *old* motion picture time. So when somebody fired a gun and I'd get twenty-one pages a day, he just fainted on us. That's when Harry Thomas came in.

Was it Stanhope who did the makeup for Sandra Knight's she-monster?
  Cunha: No, that was Harry Thomas.

Harry Wilson, who played Frankenstein's Daughter, had been Wallace Beery's stand-in for twenty-five years and had dubbed himself "The Ugliest Man in Pictures." Can you tell us about him?

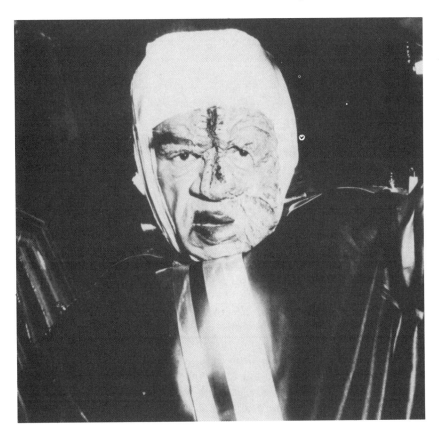

The female monster in Cunha's *Frankenstein's Daughter* was played by Harry Wilson, a one-time stand-in for Wallace Beery.

Cunha: He was a very patient man, and he suffered a great deal with that makeup and the suit that was required for him. And with the speed that we had to shoot at, it wasn't like he could rest between takes. He was always right on call and, as I recall, he was right there all the time. George Barrows played the monster in the scene where he was on fire. Barrows also did a lot of the fight scenes in *She Demons*.

Was it Paul Stanhope or Harry Thomas who did the—very unusual Frankenstein's Daughter makeup?

Cunha: Stanhope. That wasn't an unusual situation at all, it was a situation where we just got trapped, again, without any money. We had no preparation time, and Frankenstein's Daughter was designed on the set on the first day of shooting. And suddenly someone came up to me and said, "Look—here's your monster!" And I nearly *died*. We said, "No, that's not quite what we need, but by God we can't do anything about it!" And we pushed the guy on the set and started shooting — the show must go on. So the monster wasn't designed like that, it just . . . ended up like that, and once we achieved that *[laughs]*, we had to keep it!

One of the best elements from Frankenstein's Daughter *and* Missile to the Moon *is the Nicholas Carras music.*
   Cunha: He was introduced to us, and we liked his style. He was a swinger, and as eager as we were to try and accomplish something on a minimum budget. It seems to me that we paid him about nine or ten thousand dollars for the total music score on each of those two pictures — that included the writing, the musicians and everything. He did a fantastic job.

Whose idea was it to have you remake the earlier Astor release Cat Women of the Moon *as* Missile to the Moon?
   Cunha: It was Astor's idea. They thought, well, shucks, it'd be a good idea to redo the movie, they could get a little bit of sex in and have some pretty girls wandering through the scenes. And it *was* patterned after their movie.

Where did you get the giant spider used in Missile to the Moon?
   Cunha: We rented it from Universal Pictures. In those days we used to go around to all the prop shops, nose in the back rooms and see what we could get cheap. That spider was in Universal's prop shop, and it was in terrible disrepair; we just managed to put it together the best we could. As I recall, we paid practically nothing for it, and they were kind enough to let us use it. It wasn't even written into the picture until we found it in pieces at Universal.

Who designed the Rock Creatures, and what were they made of?
   Cunha: They were made of sponge rubber that was cast. Harold Banks made those for us. He was the very creative man who made the fiberglass outfits for *Giant from the Unknown.*

Wasn't it tough on the people who played those monsters — working in Red Rock Canyon in midsummer?
   Cunha: The worst — absolutely the worst. And if you'll remember we had one scene where we had to plaster them to the sides of giant rocks, for them to break out. And, you know *[laughs]*, it took a while for the plaster to dry with them in there! They'd be yelling, "Get us out of here, get us out of here!" So, yes, that was very, very difficult for them, but they were all good guys. We laughed over a beer about it later.

What was it like working with so many beauty queens in one picture?
   Cunha: A real pain. None of them were actresses as such, they were all beauty queens who couldn't hit marks and couldn't say lines — it was quite frustrating.

Was any inspiration derived from a then-current Allied Artists release, Queen of Outer Space, *which had the same premise as well as some of the same players?*

Cunha: No. I don't remember the picture, and I certainly didn't go see it.

Of your four horror films, which one is your favorite?

Cunha: My favorite was and always will be *Giant from the Unknown* because that was the most fun to make. We did it in a spirit of fun, we had the most cooperation — that was a ball.

Were you disappointed with any of these films?

Cunha: I think the biggest disappointment to me was *Frankenstein's Daughter,* only because of our monster creator; I can't blame anyone for that, we just didn't have enough money to create a monster that would represent Sally Todd. So that was my biggest disappointment. And, as far as *Missile to the Moon* is concerned, again, the money was so meager that it was just impossible to create the proper atmosphere for a spaceship — although I think, on the money we *did* have, the interior of the spaceship worked well. It included many pieces of grip equipment, as I recall, and we used a big dimmer bank for some of the controls on the missile. And we just scraped together whatever we could to make do, and that's all there was. There was X number of dollars, and you don't run over on these low-budget films — you shoot the opening scenes and the end scenes, and then fill in the picture in between. And so if you run out of days, somehow they'll dissolve between what you missed and the next scene in there. Fortunately we didn't miss anything, or if we did, it wouldn't have *been* missed. *Believe* me.

H.G. Wells' The Time Machine *is a classic of science fiction.
I first read it when I was about fifteen years old
and it has always been one of my favorite stories.
So it was a challenge to turn it into a film
without degrading the quality.
I hope I did so.*

David Duncan

AS IS THE CASE in all other types of moviemaking, the screenwriter of a science fiction film is often overlooked in favor of the director. To help correct this common oversight, we present an interview with David Duncan, a novelist turned screenwriter who has contributed to many well-remembered science fiction/horror films of the late 1950s and early 1960s. His credits include *The Monster That Challenged the World, The Black Scorpion,* the Americanized version of *Rodan, The Thing That Couldn't Die* and *Monster on the Campus.* His best work is the script for George Pal's science fiction classic *The Time Machine.*

Duncan didn't start to write full-time until the age of thirty-three, in 1946, after around ten years of work in government administration and public services. He began screenwriting in 1953 but "did not start writing science fiction for the movies until one of my SF novels, *Dark Dominion,* was serialized in *Collier's,*" Duncan recalls. "You know how they categorize people in Hollywood: suddenly I was a science fiction writer, which I had never been before."

Did you write most of these sci-fi pictures on speculation, or were you brought aboard by producers who told you basically what they wanted?

I wrote either on a salary or a contract basis. For my original screenplays I wrote what I pleased. Others were based on books or other material where the producer owned the motion picture rights.

What exactly did you contribute to The Monster That Challenged the World?

When I went to work on the story and screenplay the plan was to make the picture in Japan, and so everything I wrote was done with this in mind. As well as I recall, everyone including myself was pleased with the finished screenplay. I was paid off and had lined up another assignment when the blow fell. For reasons I don't know, the Japanese filming had to be called off, which meant that the screenplay had to be completely rewritten for a local setting. I labored at it for a few days free of charge but everything I wrote was dead, dead, dead. Pat Fielder, a very attractive young woman, was doing secretarial work for the producer at the time and asked if she could have a shot at it. Her request was granted, with very happy results for Pat.

Pat Fielder claimed that you wrote an article about ancient shrimp eggs for Life, *and that was what inspired the movie.*

No, I didn't write for *Life* about shrimp eggs. It may have been the writer-photographer David Douglas Duncan, with whom I was sometimes confused in those days. I recall that he did a book on Picasso and *Publishers Weekly* ran a review of it headed by a picture of me.

Them! *had a large influence on sci-fi films of the '50s, especially* The Monster That Challenged the World *and* The Black Scorpion. *Do you recall whether you saw the film and used it as inspiration?*

Previous page: **David Duncan today.**

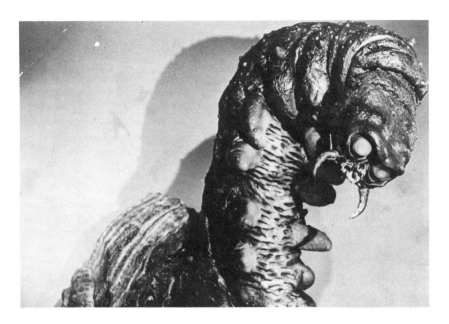

Ten feet, fifteen hundred pounds and $15,000 worth of fiberglass fury, this giant mollusk prop provided more-than-ample menace in the David Duncan-scripted *The Monster That Challenged the World*.

Yes, I saw *Them!*, one of the best. And I certainly used it to the extent that it demonstrated that the longer one could keep the nature of the menace a mystery, the better.

Some film experts insist that parts of The Black Scorpion *were "written around" certain special effects shots which were filmed before a script existed. Do you recall whether you were told to incorporate any specific scenes into your screenplay before you even began writing?*

After almost thirty years, my memories of the actual writing of these screenplays is pretty dim. I seem to recall that there was an unusable script on hand in the case of *The Black Scorpion,* and I remember a huge floppy spider that producer Jack Dietz insisted on introducing far sooner than I thought it should be. I've never seen the film.

Did the men who would eventually direct your screenplays — Edward Ludwig, Will Cowan, Jack Arnold, etc. — meet and consult with you prior to filming?

The only one of the three directors you mentioned that I knew personally was Eddy Ludwig *[The Black Scorpion]*. Directors don't like to have writers around when they start filming. At least no director ever wanted me around or bothered to consult with me. Except George Pal.

I had written a historical drama called *Sangaree* [1953] for Bill Pine and Bill Thomas—"The Two Dollar Bill"—and I went back to work for them again about two months later, when they were shooting the film. I took a break and walked down to where they were filming to see what was happening, and on the set I noticed a sign in a window, "George Washington for President." I tore back to the office and told Bill Thomas, "My God, they've got a sign out there, 'George Washington for President.' He wasn't president until three or four years after this picture is set, and he didn't have to run for president anyway—he was elected unanimously and had no opposition. This'll make the whole picture look silly."

So Bill Thomas grabbed the phone, called the set and stopped them from shooting. Then he went out there to see what was going on. I don't know what this delay cost him, but they stopped production for an hour—it must've been quite a lot. He came back, gave me a glowering look and said, "That sign isn't even in camera range—some extras put it up for fun!" That's one reason they don't like writers on the set.

What are some of the ins and outs of writing dialogue for dubbing into a foreign film like Rodan?

Working on *Rodan* was the most boring job I ever had in my life. The film goes into a Moviola that can run it forward or backward and repeat scenes as many times as needed while the operator stares at the mouths of the Japanese actors and attempts to find English words that fit the mouth movements. There are only three letters in the English alphabet that close the mouth completely—B, M and P—but there must be *dozens* of Japanese characters that do the same thing because when the sound was turned off the actors appeared to be saying something like, "Mama, mama, mama," over and over again. Actually, most of the dubbing was done by a co-worker whose name, I think, was O'Neal. *He* should have received the credit.

Most of your other sci-fi credits around that time were for Universal-International.

Howard Pine, son of Bill Pine, was working as a producer at Universal studios, and he had them put me on salary to come up with some original science fiction screenplays. I wrote *The Water Witch*, which became *The Thing That Couldn't Die*, and *Monster on the Campus*.

Where did the idea for The Thing That Couldn't Die *come from?*

Not long before I wrote *The Thing That Couldn't Die* I'd read a book on dowsing [finding water through the use of a divining rod] by Kenneth Roberts and tried to do a little dowsing myself, in the backyard of our Los Angeles home. Nothing happened. So I turned on the garden hose and carried my wand over it a few times. Nothing. About that time my youngest daughter, six or seven years old at the time, came out of the house. Without telling her

A real-life scientific discovery helped sow the seeds for Duncan's *Monster on the Campus* screenplay.

what I had in mind, I placed the forked wand in her hands and asked her to walk over the hose with it. She did so several times and started giggling. "How funny," she said. "Every time I cross the hose the stick tries to jump out of my hands." I was quite impressed. I think that was the genesis of the screenplay. No, my daughter didn't become a dowser. She's now an attorney living in St. Louis.

Can you tell us how Monster on the Campus *was conceived?*
 Not long before writing *Monster on the Campus* there'd been quite a lot in scientific publications about a live coelacanth having been caught off the

coast of Madagascar. The coelacanth was a species of fish thought to have been extinct for several million years. It was that which suggested the story.

One of the weaker elements in Monster on the Campus *is the utterly careless way Arthur Franz infects himself—getting the dead fish to "bite" him, dripping its blood into his pipe and so on.*

I didn't know the fish bit Arthur Franz, I thought it was only the blood in his pipe that turned him into Pithecanthropus. But you're quite right, that could have been done much better.

Did you also write The Leech Woman *around this same time?*

No, I wrote that long after I had done *Thing That Couldn't Die* and *Monster on the Campus.* Apparently someone at Universal liked what I had done on those two, and a producer by the name of Joseph Gershenson re-hired me.

Unlike Thing *and* Monster, The Leech Woman *was not an original.*

Oh, no. They gave me some material—in fact, I think they gave me a screenplay that had been written by somebody named Ben Pivar. It wasn't a very good screenplay—really, it was unshootable. In redoing it, I suppose I changed the story somewhat. I rewrote it on a two-week assignment and never saw it until a couple of months ago, when I happened to catch it on TV. Isn't it *awful?*

Several of your sci-fi films are surprisingly violent for their time.

I never cared for violence in movies, although I love suspense. In science fiction monster films, it's the special effects guys who have all the fun and are usually responsible for the gruesome stuff.

Did George Pal give you enough creative freedom when you worked with him on The Time Machine?

It was great working with George Pal, and there were no restraints on my writing. The only restraint was that I had to write the screenplay in the upstairs bedroom of my house, whither George came occasionally for discussion. He didn't want anyone to know what we were doing; on some previous occasions, his ideas had been preempted by quickie producers before he could get them on film. However, I liked the bedroom. I could work in my pajamas.

Tell us how you went about adapting the original H.G. Wells novel into a screenplay.

Like most of Wells' science fiction novels, *The Time Machine* was as much a social document as a tale of science adventure. It was written around the turn of the century—about 1895, as I recall. Anyhow, the Industrial Revolution was in full swing at the time, with laborers working long hours at low pay in underground mines and dingy factories while the elite basked in the sunshine at the workers' expense. Wells was something of a socialist; he conceived a future where this industrialization brought about, through the forces of evolution, a split in the human race. The proletariat became a race of underground Morlocks while the elite, being utterly dependent upon them, lost all incentive for anything except pleasure. While remaining human in appearance, they degenerated mentally and morally into thoughtless childishness.

However, by 1959 when the screenplay was written, this forecast of the future no longer carried any plausibility — if it *ever* did. Labor unions were strong, wages were high, while shorter hours, vacations with pay, pension plans and a host of other fringe benefits had moved most blue-collar workers into the middle class.

Fortunately, however, the ill wind that was blowing then and has been blowing ever since, blew *The Time Machine* some good. The '50s and '60s were the years when schoolchildren were being taught to hide under their desks (unbelievable!) and the populace at large encouraged to dig backyard bomb shelters and prepare to dive into them when the air raid siren warned of an impending attack by atomic bombs.

So you substituted that situation for the economic one in the original story?
Right. Over a period of time the people above ground became conditioned to seeking the lower regions when the air raid siren sounded; over the same centuries those who had originally constructed the vast underground shelters became the carnivorous Morlocks. That was a principal change from the Wells novel.

Then you added a great deal to the story.
Of course. In the novel the only truly human character is the Time Traveller, to whom Wells didn't even bother to give a name. George Pal decided to call him George. A number of other characters then had to be created for the opening and closing scenes of the play. One of them Pal kindly gave the name of David.

For the rest, the action generally followed the Wells novel, or at least what was suggested by the novel. In the novel, for example, the Time Traveller descends into the realm of the Morlocks only long enough to realize that if he remains there he's likely to be eaten, and so he beats a hasty retreat. This would never do for a motion picture. There had to be a major underground sequence.

It's impossible for me to write dialogue and stage directions without knowing what the stage looks like, and no scene designers had been put to work yet. So I spent a couple of hours with pencil and paper sketching out a picture of the Morlocks' underground world. When George saw it he took it home with him. The following Sunday morning, when I went to his home for a

Rod Taylor lashes out at attacking Morlocks in 1960's *The Time Machine*. Duncan considers his screenplay (adapted from the H.G. Wells novel) for this George Pal classic his best work in the genre.

conference, I was flattered to find him out on the lawn before his easel translating my sketch into a full-color finished version upon which the actual set was later based.

Didn't you and Pal discuss the possibility of giving the film's framing sequences a contemporary setting?

Yes, but only briefly. We both agreed that the Victorian beginning made the film more believable by allowing the Time Traveller to pass through that part of the twentieth century with which the audience was already familiar. That made it possible to bring it *real* history, such as the world wars. It also gave viewers the pleasure of witnessing the Time Traveller's astonishment at technological advances which, to them, were already commonplace.

Did you have a hand in designing the Morlock makeup?

No, I had nothing to do with that. But I do remember being on the set one day during shooting when the Morlocks had everyone roaring with laughter at their offstage antics. I recall George saying something to me to the effect, "My God, do you think the motion picture audience will react that way?"

Did The Time Machine *reach the screen exactly as you had written it?*

No, there was some tampering with the script after I was finished with it.

I recall going to the premiere with my wife Elaine, and at some point in the far-future part of the story the Time Traveller came out with a line to the effect that the Eloi were at a cultural level on a par with the people on the isle of Bali. Elaine gave me a ferocious jab with her elbow and I whispered frantically, "I didn't do it! I didn't do it!" The Balinese were building temples while the Time Traveller's ancestors were still chasing deer with stone-pointed sticks.

You received the Georges Méliès Award for your Time Machine *screenplay.*
I didn't receive that award until the mid-'70s, long after we'd moved to Oregon and after I'd stopped writing for films or TV. My reaction was, "Why the hell didn't they give it to me while I was still active and it might have done me some good?"

Many fans see The Time Machine *as George Pal's best feature. Did Pal ever try to seek out your services for any other collaboration?*
We talked of other projects several times but nothing more developed.

Did writing Fantastic Voyage *entail much anatomical research on your part?*
I do remember having a number of anatomical books on hand while working on it. I also remember taking my microscope to the studio one day to show the art director what living red blood cells look like. I insisted that he examine his own cells rather than mine.

Would you care to elaborate on the way that film was, according to many, mishandled?
I think the big mistake in making *Fantastic Voyage* was in trying to integrate a spy story with what should have been purely a pictorially beautiful science fiction picture. The spy-sabotage element was added by the second writer, who received the screenplay credit. I believe another mistake was the abrupt manner in which the human body was entered. This was like introducing the monster of a monster movie in the opening scene.

Did you go to see your own movies when they were released theatrically?
The only one of my movies I ever saw at a premiere was *The Time Machine*. I've never seen *The Monster That Challenged the World* and didn't even know that was its final title until you mentioned it. Nor have I ever seen *The Black Scorpion. Rodan* I had to see at least twenty times while dubbing it and never want to see it again. The others I've seen on television.

What occupies your time nowadays?
You've been keeping me busy quite a while now. For the rest, I garden a lot, especially in the spring, spend quite a bit of time with my microscope

studying the Protozoa I culture in a tiny artificial pool on the hillside, take an auto trip with my wife every now and then, read a lot and once a year watch the World Series on television.

Which of your science fiction films is your personal favorite?

The Time Machine, by a huge margin. The Wells novel is a classic of science fiction. I first read it when I was about fifteen years old and it has always been one of my favorite stories. So it was a challenge to turn it into a film without degrading the quality. I hope I did so.

*I finally got to the point where it was like,
"Oh, well—some people work at the shoe store,
some people work in the butcher shop.
I'll work in the studios, and a job's a job."
There are naturally aspirations and so forth that you have,
but it's better than working in a restaurant!*

Anthony Eisley

ALL TOO UNDERSTANDABLY, Anthony Eisley prefers to be remembered as the suave, stalwart star of television's *Hawaiian Eye,* rather than as leading man to insectivorous ingenues *(The Wasp Woman),* walking trees *(The Navy vs. the Night Monsters),* giant apes *(The Mighty Gorga)* and mustachioed sea serpents *(Monstroid).* But as the 1950s horror boom extended into the 1960s, the mantle of monster exterminator formerly worn by the likes of John Agar, Richard Carlson and Kenneth Tobey was inherited by Eisley when he starred in a long succession of low-budget sci-fi/horror adventures.

The future stage, screen and TV star (real name: Fred Eisley) was born in Philadelphia. His father was general sales manager and "trouble-shooter" for a large company, and his work kept the family on the move, up and down the East Coast, throughout Eisley's young life. As early as the days of school plays, Eisley knew that he wanted to be an actor, but because he lacked show biz contacts he felt nothing would come of his aspiration. He later took drama courses at the University of Miami, "not because I thought I could really be an actor, but because I was taking the easy way out to get a degree."

Finally following up on his longtime ambition, Eisley landed a job with a stock company in Pennsylvania, where he worked opposite James Dunn in a stage production of *A Slight Case of Murder.* Later roles in long-running plays like *Mr. Roberts, Picnic* and *The Desperate Hours* ensued, along with some early movie *(Operation Pacific, Fearless Fagan)* and TV *(Racket Squad)* work. His first genre assignment was in Roger Corman's mini-budgeted *The Wasp Woman,* and the rest is exploitation history.

How did you enjoy working with the legendary — notorious — Roger Corman on The Wasp Woman?

This reveals some lack of depth in me, I suppose, but I thought it was fun — a hell of a lot of fun — because he worked like a house afire and I like to work fast. On the stage I had spent eight years playing four parts; I'd had a great deal of luck in being in hit plays that consumed a lot of time, but after that period was over I found it much more enjoyable to learn something, do it, forget it and go on. So whipping through that picture with Corman was a lot of fun; in fact, he did some pretty strange things. He would set up one camera angle on a particular setting that may appear in the picture five times. And then you would do all five scenes, changing your clothes between each scene. Then he'd set up the *other* camera angle, over your shoulder, and you'd do the five different scenes *again,* changing your clothes five times again! There was no sense of continuity or anything, but to me it was fun to do it in little bits and pieces.

What do you remember about your leading ladies Susan Cabot and Barboura Morris?

Susan Cabot was one of Roger's stock company at the time, and I don't think she was happy with the picture. And not being happy, she was more

Previous page: Anthony Eisley strikes a ready-for-action pose in the zero-budgeted *Journey to the Center of Time.*

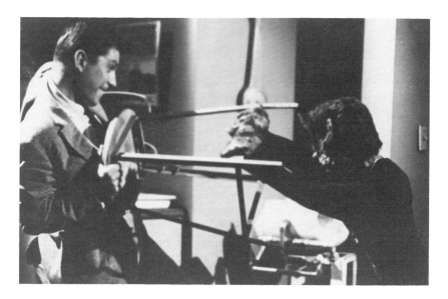

Eisley and she-monster Susan Cabot battle it out at the climax of director Roger Corman's *The Wasp Woman*.

inclined to go sulk in a corner rather than converse with anybody. I think she was unhappy, probably just fulfilling some contractual obligation, and she was not that sociable because I think she was pretty p.o.'ed at Roger most of the time — for what reasons, I don't know. Barboura Morris was just a sweet young girl; she had done quite a few pictures for Roger, and I've often wondered what happened to her career after that.

Any other Wasp Woman *memories?*
There is one funny thing I remember. At that time I was very gung-ho, and any time something came up that involved any element of danger I thought, "Hey, man, this is great, I'm gonna show 'em" — which is something you grow out of eventually. There were no stunts, per se, on *The Wasp Woman,* but they had a scene where I had to break through a glass office door and rescue the heroine. They shot that very early on and I insisted that I would kick through the glass door for real, which I did. And it was real glass — budget-wise, they didn't even have the money for candy glass. But thereafter they put opaque paper over the door — glued it on, instead of replacing the glass — and shot many scenes which preceded that breakthrough in the picture. So if you look, you'll notice that whenever the door opens or closes, the "glass" balloons back and forth like the jib on a sailboat! Talk about low-budget, I had never seen such cost-cutting as Roger Corman did. But there was no question that that guy really knew what he was doing — he was miraculous at turning out acceptable product in no time at all.

Early on, what sort of niche did you hope to fill as a movie/TV actor?

I was hoping to be a light comedian, which of course didn't happen. What actually brought me to the attention of Warner Bros. is that I did the play *Who Was That Lady?* at the Players Ring Theater in Los Angeles; Jerry Paris and I were the co-leads in it, and we were very, very funny. Then when I got a Warner Bros. contract which more or less came from that show, I had visions of being the next Jack Lemmon. Instead they put me in *Hawaiian Eye,* and I have no complaints about that, but it wasn't what I thought they would have in mind for me. So I never really got to do what I felt that I did best.

Why did you leave Hawaiian Eye *after the third season?*

It was a political thing. A guy at an ad agency who handled one of our sponsors never liked me, for what reason I don't know. When *Hawaiian Eye* was about to be picked up for the fourth year, the ad agency guy said that the sponsor would pick up the show only provided they bring in Troy Donahue. At that time Troy and Connie Stevens were hot on the big screen. Well, now you had Bob Conrad, Grant Williams, me and, in order to be picked up, they had to have Troy Donahue come in. At that point it simply became a question of seeing whose option came up first. My option came up like three weeks after this edict was handed down, so they just dumped me. Of course it wasn't that simple, but that's the basic story.

Shouldn't a popular series like Hawaiian Eye *have led to a career in a better grade of film than those you ended up in?*

Yeah! *[Laughs.]* You're right, my career never took off again like I felt that it should have. I think the big thing was the image that I came out of *Hawaiian Eye* with. It was a very limiting image.

Were there some lean years after Hawaiian Eye?

Oh, yeah, it was always up and down. Then I had some years where I made a hell of a lot on commercials, which I never thought were great fun, but it kept things going for me. It was always a seesaw ride, it was never what it should've been. But I have no complaints.

What recollections do you have of The Navy vs. the Night Monsters?

The producer recut that picture after it was made, and totally destroyed any validity it might have had. That picture, as Michael Hoey wrote and directed it, would have been a very good little thriller. First of all, you never saw these trees in explicit detail — you had a sense of mystery about what was killing the people on this island. As originally shot, the island radio tower was destroyed by a plane crash, and there was no contact between the island and the outside world. I, as executive officer of the island military base, was not prepared to assume command, and I had nobody I could turn to. So we played it at a level of fear and panic that wouldn't exist if we could have contacted

The Navy vs. the Night Monsters pitted Eisley against walking trees, a hostile sex kitten and a blundering executive producer.

some base on the outside. Then, months after the picture was shut down, the producer put in this stupid stock footage of bombers blowing up the island at the end and shot these monotonous talking scenes of generals on the telephone that were not at all germane to the original story. As a consequence, in the final cut we actors were playing at a level that the situation didn't call for at all! That was very, very upsetting.

When you talk about the producer, you mean Jack Broder?
   Right. He wanted more running time, I guess, but mainly he wanted to use that stock footage of the airplanes. The picture should have ended on a note of mystery: Will they be able to overcome this menace or not? But he had to continue the picture with all that airplane stuff. I'm not saying that the picture ever could have been any kind of a gem, but it had a validity that it subsequently lost because of the stuff he added.
   Jack Broder had produced quite a few low-budget pictures, and I was always mystified as to why he never made any sense—you'd normally figure that a guy who produces pictures must know something *about* them! Because he felt we had been taking too long and because he was so concerned about his schedule, he would walk in, in the middle of a scene, and insist that the set be torn down—which would happen! And then a few days later he'd realize the scene had to be finished, and they'd have to put the set up again! He did things like this constantly! Another time he was sitting in the projection room

looking at dailies—Michael Hoey and I were there, too, watching this fight scene that I had with Ed Faulkner in the picture. After it was over Jack said, "That was terrible!" Mike said, "I thought it looked all right—what's the matter with it?" and Jack said, "I can't hear the punches!" *[Laughs.]* I don't know what the hell he was ever doing making pictures.

Who directed all those extra scenes you talked about?

I think they were directed by Arthur C. Pierce, who also directed *Women of the Prehistoric Planet*. The opening scenes in the airplane, scenes of the guys with the weather balloons, all this was thrown in after the fact. I don't know what the hell any of that stuff was, it was totally boring.

What do you remember about star Mamie Van Doren?

Her nose was out of joint about everything in the world at the time. I have no idea why, but she wouldn't even say hello! You'd play a scene with her and it was like she was in another world, and she was offended at people talking to her even when you were just doing dialogue! It was just incredible; I don't know what her problem was, but she couldn't wait to leave. That was very uncomfortable.

One of our favorites among your films was your Italian-made James Bond imitation Lightning Bolt.

To me, that was sort of a disaster. Again, we're not talking great art here, but we made that picture two or three years before it was released over here, and by the time it came out it was too late to capitalize on the early success of the Bond pictures. By the time they brought it over here they had lost the interpositive or something, and they had to go back to Italy and piece something together—they had to reassemble it like it had been a decayed old silent picture they were restoring! They got it here a year or two too late to release it successfully—at least that's my opinion. Also, in having to piece it together like a puzzle, the editing became pretty jumbled and ragged. I understand that *Lighting Bolt* was a moneymaker in Europe, but it did miserably here. As a matter of fact, in the L.A. area they released it on the bottom of a double bill *with* a James Bond picture, which was sure death!

I always thought that picture was a lot of campy fun.

Oh, that's exactly what I thought. It made no sense, but campy fun, yes! And that was one of the most fun experiences that I ever had. First of all, at the time we made it I felt that it could possibly be a success in the U.S.—I thought it would make more sense than it ultimately did, and I thought that I could do my own looping well enough to make it come off. But in terms of the action in it, I thought it was a gas. I was still young enough to enjoy all the running and jumping, and except for one diving tackle and a few cuts that were reshot with a double after I'd returned to the U.S., I did it all myself.

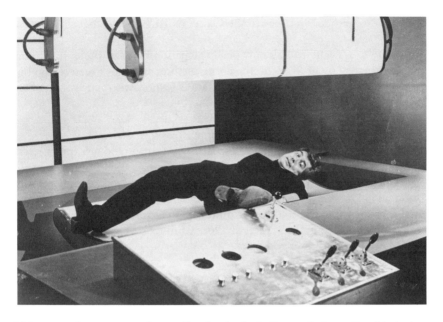

Eisley struggles to escape a frozen-alive fate in the Italian-made James Bond imitation *Lightning Bolt*.

The scene at the bottom of the water-filled silo was actually shot sixteen feet underwater, at the bottom of what had once been an official Olympics pool in Rome. I worked in short cuts, occasionally getting a gulp of air from a garden hose dangling from the surface and just out of frame.

A day or two before that sequence, we had been shooting some scenes at an actual brewery in Rome. Between shots the Italian stunt guys and I were playing a makeshift "tag" game on moving conveyor belts. I got a foot stuck in a roller on one of the turns and screamed bloody murder till they threw the "stop" switch. Nothing was broken, but my foot swelled up terribly. So, in the underwater sequences, a sharp eye can detect that I'm wearing a shoe on one foot, and a painted sock on the other! Another thing that was fun was that gantry sequence — they tore the roof off the studio and built an actual gantry, about eighty-five feet high. I think more than anything else I enjoyed the riding up and climbing on that thing, and the fight at the top. As I said, I don't think I've had more fun on a picture than on *Lightning Bolt*.

Why did you have red hair in that picture?

[Laughs.] It was a co-production with the Woolners in the United States; the Woolners brought me over there to do it and the director, "Anthony Dawson," who is really Antonio Margheriti, thought I looked too Italian! He insisted upon the hair. It was supposed to be blond, but it came out wrong.

Would you agree that Journey to the Center of Time *is probably your dullest film?*

[Laughs.] Yeah! There's only one explanation for that whole thing, and that is that they spent $1.95 on the entire picture, and shot it in a studio the size of your den! But under the circumstances I think everybody did the best they could.

What kind of director was Center of Time's *David L. Hewitt?*

David Hewitt at one time was a special effects man, and he's the sweetest guy in the world. I really like Dave, and we always had a lot of fun. He made these pictures for nothing, and when you look at them you say, "My God!" But if anybody would ever give this guy enough money to put what he wants on the screen, I think he could make quite a good picture. He's always operated totally on a shoestring; he's a hell of a lot of fun to work with, but you don't do it with any kind of expectations.

You later did another picture for Hewitt, The Mighty Gorga, *which is very rarely seen.*

I know of a guy who at one time got ahold of it and was apparently peddling it in Europe, but to my knowledge the picture was never finished. It was basically a *King Kong* rip-off, but I don't think they ever finished the special effects. The guy who was selling it probably sold it in packages, and then ran like hell!

Where was that shot?

I think we shot that out in the Simi Valley somewhere. As I said, Dave Hewitt used to be a special effects man, and he would fake all sorts of things. I think we were just out in some field that he rigged up to look like a jungle somehow, and I remember he got some animal shots by having me walk around a zoo! Dave's a hell of a good guy, and a talented guy, but I don't think anything he's ever tried to do ever translated on film 'cause he's never had the wherewithal to do it.

Were you interested in horror and science fiction films, or were these just jobs?

Jobs. I enjoyed them—had a hell of a lot of fun with them—but I didn't seek 'em out!

What do you remember about The Mummy and the Curse of the Jackals?

I don't mean this disrespectfully, but the director was quite senile at the time. Putting together the cast for that film, he contacted me and Scott Brady. Scott was to play the guy who becomes the Jackal Man, which of course was just a rip-off of the Wolf Man, and I was going to play his friend. But what happened was that Scott got something better, I wound up playing the Jackal

Man and they got Robert Allen Browne to play the friend. I was very glad to have a job—and making these low-budget things was always fun because it's like playing cowboys and Indians rather than working. But when I found out I was going to be the Jackal Man, the one thing I instantly thought was, "Oh, God, I can't sit through all that makeup stuff!"

Early in production they shot a transformation scene where I was lying on a table; they were putting one layer of makeup on at a time, shooting a few frames of film at a time, and that took all day. Well, as I said, the director was sort of losing his faculties, and I realized after a few days that he really didn't know what the hell was going on at all times. They had a second mask—just a quick pull-over thing, for my stunt double to use—so, to be very honest, the stunt double and I got to be friends, somewhere along the line I realized the director would never know, and I never put that makeup on again! Every time I became the Jackal Man, it was the stunt double. And the director never knew it! That took the curse off of that picture.

That film was never released, and has only recently come out on video.
To my knowledge the picture was never finished, and I have no idea what's out on tape. What I always understood was that it was uncuttable—there was so much stuff that did not match at all. For example, the director shot one sequence at midnight, an exterior, that was supposed to be *high noon*—and that was a plot point! We knew as we were doing it that this was never going to make it.

Were you involved in the monster scenes shot on the Las Vegas Strip?
No—but that's another story! I was shooting out at a shack someplace one afternoon when the director became frantic about being behind schedule, turned to the assistant director and said, "Let's set up a second unit downtown and get that stuff with the monsters running around." So the assistant called downtown, got all the permits and everything, they split up the crew and sent 'em downtown. I still had a whole day's shooting left to do where I was. An hour later a call comes from downtown to tell the director that they needed me. He had set up a second unit to save time, and I was supposed to be working both places! So I never went down there, and I have no idea what they shot. That was the absolute epitome of total confusion.

Why was the film never finished?
It just became hopeless *[laughs],* and I'm sure they ran out of money and everything else.

What can you tell us about your frequent co-star John Carradine?
John is the sweetest guy in the world, just a delightful man. He's a true product of the old theater—Shakespeare and so forth—and he has anecdotes that are simply priceless. You know he is so crippled and pained with arthritis

it's amazing to see him rise above it and triumph over it. He's the oldtime trouper through and through, and as such you have to respect and admire him. He definitely will die with his boots on—that's the only way he would have it. It's that kind of thorough professionalism that just makes him a joy to be around.

How did you become involved on The Witchmaker?

That was made by friends of mine, and it was sort of a mutual project. I was not one of the instigators—Alvy Moore and L.Q. Jones, both of whom are actors, scared up money and actually did a film, which very few people can do. That was made on location in Marksville, Louisiana, and that again was a hell of a lot of fun. Not because we had a great script to work with or any particular budget or anything like that, but because practically all the people involved there *were* actors, and we could all share the experience of trying to make something out of what little we had.

Was that all shot in Louisiana?

Yep. From the motel where we stayed, it was about a half mile by motorboat, through the bayous, to the cabin location. So we had the advantage there of being in an authentic locale, which sort of gives you a little edge to start with.

Dracula vs. Frankenstein *was no better than a lot of these other cheapies, but at least it had some strong cast values.*

That, to me, has to be the absolute worst. I made a picture called *The Blood Seekers* which did not involve Dracula, Frankenstein or several of the other elements that are now in there. J. Carrol Naish and Lon Chaney were in it, and it was about the pair of them killing girls to use their blood for some kind of experiments—we've heard *that* plot before! It was a pretty raunchy little picture, but it made sense. Director Al Adamson and Independent International started cutting, reshooting, adding more and more plot elements, pieced it all together and tried to make a story out of it. I had no idea what the hell they had in mind. When I finally saw the picture I can't say I was terribly shocked, 'cause I didn't expect it to be a work of art in the first place, but between that half-assed looking Frankenstein and the strange young man who played Dracula and some of the other elements they brought in, I thought, "Well, there's one picture that I would rather nobody *ever* see!"

Can you tell us about working with Chaney?

Lon Chaney died a few months after we finished that; he was probably the most fascinating man I had ever worked with. He was very, very ill then—he would have to lie down after every take—but to talk with him and to hear his stories was just incredible. He was a wonderful, lovely, unbelievably interesting man. I think in the few days that we were on the set he was very ill,

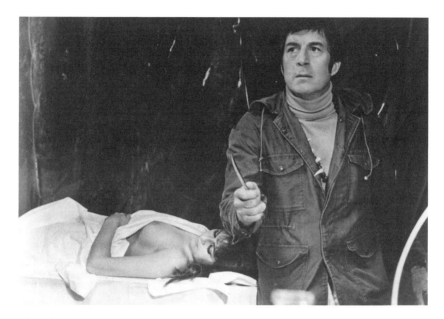

Eisley feels he reached his professional nadir with the execrable *Dracula vs. Frankenstein*.

but for that short period of time we became friends, and I was terribly saddened when he died.

Wasn't his voice pretty much gone by this point?

Yes, he spoke in a whisper, which is why they made his character a mute. You may recall that he and I had a little bit of a physical encounter in the picture. Lon was going to be doubled in that sequence, because he really was ill. Some time before they were supposed to do that sequence, he whispered to me that, once more before he — he didn't say *died,* but that's what he meant — he would really like to do a fight scene, and that they wouldn't let him do it. I thought, jeez, this guy has been around so long, he's a legend of a sort — why not give him his last wish? Back in my *Hawaiian Eye* days Bob Conrad and I had done a good portion of our own fights and so forth, so we knew the basic techniques. I went to Al Adamson and told him we could shoot this thing in really short cuts, and there was no reason that Chaney couldn't do it. So we did do the fight that way, and he was exhausted. The next day he came to the set and told me he'd gone home the night before and almost drowned in the bathtub, he was so tired — his wife had to wake him up! But he told me, "I'm so glad we did it, because that was the most fun I've had in ten years."

What do you remember about Al Adamson?

I had never gotten that close personally to Al; I never disliked him, but I kept an emotional distance from him because I felt that he had excruciatingly

Ad for *Dracula vs. Frankenstein.*

bad taste. I wanted to reserve the right to say, "No, thanks, Al, I won't do that." So I never warmed up to him too much.

What do you recall about the unreleased 1,000,000 A.D. *[1973]?*

[In stitches.] That was a scam—although not on my part! This was the same film salesman who was selling *The Mighty Gorga* overseas; he came up

with a scheme to shoot a trailer for a nonexistent picture, show it in Europe, take advance orders on the picture, get the money and then come back and make it—which never happened. John Carradine, Jo Morrow and I went up to Victorville, California—we were there two or three days—and what we were shooting was this *trailer*. I don't know whether he even had a story! I remember us crawling out of a plane; being chased by a bunch of prehistoric women; and Carradine, as some sort of an old sage, making a speech on a rock. But that's it—there *is* no picture!

Monstroid *was really rock-bottom, and even you looked unhappy.*
I was—that was a disaster. The producer, Ken Hartford, raised enough money to get us on location and buy ten feet of film, I guess, to start out—it was one of those situations where there was just no way of ever really doing it right. Most people going in felt that they could get a few bucks out of it and forget it, and that nobody would ever see it. Of course the only flaw in that theory was that apparently he did get it finished to some extent and some people have seen it—but you can only hope there aren't that many! That was a terrible experience.

What made it so bad—poor working conditions?
That, and total idiocy on the production end. Expecting people to do things that are impossible, and having no understanding of what the quote-artistic-unquote people are trying to do. All Hartford cared about was his cockamamie monster—if he could have had ninety minutes of the monster swimming in the pond there, everybody could have gone home and he'd have been very happy.

Hartford gets director's credit, but Herbert Strock told us that he *directed it.*
Strock directed everything. Then later Hartford shot a couple scenes in Griffith Park with his own kids and claims to have directed it. It's totally falacious.

Your newest sci-fi film is Fred Olen Ray's Deep Space. *How did you become involved with him?*
You won't believe this. Through my agent, I got a call to go see Fred Olen Ray, whom I had never met before. Fred said that he had always liked my work, so on and so forth, and that he had just run a tape of one of my pictures. I asked him which one, and he told me it was *The Mummy and the Curse of the Jackals!* Can you imagine? Some guy sees that and says to himself, "I want to use that actor!" *[Laughs.]* But at any rate, he went on to say that he makes two or three pictures a year, and that he just wanted to meet me. A few weeks later, he called my agent again and offered me a part, with star-type billing, in *Deep Space*.

I really enjoy seeing you in pictures, but I get so depressed at the pictures themselves.

   [Laughs.] Me, too! I finally got to the point where it was like, "Oh, well — some people work at the shoe store, some people work in the butcher shop. I'll work in the studios, and a job's a job." There are naturally aspirations and so forth that you have, but it's better than working in a restaurant!

What are you doing to keep busy nowadays?

   Up until this past year or so I've kept comparatively busy doing guest star shots on TV. Then in the last year I just got tired of the rat race in general and I moved down here to Palm Desert. Also I became a stunt driver a couple of years ago; I don't publicize it because you don't have to work a lot to make a good living, and because I want people to continue to think of me as an actor. I guess I've become philosophical about it: I enjoy the sunshine, it's a healthy place to live down here, and I've gotten out of the rat race completely. I don't feel like going around any more to casting offices where they have a twelve-year-old kid in charge and he wants to know who you are. So I decided I'll work quietly as a stunt driver, two or three days a month, and that's all I need. The rest of the time I'm gonna sit down here and relax, where people aren't so crazy.

   I really probably shouldn't say that — it may sound a little bitter. And while I don't mean to say that there aren't areas of bitterness in my memories of my career, all in all I've had a lot of fun, and I've met and worked with some great people. And if a great part came along and somebody would let me do it, I'd love to. But I've gotten beyond the point of really feeling any great concern about it. I've had a good time and I've got a lot of years left just to sit back and enjoy myself.

*It disturbed me for a while [that Ray Bradbury got
all the credit for writing* It Came from Outer Space*];
all my friends and all the people "in the know" knew
what the facts were, but I doubted that the public knew.
When Bernard Shaw and Joe Blow write something,
they're going to give all the credit to Shaw!*

Harry J. Essex

AT THE HEIGHT of the 1950s science fiction boom, writer Harry J. Essex was involved with two of the best-remembered and most influential films of that period: director Jack Arnold's 3-D productions of *It Came from Outer Space* and *Creature from the Black Lagoon*. Although these two credits alone would assure Essex's place in sci-fi history, he also contributed to *Man Made Monster* and *What Ever Happened to Baby Jane?* as well as handling writer-producer-director chores on the more recent *Octaman* and *The Cremators*.

New York–born, Harry Essex planned on a writing career throughout his young life. Among his first jobs were stints on the New York newspapers *The Daily Mirror* and *The Brooklyn Eagle*, short stories for *Collier's* and *The Saturday Evening Post* and even a Broadway play entitled *Something for Nothing*. "It was a resounding *failure*, both out of town and in New York, but it was an achievement for a kid who was not even twenty-one to have played on Broadway." Writing for the movies was uppermost in Essex's mind throughout the period, but the big break never came, and World War II intervened. Then, five or six days after his discharge, he ran into an old acquaintance whose new job was finding playwrights to turn into screenwriters for Columbia Pictures. His friend greeted him with the question, "How would you like to go to Hollywood?" and Essex was off and running.

Several years before your Hollywood career officially began, your name turned up in the credits of Universal's Man Made Monster. *How did that come about?*

That was written while I was still working at *The Daily Mirror*. There were three of us sitting around an office—myself, Sidney Schwartz, who also worked for the paper, and Len Golos, a press agent. We were bouncing story ideas around, and I came up with the notion to do a thing called *The Electric Man*. It was based on a true story I'd read about: A government organization was performing tests on the electricity in the human body, how much we use up throughout the day and how we "recharge the batteries" by sleep at night. Out of that was born the idea of *The Electric Man*—if there was some way to recharge the body's electricity, we wouldn't have to eat or sleep.

Were you writing with the intention of selling it to the movies?

Yeah, it was a movie treatment. The three of us sat there and developed the story. Well, actually, Golos wasn't much of a writer, he was a press agent, and just in for a free ride. It was really Sidney and I—we'd been collaborating on stories prior to that, and we kept thinking about the movies, of course. The story was submitted to an agency, under the title *The Electric Man*, and sold to Universal. We didn't get much money for it at the time—I think we got something like $3,300—but it was my first big sale. *Man Made Monster* got some excellent reviews—I remember that *Time* and *Life* liked it very much—and it was pretty much exactly what we had written. That was my very first screen credit.

Previous page: **Harry J. Essex.**

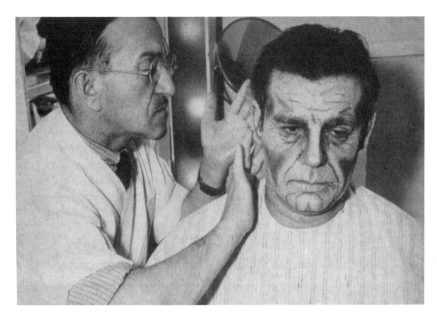

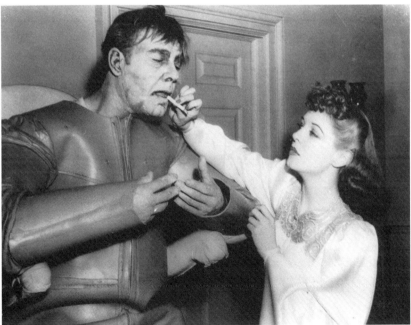

Top: Universal's resident makeup genius Jack P. Pierce puts some finishing touches on *Man Made Monster* Lon Chaney, Jr. This 1941 thriller was Harry Essex's first screen credit. *Bottom:* Leading lady Anne Nagel helps an encumbered Chaney take a drag on a cigarette behind the scenes on *Man Made Monster*.

Was it producer William Alland who took you on as a writer on It Came from Outer Space?

Really, it was the studio that assigned both Alland and me to the job. But of course I'd have to meet with Alland first, to see if we got along. A couple of years ago I ran into him at a marina out here; we stopped and talked, and I asked him why he was no longer in the business. He said he couldn't tolerate it anymore, it was an impossible business. Well, the truth is that I always found *him* a little impossible! He was an ambitious man, very sensitive — he'd weep at the drop of a hat — but underneath it all he was ruthless. But he never achieved enough importance or power that he could practice at *being* a ruthless man! But when I ran into him at the marina he was very gentle and very sweet; we talked about the old days and that was about it. He was a very strange little guy — he's no longer around, and I have no idea where the hell he is.

Since Ray Bradbury wrote some treatments for It Came from Outer Space, *why wasn't he allowed to do the screenplay?*

Ray never did a treatment, he did a three-page short story.

I've seen copies of full-length It Came from Outer Space *treatments, with Bradbury's name on them as author.*

No, it's *my* treatment. Ray's story was a very short piece, and I did the treatment, which was accepted. Some time later, when we were invited to attend the preview, some very formal invitations were sent out, and there was Ray Bradbury's name above mine, which would generally not be the case. But of course I could understand what the situation was — I mean, we're talking about an internationally popular writer, a famous man! There was enough credit for everybody; the people inside the business knew that I had written the screenplay, and that was all that mattered.

Did Bradbury even attempt to write a screenplay?

Yeah, he tried to write a screenplay, and it was just no good. He's not a screenplay writer. But as a matter of fact it was through *It Came from Outer Space* that Ray got a very important job, writing *Moby Dick* [1956] for John Huston, who probably thought that he *had* written the *Outer Space* screenplay. And *Moby Dick* was a fiasco and a disaster. Ray is primarily a novelist and short story writer, and there's a difference between dramatization and just pure narrative writing.

It didn't bother you at all, that so much of the credit for the success of It Came from Outer Space *was heaped on Bradbury?*

Well, it disturbed me for a while, yeah; all my friends and all the people "in the know" knew what the facts were, but I doubted that the public knew. When Bernard Shaw and Joe Blow write something, they're going to give all the credit to Shaw! There was nothing I could do about it, but it did bother

Telephone linemen Joe Sawyer (left) and Russell Johnson are attacked by the xenomorph in *It Came from Outer Space*. Writer Harry Essex insists that, contrary to reports, it was he and not novelist Ray Bradbury who was responsible for the screenplay.

me. But Ray and I remain friends to this day; in fact, we tried recently to do something together called *Chrysalis,* based on a short story of his. But we never could sell it. We came close several times, and on one occasion we almost had a deal, but I think we outpriced ourselves. We asked for something like $300,000 for it, and that soured the entire deal.

Did Universal treat It Came from Outer Space *as a picture with strong potential?*

Yes, they knew immediately that they had something important. And it *was* — it turned out to be an extremely successful picture, especially considering the fact that it cost very little to make and didn't have any important stars.

Your Outer Space *script calls for "an instant's sight" of the alien creature, but in the picture itself the aliens are clearly seen on several occasions.*

That's something the director decides on. I don't know why Jack Arnold decided to show it several times; I will say that he was a very bright, very careful man, and I'm sure that if he thought it had to be seen several times, then it was probably to the picture's benefit. How can you fault anybody who makes a successful picture for what he does? We called that monster "The Fried Egg," by the way. The big trick in *It Came from Outer Space* was that the aliens could assume the features and physical shape of humans. That idea, as you know, has since been used a hundred times by other people.

Were you a visitor to the set of It Came from Outer Space?

I was there constantly. Jack Arnold was a very dear friend and a very gentle man. And the star, Richard Carlson, and I also became good friends. Later on in the '50s, as a matter of fact, Carlson was supposed to do a picture based on a piece of mine called *The Dune Roller*—a science fiction story—and when that came to naught he bought the script. And then when he didn't do it I bought it back from him and eventually did it myself [as *The Cremators*]. Carlson had great problems, he drank a lot—really, he was a terrible drunk, but a very sweet, kind man. I liked him very much.

Was he already a drinker when you did It Came from Outer Space?

When I first met him he was already involved in drinking, how deeply I don't know. I didn't socialize with him, we were just good friends on the set. They all liked me at Universal, since I had had two of the most successful pictures there [*It Came from Outer Space* and *Creature from the Black Lagoon*]. And we're talking about days when these pictures cost less than a million dollars—we're talking about three, four, maybe five hundred thousand dollars for a movie that would make millions, and are still making money to this day.

What can you recall about Creature from the Black Lagoon?

I remember that when I was assigned to do *Creature,* it was a very, very poorly written short story—just the basic idea of a fish that had been discovered in the jungle. Universal had bought the story for very little money and assigned me to it, and I was bitter and angry. I didn't want to do anything with a title like *Creature from the Black Lagoon,* it was an embarrassment to me! But they pleaded with me to do the picture, and so I began to redevelop the whole damn thing. It's pretty much formula, for the kind of horror stories we used to do in those days, except in this particular case I added the "Beauty and the Beast" theme. The whole idea was to give the Creature a kind of humanity—all he wants is to love this girl, but everybody's chasing him! It's an old formula of mine that I've used with great success.

Did Universal have the same high hopes, going into Creature, *that they had for* It Came from Outer Space?

No, *Creature from the Black Lagoon* was a picture they just wanted knocked out, and that was that. But it grew and grew. Jack Arnold again was the director, and we had Dick Carlson in this one, too—they gave us the same company! Universal wanted the same success, and it turned out to be even more successful than *It Came from Outer Space!* They didn't anticipate it—

The one classic movie monster to emerge from the 1950s, the *Creature from the Black Lagoon* was the brainchild of scripters Harry Essex and Arthur Ross.

Ray Bradbury wasn't involved this time—but it broke through, it just played forever and it's playing now. I don't know why it should have been that successful, but to this day it's kind of a cult picture.

Were you a fan of the 3-D technique that was in vogue at that time?
  For some strange reason, so many of my pictures—more than anybody

Essex revamped the popular "Beauty and the Beast" theme in fashioning his screenplay for the 1954 thriller *Creature from the Black Lagoon.*

else's, I guess—*were* 3-D. I was involved with three of the most successful 3-D pictures: *I, the Jury* [as writer-director; 1953], *It Came from Outer Space* and *Creature from the Black Lagoon*. I found 3-D kind of a novel thing—although it gave me a headache, looking through those damn glasses!—but I felt at the time it couldn't be successful. While it was interesting, and gave the pictures another dimension, there were too many problems, and I knew that eventually the idea of the double cameras and the double projectors and the need to revamp the movie houses would be too much. And I was proved right.

Weren't you involved, without credit, on What Ever Happened to Baby Jane?

That's one of the bitter memories of my life. I came across a story by a man named Henry Farrell, *What Ever Happened to Baby Jane?,* and I thought it would make a hell of a play. I went to an agent, Sid Beckerman, and told him my idea. I had a good reputation and people were willing to take me at my word, so he optioned the book and gave me a minimal amount of money to sit down and prepare a play. I finished the first act when Beckerman called me up and said that somebody was offering me $10,000—*not* to bother finishing it, but just for the material, because they wanted to do it as a movie. Who the man was, he wouldn't tell me. I said, "No, I want to do it as a play." Later he called me back and offered me $15,000, and I still said no. Finally it got up to $28,500, and Beckerman told me, "Look, I want you to know now that I'm not going to produce it. I think you ought to take the money." So I took the 28.5 and turned in my play. Well, I was later to find out that the man was Robert Aldrich. He was getting the material as I was turning it in to the agent and loving it, and was talking to the two stars, Bette Davis and Joan Crawford. They literally gave me the business. But I was greedy, and a lot of it was my fault. So I took the 28.5 and I turned in my play.

Why no screen credit at all on the film?
Because what I wrote was a play and was not done in screenplay form, the [Writers] Guild had no jurisdiction. If I had written "Dissolve in" and "Dissolve out" a few times I could have demanded credit.

In 1971 you wrote and directed a semi-remake of Creature from the Black Lagoon *called* Octaman.
Octaman was a chance for me to direct and to become co-producer — with this same man Beckerman, as a matter of fact *[laughs]!* He called and asked me what I was doing, and why don't we get together, etc., etc. I said, "Let's do some kind of a takeoff on the science fiction junk that's around." So we went and did *Octaman*. But that, too, came a-cropper; it didn't turn out the way I wanted it to, there just wasn't enough money for the thing. You can't do these things for ten dollars, you just can't. Our shooting schedule was probably sixteen to eighteen days, and the budget was about $250,000. We shot it on the Universal lot and in Griffith Park.

Were you pleased with the Octaman outfit used in the film?
No, I wasn't. But the people who did the Octaman outfit were the same people who were later to become famous because they did *E.T.* and all the other important science fiction stuff. But their Octaman suit was too cumbersome, too difficult, and just wasn't good enough.

And how did The Cremators *come about?*
I really did *The Cremators* because I wanted to give my son David another shot at acting: He had played the Indian in *Octaman,* and he was in this one as well. I wrote, produced and directed *The Cremators,* which was shot in Westlake, in Griffith Park — the caves again — and in Agoura. Shooting took thirteen days, maybe less.

The Cremators *was based on the short story* The Dune Roller, *which we talked about before.*
The original short story was written by a woman named Judy Ditky. I bought the story from her — for $500, I remember *[laughs]* — but I couldn't get a major studio to do it. Richard Carlson bought it from me and had plans of doing it, as I told you, but nothing came of that and I ended up with it again. Eventually my agent made a deal for me with Roger Corman, who was running

New World Pictures at the time. Corman and I didn't get along from the beginning—I mean, we just couldn't stand one another! He knew we were going to do the film for very little money, and I felt he just didn't give the picture a fair shake. I produced and financed *The Cremators,* figuring that I would control it that way. Well, what I had forgotten was that Corman would control it by distributing the thing—he'd put some of his own pictures as the main feature in a double bill, and put *The Cremators* in as a second. That meant that I'd get a flat fee, $100 or $150 a night, while he played his own pictures on top for the percentage!

What kind of money were you working with this time?
   We did *The Cremators* for $50,000—the fact that *anything* came out of it was a miracle! We shot the thing in a hurry, and for very little money. But if we had had the right money and the right sets and the right everything, we could have had a very interesting picture.

Looking back over your career, which would you say is the picture you're best known for?
   I would have to say *Creature from the Black Lagoon.* As I mentioned, it was based on the "Beauty and the Beast" legend, a fairy tale that's been in existence for hundreds of years and has always been a successful story. Basically, I suppose, most of the public thinks of itself as the Beast, and when Beauty comes along we all hope to achieve what these symbolic characters did. And so *Creature* has become the sort of cult picture that young people just love and accept.

The memories of working with Roger Corman are pleasant because I got along with him very well. He was fun to be around and work with. We always did these films on a cheap budget, and people were always mad at Roger because he'd hardly feed us! And no matter what happened to you, you worked regardless.... You could be dead and Roger would prop you up in a chair!

Beverly Garland

For most fans of '50s horror there are just no two ways about it: Beverly Garland is *the* exploitation film heroine of the period. A principal member of Roger Corman's early stock company, she was the attractive, feisty leading lady in such Corman quickies as *It Conquered the World, Gunslinger, Naked Paradise* and *Not of This Earth*. In between Corman assignments she braved the perils of the Amazon River on writer-director Curt Siodmak's *Curucu, Beast of the Amazon*, and a less-harrowing Hollywood backlot swamp in Fox's *The Alligator People*. Her 1960s film work included *Pretty Poison, The Mad Room* and the multi-storied *Twice Told Tales* with Vincent Price. Overall, this list of titles is unmatched by any other '50s genre actress.

Born Beverly Fessenden in Santa Cruz, California, Garland made her feature film debut in a supporting role in the film noir *D.O.A.* (1949) with Edmond O'Brien and Pamela Britton. During the next few years she appeared in many small parts and acquired the screen name she is now known by when she married actor Richard Garland. Her first experiences in science fiction were small parts in *The Neanderthal Man* (1953) and *The Rocket Man* (1954). Her exploitation film career went into full gear in 1955 when she signed to star in Roger Corman's Louisiana-made *Swamp Women*.

What do you remember best about the five films you made for Roger Corman?

Roger made us work hard and long, I remember that! He was always fascinating to me, a fascinating man—and a good businessman! He had such incredible energy, it was tremendous—he was a dynamo to be around. I always knew he was going to be a huge success because there was no stopping him. He just made up his mind that he was going to be a success and that was it! I think his real talent is getting the money together and producing. But he also knows his craft. He knows how to direct, he knows just about everything there is to know about films. If the picture broke down and everybody went on strike, I'm sure Roger Corman could put it together one way or another. He could probably write the script, cut the film, write the music—maybe the only thing I think Roger couldn't do was *act!*

Did you enjoy working with him on these films?

The memories of working with Roger are pleasant because I got along with him very well. He was fun to be around and work with. We always did these films on a cheap budget, and people were always mad at Roger because he'd hardly feed us! And no matter what happened to you, you worked regardless. But that was all right with me because that was the type of person I was anyway—I don't like to fool around, I like to get the work done. I found Roger to be very professional—except when it came to putting us up in a good hotel or feeding us a decent meal or paying us any money! But that's how he got

Previous page: Scream queen Beverly Garland was the spunky and attractive leading lady in such '50s favorites as *It Conquered the World, The Alligator People* and *Curucu, Beast of the Amazon* (pictured).

With her second husband, Richard Garland (left), Beverly Garland appeared in the 1951 stageplay *Dark of the Moon*. The spooky guy is Lloyd Meyer.

started in the business so you can't fault him for that. After all, you didn't have to work for him. People shouldn't have complained — it was their own decision to work for Roger, no one forced them. I didn't ever bitch because I could see what he was trying to do. And he had a lot of people around him that were not particularly professional, so he really *had* to have the whip out to get the work done.

Roger and I had a good relationship, and we worked very well with each other. I think he made some of the best B movies around, and they weren't all monster films. Roger had, and still has, a sense of what the public wants, and he was right there to supply those types of films. He's become a very wealthy man and I think he is married to a great gal. I've never met her but she's a director, too, I believe. She has babies and continues to work, and that's the kind of high-powered, bright woman that Roger would need.

In your Corman movies you yourself generally played plucky, strong-willed, sometimes two-fisted types.

I think that was really what the scripts called for. In most all the movies I did for Roger my character was kind of a tough person. Allison Hayes always played the beautiful, sophisticated "heavy," and I played the gutsy girl who wanted to manage it all, take things into her own hands. I never considered myself very much of a passive kind of actress — I never was very comfortable in love scenes, never comfortable playing a sweet, lovable lady. Maybe if the script wasn't written that way, then probably a lot of it I brought to the role myself. I felt I did that better than playing a passive part.

What do you recall about your first Corman film, Swamp Women?

Swamp Women! Oooh, that was a terrible thing! Roger put us up in this old abandoned hotel while we were on location in Louisiana — I mean, it was really abandoned! Roger certainly had a way of doing things back in those days — I'm surprised the hotel had running water! I remember that we each had a room with an iron bed. Our first night there, I went to bed, and I heard this tremendous crash! I went screaming into Marie Windsor's room, and there she was with the bed on top of her — the whole bed had collapsed! Well, we started laughing because everything was so awful in this hotel, just incredibly terrible, and we became good friends.

You did all your own stunts in these films, didn't you?

At the end of *Swamp Women* I was killed with a spear and fell out of a tree. They got me up in this tree and Roger said, "When you're killed, you have to drop" — and this was a big tree! I'm not exaggerating when I say it was at least a twenty foot drop. I said, "Well, will somebody be there?" and Roger said, "Yes, they'll catch you." And by God, they had three guys underneath. And when they "killed" me, I just fell — dead weight on these three poor guys! Roger said to me, "You're really one of the best stuntwomen I have ever worked with."

But you actually did get hurt doing your own stunts in Gunslinger *[1956], didn't you?*

I will never forget that. I was supposed to come running out of a saloon, get on a horse and ride out of town as fast as I could. I looked at this horse, and it was quite large! And I said to myself, the only thing I can do is to make a flying leap and get on him and go. So I come out of the saloon, down the stairs and I leap — and *over* the horse I go! I went right over the other side of the horse! Roger said, "Okay, let's do it again." *Oh, God,* I thought! So I came running down the stairs again in those boots, and as I did my ankle just twisted underneath me and I sprained it badly — but I managed to get on the horse!

When I went home that night I thought it would feel so good to put my ankle in a warm bath, so I did — and I left it there for about an hour. And the next day, my ankle was about twice its normal size! And I had to work! This was toward the end of the picture, so I couldn't be replaced, and practically all the remaining scenes were fight scenes — you know, with all the prostitutes, getting them out of town and such. Somebody had to drive me to work. When I got there, Roger looked at it and said, "Well, we have to start shooting."

Top: Garland is about to encounter the claw of the carrot creature in a tense scene from *It Conquered the World. Bottom:* Garland struggles in the grip of space vampire Paul Birch in the cult favorite *Not of This Earth.*

Naturally, Roger! You could be dead and Roger would prop you up in a chair! So I said, "All right, what do we do? There's no way I can walk." I couldn't even get my boot on! So Roger agreed then to call a doctor, and the doctor brought this giant novocaine needle. They shot the novocaine into the bone, which was the most painful thing. Breaking an ankle is nothing, but shooting novocaine into the bone is absolutely out of this world! If you ever want to feel pain, just have someone do that to you. But then I felt marvelous! So they took the boot and split it in the back and taped it on my foot, and I worked all day. I did all the fight scenes, and I ran and jumped and did whatever—and I couldn't walk for a week after that! I had screwed up my ankle so bad!

The first scene we shot of *Gunslinger* was another unforgettable one. It was a love scene where John Ireland and I were leaning on this tree. It was 6:30 in the morning, we were colder than good God's head and our teeth were chattering. When it was time to say our lines we somehow had to manage to stop the chattering. And as we started to do our love scene, these huge red ants began crawling all over us—so not only was it freezing cold, but these ants were biting the living hell out of us! You can actually see the ants on us when you watch the film!

Do you recall seeing the smaller version of the Venusian monster which Corman initially planned to use in It Conquered the World?

I remember the first time I saw the *It Conquered the World* monster. I went out to the caves where we'd be shooting and got my first look at the thing. I said to Roger, *"That* isn't the monster...! That little thing there is not the monster, is it?" He smiled back at me, "Yeah. Looks pretty good, doesn't it?" I said, "Roger! I could bop that monster over the head with my handbag!" This thing was no monster, it was a table ornament! He said, "Well, don't worry about it because we're gonna show you, and then we'll show the monster, back and forth." "Well, don't ever show us together, because if you do everybody'll know that I could step on this little creature!" Eventually I think they did do some extra work on the monster: I think they resprayed it so it would look a little scarier, and made it a good bit taller. When we actually filmed, they shot it in shadow and never showed the two of us together.

Did you enjoy working with Corman regulars Dick Miller and Jonathan Haze?

They were the funnymen in It Conquered the World, Not of This Earth and some of the other films I did for Roger. They were really nice guys. They were proteges of Roger's and he always put them in his pictures. I remember them as being sweet guys, really nice young kids.

Were you and Roger dating by this time?

Well, we really weren't dating, but—*kind* of. I mean, he wanted me to find him an apartment, decorate it, things like that. At one time, Roger wanted to put me under contract. I was with Bill Hays, who was handling all my money at the time, and he said, "Beverly, I don't think that's what you want to do. If you do that, I'm afraid you'll stay in B movies and that's really not where you want to go. Let's see if you can move from there." So I didn't go under contract with Roger. But I dated him a little—nothing very serious. We were very good friends—I loved his mind, and I think he liked my mind. I loved to talk to him about his deals, and what he was doing. We seemed to get along very well. But he always had a girlfriend, and I was always dating somebody else.

Where was Not of This Earth *shot?*

We filmed that at a beautiful old Tudor-style house in Hollywood. The interiors were all done in that home, too. Oh, I remember the pool sequence! I had a scene where I had to jump into the swimming pool and everybody, the cast and crew, thought that that was very sexy, that I had that bathing suit! That was a very sexy scene back them. Really! And even I was embarrassed—it *was* very sexy then. Also the scene in the bedroom—that was a bit much for its time. I'm wearing a robe and I'm putting on stockings while Jonathan Haze is talking to me from the other side of the dressing screen. Those funny scenes that were supposed to be so sexy—oh, God!

Corman and star Paul Birch had some sort of argument during the making of Not of This Earth, *and Birch walked off the picture. Do you recall any of this?*

I don't remember a lot of it except that Paul Birch, I think, felt that he was doing a B movie and that it was a little bit below him. I think he felt, "I am an actor, and I don't need this stuff." You know, when you work with Roger Corman, there isn't time to think—I mean *[talking faster and faster]* you do it and do it fast and you better know your crap and you better get in there and get it done. That's the way Roger is. I understood that; that's how I work, and that didn't bother me. I believe Paul felt that he didn't like the pace. Also, he was very unhappy about his eyes—he had to wear those contact lenses, and you have got to realize that in those days contact lenses were not like what we wear today. Back then it was really like putting *plastic* in your eyes! I mean, it was tough! Paul could only wear them for about two minutes before he would have to take them out. Then we'd have to wait around for a while before he could continue again. We did long scenes, and he was very uncomfortable, and it was hot—it's always hot when you work with Roger Corman, for some reason *[laughs]!* So I think there were lots of things Paul didn't like, he got more and more frustrated, and finally said, "To hell with it all. Goodbye!" Luckily, there was enough film taken already with Paul so that we could go ahead without him. They dressed a stand-in to look like Paul, and used him in three or four scenes, I believe. Roger can get around just about anything.

Had you gotten to know Paul Birch during the shooting?

I didn't do a lot of talking to Paul because he was not very happy *[laughs]*. I just felt that the best thing was to stay out of his way—so I did.

Did you enjoy going on location for Naked Paradise?

Absolutely. That was the last movie I ever did for Roger, and he took us all the way to Hawaii to film it. We filmed on the island of Kauai, stayed at the Cocoa Palms Hotel and had great accommodations. Roger really did this one up the right way. I don't know if it was because we were at this beautiful location and Roger simply felt like spending more, but it was one of the best locations ever—especially for a Roger Corman film. It was just a good movie to work on.

Which of these five Corman films was your favorite?

I liked *Gunslinger* the best. I liked playing the sheriff and I loved that love scene with John Ireland. *Naked Paradise* was also good, but any actress naturally likes the movie that she has the most to do in, and *Gunslinger* was *my* movie.

In the '60s, when Corman moved on to a better class of pictures, he left most all his '50s stock players behind.

Absolutely. And I have no idea why. I guess he thought we weren't good enough for him. Too bad. We were. We were *very* good for him, and we'd worked very hard for him. And later on he never even asked me if I would be interested in doing anything. He never even *asked*.

You know, we were with him at the beginning when we would work with scripts that weren't finished. We never had dressing rooms, we never had a john, we never had anything. And we never stopped! We worked our butts off for this guy. And then when he began to move into better pictures, I don't think he had *any* of us work for him. Maybe he felt we were all B players, and he didn't want B players. He dropped us all—and I've always kind of resented that. There were times when I really needed a picture, really needed to work. A lot of us have had good years and bad years. I had some bad years, and Roger was never around. I might not have done a later picture for him, but I sure would like to have been asked.

Did you enjoy working with Curt Siodmak while making Curucu, Beast of the Amazon *in Brazil?*

You know, it was hard working with Curt. First of all, he was very difficult to understand because he had a very thick accent. He was in a hurry to do this picture—the heat was oppressive, we all got the turistas, we were all sick. He had probably the hardest job because he had to be up every morning earlier than anybody else, and he was the last one to go to bed. And he was not a

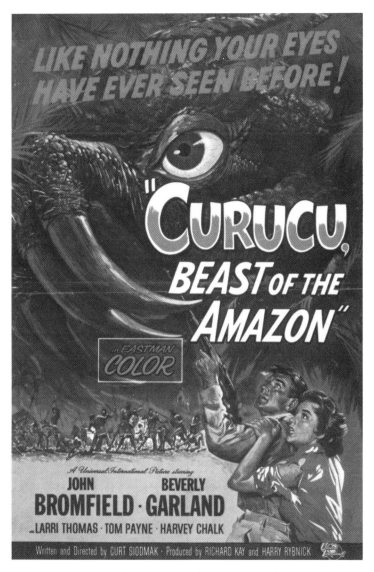

Garland braved the dangers of the Amazon River while shooting *Curucu, Beast of the Amazon* in Brazil.

young man when he did *Curucu*. As he told you when you interviewed him, he got very sick, and he came away from that picture never really feeling good again. And I can understand that.

He had a crew that was Portuguese, with just a few Germans. Between his German and Portuguese, he was able to communicate and do the best he could, but it was very hard for him. So I don't think that Curt was really thinking about trying to make an Academy Award picture—he was just trying to do the picture, get it finished and get out of there!

Where did you stay while making Curucu?

At a hotel in Belem, which is a port on the Amazon. And there were bugs everywhere! I mean, there was nowhere you could walk without bugs! And the temperature was like a hundred and twenty degrees—hotter than hell! At night you should have seen me: First I'd take the sheets and blankets off the bed so I could get all the bugs out. Then, to *keep* the bugs away, I'd light candles all around the bed—I looked like some kind of mummy that had been laid out! It was really something else!

The bathroom had a toilet and a sink and the rest of it was all shower. The shower nozzle was right in the middle of the room so when you turned it on everything was sopping. So really the shower happened to have a toilet and a sink in it! The whole room was a shower with a drain in the middle of the floor! So once you used the shower you might as well forget about going in there again—everything was sopping wet! At 4:30 in the morning I would go out on this teeny tiny patio with a coat rack, and I would hang my mirror on the coat rack and then put on my makeup by the light of whatever sun was coming up that day. Naturally *we* were on the shady side. It wasn't easy to get made up, but I did it!

John Bromfield had brought his girlfriend, Larri Thomas, down and got married—and they certainly weren't interested in having *me* around! I'd knock on their door and say, "Are you going to be doing anything tonight?" and they would go, "Oh, *Beverly!*" So I was really by myself—I had no one to talk to except Curt Siodmak. And he was really getting kind of friendly, so I thought the best thing to do was not to talk to him at all! So I spent three months in South America really all by myself. There was a darling German boy, but I never knew what he was saying to me—so I figured I'd better not get involved with *that,* either! It really was a strange picture!

Again, you did all your own stuntwork.

The thing I remember best about *Curucu* is that I had to have this huge snake wrapped around me in one scene. This snake was twenty-eight or thirty feet long! Off-camera, two native boys held its head and two more held its tail. After spending at least an hour preparing, they wrapped the snake around me, got me on the ground and started filming. So I started screaming—and Curt yelled, "Cut!" I said, "What the hell's the matter?" and he said, "Are you all right?" I said, "Yes, I'm fine—am I not *supposed* to be screaming in this thing?"

I was talking to Curt one day twenty-five years later, and he said, "You know, it's amazing you're still here." I said, "Thanks a lot, Curt! What do you mean by *that* remark?" He said, "Well, you know, that snake in *Curucu* was very dangerous." What he was saying was that the snake was a boa constrictor, and that if anybody had let go and it had constricted, that there was no way they could have freed me. Because once the snake constricts, it squeezes you to a point where it takes all the breath out of you—it's like being choked to death. Even if you kill it, it still can't un-constrict; it's stuck there until those muscles relax, which can take anywhere from twelve to twenty-four hours. And of course they had the snake wrapped around me about five times, so there would be no way to save my life. Curt said, "Gee, it was just wonderful that the snake never did that," and *[laughs]* I thanked him very much. He'd never told me that, and I never knew it! That was a wonderful little episode...!

What about the scene where the Indian village catches fire?

John Bromfield and I almost didn't make it out of there. These straw huts were built early on, when we first got there on location, and they just stayed out in that sun. And all this straw became so dry that when it caught fire it just went up immediately. John and I were way in the back and we had to run out—I thought we were never going to make it. I singed my hair and my clothes. Scary—it was a scary thing.

Much of Curucu *was actually filmed on the Amazon River.*

We were on the Amazon River in Belem. We took this horrible little fishing boat out—John Bromfield and myself, Curt Siodmak, the cameraman and one other assistant—and we shot all day on the boat. About 4:30 in the afternoon, because we were shooting and everybody was distracted, we hit a sandbar. So there we were, in the middle of the Amazon River, up on a sandbar and we couldn't get off. Someone said, "The thing to do is to stay here until the tide comes up. That'll probably be about 11:00 tonight." Well *[laughs]*, I didn't think I wanted to wait! Another boat came along and stopped a good distance away, in deeper water. They offered to take us back with them, but we'd have to get *in* the water and swim over *to* them. John and I looked at each other; we didn't know if we really wanted to go into the Amazon River, but on the other hand, if we didn't, we'd be there until eleven, twelve, maybe one, two a.m. A *l-o-n-g* time. So we got in the river and swam to the other boat. When we climbed out of the water, I had all these red spots all over me that itched like mad! I was just covered with little red marks left by the millions of bugs in the Amazon River.

After all this grief, Curucu *didn't even turn out all that well.*

We had a South American actor named Tom Payne who thought he was magnificent, and he chewed the scenery up like nobody's business. And John Bromfield, God love him, was certainly not an actor—a good-looking, wonderful person, but I really don't think he was much of an actor. Larri was good, but she only got to dance and that was the end of her. And the rest were just *peasants* who were *starving* to death, that we dressed up as Indians! They didn't know what the hell they were doing!

But it was probably one of the most exciting things that I ever did. I mean, I look back on it now and think about all the junk we went through, but it was thrilling and great fun. It was awful but it was wonderful, and I would never trade the experience for a million dollars. I loved every bit of it.

Outside of The Joker Is Wild *[1957] with Frank Sinatra, you've never had a strong part in a major film. Is that a sore point for you?*

Yes, it is. I did *The Joker Is Wild* for Paramount, and I had a very strong part, as you say. I think that if I'd stayed in this town and gone from Paramount to somewhere else and built that career, I might have climbed a few more steps up the ladder in the motion picture area. Instead I went to New York and did a TV series called *Decoy,* the story of a New York policewoman. It was syndicated instead of being sold to a network. But it was not sold in California and it was not sold in New York. For all intents and purposes, I had disappeared from this town, and everybody here must have thought I had died! Nobody knew where I was or what I was doing—they never saw *Decoy,* because it wasn't playing here. When I came back after a year in New York, people didn't even know I *was* back. It was almost like starting all over again.

What were some of your experiences on The Alligator People?

The hardest thing in that movie was simply to keep a straight face. I was all right from the beginning of the film up until I found my husband in the sanitarium, and then I just fell apart. That was the end of me! There was that one scene where I had to be a bit romantic and console my poor husband, and this was probably the most difficult scene I had to do in the film. This was when he was pretty much an alligator, and I had to say to him, "I'll love you no matter what," which I think took me a good half day to say. Laugh? I thought I'd *die!* They almost had to film that on the back of my head, but I managed to get through it. That was very hard.

Like E.A. Dupont, who directed you in The Neanderthal Man, *Roy del Ruth was a director who had seen better days.*

I liked him—he was a sweetheart of a guy and a good director. *The Alligator People* was a fast picture, but he really tried to do something good with it. And I think that shows in the film. It's not something that was just slapped together; I think he really did his best. It was such a ridiculous story, and some of that dialogue was enough to drive you crazy! But we all worked hard and we all knew that if we didn't do our job it would be the comedy of the season! So we had to really get in there and make it as honest as we could. I feel that Roy del Ruth really tried to do that, also. I had a lot of respect for him, and I liked him.

What else did you find funny in Alligator People?

I remember that when all these people started turning into alligators, they

Beverly Garland resists the romantic advances of one of *The Alligator People*. "The hardest thing in that movie was simply to keep a straight face," the veteran actress recalls.

had a place to go — a clinic or doctor's laboratory or something. So, that day of filming I walked onto the set and we were about to do the scene where I go to the hospital to see my husband who is slowly turning into an alligator. I walk in and here they have these guys in long white robes with some kind of hat thing over their heads — and, I tell you, they all looked like they had *urinals* on their heads! I started to laugh — I laughed so hard that tears came to my eyes! I said, "You've got to be kidding, fellows! All of these tall urinals walking around!" Well, we did not film for three hours, I was in such hysterics! Every time these things would walk down the hall, I would just crack up! I couldn't recite a line of dialogue! Then Roy del Ruth began to look at them, and it started to get to him, too! I guess we must have lost close to half a day of shooting time. Great control — that's what you needed in order to do some of these monster pictures without a smirk on your face! It was really too much!

Many viewers are disappointed with the way that film ends.

I felt when I read the script and when I saw the film, which was a long time ago, that it ended very abruptly. It all happened too fast; it was kind of a cop-out. But there really was no way to end it. What were they going to do — were they going to have us live happily ever after and raise baby alligators? There was just no way! So this was what they had to do.

Did Lon Chaney's drinking problem cause any difficulties?

I thought Lon Chaney was fabulous, fun and easy, and he certainly never drank on the set as far as I remember. It was fascinating to hear him talk about his dad and all the things he remembered about his father's career. He was a favorite person of mine. Maybe he worked with other people that made negative comments about him, but I just adored him and thought he was great.

Stark Fear *was advertised as a* Psycho-*style shocker, but it didn't live up to any of its publicity.*

Oh, my God—*that* awful movie! That was made in Norman, Oklahoma, by Ned Hockman, the head of a drama department there. We kept saying to him, "This script doesn't make any sense," and he said, "No scripts at the Cannes Film Festival make sense, and they all win. This'll be fine." We didn't think that his logic was too sharp *[laughs]*, but *he* seemed to believe so. It was a disaster. Although he was a teacher, for some reason he just didn't seem to know what he was doing. Skip Homeier finally ended up taking over the direction, and Skip didn't know anything about making a movie, either! It just got to be more and more of a mess, but we finished it. I remember seeing it in a theater here, and there were three people in the audience. The next day I came back to bring some more people, and the theater owner said he'd pulled it and was not going to show it any more. That was the worst movie that ever came out.

Did you enjoy working on Twice Told Tales?

Oh, I loved it because I loved Vincent Price. He is the most wonderful, sweet, adorable man! I don't remember much about that movie, I just remember working with Vinnie and how wonderful he was.

How well do you feel your Twice Told Tales *segment,* The House of the Seven Gables, *turned out?*

I didn't like it that well. There were a lot of scenes where I was just staring, in a trance, thinking back into my other life or some damn thing. A lot of that could've been cut, or directed differently. I didn't think it was the best movie I'd ever seen in my life, no.

How did you land your part as Mrs. Stepanek in Noel Black's Pretty Poison?

Someone had seen my work in something else and felt that I would be very good as Tuesday Weld's mother. Mrs. Stepanek was a marvelous character—I loved the part. I felt it was one of the best things I'd done.

Pretty Poison *has attained cult status in certain circles, but it flopped when it came out theatrically.*

I thought it was a great movie, well-directed. Noel Black did a great job.

But the studio got very upset with him because it took a long while to shoot. Studio people kept arriving and saying, "You're taking too long," and they had him under a lot of pressure. *Pretty Poison* was done on location in Great Barrington, Massachusetts, and any time you go shooting on location it's hard. Noel had some wonderful ideas, and some camera stuff that took time. He went to great pains with that movie and the studio got very upset with him. But I think the movie shows that he took the time.

So why wasn't the film more successful than it was?
   Pretty Poison came out a few years ahead of its time — people were really not ready for that sort of movie. It was one of the first of its kind, and it's been copied many times since.

Were you really pregnant when you did The Mad Room?
   Yes, I was — I was very pregnant! When they asked me to do this movie, I was three months pregnant and I didn't show. By the time they got around to me I was *six* months pregnant and I *did* show! And I certainly wasn't supposed to be pregnant in the film! So they had me in A-line dresses with lots of ruffles and things like that. I don't think it showed as much as I thought it was going to.

Your suicide scene in that film is one of the best parts of the picture.
   They really wanted the blood to flow when I slashed my wrists in that scene. So I was rigged with tubes that went up my dress and down my arm. It was late at night — this was the last shot we did — and something would go wrong every time. I had to do the scene over and over, each time having the tubes removed and adjusted, the "blood" cleaned off my dress, off of me — *ai-yi-yi!* We did this fifteen times, I guess, before the blood came out, and, you know *[laughs],* it's always the time the blood comes out that you don't think your scream was as good as it would have been if the blood had come out the first time!

Wasn't there a great deal of behind-the-scenes feuding on The Mad Room?
   Well, the director, Bernard Girard, wanted to shoot it one way, the studio wanted him to film it another way — and Bernard did shoot it his way. Then when they edited it, they wanted to cut certain things out and Bernard wanted them in, and he got very upset with the cutting. So I think that he decided that if they were going to cut it their way, that he would like to have his name taken off of the film. And there are some things in the film that don't make any sense to me; I think that some scenes were cut very badly. When I saw the picture there were lots of things at the very end that I felt did not fit together right.

Do you ever look back on your B movies and feel that maybe you were too closely associated with them? That they might have kept you from bigger and better things?

No, I really don't think so. I think that it was my getting into television; *Decoy* represented a big turn in my life. Everybody did B movies, but at least they were movies, so that was okay. In the early days, we who did TV weren't considered actors; we were just horrible people that were doing this "television," which was so sickening, so awful, and which was certainly going to disappear off the face of the earth. *Now,* without TV, nobody would be working. *No-bod-y.* But I think that was where my black eye came from; I don't think it came from the B movies at all.

Which of your many horror and science fiction film roles did you consider your most challenging?

Pretty Poison. It was a small part, but it had so much to say that you understood why Tuesday Weld killed her mother. I worked hard to make that understanding not a surface one, but tried to give you the lady above and beyond what you would see in such a short time.

*In the early days when I was representing Bela Lugosi, I used to have
autographed photographs of all the people with whom I was associated
hanging in my office. And I discovered early on that when Bela came to
my office and saw his picture hanging next to Boris Karloff's,
that he got very upset about the idea! So after that, whenever
there was an appointment for Bela to come to my office,
I would take down the picture of Karloff
and substitute somebody else — and then
hang it up again after Lugosi left!*

Richard Gordon

170　B Movie Makers

OVER THE WATER and far away from the bustle of the Hollywood B-hive, Richard Gordon was busy carrying on the grand tradition of 1950s exploitation on his native English soil. Producer of such '50s favorites as *The Haunted Strangler, Fiend Without a Face* and *First Man into Space,* the London-born Gordon became interested in the movies at an early age and, together with his like-minded older brother Alex Gordon, became involved in film societies at school. Detecting greener grass on the other side of the ocean, the brothers Gordon relocated to the United States in the late 1940s. While Alex ended up in California (where he later helped to found American International Pictures), Richard remained in New York and started his own company, Gordon Films, importing and distributing British and other foreign pictures in the United States. This gradually led to his involvement in the setting up of co-production deals, at which point he decided that, "if I was going to do it for somebody else, I could do it myself!"

How did you get to know Bela Lugosi in the late '40s?

My brother Alex and I were both in New York, and one of the things we were doing was writing articles for British fan magazines. We were interviewing actors we could get hold of—people like Chester Morris, Kay Francis, Richard Arlen and William Boyd, who were appearing in summer stock or visiting the city. In fact, we interviewed Boris Karloff, who was appearing in New York in the plays *The Linden Tree* and *The Shop at Sly Corner.* And we went out to a summer theater on Long Island where Bela Lugosi was doing *Arsenic and Old Lace,* playing Jonathan Brewster. We managed to contact Lugosi and he agreed to an interview, and he and his wife took us out to dinner after the show! We hit it off very well, we developed a great friendship, and the result, shortly thereafter, was that Bela asked us if we would like to represent him in New York—sort of on a management basis—and try to arrange some deals for him. That was how I developed my relationship with him.

What sort of work did Lugosi end up doing in New York?

He did several television shows—he appeared on the Milton Berle show as a guest and he did a live Edgar Allan Poe adaptation of *The Cask of Amontillado* with Romney Brent. Meanwhile, we were trying very hard to set up a revival tour of *Dracula* for him in England, which I eventually succeeded in doing in 1951. Bela went over to England with great expectations. Unfortunately, the management that we set it up with turned out to be a very unreliable company which was very badly underfinanced. They figured that if they had Bela Lugosi, they didn't have to spend any money on anything else, and that Lugosi would sell himself! The result was that the production was very poor, the supporting cast amateurish, and the whole thing turned into a disaster. The tour closed before it hit London and Bela was left stranded

Previous page: Horror great Bela Lugosi indulges in some behind-the-scenes clowning with an "unsuspecting" Richard Gordon on the set of *Mother Riley Meets the Vampire.*

without any money. To get him sufficient money just to get back home, I was able to arrange for him to do the film which became known over here in the U.S. as *My Son, the Vampire*. The original title was *Mother Riley Meets the Vampire*. That at least got him the money for him and his wife to get back to the States. Then, of course, he moved back to Hollywood and I sort of lost contact with him, but Alex remained in touch with him right through the years of Eddie Wood, Jr., right up to the time that Bela died.

What more can you tell us about Lugosi himself?

He was a very charming, very generous person. Although he was in severe financial straits at the time, if he suddenly got a job and a good check, like he did for the Milton Berle show, he'd go out and spend it all the next day having a big party and entertaining everybody. We had a very good time with him. The principal problem was that he was bitter about the way his film career had deteriorated. He had a slight resentment toward Boris Karloff, because he felt that Karloff had succeeded so much better than he had—not realizing, of course, that he himself was limited by his accent, which was something he could never overcome. He also never stopped reminding us of the fact that he had originally been selected to play the Frankenstein Monster [in *Frankenstein*] and was replaced by Karloff, and if that hadn't happened Karloff would probably still be a bit player on the Universal backlot. But what he never did mention was that in fact he *refused* to play the Monster—after *Dracula* he thought it was a demeaning role in that it had no dialogue and his face would be covered by makeup. So in some respects it really was his own fault.

How did your first science fiction film, The Electronic Monster, *come about?*

The Electronic Monster came about at a time when I was doing co-productions with Anglo Amalgamated Pictures, with Nat Cohen. The first picture we did was called *The Counterfeit Plan* [1957]. I got Zachary Scott and Peggie Castle to go over to England for it, and it worked out nicely: The picture turned out well and it was quite successful, so we decided that we wanted to do a couple of other pictures together. Nat Cohen had a lot of properties under option and in development, and one of them was *Escapement,* a novel by the English science fiction writer Charles Eric Maine. When Cohen sent me that to read and suggested it as one of the films, I liked the idea very much, and that was how *The Electronic Monster* came about.

When Nat sent me the first proposed story outline, I thought that it was an ideal opportunity to try and get Basil Rathbone to return to England to make a film by offering him the role of Paul Zakon. Nat enthusiastically endorsed the idea, and as Rathbone was living in New York at the time, Alex and I arranged to meet him for lunch. Unfortunately, Rathbone had very different ideas about the possibilities of a screen or stage comeback in England. Having not made a British film since the Frank Vosper adaptation of Agatha Christie's *Love from a Stranger* in the 1930s, he wanted to go back only if he could star in a prestigious vehicle that would have a chance of critical acclaim and surround him with the proper publicity of a Hollywood star returning to England in triumph. He was too much of a gentleman to say that he wouldn't consider doing a B movie for us, but he very definitely said that he wouldn't do a horror picture or anything as melodramatic as *The Electronic Monster*. When pressed as to what he would consider a worthwhile vehicle, he admitted that his ambition was to do a role originally played by George Arliss, and the subject he had in mind was *Old English*. There was of course no possibility for us to set up a remake of such a production, so we parted on good terms but with no chance of a deal. The role of Zakon was eventually played by Peter Illing.

If Rathbone had accepted the part, would you still have cast American stars Rod Cameron and Mary Murphy in the hero/heroine roles?

Had we obtained Basil's services, the film would have been structured quite differently. The role of Zakon would have been developed into the central character, and we probably would not have used any American players in other parts since Rathbone's name had sufficient box-office value for the American market. I did not see Rathbone again until many years later, during a visit in Hollywood. I ran into him at the Hollywood Roosevelt Hotel where he was then living and appearing in films for American International — films not so different from what we had wanted to do! We did not refer to the subject of our luncheon conversation in New York.

What were your budgets on pictures like The Electronic Monster?

The production budgets on those early films were in the range of £50,000, which at that time was about $125,000. The shooting schedules were generally four weeks.

The Electronic Monster *is set on the French Riviera, but where was it actually shot?*

The whole thing was shot in England. Anglo Amalgamated had a long-term production arrangement with a studio in London called Merton Park Studios, and the entire picture was shot there, with some location work outside London.

Why did you have a different director and a different photographer in shooting the film's dream sequences?

To the best of my recollection it was because those sequences were being shot simultaneously with the rest of the film, and it was a sort of second unit operation. For economy's sake it was necessary to do it that way.

Except for the dream sequence, there was nothing science-fictiony about that film. Did you approve of Columbia's misleading title The Electronic Monster?

To be quite honest with you, *I* came up with that title *[laughs]!* Certainly I didn't want to call it *Escapement,* and I thought it needed something to sell it—particularly as there wasn't that much science fiction or horror element in the picture. I screened the picture for Columbia and they expressed some interest in it, *if* it could be combined with something else in a double horror show. So I acquired the picture *Womaneater* with George Coulouris and Vera Day and made a combination out of those two, to release it through Columbia. But, getting back to your question, we then felt that we needed a much stronger title for our top picture, so I came up with *The Electronic Monster.* In England it was known as *Escapement,* and then eventually reissued there as *The Dream Machine.*

Probably the best film from this early era was The Haunted Strangler *with Boris Karloff.*

The Haunted Strangler was actually my first solo production. I had gotten to know Boris Karloff when we interviewed him in New York and had remained in contact with him. A writer in England by the name of Jan Read had written a story called *Stranglehold* specifically for Karloff, and had submitted it to him and suggested it as a starring vehicle. One time when I was speaking with Karloff and talking about the fact that I was getting ready to go into production on my own, he suggested that he would send me the story to read, and if I liked it he would be willing to commit to doing it. He sent me the story and I liked it very much. I got in touch with Jan Read, Boris and I agreed on a deal, and that's how the whole thing got started.

How did you raise the money to produce Haunted Strangler?

Part of the money came from Eros Films in England, who had an agreement with me to distribute the film in the United Kingdom. The rest of the money I arranged through my own resources. We did two pictures that way, *Haunted Strangler* and *Fiend Without a Face,* which were shot back-to-back in England, had much the same crew, and used the same studios [Walton Studios]. They were designed as a double bill for distribution by Eros in England. *Haunted Strangler* was called *Grip of the Strangler* over there.

How did you like working with Karloff?

Very much. He was a charming, delightful man, a complete professional, couldn't have been more cooperative. He was anxious to do everything himself if it was at all possible. There was a sequence in *The Haunted Strangler* where Karloff appears at a dance hall, kills a girl and jumps from a box onto the stage. Of course we had a double for him. Karloff took me aside and said, "You know, I'd really like to try to do this myself." I told him, "It's out of the question. First of all, with all due respect, I don't think you could do it, and secondly, even if you can, the risk of injury to the star of a picture is far too great." Well, he persisted and finally persuaded me that he should at least be allowed to try to do it, and he did in fact do it! But it didn't play well—he lost his balance when he landed on the stage—and so in the film it is done by a double. But this was Karloff's attitude of complete professionalism, that he wanted to try everything, and was willing to extend himself to do whatever he could to make it a good film.

I'd been told that Karloff was spending a great deal of time in a wheelchair, even as early as the 1950s.

No, that's totally untrue. Karloff did not end up in a wheelchair until much, much later—not until the time when he made *The Sorcerers* in England and started having this terrible emphysema problem. Also, his leg had given him trouble all his life, ever since he broke it during the making of *Bride of Frankenstein*. That's why he had that peculiar walk which became his trademark—he never really recovered completely. That was giving him trouble in those later years, and then, as I said, around the period of *The Sorcerers* he started using a wheelchair. But when I was working with him in 1957 and 1958 he was in perfectly good health.

Karloff's performance in Haunted Strangler *is a very good one amidst many very hammy ones. What prompted this extra effort?*

I think first of all that he liked the story very much. I think he felt that it was a picture which could be something more than just a horror film, and that we were treating it as a serious picture and not just a schlock horror movie. And he entered into the spirit of the thing. Also, think of the professional people he was surrounded by—Anthony Dawson, Jean Kent and Elizabeth Allan. It was really a very fine cast for a picture of that kind, and in that budget category. Karloff just felt it was worth the effort to try and really make something out of it.

Much as I admire Karloff, it's almost embarrassing to watch his work in pictures like Voodoo Island, Frankenstein 1970 *and others he made around that time.*

Karloff's attitude, once he agreed to do a picture, was that he should always act to the best of his ability and give it everything he had—even if he knew it was going to turn out to be a rotten movie! On the other hand, I suppose it also depended on the directors that he had and the shooting schedules—maybe they didn't have enough time for rehearsals, maybe they rushed them through too fast. We were fortunate in having a very good director, Robert Day, who wasn't well-known at that time but has since made a big career for himself in Hollywood. He and Karloff worked very well together on *The Haunted Strangler*.

Producer John Croydon, writing in Fangoria, *mentions Karloff's "aversion to the film" and that he later denigrated his own performance in it.*

Boris Karloff volunteered to remove his own false teeth to create the ghoulish visage of *The Haunted Strangler*.

I read that, of course. But I must say that in all the years I talked with Karloff after *The Haunted Strangler*, he never said anything to me about it, and I never had the feeling that he was dissatisfied with the film.

Croydon also describes problems with Robert Day.

Actually, what happened was that John Croydon had a falling out with Karloff, and that was the real basis of the problem. It wasn't so much in *The Haunted Strangler* as it happened later in *Corridors of Blood*, but there *was* a personality clash between Croydon and Karloff, and it was that which really created some of the problems rather than Robert Day, who was just trying to do a good job as director.

What was your budget on The Haunted Strangler?

The sterling budget was approximately £70,000. We paid Boris Karloff $25,000 for *Strangler* and then $30,000 for *Corridors of Blood*.

What can you remember about Karloff's makeup in the horror scenes of Haunted Strangler?

The facial expression on the mad killer was very largely devised by Karloff himself. We didn't want to have to spend a lot of money on the type of trick photography that was used in films like *Dr. Jekyll and Mr. Hyde;* we were trying to find a simple way of doing it. And Karloff came up with the answer: With a few simple tricks like putting cotton wadding in his mouth and distorting his features, he came up with what you see on the screen in the finished picture. It worked very successfully and is done almost entirely without makeup.

Is it true that he removed his false teeth?

Yes, that was one of his ideas—even as a producer I would never have *dared* to ask him to do that *[laughs],* had he not volunteered! We were standing there talking with him and he suddenly said, "Let me try something." He turned his back to us, and when he turned 'round again he'd removed his teeth and distorted his face—and that was the beginning of it!

While Haunted Strangler *was in production, you announced that your next picture would be* Dracula's Revenge *with Karloff.*

We obviously wanted to publicize the fact that we would do another picture with Boris Karloff. I had been mistakenly informed by lawyers in New York that by that time the property *Dracula* was in the public domain, and that if we wanted to produce a version with Karloff we would be free to do it. So we announced *Dracula's Revenge,* and in fact we had a screenplay written by Jan Read. But then in the eventual research and in talking with MGM, we found that our information wasn't correct—the property was still controlled by Universal, who in fact had struck a deal with Hammer Films to do the Christopher Lee *Horror of Dracula.* So we abandoned the idea.

Would Karloff have played Dracula?

Karloff would have been Dracula, and he was quite keen on the idea. It would of course have been very different from the Dracula that Bela Lugosi played; perhaps if anything it would have been more like the *Nosferatu* character. Karloff thought it was a very good and challenging idea, but for legal reasons it wasn't possible to do it.

Your next film was Fiend Without a Face.

In those days everything, particularly genre pictures, went out in double bills. So we figured that in order to do well with *The Haunted Strangler* we

Gordon ran into troubles with both British and American censors over the grisly special effects of *Fiend Without a Face*, as in this scene where the title character attacks Launce Maraschal.

really should have a picture of our own to go with it; otherwise we would get double-billed with somebody else's picture and forever have to worry about allocations and so on. So that was the *raison d'etre* for *Fiend Without a Face*: it was simply designed for the double program with *Haunted Strangler*.

How did Fiend *come about?*

In my constant search for properties I received from my brother Alex a copy of a magazine called *Weird Tales,* published in the early '30s, that contained a story called *The Thought Monster* by Amelia Reynolds Long. This was given to Alex by Forrest Ackerman, who at that time was representing some of the *Weird Tales* writers and trying to sell film rights for them. I read the story and liked it very much, and I thought it'd be a great idea for a low-budget science fiction movie. So, through Ackerman, I acquired the rights from Amelia Reynolds Long. Herbert Leder, who later went on to write and direct a few low-budget horror films on his own *[The Frozen Dead* and *It!],* did a screenplay for us which became *Fiend Without a Face.*

Your star this time was Marshall Thompson.

Through my co-production activities I'd had dealings with people like Richard Denning, Wayne Morris, Zachary Scott, Rod Cameron and so on. Marshall Thompson was one of the available people, and I made a deal with him. He was a very quiet, reserved guy, and it was difficult to get to know him because he kept mostly to himself, but I liked him and had no problems with him at all. In fact, I ended up making three pictures with him—*Fiend Without a Face, First Man into Space* and *The Secret Man* [1958].

What about your budget on Fiend?

Our original budget was only about £50,000; *Fiend* was supposed to cost less than *Haunted Strangler* and be the supporting part of the program. But because of the complexity of the special effects and the amount of time it took to do them, it eventually ended up costing about the same as *Strangler*. As I mentioned earlier, we shot it back-to-back with *Strangler*—we had, for instance, the same production manager, Ronnie Kinnoch, and largely the same crew. We had to have a different director, because Robert Day couldn't have shot both pictures at the same time. So we got Arthur Crabtree, who was quite a well-known director in England and had done some very good pictures.

Did special effects men Ruppel and Nordhoff help shape the story, or did their effects simply meet the requirements of a finished script?

When Ruppel and Nordhoff came into it, we had a finished screenplay and they pretty much had to stick to it. They were working on their effects continuously while we were shooting, and then most of the special effects scenes were finished after the principal shoot was over. It did take rather longer than we expected, and the picture went way over schedule in the postproduction because of the special effects. But it all worked out in the end. And certainly we were very satisfied with Ruppel and Nordhoff because in fact we used them again on *First Man into Space,* although the effects there weren't nearly as extensive as on *Fiend Without a Face.*

Did the gruesome special effects in Fiend *cause any censor problems down the line?*

They did cause some problems with the censors, yes; in fact, we had to make a cut version for England because the British censor didn't want to pass it the way it was. The censors in the United States also trimmed it slightly, for the MGM distribution, before we could get the Code seal.

After the two pictures were finished I screened them for MGM, they liked them very much and I made a deal with MGM to distribute them throughout the rest of the world outside the United Kingdom. And as a result of that, when it came to doing my next pictures with Marshall Thompson and Boris Karloff, which were *First Man into Space* and *Corridors of Blood* respectively, then MGM put up the money for those pictures.

How did the Haunted Strangler/Fiend Without a Face *double bill do at the box office?*

It did very well for us, particularly in England. Both pictures performed very well all over the world, and we were satisfied. If they hadn't been successful, MGM wouldn't have agreed to do *First Man into Space* and *Corridors of Blood* with us, so they obviously felt that it was worthwhile and that the profit potential was there.

Who came up with the idea for First Man into Space?

First Man into Space was an idea that actually was conceived by my then-partner Charles Vetter. He came up with the original story idea, which he wrote himself, and we sold the idea to MGM.

How much did First Man into Space *cost compared to the others?*

Our budget on *First Man into Space* was a little higher. This was partly because of the involvement of MGM, which meant that there were certain overhead and interest charges, etc., to be added to the budget. The budget came up to around £100,000. Of those four films it was the one that cost the most. Most of *First Man* was shot in a mansion near Hampstead Heath, which is an area similar to New York's Central Park. Some of the exteriors, like the scene where the police car is chasing the monster, were shot on Hampstead Heath itself. And then finishing touches were done at the MGM Studios.

Bill Edwards, the actor playing the astronaut who becomes a monster, sounds as though he's been dubbed throughout the picture.

It's postsynched, not dubbed. It was too difficult for him to maintain the American accent while he was actually doing the acting.

Did Edwards also play the monster, or was that a stand-in?

He did play the monster—the budget wasn't *that* big that we could afford to have an extra monster actor! It was basically a suit that Edwards was put into, with small holes in the mask for him to see out through. One problem we did have was that he couldn't wear the outfit for very long because not enough air was getting through. It was extremely hot and uncomfortable, and would have given him breathing problems after a while, so he could only wear it for limited periods of time.

Was First Man into Space *shot entirely in England?*

No, there was some shooting done in the United States—not footage involving the actors, but some of the car run-throughs and things like that. Alex did this for me—he got a cameraman to go out to a location in New Mexico and shoot some long-shot car scenes. We also got a couple of establishing shots at an Air Force base in Brooklyn. And then we reconstructed the rest of it in England.

The funny thing was that when we eventually delivered the picture to MGM, they turned it over to their distribution department, which of course had no idea what the background of the picture was—they were just presented with the finished film and told to release it. Someone in the publicity department looked at it and said, "It would be a great idea if we had the world premiere in Albuquerque, New Mexico, because that's where the film was shot." So they staged an opening in New Mexico and it got a somewhat sarcastic reception *[laughs]*, because the people recognized immediately that it *wasn't* shot there!

Mightn't you have been better off releasing the film under the shooting title, Satellite of Blood?

Satellite of Blood was not our shooting title, it was the title of a Wyott Ordung screenplay that Alex had sent me to look at. Ordung's ideas seemed to mesh very well with Chuck Vetter's, so we acquired Ordung's screenplay and incorporated elements of it into Chuck's. Ordung seems to have been very pleased with it, because I read an interview with him in *Fangoria* where he said that *First Man into Space* was his favorite among his own films. Getting back to your question, I *don't* think *Satellite of Blood* would have been a good title for our picture. I think *First Man into Space* was an excellent title.

Why were the horror and monster elements played down in the First Man into Space *ads?*

MGM thought it would have more appeal to a general audience and that it could play much more widely than a horror picture might. So they decided to play up the science fiction rather than the horror or monster angles.

Why doesn't your name appear in the on-screen credits of these early pictures?

There were two reasons. First of all, I had a line producer, John Croydon. The second reason has to do with the British Quota, which is a very complicated thing I'm not sure we want to get into now! Since I was no longer a resident in England and since we had to conform to certain British Quota requirements, it wasn't really feasible to put my name on these pictures. So just my production company's name is on them, and I didn't take the individual credit.

And whose idea was Corridors of Blood?

We were looking for another subject for Karloff, and John Croydon came up with the original story idea for *Corridors of Blood*. A woman named Jean Scott Rogers wrote the screenplay. Her idea was to make a very serious picture about surgery in the days before anesthetics, which of course wouldn't have made a very commercial picture. So we tried to inject horror and melodramatic elements into it.

Why was Karloff paid more for Corridors of Blood?

The start of production was delayed after Karloff had committed himself to the picture. We had a lot of problems getting *Corridors of Blood* off the ground, and he received $5,000 more because of the extra time.

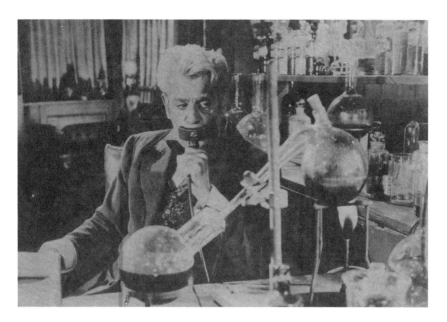

Early experiments with anesthesia lead to tragic consequences in Gordon's *Corridors of Blood* with Boris Karloff.

What were the problems in getting Corridors *started?*

We were in the middle of our negotiations with MGM for the financing of the picture when there was a complete change of management there. We were caught right in the middle—the picture was scheduled to start shooting at the MGM Studios in England, and then at the last minute it had to be postponed because MGM wasn't going to put up the money until all the documents were completed.

Corridors' *lurid title and ad campaign added up to audience disappointment in the film when people got a movie about anesthesia.*

I think the problem with *Corridors of Blood* is that it's really a hybrid film which isn't one thing or the other. It's not enough of a horror film like, let's say, *The Haunted Strangler,* and yet it's too *much* of a horror film to be regarded as a picture dealing seriously with surgery and with the medical profession in that era. To my mind the finished film falls in the middle, and I wasn't too happy with the way it turned out. But I thought that Karloff gave an extraordinarily good and convincing performance in it.

One impressive aspect of the film is its attention to period detail; it almost has the look of a Dickens film.

Because we were making it for MGM, it was shot at the MGM Studios in London, where we had the facilities of the MGM wardrobe department, carpenters, backlot and everything else. I doubt that we would have been able to reproduce that as effectively if we'd still been shooting at a smaller, independent studio like Walton, where we'd made *The Haunted Strangler* and *Fiend Without a Face*.

What were Karloff's true feelings about horror films? Toward the end it began to seem that he really didn't have that much affection for them.

No, that's not true. First of all, he was very grateful for the opportunities they gave him to become a star. He wasn't at all resentful; he was very proud of his work in *Frankenstein* and some of the other films. And he had a great, affectionate regard for them. Naturally, he regretted some of the lower-budget horror films he was forced to make because of economic reasons. And later, when horror films started to turn into ultra-violent, slasher/gore movies, *then* he turned against them completely, and felt that it was a betrayal of the whole idea of making horror films. He thought that they were disgusting, and possibly something that he no longer wanted to be associated with. But certainly in the early days he was very appreciative of the horror films, and he felt that they provided him with just as good an opportunity to perform his craft as any other kind of film.

Also, he wasn't completely typecast in horror films, not like Lugosi.

Right. In fact, Karloff felt sorry for Bela Lugosi because Bela *had* been typed in that area. As horror films dropped in popularity in the late '30s Bela was forced to do cheaper pictures, and he really never got the opportunity to do anything else. Karloff was never resentful of Bela, he just felt sorry for him.

In the early days when I was representing Bela, I used to have autographed photographs of all the people with whom I was associated hanging in my office. And I discovered early on that when Bela came to my office and saw his picture hanging next to Boris Karloff's, that he got very upset about the idea *[laughs]!* So after that, whenever there was an appointment for Bela to come to my office, I would take down the picture of Karloff and substitute somebody else — and then hang it up again after Lugosi left!

Which film did Karloff prefer, Haunted Strangler *or* Corridors of Blood?

He much preferred *Strangler*. He was also unhappy about the mix in *Corridors of Blood*, and in fact that was where a lot of the real problems between him and John Croydon arose. Karloff blamed Croydon, but it wasn't Croydon's fault; if it was anybody's fault it was MGM's, because they said, "You've got to put more lurid stuff into it and you've got to build up the scenes in Black Ben's Den in the Seven Dials" — kind of create a little sex element, with the girls dancing and all of that. Of course that had nothing to do with the story, and it took away from the seriousness of the picture. Karloff was very disappointed with that — we all were! But when you're making a picture for a major

Devil Doll principals meet with members of the press on the first day of shooting. *Left to right:* Bryant Haliday, Sidney J. Furie, newsman, Kenneth Rive, Richard Gordon, newsman, and Lindsay Shonteff.

company and they're financing it, they call the shots. The picture didn't turn out the way any of us would have liked, and it also wasn't as successful as any of us would have liked. We had a very hard time getting it properly distributed.

Why such a long delay before U.S. release?
Because MGM didn't know quite what to do with it. They didn't have a picture to go with it; naturally I suggested that *we* would make another picture for them, but by that time, with the changes of management and everything else, they were trying to get away from that type of filmmaking in their own schedule.

And since they had financed it, you were in no position to force the issue.
Right. So *Corridors* sort of languished until MGM set up a separate unit, headed by Fred Schwartz, to distribute pictures that they didn't feel the mainstream of MGM distribution could properly handle—or perhaps didn't want to be associated with! Fred, who was formerly an exhibitor, came up with an Italian import called *Werewolf in a Girls' Dormitory* as the second feature, and the whole thing was a disaster. But that's how *Corridors* got released.

After a lapse of several years, you jumped back into production with Devil Doll *and* Curse of the Voodoo.

Devil Doll was a favorite project of mine. After we had finished the association with MGM and a suitable interval had elapsed, I was looking to get on with something else. I came across this short story called *Devil Doll* in *London Mystery Magazine*, liked it very much and acquired the rights for it. Then after we had the screenplay written, I made a deal with Ken Rive of England's Gala Films, to do the film in association with him.

Gala at that time had a contract with Sidney J. Furie, who had directed for them pictures like *During One Night* [1961] and *The Boys* [1961]. The original intention was that Sidney would direct *Devil Doll,* but while we were still in the early stages of preparation, he suddenly got an offer to do a big film with Cliff Richard. That film, in turn, led to his going to Hollywood and making *The Appaloosa* [1966] with Marlon Brando for Universal. So his career suddenly took a great jump. By mutual agreement we let him out of the commitment to direct *Devil Doll,* because he would have lost his other deal if we had held onto him. He suggested that a protege of his, Lindsay Shonteff, should take over the direction of *Devil Doll.* Lindsay *did* direct it, but Sidney, to his credit, was still very much around, kept an eye on things and guided Lindsay, because it was Lindsay's first actual directing job. So I would say — particularly if you look at the difference between *Devil Doll* and Lindsay's next picture *Curse of the Voodoo [laughs]* — that part of the credit for *Devil Doll* goes to the fact that Sidney Furie was on hand during production and guided it behind the scenes.

What can you tell us about your frequent star Bryant Haliday [Devil Doll, Curse of the Voodoo, The Projected Man, Tower of Evil]?

Bryant and I have had a lifelong friendship, and we still are very close friends — he lives in Paris now, and whenever I'm over there I always see him. Bryant was a stage actor and was the founder of the Brattle Theatre in Cambridge, Massachusetts — he was both an actor and a producer there, and was responsible for bringing some of the leading European theater companies to America, to appear at the Brattle. Together with a man named Cy Harvey, he was also the founder of Janus Films, the foreign film distributing company. They operated a movie house in conjunction with the Brattle in Cambridge — that was where a lot of these films had their first showings — and I actually got to know him through the distribution business of Janus Films.

And you used him in your pictures.

Bryant had made a couple of action pictures and thrillers in France, and he was always interested in trying to keep his acting career going. So it seemed a logical idea to me, when we were preparing *Devil Doll* and we were not really looking for a big American star to play in it, that he would be ideal for that part, and I think it turned out very well.

What became of your policy of putting American stars in your pictures?

It didn't seem necessary any more. By then the whole trend of the business was changing—pictures that were made overseas with less-than-big-name American stars came to be regarded as television fare rather than theatrical fare. The idea of doing low-budget movies overseas and using American actors went out of style. Also, the actors became less available because of the amount of television work they were doing.

Were you inspired by older pictures like Svengali, The Great Gabbo *or* Dead of Night *in shaping your* Devil Doll *screenplay?*

Naturally I was very familiar with those pictures, particularly *The Great Gabbo,* which has always been a big favorite of mine. Of course the ventriloquist sequence in *Dead of Night* has a strong bearing on *Devil Doll*. But what we used was what was in the original published story in *London Mystery Magazine*—we didn't try to plagiarize *Dead of Night* or any of those others. There's a limit to what you can do with the situation of a ventriloquist who eventually is dominated by his dummy, as you can see in the film *Magic* with Anthony Hopkins. Where our film is different was that in a way it was fantasy or science fiction—Bryant Haliday actually kills somebody and imprisons his soul in the body of the dummy, and this activates the dummy through some mysterious Eastern process. When the dummy talks back to Erich von Stroheim in *The Great Gabbo* or to Michael Redgrave in *Dead of Night,* it's because the ventriloquist has developed a split personality, and it's really *himself* projecting the voice *onto* the dummy.

Why have you never made a movie in America?

I suppose it comes about through the fact that I started out making movies in England, became reasonably successful at it, had a British production company and had financing sources available to me in England. When you're onto something that seems to work, I always think it's logical to stay with it, rather than to try and make any drastic changes. Of course, there were certain advantages to working in England. First of all, production costs in those days were substantially lower in England than in the U.S. Also, there was something called the Eady Fund, which was a government subsidy that was available for British productions. It derived from a levy on cinema admissions: A certain percentage of the tickets sold at the box office was returned to the Eady Fund, and this money was paid out as a kind of bonus to British production based upon the box-office gross of the film in England. This helped to assure investors that they would get a return on their money.

What was your budget on Devil Doll?

The actual British production cost, without my own services or those of Bryant Haliday, was about £25,000—it was a *very* low-budget film. I flatter myself that it doesn't show it....

And it remains a favorite of yours?

Yes, it does—in fact, one of my future projects is to remake the picture, in color, as a much bigger film and in a modernized version. That's something I've been working on for some time.

And how did Curse of the Voodoo *come about?*

That started out as a finished screenplay called *The Lion Man* that came across my desk. Both the people at Gala Films and I liked it; it seemed to fit into the pattern of what we were doing, and also seemed like a very good follow-up vehicle for Bryant Haliday. So we went ahead and did it.

Curse of the Voodoo *always seemed like a picture with too much footage for so little plot.*

I'd go along with that. But that is, of course, one of the ways to make low-budget pictures—to have plenty of extra footage that takes up a certain amount of running time, without your having to do a lot of complicated shooting. The budget on *Curse of the Voodoo* was approximately the same as *Devil Doll,* and the whole picture was shot in England. A lot of the exteriors were shot in Regent's Park, in the center of London. The African footage, naturally, was stock footage that we incorporated into the picture.

What recollections do you have of the film Naked Evil?

Naked Evil came about through my friendship with Steven Pallos, who is a very successful English producer. It was originally a radio play by Jon Manchip White called *The Obi;* Steven sent it to me and said he thought it would make a good film.

This time around, I had very little control over the production and very little to do with the actual making of the film. I was really more of a co-financier/partner than actual producer. Steven was a very experienced producer, and I really was not of a mind to interfere with him. The big mistake that we made with *Naked Evil* was that we made it in black-and-white at a time when everything was switching to color. It was like those last silent films that were made when the industry had converted to sound! The year that we made *Naked Evil* was the year that black-and-white really went out of style.

So why wasn't it made in color?

Steven made a deal with Columbia Pictures to part-finance the film and to distribute it in the United Kingdom and the Eastern Hemisphere. When he went to Columbia and suggested that we should make it in color instead of black-and-white, and that we would need a certain amount of additional money to do it, they rejected the idea—they were only interested in using it as a second feature with one of their own films, and for that, color was not justified. Steve and I decided we were not going to do it on our own without their participation, so we went ahead and did it in black-and-white. But that was a mistake, and the picture did very little business as a result.

What inspired Independent International to later pick up Naked Evil?

Well, I suppose it was my salesmanship *[laughs]*! Sam Sherman, the head of Independent International, saw something in *Naked Evil* and felt he could turn it into a viable picture with some additional shooting. And I think he's been quite satisfied with the results.

Was it Independent International that added the color tint to the film?

The tinting was actually something that Alex had already devised in Hollywood for me — we tried it, but it still wasn't enough to get the picture off the ground. It was the addition of extra scenes that Sam Sherman came up with.

Your next two films were Island of Terror *and* The Projected Man.

Island of Terror came to me when Gerry Fernback sent me a screenplay called *The Night the Silicates Came*. I read it and really thought it was one of the best finished science fiction/horror screenplays that I'd read for a very long time. Gerry suggested that we should make the picture, and that Tom Blakeley of Planet Films would be a good partner to do it with. We went ahead and did it, and it's one of my favorite pictures.

How did you enjoy working with Hammer Films alumni Peter Cushing and director Terence Fisher?

I enjoyed working with them very much, but there's not too much I can tell you about them. We were shooting *The Projected Man* at the same time, and I ended up spending more time on *Projected Man* than on *Island of Terror* because *Island* ran very smoothly while on *Projected Man* certain problems arose: It started to go over budget and there were problems with the director. So I found myself trouble-shooting on *Projected Man* rather than worrying too much about *Island of Terror*.

How were the giant slugs in Island of Terror *motivated?*

Mostly with wires, being pulled along the ground — there was no stop-motion photography or anything like that. I thought *Island of Terror* turned out well — in fact, even when I look at it *now*, I must say that in my opinion, for a picture of its era it worked extremely well. It had a few really good shock scenes, and I was very pleased with the finished film. The first company I showed it to in the United States was Universal, and they bought it immediately for a very large sum of money.

You showed it to them singly, or on a double bill with The Projected Man?

Bryant Haliday makes a dramatic entrance in producer Gordon's *The Projected Man*.

I showed it to them singly, but I told them that I had *The Projected Man* coming along shortly. I also let them know that if they were interested in buying *Island of Terror*, I would really like to think in terms of providing my own co-feature. By the time we had negotiated the deal, *The Projected Man* was ready, and Universal accepted that as the other film.

What was the genesis of The Projected Man?

The Projected Man was a screenplay that Alex found in California. It was written by a man named Frank Quattrocchi, a Hollywood writer, and was of course written to take place in the United States. Alex sent it to me and I liked it; I sent it over to Gerry Fernback and *he* liked it, so we decided to have it rewritten for London locations.

One complaint fans have with The Projected Man *is that it's too similar to the earlier films* The Fly *and* 4D Man.

Well, I would certainly go along with that as far as *The Fly* is concerned; I haven't seen *4D Man*. *Projected Man* does have a very strong similarity to *The Fly*, but it came to us as a finished screenplay and seemed to be a perfectly logical film to make.

Earlier, you mentioned problems with your director on Projected Man.

The director, Ian Curteis, who had come out of television and had not had any real experience shooting feature films, got into trouble toward the end of the picture. In fact, on the last few days the direction was taken over by John Croydon, who actually finished the film.

Why is the American running time on Projected Man *thirteen minutes short of the original British running time?*
The whole of our opening sequence was cut by Universal because they felt it took too long for the picture to get going. The sequence was a rehearsal for the experiment that comes later, so it *is* kind of a repetition, and Universal felt that it was unnecessary. Also, Universal didn't want a double-bill that ran three hours, and they didn't want to cut anything out of *Island of Terror,* so they decided to make the cut in *The Projected Man* to bring it down to a manageable double-bill running time.

Why after the 1950s have all your films been sci-fi/horror?
I've always tended to like that genre—I was successful with it, I told myself I'd become a sort of specialist in it, and it seemed to be better to stay with something you know you're good at, rather than experiment in other areas. Also, because I'd been successful at making horror and sci-fi pictures, I found it was easier for me to arrange financing and distribution making that kind of picture, rather than going off on a completely different tangent. And then, of course, operating within low budgets, horror and science fiction really were two of the best categories to be involved with because you don't necessarily need big stars, elaborate sets or complicated special effects. You could achieve something that would hold audience interest even if it was done on a low budget, without recognizable names and so on.

What were the beginnings for Secrets of Sex?
I had a very close friend in London, Antony Balch, who was a film distributor in England and was in fact the man who put out *Freaks* in England, when it was finally passed by the British Board of Film Censors 35 or 40 years after it was made. Antony had produced and directed some short films and done some experimental work, and he wanted to get into feature production. I had a lot of confidence in him as a director, and I thought it would be worthwhile to do something with him. He had an idea to do a low-budget film that would be an anthology of horror and sexy stories—he called it *Secrets of Sex.* We decided to do it together, with me producing and Antony directing. We made the film for approximately £40,000, which by then—1970, '71—was a *very* low budget.

Was the film successful at all?
It was very successful in England: It opened in a theater off Piccadilly Circus in London, where it ran for approximately 28 weeks! Between the money that it earned at the box office, plus the Eady Fund money, the entire

Richard Gordon, behind the scenes on 1971's *Tower of Evil*.

production cost of the film was recouped out of the one run in the West End of London! However, when I brought the film over here, I found that I couldn't get a Code seal on it—there was a certain amount of nudity and some erotic scenes, and the MPAA wouldn't pass it. Also, it was "too British"—it didn't appeal to the American distributors I showed it to. I made a deal with New Line Cinema, who tried to put it out nontheatrically, in 16mm, as a sort of midnight or cult movie, but it really didn't work. So I had it "on the shelf" for a year or two. Then, after I produced *Tower of Evil* and arranged for its American distribution, I suggested *Secrets of Sex* as a second feature for *Tower of Evil*. Of course that meant we had to reedit it, eliminating the sexy and erotic scenes and concentrating on the horror stuff, get it down to a shorter length, get it passed by the MPAA and change the title, and that in fact was what we did. We changed the title to *Tales of the Bizarre* and put it on the double-bill with *Tower of Evil*.

How did that particular film get started?

At that time I was friendly with George Baxt, the writer of such films as *Horror Hotel, Circus of Horrors,* Hammer's *Shadow of the Cat* and *Burn, Witch, Burn*. George and I were friends in New York and he knew I was always looking for subjects, so he came up with a story called *Tower of Evil*. I bought the story from him and then had him write the screenplay. Eventually that screenplay was rewritten by [director] Jim O'Connolly to fit the locations, the budget and the circumstances of the shooting. But it was George's story.

I showed the screenplay to Joe Solomon, who also liked it very much. Joe was the man who produced *Hell's Angels on Wheels* [1967], *The Losers* [1970], *Run Angel Run* [1969] and pictures like that, and I had been his foreign sales distributor ever since he started in business as a producer. He said he'd like to go in with me on it, and we went about setting it up.

Where exactly was Tower of Evil *photographed?*

Except for a few location shots that were done on the South Coast, it was shot entirely at Shepperton Studios. The island lighthouse was a set that was built at Shepperton. The establishing long shots of the lighthouse and the island in the water are actually all glass shots.

In 1973 you collaborated with Antony Balch again, on Horror Hospital.

After the success of *Secrets of Sex* in England and elsewhere in Europe, Antony and I decided that we certainly wanted to do another picture together. He was a great fan of horror movies—in fact, he used to say that his favorite movie was *The Devil Bat* with Bela Lugosi! We were both at the Cannes Film Festival in 1973, sitting around on the beach, between activities, throwing ideas around, when Antony suddenly said, "Why don't we make a picture called *Horror Hospital?*" I said, *"Fine,* I think it's a great title but where's the script?" He said, "Well, first let's decide on the title, and if we agree that it's a good idea to make a picture called *Horror Hospital* then we'll get somebody to write us a script that'll fit that concept." So we kicked it around for a few days and came up with a storyline. There was a writer friend of Antony's who was also at the Cannes Festival, a fellow by the name of Alan Watson; we got him in on the meetings, and he seemed to be thinking along the same lines as we were, so we made a deal with him. While the script was written by Alan

Watson, I would say that there was a lot of input from both Antony and myself—perhaps more script input than I've ever had on any other picture.

It was a lot of fun making *Horror Hospital*—there was a picture where we had a wonderful time all the way through production. All the people involved—Michael Gough, Robin Askwith, Skip Martin, Ellen Pollock and so on—were all delightful to work with.

Can you tell us a little more about horror star Michael Gough?

Michael Gough was an actor with great classic background and stage training. Like Boris Karloff years earlier, he was the type of person who, once he agreed to do the thing, entered into the spirit of it and treated it just the same way as if he were appearing in a production of *Macbeth!* He didn't regard it as beneath him or as a joke or anything else. He was really very cooperative: He knew that Antony had had limited experience and that this was really his first proper feature film, and he went out of his way to be helpful to everybody. I can only say the nicest things about Michael Gough.

How did The Cat and the Canary *come about?*

The Cat and the Canary came about through my friendship with Radley Metzger, whom I've known for many years from the distribution side of the business. Radley and I had also talked about the possibility of doing a picture together and had been kicking around ideas. One of the things we talked about was the possibility of remaking some well-known horror picture, and it seemed a very good idea to try to do *The Cat and the Canary*.

What qualities led you to that choice?

Well, it hadn't been done since the Bob Hope version, it had never been done in color, it was a well-known title, had a certain reputation, and it was something that logically could or in fact *should* be made in England. It also invited the idea of getting together a sort of all-star cast—of course, the cast that *we* could afford was not on the level of *Murder on the Orient Express* or *Death on the Nile [laughs],* but let's say on the next level! We made a deal with Raymond Rohauer, who owned the literary rights, the screenplay was written by Radley Metzger, and that's how the production got set up.

Did your "all-star" cast take a big bite out of your budget?

The Cat and the Canary was certainly the most expensive picture I'd done up to that time, not only because of the cast but because of the circumstances of the production—it had a somewhat longer shooting schedule and required a more elaborate set-up. We *were* able to put together what I think was an exceptionally good cast: Carol Lynley, Michael Callan, Edward Fox, Olivia Hussey, Honor Blackman, Wendy Hiller, Wilfrid Hyde-White, Peter McEnery, Daniel Massey and Beatrix Lehmann. The casting itself wasn't all that expensive because, by the nature of the story and the way we scheduled the production, most of the cast we only needed for certain limited periods of time, and we were able to shoot all their scenes together. In fact, Wilfrid Hyde-White only worked one day!

How did Inseminoid *come about?*
  Inseminoid was a project that Norman Warren brought to my attention. Norman, who had made a number of low-budget horror and exploitation films in England, sent me a script which had been brought to him by Nick and Gloria Maley, the special effects people. They had in fact written it with the idea that if they could get the production set up, it would be a showcase for their special effects abilities. Norman and I both liked the script, so I went to England and made a deal with Nick and Gloria. The Shaw Brothers in Hong Kong agreed to put up half the money and become partners in the picture, and that's how *Inseminoid* began.

Where was that film shot?
  Most of it was shot in the underground caves at Chislehurst, which are just outside London. It's a network of tunnels and underground caves that go back hundreds of years, and has become a sort of tourist attraction. Rather than try to build the underground settings in a studio, we decided that we would make a deal for the use of the Chislehurst Caves and build our sets there. The rest of the picture was shot at Lee Studios in Wembley Park — some of the interiors, closeups and whatever else we needed.

Did shooting in actual caves cause any problems?
  It caused a *lot* of problems. We had to go fairly deep into the tunnels to get to cave areas that were sufficiently large and open for us to be able to build the sets and to get the camera equipment and everything in there. As you can imagine, the air down there was not very good — there was a constant dampness and it was very cold — and by the time we had the lights and camera crews and everything else down there, it really was difficult for people to work without getting claustrophobic, and becoming somewhat neurotic about being buried under the ground! I don't know if this added to the performances or detracted from them *[laughs]*, but it was very hard, and at intervals people had to go back outside for a breather — it really was tough to work there all day long. In addition to that, the caves were constantly wet, and the sets had to be repaired again and again because everything was dripping with water.
  I think all this paid off in terms of what we got on the screen for the budget, but the circumstances were very difficult. It was much easier, of course, when we eventually went into Lee Studios, which is a regular motion picture studio, for the finishing work.

You also assembled what would, in time, become a much stronger cast.
  We got our stars Jennifer Ashley and Robin Clarke through a Hollywood

agency, and then of course we had Judy Geeson; Stephanie Beacham, although this was long before *The Colbys;* and Victoria Tennant, and this was long before *The Winds of War.* So as it's turned out, when you look at it now it really *is* an all-star picture!

But what a demanding, demeaning role for Judy Geeson!
  She didn't regard it that way; she thought it was a very interesting part. She's a very professional young lady and a good actress, she thought it was a challenging role and she was happy to accept it.

And Inseminoid *remains your biggest budgeted picture to date?*
  That was my most expensive picture, yes. *Inseminoid* was the original title and the title under which it was released in the whole world outside the U.S. and Canada. When we made a deal with Almi Pictures for the distribution in the U.S. and Canada and they didn't like the title *Inseminoid,* they came up with the title *Horror Planet.*

While doing a gratuitous horror film like Inseminoid, *do you miss the days of black-and-white, Lugosi, Karloff and implied horrors?*
  Let me say that if I had my choice I would much rather make the more subtle kind of horror picture, a *Haunted Strangler* or *Devil Doll* or something like that. I don't really enjoy the slash-and-gore or slice-and-dice kind of picturemaking, I don't think it's any fun, but *if* I make another picture I think I will have to conform to the requirements of the box office.

What are your plans for the future?
  There are two projects that I'm particularly interested in at the moment. One, as I mentioned before, is a modernized and updated version of *Devil Doll,* in color, on a bigger scale and with a bigger artist. That would *have* to be the more subtle kind of film, because it doesn't lend itself to an out-and-out gore approach. It wouldn't even be a "horror film" today, it would be a psychological thriller in the vein of *Magic* or what people call the Hitchcock type of movie. The other thing I've been thinking about is a remake or sequel to *Fiend Without a Face.* I've had several companies approach me about the possibility of doing a remake or sequel—because it's such a well-known title, it's become a sort of cult movie. I've been considering it very seriously, but I haven't got down to either devising a new script or making any active plans yet. I *have* had a new script written for the remake of *Devil Doll:* It was written for me by Stanley Price, who wrote *Arabesque* [1966] for Stanley Donen and who is quite a well-known writer in England. I think it's a very clever script that gives the story a different twist, and this is one of the things I hope to get off the ground within the next twelve months.

*When I'm introduced to someone who knows my name
but doesn't know what I've done, they hear* The Blob
and a sparkle comes into their eyes. The Blob *just goes
on and on and on; it's a respected movie and I've got to
think of it as the best thing I've ever done.
I will top it, but I haven't done it yet.*

— *Jack H. Harris* —

ONLY THE SMALLEST HANDFUL of '50s science fiction films can rival the unique appeal of *The Blob,* 1958's phenomenally popular saga of drag-racing youth versus flesh-eating outer space slime. The pet project of first-time filmmaker Jack H. Harris, *The Blob* has achieved classic status, while the man behind it has parlayed his initial success into a long and lucrative career as a producer-distributor, seldom straying too far or too long from his sci-fi roots.

The Philadelphia-born Harris first entered show business by way of vaudeville, singing and dancing with "Ukulele Ike" Edwards' Kiddie Revue at age six. Working his way up from an early job as a theater usher, Harris went into publicity and learned distribution, eventually opening his own offices.

Dissatisfied with the minor black-and-white films foisted upon him, Harris quickly developed an itch to produce his own pictures. Linking up with the moviemaking ministers of Pennsylvania's Valley Forge Film Studios, producer Harris and director Irvin S. Yeaworth collaborated on *The Blob,* a film which eventually grossed more than a hundred times its $240,000 cost.

Harris followed up on this early success with *4D Man* and *Dinosaurus!* before circumstances temporarily curtailed his producing career in the 1960s. Returning to distribution, he has provided U.S. release for the British Bela Lugosi vehicle *Mother Riley Meets the Vampire* and the Argentinian Poe anthology *Master of Horror,* as well as for such home-grown fodder as *The Astro-Zombies,* the John Newland–directed *The Legend of Hillbilly John* and student films like *Equinox* and *Dark Star.*

Years later, Harris's own *Beware! The Blob* (a.k.a. *Son of Blob)* encored the '58 original, and in 1978 he exec-produced the stylish but sterile Faye Dunaway thriller *The Eyes of Laura Mars.* In this exclusive interview, Jack H. Harris talks candidly about his quarter-century's worth of fantasy fare and a business *The Blob* helped build.

Although made in Pennsylvania, The Blob *has the polished look of a Hollywood production.*

Absolutely. I had distributed five hundred pictures by the time I got to *The Blob,* I knew what I wanted and I insisted upon it. We were lucky enough to have a group of people I don't think you could ever assemble again. These people had done about a hundred and fifty short films, ranging from three to twenty minutes in length; they'd never done a feature film. But at least they did have the technical facility to understand what a camera was, and to know enough not to split somebody's skull with a microphone boom. Whenever we had a problem, we solved it with good, clear thinking.

You're talking about the people at Valley Forge Film Studios.

Right. The guiding light there was a guy named Irvin S. Yeaworth, Jr. He was a Methodist minister, and he had a group of strong believers in Jesus working with him. Their basic mission was to promulgate the Word. They were doing that pretty well, but starving to death at the same time. I convinced

Previous page: Jack H. Harris schmoozes with starlets Sandy Brooke (left) and Susan Stokey during a break in the shooting of Harris' *Star Slammer* (1986).

Veteran Hollywood character actor Olin Howlin played his last (and best-remembered) movie role as the first victim of *The Blob*.

them that we could take what facilities they had, add certain equipment I could bring in from New York and L.A., upgrade the actors and come up with films that a lot of people would come and see. And if they did it right, we'd do it again; and the more notice they got, the more Word they'd be able to transmit. It was not a sales pitch, it was a *fact*. And as things worked out it did them a lot of good, because they were able to do their primary thing, which was spreading the Word, because of the association that they had with Hollywood.

I knew a lot of pros and so did they, through religious connections, and everybody helped. But nobody could do anything about the twenty-two hour days we put in, seven days a week. But that's what made the difference. I believe that success is a combination of clear thinking, creative ability and hard work, and *[laughs]* I guess hard work is 90 percent. *The Blob* took thirty-one days to shoot and nine months to do the effects. And we invented a lot of things; some of them are still being used, and a lot of others we never bothered to tell people about.

Who originally came up with the idea for The Blob?

The original notion was put together by a guy named Irvine Millgate. He was a consultant to the Boy Scouts of America, for their Visual Aids Department. With the help of the Cecil B. DeMille office, he had put together a film on the jamboree that took place in Hollywood in 1953. Every star in Hollywood was in it, but the Boy Scouts had a problem getting the picture out. They wanted it to play in theaters, so they came to me and used my distribution expertise to get it out in the marketplace. Millgate and I covered the country and got it played; we traveled together, on and off, for a year or more. He knew I wanted to make pictures, and he used to ask me what I wanted to make. I finally said, "Listen, what I want to think up is a movie monster that is *not* a guy dressed up in a suit—*not* a puppet—but some kind of a form that's never been done before. I want it to do things that will undo mankind as we know it if it's not arrested or destroyed. But I want the destruction to be something that Grandma could cook up on her stove on an experimental Sunday afternoon." We kept throwing things back and forth, back and forth, and I must admit we didn't come up with anything. One night, the phone rang at three a.m.—I was in New York, sleeping at one of the hotels there at the end of a long day—and it was Irvine. I said, "What is it?" and he said, "A *mineral* monster." I said, "I'm hanging up."

He said, "No, no—don't hang up! This mineral, if you get involved with it, can absorb your flesh." I liked it. But I wondered, if you were wearing a nice suit, does it spit it out or eat that, too *[laughs]*? And how do you do it in? We had to work those things out. But I'd never seen anything like a mineral monster, so I knew we had better get serious. The next day he flew into New York and we worked on it all day. We figured out we couldn't burn it, shoot it or destroy it with acid, but we could immobilize it if we froze it. And that was our basic synopsis for a film we initially called *The Molten Meteor*.

I introduced Irvine to the guys out at Valley Forge and they worked with us on the story. We built the story on a storyboard basis before a script was written; that was great because it gave us our major sequences and blocked everything out for the director [Yeaworth]. Theodore Simonson and Kate Phillips did the screenplay. Ted Simonson was a guy who's always written— he's another minister—and his writings were all religious in content until *The Blob* moved him in another direction. He's done a series of teleplays and other things since that time. Simonson could probably have turned it out, but we were all running scared. Kate Phillips and her husband, whose name I forget, had done a lot of good things on television and were good friends and wanted to help, so we brought them in to do a polish.

Tell us a little about your casting of Steve McQueen.
   The summer before, Neile Adams was doing a little favor for Yeaworth — she came down and appeared in a twenty-minute religious film that took 'em two days to shoot. There was this dirty jerk, an opinionated pain in the ass — her husband — who decided to be there at the same time. They couldn't *wait* to get him out of there, so they finally kissed *her* goodbye and kicked *him* out. I don't know anything about this; all I know is, I go to see *A Hatful of Rain* on Broadway because I had my eye on Tony Franciosa for the lead in *The Blob*. Ben Gazzara got sick and his understudy Steve McQueen — Neile Adams' husband — played the part. He was superb. I was all excited, and I told Irvin Yeaworth, "We found our leading man — Steve McQueen." Yeaworth cried out, *"What?!"* and told me the whole story — "He's a dirty guy, he's an opinionated ass, he's this, he's that." They all hated him — the idea of him going back there and living with them for week after week was unthinkable. They told me, "We know he's gonna rot in hell 'cause he's no good, but besides that we may kill him!"
   I told them I wanted to think it over. That night, I went home and *Studio One* had a two-parter on about a father-and-son law firm. Steve McQueen had a role in that, too, and by the time it was over I was convinced, McQueen was the guy for our picture. So the next day Steve McQueen was signed to play the lead in *The Blob*.

Were you pleased with his work in the film?
   He had done a little part in a Paul Newman film, *Somebody Up There Likes Me* [1956], and he had starred in a small picture for Allied Artists called *Never Love a Stranger* [1957]. So he did have some experience in front of a camera, and his stage presence was excellent. Really, the long and short of it was that he played Steve McQueen in everything — the same gestures, the same little smile, the same excitement level. That indicated star quality to me. But it didn't indicate it enough, because I had agreed to star him in two more pictures which were coming up — yes, *4D Man* and *Dinosaurus!* would have been the pictures — but he was such a royal pain and I hated him so much I didn't use him. I'm sure sad that I didn't — I've regretted that decision — but he was so impossible I wouldn't hear of it at the time. And not only that, I couldn't foist him upon the same people — I'd have had to find a whole new crew and director in order to use him. It was more important to get the pictures done, because I had commitments. I believe it was his insecurity that made him difficult to deal with. I must admit, the later productions went a lot smoother, but boy — as Walter Mirisch said, he's a pain in the ass but worth it.

What was the Blob made of?
   The Blob was made of silicone, which was kind of a new thing at that

time. We discovered that we could achieve varying degrees of consistency, from that of running water to hard glue, and we varied our consistencies to meet the requirements of each scene. There were a couple of scenes in which we used a barrage balloon, covered with goop and pulled along on a fishing line. And there were times when the Blob was air-brushed and animated—it all depended on the situation. Vegetable coloring gave it the red color; it got redder and redder as it grew and consumed more people. One thing we never resolved was, how do you keep the color in there? We just had to keep mixing it, like cake batter, otherwise it would all settle to the bottom.

How much Blob were you working with?
    The most we worked with was about a washtub full. Naturally we couldn't afford to cover a diner with the Blob, so what we did there was photograph the diner through a bent bellows to give it dimension. To correct any minute flaws we enhanced the photograph with touch-up and air-brushing. We then mounted it on plywood, set it up on an eight-foot-square gyroscope-operated table and tied cameras to the table, rock-steady. Then we were able to move the table in any direction we wanted; the Blob, of course, would always follow gravity. When we wanted the Blob to jump *on* the "diner," we put it on there and got it to jump *off* with a quick movement of the table. That footage, shown in reverse, gave us our effect.

From the original Paramount release through all your various reissues, how many box-office dollars has The Blob *pulled in?*
    My guess is that it's somewhere in the forty mill category. That took a lot of years, but it goes back to the days when admissions were a buck. So that's pretty good.

How did you come up with the idea for 4D Man?
    I was in a restaurant looking through a little pamphlet on the fourth dimension. It went into the molecular structure of matter, and said that if we could figure out how to arrest the molecular structure of two foreign pieces of matter, that these molecules could be allowed to intertwine. In other words, you could put a pencil through a table, why couldn't a person walk through a wall?
    So you walk through a wall, who gives a damn? We had to make it interesting, we had to provide menace. That's why we came up with the idea that, as a result of walking through walls and the like, our 4D Man was rapidly aging and could die very quickly of premature old age. *That* notion I gleaned from a book of *Ripley's Believe It or Not;* I remembered reading about kids who died at the age of seven of old age because of something peculiar in their physiological makeup. Through his touch, the 4D Man could kill a person and replenish his own life energy. We applied that to the storyline to provide conflict.

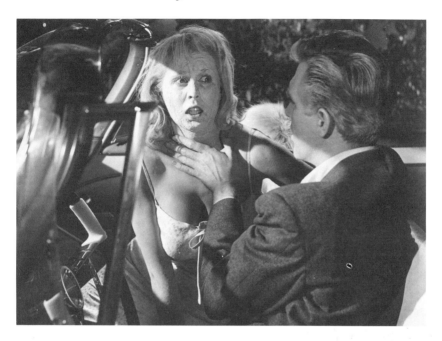

A prostitute (Chic James) withers from the life-robbing touch of Robert Lansing in Harris' *4D Man*.

Who cast Robert Lansing?
 I picked up Bob Lansing from Broadway; I found myself choosing between him and Jason Robards. I thought Lansing had more of a romantic leading man–look about him. Robards went further in his career, although he's never been a command ticket seller, but Lansing's always been solid, and has never given a bad performance.

What were your budget and shooting schedule?
 4D Man had about the same budget and shooting schedule as *The Blob*. The special effects took a hell of a long time.

Can you elaborate on how you achieved the 4D effects?
 [Laughs.] Tediously! The color robin's-egg blue can be blotted out by an image if you combine two negatives and print the positive from them. We shot some of the scenes of Lansing against a blue backing, and then laid that over the live scenes. To have him reach *through* somebody, we photographed him and then photographed the victim, and put the two negatives together. And as his hands were going *into* the victim, we would scrape away emulsion, losing more and more of his hands as his arms moved forward. Then, as his arms pulled *out*, we scraped less and less. It's called rotoscope. Again, as with *The Blob*, the special effects took about nine months.

You sponsored a contest offering a million dollars to anyone who could duplicate the 4D Man's feats on a theater stage. What would have happened if someone pulled it off?

I'd have given 'em a million — because I'd have owned the method! We had a hell of a time getting a backer for the policy — we had to go to Lloyds of London, who brought in fifteen co-insurers to lay off their bet. Everybody was afraid somebody could do it, and I kept saying, "Let 'em do it! I'll cut you in!" I was hoping somebody would do it, but nobody ever tried. Never a phone call or a postcard — nothing.

Why did you switch distributors for 4D Man?

Universal gave me the kind of arrangement I was happy with; Paramount wouldn't, on *4D Man*. While we were at Universal with *4D Man*, I told them I intended to make *Dinosaurus!*, and they said, "Let's put them together." It was that simple.

What was your original concept for that film?

The original idea was a dinosaur picture, but I didn't want to do a prehistoric film. The basic concept was that dinosaurs find their way into contact and conflict with contemporary man. I brought in a consultant, Alfie Bester, who had written a number of science fiction things, and we spent a day in a New York hotel suite bruiting over how to get the dinosaurs from where they were to where we are. He brought up the touch of having them long-buried under the sea and blasted out by men building an island harbor. Then I worked with Algis Budrys, who was a famous science fiction writer; he stayed at my home for two weeks and we came up with all the characters and how they interplayed. In fact *[laughs]*, he came up with a six hundred page synopsis — unbelievable! Dan Weisburd was brought in to write the screenplay, 'cause Budrys was all wrote out.

Where did you shoot?

The location work was done at St. Croix in the Virgin Islands; the balance of it was done at a studio in Hollywood. The budget on that was almost double what the others were; *Dinosaurus!* came to about $450,000. Shooting took about five weeks. The effects, once again, took one hell of a long time. This time we had to build puppets as well as life-size parts for contact. The puppets were motivated through stop-motion animation, which takes a long time.

How did you hook up with the special effects team of Tim Barr, Wah Chang and Gene Warren?

By process of elimination. I had gone all over town — I even hired Willis O'Brien to be my consultant. He kept trying to sell me on stop-motion and I kept saying I didn't want to do it that way. I found some nut that was going to build me two life-size dinosaurs, with three men operating them with pulleys and wires from the inside. He showed me a leg with armatures, real Rube Goldberg stuff—I crossed him off. The next thing we went to was animation, but I just couldn't believe that anybody could animate something that would look like more than a cartoon. One guy wanted to take lizards and stick them in there, but I wouldn't hear of that.

Now I was down to stop-motion, and I went through the list of people that knew how to do that. I met George Pal and he said I ought to talk to these guys, because they had done things for him—some of the Puppetoons, and all the special effects for *The Time Machine*. I went to talk to them, they were excited and I was excited, so we got together.

Were you happy with their effects?

I thought they were excellent for that point in time. The state of the art has improved a lot since then, of course.

The Blob *and* 4D Man *are such sincere, straightforward films, it's disappointing that* Dinosaurus! *spoofs itself.*

Dinosaurus! did have a humorous central portion; Irvin Yeaworth and his wife, Jean, came up with that. I was sort of on the fence about it, but it tickled me so much that I gave in. I was experimental because until that time nobody ever really tried anything like that—mixing this sort of monster movie with humor. I just figured it was new enough to give it a shot, so I did. I take responsibility for it; I could've put my foot down and said, "Nothin' doin'." But I laughed when I read it—I thought it was cute. Looking back on it, it would have been better if we didn't do it.

Why is Mother Goose a Gogo *your only directorial credit?*

A lot of times a movie's credits will say, "Produced and directed by...." I found out on that picture that that was bull. You really can't do both jobs. On *Mother Goose a Gogo* I did both jobs, and I worked myself into a state that it took me about three months to climb out of. I was in on all the arguments with the agents and the managers and the unions, and I was also trying to get performances out of the actors and trying to get the thing to make sense. It ain't easy.

Tell us how you kept busy throughout the '60s.

I was suddenly thrust back into distribution. I was getting my own pictures back and doing very well, and then friends of mine that had made pictures but couldn't find anybody to release them would come to me and I'd help *them* out. And the next thing I knew I was building a distribution organization.

For instance, Wayne Rogers was an acquaintance of mine, and he walked into my office one day tearing his hair out. "I put money in this turkey of a film and now I don't know what to do with it," he told me. "Take it off my hands—just get me out!" I asked him what the title was and he said, *"The*

Producer Harris and director Irvin Yeaworth mixed up an uneven blend of sci-fi thrills and broad comedy in 1960's *Dinosaurus!*

Astro-Zombies." Well, I got turned off by the title. Then when I saw the picture I *really* wanted to vomit! But then I saw an angle: The key art had a zombie—sort of a Frankenstein Monster type—holding this great big machete and grabbing a girl. I felt that had a little marketability about it, and I also could have used a second feature for *Equinox.* So it made good sense for me to pick it up.

How did you latch onto Equinox?

Equinox was a completed 16mm film brought to me by a student named Dennis Muren. You've seen his credits since that time; he got the Academy Award for *Indiana Jones and the Temple of Doom* in 1984. *Equinox* was his demonstration film, and it was *horrendous*—just God-awful. It had a storyline that made no logical sense. I had my son sit down with me one night to look at a print and he walked out after about ten minutes. But I stayed there and went through it, and I saw the seed of something good in it. I bought the picture from him and threw away 70 percent of it. Then I brought in Jack Woods, who is a director, an actor, a writer—really one of the unsung great people of this town. We sat down and tore the picture apart, and came up with the ultimate storyline. We then began reshooting, with Jack Woods directing. Some of it we shot in 16mm, but most of what we did was in 35.

How about Schlock?

Schlock was a film that John Landis had made on spec, and he was taking it all over town. It was rejected by American International, who called me and said I should take a look at it. They thought that maybe I could figure out something and turn it into a movie — I was getting a pretty good name around town for doing that. I took a look at it and I was frightened to death of it, because I had never seen anything like it *[laughs]!* I took the picture into a Hollywood Boulevard sleaze joint and "sneaked" it, and the poor people didn't know what the hell they were looking at. However, enough of it worked to convince me that it was worth pursuing. We dropped some garbage that was in there, went out and shot new sequences, and the picture started to come together. I *still* think it's a strange little "off-center" movie, and it's become a sort of collector's item.

And Dark Star?

Dan O'Bannon knew John Landis, and he asked him to have me look at the film he had done. *Dark Star* was a forty-minute 16mm student film made by O'Bannon and John Carpenter when the boys were going to U.S.C. But what were they going to do with a forty-minute film? They took it around but everybody said it had to be ninety minutes. So they went out and shot fifty more minutes. And it was dreadful, it was *death* — I mean, the opening scene was four guys laying in their bunks, snoring, for five minutes. The bunks looked like Russian army cots, they didn't look like anything on a spaceship. But I felt there was enough *something* there. First of all, it was space; I had never done a space movie, and I figured I wanted to. So at least we had a framework. We threw away a good 60 percent, cutting it way down even below their original forty minutes — some of *that* was padding. We constructed some sets, literally started all over again, shooting in 35mm, and built it back up again. We even shot the meteorite storm and a number of special effects things that weren't in the original picture. And the final result turned out better than I thought it did, because at that time I laid the picture off with Bryanston Pictures, which was emerging, and it turned out to be a cult movie. It's still popular.

Based on his work in Dark Star, *did John Carpenter's later success come as a surprise to you?*

A little bit. I knew he had something, and when he came forth with *Halloween* I was very thrilled for him. And as he proceeded, I was delighted. I think he's a very literate, astute person.

Why did you wait fourteen years to come up with a sequel to a big money-maker like The Blob?

I didn't think it was necessary to make one. My son Tony had graduated from U.S.C. with a degree in music, and he went from there into A&R for a small record label. He was making a lot of money, but he got fed up with it, and he came to my office one day and said, "I'm putting myself under your direction." I said, "Why? I'm not in the music business." He told me that he *wanted* to work with me, that he felt remiss because we had not worked together before. I said, "Well, come in and hang out, see what's going on." After a week, he came to me and said, "Let's make a movie," and I said okay. He reminded me that I had in my drawer a script by Richard Clair called *A Chip Off the Old Blob*. I reread it, it was cute, and *Son of Blob* was the result.

How did Larry Hagman get the job of director?
   I had a beach house on the Malibu colony, next door to Larry's. He came over one afternoon, heard us talking about making *Son of Blob* and said, "Boy, I'd love to be in that." He told me that everybody wanted to be "blobbed," every actor wanted to be in a picture like that. He told me that he could put together a cast for the thing, *but* — he would like to direct it. So that's how it came about.

Was the Son of Blob made of silicone as well?
   The special effects were done by Tim Barr, of *Dinosaurus!* fame, and they came up with new ways to do them. They were not as effective as the original's. We used a newly developed powdered substance that, mixed with water, gave us a jelly-like consistency. It came in various colors, too, so we didn't have to worry about silicone, vegetable dye and all those other things. We put it on rollers and mounted it right in front of the camera, and it looked like the Blob was rolling right onto the people.

Do you think Son of Blob *was a worthy sequel?*
   No. It was too funny and not scary enough.

How did you get involved on Columbia's Eyes of Laura Mars*?*
   That was an idea that John Carpenter came to me with; I was able to take it and get it turned into a picture. That was shot entirely in New York, and the budget was about six and a half million.

Wasn't Barbra Streisand up for the lead in Laura Mars*?*
   She was — for about twenty minutes *[laughs]*! But at the crucial moment she ducked out. She's really frightened of "fright" movies, and when she saw the way the script was going she changed her mind.

Were you happy with the finished film?
   I was ... *fairly* happy with it — not ecstatic. Even though Faye Dunaway had just come away with the Academy Award and it was a coup to have her, I felt she didn't get her face dirty enough, she wore high heels when she should have been wearing sneakers and she didn't look as vulnerable as the gal should have. *Eyes of Laura Mars* was too glossy and too chic, and it lost heart by doing that.

As executive producer, couldn't you have pushed for a grittier look?

I pushed for everything I could, but when you make a picture with a studio it's a combined effort of so many things. And then we went through three changes of administration before the picture got finished; we had a different production supervisor every six months starting from the writing stage forward. About the ninth rewrite, I went in and complained to the production head and he said, "What the hell are you worried about? We still don't have a half million in the script." *Oh, my God!* I thought to myself. And on the other hand, the head of physical production was on my tail about the budget!

You've played small roles in most of your own films, haven't you?

I ran out of the theater in *The Blob;* I was a nightclub extra in *4D Man;* in *Dinosaurus!* I was one of the tourists on the boat; in *Equinox* I was the detective; in *Son of Blob* I ran across the skating rink as the ice was forming; in *Schlock* I was sitting in the movie theater in front of Forry Ackerman, reading a horror cartoon book; and in *Eyes of Laura Mars* I was a dress extra in the gallery.

Can you name a favorite among all your films?

Well, there can't be a contest there, it has to be *The Blob*. When I'm introduced to someone who knows my name but doesn't know what I've done, they hear *The Blob* and a sparkle comes into their eyes. *The Blob* just goes on and on and on; it's a respected movie and I've got to think of it as the best thing I've ever done. I *will* top it, but I haven't done it yet.

I guarantee you, these cheap pictures will stand up against any two-hour movie made today. There's more care and thought in them; even though they were low-budget, we really cared what we were making, we really tried. It was such a ball, and we had so much fun.

——— *Howard W. Koch* ———

SOME BIG HOLLYWOOD PRODUCERS might act like they don't remember their low-budget roots, but Howard W. Koch is not one of them. A former head of production at Paramount and the producer of such major films as *The Odd Couple, Airplane!* and *Dragonslayer,* Koch recalls fondly those days back in the '50s when he was producing and/or directing horror staples like *Frankenstein 1970, Pharaoh's Curse* and the all-star terror show *The Black Sleep.*

Getting his start in the movie business in Universal's contract and playdate department in New York City, Koch moved on to Twentieth Century-Fox as a film librarian and then entered production as second assistant director on *The Keys of the Kingdom* (1944). After many films as assistant director, Koch joined forces with his professional benefactor Aubrey Schenck, as well as Edwin Zabel, to strike a three-picture production deal with United Artists that was to start with the Western *War Paint* in 1953. The success of these pictures opened up the deal for more United Artists films by Koch, Schenck and Zabel under the company title of Bel-Air Productions. Koch's first horror films were made at this time.

Following this string of Bel-Air movies, Koch went on to work in TV. With Schenck, he produced *Miami Undercover,* and also worked extensively as a director on such shows as *Maverick, Hawaiian Eye, Cheyenne* and *The Untouchables.* From 1961 to 1964 Koch was vice-president in charge of production for Sinatra Enterprises, and among his many executive-producer credits during this period was the chilling *The Manchurian Candidate.* He became the production head at Paramount in 1964 and then shifted gears two years later to form his own production unit, which has been supplying major features to Paramount ever since.

Did Aubrey Schenck, Edwin Zabel and you have specific functions within your organization, or was everything done collaboratively?

Aubrey Schenck was the story man—a brilliant story man, and a wild, enthusiastic kind of a guy. He gave me every opportunity I had in my life—whatever break I got was from him. I owe him everything. I was the down-to-earth guy that made the pictures—either I directed them or produced them. I was a "factory picture" maker—I knew what it took to make a film. A lot of producers in those days only knew about finding a script, casting, hiring a director. They didn't know one thing about how the below-the-line was done. Having been an assistant, I knew that pretty well. Edwin Zabel was chief buyer for Fox West Coast Theaters, which was the best chain of theaters in California. He was really our "trigger man," helping us get our pictures distributed right.

What sort of arrangement did you have with United Artists?

Our deal with UA was open-ended. What we would do was, we'd get a title, we'd show it to United Artists, and they'd say, "Here's x number of dollars, go make it." Then we'd write a script for it, check one member of the cast with UA, and then shoot the picture. That was the time of exploitation films—second features were still hot then. All of our pictures, except maybe

Previous page: Director Koch provides some last-minute instructions to horror legend Boris Karloff on the set of *Frankenstein 1970.*

Left to right: John Carradine, Lon Chaney, Jr., Tor Johnson, George Sawaya and Sally Yarnell comprised the ghoulish gallery of mutants in Koch's 1956 production *The Black Sleep*. (Photo courtesy Steve Jochsberger.)

three of them, were second features. We'd come up with a title and then write the story; that's precisely how *The Black Sleep* came about.

When you announced The Black Sleep, *Allen Miner was scheduled to direct.*
    Allen Miner had directed a picture called *Ghost Town* [1956] for us and he did very well—five days, $100,000. We had a nice relationship with him and announced him for *The Black Sleep,* but then when we got deeper into the picture we figured it would take a guy who had done that kind of stuff, knew that genre better. So we switched over to Reginald LeBorg. I'd met Reggie when I was an assistant director at Eagle-Lion, when he was directing a picture with Alan Curtis and Sheila Ryan called *Philo Vance's Secret Mission* [1947].

He'd also done a good job on several of Universal's '40s horror films.
    Reggie LeBorg is a fabulous director—even today he can direct rings around most directors—but he never had the chance to really prove himself. But if you look at *The Black Sleep* and see how slickly that was done—in twelve days!—you've *got* to say he's one hell of a director. And look at the cast we got together for no money—the whole picture cost $225,000.

Horror greats Tor Johnson, John Carradine and Bela Lugosi indulge in some behind-the-scenes buffoonery after shooting *The Black Sleep*.

Can you tell us about the great horror stars you worked with on The Black Sleep: *Basil Rathbone, John Carradine, Lon Chaney and Bela Lugosi?*

Basil Rathbone was the dignified Englishman, just wonderful. I loved to talk to him just to hear him speak. He'd talk to me about his days on Errol Flynn pictures, and how much he loved doing them. He said he did a lot of the swordfights himself. A lovely gentleman, just like Boris Karloff — they were cut from the same kind of cloth. They were hard-working, lovely guys, nothing like the characters you'd see them play.

I had known John Carradine for years, from the days when I was an assistant director at Fox. Carradine had done another picture with us before *The Black Sleep,* an action film called *Desert Sands* [1955]. He was always a shifty kind of guy in life, and by "shifty" I definitely do *not* mean that he was dishonest. But he *lived* the make-believe world of the actor. He really lived in a world of his own, in a dreamworld, and never faced reality.

Lon Chaney I had just directed in *Big House, U.S.A.* [1955], and we really had a great relationship. He said to me, "Look, I'll do anything you want. I know you guys have no money — just tell me how much and I'll show up." Lon was also an amateur chef — he made the best chili in the world. If you loved his chili, he loved you. On the screen you always saw him as a horrible kind of guy, but in life he wasn't at all like that. He was anything *but* — he was a sweet, compassionate, wonderful man. He was great with me, and I was really crazy about him.

Bela Lugosi? Well *[laughs]*, I couldn't figure him out. I don't think he knew he was there! When we opened *The Black Sleep* in San Francisco, we sent Lugosi and a press agent, Chuck Moses, up there for the opening of the picture. Chuck walked into the hotel room one night, and Lugosi was standing on the sill overlooking San Francisco, with the window wide open, saying, "I'm gonna fly!" Chuck cried out, "Wait a second! You *can't* fly!" Lugosi was so drunk, he was going to jump out the window of the hotel! Chuck nearly fainted—he didn't know whether to run and grab him, or to stand there and not disrupt Lugosi's thinking. Anyway, Chuck got him in, called me and said, "What should I do?" I told him, "Put a handcuff on him, take him to the theater, put him on a plane with you and *come home!*"

Both The Black Sleep *and* Pharaoh's Curse *carry an unusual credit line, "Characters Designed by Volpe."*

Volpe is an artist out here in California. He'd read the scripts and then he would draw the characters. Then we'd dress and make up the actors the way he drew them. A very interesting guy; he worked for no bucks, too, very inexpensively. But it helped us—we weren't the great talents of all time. We really needed his direction.

You know, that *Black Sleep* script was really fun to play with; I think more people laughed at it than went with it, although I'm sure there are scary moments in it. I got one of the top brain surgeons in America, who lived in Los Angeles, and used his hands for the brain operation. To this day he's still a neurosurgeon at Cedars of Lebanon out here, and every time I see him he asks, "Where's my second movie?"

The makeup jobs in Black Sleep *are very effective.*

We had more fun doing that makeup; today'd we'd have gotten an award for best makeup, because it was made for spit. We didn't have a lot of money to spend on that.

Bel-Air did pretty well with The Black Sleep, *didn't they?*

When the picture opened, we got some damn good reviews; it did business which was much above what our usual pictures did. In Illinois it played in a double feature with a picture called *The Creeping Unknown,* and a little boy died of fright watching that picture.

Right after The Black Sleep *was finished, you announced that you planned a second horror film,* The Lizard Man *with Lon Chaney.*

I remember the title, but I don't recall what happened with that. I think Lon *wrote* that script, maybe with his wife.

Outwardly, Pharaoh's Curse *seems the most modest of your four Bel-Air horror films, but in many ways it is the most effective.*

The mummy closes in on victim Kurt Katch in a scene from Koch's *Pharaoh's Curse*.

We had planned to make that as a "parasite picture" — to shoot it on location, for around $100,000, after one of our bigger-budgeted features had wrapped up. We had a script developed and we really liked it. But then we had no location picture to put it behind. So we got a little more money — I think that cost $116,000 — and we went back to Death Valley, where we'd made our first success, *War Paint*. The interiors were shot at an old studio on Santa Monica Boulevard. Originally that studio was called Educational, then it became Eagle-Lion, then American National, then Ziv. I think it was during the American National time that we were doing our shooting. *Black Sleep* we shot there, too.

Lee Sholem did a good job of directing Pharaoh's Curse.

In Hollywood they call him "Roll 'Em" Sholem, because he had cameras rolling all the time *[laughs]!* That picture was made in six days, and it really was a good horror picture. Again, Aubrey had developed a good script, and all the actors worked hard.

While the film's mummy looks good in close-ups, in long shots it resembles an old man in pajamas.

[Laughs.] That's all we could afford! One hundred sixteen thousand dollars, what the hell could you do? By the way, every once in a while I still see the guy that played the mummy — he's in the State Department or something now! Every time he sees me, he hugs me and says, "See what you did to me? You got me out of acting!"

Unlike your other early horror films, Pharaoh's Curse *has a cast of comparative unknowns.*

We knew what we had to make it for, and that we couldn't afford to pay anybody who was *some*body any real money to be in it. Remember, our deal with UA was, as long as we could make our pictures for price, we'd just give them the title, the lead in the cast, and go on. On *Pharaoh's Curse* I think all we did was give them the title, 'cause at that cost they didn't care who was in it *[laughs]!* It could have been you or me.

How did Boris Karloff enjoy the location trip to Hawaii for Voodoo Island?

He had a ball, he really did. Again, he was the opposite of everything he was on the screen: He was very congenial, worked hard and loved it. We had signed him to a three-picture deal, at $25,000 each, and *Voodoo Island* was our first film with him. We lived very well over there in Hawaii: We stayed at the Cocoa Palms, on the island of Kauai, and Karloff had a nice bungalow. We did all the interiors there, too, because we couldn't afford to do it any other way—coming back and forth was out of the question, we couldn't afford the travel time between.

Two surprising things in Voodoo Island—*first, that actress Jean Engstrom plays a character who is clearly a lesbian. Did you have any trouble getting that past the censors?*

No, I don't think they understood it. And I don't know how much *we* understood it!

The other thing is, you shot a nude bathing scene for the foreign version.

We thought the foreign market would be able to play it, because nudity could be shown in France and several other countries. We planned on putting that scene in the foreign version, but everybody liked the picture the way it was and we weren't going to gain any mileage showing it, so we didn't use it.

Reginald LeBorg told us he was unhappy with the plant monsters used in Voodoo Island.

We had a fellow named Milt Rice who did those plants; he turned out to be one of the best special effects men in the business, and probably is still working. But, again, *money*. He did the best he could with 'em, and I think they made the point.

Effective musical scores helped Voodoo Island *and all the other pictures quite a lot.*

Les Baxter did the musical score for *Voodoo Island;* Les and Paul Dunlap did all our work. I think the music makes the horror work, so thank God for Les and Paul. You know what our deal would be? We'd give Les or Paul $5,000

Boris Karloff as the disfigured monster maker in *Frankenstein 1970.*

and say, "Write the score, pay for the musicians, the stage and everything, and deliver the score to us." How the hell they ever did it, I don't know. Les did one of our Westerns, *The Yellow Tomahawk* [1954], in three hours — *three hours* on the music and scoring time! Today's guys get six weeks and $90,000 to do a score.

How did Frankenstein 1970 *come about?*

Remember, we had made the three-picture deal with Karloff — we didn't want to have to pay him, and *not* have a picture. We tried to make a deal to make this second Karloff film for United Artists, but they didn't like the idea. So Ed Zabel got ahold of the president of Allied Artists, a fellow by the name of Steve Broidy, and said, "Steve, would you put up the money for this picture? We'll get a CinemaScope lens, which is a selling point for the theaters, and we'll make it for $105,000." Allied Artists said okay, go.

We were making pictures at Warner Brothers around that time, 1957–'58. I had seen a fabulous set there at Warners from an Errol Flynn picture, *Too Much, Too Soon* [1958], and I knew it was still standing. I went to the production manager and said, "Would you give us this whole stage and the backlot for $20,000?" He said, "What are you, crazy? That set cost $90,000." I said, "Yeah, but it's all rigged and there it is, just sitting there." He said, "Let me talk to J.L." Well, J.L. [Jack L. Warner] happened to like me a lot, I guess because of the few pictures we had done there at Warners — *Untamed Youth* [1957] he *really* liked. He said, "Okay, what the hell, give it to 'em." So we paid them $20,000, Karloff $25,000; that left us $60,000 to make the picture. CinemaScope lenses we got from Twentieth Century–Fox for nothing 'cause Aubrey Schenck is a Schenck and Fox was Joe Schenck. I directed. Nine days' shooting—and I never had nine tougher days in my life, to do that picture in that time. I like directing—in fact, I enjoy directing more than producing—but as a director I don't feel I did such a great job on *Frankenstein 1970*, because I didn't have much time to really think.

By this point in his career, Karloff had begun indulging in a rather overdone, almost self-spoofing style of acting out his "heavy" roles. Did you encourage this broad playing?

No, but it was very hard for me to direct him because he was really not directable. I was in awe of him, and we just let him go. At that time Boris Karloff had a standing in life, and whatever he did you thought was right, you were afraid to say it was wrong. I was *afraid* to say to him it was too much! That's not right, but again I tell you we weren't great talents, we were just trying to make movies. All I was really concerned about was schedule—which is not a good thing to admit, but I had the pressure of the fact that we couldn't go over the $105,000. I just was glad to get the scenes done.

Did Karloff present that problem for LeBorg on Voodoo Island?

I think Reggie's a little tougher than I am; I think he stood up to Karloff a little bit. Reggie probably got it more the way he wanted it. He's a brilliant director, so overlooked in his life. And at this stage in his life he *still* wants to direct a picture! And I wouldn't be afraid to give him one.

Frankenstein 1970 *is an oppressively "indoorsy" picture, but there are several gruesome highlights.*

In one scene, when Karloff transferred the heart from the living man to the monster, you could see that cow's heart and the blood going through the tubes. That heart looked just like chicken liver. I'd never had chicken liver for dinner. But that night when I came home my wife had chicken liver, and I damn near *died*. I couldn't eat after seeing that heart all day long! And remember when Karloff carried the body parts over to the garbage disposal, dropped them in and turned it on? When we showed that to the Code, they said, "You can't have that sound effect in there, you've got to take it out! Christ, it's the most gruesome thing we ever heard in our lives!" The sound effect now is way down from what it was when we showed it to them.

Now it sounds like a toilet flushing!

Right! We had to get rid of our original, *crunching* sounds.

Shortly after Frankenstein 1970 *was completed, your third Karloff film,* King of the Monsters, *was announced, but it was never made.*

Zabel and Aubrey didn't live up to the agreement with Karloff. By that time I had left them and gone to work for Frank Sinatra's company. They never made a third picture *or* paid Karloff, and I think it was an unhappy relationship at the end. Maybe Karloff felt badly toward me, too, but as I said I had already gone on with Sinatra and was not responsible. I do think, unfortunately, that before he died Karloff was unhappy with us, that we hadn't lived up to our agreement.

You know, Aubrey Schenck and I made a horror picture that you might not see on our list of credits. I had a friend named William Castle—Bill and I grew up together in New York, where we lived right across the street from each other. One day he called me and said, "Howard, I've got the greatest idea in the world, but I'm afraid to tell it to anybody." I told him to come over to the office. He came over and said, "I want to make a picture like you guys do. I want to call it *Macabre,* and I want to make it with a hook. I got ahold of Lloyds of London, and I made a deal with them: Everybody that buys a ticket automatically gets a life insurance policy for $5,000 against death from fright by watching the picture. That'll be the campaign." I said, "That's the greatest idea I ever heard in my life." Aubrey and I produced it with him, but we didn't take any credit or pay because he had no money. We made the picture for $102,000, then we broke the story about how we would sell it. That's when Allied Artists bought it. All over the United States, the thing did business. *Macabre* grossed over a million dollars, and we all made a few bucks. Bill and I went on from there—I brought him to Paramount when I got in, and of course *Rosemary's Baby* and all those things developed.

Which one of these early horror films is your personal favorite?

Oh, I liked *Voodoo Island* the best. I enjoyed the experience, and the dealings with Karloff. And I like that picture's ambience—the background of the Hawaiian Islands. I just liked the look of it, and thought Reggie LeBorg did one hell of a job. I *love* that picture, I think it's a classic.

Whose idea was it to bring the novel The Manchurian Candidate *to the screen?*

[Sighs.] I wish I could say it was mine. I made a deal to run Frank Sinatra's company: Max Youngstein, an executive at United Artists, had recommended me because of all the pictures I had made for them. Frank, who was not a picturemaker, was supposed to make four pictures for UA, two with him and two without him, over a couple-year period. The day I met Frank he said, "Howard, there's this book I read, I love it, I want to do it. See if we can buy it. It's called *The Manchurian Candidate.*" So I tracked it down and found out that John Frankenheimer and George Axelrod had bought it. It took us a while to negotiate a deal with them as a package, George to produce and write it, John to direct it, and myself to be the executive producer—which *was* the producer, 'cause George was busy enough writing. Frankenheimer's career was

really just starting; this was his third or fourth picture, I think. He was a flamboyant, wonderful kind of kid.

What was your budget on that one?

The picture cost $2,200,000 in 1962—a *lot* of money. Of course, Frank got a million dollars himself, and Larry Harvey got $200,000. So we didn't have much left to make the picture.

One Communist newspaper speculated that Sinatra took the leading role to dispel rumors of his being a Red sympathizer.

Hogwash. Frank thought as an actor he had a chance to play a very confused kind of guy, a character who was brainwashed, had bad dreams, and finally managed to figure it all out. He thought that was a great acting challenge. And Frank worked harder in that picture than in any we had done before or since. He gave it everything he had. And Larry Harvey was a delight. Larry jumped in the lake in New York February 12, and it was twenty degrees above zero the day we shot that scene. I thought he'd die when he hit that water! He had all kinds of rubber clothes on underneath, but he was so shaken I think he drank a bottle of brandy in a minute.

Manchurian Candidate *is easily the most frightening film you've done.*

Oh, I would say so—God, yes. The whole idea of the power of Khigh Dhiegh, that the mind can be controlled—and it *can,* it's been proven. It's such a frightening thing.

I thought that picture was wonderful, and it's a cult favorite to this day. But UA didn't know what the hell to do with it. The word-of-mouth was good but unfortunately not strong enough. You know, that picture took fifteen years to get into profit!

How did you enjoy collaborating with the Disney organization on the recent fantasy film Dragonslayer?

You know, it's funny—we didn't have any real collaboration. The only time I ever saw anybody from Disney was at the preview *[laughs]!* Paramount was in control of the picture, and Disney put up 50 percent of whatever it cost. So the "collaboration" was really nil.

How much creative input did you have on the picture?

I got in so late that I didn't get into the picture until two days before shooting. Most of what I provided was advice and directions, so they wouldn't get themselves into positions they couldn't get out of. Our budget was $12,000,000; we went to $18,000,000. Most of it was because of the cost of the miniatures that were done by Industrial Light and Magic. Not that it was I.L.M.'s fault; it's just unfortunate that we got into heavy expense. I thought they did a fabulous job on the visuals.

Looking back, did you enjoy making the older pictures more than you enjoy working on your newer, "bigger" projects?

I did, absolutely. It was a different time of my life, it was fun, it was challenging as hell. And I guarantee you, those cheap pictures will stand up against any two-hour movie made today. There's more care and thought in them; even though they were low-budget, we really *cared* what we were making, we really *tried*. It was such a ball, and we had so much fun.

*These kinds of shows are made as a collaborative effort.
Everyone did everything, which is a wonderful way to work;
I mean, everyone's totally involved, everyone cares.
Though they were seven-day shows and the titles were exploitative,
we wanted them to be the very best we could possibly make them.*

——— *Bernard L. Kowalski* ———

YET ANOTHER SUCCESSFUL DIRECTOR who got his career going with the help of Roger Corman, Bernard Kowalski made two of Corman's most luridly titled and enjoyably cheap productions from the '50s: *Night of the Blood Beast* and *Attack of the Giant Leeches*. Although not as visibly successful as other Corman proteges like Francis Ford Coppola and Peter Bogdanovich, Kowalski went on to direct such films as *Krakatoa, East of Java* [1969] and *Macho Callahan* [1970], and, more significantly, to establish himself as an important figure in television with a long and impressive list of credits. To mention a select few, he directed the pilots for *Richard Diamond, N.Y.P.D.* and *The Monroes;* executive-produced *Baretta;* and was co-owner of *Mission: Impossible*. In 1973, he took a break from all his TV work to return to the horror genre with the entertaining thriller *SSSSSSS*.

Kowalski got his first job in the movie business at the age of five as a Warner Bros. extra in *Dead End Kids* pictures, as well as such Errol Flynn vehicles as *Dodge City* and *Virginia City*. His experience behind the camera began at age sixteen when he worked as a clerk for his father, who was an assistant director and production manager. Early TV provided Kowalski's first opportunity to direct on such Western series as *Frontier* and *Boots and Saddles;* he then made the transition to feature-film directing in 1958 when he was hired by Gene Corman (Roger's brother) to make the teen exploitation feature *Hot Car Girl*.

How did working for Roger and Gene Corman compare to working at the larger studios, and in television?

It was a tremendous learning ground. I found that the Corman brothers were the type of producers who would make very tough deals with people in the sense of protecting *their* dollar investment. But I found them to be full of integrity and honesty. I know that no one worked harder than either Roger or Gene on whatever the project they were involved with. Their input was tremendous, and they were very tasteful gentlemen. I'm a big fan of both of them.

Volume upon volume has been written about Roger Corman and his films, but little mention is ever made of Gene. Can you tell us a little more about this lesser-known Corman?

Gene has a tremendous sense of humor, and he is a very highly competitive individual. He's an art connoisseur and a man of extremely fine taste. We were making these movies for sixty-five and seventy thousand dollars, and Gene would practically go to the hospital after each show, such was his total dedication and involvement. He's someone who does know film, does know costs, and is truly a class act.

Any guesses as to why he's been overshadowed by his older brother?

I think it's just that Roger started off and brought Gene into the company. Roger's was just a huge success. Later, Gene made a few attempts at producing

Previous page: Kowalski allied himself with the Corman brothers for his first science fiction effort, *Night of the Blood Beast*. Ross Sturlin flexes his talons in this posed shot.

other kinds of movies, and by that I mean a more expensive, major-feature type of film such as *Tobruk* and *F.I.S.T.*, which were near misses.

Did Roger have any creative input on Night of the Blood Beast *and* Attack of the Giant Leeches, *or was his involvement strictly financial?*
  He was involved creatively *and* financially. Roger would supervise the shows, Gene was running the shows. It was an embryonic period for Gene in that area, and Roger, with more experience, was standing back and just guiding Gene as well as myself.

Did you have any choice of material during your time with the Cormans?
  It was a matter of reading the material and then agreeing to do it or not. That was the only choice involved.

What were your budget and shooting schedule on Blood Beast?
  Shooting schedule was seven days, budget was around $68,000. We shot *Blood Beast* in and around the Bronson Canyon area, and operated out of what was then the Chaplin Studios, which were on Sunset and LaBrea.

Did you have to do any rewriting of the Blood Beast *or* Giant Leeches *scripts, to make them fit in with the way you wanted to do them?*
  We did some rewriting as we got into it. These kinds of shows are made as a collaborative effort. Everyone did everything, which is a wonderful way to work; I mean, everyone's totally involved, everyone cares. Though they were seven-day shows and the titles were exploitative, we wanted them to be the very best we could possibly make them. For instance, Danny Haller, who's been directing for some time now, was the art director, and he would pull a trailer onto the sound stage and sleep there, and do a lot of the sawing and hammering himself. It was tremendous fun, because everyone was just doing their best.

The Blood Beast *screenplay was reminiscent at times of Howard Hawks'* The Thing from Another World, *and also used elements from the earlier Corman films* It Conquered the World *and* Attack of the Crab Monsters. *Were these films drawn upon for inspiration?*
  I'm sure that the writers were aware of them—we all were. I did not sit down and write with them, but to my knowledge those were probably springboard ideas. I don't think that the writers were intentionally imitative.

Conversely, the 1979 film Alien *seems derivative of your* Blood Beast *and another '50s film,* It! The Terror from Beyond Space.
  I'm sure that the same kind of thing happened with that. There were pieces here and there that were springboarding ideas.

What's your reaction when a film like Alien *borrows elements from your early pictures and becomes a huge success?*

You're pleased that you were right in what you were attempting to do. I personally harbor no angers within me. I know it's a creative field and that there are many ways of doing the same thing. Sometimes they're better and sometimes they're not. I thought *Alien* was quite good.

Did you have any say in the casting of these films?

I cast them with the Cormans, who were using a lot of the people that they normally used—an ensemble group. I was happy to use them. If there was anyone I didn't want, I would not be forced to work with them.

What can you tell us about Michael Emmet, who starred in both Blood Beast *and* Giant Leeches?

Michael Emmet and I had worked together on the series *Boots and Saddles;* he was a regular on it, and I had experienced maybe eight of the thirteen shows with Michael having a major role. He was a good, hard-working actor. Coming over to the Corman shows after having worked with Michael, I thought that he was a leading man type that we could afford. I have not kept up the relationship with Michael through the years, so I am not in a position to say where he is now, but he was always just terrific to work with and a thorough gentleman. I still see Ed *[Night of the Blood Beast]* Nelson every now and then; Ed was somebody that was always working very hard, a very decent person and a family-man type of guy. Ed did so many of the Corman pictures, he was a valuable part of the ensemble group.

The alien monster costume seen in Blood Beast *was left over from a previous Corman,* Teenage Caveman.

To save money, the Cormans would often utilize anything that was existing, and incorporate it into one of their new films. One of the philosophies that they approached their filmmaking with was, whenever they could minimize their risk, they had a better chance to have a financial success. So if they had expensive costumes already made, they would try and doctor 'em up; if there were standing sets at the Chaplin Studios from another film, they would paint 'em a different color. A very heads-up approach to being practical in the dollar area.

Did you have a better budget and shooting schedule on Attack of the Giant Leeches?

Giant Leeches went eight days, and that was about $70,000. It was the same general crew as *Blood Beast,* with everybody pitching in together. Now, looking back, there was a funny example of that on *Giant Leeches.* When you're shooting with your camera platform from the water to the shore, you get a water raft that you put your equipment and your people on. It's a rather

Divers (Ken Clark, left; unidentified, right) defend themselves against mutated swamp creatures (Guy Buccola and Ross Sturlin in suits made of raincoat material) in Kowalski's *Attack of the Giant Leeches*.

cumbersome and awkward thing, and it requires somebody *in* the water to propel it.

We were out on a water raft at the Pasadena Arboretum, and I turned to the grips on the show and said, "Push me across to that area over there." They said that Gene Corman wouldn't pay the water rate and that, though they were friends of mine, they just weren't going to get in the water. I understood that and I didn't blame them. So I turned to my brother, who was the script clerk on the show—we both had our bathing suits on—and I said, "Let's go." So while I was directing the show, the two of us were pushing the water raft that day. Later, I went to Gene and said, "Pay these guys the water rate tomorrow. I'm through pushing that raft all over." The next morning Gene was there, took off his clothes, got his bathing suit on, jumped in and pushed the raft all day. He didn't think it was right that he should have to pay the grips more money to get in the water, so the principle of the thing was involved. And I say, Gene would go out and spend $250 for dinner, but instead of giving in to their position, he just did triple-duty all day. And *again,* at the end of the show, Gene, who was so involved and worked twenty-two hours a day, went into the hospital for three or four days, just to get himself healthy, before he'd come back and finish the movie up in postproduction.

We shot all the swamp scenes at this Pasadena Arboretum, a beautiful refuge for ducks and geese. The interiors were done at the Chaplin Studios. The underwater scenes were done in a private home in Studio City. It had a private pool with a viewing glass; we would dress it up with plants and things, then bring the actors in and shoot the underwater scenes there.

Didn't you have some sort of mishap with one of the studio tanks?

We were shooting some scenes on a sound stage, with the leech actors coming out a three-foot tank and into a cavelike area, when the tank *collapsed.* The danger was not of anybody being in the tank or of us possibly getting a little wet, but it happened while all the lights were hot and everything was on. Had anyone been holding onto something and gotten water on them, we could've had an accident. We were all really very fortunate that no one got electrocuted.

Were you happy with the leech costumes used in the film?

No. The two actors playing the leeches were Guy Buccola, a basketball player from U.C.L.A., and Ross Sturlin, a young man that had done stunts on *Boots and Saddles* and played the alien in *Blood Beast.* These two fellows were forced to build the leech costumes in order to get the job. They *were* paid money for the building of them, but the job did come "with costumes." They were made out of cheap, rubberized raincoat material, sewed in a capelike form. Very little money was spent on them, they were always tearing, so as a result they did have a number of problems in trying to maintain the look. Of course, when we'd go underwater, that was difficult because they'd get air pockets in the suit.

You can also see their legs and flippers protruding from the suits.

It was the best that we could do with the time that we had. Unfortunately, on a seven-day feature like that, you don't have an awful lot of time once you've started to make these kinds of corrections. To go back to your original question, "Were you happy with them," in no way were they totally satisfactory at all.

Part of Giant Leeches' *appeal springs from Yvette Vickers' presence in the cast.*

All of us doing the show were really impressed with her, because she had been a *Playboy* centerfold, and we understood why—she had a gorgeous figure. She was hard-working, willing to do whatever she had to do, including some things she didn't like, like going underwater and being dragged around. She was a first-class trouper and a good actress, and someone that we were very happy to be working with. I could say nothing but positive things about her. I worked with her later on *M Squad,* and I saw her again several years ago when I was executive producer on *Baretta* and she was doing one of the episodes.

The grimmest scenes in Giant Leeches *— or, for that matter, in* any *horror film from that era—are those in which the leeches attach themselves to their victims*

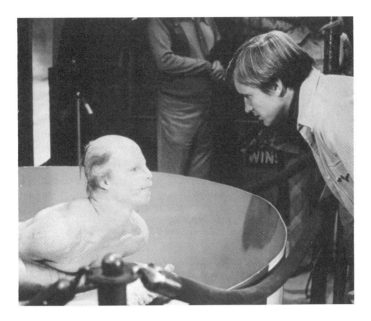

Dirk Benedict marvels at the sideshow snake-man in Kowalski's 1973 sci-fi chiller *SSSSSSS*.

and suck their blood. Did you have any trouble getting those scenes past the censors?

Not really. In those days, Roger and Gene Corman would deal with the censors. They were very effective, total film buffs who knew what the censors had allowed other people to do. They would be about the finest representatives in that area that you could have. They would know what limitations had been imposed on most of the shows that were out, and then they would fight for parity.

How did SSSSSSS *come about?*

It was an original story idea that Dan Striepeke had; Dan had been a makeup artist, and he and John Chambers were credited with *Planet of the Apes*. Dan went to see Dick Zanuck, and Zanuck had responded to the story. It ended up being the first movie that Zanuck and David Brown made at Universal.

And that's where the film was shot?

We did it entirely at Universal — the backlot and a few of the street areas around it; back near the *Psycho* house; we used the *Virginian* ranch as Strother Martin's place. We shot it, I think, in about twenty-two days.

And your budget?

Since we made it at Universal, with their overhead factors and everything else, it came to $1,030,000. We had high hopes for *SSSSSSS;* we owned a good piece of it, so there was a chance to be in a profit participation basis that might have proved quite lucrative. We've never really received any money on it in the way of profits, but that's a tough thing to do at a major studio. It was quite well received in Europe.

Were you happy with the unusual title, SSSSSSS (Don't Say It, Hiss It)?

Yes. I found it to be a title that created a lot of word-of-mouth. Part of how the title came up was, Dan Striepeke and I went to the Hermosa Beach Reptile Emporium during our initial investigation on cobras. The store owner pulled a cobra out — a totally poisonous, lethal cobra — and put it down at his feet. He was between us and the cobra, but it was a very small room, and we heard the sound that it made. That's where we picked up the title of the show. It worked for us.

Did you enjoy working on this one as much as you did the Cormans?

We had a good time making it. Dan Striepeke was a very bright, honest man, full of integrity; Zanuck and Brown were wonderful to work with, thorough gentlemen who had a lot of input; and Strother Martin was just a wonderful human being, a lovely actor and a very funny man.

Did the snakes present any threat during production?

We had a hundred and fifty-five reptiles, and of that, we had like sixty or seventy that were lethal. The King Cobra that we used was absolutely *regal* in the sense that it didn't make mistakes twice. All the other snakes would hit the glass any time you'd go near them, but the King Cobra did it *once,* and then he'd just *look* at you. There were a lot of silly, fun things that we shouldn't have done but we did. The very first day, for instance, I said to my assistant Gordon Webb, "I want you to tell everybody here there'll be no games, no playing around. We're in a position where it could be dangerous, and we'll deal very heavily with anyone that fools around with this." Well, he makes this speech, and the minute he gets done somebody throws a rubber snake at him and he screams at the top of his lungs! *That* was the end of it; after that, everyone was doing terrible things to everybody else all the way through.

One story I enjoy telling on Dick Zanuck: Dick, who was very athletic, very much his own man, would come up to the set every day to offer his comments on dailies, but he never got too close to the snakes. So one of the young snake trainers, who didn't know or care who anybody was, walked up to him and said, "You're one of the big shots with the company, huh?" And Dick said, "Well, I'm the executive producer." And the kid came back, "You're also scared shitless of the snakes, huh?" Dick just looked at him. The kid went on, "Yeah, I could tell. You haven't come anywhere near 'em, and you get away as fast as you can." Dick is the type of person that would swing on someone who would call him that, but he got in his limousine and left. He came back in two hours, walked up to this kid and said, "Put the boa constrictor around my neck." The kid looked at him and said, "You had a couple of drinks, huh?" Dick said, "Uh-huh. Put the boa around my neck." And so they did it. That was kind of fun.

What precautions did you take to safeguard your cast and crew against the snakes?
We had a doctor there at all times, in case anyone had gotten bit by accident. I'd had all of the people that were going to be dealing with the snakes exposed to the hazards, dangers and limitations of the snakes prior to our filming. Everyone was informed as to what we *could* fool around with and what we *couldn't* fool around with. We had no problems, I'm very pleased to say.

One of the highlights of SSSSSSS *is the effective makeup on Dirk Benedict.*
It was done by the best people in the makeup business, Dan Striepeke and John Chambers. At that time they were the very finest—they were Academy Award winners. Dirk Benedict was very patient—some of that makeup that they put on him took six to eight hours to apply. He was a wonderful person, by the way, a super guy. Heather Menzies and he were a wonderful team. It was a little family; all the way through working the picture, we did everything together, Strother and them, all of us. We shared all the good and bad moments.

The most disappointing thing about SSSSSSS *is its too-abrupt, let's-get-this-thing-done ending. Was that a last-minute, money-saving measure?*
No, that *was* the original writing. We didn't know where to go with it from the time that Dirk Benedict was killed. Being of the genre that it was, the intent was to go out on the girl, Heather Menzies, screaming, and the terror of it. I can appreciate where you feel that it was abrupt. Obviously, in some senses, it didn't work for us, but that was *not* done through an economy-cut process.

Which is your personal favorite of the three horror/sci-fi films you directed?
The most recent one, *SSSSSSS*, because the memories are more alive and fresher for me. I'm a giant fan of Strother Martin, and it was one of the latter experiences he had in films. He was such a joy to work with.

*There was a rivalry going on between
Lon Chaney and Bela Lugosi from the Universal days
when they both played Dracula. You see, Lugosi
was the great Dracula, but then something happened
at Universal and they gave the part* [Son of Dracula] *to Chaney.
It came out on* The Black Sleep:
*Chaney was sore at something Lugosi brought up
and it nearly came to a fight. Chaney
picked him up a little bit, but put him down —
we stopped him. We kept them apart quite a bit.*

Reginald LeBorg

LOOKING BACK over a career which has spanned a full half-century and encompassed hundreds of credits, Reginald LeBorg is understandably discontent with his too-close identification with "monster movies." He is quick to point out the many different genres his career has embraced, from comedies to musicals and Westerns, as well as the many different positions he has held within the industry itself; to be remembered primarily for films such as *Calling Dr. Death, Jungle Woman, The Black Sleep* and *Diary of a Madman* seems somewhat of an injustice that perplexes and amuses the octogenarian director. Nonetheless, only a handful of directors can equal his output and longevity within the genre (from 1934's *Life Returns* to 1973's *So Evil, My Sister),* and no other director could claim to have worked with as many of the famous horror personages that LeBorg has known. His contribution to the genre is unique and unmatched.

The oldest of three sons, Reginald LeBorg was born in Vienna in 1902. He majored in political economy at the University of Austria and studied musical composition for a year at Arnold Schoenberg's Composition Seminar. His education completed, LeBorg entered his father's banking business and, acting as the senior LeBorg's representative, he traveled to Prague, Hamburg and Paris to transact family business negotiations. During his extended two-year stay in Paris, he studied at the Sorbonne. In the mid-'20s LeBorg traveled to New York to dispose of a collection of paintings in his father's behalf. Remaining in New York, he was employed in several banks and brokerage houses and at an advertising agency. The stock market crash of 1929 wiped out the LeBorg family fortune, and Reginald's interest in the financial world waned. He returned to Europe and his first love, the stage. He worked at the Max Reinhardt School in Vienna, and later devoted much of his time to directing operas and musical comedies for provincial houses throughout Central Europe.

Arriving on the Hollywood scene in the early '30s, LeBorg appeared as an extra in pictures at Paramount and Metro and later staged opera sequences in the Grace Moore hits *One Night of Love* and *Love Me Forever,* as well as other films with operatic themes at Fox, Paramount and United Artists. After a number of second unit assignments at Metro, Goldwyn and Selznick, LeBorg joined Universal, where he turned out band shorts. An eighteen-month hitch with the United States Army interrupted his Hollywood career, which resumed in 1943 with his return to Universal and his promotion to feature film director.

How did you become involved on 1934's Life Returns?

I met the producer, Dr. Eugene Frenke, socially, we started to talk and he told me about the story. I began to point out to him things that I thought were wrong with the story and to offer suggestions, and he asked me if I wanted to write a little bit. He gave me the story and I started to do the screenplay. I didn't do very much on it; I worked only a couple of weeks, a couple of things that I did *he* didn't like. So we had disagreements and so forth.

In 1943 your Hollywood background was largely confined to musical comedies and shorts. How did Universal happen to assign you to The Mummy's Ghost?

Previous page: LeBorg strolls with horror great Lon Chaney, Jr., on the Universal backlot as they discuss their upcoming joint project *The Mummy's Ghost.*

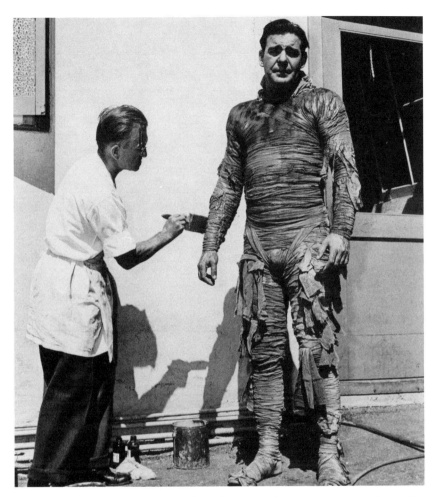

Makeup wizard Jack P. Pierce works his magic on an unhappy-looking Lon Chaney, Jr., in this behind-the-scenes shot from LeBorg's *The Mummy's Ghost*.

The first feature I made at Universal was an overgrown short musical, *She's for Me* [1943]; it had no stars in it, just their stock players. I was supposed to get a comedy afterwards, because I had some comedy in *She's for Me* and Universal liked it very much. Ben Pivar, an associate producer at Universal, had a director assigned to *The Mummy's Ghost*—I don't know who the man was— but I think he had an accident or something, and they had nobody there right then to take his place. Pivar seemed to like me and he said, "How 'bout reading the script?"

What was it like working with Lon Chaney, Jr., in the heyday of his career?

Chaney, Jr., in complete makeup for *The Mummy's Ghost*. (Photo courtesy Steve Jochsberger.)

Well, I *liked* him, he was a nice guy. The only thing is, of course—he drank.

What sort of problems did his drinking create?
No problems, I just had to change my way of shooting. I shot with him mostly in the morning—I tried to get everything in up to 2:00. Then he had his lunch and started on the bottle. He couldn't shake it.

There was a scene in *The Mummy's Ghost* where Frank Reicher brewed tana leaves and inadvertently attracted the Mummy. Chaney limped into the room and Reicher backed against the wall. Chaney's hand went up to Reicher's throat and squeezed so forcefully that Reicher nearly *fainted*. Reicher was an old man, and frail, and Chaney got carried away. Reicher cried out, "He nearly *killed* me! He took my breath away!" After the shooting, I took Chaney to one side and said, "Look, Lon—don't *do* that...!" He said okay, but I could tell that he was very happy about it. Chaney always was very—I don't want to say rough, but—he *was* an action man. It was doing it like his father would have done—he was trying to emulate Chaney, Sr., or better him.

In another scene, Chaney broke into a museum at night to steal the body of the Princess Ananka. After a scuffle with a guard, he was supposed to crash through some plate glass doors. I didn't want to endanger an actor by having him go through glass, so I told the prop department to install breakaway glass. The prop man forgot to give the order, and the next day we arrived on the set and the job wasn't done—it was still plate glass. I told Chaney, "Look, the plate glass is still here and I don't want to hold up production. Just push the door open with your foot or elbow." He didn't say anything, he just nodded his head. And when it came time to do the shot, he went *right through* the plate glass. He even injured his hand—of course the Mummy is fully bandaged, but even through the bandages glass penetrated and there *was* a little blood. I said, "See what you did?!" and he said, "I wanted to show you that I had the courage." He was trying to show off his bravura.

In a mid-'60s interview, Chaney said that the Mummy was his least favorite monster role of that era.

Well, sure, because Chaney wanted to act, and the only thing that he invented for the Mummy was the walk—which was very good, incidentally.

What about rumors that Chaney allowed a stand-in to take his place throughout much of the production?

Chaney never had a stand-in during *The Mummy's Ghost*. He was doing it himself, all the time. He may have done this in some of the other *Mummy* pictures but he didn't do it with me. In fact, I baited him a little bit—he wanted to do a picture as a gentleman, and in our next picture, *Calling Dr. Death,* he played in an excellent wardrobe, had a mustache and he was a dandy.

John Carradine really hammed it up as the new High Priest.

Yes, but considering the character he played it wasn't too much of a fault. There were no heavies in that picture other than him—Chaney was no heavy, playing that poor mummy—so we had to have somebody fill that slot. Carradine's voice was sonorous and excellent, much better than the average actor's, so I let him go on. In a picture like that you *can* be a little hammy—it was usually kids and teenagers that went to see that kind of picture.

The role of Amina/Ananka was originally assigned to Acquanetta. Why was she replaced by Ramsay Ames?

In the morning of the first day of shooting [August 23, 1943], Acquanetta was on the set at 9:00 but she was walking very awkwardly — she was scared, I think because this was her second or third film. In the second shot, she was supposed to walk from a lawn, up a couple of stairs and into a house. She slipped and fell, and hit her head, and for half an hour she was unconscious. They took her to the dispensary and gave her smelling salts — she was all right, but she had a slight concussion. Pivar didn't want to take any chances, so the role was recast with Ramsay Ames.

Were you satisfied with the performance Ramsay Ames gave on such short notice?
No, no, no — it was very bad. She was not a very good actress. She later developed, but again, as with Acquanetta, this was her first or second picture.

Did you have any say in the casting of these early pictures?
No, unfortunately, none at all. I got all the stock company. I could only complain. And I wasn't very well liked by some of the people there for that reason — the executives said I was a complainer and a tough guy to work with. There's an old Latin proverb that says, *"De mortuis nil nisi bonum"* ("About the dead, speak only the good"), and Ben Pivar is dead — but I had a lot of run-ins with him.

One of the weak points of The Mummy's Ghost *screenplay is that Kharis is introduced simply wandering out of the woods, with no explanation of how he survived the* Mummy's Tomb *fire or where he spent the years between.*
To me, that seemed ridiculous at first; in fact, I had a fight with Pivar about it. I said to him, "There's no reason! We have to have a motivation!" He said, "Motivation? We've made two *Mummy* pictures already and the Mummy *always* comes out of the woods! Just *shoot* it!" I said, "Well, let me try and find a motivation." So I ran the old *Mummy* films, including the original one that Karl Freund made, and in one of them I found a long shot where a frocked man with a fez goes into an Egyptian temple in Memphis. So I said, "Let's have a scene where John Carradine, the caretaker of the Mummy, goes in there and gets an order to hunt for the Mummy." Pivar liked that idea, and so we took that one long shot, made a negative dub, put it in my picture, and then I shot close-ups in the temple with Carradine and George Zucco as the High Priest. Pivar liked it.

Did you have a hand in the writing of your other pictures?
Every one I did, because I pride myself on being a writer, too. I find a lot of scripts pretty much the same as the others — too much *déjà vu.*

We've always liked the surprising finale of Mummy's Ghost, *with the heroine sinking into the quicksand in Kharis' arms.*

We discussed the finale with Pivar and I said, "Why not let Ananka sink with the Mummy? Why should there always be a happy ending?" Somebody else said, "No, we might make a sequel." I told him, "The Mummy is *always* coming up—Ananka doesn't have to!"

So that downbeat ending was your idea?

It was a steal from the Frank Capra picture *Lost Horizon* [1937], so I can't take all the credit for it. I did take time to shoot it—it took me two or three hours to shoot that climactic chase when I should have only had one shot. I took shots from the back and from the front, shots of the feet and the hands and all that sort of thing. Ramsay Ames was Ananka at the beginning, but after that it was her stand-in, who we dressed the same way and put the makeup on. Incidentally, I shot that chase differently than what Pivar was used to. Chases always ran left-to-right, left-to-right, all the time. I mixed it around. When Pivar saw the rushes, he started to fight with me! He said, "How could you shoot it this way? This has to be a progression!" I went into a cutting room with a cutter and after I pieced it together it was a beautiful chase. Pivar was very satisfied and he asked me to direct his next picture.

That next picture was Calling Dr. Death?

Right. Pivar had confidence in me because I was a fighter who tried to get better and better material. Pivar was sometimes afraid that I would go over budget, but whenever he saw that I *was* on budget, he didn't worry anymore—he stayed in his office and played gin rummy.

Calling Dr. Death was supposed to start a series of *Inner Sanctum* films, *if* it hit. Universal had an option on further stories. We did *Calling Dr. Death* and it got very good reviews.

When Universal initially mapped out the Inner Sanctum *series, they announced that Lon Chaney and Gale Sondergaard would co-star in* Calling Dr. Death *and in all further installments. As it turned out, Sondergaard never appeared in a single one!*

I don't know whether this was the real cause of it or not, but she was a leftist and she and her husband were shooting off their mouths quite often. The war was still going on, of course. Executives there at Universal may have decided to recast it—but I can't be sure, I was not in on any such conference. I just heard one day that she was out, and that they were going to cast somebody else—that's all. They didn't say why, you could only speculate. It happened later on that she *did* find it difficult to get work, and then it *was* due to that situation.

Screenwriter Edward Dein, who wrote Calling Dr. Death, *told us that Chaney could not cope with some of the complicated scientific dialogue that he was asked to deliver in the picture, and that the "stream-of-consciousness" voice-over narration was the result of his inability.*

We had to do a little bit of simplification, that's true, but I think it was not only Chaney but Pivar also. Pivar was very, very crude, not very intelligent, and he couldn't read very well.

Was there a more conscious effort on your part to stylize Calling Dr. Death *as opposed to the other films you directed in this series?*

I put a few different visual effects in there which were absolutely fresh at that time. In one sequence, I had the camera *become* Lon Chaney, with everybody else looking *into* the camera. That's the sequence where Chaney is brought to the house where the wife was murdered—the reporters look into the camera as it moves forward into the house; then J. Carrol Naish, playing the detective, also addresses the camera. Then, the camera pans down to the floor where the coroner is examining the body. The whole sequence was shot this way until Lon Chaney is accused, and *then* you see his face. That was one sequence in the whole film which I thought was a novelty at that time. It was so fresh and new that when Robert Montgomery, who was also directing at that time, saw *Calling Dr. Death* he made a whole picture this way—

Lady in the Lake! *[1946.]*

And that was a *flop!* For one sequence that was all right, but it couldn't sustain an entire film. One critic wrote about *Lady in the Lake* that it was a copy of *Calling Dr. Death* but Montgomery made the mistake of doing the whole picture that way.

In your second Inner Sanctum, Weird Woman, *Evelyn Ankers is cast against type in the role of the sinister Ilona. Was she pleased with the opportunity to play a villainess for a change?*

Evelyn Ankers was a very sweet girl and a very good actress, but no, she wasn't very happy about her part in *Weird Woman*. She was a good friend of Anne Gwynne's, and she had to play Gwynne's enemy in *Weird Woman*—to torment her—and they even had to have a fight at one point because they were competing for Lon Chaney in the film. When Ankers had a scene with Gwynne that was rather macabre, she couldn't do it very well because she loved Gwynne so much that she *couldn't* be mean to her. I gave her a few pointers, and after three or four takes she did it very well.

In preparing Weird Woman, *did you read the original Fritz Leiber story* Conjure Wife?

No, I only read the script. I got the script on a Friday and was told to start shooting a week from Monday. So I had to read it over the weekend and then come in and prepare. That was the norm at Universal: sometimes you'd get two or three weeks in between, if they had no script, but sometimes they had to rush these things out. Of course, me being a hard worker and a fast worker, they gave me the dirt—when they had something they wanted done fast, they rushed me in.

Lon Chaney learns the hard way that acid is no substitute for eyewash in *Dead Man's Eyes,* a Universal *Inner Sanctum* mystery.

Your third and last Inner Sanctum, Dead Man's Eyes, *boasted no supernatural elements, but it is an effective B mystery.*

I think so, too, because I like stories that have a basis in medical fact. I think *Dead Man's Eyes* did have pace, and Paul Kelly was very good in it.

What did Lon Chaney think of your leaving the Inner Sanctum *series?*

At the beginning Chaney thought I would be his *pal,* and when after three *Inner Sanctums* I wanted to do a musical—a Deanna Durbin picture or something—he said to me, "You traitor! We were supposed to do big things together!" I told him, "We'll get together again, don't worry."

Part ape and part woman, Acquanetta contemplates some unsightly leg hairs in this posed shot from *Jungle Woman.*

How did you like working with your Mummy's Ghost *casualty, Acquanetta, on* Jungle Woman?

She was a nice-looking girl, but she had a squeaky, high-pitched voice. A lower-class Maria Montez. Again, as with Ramsay Ames, she developed a little later, after a few pictures, but unfortunately...

You had to have her at the beginning!

[Laughs.] Right! At that time, the casting couch was important for the women players, especially for the young starlets. They were put on short money contracts—if they made out, fine; if they didn't, they were let go after six months or a year. In the meantime, the producers had a nice interlude.

What hurt Jungle Woman, *more than Acquanetta's performance, is its surprisingly weak script.*
   It was an atrocious script, and a silly idea anyway. But, again, I was under contract. If I had refused it, I would have been suspended without pay, and I wouldn't have gotten *anything* good any more. You had to play ball with the front office.

Jungle Woman *is such a short film, and it uses so much stock footage from* Captive Wild Woman, *you must have been able to get it "in the can" in a very short time.*
   I think we made it in one week. Most of these pictures were done in ten days, and this was practically done in seven.

One interesting aspect of the screenplay is its tendency to suggest the presence of the Ape Woman through shadows, moving bushes and branches, etc., and not show the monster until the film's closing seconds.
   I tried that especially, because I think you have more suspense that way. If you'd seen the Ape Woman immediately, you wouldn't care about it any more. The story was so bad, I felt I had to do *something* — if I gave it away in the first reel, I would have no more picture.

Were you inspired to do that by the Val Lewton films that were being made at RKO at the time?
   Well, I knew Val Lewton very well, and I wanted to work with him, but we never got together. Naturally I saw his pictures and they were good, and there *was* an inspiration, there's no doubt about that. I think that was the only way to make the script palatable.

Was The Black Sleep *conceived as an all-star horror show?*
   No. When the script came to me, we had no idea what the cast would be like. Howard W. Koch and Aubrey Schenck, the executive producers, told me they were negotiating for Basil Rathbone and Lon Chaney.

With its all-star cast, The Black Sleep *seems a poorly structured film: Rathbone gets the only sizable role, the others are left to fight for the crumbs.*
   Well, Basil Rathbone had a big name. John Carradine was getting old; Chaney was already a sick man — drinking, you know; and Bela Lugosi was practically a wreck, under the influence of drugs. He had a man with him continuously who had to hold him up.

Lugosi's biographers claim that he had been cured of drug addiction by that time and appeared a healthy man.
   He was in very, very bad shape. He died a year later.

Were Chaney and Lugosi given mute parts because of their health problems?

Lon's character wasn't mute, he was brain-damaged. And Lugosi's tongue was supposedly cut out so that he couldn't speak, either. The funny thing was that Lugosi came to me all the time asking, "Herr Director, give me more to do—I do not speak!" I laughed, "Well, your tongue is cut out, I *can't* give you more, you can't speak!" He said, "Give me more lines! I've got to do more!" I told him, "You *can't* do more—you're Basil Rathbone's valet, and all you can do is stand next to him and nod." Finally, I compromised: I told him I'd put him into some shots where Rathbone was speaking. So when Rathbone had a discussion with Akim Tamiroff, I put Lugosi in there with them. And he started to *grimace,* while Rathbone spoke—that spoiled the shot! But to placate Lugosi, I took a couple of close-ups of him, knowing they would end up on the cutting room floor. But that satisfied him, and he thanked me.

Lugosi was quoted on the set as saying, "There is Basil Rathbone playing my part. I used to be the big cheese. Now I'm playing just a dumb part."

That's possible. But even Basil Rathbone played better parts than *The Black Sleep*—he was a leading man. Even the greatest stars get old and play character parts when they had played lovers before. That was typical silliness for Lugosi, to be petulant like that.

There was no antagonism between the members of the cast, but each one wanted to steal the scene from the others. When they were together in a scene, each one tried to overact, and I had to hold them down because that would have spoiled the picture. At the end, when the monsters escape into the tower with Carradine shouting, "Kill! Kill! Kill!" they were all overacting in some way, but I let it go because it was an exciting scene and the end of the picture, and there had to be retribution against the mad doctor [Rathbone].

Is is true that, one day on the set, Chaney grabbed Lugosi and hoisted him up in the air over his head?

There was—I won't say *hate*—but a rivalry going on between Chaney and Lugosi from the Universal days when they both played Dracula. You see, Lugosi was the great Dracula, but then something happened at Universal and they gave the part to Chaney *[Son of Dracula]*. There was a terrible rivalry between them before I even arrived at Universal. It came out on *The Black Sleep*: Chaney was sore at something Lugosi brought up and it nearly came to a fight. Chaney picked him up a little bit, but put him down—we stopped him. We kept them apart quite a bit.

Chaney was physically effective as the afflicted Mongo, but his performance was awfully derivative.

Chaney used the walk he had developed on his own for the *Mummy* films, and his whining was from the one good part he had—Lennie in *Of Mice and*

Men [1939]. Lennie became part of him—he was Lennie in a lot of pictures where he shouldn't have been. Whenever there was a petulant scene, he became Lennie again.

Many horror fans are put off by the way The Black Sleep *tries to pass off Akim Tamiroff as a top horror star, even though this was his first genre credit.*

He played Odo, the gypsy, and was supposed to act as comic relief from the horror. He played it very well. We tried to get Peter Lorre for that part, but he wanted too much money. If Lorre had been in it, we would have built the part up.

Herbert Rudley played the part of the young doctor. After the shooting, he showed me one of his own stories, which was well written, and I showed him one of mine. I asked him if he would like to collaborate with me, he said he would love to, and together we wrote a script, as yet unfilmed. It's called *The Flesh and the Spirit,* and it's a new slant on the Mary Magdalene story. It tells how Mary of Magdala and Levi of Jerusalem met when they were teenagers and fell in love.

Where was The Black Sleep *shot?*

It was shot right in the Ziv Studio, the whole thing. The budget was around $200,000, give or take ten. I wanted to do that picture in color; in color it would have made five times as much money. I asked, but they couldn't afford it. It would have cost about 20 percent more.

Did you also have a hand in the Black Sleep *screenplay?*

I always try to bring out the motivation for someone who is "bad"—*why* does he do it? Rathbone played a doctor who mutilated people by experimenting with their brains. The average horror picture does the horror and doesn't explain why. So I wrote the scene where Rathbone vows to his comatose wife that he is going to do everything he can to bring her back to life, even if he has to kill people to do it. You *have* to get empathy for a person like that. I think the scene helped the picture because it gave him stature—he wasn't just a madman. Later on *[laughs],* Aubrey Schenck told me that the writer, John C. Higgins, was furious that I didn't call and consult with him. In fact, I did call him, but he wasn't available so I left a message. He never called back.

One of the best-remembered scenes in Black Sleep *has Rathbone and Herbert Rudley operating on the sailor, peeling back his scalp to expose the brain.*

I called a neurosurgeon and asked him to be technical advisor. He told me exactly how to do it and that, when the brain is exposed, it seeps fluid. So we had a special effects man put a sponge and a hose beneath the operating table and, on cue, he had to squeeze the fluid out of the sponge through the hose and out the brain. That was a different type of horror—it wasn't bloody, as they do it now.

Did anyone ever consider engaging Boris Karloff to play a role in The Black Sleep?

No, I don't think so. I think Karloff was out of the country at the time. I did enjoy working with him on *Voodoo Island* very much. He was not only a wonderful actor, but also a gentleman, very well educated.

Did working on an essentially all-outdoor film like Voodoo Island *present any problem for Karloff?*

No, because the weather was very nice in Hawaii — very mild. It was all shot on Kauai. There was a strip of land in a certain garden there where the flora in each direction was different. All we had to do was turn the camera, and there was a different location. So it was done very economically and efficiently. The budget was, I think, about $150,000.

What about the nude scene that you shot for the foreign version?

Jean Engstrom was playing a character who was supposedly a bit of a lesbian. In the dialogue it wasn't obvious, because we weren't allowed to do it at the time, but there *was* an intimation that she wanted to make it with Beverly Tyler, who played Karloff's secretary. So we had Engstrom swimming in the nude. At that time, we had censorship, but in Europe they allowed nudity.

How did the scene come out?

It didn't come out as well as we had wanted. She said she'd do it, but when the time came she was afraid she wasn't sufficiently well built. I guess we should have looked at her first *[laughs]*! She put on false bosoms and a type of bathing suit that, when it got wet, looked like skin. So it *looked* like she was nude, but she wasn't. Naturally it never looked as good as it could have.

The man-eating plants in Voodoo Island *were also unconvincing.*

The special effects man showed us in a pool in Hollywood how these plants could wind themselves around the feet and legs of swimmers. It wasn't too good an effect, and I told him it had to be better. He said he knew then how they worked and that when we got to Hawaii it would be all fixed. They *never* worked very well at all.

Your next fantasy film was The Flight That Disappeared, *a preachy science fiction meller.*

I'd agree with that. It was a good idea that could have been developed — it was a "message picture." It could have been much bigger, with more money, but it was done in eight days, on a budget that was nothing. It was just an idea that somebody brought in and said, "We can make a cheap picture that has something to say." I like to make pictures with something to say, so I accepted it.

A brutal and graphic knife attack was a high point of LeBorg's *Diary of a Madman* starring Vincent Price and Nancy Kovack.

How would you have improved it with extra money?

We built a set that was just a platform, with smoke and mist around it. With more money, I could have built a bigger set, had more characters in the plane, and had a real political debate. But they didn't want to go into that.

The Flight That Disappeared was an Eddie Small production. I did three pictures for him: *Flight That Disappeared*, *Deadly Duo* [1962] and the Vincent Price picture *Diary of a Madman*. First I did the two cheapies, *Flight* and *Deadly,* and Small liked them very much, so he gave me the Vincent Price assignment.

Diary of a Madman *seems to have been inspired by the success of the Roger Corman–Edgar Allan Poe films then popular for AIP.*

Possibly. The producer Robert Kent liked this story, *The Horla,* by Guy de Maupassant, and he sold Eddie Small on the idea of making the film. Kent wrote the script and I got the assignment. I felt that the story was a good one and it came out very well — except for the voice of the Horla, which I wanted to distort quite a bit. We made a test of the voice, the way I wanted it, and Eddie Small said, "I can't understand a word!" He wanted the Horla to speak normally, which was wrong.

Did Vincent Price have any enthusiasm about the film or his role, or did he treat it as just another job?

Top: LeBorg displays the poster from 1944's *Dead Man's Eyes* in the living room of his Hollywood home. *Bottom:* LeBorg and Acquanetta display the poster from *Jungle Woman* at a 1987 Universal Pictures reunion.

It was just another job for him. But he did become conscious that I was holding him down. I had looked at some of his other pictures, and I thought he overacted in some. On *Diary of a Madman* I held him down — he started to gesticulate and raise his voice in some scenes, and so I took him aside and whispered, "Tone it down, it'll be much more effective that way." He did, and he thanked me very much afterward. Even the producer, Eddie Small, said afterward that this was the best performance he'd seen Price give.

What kind of budget were you working with here?

Three hundred or three hundred fifty thousand, all shot at Goldwyn

Studios. *Diary of a Madman* was very well received, had good reviews, and did very well. I was very sorry when Eddie Small died right after *Diary,* because he promised me that he might want to use me on other things. You miss out a lot of the time, but that's life, I suppose.

In 1973 you made your last horror film to date, So Evil, My Sister *with Faith Domergue and Susan Strasberg.*

I thought that picture turned out well, but I got cheated on that. I was called in by the producers to direct; the money was not great, but they promised me a percentage. We shot everything out of the studio, on location — on the beach in Malibu, in actual offices and so on. It came out good and I was paid the minimum — the amount they *had* to pay — but I had high hopes for the percentage. Four weeks later one of the two producers died; the other one, who was just a money man, thought he knew everything, and he came in and started to recut, despite all my protests. Then, eight or ten weeks later, I talked to the cutter, Herbert Strock, and he told me that for the most part they had gone back to the old cutting, what *I* did. Then the producer took the negative and *left;* suddenly nobody knew where he was, nobody could find him. And I'm still today waiting for my percentage, which should have been a fair-sized amount of money — Strock told me that the producer went around with the film, distributing it himself, and then went to Europe, and made a lot of money with it.

You've known and worked with all the great horror stars. Who was your favorite?

Karloff. He was a gentleman; it was nice to talk with him and to work with him professionally.

Basil Rathbone was a friend of mine; I knew his wife, Ouida, and used to get invited to her parties. It was very nice to work with him, and he was very receptive to me. We got along very well. In fact, after *The Black Sleep,* he wrote me a long letter from New York. He was being considered for another horror picture by a New York company, and said he would do it only if I directed.

I liked Lon Chaney personally because he thought I had talent. After our first picture, he was very enthusiastic about my direction and my handling of him. He wanted to become *chummy* — he always called me "Pappy" or "Pops," although I was not much older than him. I didn't want to become too chummy, because I'm not a drinker — whenever he wanted to discuss things, it was, "Come on, have a drink." Well, I can have one beer and that's about all. I had to say no. He even invited me to his home, and I backed out. He thought I was arrogant or something, gradually his idea of the "great friendship" that he would get from me left him, and we drifted apart. Again, I liked him personally, but I couldn't help him emotionally; he wanted to be bigger than his father. Whether this was the only thing that drove him to drink or not, I couldn't find out — I wasn't a psychiatrist. But I wasn't about to baby him or sit down and drink with him.

Vincent Price I found to be entirely professional and very, very nice, and I enjoyed working with him very much. I was surprised how brave he was in the fire scene in *Diary of a Madman* — I was scared for him, because there was fire all around him in that scene. I had asked him if he wanted a double, and he said no. I said, "Well, it might get really hot, so be careful," and he said, "Don't worry, I've done things like this before." He was a brave guy.

John Carradine I enjoyed working with, because he'd also drink and then start spouting Shakespeare. When we finished shooting *The Black Sleep,* we had a party on the set and he imbibed quite a bit and started to do Shakespeare. I knew a little bit of *Hamlet* and joined in myself. He took me around and we spouted together. It was funny; he does become boisterous.

Bela Lugosi was a typical Hungarian. When he came to me and said, "Herr Director, give me something to do" — when he *begged* me — I placated him; that was all I could do. There are always things that are difficult to do, but you have to overcome them. That's part of the business.

*No, [Ed Wood] wasn't flaming around, like I've heard stories of,
wearing this and that and using a megaphone and
acting like an idiot.... He never pranced around
on the street in high heels and a wig, he
did it in his own home, and he
was never embarrassed about it.*

Paul Marco

CLOSE FRIEND and associate of the late Edward D. Wood, Jr., actor Paul Marco is content in his niche as monsterdom's favorite cop in Wood's low-budget '50s productions of *Bride of the Monster*, *Plan 9 from Outer Space* and *Night of the Ghouls*. Best known for his role as the clumsy, cringing Kelton in Wood's notorious horror trilogy, the veteran actor has fond memories of his experiences with Eddie D., Bela, Tor (and more!).

Born and raised in Los Angeles, Marco planned on being an actor all his life, taking dancing, singing and drama lessons in high school and later appearing in little theater productions. His work was brought to the attention of television prognosticator Criswell, who predicted on his TV show that Marco would go far in the picture business. A showbiz friend introduced Marco to Criswell and later to Ed Wood, who made Marco part of his entourage. Capitalizing on the resurgence of interest in Ed Wood and his films, Marco keeps busy today appearing at science fiction conventions, hawking Kelton the Cop merchandise and pitching himself and his Kelton character to movie and TV producers.

Were Ed Wood and Bela Lugosi friends, or was it just a professional relationship?

Ed was basically interested in old cowboy actors; he'd be up all night watching Tom Mix and Tex Ritter and all those old Westerns on TV. Ed met Bela, who was down on his luck, and he got the idea to help him — that's when they did *Glen or Glenda*. I didn't know either of them at that time, I came in right after that.

But they did get along well together?

Ed and Bela liked each other instantly — they were like brothers. Eddie was such a likable person, you couldn't say no to him if you wanted to! He was just a real wonderful promoter that would offer you everything — and although he wouldn't always live up to everything, he sure tried like hell.

Who came up with the idea for your recurring character, Patrolman Kelton?

Ed was about to do *Bride of the Monster* and he was wondering what kind of part was in it for me. Actually, there *was* no part that really fit me except for a desk sergeant called O'Reilly. Ed said, "Well, you're not Irish, and you're too young for a sergeant. Let's make you just an office boy, an assistant to the captain." All of us put our heads together to think up a name for this new character; my agent, Marge Usher, said, "How 'bout Kelton?" We all looked at each other — it sounded *so* right that we asked, "Gee, where'd you get that?" She said, "Well, I *live* on Kelton Avenue!" So I was christened Kelton the Cop right then and there. Ed rewrote the part for my personality, which was younger and, shall I say, a bit on the clumsy side — not knowing my work as a policeman. That's how Kelton was born.

Previous page, left to right: Ed Wood, Vampira, Paul Marco and actress Meg Randall attend a 1955 testimonial benefit for the ailing Bela Lugosi.

Left to right: Allan Nixon, Vampira, Tor Johnson, Stepin Fetchit, Bela Lugosi, Jr., Paul Marco and Dolores Fuller line up at Bela Lugosi's testimonial benefit.

Makeup man Harry Thomas told us that Lugosi seemed pretty lost on the sets of these films.

I never got that. Bela was always a real sweetheart. He wasn't what you'd call a *loner,* but after all he was quite old when he made *Bride of the Monster.* I remember that he had this tremendous speech to deliver to George Becwar — lots of dialogue. Ed didn't use too many closeups or different kinds of set-ups, and he was afraid that this was a bit too much dialogue for Lugosi. Bela was not sickly, but he *was* tired, and not 100 percent well. So we put all his dialogue on cue cards. Lugosi sat there, me sitting next to him, solemnly studying the lines while I held the cards.

Then came time to shoot. Eddie was very sweet — he treated Bela with all the respect that he deserved. Ed was escorting him to the sofa where he was going to play the scene when suddenly Bela came out with, "Oh, take those cards away. *I'm* going to *do* it!" By this time, the picture was running short on time and money, and allowing Bela to try it without benefit of cue cards seemed somewhat risky. Bela continued to insist that he could do it.

Well, he did it, without even looking at the cards, and the whole crew burst into applause and told him how great it was. Some critics have written that Bela was hammy in that scene, but he was really *feeling* it. This was the last big movie speech that Bela did before he died — his few remaining pictures saddled him with nonspeaking parts. I was there, and helped him. Sometimes when he was acting and doing a very dramatic scene, you could see the tears well up in his eyes. And when in his pictures he would say, "Come to me, I want to suck your blood!"—you'd just go *[laughs]!* Of all the stars that became my friends, he was one of the few that had that magnetism.

So you and Lugosi did become friends?

We became very close friends—I knew the man's warmth and his feelings, and he had so much heart. One night we were shooting in Griffith Park, and he really didn't feel well and he *needed* his shot [dope]. It was very damp and a real black night up there in the hills. Bela walked over to Ed and said, "Eddie, take me home. I've *got* to take my 'medicine.'" Bela didn't call it dope, he called it his medicine. Well, Eddie couldn't go. And Bela didn't trust drivers—you either had to be a perfect driver or a friend he *really* trusted before he'd get in a car with you. We did have a driver on hand, but Bela said, "No, I don't want that stranger! If you won't take me, you have to let me have Paul!" Eddie cried out, "No, he's in the next scene, I can't!" And Bela said, "Okay, then you don't have me either."

Eddie gave in and so I drove Bela home, which wasn't too far away—he lived in a small two-story apartment building somewhere in the vicinity of Griffith Park. It was dark and nobody was there. We entered his apartment and turned on the lights, which were very dim, and Bela said, "Paul, make yourself at home." He motioned for me to sit down in a very old-fashioned type of loveseat. Above it was a huge oil painting of him, from the sofa all the way up to the ceiling. "You're not going to like to see this, Paul," he said. "It's not very nice to watch, but I *have* to have my medicine." I told him, "Please, Bela—do what you have to do, nothing will upset me."

Directly in front of me there was a walk-in closet, and Bela pulled back the drapes and I saw that it was like a small room—I could see a little sink, a table and a hatrack. Off the hatrack Bela took an apron, and he wrapped it around himself very daintily and slowly tied a bow. And then he rolled his sleeves and washed his hands, took a clean towel from a drawer and wiped them dry. Then he opened the sterilizer and took out his hypodermic and his "medicine." This was all so dramatic, it was like I was in a daze, in a fog. This whole heartbreaking ceremony that I was witnessing was so beautifully done, I was spellbound. He put the needle in his arm and took it out—I sat motionless, I just couldn't move. When he was finished, he reversed the process—sterilizing the needle, taking off the apron and so on—just as cleanly and precisely as it was done to begin with. He turned off the light, drew the drapes closed, then turned and smiled at me like nobody but he could ever do. "Now," he said with a laugh, "I think we are ready to go!" And so we went back; it was a long, damp evening up there at the park, but Bela's medicine got him through the night. It was an experience I'll never forget.

Shortly after Bride of the Monster *wrapped up, Lugosi committed himself for treatment of his drug addiction.*

Eddie was very, very concerned about him, and so was Alex Gordon — we all were, because we'd all worked so hard on *Bride of the Monster*. When Lugosi did give himself up for dope addiction, I think it ran in the papers for about five days, and every day the headlines were bigger. Apparently there was *nothing* happening in the world at the time and they had nothing else to write about! It was while Bela was in the hospital that we approached him with the script for *The Ghoul Goes West*, a Western horror film that Eddie was planning. Then Ed changed his mind, and thought it would be better to do a picture called *The Vampire's Tomb*. It was for that picture that Ed shot all that miscellaneous footage of Bela [later used in *Plan 9 from Outer Space*], which had no purpose whatsoever outside of maybe *The Vampire's Tomb* would take advantage of *some* of this material.

What sort of budgets was Wood working with?

I don't think we ever *had* budgets, funny as that sounds. We made these movies for the money we could get or the money that we had. We raised the money as we went along. We'd shoot till we were broke, then Eddie would say, "Gee, I'm going to need $5,000 more" — or $2,000 or $1,000, or whatever — and then he'd go about the business of scrounging up that extra cash. He did everything on a very, very small budget, but it was in his blood — he had to go, go, go.

Bride of the Monster was not made as cheaply as people assume that it was; when [leading man] Tony McCoy's father took it over there was quite a bit of money owed. It isn't the $20,000 picture people think it is, I would say it was more in the $60,000–$70,000 range. Now, *Glen or Glenda* might have been $20,000, but I think *Bride* was considered Ed's first "biggie."

How would Wood go about raising the additional money?

Oh, sometimes Marge Usher would bring in another investor, or a couple of actors would come along who wanted some film on themselves, and so Eddie would write 'em a part. Eddie once told me that he made over a million dollars, and he had nothing to show for it.

What can you remember about the Bride of the Monster *premiere that was staged to raise money for Lugosi?*

Bela wasn't there, he was still in the hospital, but his son Bela, Jr., and Ed Wood were both there, and they each gave a little speech. I took Vampira to that premiere — I was dressed in a tuxedo and she was done up in her costume; Nicky Hilton, from the Hilton chain, drove us there in his Cadillac. When they opened the car door and we stepped out, we stopped the show.

How much money was raised for Lugosi?

Sales were very, very bad and we were all disappointed that more money wasn't raised, because Bela really did need it. Ed tried very hard selling blocks of seats, and Universal didn't even buy any. You'd think, after all the money Lugosi's pictures had made for them, they'd buy a block. We raised very little money, and that was very, very disheartening.

What can you tell us about Lugosi's marriage?

He married a very lovely lady; Hope and I became good friends, and remained so even after Bela died. She was a wonderful girl. When Bela got out of the hospital, they went around for a while and I think they got married within a week! It was done very hurriedly—so hurriedly, in fact, that one day Ed Wood just slapped me on the back and said, "We're gonna go to Bela's, he's getting married." Eddie was running around with a little singer named Jo at the time; the three of us piled into Eddie's beat-up convertible and we were rushing down Los Feliz Boulevard when Eddie suddenly said *[babbling]*, "We've gotta bring something, we've gotta take 'em something! Paul, have you got any money?" I had *some* money, and I said, "Let's take 'em some flowers!" We went into this big Japanese orchard and I gave the guy all the spare money that I had, and we ended up with this huge bunch of long-stemmed gladiolas. As it turned out, this wedding was arranged in such a rush that neither Hope nor her sister Pat had remembered to order flowers. I walked in with the gladiolas, took this big vase into the kitchen and arranged the flowers in it, and set it in front of the fireplace, which is where the ceremony took place.

There must have been at least fifty photographers there, all over the room. When you walked in, all you saw was cameras—*very* few guests. Later on I counted—there were 13 guests, appropriately enough, and *I* was the thirteenth person! Bela was late; he'd had a few drinks, I imagine, because he was—not *drunk,* but—*happy*. Eddie and I met him at the door and escorted him in while Hope put the finishing touches on her makeup and Pat, her sister, set the champagne out. Then we had the ceremony; the photographers were flashing pictures like crazy. It was really very, very touching, a beautiful ceremony. Bela acted wonderfully and Hope just looked so lovely—she was so blonde, and there was such love in her eyes it was just fantastic.

After it was over, all of the photographers left, and eventually the only ones there were Bela, Hope, Eddie, Jo and me. So here we were, driving Bela and Hope to their wedding apartment. We were coming down Western Avenue when Bela spotted this big Italian deli and cried out, "We *gotta* stop here!" Eddie stayed in the car with Jo and Hope while Bela and I went into the store. There were half a dozen people in there, everyone started congratulating Bela on his marriage and he was feeling *good*. We walked out carrying jugs of wine, long loaves of French bread, long salamis, jugs of olives, provolone cheese—my arms were full! They were giving us this, giving us that—I don't think we paid for much of anything, everybody was *giving* us things to congratulate Bela on his getting married.

We arrived at Bela's apartment and walked in—pitch black! Either they

Duke Moore, Mona McKinnon (hidden behind Moore), Gregory Walcott, Tom Keene and Paul Marco greet the Ghoul Man (Tom Mason) with a hail of bullets in Ed Wood's *Plan 9 from Outer Space*.

hadn't had the electricity turned on yet or they didn't have enough bulbs, but there was very little light in this huge, old-fashioned Spanish living room. There was practically nothing in the room except a huge trunk right in the middle of the floor — it looked like a coffin, it was that big! We moved some boxes and chairs around the trunk while Hope got some kind of a tablecloth to spread over the top. Then we brought out all the wine and bread and cold cuts, and we all sat around this trunk like picnickers, laughing and telling stories. That was Bela's wedding dinner.

After Lugosi died, whose idea was it to use this Vampire's Tomb *footage in* Grave Robbers from Outer Space *[shooting title for* Plan 9 from Outer Space*]?*

We were all sitting around, having a few drinks and talking about what to do with this Lugosi footage that Ed had shot. Ed said, "Let's make a monster picture!" We all laughed, "How much footage have we got? Not very much!" But Ed was very, very clever in his writing, and that's how *Plan 9* started.

Can you tell us a little about assembling the cast of Plan 9?

It was me who suggested Vampira for *Plan 9,* and Ed went along with that right away. He said he was only going to use her for a day, for about two hours, and I do think that's about all it was. She did it as a favor to me, because I was her friend, and because it was a Lugosi film—she was a great admirer of his. And now she's more known for *Plan 9* than for anything else she's ever done. I also suggested using Criswell; I had become his close friend and right-hand man, been on his television shows and done personal appearances with him. Criswell wrote his own narration for *Plan 9* and *Night of the Ghouls*—partly because he had a speech impediment, and there were so many words he couldn't quite get out. Ed would tell him basically what he wanted conveyed, and then Criswell would write it to fit his speech.

Now that I had lined up two stars for Ed, I told him, "Now there's something you can do for *me*—I've got two houseguests that are driving me crazy. You've got to do me a favor and write them each a part." It was John Breckinridge and his secretary, David De Mering. Breckinridge was a big socialite from San Francisco—his family owned the Palace Hotel and the Comstock Lode, and his great-great grandfather, John Cabell Breckinridge, was at one time [1857–1861] vice-president of the United States, under James Buchanan. "He's a very flamboyant, articulate and highly educated man," I told Ed. "Why don't we make him the man from space?" And that's how he played his part of the Ruler—he's actually like that in person. His secretary, David De Mering, played the co-pilot of Gregory Walcott's airplane. When Ed Wood died, in 1978, David, who was an ordained minister, presided over the services. And Ed's wife, Norma McCarty, played the stewardess in that same airplane scene.

And the rest of the players came from Wood?

Dudley Manlove, who was a radio man, was Ed's own "find"; "Duke" Moore was a drinking buddy of Ed's. And people like Tom Keene and Lyle Talbot were friends of Ed's, and their little "guest star" scenes were shot in a couple of hours. Tom Mason took over for Lugosi in *Plan 9;* he was also in *Night of the Ghouls.* If you want to see *that* particular "man behind the cape," he was the atrocious actor that shoots it out with the police in the drape room at the end of *Ghouls.*

I think Ed did a masterful job of putting all these little bits and pieces of film together and making a movie out of it. Although he preferred working on *Bride of the Monster* because that was more of a movie, he called *Plan 9* his "little gem."

How did it happen that Plan 9 *was taken over by the Baptists?*

Ed's neighbor J. Edward Reynolds happened to be with the Baptist Church, and in talking with him, Ed mentioned the picture and that he needed x amount of dollars to finish it. Reynolds got involved and brought in other Baptists, and eventually they took it over. Naturally some of them wanted to be actors—everybody does!—and so the two grave diggers in *Plan*

9 are Reynolds and Hugh Thomas, Jr., another fellow from the Baptist Church. Reynolds is the stout one.

One condition had to be met before the Baptists would become involved: Everyone had to be baptized. Eddie had to be baptized, and Tor Johnson, too. Tor was too big to be baptized in the tank, so they had to baptize him in a swimming pool! Then the Baptists took complete control; Ed was in hock up to his eyeballs, and they took over *everything*. Also, they didn't like the title under which we had made the film, *Grave Robbers from Outer Space,* so they changed it to *Plan 9* — which Eddie *hated*. No one really liked that title.

On Plan 9, *you were promised a producer's credit that never came about.*

I was promised the title of executive producer, which is a title usually left in reserve for whoever invests the most money; well, I lost that to Reynolds. And through an oversight my name did not appear in the credits as prominently as Ed had promised. That really teed me off, and I told Ed that *Plan 9* wouldn't have been done if it wasn't for me and that I felt very, very bad about how I had been treated. I was very hurt that he would do this to me, because I was really the closest friend he had. I was very perturbed and I just didn't see him for a while, but then I simmered down and realized, with Reynolds taking over and all, that Ed was caught in the middle. Once we'd patched things up, we stayed close friends until he died.

Your last Wood film, Night of the Ghouls, *teamed you for the third time with Tor Johnson. What do you remember about him?*

He was just a big teddy bear. He didn't speak too well, as you can see in *Plan 9,* but personally he was a pussycat — sweet, generous, charming and a lot of fun to be with. His son Carl, who was a police officer in the San Fernando Valley, was also very nice; he had a small part in *Plan 9,* and he was one of the dead men in *Night of the Ghouls.*

Did Wood ever appear in any of these films?

In *Night of the Ghouls,* Eddie dressed up as the Black Ghost in one sequence! When we couldn't get the girl who had played it in a couple of scenes, *he* put on the same outfit. In fact, he had even doubled for Mona McKinnon in *Plan 9* — he dressed up as her for the scene where she — *he* — is running and falling down, being chased by the Ghoul Man, just before the convertible comes along.

What about the stories that Wood directed in women's clothes?

[Emphatically.] No, he wasn't flaming around, like I've heard stories of, wearing this and that and using a megaphone and acting like an idiot. *I've* never seen that stuff. I'm not saying that I was on the set of every picture he ever made, all the time, but I *never* knew of him getting out of line. He always wore a shirt and tie, always was in a suit when he was directing, to my

Marco (seen here in a 1986 pose) hopes that the renewed interest in the films of Ed Wood will revitalize his own acting career.

knowledge. I never saw him in anything that made me ashamed. Certain people like to knock Ed down because these pictures have notorious reputations nowadays; nobody wants to hear all the good things, they only want to hear the bad. Now, some of the "bad" things you hear about *are* true, but there were also certain little aspects of these films where credit is due. I think Ed deserves a lot more credit than he's gotten from these people who've made a lot of money by deriding him.

Would Wood have been embarrassed to learn that his being a transvestite is now a well-known fact?

No, he was *never* embarrassed about that. If he was sitting at home with his negligee on, and a wig — *and* a mustache, smoking a cigar, with a bottle of vodka nearby, pounding on his typewriter in a most *un*ladylike fashion — and somebody walked in, he'd say, "Hi, sit down, I'll be right with you." But when he went out, he'd always be dressed in a shirt and tie; he never pranced around on the street in high heels and a wig, he did it in his own home, and he was never embarrassed about it.

Why was the release of Night of the Ghouls *held up for so many years?*

According to what Ed told me, the backers decided to use it as a tax write-off. Ed talked about *Night of the Ghouls* quite a bit and tried to get all the rights to it, hoping to get it out, but he never could. And then it began piling up an awful lot of storage fees.

For all its inadequacies, Bride of the Monster *was probably the best picture of the three.*

For Eddie, the favorite was *Plan 9;* as I mentioned before, he called it his "little gem," believe it or not.

Which was your favorite?

I enjoyed doing them all, but *Bride of the Monster* was perhaps my favorite experience. Naturally, since we were working with Bela there was a certain magic on the set, and production-wise and so on that was a bigger picture. And Eddie really *felt* like a director on that one: it wasn't a hodgepodge, he had a script, a *good* script — I think Alex Gordon did a fine job. We all worked hard, and it was more of a movie than, say, *Plan 9,* which was made up of pieces. And it really did get a lot of play — it showed in hundreds and hundreds of theaters and drive-ins, all over the world.

What are your feelings about the Worst Films *people who've taken their potshots at Ed Wood, Bela, Tor and all the rest?*

Well, naturally, it hurts me very much — in fact, it makes me sick to my stomach. Bela was such a fantastic person, yet people say such awful things about him. And the same for Ed — all these weird things you hear about him directing, they didn't ever happen on the movies I made with him. But through these *Worst Films* people, Ed has finally become a name; he'll live a long, long time in the books, and I hope there'll eventually be a lot of good things said about him, not just the bad.

*I think good science fiction is really one of the untapped frontiers.
Look how much sci-fi has later turned up as fact. One of the
very early science fiction things that I did was
an episode of* Men in Space, *and I designed a spacecraft
that was exactly like what turned out later on!
Science fiction is really looking into the future in a way,
and I have no quarrel whatsoever about being identified with that.*

Ib J. Melchior

THE SON of the late Wagnerian tenor and film star Lauritz Melchior, Ib Jørgen Melchior was born and educated in Denmark. After graduating from the University of Copenhagen he joined the English Players, a British theatrical company, and toured Europe with the troupe, first as an actor and later as stage manager and co-director. Just prior to the outbreak of World War II Melchior came to the United States with the troupe to do a Broadway show. After 1941's "Day of Infamy," he volunteered his services to the United States Armed Forces, operating with the "cloak-and-dagger" O.S.S. and the United States Military Intelligence Service. He also served in the European Theater of Operations as a military intelligence investigator attached to the Counter Intelligence Corps. For his work in the E.T.O., Melchior was decorated by the United States Army as well as by the King of Denmark.

After the war Melchior became active in television, directing some five hundred New York–based TV shows ranging from the musical *Perry Como Show* to the dramatic documentary series *The March of Medicine*. In 1959 he collaborated with producer Sidney Pink on the independent sci-fi adventure *The Angry Red Planet*, and he followed up on this early genre credit with screenplays for Pink's *Reptilicus* and *Journey to the Seventh Planet*, Byron Haskin's *Robinson Crusoe on Mars*, Mario Bava's *Planet of the Vampires* and his own *The Time Travelers*. In 1975 his short story *The Racer* furnished the basis for director Paul Bartel's cult favorite *Death Race 2000*, and the following year he was awarded a Golden Scroll for Best Writing by the Academy of Science-Fiction (for body of work). Taking time out from his new career as a novelist, Melchior reminisces about the days when he helped to usher in a whole new Eastern-colored era of AIP terror.

How did you first become associated with Sidney Pink, producer of The Angry Red Planet?

I met Mr. Pink at a party, and he was telling me that he had a story called *Invasion from Mars*. He had had several screenwriters try to write a script on it, and he hadn't liked any of them. I was interested in science fiction at that time, and I'd had a lot of trouble getting directorial assignments because I came from New York and they wouldn't let me work in the Guild out here. The only way you can get in is if a producer says, "This man *must* do my film." So I made a deal with Pink: I said, "I will write a screenplay for you, at scale, provided that if you like it, you also have me direct it, also at scale." So I wrote the screenplay, he liked it and I directed the film, which was released as *The Angry Red Planet*. That's how I started.

Tell us a little about Cinemagic, and what Pink's hopes were for that process.

He really hoped to kind of *invent* a process which would, as he said at that time, revolutionize animation—a process where you just simply photograph people, and they come out as animated figures. Norman Maurer, who later married the daughter of Moe from the Three Stooges, was the inventor of it.

Previous page: Ib J. Melchior earns a living today as the writer of novels with foreign intrigue backgrounds.

The story that I heard is that they were working out of Maurer's garage, and they couldn't get it to work. It did work when they did it slowly, frame by frame, but it never worked the way they really wanted it to. At one point, according to the story that Sid told me, Maurer got so disgusted that he took the lens and threw it against the wall, and it cracked. So they tried it with the crack and it worked *[laughs]!* And *that's* Cinemagic!

What was the advantage of Cinemagic, though?

The advantage, I really don't know. Frankly *[laughs]*, I never knew exactly *what* they had intended! In my opinion, what finally came out as Cinemagic wasn't at all what they had in mind when they started. It *was* an interesting effect, but I don't think it was something that could be used other than for very limited things, like *The Angry Red Planet*. The proof's in the pudding—Cinemagic never caught on or amounted to anything.

What were your budget and shooting schedule on Red Planet?

The budget I'm not really sure of; in those days it would have been very small, probably around $250,000. The shooting schedule was very short, only seventeen days. We shot it out at the Hal Roach Studios in Culver City.

Since your list of film credits leans heavily toward science-fiction subjects, can we assume that you're a fan of sci-fi?

Well, I never read science-fiction, outside of Jules Verne and H.G. Wells, until I came to this country. Then I started reading it, and I got fascinated by it. I was really more of a reader than a writer of it; *The Angry Red Planet* was simply the key to becoming a director. But then, once you have done a science-fiction film, that is what you are—you are now a science-fiction filmmaker and that's *it*. Other films that I wrote were more along the lines that I am working in now; they were adventure stories like *When Hell Broke Loose* [1958] and *Ambush Bay* [1966].

There were several interesting special effects in Red Planet.

Like people on short budgets usually do, we ran out of money before the special effects were done. We were planning to shoot the scene where the giant monster's claw crushes the rocks with [actor] Les Tremayne between them; that claw was supposed to have been on a big rig with motors and everything else. The special effects technicians said, "That's going to cost $13,000, we can't do it," and *I* said, "The hell with that, we're going to do it anyway!" So I took two two-by-fours and put them into those claws that we had made—like a scissors. Then we put them on a little cart and just wheeled the cart in! The shot is tight and it looks terrific, but instead of $13,000 it cost $13!

In another scene, we wanted to achieve the effect of the giant amoeba enveloping the spaceship; we wanted a sort of mass to slowly crawl up the sides of the ship and engulf it. What we did was, we took a lot of multicolored Jell-O

Melchior's first science fiction film, *The Angry Red Planet,* featured high-concept advertising and low-budget special effects.

and poster colors and mixed them together. Then we stuck a small model spaceship into that Jell-O and melted it on a hotplate. That, shown in reverse, gave us our effect.

Norman Maurer used to describe you as "a highly excitable young man." Is that a fair assessment?

Excitable? I don't know about that—maybe so. That's hard for me to judge. Of course, *The Angry Red Planet* was a transition, from having done musicals into something which at that time interested me enormously. I *was* enthusiastic—perhaps more so than normally *[laughs]!* I tried to do the best I could with what I had at the moment, which was limited, as you know.

Did you go along to Denmark when Sid Pink shot your scripts for Reptilicus *and* Journey to the Seventh Planet?

No, I just wrote the scripts, which were rewritten to some extent—quite a bit, in fact, in some areas. I have always felt that I would just as soon *not* be that closely associated with those two films. Few people knew that my only connection with them was writing scripts which were considerably altered. I had absolutely nothing to do with the directing of them, or anything else.

Of the two, Reptilicus *seemed to have the greater potential.*

Sid had a lot of good production values in *Reptilicus* because he got everybody to cooperate. Do you remember the scene where Reptilicus chases the people off the bridge? Sid rounded up about twelve hundred people that belonged to an athletic club—those are all the people that ran and fell down into the water. He got them by simply promising some equipment for their club *[laughs]*—he was a *tremendous* promoter. He had five or six cameras set up to cover this whole thing—and he forgot to run them! "Action" was called and the people began running; somebody was supposed to tell all the cameras to start rolling, but nobody did! Luckily, one of the cameramen said, "Hey, I'm going to shoot anyway," and that's what they got.

I have now been to Denmark several times; *Reptilicus* is a cult film there, and the audience has actually memorized the lines! When Sid shot the film, he had Danish actors and he had German actors, and everybody spoke English with a different kind of an accent—some of them very, very badly. Sid knew it was going to be dubbed when it came over here, so he told his actors, "When you speak, be sure to speak distinctly and move your mouths distinctly so that we can dub this." This, of course, is not necessary at all, but that's what he told them. As a result, you have people like Carl Ottosen, the general, saying, "Come . . . on . . . let . . . us . . . hur-ry"—it became ridiculous! So now in Denmark they screen it and the entire audience says, "Come . . . on . . . let . . . us . . . hur-ry." It's hilarious!

Is is true that AIP initially felt that Reptilicus *failed to meet their standards?*

The Melchior-scripted *Robinson Crusoe on Mars* pitted a human and an alien (Paul Mantee and the kneeling Vic Lundin) against the perils of the Red Planet.

That's right; they weren't happy with it and we had to do some doctoring here. I dubbed it; in fact, six of the voices in *Reptilicus* are mine. I'm a reporter, a police officer, a mayor ... six small parts. And we did shoot some additional scenes here—some of the early stuff, some of the close-up stuff, close shots of the monster's tail and so on. One scene in there, where Reptilicus destroys a farmhouse, didn't come off at all, so *we* shot the scene of the farmer being eaten by Reptilicus—in fact, the farmer was played by my own son Dirk *[laughs]*! He was about twelve years old at the time, we needed a small person, so we used him. He's always been very happy about having been swallowed by Reptilicus.

Were any of the original Reptilicus *cast brought over for these extra scenes?*
　No, none at all—it was all close shots and things that could be done without bringing anybody over. We had next to no money to do it with; Sam Arkoff asked me to try and fix it up, and that's what I did.

And then the same thing happened with the monster scenes in Journey to the Seventh Planet.
　That's correct. I saw the original 35mm print that came over here—in fact, I still have it out in my garage!—and *[laughs]* believe it or not, you see the chicken wire on the monsters! Those scenes were all redone; in fact, they even replaced one monster with stock footage of a giant spider from an earlier, black-and-white film *[Earth vs. the Spider].*

The most ambitious and well known of your early films is Robinson Crusoe on Mars.
　Robinson Crusoe on Mars was a big project of mine. I submitted it to [producer] Howard W. Koch and he said, "I am busy at the moment, but I know this is something that Aubrey Schenck would like." Aubrey Schenck and Edwin Zabel were longtime associates of Koch's; they got excited about it and they wanted, believe it or not, a three-and-a-half-hour movie out of it. And I *wrote* a three-and-a-half-hour script! At the same time, I was brought this other property, *The Time Travelers;* I developed that into a script, and started directing it just as *Robinson Crusoe on Mars* was ready to go into production. So I had nothing whatsoever to do with the production of *Robinson Crusoe on Mars.*

Was it Schenck and Zabel who changed their minds about the length?
　Right. They got a writer named John Higgins—whom I've never met—to cut it down. He changed a couple of things that I was very unhappy about; for instance, I wanted to show the meeting of two totally alien people that could *respect* each other—*not,* "Me master, you slave." Unfortunately, a line was put in that said precisely that—*exactly* the thing I wanted to get away from! I was very unhappy when I discovered that, but there was nothing I could do about it.

Do you feel that Robinson Crusoe *could have used a better grade of star?*
　No, I had nothing against using unknowns; I thought they did a good job. There is some advantage, when watching a film of this sort, in *not* seeing a major star in it. For example, I remember about three or four pictures that were made at the time of the Entebbe incident, and the one that was *real* to me was the one made with Israeli actors—because I didn't know any of 'em! When I see Kirk Douglas or Elizabeth Taylor, it is a *film;* the other way seems so real. I think this is what they tried to do in *Robinson Crusoe on Mars;* they were actors you were not familiar with, and the film was more believable that way. I liked that.

In a book-length interview, Byron Haskin had some very disparaging things to say about your contribution to Robinson Crusoe on Mars. *What might have prompted him to do this?*

I don't know. I knew Byron very, very slightly; before the picture was begun he came to my home a couple of times and I gave him all my ideas on what I had meant to convey in my screenplay and how I saw the whole picture. We got along just fine. What made him say those things later on, I do not know.

Haskin claimed that he picked out all the Death Valley shooting locations.

Every location was picked by me—I went there, and I gave Byron a map with every location, and told him which scenes should be shot where. For him later on to say that he did all that is kind of sad, but it happens—there are people who do that.

According to Haskin, your original script was crammed with Martian monsters.

Absolute nonsense! Total, complete and utter nonsense! If he said that, it is an obvious lie. This is no longer something I can accept as having been a mistake. This is a deliberate belittlement. Obviously, in his later years he became terribly insecure. Insecure people have to do that sort of thing. I feel very sorry for him.

He also said the title Robinson Crusoe on Mars *was the only single thing of yours that remained in the picture.*

That is totally and completely and ridiculously wrong. I can only say that I am shocked, that a man with that kind of reputation would belittle himself by saying something like that. Every single solitary person who was involved with *Robinson Crusoe on Mars* will know how wrong that is.

Your Robinson Crusoe *premise seems to have been pirated for a recent film called* Enemy Mine.

And the interesting thing to me is that some of the things in *Robinson Crusoe on Mars* that were not shot, but were only in my original script, turned up in *Enemy Mine*. Almost word for word! It was incredible!

Getting back to The Time Travelers, *how exactly did that come about?*

A young man named David Hewitt had the idea for that film; he and [producer] Bill Redlin came to me and asked me to write it, which I did. Then I became very involved in the project, and David and I evolved the special effects for the film. We used actual magician's illusions—David had been involved in that sort of thing—and we were able to do some absolutely marvelous things, right on the stage, without any optical work. If you had stood where the camera stood on our stage, you'd have seen the same effect that you saw

Melchior and special effects man David L. Hewitt used an actual magician's illusions in lieu of conventional effects on *The Time Travelers*.

on film. They were just simply an illusionist's tricks that we modified for our purposes.

We had some fun moments on *The Time Travelers*. Our mutant-actors were actually a basketball team — some of them were Lakers — and I think the biggest guy was about 7'2". These were *huge* guys! We had them running across this field of dead trees, right next to a road that ran through the desert; we were set up in some bushes on the opposite side of the road, shooting these guys running toward us. As we were doing this, a car came along — just as our mutants started running across the road! It came to a *screeching* halt, and there was this little lady inside. And this 7'2" guy went over to her and said, "Lady,

Melchior (left) coaches actor Steve Franken (center) and an unidentified "mutant" on the set of *The Time Travelers*. (Photo courtesy Robert Skotak.)

take me to your leader!" She took off like a shot! And I've always wondered, *what* stories did she tell, and *what* psychiatrist is still saying, "Lady, you are crazy!"

The battle between the androids and the mutants was one of the highpoints of that picture.

We had one guy whose hand was missing in real life; we put a false hand on him, he grabbed somebody's throat and then, *whap!*, someone else hacked at his arm so that his hand stayed around the throat while he pulled his stump away.

Any other memories of the battle scenes?

Well, we had a troublemaker amongst the extras. Remember the scene where the workmen are carrying big boxes to load the spaceship? Those were empty cardboard boxes, you could lift them with one little finger. Just as we were about to shoot, this extra came to me and said, "Mr. Melchior, we have to carry these heavy boxes, and that is time-and-a-half." I didn't have the money for that! And I visualized the battle scenes that were coming up later — were they going to want *triple* time for those? I said, "We've changed our schedule, and we don't need any more extras today. Good-*bye!*" And they left. So then *we* went out and rounded up all the relatives and friends that we could find — we literally got people off the street! We put them in the costumes and shot the whole damn thing. These were the people who did most of the fighting in the battle scenes! By the time the union found out about it the picture was already done; the producer settled with them and that was that. But we would not have been able to finish the picture if it hadn't been for that.

What can you tell us about the actor who played The Deviant?
That's a fascinating story. That man, Pete Strudwick, is a brilliant fellow, a Mensa, in fact. He was born without feet; one hand is like a knob, and the other hand looks like a lobster pincer. I got a telephone call from him one day; he said, "I understand you're doing a science fiction picture and you need, maybe, a monster?" I told him, "Possibly," and he said, "Well, I happen to *be* a monster. Could I come and see you, and possibly get a part?" He showed up at my house, took his shoes off and all, and so we wrote in a part for him—and he did a very, very good job in it. I think he is an inspiration—he has run the marathon several times without feet, he has run up and down Pike's Peak, and he even competed in a marathon against the Marines where half of the Marines did not finish but he did!

How did you get involved on Planet of the Vampires?
That was a story idea that someone, or several people, had worked on in Italy. AIP brought it to me and said, "Do something with this property—it's unusable." I wrote the screenplay, and it was directed by Mario Bava—Mario was very complimentary about that script, by the way. I went to Italy and spent a few days on the set with Mario and Fulvio Lucisano, who was the producer, and ironed out a few problems and what-have-you. I think Mario made a good, moody piece out of *Planet of the Vampires,* and I rather liked it.

Was AIP an agreeable outfit to work for?
I have had excellent relationships with Jim Nicholson, before he died, and with Sam Arkoff, who is still around. They treated me about as good as anybody. The same thing, as a matter of fact, went for Roger Corman, who also had a reputation for sometimes not being the easiest person to work with. He, too, treated me very, very fairly on *Death Race 2000.*

That was based on your short story The Racer?
That's right. I wrote that around 1958, and it's been in at least six anthologies and reprinted in all kinds of magazines both here and in Europe. I had been to the Indianapolis 500 somewhere around 1939, and I sat in the box with the wives of the drivers. There was an accident, and one of the drivers was killed. And the juxtaposition of watching the horror on his wife's face and the excitement of the fans—this, after all, was what they really came to see—struck me enormously. That became *The Racer*—I wrote it as a short story, a serious kind of piece.

Did you approve of New World's black comedy approach?

At first I was *appalled* — after the first ten minutes, I said, "My God, what have they done to my story?" Then I started laughing, and by the time the film was over I thought it was one of the funniest things I had ever seen.

So when you talk about being well treated by Corman, you mean financially.

Right. But also we had some kind of a sequel contract, and although he did not make a sequel, he did do another film which was called *Deathsport* [1978]. It had nothing to do with *Death Race 2000,* but he said, "Look, if it hadn't been for *Death Race,* we would never have done this other one, so I think you're entitled to some money," which he paid me. I thought that was very good of him.

Robinson Crusoe on Mars *is probably your best-known film. Is it one of your favorites, or did the tampering you spoke of spoil it for you?*

Robinson Crusoe, and *The Time Travelers,* are my two favorites among the science fiction things. I would have liked very much to have been more involved with *Robinson Crusoe,* although I do think that Byron Haskin did a good job in directing it and taking advantage of the Death Valley locations that I had picked out. There were a few things that I would have done differently — *differently,* not necessarily better — but I was pleased with what they did with it. *Robinson Crusoe* had a fairly small budget, I think it was about a million and a half, and the same was certainly true of *The Time Travelers* — that was done for under $200,000!

What keeps you busy these days?

In 1973 my wife nagged me to write a novel that was based on one of my own experiences as a counter intelligence agent in World War II. I wrote it, it came out and became a best-seller! Since then I have been writing novels with a foreign intrigue background. They have been very well received; they are published, incidentally, in twenty-five countries, which is rather interesting.

Do you mind remaining best known for what you've done in science-fiction?

I don't mind. I think *good* science fiction is really one of the untapped frontiers. Look how much sci-fi has later turned up as fact. One of the very early science fiction things that I did was an episode of *Men in Space,* and I designed a spacecraft that was *exactly* like what turned out later on! Science fiction is really looking into the future in a way, and I have no quarrel whatsoever about being identified with that.

*If [Edgar] Ulmer had a little more
money in his budgets, more time in his schedules,
he would use it. When he had to turn out
the best possible film he could with his back to the wall,
he was marvelous. Turn Ulmer loose,
and God only knows what would have happened!*

Jack Pollexfen

JACK POLLEXFEN may not be a household word, even amongst horror fans, but as producer and writer he was responsible for a number of sci-fi and monster movies from the '50s that are remembered well even if the creator's name doesn't spring immediately to mind. At the beginning of the horror/sci-fi cycle of the '50s, Pollexfen produced the moody cult favorite *The Man from Planet X*, directed by B-movie master Edgar G. Ulmer. Other Pollexfen films include *Captive Women*, a postholocaust adventure; *The Neanderthal Man*, a variation on the Jekyll-and-Hyde theme; and *Indestructible Man*, starring Lon Chaney.

Pollexfen began his professional life in the newspaper business, working his way up from copyboy at the *Los Angeles Express* to reporter on several other dailies. During this period, he also found time to write and produce three plays that he says could be classified today as "off-Broadway—a *long* way off!" He found himself in the movie business when MGM offered him a contract to turn one of his magazine articles into a screenplay. Four years in the Air Force writing training films and manuals during World War II interrupted his movie career, which then got back on track with a series of screenplays for such adventure pictures as *Treasure of Monte Cristo* (1948), *The Desert Hawk* (1950) and other B movies— "sheer assembly-line junk," Pollexfen recalls. Around this time, Pollexfen's producing career got started, in cooperation with his co-writer Aubrey Wisberg.

Our favorite of your science fiction/horror films has always been your first, The Man from Planet X.

The Man from Planet X was always a favorite of mine. One reason, possibly it was the only space film then where Earth people are more or less the heavies. My partner Aubrey Wisberg and I wrote the script with the idea of selling it, but realized it could be made on a very low budget, so we decided to take the production plunge.

A recent book on sci-fi films insists that the most intriguing part of the story— depicting X as a harmless visitor and certain Earthmen as heavies—was not written into the screenplay and therefore must have been introduced into the story by director Edgar Ulmer.

Wrong. Making the Earthlings—or some of them—the heavies was a key part of the script from the first. Oddly enough, the idea has been seldom copied. Edgar Ulmer had begun as an art director, working with such personages as Max Reinhardt. His flair was mood. I think if silent films had lasted, he would have become one of the greats.

What was Ulmer like to work with?

No problems for me with Edgar. I thought that, considering the handicap of a six-day shooting schedule and a budget of $38,000, he did a remarkable job. But Edgar and Aubrey developed a feud. Both had that habit.

Previous page, left to right: Jack Pollexfen, Edgar G. Ulmer and Aubrey Wisberg relax during a break in the shooting of *The Man from Planet X*. (Photo courtesy Robert Skotak.)

I think Edgar could get more on the screen, with less time and money, than any director I worked with. He had a reputation in Hollywood, not wholly unjustified, of being difficult. Incidentally, so did E.A. Dupont [director of *The Neanderthal Man*], who had shot *Variety* [1925], one of the silent screen's all-time classics. Both Ulmer and Dupont, under pressure of time and budget, could get more values than any of the B-budget specialists. But when studios had any say, they generally wanted to settle for the handy hack.

Did Ulmer bring it in for $38,000?
It actually came in at $41,000.

How much creative leeway did you allow the directors who made your films?
On our schedules there was no story leeway on the set. In preproduction I always worked with the director on any problems he thought might arise.

Were you a frequent visitor to the sets of your own films?
As I was generally the production manager as well as co-producer, I was on the set from well before the day's shooting started, to sometime that night when we looked at the previous day's rushes.

Can you tell us about your Planet X *stars, Robert Clarke, Margaret Field and William Schallert?*
We probably looked at a hundred players before selecting Bob and Maggie. Both did excellent jobs. To be truthful, sci-fi does not give the male player too many opportunities, and less to the girl—unless each is lucky enough to have two heads! Bob and Maggie came along at the wrong time in Hollywood's history. Studios were no longer building up contract players, and independents were confined to low budgets for the bottom half of the bill. Incidentally, it was Margaret Field's daughter Sally who won Academy Awards for *Norma Rae* [1979] and *Places in the Heart* [1984].

Both Bob Clarke and Bill Schallert were first-rate, both on and off the set. I suppose you know that some years later Schallert became president of the Screen Actors Guild.

Can you recall anything at all about the actor who played the alien?
He was out of vaudeville, where he did a slow-motion act that combined dance and acrobatics. And he was quite small, about five feet tall. I *don't* remember his name.

The conception of the diving bell–shaped spaceship was quite original and effective.
Ulmer did both the spaceship and the model of the moors. The actual moors we shot were in southwest Los Angeles, and are long covered by tract

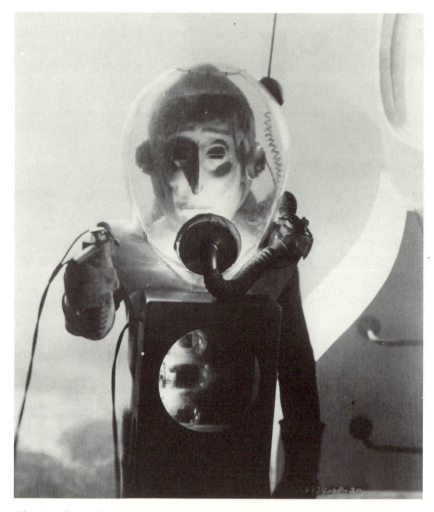

The Man from Planet X. Pollexfen does not remember the name of the actor who played this part—only that he was a vaudeville performer and that his height was "about five feet."

housing. The L.A. Griffith Park Observatory was the telescope location. We also used, somewhat redressed, some of the standing sets at Hal Roach Studios from *Joan of Arc* [1948].

Did you encounter any problems or delays during production?
  The most particular problem we had was that we shot nine-tenths of the picture on the studio stage, and we were using tetrachloride for our fog. Tetrachloride sticks fairly low, which is quite an advantage when you're shooting, because other fogs will circulate around and get up to the tops of the

sets and things like that. But its disadvantage is that, after you've been shooting in it for a few days, you are coughing for the next couple of *weeks!*

Who was Sherrill Corwin, and how was he instrumental in getting The Man from Planet X *released?*

Sherrill Corwin owned a chain of California theaters and drive-ins, and was also one-time president of the Motion Picture Theater Exhibitors. He saw the picture after it was finished and paid us $100,000 for 75 percent. We retained 25 percent. He arranged for the United Artists release. The picture went on to gross well over a million in rentals. Corwin, a most ethical man in the jungles of Hollywood, is now dead. He was not involved in any of our later projects.

Were you completely pleased with the results on Planet X?

If we had had more money to spend on it, there would have been a lot of things that we would have liked to have done. But we were making it on a very, very low budget and had some of our own money in it. So we shot in six days, and I think it was a pretty good picture for six days. Ulmer was an extremely good director for a *fast* picture. He did *not* work out too well if he had any time. His English was pretty shaky, and if he had time enough he'd sit down and try to direct the cast in their dialogue. And his English was, as I say, quite shaky. Ulmer was a difficult person, but a very talented person.

In what way was he difficult?

If Ulmer had a little more money in his budgets, more time in his schedules, he would use it. When he had to turn out the best possible film he could with his back to the wall, he was marvelous. Turn Ulmer loose, and God only knows what would have happened!

What sparked the Ulmer–Aubrey Wisberg feud you mentioned earlier?

I don't remember. Wisberg got into feuds with an awful lot of people — that was probably the main reason I finally broke up with him. He would be irritated if, say, a cameraman who'd worked for us once was not available on the next picture, and things of that nature. Very touchy.

What can you tell us about The Son of Dr. Jekyll, *which was based on an original story co-authored by Mortimer Braus and yourself?*

Not much. Mort Braus and I were kidding one day about outlandish film titles, and we came up with *The Son of Dr. Jekyll*. We thought about it for a moment, thought it might sell, and knocked out a quick story. Columbia bought it at once. We had nothing to do with the production.

Did you or Braus contribute to the screenplay of She-Wolf of London, *which has a plot similar to* Son — *and* Daughter — *of Dr. Jekyll?*

No—neither Mort nor I passed by the *She-Wolf of London*. I never saw it and I doubt if Mort had.

Tell us how you became involved with Albert Zugsmith's American Pictures Corporation, and how the films Captive Women *and* Port Sinister *came about.*

Aubrey and I had a deal to make three pictures at RKO *[Captive Women, Port Sinister* and a Robert Clarke swashbuckler, *Sword of Venus]* when Al, who had been a newspaper and radio station broker, came on the scene. Howard Hughes had been muttering about selling RKO, and Zugsmith conned a couple of RKO executives into thinking he could put together a syndicate to buy the studio. Al didn't have the syndicate, *or* the money, and Hughes at that time had no real intention of selling. However, we found ourselves with a new partner—Al convinced the executives that he should take 25 percent of our deal, leaving Aubrey and myself the other 75 percent, and in return he guaranteed RKO against any losses. We had no losses, which was fortunate, as Al had no money, according to one RKO attorney. Al tried to talk us into an American Pictures partnership, but fortunately we wanted no part of it.

Captive Women *is slow-paced and overly talky, but we've always been fans of this film, with its odd conception of a postatomic world where man has been reduced to near-savagery.*

Our main problem in *Captive Women* was that we were battling Zugsmith too much to pay attention to the production. More serious, Howard Hughes, who normally left us to ourselves, insisted we take Stuart Gilmore as director. Stuart was one of Hollywood's top film editors—had done some of Hughes' most important films—and Hughes had promised him a chance at directing. While there have been exceptions, film editors generally don't work out well as directors. It's one thing to sit before a Moviola and see all the director's mistakes and consider them at your leisure. It is quite different to knock out a low-budget picture where you don't have time to go to the bathroom, let alone do any thoughtful pondering.

Did Captive Women *really have the $100,000 budget—two and a half times that of* Man from Planet X—*announced by Wisberg at the time of the film's inception?*

Never believe *anything* published about budgets. From *The Birth of a Nation* to the latest George Lucas epic, the practice has always been to add a zero or two so the exhibitor won't feel so cheated—as *he* cheats the producer. If I remember, *Captive Women* came in at about $85,000, including a $15,000 writer-producer fee to myself and Wisberg. Zugsmith got $2,500 as associate producer.

The other pictures—*The Neanderthal Man, Indestructible Man, Daughter of Dr. Jekyll* and *Monstrosity*—were independently produced and usually sold outright to a studio.

Why was the release of Captive Women *delayed for almost fifteen months after the film was completed?*

I think some of the delays were hopeless attempts to patch its flaws in the cutting room. It seldom works. However, I was gone from RKO, making some swashbucklers for United Artists.

Captive Women *is really a meaningless title. The picture might have done better if released under its shooting title,* 3000 A.D.

Captive Women was a *god-awful* title. It killed any chance the picture might have had.

Was Port Sinister *initially conceived as a straight adventure film, with the sci-fi angle of the giant crab added as an afterthought?*

The main trouble with *that* epic was that we never licked the story. Actually, it had been initially conceived as sci-fi, with the giant crab in from the start.

What can you tell us about those giant crab scenes?

The crab was a spider crab—tiny body, but legs and claws about three feet long. Not much meat on them, so they are not fished commercially, but they are fairly plentiful on the Southern California coast. In some special effects shots we blew it up to the gigantic monster. It worked fairly well, provided we did not hold on the shot for too many frames. The crab's legs were operated by nylon thread against a dark background. And how it began to *stink!*

In what fashion was Marineland of Florida used during the production?

The pressbook item reporting the participation of Marineland of Florida was strictly a press agent's daydream. The picture was shot at RKO-Pathe Studios in Culver City. The location shots were in Palos Verdes, near Long Beach, California, at a cove called Portuguese Bend.

In a 1973 interview, Albert Zugsmith complained that the casts of these films were forced on him, and that the pictures suffered as a result.

Zugsmith actually had no part in any of our RKO films. The first picture I know of his making was *Invasion, U.S.A.*, released through Columbia. RKO had to approve the two leads and the director. I wasn't enchanted with their choice of players, but the real problem was the directors they dug up.

E.A. Dupont seems a rather offbeat choice for director of The Neanderthal Man.

Ulmer would have been the better director for *The Neanderthal Man*, but he was in Europe at the time. Dupont, considering budget and time, did a decent job. A horror picture is really more of a suspense film than a science film. What you suggest is more than what you show.

I got along very well with Dupont. I much preferred working with directors who had a lot of talent, and also could be rather difficult. I either had to use someone like that, someone the major studios wouldn't touch because they *were* difficult, or I had to use a hack.

Can you comment on the effective man-into-monster sequences in Neanderthal Man?

The transformation scenes were shot in a small special effects room, using a cameraman and a makeup man. It took about half a day. We used red and blue filters, cutting from face to hands, adding a bit more hair, fangs, etc., as we cut back and forth. When the transformation was complete, we switched to a stuntman wearing matching makeup.

Why doesn't that film's saber-tooth tiger have saber teeth?

We were dealing with an amiable but rather large Siberian tiger, and our makeup man became somewhat bashful about adding fangs—especially after the tiger shook them out the third or fourth time! If I remember correctly, we then got a tiger skin rug, added saber teeth to the jaws and put a few quick—*very* quick!—shots into the fight scenes. In shooting monster films, one must be flexible—very flexible.

What hurts many of your early films is the overwritten and unnatural dialogue.

Normally I would write the first draft of the script; Aubrey would *enhance* the dialogue. Another of the reasons we split!

Actually, both horror and science fiction generally need a minimum of dialogue. It is rare that the stories are not, fundamentally, ridiculous. The visual is all-important—which is one reason for the quality of the best of Ulmer's direction. Music, sound effects and so on, all combine.

Indestructible Man *bears a certain resemblance to an earlier Lon Chaney movie,* Man Made Monster. *Were your writers inspired by that older film?*

Man Made Monster played no part in this picture. I wrote the first draft. Sue Bradford and Vy Russell, who get the screenplay credit, were wives of Bill Bradford and Jack Russell, cameramen on many of my pictures. They helped on the second draft.

What prompted you to take on the responsibilities of directing on Indestructible Man?

No director I wanted was available. I had been doing some directing and had my Directors Guild card, so I made the picture. However, I did not want credits as producer, director *and* writer—I thought I would leave such credits to Chaplin and Welles.

John Agar (left) and Arthur Shields comfort a blood-spattered Gloria Talbott in Pollexfen's *Daughter of Dr. Jekyll.*

Many of Lon Chaney's later film roles were of the mute strongman variety.

Chaney could handle dialogue reasonably well. Of course, a talkative monster would tend to be ridiculous. I found him intelligent, probably more so than many actors. He warned me before we started shooting, "Don't make any changes in dialogue, or add new dialogue, after lunch!"—which he drank down rather liberally.

Were you happy with the results on Indestructible Man?

I was reasonably satisfied with it. I thought I did about as good a job of directing as a number of directors we'd used—but I was *not* as good as an Ulmer or a Dupont!

Was it Edgar Ulmer's fine work on Man from Planet X *which prompted you to rehire him for* Daughter of Dr. Jekyll?

Yes, Ulmer, as I have said, was an excellent director, at his best when he had his back up against the wall budget-wise. We shot *Daughter of Dr. Jekyll* in an old L.A. mansion, and the establishing shot of the mansion and the car driving up were done in miniature.

Did you have to secure permission from Columbia to remake, in a distaff version, the story [The Son of Dr. Jekyll] *you had written for them?*

The Son—and the Daughter—of Dr. Jekyll carefully ducked anything in common that could not be traced back to Robert Louis Stevenson's original story, which was in public domain.

Did you use doubles for the monsters in Daughter?

Stuntman Ken Terrell doubled for Arthur Shields in the fight scene. His guttural, animal-like roars came out of a sound effects library. The fanged girl-monster was also played by a double. We shot the scene in a recently burned-over woods, using ultraviolet film to get a weird effect.

What in Daughter of Dr. Jekyll *could possibly have inspired its surprising Legion of Decency "B" rating?*

I don't know why that picture got the "B" rating. The mental processes of the Legion at times verged on fantasy.

What became of two sci-fi/horror thrillers you announced in 1958, The Astonishing 12-Inch People *and* The Brain Snatchers? *Did* The Brain Snatchers *evolve into the much-later* Monstrosity, *which has a brain-transplanting premise?*

The Brain Snatchers did turn into *Monstrosity* — certainly the worst picture I was ever involved with, and incidentally the only one that did not eventually climb into the profit column. Alas, I have to confess I did the first draft of the script. B films were collapsing; the studio financing the film turned out to be heading into bankruptcy. We had shot about half. Tried to patch it together in the cutting room — but that was a task beyond human hands.

When was that film made? It wasn't released until around 1964.

I guess that was shot around '58, with fundamentally an amateur crew. *Everything* went wrong with it. The major reason for this was that it was the only picture I ever tried to make without a first-rate, professional crew. That was a lesson to me.

Did you at least save money by using amateurs?

Not really. The budget was about $25,000, but it ran up to around $40,000 by the time we finished it. Joe Mascelli was a pretty good cameraman, but he was no director. I ended up doing most of the directing.

Isn't that Bradford Dillman doing the narration?

Dean Dillman, Jr. [co-writer and co-producer] is his brother. Brad did help out on the narration.

And The Astonishing 12-Inch People?

I simply dropped that. The handwriting on the wall was clear. B movies were dead.

Of your many sci-fi and horror films, do you have a favorite?
   The Man from Planet X, because it was my first production, and one of the first sci-fi films made with sound.

A least favorite?
   Monstrosity. The name describes it.

*My pictures were great, they were fun....
It was a great life—but, I sure wouldn't want
to be doing it now. The pressures are too great....
I've had it—forty years is plenty. It's fun to reminisce,
but I don't want to get back into that routine.*

Lee Sholem

IF THERE'S ONLY one Hollywood name that's synonymous with speed and efficiency, then it has to be Lee "Roll 'Em" Sholem. In a forty-year career Sholem has directed upwards of 1300 shows, both features and television episodes, without once going over schedule—a feat practically unparalleled in Hollywood history. In the 1950s he turned his talents toward the area of science fiction when he took the directorial reins on the feature *Superman and the Mole-Men,* the film which introduced George Reeves in his best-remembered role as the Mighty Man of Steel. After helming nine episodes of the *Adventures of Superman* teleseries during the '51 season, he returned to the genre for 1954's *Tobor the Great* and then branched off into horror with 1957's *Pharaoh's Curse.*

Sholem learned the motion picture business by starting out in the cutting room some time in the 1930s. "The first week I worked a hundred and eighteen hours, the second week a hundred and twenty-six, and the third week a hundred and thirty-eight, and then passed out!" he recalls. A lengthy association with *Tarzan* producer Sol Lesser brought Sholem in contact with the celebrated William Cameron Menzies, from whom he learned the key to expedient production, and later led up to his first directorial assignment on Lesser's *Tarzan's Magic Fountain* (1949).

Do you remember how you became involved on Superman and the Mole-Men?

I got involved when the guys who were writing and producing the show asked me to do it, and so I went to work on it. That was Bob Maxwell and company. National Comics owned *Superman,* and they're really the ones that got the whole thing going. It was an interesting movie, a cute little show.

Was George Reeves cast as Superman before your involvement in the production?

Yes, he was. It was a lot of work building him up to play the Superman character—he had a good physique, but his shoulders needed padding and so on. But what a sweetheart—everybody loved him, you couldn't help it. He had no ego, none of this crap that you get from most of these guys. And he could tell stories—I mean, he really could rattle 'em off, one after another. He was very much like another actor that I used to work with, Alan Mowbray. Alan would start telling a story, he'd get about three-quarters of the way through, and the cameraman would interrupt and tell him that everything was ready. He'd stop right there, I'd yell, "Roll 'em!" and he'd go right into his lines. And when I'd say, "Cut!" he'd go right on with the story just as though nothing had happened *[laughs]!* It was remarkable, *incredible,* and George was very much like that.

Where was Superman and the Mole-Men *shot?*

At a studio out in Culver City, RKO-Pathé. The oil fields seen in the film were within a stone's throw of the place—they were within two hundred yards

Previous page: Lee Sholem in a 1987 pose. (Photo courtesy Ed Watz.)

The low-budget feature *Superman and the Mole-Men* introduced George Reeves as the Man of Steel and spawned the popular *Adventures of Superman* teleseries. And, yes, that *is* an Electrolux vacuum cleaner the little guys are aiming.

of the studio lot. We'd shoot *Tarzans* there, too, and we had a hell of a time keeping those derricks out of the picture! The budget on *Mole-Men* was, I guess, about $275,000, and I think it was shot in approximately four weeks.

How much input did National Comics have in the production?
They had nothing to do with it. A V.I.P. from National Comics came out to visit one day, and I was introduced to him. He was a very nice man. But that was the only visit that I saw from National Comics! From then on, *never* during the shooting was anybody representing the company out here.

How did you earn your nickname "Roll 'Em"?
[Laughs.] When I'd be waiting on the set and my assistant would say that we were ready, I'd get the cast out and I'd yell *[loudly]*, "All right—r-r-r-roll!" And everybody in the place knew it! Then when the scene was over, I'd yell *[loudly and very sharply]*, "*Cuh*-hut!" And they could tell by the way I would yell *cut* whether it was a print, or if we were going to do it again.

On the average, how many takes would you go before you'd print?
Normally I would get any scene within three or four takes. You *have* to. You can't go ten, twelve, fifteen takes, waiting to get something absolutely

perfect—none of the shows I made required that. They were all action shows, and so if some guy missed a beat or something like that, it really wasn't all that important.

Do you prefer to work that fast?
[*Emphatically.*] I sure do. Also, by knowing exactly what I was going to do, I could walk on the set in the morning and say to the crew, "Eleven shots from now I'm going to make a dolly shot, from *here* to *there.*" By knowing and telling them that, it gives them a chance, whenever they have a few minutes' break, to go ahead and lay the track, put the dolly on there, and set a camera and tripod on it. So by the time we got to that eleventh shot, everything was ready! *This* is where you save the time. If you wait until you're just about to do that particular shot, your company could sit on its ass for anywhere between forty-five minutes to an hour and a half while they're preparing the damn thing.

How did you like working with Phyllis Coates in the Superman *movie and TV show?*
She was just a very, very nice gal, willing to do anything. I'll tell you an anecdote that concerns her: We had stuntmen doing fights on that show somewhat often. We had both George Reeves and Phyllis Coates in fight scenes in one day—and this one day was *not* a lucky day for us. *Both* of them got knocked cold. These stuntmen would throw a right or a left hook, and if their timing was off, even just a little bit, look out! That day it was; one of the stuntmen actually punched Phyllis Coates and knocked her out! Later we were shooting a scene where George was supposed to run and crash through a door. The prop man or the construction man who made the door made it out of balsa wood, but he put two-by-fours in the son of a bitch *[laughs]*! And George was knocked cold! He was supposed to go right through, but he hit those damn two-by-fours dead on!

Any mishaps during Superman's *flying scenes?*
We never had an accident with any of that—we did a hell of a lot of testing. The takeoffs we achieved by yanking George up into the air on piano wires. We had the same guy who worked with Betty Bronson on *Peter Pan* [1924] involved on *Superman,* and the effect was marvelous. In most cases, the tricky part is the lighting—those piano wires had to be painted to cover up their shine, and also so that they would blend into the background. When George would leap out a window, he was simply diving onto cardboard cartons which would break his fall. We got the actual flying scenes by having him lie on a body cast—it looked like a spatula, almost. He'd lie on this thing with his arms out and we'd have the wind machines going. Later, of course, that body cast had to be masked out, and it would look as though he was actually flying.

What do you think of the new Superman *movies?*
   Good. But, I mean, when they spend money like that, they can do a *lot* of things that we couldn't do. These new pictures cost twenty million, thirty million, forty million...! I mean, what the hell, if you've got *that* much money—

You'd better *end up with a good movie!*
   And how!

How many days did it take you to shoot an average Superman *episode?*
   Two and a half.

And how many set-ups a day?
   I've *done* ninety *[laughs]*...! I can give you an example of how we used to work: We were doing a *Superman* episode, and we did ten pages without a break. We started with an insert and pulled back to a shot of a man picking this object up off the floor. As he started to look at it, another person came in, and it kept building until there were ten people in the room! The scene just flowed right on till, toward the last couple of pages, everyone had left but two guys, and *they* walked from that one room, which was a sort of a living room, into a laboratory which was next door. And the scene went on in *there* until the ten pages were completed; we did it in one take!

Where did you learn to work like this?
   I learned by working with a man by the name of William Cameron Menzies. He was an art director, and he was the best. He was *miraculous*. He couldn't direct, but he could sure lay out the show. Bill Menzies was working on a picture called *Our Town* [1940], produced by Sol Lesser. Menzies was brought in as the art director, and he sketched the entire show. But he had a problem, and that was drinking. I was the assistant director on the show, but my biggest job was to keep him off the booze, *or,* to keep him off it at least long enough for him to get the job done, and then let him go out and have his drinks. I learned to block my shows, so that I knew where I was going. Blocking means to lay out the show with *hieroglyphics,* more or less *[laughs]*—laying it out with pencil and paper, and knowing where your camera is going. As long as you know your sets, you can plan your action. That way, when your actors show up in the morning, you can walk through the entire scene with them, and they'll know exactly what lines they're going to move on, what props they're going to use, where they'll hesitate, where they'll pick up the tempo and so on. All these things are figured out prior to any actor appearing on the set, and it's so much easier that way to explain to them what you want done. I literally could do a show backwards—I could go from the back page of the script to the front, and know exactly what I was doing.

Did Menzies actually sit down and teach you this, or did you learn by observing him?

Menzies taught me the idea of blocking. He was a great artist; I'm not *[laughs]*! I would sketch things the easiest way possible, but *he* could draw; he did everything in charcoal, and it was magnificent. His artwork was so great that I would guess that a museum could be filled with it.

How did you get started in the business?

I got started as a director of plays when I was with the *New York Times*. We started a little group back there called the *New York Times* Theater Guild, and we put on thirty-two different plays. I directed about half of them, and acted in a few. I'd been brought up in California, and we had a lot of friends in the picture business, one of whom was a director named Hobart Henley. Henley said to me, "Lee, if you want to go into directing, it's all well and good, go for it. But quit when you're ahead—when you have done as much as you feel that you ought to—and *relax*. The pressures are great." And they are—it's a tough racket, a tough business. I was in the business for forty years, I directed 1300 shows and I never was late. I always brought 'em in on time.

Many of your early credits were on the Johnny Weissmuller Tarzan *series. How well did you get to know Weissmuller?*

Very well. Weissmuller was just a doll to work with, just a hell of a guy. He wasn't the most intelligent guy in the world, and so those *Tarzan* and *Jungle Jim* parts were perfect for him. They didn't require a lot of brains, they just required a good physique. And Weissmuller was a master at swimming, and at keeping his trunk out of the water when he'd swim. Even in his older age—he was still playing Jungle Jim when he was in his fifties, and that's pretty damn good. His body wasn't *great* anymore—he did do a little drinking, and when you do that, something's got to give!

The first Tarzan *film you directed was* Tarzan's Magic Fountain *with Lex Barker. What's the story on him?*

He was an egomaniac—I mean, *really* an egomaniac. He had a birthday while we were shooting one of these *Tarzan* pictures, and the crew got together and purchased a great big mirror for him *[laughs]*! He was *built*—God, he had a nice physique—and he did very well in the business; he made a lot of pictures in Europe after he finished playing Tarzan. He was a real egotist, and that's about as much as I can say for Lex.

You know, my *wife* discovered one of the Tarzans. We were up at the Sierra in Las Vegas: I was looking for a Tarzan and she knew it, and she looked over and saw this handsome hunk of beef who was a lifeguard there. His name was Werschkul. I asked him if he was thinking that possibly he'd like to be an actor; he hadn't thought about it. I said, "Well, you'd make a good Tarzan, and they're looking for one in Los Angeles. I'm going to try and set up a meeting with you and a man by the name of Sol Lesser, who is producing."

That was Gordon Scott, right?
 Right. My wife also gave him that name. He came up to our house one day and we agreed that the name Werschkul didn't sound too good for a Tarzan — or for *any* actor, for that matter! So she suggested the name Gordon Scott, and he grabbed it.

Did you ever help discover any of the Janes?
 At one point, Lesser was looking for a new Jane and I found a young gal that I thought was just *marvelous* for Tarzan's mate. She didn't have to be a great actress, but she had to be attractive. A girl by the name of Marilyn Monroe. I just thought Marilyn would have been perfect. Well, Lesser didn't think so. I had her out *eight times* to see him, and eight times Lesser remained undecided. And, needless to say, he never did cast her.

Who ended up with the part?
 He finally ended up with a gal by the name of Vanessa Brown for that picture *[Tarzan and the Slave Girl,* 1950]. She was a quiz kid, and Lesser had fancied himself as a man who had a great knowledge of words. He'd put long words into his scripts so that you'd literally have to look 'em up in the dictionary to understand what the hell he was writing about. He'd get the thesaurus out and find words that he thought would work, and he'd throw 'em into the script to make everybody think he was a genius! And he was more of a horse's ass *[laughs]*! Anyway, he chose Vanessa Brown because of her knowledge of words and her diction. And she was no bargain herself. There was a situation one day where she had about three words to say, and she asked, "What is the underlying *meaning* of this?" In a *Tarzan* picture *[laughs]!* "What is my feeling here? What is my attitude?" Oh, you never heard such shit!

After Superman and the Mole-Men, *your next science fiction film was 1954's* Tobor the Great.
 Tobor was not an easy picture to make. There was a lot of action, a lot of hard work, a lot of nights and lots of days. I think we shot it in about two weeks.

What do you remember about your robot suit?
 The suit that Tobor wore was expensive — I think the guy who put that together had been working on it for probably five months. It was utilitarian. The guy that worked in it had a tough time — it wasn't easy for him at all. It was no big problem, though, because we really didn't have him doing very much. But the guy worked out in the suit for about four weeks — what for, I'll never know! One *day* would have been enough.

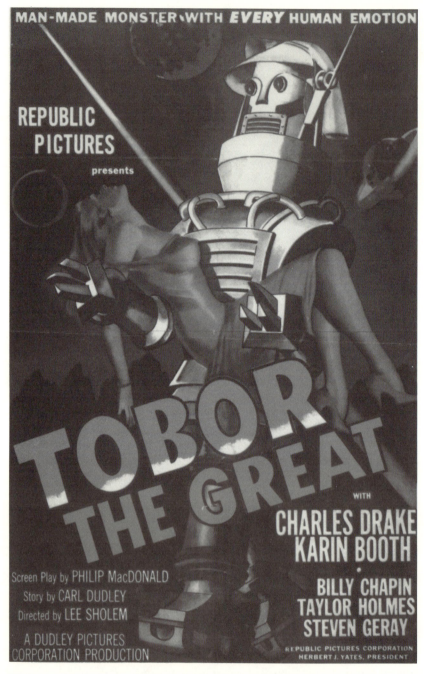

Made on a low budget at Republic Studios, Sholem's *Tobor the Great* was a kiddie-oriented sci-fi adventure remembered mainly for its mechanical star.

Unidentified man, director Lee Sholem, makeup man George Bau and assistant director Paul Wurtzel gang up on the shrivelled (and unidentified) star of *Pharaoh's Curse*.

And where was Tobor *shot?*

At Republic, in the Valley. But that wasn't made by Republic; the producers of *Tobor the Great* simply rented the studio space and the crews and everything else.

Then, in 1957, you made your only horror movie, Pharaoh's Curse.

I made *Pharaoh's Curse* for a producer by the name of Howard W. Koch. Howard is a doll of dolls; I've known a lot of guys in this business, and there *isn't* a nicer guy than Howard Koch. He used to work with a guy by the name of Aubrey Schenck, and I directed three pictures for them.

How did you get hooked up with Koch and Schenck?

I was shooting a show with Jon Hall, and the operating cameraman said to me, "Lee, when you get finished today, what are you doing?" and I said I was going home. He said, "Well, I've got somebody you ought to meet, a producer named Howard Koch. I'm going to go down and talk to him, and you'll probably be hearing from him." I got home and the phone rang, it was Howard Koch, and he said he'd like to have me come down and pick up a script for a picture *[Crime Against Joe,* 1956] he wanted made in Arizona. So I picked up the script, came home and read it, and called him up. He asked me, "Can you shoot it in seven days?" and I told him, "Yeah, I think so." And he said, "Well, then you'll be leaving for Arizona day after tomorrow."

So we go to Tucson, where [director] Les Selander was already shooting a Western for Howard. He was shooting first, and then after he was finished I'd move in and do my show. I had a week to prepare, and in that time I blocked my show. Now came time to shoot, and Howard came on the set. He'd never seen me shoot; up until a few days before he'd never even *heard* of me! He came on the set as I was shooting my first scene. He watched, and then he came up to me and shook my hand and said goodbye. I said, "Where are you going?" and he said, "Back to Los Angeles." I said, "Well, that's a hell of a thing — I'm just starting your show, and you're taking off." And Howard said, "Lee — you're going to do *fine*."

P.S.: we finished that picture in *five days [laughs]*! And then he gave me another one *[Emergency Hospital, 1956]* and *another* one *[Pharaoh's Curse]*. The total for these three shows: seventeen and a half days, for three features.

Where was Pharaoh's Curse *shot?*

The exteriors were done in Death Valley. We flew out of Burbank, early in the morning, and landed in the desert just as the sun was coming up. The company and cameras and all the equipment were all on trucks, and they were there already. We started at one end of the canyon in Death Valley and worked all the way down to the other end. We moved with the sun. We shot all the desert exteriors, finished the day's work and came home. One day! That was really one for the books.

You created lots of atmosphere in the tomb scenes.

Those were shot at American National. And you'd be amazed how little area we used in shooting those scenes. We did that by constantly redressing the sets: We'd put a piece or a prop in front of the camera, in the foreground, and we'd have a couple of run-bys. Then we'd move the pieces around, and you'd think it was a whole different area — but we'd only lit *one!*

What can you tell us about Doomsday Machine?

Oh, Christ — I didn't even know that was *released!* I kid you not! I'll tell you what happened on that damn thing: They had two directors in on that show, and they called me in to see if I could make anything out of it. Everything was just a hodgepodge — I don't know why they let the director carry on as long as they did. They had nowhere to go, they didn't know what to do. They knew they had nothing, the cutter was proving that — they couldn't even cut what they had! It was a monstrous job — it was a patch-job more than anything.

You get a director's credit, though.

Well, I guess because I saved it — as much as it could be saved *[laughs]*! I really don't remember how I got hired for that; I know the guy behind that picture was using his own money. And a lot of money had been spent. I had my own ideas about how to fix and finish the thing, and when I told him he asked *[sheepishly]*, "Can't we get away with just doing it *this* way...? I haven't got that much dough." And then they had to go out and borrow more money—he had a very tough time.

Doomsday Machine was a tough job. When you go in to patch a show, you find that you've got certain sequences that *haven't* been shot and others that *have*. And you've got to shoot added scenes, and retakes, and God knows what else. That was a *mess* when I got ahold of it.

Do you have any particular favorites among your 1300 credits?
No, no—I enjoyed 'em all. They were great, they were fun. It was enjoyable, it was a great life—*but,* I sure wouldn't want to be doing it now. The pressures are too great. Everybody wants a picture done in so many hours, and you're under the gun from the time you get there in the morning till you leave at night. I've had it—forty years is plenty. It's fun to reminisce, but I don't want to get back into that routine.

*I'm a writer, and to write the right things
is more important than getting a lot of dough for it....
Today, nobody lives better than I do.
I have an estate, fifty acres overlooking the mountains,
and every night I say "Heil Hitler!"
because without the son of a bitch,
I wouldn't be in Three Rivers, California,
I'd still be in Berlin!*

Curt Siodmak

AN INTERVIEW with Curt Siodmak offers the rare opportunity to speak with a man who was an important contributor to both the classic Universal horror pictures of the '40s and the sci-fi/horror cycle of the '50s. As writer or director, Siodmak has been associated with the superb *The Wolf Man*, the Karloff-Lugosi vehicle *Black Friday*, *Son of Dracula*, the all-star horror show *House of Frankenstein*, the Val Lewton masterpiece *I Walked with a Zombie* and, in the 1950s, such sci-fi standards as *Earth vs. the Flying Saucers* and *Donovan's Brain*. A prolific novelist and short-story writer as well, he is currently working on a novel called *Siblings*, inspired by his relationship with his brother Robert Siodmak, the great director who made such *film noir* and thriller classics as *The Killers*, *Phantom Lady* and *The Spiral Staircase*.

Born in Dresden, Germany, in 1902, Curt Siodmak worked as an engineer and a newspaper reporter before entering the literary and movie fields. It was as a reporter that he got his first break of sorts in films: In 1926 he and his reporter wife hired on as extras in Fritz Lang's *Metropolis* in order to get a story on the director and his film. Siodmak's first film-writing assignment was the screenplay for the German science fiction picture *F.P.1 Antwortet Nicht [Floating Platform 1 Does Not Answer]*, based on his own novel. Compelled to leave Germany after Hitler took power, he went to work in England, where he adapted the novel *Der Tunnel* for the film *Trans-Atlantic Tunnel* and co-wrote the script for *Non-Stop New York*. He then moved to Hollywood in 1937 and got a job at Universal on the picture *The Invisible Man Returns* through his director friend Joe May. "It was one of the first pictures that Vincent Price starred in," Siodmak recalls. "It went over well, and I fell into a groove."

While writing your three Invisible Man films — The Invisible Man Returns, The Invisible Woman *and* Invisible Agent — *were you limited in what you could write by what the special effects department was able to do?*

No, *I* told the special effects department what they *should* do. We had a kind of competition: I thought of the most impossible things, and John P. Fulton really came through with it, every time.

Were you comfortable with sci-fi/comedy on The Invisible Woman?

That was charming. Yes, I like comedies, and I also wrote a lot of musicals for Universal, for people like Ginny Simms and Susie Foster. John Barrymore was in *The Invisible Woman*, and he was at the point where he couldn't remember one line anymore. He had to hold the pages of dialogue at his side so he could read them.

On Black Friday, *Boris Karloff was originally slated to play the college professor who is turned into a Jekyll-Hyde character, and Bela Lugosi was supposed to portray the brain surgeon who is responsible for the transformation. When the film was made Karloff became the surgeon, Stanley Ridges played the*

Previous page: **Curt Siodmak is flanked by twin female fans in a '50s photo. (Photo from the archives of Forrest J Ackerman.)**

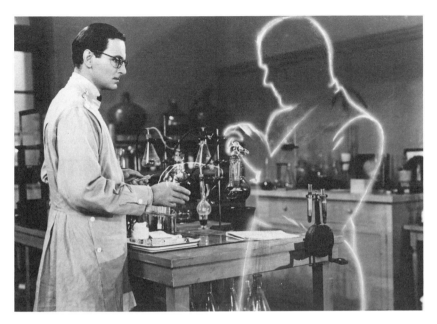

The Siodmak-scripted Universal film *The Invisible Man Returns* went over so well that Siodmak was instantly typed as a sci-fi/horror writer. John Sutton and a not-quite-invisible Vincent Price share this posed shot.

professor, and Lugosi took on another villainous role. What prompted this role-switching?

Karloff didn't want to play the dual role in *Black Friday*. He was afraid of it; there was too much acting in it, it was too intricate. So they took Stanley Ridges, who was a stage actor, and he filled the part. Karloff was smart enough to know that he might not come off too well in the role. Karloff had a very dark complexion, and I've often wondered where it came from. I think he had a little shot of Indian blood or something. A very friendly, very kind Englishman.

Bela Lugosi ended up playing a gangster in *Black Friday,* and that didn't turn out well at all. Bela never could act his way out of a paper bag. He could only be *Mee-ster Drac-u-la,* with that accent and those Hungarian movements of his. And he was a *pest!* He would call me up and say, "Curt! Please! Put me in your picture!" He was very unrealistic.

When you wrote The Ape *for Monogram, you made a lot of changes from the play and the first film version.*

Oh, sure. Whether it was *The Ape* or *The Climax* or even *I Walked with a Zombie,* I never used the original material. I used my own stories. In *The Ape,* Karloff played a scientist who discovers that fluid taken from the human spine can be used to cure a crippled girl, played by Maris Wrixon. That was an idea which *I* had.

While writing movies for Universal, did you know in advance who would be playing the various roles?

Yes, they told me who would be in the pictures before I would even start to write them. On *The Wolf Man*, for instance, I was told, "We have $180,000, we have Lon Chaney, Jr., Claude Rains, Ralph Bellamy, Warren William, Maria Ouspenskaya, Bela Lugosi, a title called *The Wolf Man* and we shoot in ten weeks. Get going!"

Was The Wolf Man *written as a vehicle for Lon Chaney, Jr.?*

Yeah. Well, actually Boris Karloff had originally been assigned to that title [in 1932], and he wanted to play it, but then another job came along and *The Wolf Man* with Karloff never came about. But I created the *character* of the Wolf Man. Of course there were some werewolf films before—not many, but some—but none with that sharp definition of character.

Was any research required in writing The Wolf Man?

A tremendous amount. Books and books on lycanthropy. Every time I write a story, you wouldn't *believe* how many books I read. Then, if it's a science fiction story, before I write I pick up the telephone and I call the most important men I can think of in their fields. And all the things are checked and rechecked.

You know, I have the bad luck in life of always being ten or twenty years ahead of my time. I wrote a book called *F.P.1 Does Not Answer,* the story of a floating platform in the ocean where the airplanes land between Europe and America, to refuel. I wrote that in 1931, and there's *radar* in it. And the weather stations of today are exactly the same construction. I wrote another book about twenty years ago called *I, Gabriel,* and in it I had *microchips*. Ten years before they *invented* microchips!

The Wolf Man *is such a definitive treatment of the werewolf theme that today it's difficult not to confuse the actual legends with your film's innovations.*

That's right. I wrote that little four-line ditty for *The Wolf Man*—"Even a man who is pure in heart..."—and nowadays, film historians think it's from German folklore. It isn't. I made it up!

A few years ago, I got a letter from a Professor Evans, from the University of Alabama, citing the parallels and similarities of construction between *The Wolf Man* and the Greek plays. At first I thought to myself, "This guy is nuts," but it was true. In the Greek plays, the gods tell a man his fate, and he cannot escape; in *The Wolf Man*, when the moon comes up Lon Chaney knows there's going to be a killing. In the Greek plays, the gods are domineering; in *The Wolf Man,* the father of the family is domineering.

The movie certainly made a lot of money for Universal.

After *The Wolf Man* made its first million, [producer-director] George

Lycanthrope Lon Chaney, Jr., hovers over an unsuspecting Evelyn Ankers in a posed shot from Curt Siodmak's *The Wolf Man*.

Waggner got a diamond ring for his wife, and [executive producer] Jack Gross got a $10,000 bonus. I wanted $25 more a week, and they didn't give it to me.

I never got a raise from Universal — *never*. "You get your raises outside, and *then* we'll pay you more," they told me. Basically I never pushed it because — this may sound silly — money doesn't mean as much to me as an objective in life. I'm a writer, and to write the right things is more important than getting a lot of dough for it. The other people make the money, and try to cheat you out of yours. I cannot be bothered. I mean, my time and my mind are much more important to me than fighting to get money out of some lawsuit. Today, nobody lives better than I do. I have an estate, fifty acres overlooking the mountains, and every night I say "Heil Hitler!" because without the son of a bitch I wouldn't be in Three Rivers, California, I'd still be in Berlin!

How much creative input did George Waggner have on The Wolf Man?

I never talked to George except on Thursdays. I'd go into his office and give him all the honey I could think of—told him how big a man he was—and I figured, "The guy *must* know that I'm kidding." He never found out. I couldn't really sit down and talk to him about these pictures, because he'd say, "I don't want *my* ideas, I want *your* ideas!" So he never talked to me. But he was a nice man, and we had a good relationship. His idea of fun was to drink beer, sing songs—he was very German in his tastes. My brother Robert did a picture for him called *Cobra Woman* [1944], and they couldn't get along at all. Robert was much more individualistic than I am. For me it was a *job*. I went from one picture to the next.

What kind of relationship did you and your brother have?

We had a sibling rivalry, Robert and I. When I was born, my father took little Robert to my crib and said, "Here's your new brother." And Robert said, "I don't want your new brother!" You know, like a dog who doesn't want a second dog around *[laughs]*! When we were in Germany, Robert had a magazine, and when I wrote for it I had to change my name. He wanted only one Siodmak around. This lasted seventy-one years, until he died!

And you only worked with him on one picture in America?

I *never* worked with him in America.

What about Son of Dracula? *You get a story credit.*

That's another story. Robert got his start in Germany, became very famous, made the big pictures, and then Hitler threw us out. He started in France and became very famous there. Then he came to America, where nobody knew of him. Finally he got a job at Paramount making B pictures—*West Point Widow* [1941], *Fly by Night* [1942], things like that. They forced him to do *this* shot and *that* shot, and Robert didn't want to do it. One day an assistant said to him, "I thought you were such a big director! Why don't you fight to do it your own way?" Robert said, "Because this is Paramount shit, this is not a Siodmak picture!" So they fired him. That's when Robert got a job at Universal directing this picture I had written, *Son of Dracula*. Next thing I knew, I was out. He had me fired and took on Eric Taylor as a writer!

We've been told that Robert Siodmak concentrated on getting one "perfect" sequence into every movie. The rest was just framework for it.

Yes. Robert once said, "Only five minutes of my pictures are okay. The

Spooky posed shot of Lon Chaney, Jr., and Louise Allbritton from *Son of Dracula*. Siodmak had a writing job on this Universal film until his brother Robert came in as director and had him kicked off the picture.

rest is routine." I think Robert was one of the best directors you have ever seen. His pictures, they are classics.

We've heard that your brother and Lon Chaney had a dispute on the set of Son of Dracula, *and—*
 —and Chaney took a vase and hit him over the head! Chaney was drunk—or at least I imagine he was drunk. Secretly he must have sneaked a few, then went up behind Robert, took a vase and hit him over the head with it!

All these people, if you knew them, had sad stories behind them. The father of Lon Chaney—the old man, Chaney, Sr.—was a very cold man, and he used to beat the boy all the time. Lon told me he had to go into a shed and be beaten with a leather strap, sometimes for things he hadn't done. This *killed* him, mentally—he became an alcoholic, and always needed a father figure to tell him what to do. He'd drink on the set. I stopped that when *I* directed him.

Tell us how the Wolf Man *sequel,* Frankenstein Meets the Wolf Man, *came about.*

Never make a joke in the studio. I was sitting down at the commissary having lunch with George Waggner and I said, "George, why don't we make a picture, *Frankenstein Wolfs the Meat Man*—er, *Meets the Wolf Man?"* He didn't laugh. This was during wartime; I wanted to buy an automobile and I needed a new writing job so I would be able to afford it. George would see me every day and ask me if I had bought the car yet. I said, "George, can I get a *job?"* He said, "Sure, you'll get a job, buy the car." Well, the day finally came when I had to pay for the car. George asked me that day, "Did you buy the car?" and I said, "Yes, I bought it." George said, "Good! Your new assignment is *Frankenstein Wolfs the Meat Man*—er, *Meets the Wolf Man!* I'll give you two hours to accept!"

And then you had to sit there and think, "What can I do?" Now is when you need a basic idea. My idea was, the Wolf Man, as was the tradition now, wants to die—he doesn't want to be a murderer. And Dr. Frankenstein knows the secrets of life and death. So he wants to meet Dr. Frankenstein. The Monster, on the other hand, wants to live forever. In an early script I wrote a scene which I knew definitely would be thrown out. The Monster is walking along with Chaney and Chaney says, "I change into a wolf every night." And the Monster says, "Are you kidding?"

One weak aspect of the Universal horror films is that the monster characters would turn up in sequels, often with no explanation of how they escaped destruction at the end of the previous picture.

That became a kind of gag. We finished the pictures in such a way that the next writer *couldn't* revive the characters. We'd freeze them in ice, cremate them, whatever. It was a game. Then *you'd* get the assignment, and you had to do it yourself!

It's never clear what happens to Maria Ouspenskaya at the end of Frankenstein Meets the Wolf Man. *Are we supposed to assume that she dies, or not?*

She died in the meantime *[laughs]!*

What can you tell us about House of Frankenstein?

The idea was to put all the horror characters into one picture. I only wrote the story. I didn't write the script. I never saw the picture.

Most of your early films lack a conventional hero type. They either have tragic heroes, like Chaney in the Wolf Man pictures and Robert Paige in Son of Dracula, *or unsavory or unscrupulous protagonists [Karloff in* The Ape *and* Black Friday, *Robert Alda in* The Beast with Five Fingers *and several more].*

This comes again from Greek mythology: a man who is guilty without being guilty, through some inequity, a defect in character, or something like that. My heroes are never *bad* people. I wrote a play called *Song of Frankenstein*—a musical—and in the story, everybody is a monster, *except* the Monster! The Monster is only twenty-four hours old, so why should it be mean? Nobody has hurt it. But *people* go through life and *they* become mean, see? That was the theme of it.

How did you get involved on The Beast with Five Fingers?

They had a few different scripts for that film, but they couldn't lick it. So they called me in. I had the idea that the hand was only in the man's mind. *This* made it, so they gave me the assignment, and a year's contract afterwards. I had Paul Henreid in mind for the [Hilary Cummins] part. "I won't play opposite some goddamned hand!" he said, so they took on Peter Lorre—which was, to me, too obvious. With Paul Henreid, it would have been a better picture. The special effects department did an excellent job.

Were you pleased with director Robert Florey's handling of the film?

I wanted to direct it; that was my whole objective. They wouldn't let me. Florey supposedly was very unhappy about the thing, and didn't want to do it. Luis Buñuel supposedly worked on it; I don't believe it. I never met the man.

You used some of the better situations of the short story, and built a very interesting and largely original film around that framework.

The widow of William Fryer Harvey, who did the original story, hated the film. She had sold the short story to Warner Bros., and it didn't turn out exactly as her husband had written it. But it was a very short story, so how can you make a big picture out of it? You have to add to it.

How did you enjoy working with Peter Lorre?

He was really a sadistic son of a bitch—liked to look at operations. He really was the type, a very weird character.

Jack Warner reportedly was unhappy over the way The Beast with Five Fingers *turned out. Did this ever get back to you?*

I only met the man once. One day he called me into his office and asked me not to become a Communist. That was all he ever said to me.

Val Lewton was known for his contempt for the kind of horror films being made at Universal during the 1940s. Did that cause any initial tensions when you worked with him on I Walked with a Zombie?

Oh, no. Why would he engage me if he had so little respect? He certainly liked my stuff, or obviously I wouldn't have gotten the job.

What was Lewton like?

He seemed like a lovely guy, very erudite, very interesting. But later I gave him *Donovan's Brain* to read, and when I came back to him he said, "It's not a good book." There was already a kind of friction between us, because he liked people he could dominate. He couldn't do it with me, because I was independent.

How did working with him compare to working at Universal?

Oh, he was brilliant, constructive and intelligent — much more interesting than any of those Universal guys. Producers at Universal were businessmen who would see that pictures came in on time and for the money. They never contributed anything of any literary value.

Did Lewton have a hand in the writing of I Walked with a Zombie?

Nobody helped me with *I Walked with a Zombie*. Of course, Lewton and I discussed scenes, and if he objected to something, I came up with an alternative suggestion. Ardel Wray came on the picture after I left; I never met her. Maybe Lewton had had enough of me, and that was why he hired somebody else.

Which of the three major movie versions of your novel Donovan's Brain *do you like best?*

I have not seen them. I saw half of one, and walked out. Republic made the first version. Herbert Yates [president of Republic Pictures] called me one day and said, "Siodmak, you are crazy!" I said, "Why am I crazy?" He said, "A scientist like Dr. Cory, he doesn't live in a little hut in the desert. He lives in a *castle!*" He put a damn castle in the story, and von Stroheim running around it like a rat! "And," Yates went on, "I have a new title for you — *The Lady and the Monster*. And *The Lady* will be *Vera!*" — Vera Hruba Ralston, the ice-skater, Yates' girlfriend. So I quit. And I never saw the picture.

Then they did it again — Allan Dowling made it, and it was called *Donovan's Brain*. Nancy Davis Reagan was in it. And in this one *God* destroys the brain with a lightning bolt! So I didn't see it. Then they did it again in England. The title was *The Brain*, with Peter Van Eyck. In that one, he invented a cancer cure. Why a cancer cure?!

If I had to be reborn, I would like to be John Huston. John Huston was about to do *The Maltese Falcon* [1941], so he took the Dashiell Hammett book to his friend Allen Rivkin, who was a writer, and asked, "How do I write a screenplay?" Allen Rivkin took the book, marked the scenes in continuity and said, "Take the book and shoot it." And so he did. I never wrote *any* of those *Donovan's Brain* scripts — they wouldn't let me. I had a contract to *direct* the

Allan Dowling version, but they paid me off. There was a guy over there, Tom Gries, that didn't like me. He had these advertisements made for the film saying, "Based on the famous book." Period. He didn't want to mention my name! Gries was the producer and he wouldn't let me direct it because of a personal dislike. He was the meanest son of a bitch I had ever seen.

Why did you decide to become a director in the 1950s?
  I wanted to show my brother Robert I could direct. My first film, *Bride of the Gorilla,* is one of the pictures I like most for some reason. It was a marvelous idea: Raymond Burr has an affair with Barbara Payton, who has an older man for a husband. The husband gets bit by a snake and Ray Burr doesn't help him, lets him die—so he's a murderer. But his conscience doesn't permit that, so every time he looks in a mirror he sees an animal. Because an animal can kill without being punished, he's free of guilt. *They* made a gorilla out of it—I didn't even want to show that. *They* called the film *Bride of the Gorilla;* my title was *The Face in the Water.* It had real characters, and a story. Today's horror film directors, they have a mattress with two hundred and fifty gallons of blood coming up out of it, and *that* they call a picture *[laughs]! This* was development of a character.

There is one shot, toward the end of the movie, where you do see the gorilla, and not through its own eyes.
  They forced me to do that—sometimes you can't fight 'em. But I like that picture anyway. And, can you believe, only seven days' shooting? Wow! And I got good performances out of them. Directing is 80 percent public relations and 20 percent directing. You have to put your people at ease. I made my people as comfortable and happy with their scenes as I could, and I got better performances out of them.

There are some interesting parallels between Bride of the Gorilla *and* The Wolf Man.
  Possibly there are. I wrote the script on speculation, because I wanted to direct something.

How did The Magnetic Monster *come about?*
  Ivan Tors came to me with ten minutes of a German picture called *Gold,* which had tremendous special effects shots, but he had no story. So we formed a company and I wrote a script around the footage and directed the picture. It cost $105,000.

Richard Carlson was a partner in that company also, wasn't he?
  Yes, he was. He died of alcoholism, too. They're all unhappy people, actors. Most of them start to fade, and they cannot take it. I later wrote a picture for Carlson to direct, *Riders to the Stars.*

What can you tell us about Curucu, Beast of the Amazon?

I had no money at that time, so I wrote *Curucu*. The idea behind it was very interesting, actually: The people in the Amazon jungle can shrink heads, and a girl who studied medicine realizes that if she can find out the process, she can use it to shrink cancer tissues, tumors and what-not, by injection. My agent got a couple of other guys, Richard Kay and Harry Rybnick, aboard to produce. It was done in Brazil for $155,000. I shot it down there, in the jungles. I never recovered, physically.

Beverly Garland's presence in the cast really enhances that picture.

I'll tell you a story about her. I remember I wanted to shoot a scene by the big waterfalls in Argentina. I figured I could make rubber face masks of my stars and put them on extras, then shoot some long shots by the falls in Argentina without having to bring the stars along. We went to this company, Beverly Garland and I, to have a mask made. It was a horrible process. I couldn't have done it, to have your face covered up with all this stuff and to have straws up your nose so you could breathe. Beverly didn't want to do it either, but there was already a naked rubber body of an actress, Carolyn Jones, made for *Invasion of the Body Snatchers*. Beverly saw it and said, "Well, if *she* can do it, *I* can do it!" and she went through with the thing. She's a brave, tough lady.

You had an entirely Brazilian crew on that one, didn't you?

Portuguese. And I learned Portuguese very quick, to see what those sons of bitches were saying behind my back!

What about your follow-up film, Love Slaves of the Amazon?

That was very tough, because I never knew what I had. I had forty thousand feet of film. You couldn't import film. By law, you could only develop *in* the country, and they had no color labs. So what do you do? At one point I asked my production manager, "How much film do I have left?" and he said ten thousand feet. I said, "Wait a minute! I'm not half through yet!" So I rehearsed every scene and got it in one take, and came back with the picture. I could never see dailies, and so by *memory* I knew where to put the shots.

About this time you also got involved with some television horror programs.

I directed the pilot for *Tales of Frankenstein*, but no one ever picked it up. I *told* them, "You cannot carry a whole show with nothing but Frankenstein stories!"

How about the made-for-television No. 13 Demon Street?

I had a title, *No. 13 Demon Street,* and I knew a guy named Leo Guild, who was connected with an outfit called Herts-Lion. I met Kenneth Herts, who

Director Siodmak (with hat) checks the pulse of Frankenstein Monster Don Megowan in this candid shot from TV's *Tales of Frankenstein*.

made a deal for the pictures to be made in Sweden, and so I went over there to direct them. Twelve or thirteen episodes I shot. Herts-Lion showed them to CBS, but CBS didn't take them. Half a year later, NBC came out with *Thriller* with Boris Karloff — same idea, everything. Then Herts-Lion double-crossed me — they took three of the shows, put them together, put a frame around 'em and put Herbert Strock's name on it as the director. They made a feature out of it, and called it *The Devil's Messenger*. I wasn't even mentioned in the credits, but I'm glad of that. I never saw it.

Actually, some of those episodes did come out okay. I think they were better than the *Thriller*'s, in story values.

Lon Chaney worked on that series, too.

Chaney went over to Sweden also, but he only played in the framing device. The frame was very interesting: The camera was on a house, and a storm was brewing. The camera went into the house, and a strange guy in a hirsute suit came forward — you never saw who it was — and he talked to the camera about the worst crimes he committed in his life, and how he is condemned to stay there in that room for eternity. He was a Wandering Jew. Then the camera went to the window and we'd show the show. At the end the camera would pull back through the window, out the door, and the wind would blow it shut. It was a good frame.

Compare the Lon Chaney of 1941's The Wolf Man *to the Chaney of* No. 13 Demon Street.

Well, he was already deteriorating, believe you me. He was a drunk, an alcoholic.

What is your opinion of the horror films of today?

Today, the approach is different. The special effects have taken over. There's no humanity in it any longer, no personality. We have drifted now into a soulless picturemaking business which is based on effects and cruelty. The pictures we did had no violence, only implied dangers.

You know, there's a parallel between time, history and horror pictures. When we made those pictures throughout the Second World War, we couldn't show an American with a machine gun mowing down five thousand Japanese. Nobody would believe it; it wouldn't work. So we had the Gothic stories. People would get rid of their fears and walk out of the theaters *knowing* it was a fake, a fairy story. When the war ended, the bottom fell out of the horror film business. Then, when they began testing the atom bomb, it all started again. And today, with the threat of a war, a *holocaust,* these films are as popular as ever. In times of peace of mind, there's no place for horror films; times of fear — like now — bring out the need for violence in people. This reflects, in my opinion, a fear of the people of *tomorrow.*

Everything seems so glamorous when you look back. It wasn't. It was a struggle for life, all the time. As soon as you finished a job, you were *out* of a job and trying to find another one. I took every job that came along in my life. I have thirty-four pictures running on television now and I don't get a penny out of them — not one cent. But look at the credits. Those guys are all dead and I'm alive. *Who's winning?*

*I remember when I was doing these pictures,
my kids were ashamed of me, they felt I was pandering.
I said, "Look, we've got to eat—they're fun to do
and I don't mind." Now they're clamoring for me
to collect the posters from these films....*

Herbert L. Strock

HERBERT L. STROCK was involved in the early years of '50s science fiction and horror, first as an editor, then as a director, and worked steadily in the genre through the early '60s. The movies he has directed have ranged from the serious-minded science fiction of Ivan Tors to the no-holds-barred exploitation-horror of Herman Cohen. For Tors, Strock worked on *The Magnetic Monster,* a sci-fi thriller that made ingenious use of stock footage from the 1934 German film *Gold,* as well as *Gog,* a story about robots and sabotage in a space-station-in-the-making. From these relatively sober thrillers, Strock then went on to collaborate with AIP's Herman Cohen on three sensationalist horror pictures: *I Was a Teenage Frankenstein, Blood of Dracula* and *How to Make a Monster.* These movies, along with *The Devil's Messenger* and *The Crawling Hand,* have established Strock as a prolific and memorable horror craftsman.

Boston-born Strock's introduction in the movie business was as director of the Fox Newsreel crew, visiting Hollywood stars in their homes. After serving with the Ordnance Motion Picture Division, he found employment as an editor at MGM and later moved into the infant medium of TV, where he produced and directed *The Cases of Eddie Drake,* the first-ever motion picture film to become a network series. His first fantasy film credit was as assistant to the producer on *Donovan's Brain,* a film initially slated to be directed by Curt Siodmak but ultimately helmed by Felix Feist. Today the head of his own postproduction facilities, Strock looks back with disarming candor on a science fiction film career that has spanned four decades.

Curt Siodmak told us that producer Tom Gries dropped him as director of Donovan's Brain *because of a personal dislike, and described him as "the meanest son of a bitch" he had ever seen. Do you know anything about this?*

Despite what Mr. Siodmak told you, Tommy Gries was a lovely, lovely man. I knew him when he used to work on the *Daily Variety;* he was a very intelligent young fellow and became a damn good director. I was very excited about the fact that Curt was going to direct *Donovan's Brain,* and I wanted him to stay on the picture. But it seems that in discussions of how things were going to be done, Curt became the stiff, Germanic, immobile person, and would not listen. Gries and the producer, Allan Dowling, became very upset; I pleaded with them to keep Curt on, that I would guide him through, but behind my back they bumped him. And it was too bad, because Curt did feel very badly hurt. I tried to explain to him what had happened, and I also very much wanted to be his friend, but he kept sloughing me off and did not want to discuss it. He was extremely sensitive and extremely hurt. I can't understand his attitude toward Tom, because it wasn't a personal dislike at all.

I replaced Curt Siodmak a few times in my life: once on *The Magnetic Monster;* once on a TV series *[No. 13 Demon Street]* that was being done in Stockholm, Sweden; and then of course there was the situation with *Donovan's Brain.* As I said, I tried to get him to stay on the picture and tried to get the

Previous page: Strock (left) enjoyed the opportunity to work with name stars like Wayne Morris (right) on TV's *Science Fiction Theatre.*

producers to keep him on, but it didn't work and he blamed me for this for the rest of the years. I haven't seen him in many years.

Siodmak places all the blame for his removal on Gries. He didn't mention you at all.

No, he told me that he blamed me for his losing *Donovan's Brain.* He also was very hurt when he was later thrown off of *The Magnetic Monster,* and that had nothing to do with me. I started out as editor on *Magnetic Monster,* and I just mentioned a few things to the producer, Ivan Tors: I told him that I thought Siodmak should get in closer with the camera, that he should do this and that, and so on. Apparently Siodmak resented these intrusions from the cutting room; he and Ivan had a fight and he was off the picture.

Curt has many negative feelings; he always had a chip on his shoulder because of the fact that he could never follow in the footsteps of Robert, his brother, who *was* a fairly good director. Curt just couldn't get his own projects going the way he wanted to do them.

What was it like working with Ivan Tors?

Ivan was charming to work with. He was a very open-minded, even-handed producer who knew his business.

Tell us about your experiences on The Magnetic Monster.

The Magnetic Monster was a picture written by Curt Siodmak. Ivan and Curt and Andrew "Bundy" Marton and Laslo Benedek were the Hungarian clan in Hollywood—there was a sign over their writing department at MGM, *Being Hungarian Is Not Enough.* They all took care of each other, and that's how Curt was working with Ivan. After two or three days into *Magnetic Monster,* Ivan was very unhappy with the dailies, and one day he called me and said, "Come on down to the sound stage." I said, "I can't—if I come down, you won't have your dailies on time." He said, "To hell with the dailies—come down to the stage." So I jumped on a bicycle and went down to the stage. Here was Richard Carlson, Ivan Tors, the cameraman and Harry Redmond, the special effects man—standing around, doing nothing! The script supervisor, a charming lady by the name of Mary Whitlock Gibsone, said, "They want you to take over the picture." I said, *"What?!* I'm not a director, I'm a film editor!" And she said, "This picture uses *so* much stock footage from the German film [*Gold,* 1934] we have, and you know *exactly* how everything must go together"—and Curt couldn't understand it. Ivan came over and said, "Don't worry, I've called the Directors Guild, you're in the Guild, take over." So *[laughs],* I was called upon to instantly become a director! I went over to the cameraman, asked him what was being shot, he told me and I said, "Well, that's not the way to do that, let's do that *this* way, and *this* matches *this"*—I didn't even have to *look* at the stock film, I knew it so well. And I directed the picture.

Speaking of Andrew Marton: When I took over this picture, "Bundy" said to United Artists, "Don't worry about the new director, because if he doesn't do it well, I will break my contract at MGM and *I* will take over the picture. That's how much faith I have in Herbie." And that's how I became a director.

Now, what exactly was the problem with Siodmak?

The problem with Siodmak occurred on the third day of shooting. He had shot some interior elevator sequences with Richard Carlson and King Donovan, and these intimate shots felt like they were shot in a barn — he used the wrong lens, he was too far away and so on. Scenes weren't playing, the man was falling behind schedule — he was *lost* somehow, I don't know what happened. That's when Ivan yanked me out of the cutting room, fired Siodmak and gave me the picture to direct.

As you can readily imagine, it was difficult to plot out the scenes at night that you were going to shoot the next day — I am a firm believer in production preplanning, which I had taught at U.S.C. for years. I would plan and come in and shoot, and then I also had to edit the film at night — so it was a real chore. However, the day after we finished, we showed what is known as a rough cut, and in fear and trepidation I ran the film with Ivan Tors and Richard Carlson, who was a partner in the project. I kept slinking down in the seat saying to myself, "Well, I gotta fix *that*," and "I gotta speed *that* up," and "That's not a good match." But when the lights came on, Carlson and Tors got up and *applauded,* and thought I had done an excellent job. They were both very happy.

Now, the upshot of this story is, I tried to get a poster from this movie recently, it was sent to me by a friend in New York, and it has Curt Siodmak's name on it as director. That was my first picture, and my name is on the film as director and film editor. And apparently no one bothered to tell United Artists — or if they did, it didn't drift down. The poster went out with Curt's name on it — which is to this day galling me. *I* directed that picture...!

I hate to be the one to tell you after so many years, but you don't receive screen credit as director. The only time your name appears is as editorial supervisor.

I just don't understand! I remember ordering — I *think* I remember ordering! — my name on it as director. However, it could be there was a legal shenanigan pulled by Siodmak against Tors, I don't know. I know I was a member of the Directors Guild, and if anything we should have had co-credit. But if I recall correctly, he only shot three days on that film, and I had to redo a lot of the stuff that he did. There was very little left that he had done; in fact, if I am right, there can't be more than six scenes that he shot.

Mr. Siodmak took the credit for directing Magnetic Monster *when we spoke with him.*

I did just about all of that movie; I don't know why he claims he directed the picture because he didn't shoot one-tenth of it.

Was the documentary flavor and the extensive location photography on Magnetic Monster *Ivan Tors' idea?*
I did all the exteriors—this was my idea, *not* a Tor-ism. We were short on the movie, and we decided to go out and get some reality. I went out with a camera crew and shot all this stuff. When Richard Carlson went to work at the Office of Scientific Investigation, that was shot at the McCullough Plant at the Los Angeles Airport. I just walked up to the door and asked them if we could shoot in there, they said certainly, and we shot it right inside that place.

How did you like working with Richard Carlson?
Carlson was a good friend of Ivan's. He was an actor with a photographic mind—he would merely look at a script, ask you what it was about, and then learn the lines that you wanted put on film immediately. He was a very pleasant man to work with.

What was he like as a director on Riders to the Stars?
He was very capable. Carlson was originally brought out to Hollywood by David Selznick as a writer, became an actor, was very astute as a writer, very astute as a director, and knew quite a bit about editing. We got along like two peas in a pod; in fact, when he later did the TV series *I Led Three Lives* at Ziv, it was he that insisted that I come over there and take over the series because he felt that he and I were most compatible. Carlson directed *Riders to the Stars*—with my assistance—and I edited and was associate producer on that picture. We went to the U.S.C. Centrifugal Force Department, and we actually photographed Bill Lundigan in a centrifuge and spun him around and got the effects that we wanted from him. I did that directing, by the way.

Your next film for Tors was Gog *with Richard Egan.*
Right. That was made in 3-D, shot with a magnificent cameraman by the name of Lothrop Worth, who I still see today. We had two cameras running simultaneously, through optics, to give it the 3-D effect which you saw when you put on the special glasses. Well, the funny part about it is, *I* can't see 3-D because I have monocular vision. So I had to rely on a Dr. Gunzburg, who was technical assistant. He guided me through this thing, and we had at that time one of the best 3-D versions that could be shot because we used it for effect and did it so it wouldn't hurt the eyes of the audience. And I'll never forget going to the preview of that picture, when Gog fired his arm of fire out into the audience and everybody screamed—and it didn't affect *me* at all!

All three of your sci-fi features for Tors were intriguing and sometimes exciting, but were belabored by talky scripts and a heavy emphasis on "science fact."

Scientist John Wengraf struggles in the neck-breaking grip of *Gog*.

That was another Tor-ism. Tors had a great intrigue for *The Scientific American* magazine, he became very over-talky in what he wanted, and you were stuck with that. The key was to try to find a way around the original talkativeness—that was *deadly*—that was written into the scripts, and you would have to fight Ivan a bit on how you wanted to rewrite those scenes. He rarely allowed us to rewrite, but when we did he went along pretty much. I completely rewrote *Battle Taxi* [1955] with a friend of mine, Richard Taylor. It looked so much like a documentary and a hurrah-hurrah for the Air Force Rescue Service that we didn't think it would make an entertaining film, and so we inserted where we could things that made it a dramatic film. We tried to do the same with *The Magnetic Monster*, *Riders to the Stars* and *Gog*—in fact, Taylor and I did a tremendous rewrite on *Gog*, and Ivan finally agreed that if we did certain things certain ways, he would go along. But he wanted that "science fact" *slammed* into the pictures, and that's the way we had to do it. He was in love with scientific facts.

The second half of Gog *is terrifically fast-paced, in contrast to the first half and to the other Tors pictures.*

We felt that *Gog* was bogging down, and I just took the bull by the horns and edited that picture a different way than was originally intended and made it work.

How were the twin robots, Gog and Magog, operated?

The robots were operated by a midget named Billy Curtis—he got inside, and was able to turn them, walk around, move the arms about and fire the acetylene torch which was in one arm. Billy was inside of those damn robots until I thought the guy would die!

We had a terrible accident in these two films, *Riders* and *Gog,* with a brilliant man—an optical engineer, I think he was—by the name of Maxwell Smith, who in making some of the special effects for *Riders to the Stars* had an implosion at his home, due to a leaky oxygen or hydrogen tank in his living room, that blew off his right arm and cut a hole in his left leg. He did recover—we all ran out and gave blood. Ivan leaned very heavily on Max and Harry Redmond. Harry was into explosive effects, whereas Maxwell was into making gadgetry work so that we could photograph it.

Do you remember your budget and shooting schedule on Gog?

I think the budget was two hundred and fifty or three hundred thousand dollars, which was *nothing*—especially shooting 3-D with two cameras running all the time—and it was up to me to save money and come in *under* budget because Carlson had gone over budget on *Riders* and we wanted to get even. The shooting schedule I really don't recall, it was probably no more than fifteen days because in those days we had to shoot extremely fast. By knowing exactly what was needed in the cutting room, I would not waste a lot of film. However, I do remember one incident when an operative cameraman left the switch on in the camera and we went to lunch, and he ran out eight or nine hundred feet of film in each magazine, which was sixteen or eighteen hundred feet of color down the drain.

Why did Carlson go over budget on Riders to the Stars?

Carlson went over because he was trying to *act* in that picture and *direct* it and *rewrite* it and so on. Also, he was not sticking to planning. He was into color and into perhaps a larger production than he expected, he needed help and he asked me—he said, "Would you come down and direct the scenes that I'm in?" I did; I co-directed with him and enjoyed it very much. I liked Dick quite a lot.

Since space mirrors are being considered for use as part of President Reagan's "Star Wars" antimissile system, it's interesting to find them an integral part of the story of Gog.

The idea of using space mirrors was Ivan's. As I said, Ivan was into the *Scientific American* magazines, and he got a lot of these ideas out of there. Ivan was a darn intelligent writer—I didn't like the *words* he used, but his ideas were always very, very good.

Did you prefer Gog's *working title,* Space Station, U.S.A.?

You know, that's something I don't even remember! I think today it would have been a better title than *Gog,* but at the time I think *Gog* was good because it was fascinating and intriguing, and referred to Gog and Magog in the Bible.

What was it like working with a cast that included Richard Egan, Constance Dowling [Mrs. Ivan Tors] and Herbert Marshall?

I must say that Richard Egan was a pleasure to work with. He was, I would say, at the height of his career at the time—he was about to get a contract at Fox, if I remember right—and he was a really good guy. Gig Young was up for this part, and I felt that Egan was right and Gig Young was wrong. Right or wrong, I met with Gig, had a long talk with him and convinced him that this picture was not for him. Constance Dowling I loved dearly, she was a sweet, lovely woman—probably not the finest actress in the world, but very competent, easy to get along with. Because she was Mrs. Tors made no difference; she was just a member of the cast, and never pulled any rank or anything. Herbert Marshall was at that time probably one of the nicest—and *biggest*—actors I had met to date. Marshall had a bad leg; I believe he had it amputated in the war, around the knee. And it pained him terribly. If you study the film, you can see his slight limp. He came to me one afternoon, on the side, and said, "Herb, is my limping too obvious? Is it bad for the scene?" And I blurted out, like a jerk, "Oh, no, no, it's a good gimmick." And he looked at me and said, "Gimmick? With this pain, I'd hardly call it a gimmick." I will never forget that as long as I live. I felt terrible, I apologized, and he, being the charming Englishman that he was, understood. I was terribly hurt when he passed away.

There was one thing I particularly liked about this cast: They did *what* I asked them to do, *when* I asked them to do it and *how* I asked them to do it. We did a lot of moves: I was on a boom, I moved around on a crab dolly so that I would get motion into this film. I remember that I had a magnificent art director whom I had stolen from MGM, William Ferrari. Despite the fact that I was busy editing *Riders and* tackling *this* one, Bill and I worked out an idea of mine about color being used to emphasize the mood of a scene. I did a lot of research at U.C.L.A. about the impact of certain colors on the emotions. Bill and I worked out the earthy colors in certain scenes, the blue in the cold scenes, and reds and oranges in the warm scenes. And we were very clever in devising ways of cutting costs on sets, and making the same eighteen- or twenty-foot passageway work for different places in the movie. He was very clever at this, a fine art director.

Why did you edit The Magnetic Monster, Gog *and, later,* The Crawling Hand, *in addition to directing?*

At that time I felt that I could edit what *I* wanted the way *I* wanted it faster, and would therefore save money and time. Having come from the cutting room, I guess I couldn't shake loose the fun of being at a Moviola and making things work.

After making these Tors films, you spent several years working at Ziv-TV directing Science Fiction Theatre *and many other shows.*

Ivan Tors also came to Ziv through Richard Carlson; he ended up on *Science Fiction Theatre*, and I worked with Ivan on many of those. I enjoyed working on that show with actors like Victor Jory, Gene Barry, Gene Lockhart and others that the studio would hire because it was a prestige series. But eventually Ivan came to resent the fact that I would want to rewrite certain things in order to make them work better. There was really no argument between us, but he resented a little bit and I was moved off *Science Fiction Theatre* onto other series—as well as doing one of those every once in a while.

Ziv, for your information, was the name of a man—it was a Midwest firm and a man by the name of [Frederic W.] Ziv was the head of it. They were big in radio, and got into TV. He had people running the outfit that didn't know anything about the picture business—one was a mattress salesman! It was very, very tough teaching these people how to make films, because they had their own ideas. I did an unbelievable number of shows over there—*I Led Three Lives, Favorite Story, Meet Corliss Archer, Men of Annapolis, Highway Patrol, Harbor Command, Dr. Christian*, one after another. I enjoyed working over there except for the fact that the people we were working for really did not have any motion picture knowledge. It was very difficult fighting them when you knew they were wrong but they insisted things be done their way. It was like banging your head against the wall.

How did you end up working for Herman Cohen?

The way I got to work with Cohen is very interesting. Herman was on the Ziv lot at the time we were doing all these television shows. He would come down, unbeknownst to me—I didn't know who he was!—and he would watch me shoot. And he would see how fast we were going—we were always on budget, always or most of the time ahead of schedule. He came to me one day and asked me if I would be interested in doing a feature with him. I said I had a vacation coming from Ziv, I was sure I could get time off and I would be thrilled to do his picture. And that was *I Was a Teenage Frankenstein*.

What did you make of Cohen at the time?

I thought Herman was a strange bug—he had an ego that knew no end. He wanted things *his* way and *that's* the way he wanted them, and he wanted a director that would do things his way. He was a very wishy-washy guy who tried to be very pontific, which he couldn't be. He had no guts. I had very little respect for him and I guess he knew this. I remember that on *Teenage Frankenstein* we were shooting at two or three o'clock in the morning in a place called Hancock Park, which is a high-class neighborhood of homes; this Frankenstein Monster was running around in the backyards, and we were hauling cable and so on. I remember Herman and I had a terrible fight over something, I don't remember what it was, and I told him where he could go

Adolescent monster Gary Conway contributes a cultural interlude to Strock's *I Was a Teenage Frankenstein*.

and what he could do with his picture, and I would quit. And everybody on the crew was behind me, they *wanted* me to quit. But when it got down to the nitty-gritty, I just felt it was the wrong thing to do and it would be spread all over town that I walked off a film, and I stuck with it. But from that day on Herman and I did not get along too well. It was strange, however, that when he wanted to do *Blood of Dracula* and *How to Make a Monster* he took me to lunch and we walked around the block and he told me of *my* shortcomings and he told me about *my* attitude, and would I want to do the pictures? It was so strange that he would even come to me! I said, yeah, I'd do the pictures, because I wanted to do some more features and get away from the sausage-grinding-out of those hundreds of Ziv television shows I was doing. We made a deal, at a little better money, and he was easier to get along with on these two.

Did you contribute anything to Cohen's scripts for these pictures?

I would receive the scripts, practically finished, and I would say, "These stink," "These are bad," "This should be done *this* way" or "This should be done *that* way"—and we would work it out together. I tried awfully hard to correct a lot of things. You find that a writer, especially of this caliber on these pictures, really doesn't read the dialogue out loud, and you have to do that because actors have to speak the lines and they have to mean something. Sometimes alliteration or sentences that are backwards are very difficult for an actor to remember, and I would rewrite those. There was never any argument with Herman about rewriting dialogue, but restructuring was a real problem. The script supervisor was the same one I had on *The Magnetic Monster*, Mary Whitlock Gibsone, and she had broken the script down and tried to explain to Herman some of the mistakes. I remember having violent arguments with Herman over story points, over illogical things in the script, over time warps that were absolutely ridiculous—you didn't know where you were or when this was supposed to happen or how it happened. And he just didn't want to listen, till finally Mary and I got together and rewrote and did things that we thought *had* to be done. After much arguing, Herman finally accepted.

Your three Cohen films, as well as quite a few Cohen films you did not direct, are all very similar in plot structure. Was Cohen helping to write these scripts, or was this pattern something he insisted his screenwriters perpetuate?

Most of these plots and basic storylines came from Herman, as I remember. I believe that he did contribute to the screenplays, corny as they were—and now that you look back at them, they were really thin. And you're right, they *were* alike—I think he insisted that the screenwriter do this, otherwise he wouldn't work with him!

The major flaw in Teenage Frankenstein *is its heavy-handed emphasis on the repulsive aspects of the story.*

All this was done for Cohen's shock value, and I tried to get things done a little differently. I tried to do things in a tasteful way. I remember when we had Whit Bissell use the electric saw to cut off the leg, what I did was use the *sound* of the saw hitting the bone and you *felt* that it went through the bone—you never saw it. And then we lifted this phony leg through the scene. I remember when the censors ran this picture, they were furious. I had to run it again and explain to them that my effect was great—they loved the effect—but I did *not* show the leg being cut off, which they insisted I did.

What about your stars Whit Bissell and Gary Conway?

I probably used Whit in more different films than anyone else in town.

He was a very capable actor, always knew his lines, always on time—he was "Old Mr. Reliable," and he could play almost anything you wanted him to. Gary Conway was not that great an actor but he was a nice kid—a little sticky at times, but I had no real basic problem.

What prompted you to end Teenage Frankenstein *and* How to Make a Monster *with color sequences?*

Herman couldn't afford to do these pictures in color, so we did them in black-and-white and then for shock value made the last reel in color. This was a Cohen-ism, if you would want to coin a term.

What was it like working with a largely teenage cast in Blood of Dracula?

The casts in all these Cohen pictures were pretty untrained, untried—some of them had never done things before, others had made a few pictures, but they were easy enough to get along with. The only problem was, you never had enough time to really rehearse and get things the way you would like to have them. I remember when I was doing these pictures, my kids were ashamed of me, they felt I was pandering. I said, "Look, we've got to eat—they're fun to do and I don't mind." *Now* they're clamoring for me to collect the posters of these films, which I have been able to do.

Do you recall anything about Sandra Harrison, who played the teenage vampiress?

I found Sandra in readings, and I tried to get her involved in doing this show because she and I had a rapport—there was sympatico between us. But Herman didn't want her. At *all.* We read many, many other people until I finally convinced him that I wanted Sandra to do it. I think she is in New York now, doing some television commercials or something. In fact, she called me a few years ago and we had a few minutes together. Louise Lewis, who played the villainess, did a lot of work in AIP pictures, and she was married, if I remember right, to Robert H. Harris, who was also in many of these pictures. She was a very good actress. I do believe she is still alive, but I don't think she's active in the industry.

Where did the idea for How to Make a Monster *come from?*

It was either Cohen's idea, or AIP's, to combine Teenage Frankenstein and Teenage Werewolf in *How to Make a Monster.* I don't know where this story came from, but at that time we were told by many people, including a man, very famous in the business, Robert Lippert, that pictures about pictures don't make money. And I had fear and trepidation in doing this thing. I think the crew and the cast enjoyed it more than I did—it was a tough one to do.

Was Michael Landon offered the opportunity to repeat his Teenage Werewolf role?

Teenage Frankenstein (Gary Conway) grapples with Teenage Werewolf (Gary Clarke) in this posed shot from Strock's *How to Make a Monster*.

I don't think Landon was offered the opportunity because I don't know whether Herman and he got along that well. Also, I think Landon had already made too much of a name for himself and Herman couldn't afford him. Gary Clarke replaced him — not a bad kid. I thought Robert H. Harris, who passed away recently, was a little heavy-handed, a little overdone, and we had to constantly sit on him to try to pull him down. He had a tendency to run away with the lines.

Where were the studio exteriors photographed?

I think they were shot right on the Ziv lot. Because I know Cohen wouldn't let us go anywhere—we had no money for location shooting—I'm pretty sure it was shot right there—that's the old Educational Studios on Santa Monica Boulevard, which by the way is now a market.

It's always seemed to us that pictures about pictures must be especially fun to do.

How to Make a Monster was not that enjoyable because I had a lot of interference from Herman; he was always hanging around and watching what we were doing, making sure it was what he wanted. On the other pictures he was busy preparing these, so therefore he didn't interfere as much. This was one of the last ones, and he had more time to hang around. I do remember that he hired a cameraman who was related, I believe, to the assistant director. The cameraman and I just couldn't seem to hit it off. I would say to him, "I want to do the following shot..." and I would walk away *knowing* it could be done. Then in a few minutes I'd come back and see I'd have a completely different setup, and he would tell me that what I wanted to do wouldn't work. I resented this, and I pleaded with Herman to replace him. He was about ready to, because he was unhappy with some of the dailies, but he decided it was dangerous and he stuck with him.

I remember we had a fire scene. The wax masks were on a wall with these curtains, and when the special effects man ignited the pilot before the camera was running, the curtains caught on fire. We had the fire department standing by but I wouldn't let them put it out. I grabbed a camera, turned it on, yelled to another cameraman to grab the other camera, and we photographed part of the wax melting. *Then* we had the firemen put it out, and I was able to use these pieces later on. That was quite a mess.

Of your three films for Cohen, do you have a favorite?

No, I don't; I never liked any of them, really. *Teenage Frankenstein* was the most fun to work on because I had Lothrop Worth as a cameraman, and enjoyed that. I think *Blood of Dracula* has been listed in somebody's book as probably the worst Dracula film ever made—which is *[sarcastically]* a great honor.

Have you worked with Herman Cohen since?

After these pictures, I *have* talked to him but I've never been able to work with him—nor would I want to work with him, I don't believe.

About that same time you worked on a TV series called The Veil, *with Boris Karloff.*

The Veil was originated by Hal Roach, Jr., and it was done at Hal Roach Studios. I remember we had a lot of fun; I started out editing these, and then finally I wound up directing them. Karloff played a wide variety of magnificent roles—in one episode he would play a policeman from India, in the next one a British bobby, in the next a maharajah, then a doctor, then a lawyer and so on. This man was absolutely sensational. He was as easy to work with as anyone I've ever known, he was like putty in your hands. He would always know his lines; he knew everybody *else's* lines. I would tell him not to show up until 10:00, to take it easy—he was no spring chicken—but he would be there, ready to be in makeup at 8:30 in the morning no matter what I told him. He would stay after I told him he was finished—I tried to finish with him earlier in the afternoon so he could get some sleep, but he would stay. I'd say, "Don't *worry* about it; when I'm doing the other man's close-ups, I'll play your part off-camera and he can react to me." But Karloff felt it was much more charming if *he* stayed and *he* did the part, and the actor could get the proper reaction from *his* eyes. I mean, they don't come like this anymore. He and Ed Wynn were the two most professional people I have ever worked with. I was very, very sorry to see that series end. After that we went to San Diego and did the pilot for a show called *Mann of Action* with John Ireland, and right after that Hal Roach, Jr., got in trouble—the studio owed money, they got tied up with the Mafia and were sold, and all the pictures went down the drain.

Shortly after that you got involved on the Swedish-made horror TV series No. 13 Demon Street.

That brings back horrible memories. This was done for a company called Herts-Lion International, which has gone bankrupt. They had a Swedish motion picture studio, Nordisktonfilm, making this series in Sweden, with Curt Siodmak's scripts and Curt directing. The first five or six came back, and I was called by a Kenneth Herts, who was the president of Herts-Lion, to come and look at them. I ran these quote-horror-unquote pictures at home and my kids were roaring with laughter all over the floor over this corny, junk film that was supposed to be exciting horror films. When I went back to Kenneth I told him these were probably the worst scripts, the worst acting, the worst assembly of anything I had ever seen in my life. I never could understand Curt Siodmak; I always thought he was a sensible man but everything I've ever seen him do has been rather pedantic and ill-advised. It was like he just didn't know what he was doing. Ken insisted that I go to Sweden and remake them—so once again in my life I am replacing Curt Siodmak. Ken had already sent one editor over there to try to straighten them out, but the Swedes did not react pleasantly to him—he was a miserable, arrogant son of a bitch. The Swedes were putting up all the money so it was dangerous, but I went.

I met with a Mr. Hammerbaek, who ran the company, and the production manager at a club over there. At first Hammerbaek pretended that he didn't speak English—he had had it with Ken Herts and also with Curt, and I think he had it in his craw to get even with the Americans. It seems the American side was constantly blaming *them* for everything that was wrong with the series, but there was nothing wrong other than the screenplay and the direction. I noticed when I was talking, there was a light in Hammerbaek's eyes, so I *knew* that this man understood English. But he was waiting to find out where I was coming from before he would level with me. I assured Hammerbaek through the production manager—the production manager interpreted until Hammerbaek started to speak English—that they were not at fault, it was strictly a matter of stupid interpretation, a drunken Chaney, Jr., and all that crap. So finally Hammerbaek decided that I knew what I was doing, and he gave me carte blanche. He put up a lot more money, we reshot, we put some exteriors and action in, put a live score in and so on. I remade four of the messes that Siodmak left.

Did you work with Chaney, Jr., in Sweden?

No, I did not have Chaney to work with over there. When I got back, Ken called me and said that he wanted to put some of these episodes together into this *Devil's Messenger* film. We took three of the shows and strung them together with the Hell sequence, which I wrote. We had what I would call a half-assed crew—everything was done for spit and chewing gum. It was no fun—we rented a cheap stage and built this Hell set and played this stupid movie, and then I had to reedit and put it all together. Herts merely took the episodes and created a feature film and reaped all the money with no expense, the Swedes having paid 99 percent of the cost. I'm *still* owed about $10,000 on that picture which I have never seen to this day.

Herts changed his name and opened up a new company, and several years ago he conned me into believing he had found God and that he was a changed man. He had a half-baked story about a monster in Colombia and he wanted me to direct this picture *[Monstroid]* if I would do it for the expenses involved plus the trip to Colombia with my wife and daughter. My wife would be in charge of wardrobe, my daughter the script supervisor. I acquiesced, figuring it would never get off the ground. When it *did*, I was conned again into letting him use half of my building for his office. We were going to shoot in 35mm color and we were going to use my cameraman. I completely wrote the script—all he had was a storyline that was just terrible. I wrote the whole movie with a friend of mine and registered it with the Writers Guild. All of a sudden we're *not* going to Colombia, we're going to New Mexico, because I didn't realize Herts had trouble with the Colombian government—he had ordered a monster built down there at a cost of $10,000-plus, and had never paid for it.

Every location that he picked was absolutely unusable. My production manager, the cameraman and I picked all new locations with the help of the New Mexico Film Bureau. Now came casting. For our star we got Jim Mitchum, who sounded and looked like his father but . . . is problems. All of a sudden, everything was downgraded. Herts doesn't want to take my cameraman, he doesn't want to take my production manager — they cost too much money. Also, we're going to shoot in 16mm. I should have *walked*. I didn't. Actors came out of sewers. The word "actor" is actually a misnomer — these were human beings that couldn't spit and walk at the same time. We didn't have the time to teach them to act, we had a cameraman who had his own ideas, we had no one on the crew we could rely on. We shot this miserable mess for almost a month. I came back, put it in a rough cut, and then Herts and I had an argument and he had an argument with some of his backers. I've never seen a dime. To this day I have not been able to collect a penny of the $60,000 for the screenplay, the editing and the direction. *This* was the same guy that did *The Devil's Messenger*.

Why does he get screen credit for direction on Monstroid?
That is also a viable lawsuit, but I don't want to get into that because I don't *want* credit on it! The picture doesn't make any sense at all because he skipped story points — this guy has absolutely no story sense, no artistic integrity.

How did you get involved on The Crawling Hand?
The Crawling Hand also came to me through this Kenneth Herts. A man by the name of Joe Robertson had brought him a script, a science fiction/horror picture, and Herts asked me if I would read it. It was just awful. Some friends of mine and I had written this *Crawling Hand* a couple of years before, and it was very visual in the writing. I said to Robertson, "Let me show you how it should be written." So Robertson looked at our script for *The Crawling Hand,* and said that the guy he had putting up the money would put up money for *this*. The budget would be $100,000, it would be in black-and-white, and he wanted me to direct it. I made a deal with the writers and we went into production. Joe Robertson was the kind of producer that left you alone — he never bothered you, you did what you wanted. In fact, he was trying to *help* and would do things that would cost you money, like taking the pieces of film left over at the end of the shooting and sending them to the lab for processing when there's nothing on them! But he was a very charming guy and I know him today — he's in the soft-porn business at the moment.

As I told you, the budget was $100,000, it came in for ninety-eight some-odd. If I remember right, that picture was shot completely on location — we never once set foot in a studio. Even the computer banks and stuff were shot at the U.S.C. Computer Division Center. It *is* a minor film, it was made for peanuts, as I said, but it was a lot of fun to do.

Were you satisfied with the performance of your star, Rod Lauren?
I was not. I felt that Rod was a one-dimensional actor with a one-octave range, and I like larger ranges between people, to get highs and lows. Also,

Strock poses with actress Sirry Steffen during a break in the filming of *The Crawling Hand*.

we had this Miss Ireland, Sirry Steffen, in the lead—she wasn't much of an actress, but she was a doll to look at. We had nude scenes to do which Sirry Steffen didn't want to do. She would only do it if *I* put the body makeup on her; she trusted me implicitly—because I'm a prude, I guess. We shot the scene, it was never used. I found it rather difficult to maneuver these people. Mechanically, it wasn't too bad, I was able to stage things the way I had envisioned them in writing the script, but I found that interpretation and subtleties were missing because the actors really didn't have the experience.

Conversely, your supporting cast included a large number of screen veterans.

We just felt we could get these people, who had some sort of a pseudo-name which would help the picture, for less money because they weren't working, and that's exactly what happened. I had worked with Richard Arlen in some of the science pictures that Ivan was doing at Ziv; a very good actor, very good friend. Alan Hale was another actor I had worked with before; also Ross Elliott, Tristram Coffin, Syd Saylor and Arline Judge, whom I liked very much. We got them all together for very little money and made this picture. Another one of my mistakes: I could have had Burt Reynolds, who read for a part, but I didn't think Burt was good enough; at that time, he was a stuntman. So we wound up with Kent Taylor, who was a bit of a problem. He was never on time and he never knew his lines.

It's hard to picture Burt Reynolds in the part played by Kent Taylor. Was the role rewritten?

No, it was the way Taylor played it. We changed a little bit of it because he couldn't remember some of the long dialogue. Apparently he hadn't worked in a long time and was out of practice. He wasn't a bad egg, but he didn't have the professional attitude of getting in there and getting the job done. He was not showing up on time; begging off at lunchtime to go somewhere, promising to be back in an hour and not coming back for three or four hours, things like that. It wasn't a drinking problem—I don't know what he was doing or who he was seeing, but he was never on time.

Who designed the mechanical crawling hand, and how was it activated?

The mechanical hand was designed by myself and Charlie Duncan, an old-time special effects and powder man. He and I worked out the mechanical hand, which had little prongs in its fingers and a battery-driven motor on wheels. We just put a torn sleeve on it. Of course we couldn't make this hand crawl up stairs and up bannisters, and at times it would get stuck. So I merely donned a glove and it was my hand that did the actual crawling in those situations.

Have you been involved on any other horror or science fiction film projects in recent years?

A few years ago I took over a picture with Richard Benjamin, Lana Turner and Teri Garr called *Witches' Brew,* which a director by the name of Richard Shorr had started. He and his partner Donna Ashbrook got the movie with an NBC show-of-the-week commitment and started to make the picture. Apparently they didn't get along too well; Shorr was taken off the movie and I was asked to complete it. I shot about a week, wrote and redirected many scenes, and edited the picture. It was a lot of fun working with Lana Turner and Benjamin and Teri, who are all very, very capable. Lana was of course full of fear and trepidation *against* Shorr; he berated her terribly. He would scream at me about certain things and I finally just barred him from the cutting room once he was taken off the movie. It *is* a good picture, it cost about six or seven hundred thousand dollars, and it was a lot of fun.

My acting days are behind me now. I saw Audrey Hepburn on TV the other night, and talking about her career she said, "I did my thing. Let the kids do it now." And that's how I feel. Thank God I don't have that burning desire that some people really have — I think that'd be horrible to live with.... My Emmys and my Oscars are my children, and I like it that way.

Gloria Talbott

IF THERE'S A LESSON to be learned from the sci-fi films of actress Gloria Talbott, it's just that you can never be too careful in picking your friends. She was the girlfriend of a rampaging one-eyed giant in *The Cyclops,* legal ward of a werewolf in *Daughter of Dr. Jekyll,* bride of an alien invader in *I Married a Monster from Outer Space* and romantic rival of an ageless murderess in *The Leech Woman.* But what the onscreen Gloria Talbott apparently lacked in discriminating judgment, the real-life one compensates for with exuberant charm and earthy wit.

Gloria Talbott was born in the Los Angeles suburb of Glendale, a city co-founded by her great-great-grandfather. Growing up in the shadows of the Hollywood studios, her interests inevitably turned to acting, with the result that she participated in school plays and landed small parts in such films as *Maytime* (1937), *Sweet and Lowdown* (1943) and *A Tree Grows in Brooklyn* (1945). After leaving school she started her own dramatic group and played "arena"-style shows at various clubs.

After a three-year hiatus (marriage, motherhood and subsequent divorce), Talbott resumed her career, working extensively in both television and films. A showy "sweet young thing" role in Paramount's *We're No Angels* (1955) failed to pave the way to top stardom, and the talented actress soon found herself a fixture in B-grade Westerns and horror thrillers. Although long retired from the acting profession, Gloria Talbott remains a '50s favorite for sci-fi fans.

How did you become involved on The Cyclops?

I think I was just simply sent the script, they met my price, and I was *in* — although I had no idea what I was in *for!* I remember that the first day of shooting was on Alvera Street, in the oldest building in Los Angeles, where we did the scene where I'm talking with the Mexican governor. Just seconds before we were going to start, Bert I. Gordon said to me, "Gloria, I want to ask you something. I saw *We're No Angels.* I just don't understand how you let Peter Ustinov and Aldo Ray so overpower you in that picture. You came off looking like a little weakling compared to their performances." I was stunned. I said, "Are you *serious?* I was playing a little girl! A sweet little girl who fainted a lot! What in the world are you *talking* about?" And he said, "Well, I just don't know why an actress would allow them to take the scenes away from her."

To this day I don't know if he just wanted me angry in that one scene — but if he did, he did a very good job! I was absolutely infuriated, and I stayed mad at him throughout the rest of the picture because I thought that was one of the dumbest things I'd ever heard. You'll remember that in that first scene my character is agitated? Well, it's *not* all acting! I was mad as hell that first day — I came very close to crying, I wanted to quit. I told Tom Drake about it — I liked him enough to confide in him that Bert Gordon had already gotten me to the point where I was ready to puke — and he said, "Oh, the hell with him, Gloria. Forget that crap and just say the lines." Thank goodness he had

Previous page: Gloria Talbott and Tom Tryon recoil from the alien menace in *I Married a Monster from Outer Space.*

Gloria Talbott fans got a double dose of their favorite leading lady when Allied Artists co-billed *The Cyclops* with *Daughter of Dr. Jekyll* in 1957.

that attitude, because that helped me a lot. I just tried to stay away from Bert Gordon as much as I could.

What kind of a director was Gordon?
 He was like a man possessed because he did have to get it finished quickly; this was all done in five or six days. But he certainly had it well organized — and I'm sure that his wife had a hell of a lot to do with that. His wife was so sweet — she was doing the script supervising, the wardrobe, making cookies, *everything* — and he was so *mean* to her, like she was "the help." He had a disregard for actresses, I do believe — or maybe females in general. He just wasn't a particularly pleasant person.

Gloria Talbott, James Craig and Tom Drake in *The Cyclops*.

How did you get along with co-stars James Craig and Lon Chaney, Jr.?

James Craig was an enigma to me. He never once said, "How do you do, Gloria?" or "My name's Craig" — he would say his lines and go away. And it wasn't just *me* — he was that way. So we had absolutely no rapport. I don't know whether he was having terrible personal problems or what, but he would do the scene, then just sit down and not talk. He was not cruel or mean, but he didn't want to have very much to do with anybody.

And Lon Chaney?

Lon Chaney was just a dear, sweet man, with such a vulnerability that you wanted to wrap him in cotton and take him home. His mama came up to Bronson Canyon and brought him lunch, which I thought was dear, and brought him an air mattress. They blew it up, and he laid out in the sun and went to sleep on it! I thought that was charming. He was a bear of a man, but kind and sweet. I loved him.

What about Chaney's notorious drinking problem?

Lon Chaney was a darling, darling man — but drunk as a skunk! I don't drink and I've never done drugs, but those things probably hurt a lot of people in the '50s — they were passing out amphetamines in the cafeterias! I remember that all the scenes that took place on the Cessna were shot in a mock-up on a little tiny stage on Melrose that I think Bert Gordon rented for the day. Lon Chaney and Tom Drake were in the two front seats, and James Craig and I were in the back. Well, both Lon and Tom were absolutely *smashed*. James Craig was nipping a little, too, but nothing like what was going on in the front! And in this *h-o-t,* tiny mock-up I was getting blasted from the *fumes!* It was such close quarters and so hot that I was ingesting alcohol through my skin, I was getting absolutely stoned, and by the time we got out of there I was *weaving* *[laughs]!* If you watch that scene, you'll see that every once in a while I look a little sick — well, I *was!* That was a funny piece of business.

Did you come in contact with the actor who played the Cyclops?
Only the time that the boa constrictor almost killed him! I did not know the stuntman; we were all so busy that I didn't even get a chance to watch them apply his makeup. But we were all there at Bronson Canyon, and I was watching them shoot the scene where he fights the snake. Well, the snake did manage to get around the actor, and it started to constrict around his throat and his chest. It got hairy — the actor went down, he was in trouble. And the handler was scared to death. What I think he did was take a stick with a little nail in it, and somehow used it to make the snake let go. There *is* a little bit of it in the film, but I'm not sure how much. That was scary.

Where else besides Bronson Canyon was The Cyclops *shot?*
There was a scene in the jungle that we shot at the Arboretum — James Craig and I are chased by a giant lizard, and we run into a pond. We tried it once, and we kept running on *top* of the pond! And we all realized that there was at least twenty years of *duck shit,* cement-hard, forming a surface that went out a good ten feet. And, I swear to God, they yelled, "Cut out a piece of the duck shit so we can get the actors in!" I actually sat there and watched them bring out a chainsaw and hack out a big area for James Craig and me to wade in, where the duck shit was still floating around in pieces. I'm amazed neither of us got salmonella — I mean, it was horrendous! And I thought to myself *[laughs],* "*This* is glamor? *This* is fame and fortune?" I just wanted to go home...!

Any other recollections on The Cyclops?
One funny thing, when it was premiered. They opened a new theater in Redondo Beach, and the first picture they played was *The Cyclops.* It was a "sneak preview spook show" — they didn't tell the people what the picture was. This theater was huge, and it was packed. I was there, with my agent, and my folks, and my little boy. The film progressed past the point where the Cyclops was seen for the first time; James Craig and I returned to camp, and I said, "I feel sorry for that giant, I pity him, and I don't know why." Beat. Beat. "There's something about his *face...*"

Well *[laughs],* when I was saying it, it made sense to me as an actress — I was seeing my old lover's face somewhere in there. But within the context of the film it was one of the funniest lines I had ever heard in my *life!* The people

Doing what a scream queen does best, Gloria Talbott lets out a yelp in director Edgar G. Ulmer's *Daughter of Dr. Jekyll.*

caught on—it started low, people tittering, and that started a roll. Pretty soon everyone was hysterical, *screaming,* stomping their feet and rolling in the aisles. And for the first time in my life I saw my agent get scared; he whispered to me, "Darling, I think it's time for us to go." He thought they might turn *angry!* And we left the theater while this was still going on! Since then, they have cut it—thank God!—but it was a classic line.

Were you happy with the results on The Cyclops?

I was amazed. There are parts that are corny, but considering the time involved; the amount of locations we went on; how quickly we did it; some of the not-too-reliable actors; and Bert I. Gordon's personality—considering all that, I think it's not bad. I'm not ashamed of the film; and I'm not ashamed of *Daughter of Dr. Jekyll,* either.

What did you enjoy about Daughter?

I felt that it had a good, interesting script; I loved Arthur Shields, I thought he was by far a better actor than his brother, Barry Fitzgerald. He was certainly a wonderful gentleman. And I worked with a *nice* director, Edgar Ulmer—I liked him a lot. He was ... *[laughs]* kind of insane, and I love people who are quirky and funny. He just was easy to work with—he was not a Douglas Sirk, who thinks he can get a performance out of somebody by scaring them to death. He was affable and fun—a pixie, sort of.

Also, I had some good lines in the film, like, "If you love me, you'll kill me"—I really *felt* it, and I can still make myself cry when I watch that scene. And I thought that the cameraman did wonders with my face. If you don't light my face just right, I look *funny*. Well, this man was indeed a photographer, and I was vain enough to be very happy with the way I looked in the film. And, again, we did it in something like five to seven days—not on a stage, but in a house. It was on Sixth Street, near Hancock Park, where there are great, *wonderful* old mansions; it must have been the Beverly Hills of seventy years ago. That house was fascinating—I'd never seen a kitchen like that, never seen a dumbwaiter, never seen such a library or such a glorious staircase. It was a real experience.

The first time we met, you told us about a "dumb mistake" you spotted in Daughter.

In the scene where I come down for breakfast, in the background is a lace curtain. If you look closely, you're going to see 1956 Chevys, Fords, etc., going by on Sixth Street—and since John Agar and I drove up to the house in an old Stutz Bearcat to establish the period, these new cars flying by spoiled the whole mood. I didn't pick up on it, either, as we were shooting, and it just drives me insane whenever I watch it. It *was* a dumb mistake.

What do you remember about working with Agar?

John was another enigma to me; I can honestly say that John didn't seem to have much personality. He certainly was not gruff or mean, or standoffish, like James Craig was on *The Cyclops,* but he would do his scene and then just go sit.

Why did a stand-in take your place in the nightmare scene?

Quite frankly, I never gave it any thought. I *think* that they didn't believe that I could turn into that rather sexy, demonic-looking creature; that would have taken a lot of makeup and a lot more time. They did that scene after I was gone, and whoever that was that they brought in was wonderful.

And overall you're pleased with the way the picture came out?

As a matter of fact, I was amazingly surprised at it. I didn't think it was going to be anything—it was another one of those "wham-bam-thank-you-ma'am" shoots—and yet it turned out to have a lot more content that I might have hoped.

I Married a Monster from Outer Space *gave you your most dramatic sci-fi role. How did you enjoy the experience?*

I loved working at Paramount, I was very much at home there; the money was terrific; and I did like the role, although in a sense it really was written one-dimensional. I tried my best to put some dimensions into her. I think there could have been more of a character development, and I was anxious to play with it. One scene I liked was when I was trying to seduce Tom Tryon into bed; I was trying to be flippant and cute, and I was getting *nada*. So there was a change in character there. And there were lots of scenes where I was scared — and I can really play scared. I've been frightened in my life — horribly frightened! When I was a kid I had an older sister who was gorgeous, and the boys would follow her home and peek in our windows. We had six years of peeping toms scratching at our windows, but we were so poor we didn't have a phone to call the police. It was like living in a horror movie — scary as hell!

Did you like working with Tom Tryon?

Tom and I had worked together in two or three *Matinee Theater*s and we liked each other a great deal. I remember a day when we were at Lake Sherwood, which is where we filmed the scene where one of the aliens drowns; we were laying on the grass, between takes, and he was watching this great big plane being refueled in midflight by a smaller one. He must have watched for about fifteen minutes, I looked up finally and started watching, too, and he said *[softly]*, "They just had *sex* — right up in the air...." Well *[laughs]*, he didn't say it to be funny, he was looking at it as a writer. He *is* a writer, of course — he wrote *The Other*, which is still one of the scariest movies I've ever seen. That movie haunts me, I thought it was wonderful. So he was very introspective, very *into* himself, but always professional, always gave 100 percent. One thing I do remember is that Tom didn't like the monster outfits. Originally they had tiny spangly jockstraps for the aliens to wear, and Tom just freaked out when he saw that. He said, "This is ridiculous — it'll look like monster Rockettes!" He was absolutely right, and they did change them.

Gene Fowler, Jr., directed seven pictures, some of them very good [I Married a Monster, I Was a Teenage Werewolf, The Rebel Set], *and then went back into editing.*

Gene Fowler put a *lot* of himself into these pictures; I know that he was worn out at the end of *I Married a Monster*, I could just see it physically. I know he took the picture home with him every night, he slept with the script — it never came out in agitation, but I could see it coming out in tiredness. But I liked doing pictures with Gene, he was a sweetheart, and it was a delight, an actor's dream, to work with him.

So everything went smoothly on I Married a Monster?

I enjoyed the whole experience, except for the first three days. One side of my face was swollen because I had an abscessed tooth, and for a few days, while we were shooting the scenes that took place in the living room, they had to shoot around that. One other thing I remember is that the man who wrote the movie, Louis Vittes, was so *intense*, and so insecure that we weren't going

Talbott's wedding party assembles in 1958's *I Married a Monster from Outer Space*.

to do it right. When we'd be rehearsing a scene he'd sit way back in a corner somewhere, but then just before we were ready to shoot he'd get on the floor directly under the camera. He knew his script inside out, and he would sit there and silently *mouth* every word! And he went absolutely insane if we left out an "a" or a "the"! He was not being unkind, I think he was just scared. But it was driving both Tom and me crazy to have the guy down on the floor saying the lines! Finally I had to go to the producer and ask him if this could be avoided — I didn't want to hurt this fellow's feelings, but it was distracting as hell.

Do you think that the notoriously silly title helped or hurt I Married a Monster?

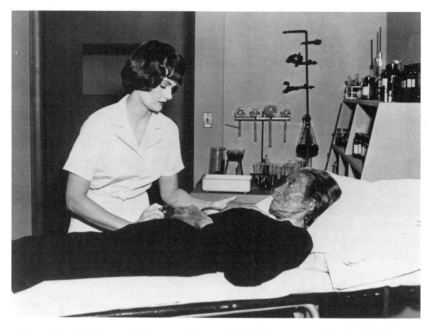

Nurse Gloria Talbott ministers to wizened Estelle Hemsley in *The Leech Woman*.

I think the title *killed* it; I think people went in expecting to see a funny movie. But now that it's so well known, I can't think of a better title—in fact, I believe now that the title has helped make the picture! But, again, at the time I thought it was sad that *I Married a Monster from Outer Space* was our title because I felt it was a better movie than that.

Was your shooting schedule quite a bit longer than on the other sci-fi jobs?

I think we had almost three weeks; compared to *The Cyclops* and *Daughter of Dr. Jekyll* this was a *big* movie *[laughs]*! And it was an enjoyable experience because we were not rushed. We did do a lot in a short period, except this time we ended up with a picture that some people now call a classic. All in all it was an excellent experience.

Can you tell us about working with the cast of The Leech Woman?

Grant Williams was a very interesting fellow—another one of those "inside-himself" people. I would come on the set and he would say, "Oh, God—pure woman!"—and then leave it at that! He was always easy to work with. Phillip Terry was another James Craig—do a scene, go sit in a corner. But the star, Coleen Gray, was wonderful. I remember that as we were getting ready to shoot the fight scene, she said to me, "I'm little, but I *am* strong." Well, about two weeks before I'd had a fight with Steve McQueen in one of his *Wanted: Dead or Alive* episodes—he grabbed me, I tried to get away from him and I really gave him a fight. It was fun because I wanted to see if he could hang onto me—it was a twirling, twisting fight where I actually picked him up on my back at one point and went around in a circle, which he couldn't *believe*. So when Coleen Gray said that, I thought to myself, "Well, if I can almost outdo McQueen, I can sure handle *you*, lady!" But, by God, this little bitty person wasn't kidding! She picked me up, *threw* me in the closet—incredible! But she was very much a lady; I liked her and she was very good to work with.

Did you enjoy the opportunity to turn "heavy" in your last scene?

Yeah, it was fun—although it was kind of weird, because I didn't get much of a chance to work up to it. I mean, it was the least of my challenges. I've got to admit *[laughs]*, I made that picture because I wanted to buy a horse for my son, and *The Leech Woman* got him a really nice horse and saddle!

The way you pull the gun on Coleen Gray, and expect to take her to the airport at gunpoint, really was ludicrous.

I know, the entire time I was holding the gun I was thinking that this whole thing was ridiculous! But I thought, "Oh, well, the horse is pretty, he's brown, I like him, so let's keep going, Gloria!" Anybody who tells you they're acting just for the love of it is in the hierarchy of 5 percent. For most working actors there's usually a monetary consideration involved in it. But how nice to be paid for something that isn't that hard, and that you like to do!

Why did you retire from acting after An Eye for an Eye *[1966]?*

I'd been working a long time, and I decided that I wanted to be with my new baby, Mia, who was born in '66. I wanted to be a mom, and I haven't regretted it—Mia's been such a joy to me. And then meeting and marrying my new husband, Patrick, has filled my life. Mia's about to get married, my son has a son, I'm a grandma—I mean, I'm *heavy* into family! The only time I miss acting is when I see a part that somebody's fluffing, or doing absolutely wrong. I get to the point where I want to scream—and so I turn the channel.

Do you ever think about getting back into the business, or are your acting days behind you now?

They're behind me. I saw Audrey Hepburn on TV the other night, and talking about her career she said, "I did my thing. Let the kids do it now." And that's how I feel. Thank God I don't have that burning desire that some people really have—I think that'd be horrible to live with. It's been fun, it's been interesting, I've enjoyed rehashing it with you—but I don't believe you've heard any mournful sounds coming from me, have you? No "my-my's" or "why didn't I get *this* part or *that* part?" My Emmys and my Oscars are my children, and I like it that way.

[The Curse of the Living Corpse *and* The Horror of Party Beach]
*opened in Fort Worth and Dallas in a multi-drive-in situation....
I remember we went to one of those back-to-back drive-ins:
on the other side of the screen from our films
were* Move Over, Darling ... *and* PT-109..., *which was
about $18,000,000 worth of pictures. And I'm thinking,
"Oh, God, what are my little black-and-white,
no-name pictures doing competing with* these?"
*The results came in the next day
and we outgrossed them. Double.*

Del Tenney

FEW HORROR/EXPLOITATION PICTURES have established as unique an appeal as *The Horror of Party Beach*. A movie with something for everyone, it combines such '60s elements as the surf craze, sports cars, teenage sex, radioactive waste, bikers, rock'n'roll, a rumble and monsters. The man behind this heady package was a resourceful Connecticut-based independent named Del Tenney, who also made *Psychomania, The Curse of the Living Corpse* and *I Eat Your Skin,* an exploitation legacy not easily forgotten.

What was your background before you began making pictures?

I was born in Mason City, Iowa, in 1930. When I was twelve, my parents moved to California, to join the war effort, so I lived in Los Angeles all my school years. I went to Los Angeles City and State colleges, got interested in the theater at the age of sixteen or seventeen, became an actor and actually made a living at it for most of my younger adult life. I worked my way through college as an actor in things like *The Drunkard,* and did extra work in films like *Stalag 17* and *The Wild One* [both 1953]. I had such classmates as Bob Vaughn, Zev Bufman, James Coburn, Alan Arkin, Bobs Watson—on and on and on. I graduated in '53 from Los Angeles State College, which at that time was considered one of the best drama schools in the United States. In '54 I came to New York with very little money, and I was going to be an actor. I worked at various jobs—working in restaurants, being a detective—but mainly I supported myself working in summer stock. You could make a decent living at it—it was nothing to write home about, but *[grandiosely]* I was a de-*vo*-ted *ac*-tor. I think by the time I finished acting in '62 I had had fourteen years of summer stock and thirteen years of winter stock.

What made you decide to quit acting and get into filmmaking?

At that point I decided that I really didn't want to be an actor anymore; the struggle was not worth it to me, and I really wanted something a little more secure. You know, when you're an actor, even though you *have* a job, you're *looking* for a job—always. I guess I wanted to be my own master—it was just a matter of growing up. I decided that I really liked the production end of the motion picture business; I'd always been on the outskirts as an actor, and I was fascinated by the technical aspects of filmmaking, editing, special effects and all that stuff.

What were your first behind-the-scenes jobs?

I started as assistant director on several very low-budget pictures—down-and-dirty stuff. Back then there was no such thing as hard porn; it was all soft porn. In those days it was pretty risque stuff; today you'd look back at it and

Previous page: Aside from handling the chores of writing, producing and directing, Tenney also played the mystery killer in *The Curse of the Living Corpse.* The bathtub victim is Tenney's wife, actress Margot Hartman.

A strong cast bolstered Tenney's first film, the mini budgeted *Psychomania*.

you wouldn't blink twice—it's done on television now! We did things like *Orgy at Lil's House, Satan in High Heels,* and a couple of shorts for what would have been considered porno producers.

How did your first horror film, Psychomania, *come about?*
My wife [actress Margot Hartman] and I started to work on a screenplay

that was based on a true story. She had gone to Bennington College, and at one point a girl disappeared—later they found her body, she had been murdered, but they never found the killer. And we thought that would be a good basis for a relatively scary murder mystery—which is basically what *Psychomania* turned out to be. My wife and I did the screenplay, which is not on the credits.

Someone named Robin Miller gets screenplay credit.

I don't even know at this point who Robin Miller is *[laughs]!* My wife and I did a treatment, and then I did the screenplay. I really didn't like it; in those days I didn't have enough confidence in myself as a writer, because that was really the first thing I'd ever done.

What were your budget and shooting schedule?

I think we did that picture on $42,000—my father-in-law put up most of the money for it. Nineteen or twenty days of shooting with actors, then maybe a week of pickup stuff.

Did you have a hand in the directing of Psychomania?

I directed a lot of it—but, again, I didn't have confidence that I could do it. A friend of mine, Dick Hilliard, was a very talented, all-around sort of filmmaker, just a few years out of Princeton. I had worked on a couple of his pictures that never saw the light of day. We really worked together on *Psychomania,* but I gave him the credit for directing it. Most of the action stuff, I did. Having my theater background, I found out as we went along that I could work with the actors better than he could, because he was really not a theater person. So a lot of the more intimate scenes I also certainly had a great hand in.

Psychomania was a nice picture to work on because our cast were all stage actors and very accomplished people. Shepperd Strudwick was, of course, a wonderful actor, and Lee Philips was quite hot at the time. I remember Roddy McDowall was also under consideration for that Lee Philips role—we knew we couldn't afford a *major* star, but we wanted somebody that people would recognize.

Many of the Psychomania *supporting players—Jean Hale, James Farentino, Dick Van Patten, Sylvia Miles—went on to Hollywood stardom.*

When we were preparing to cast after the screenplay was finished, what I did was ask myself what actors I knew that fit the roles. In those days, and today still, we use a lot of our friends—nepotism, you know. I knew Jimmy Farentino quite well, and Sylvia Miles and I had been on the road, along with Hugh O'Brian, in *The Rainmaker.* You must understand that by now I'd been in the theater and had been in summer stock, and I knew practically every actor in those days. My wife was also in that picture.

The only prints of Psychomania *that turn up today are loaded with negative splices and abrupt scene changes, suggesting some major cuts.*

Well, it was cut and then it was added to. We went back and shot a lot of the so-called "sexier" scenes with Lorraine Rogers and Jimmy Farentino, because the distributor wanted more sex in it. *Psychomania* was kind of an exploitative film—really a soft porn, I guess, although it's so mild compared to what's going on today. Our original title was *Violent Midnight*—I don't know where *Psychomania* came from.

The distributor probably came up with that, to invite confusion with Hitchcock's Psycho.

Well, that's what they were going after in their selling of it. We had a lot of fun making *Psychomania,* and it really turned me on to moviemaking. We looked at all these pictures as kind of off–Broadway filmmaking.

Did you make money with Psychomania?

Psychomania was a relative success. I didn't make a *lot* of money on it, but we ended up with a few bucks in our pockets, which I thought certainly made it worthwhile.

Tell us about Alan Iselin, your co-producer on The Curse of the Living Corpse *and* The Horror of Party Beach.

Alan Iselin's family had about thirteen drive-in theaters in and around Albany. He approached me and said, "Gee, I'd really like to get into the movie business. I have an idea: You put up half the money, I'll put up the other half, and we'll make two pictures—strictly drive-in fare. I'll come up with two titles that I know I can sell—I can even build a pressbook right out of the titles before we even start on the screenplays. Can you do it for $100,000?" I said, "Aw, why not?"—because what did I have to lose? So he came up with *The Curse of the Living Corpse* and *Invasion of the Zombies.*

I decided that I was going to try an experiment: to shoot these things back-to-back. We built a sound stage in a studio here in Stamford, the old Gutzon Borglum Studio. In those days, my father-in-law owned it—it was his summer house. He gave us the place and we turned it into a mini–sound stage. My wife and I wrote both original scripts.

Again, as with Psychomania, *this isn't reflected in the credits.*

Credits? I didn't care about credits, *nobody* cared with these things. They were always done kind of tongue-in-cheek and you never knew how they were going to turn out. And, obviously, they are not the greatest films in the world.

I gave myself seventeen days apiece to shoot with actors, and got together a bunch of people who were friends and film nuts for my cast and crew. We did *The Curse of the Living Corpse* first. As you know, that was the first film

Robert Milli reacts to a sword across the face in Tenney's *The Curse of the Living Corpse*.

that Roy Scheider was ever in; Scheider is a wonderful man. Candace Hilligoss was quite a nice actress; we had worked together on a couple of plays, and I thought she was a good choice for the ingenue role. I'd seen her in a very strange film called *Carnival of Souls,* and I think that I hired her on the basis of that.

Have you ever appeared in any of your own films?

I'm in almost every one of them! It was always a case of the-actor-never-showed-up or we-need-somebody-on-the-spot. Let's see—most of the shots of the masked character in *Curse of the Living Corpse* is me. In *Psychomania* I was in the bar and I break up the fight between Lee Philips and Jimmy Farentino. In *Horror of Party Beach* I play the gas station attendant who lets the gas spill over. And in *Zombie [I Eat Your Skin]* I did a lot of the stuntwork—the diving, and other stuff.

Curse of the Living Corpse *has some elements in common with a Roger Corman picture that was new at the time,* The Premature Burial.

Never saw it. It might be possible that I was subconsciously inspired by the original Edgar Allan Poe story, because I read all of Poe's works. Alan Iselin had come up with the title *Curse of the Living Corpse* and, realistically, there are only so many plots you can make out of that!

Where did you shoot your exteriors for Living Corpse?

Most of *Living Corpse* was shot on the grounds of the Gutzon Borglum estate — we had about ten acres there, and a river; the bog was right down the road. It was a lot of fun. The big trick was to get six or seven minutes into the can every day. Two takes was exceptional, three takes was almost unheard of. And this shows in the films — they're not good films, and were never meant to be.

Living Corpse *seems almost a prototype for today's splatter films with its slasher-killer, mutilation murders and nearly nude scenes.*

I did have some problems later with *Living Corpse*. In those days, they had the Legion of Decency, and on that board were priests and nuns and so on. They came up to me and said that they were going to give *Living Corpse* the equivalent of today's X rating — not because of the excess sex and bloodletting, but because of something that never entered my head. There's *matricide* in *Curse of the Living Corpse,* when it turns out that it's Roy Scheider who's killed the mother. I told them, "Well, I never even *thought* about that — I mean, the man's *insane!*" You get so wrapped up in these pictures that you don't think about who's killing who, you just do a murder a reel. That's the formula.

Twentieth Century–Fox saw *Curse of the Living Corpse,* which as you know has some good things about it. We told them about *Horror of Party Beach,* which I was just starting at that point, and they said, "If *Party Beach* is at all decent, we will distribute both of them, but we have to see it first."

How did Iselin's proposed title Invasion of the Zombies *wind up as* The Horror of Party Beach?

Invasion of the Zombies/Horror of Party Beach started as an evolutionary story about atomic waste speeding up evolution, changing a fish into a man who becomes a monster, "the man of the future" — big, tall, no hair, features changed. *That* was the original idea which I had for that, which I still think is a very interesting idea and someday, maybe, I will do that film. Then Alan and I tried to work the music into it, the Del-Aires and all that stuff, and tie in some kind of a beach-blanket beat. We wanted to bill it as "The First Monster Musical." I don't remember which of us changed the title to *The Horror of Party Beach.*

Are there any anecdotes you can recall concerning the production?

The third or fourth day of filming, we were going to shoot a sequence where there's kind of a drag race, using a local group of motorcyclists called the Charter Oaks — the Hell's Angels of Stamford, Connecticut. Well, as you know, people go crazy when a camera starts. This guy from the back of the pack, a crazy, decides he's going to do something different than what was planned. He puts the pedal to the ground, passes the lead guy, clips his handlebars and knocks him over! You've got to understand, there are forty of these motorcycles coming up behind them! Anyway, they start crashing off the road and into the woods and somersaulting, and one of them smashes into the camera car—! Well, to make a long story short, four or five of the bikers end up in the hospital, and one of my lead actors is among them with what we thought might have been a broken back. Obviously he was out of it for about three months, so there was no way that we could go on with him. We even had to shut down shooting for a few days.

The point I'm trying to make here is that these guys were *really* rough characters. I had made them all sign releases that if anything happened, I was not responsible for their *bikes* or their *lives*, or *anything*. We had an editing room set up in the studio so that we could look at the rushes, and late one night I was working with the editor and rewriting the script because one of my lead players was out of commission. All of a sudden I hear the motorcycles roaring in the distance, getting closer and closer. Sure enough, they pull up in the driveway and walk in with their leather jackets and their long hair and their beards, smelling like a fish market. So I grin: "Hiya, fellas! How ya doin'?" But I'm thinking, "God, these guys are *mad!*" because, after all, there'd been thousands of dollars worth of damage done to their bikes. And, since two police cars had crashed on the way to the accident, the mayor and the police department were not too inclined to help me at this point. There was this sort of pause, and they're all standing around, shuffling their feet, and I'm thinking, "You've had it, brother—you're gonna get wiped out." So one of them finally says, "We wondered whether you would show us the film...." All they wanted to do was see the film! I had shot it from three different angles, so they sat there *all night* running this footage over and over and *over,* until I wanted to throw up.

Who designed and constructed your Party Beach *monster costumes?*
Those were built by Bob Verberkmoes, who was a set designer out of the theater. I didn't like the monster suits he came up with, but he thought it was funny—campy—that people were gummed to death with hot dogs instead of sharp teeth. I didn't think it was particularly funny, but I let him have his way. The monsters' heads were well above the heads of the actors inside; the actors had to look out through a hole in the neck, if I remember correctly. And those suits were very hot—we shot that in the summertime.

What's become of them?
I have no idea. I did have one of them hanging around here, and my kids used to put it on every once in a while, and at Halloween. They're gone now. I mean, you're talking twenty years ago. I wish I still had it!

After Party Beach *was finished, you had to show the print to Twentieth Century-Fox.*

Radioactive waste spawns a band of scaly sea monsters in "The First Horror Monster Musical," Tenney's *The Horror of Party Beach*.

And I was afraid that Twentieth Century–Fox was going to see it for the piece of crap that it was! The day we were to screen it for the Fox head of distribution, I had a guy who had played one of the monsters secretly putting on a monster suit in the bathroom while we were getting ready to project. All of a sudden the distribution man says, "Excuse me, I have to go to the bathroom." So I'm thinking, "Oh, Christ, I've really blown it now!" A minute later I hear, "God *damn* you, Tenney!" And he comes tearing down the hallway into the screening room, runs up to me, shaking, red in the face, yelling, "You almost gave me a heart attack! How could you *do* that to me?!" Well, of course, everybody in the place thought that this was one of the funniest things they'd ever seen in their lives.

And Fox decided to take the pictures.
    Right. We had spent at that point, clear through to the answer prints, $120,000. Remember, our original budget was $100,000, so I was feeling a little bad about the fact that I went over budget 20 percent. We opened in Fort Worth and Dallas in a multi-drive-in situation. Alan and I flew down there with the executives from Twentieth Century–Fox because it was the first opening and a big deal. I remember we went to one of those back-to-back drive-ins: on the other side of the screen from our films were *Move Over, Darling* with

James Garner and Doris Day and *PT-109* with Cliff Robertson, which was about $18,000,000 worth of pictures. And I'm thinking, "Oh, God, what are my little $120,000, black-and-white, no-name pictures doing competing with *these?*" The results came in the next day and we outgrossed them. *Double.* Of course Twentieth Century-Fox was impressed and they really shot the works, did a big job of promotion—it was one of those flukey things. The pictures made a lot of money. Unfortunately most of the money Alan and I made went to taxes. That's the way it worked in those days.

You broke up with Iselin shortly after that, didn't you?
  Alan wanted to hire me to do his next picture, *Frankenstein Meets the Spacemonster;* he didn't want a partner, and I didn't want to work for somebody else. So then I made *Zombie [I Eat Your Skin].*

We've always felt that Zombie *lacks most of the qualities that make* Living Corpse *and* Party Beach *such favorites today.*
  After the success of *Living Corpse* and *Party Beach,* Twentieth Century-Fox came to me and said, "Listen, my friend, you've got to go union on your next picture. That's the only way we're going to distribute it." So that's why I had so much trouble with *Zombie;* it was no longer off-Broadway filmmaking. I was stuck with four makeup men, eighteen electricians, so on and so forth. That was my so-called "big" picture—it was a fiasco.

That was shot in Florida, right?
  The whole thing was shot in Key Biscayne, when Key Biscayne was nothing but a jungle. And *hot?* Oh, my *God!* We got all sorts of jungle rot and fever and malaria—you wouldn't believe it. The local doctor finally came to me and said, "What is going *on* here? Twenty people come to me every day from your cast!"
  I remember, there was one sequence where Heather Hewitt is swimming across this little inlet, way out in the jungles of Key Biscayne, and Bill Joyce dives in after her. That took about half a day to shoot. Well, we later found out that four of the largest sharks ever found in that area were seen in that bay the next day! That scared me a bit—I never did tell Bill or Heather.

Zombie went through a lot of different titles before it ended up as I Eat Your Skin.
  It was originally called *Caribbean Adventure.* The reason I called it that is, I didn't want the people of Biscayne Bay to know I was making a horror picture. We knew that we were going to call it *Zombie,* or *Zombies,* or maybe even *Invasion of the Zombies,* but *Caribbean Adventure* was our shooting title so that everybody would think it was a James Bond-ish kind of thing. I remember calling that film *Voodoo Blood Bath* for a time, too.

What were you planning to do about a second feature to go with that film?

I was going to make another picture to go along with *Zombie;* I had a cute screenplay called *Frankenstein Meets Dracula*. Unfortunately I had trouble getting a distributor for *Zombie*. The whole market fell apart at that point: Hammer was making big pictures with Christopher Lee and Peter Cushing, and then the big, color, star-studded horror/disaster film cycle started. And I knew it was time for me to get out of this business—I could see investing $100,000 but I couldn't see sinking two, three million into a picture. Then it stops being fun and it becomes big business. So I got away from low-budget filmmaking—but I will say that it was quite a wonderful, rewarding experience, because I learned a lot about all aspects of the business.

Of your four horror films, which would you say is your favorite?

I think *The Curse of the Living Corpse*. It makes a lot more sense than the others, and I think it has a little more artistry in the photography, and in the direction. I took some extra time, had good actors working for me, and the story sort of fit together. Plus, I knew more about filmmaking at that point, having had the *Psychomania* experience.

Were you discouraged by the unfavorable reviews your films got at the time, or by their presence on Worst Films *lists today?*

Those kinds of things don't bother me. I didn't make these films for art, I made them because I thought it would be fun and we could make some money on 'em, which is exactly what happened. Goodness knows, I found it amusing when my friends used to come up to me and gasp, "How could you *do* all these terrible films?" I told them, "Listen, I cry all the way to the bank."

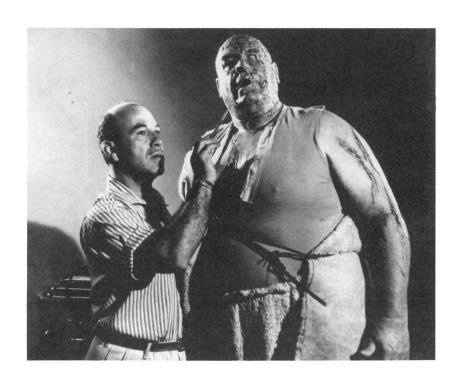

*Everything is pressured on these low-budget pictures.
Sometimes they'd say, "We've got to get this thing done today,"
and they'd start cutting pages out of the scripts.
And this hurt me, because I figured that someday
the makeup was going to sell these pictures.
It wasn't the hackneyed stories or
the poor acting; it was the* makeup.

Harry Thomas

DURING THE exploitation/horror boom of the 1950s, makeup man Harry Thomas was associated with some of the most memorable personalities and pictures of the period. He worked with Roger Corman, Edward D. Wood, Jr., Tor Johnson and Richard E. Cunha, and contributed to such films as *Frankenstein's Daughter, Cat Women of the Moon, Killers from Space, The Neanderthal Man, Port Sinister, The Little Shop of Horrors* and many more.

Thomas began his career in the 1930s when one of his first jobs was at MGM working under the renowned makeup artist Jack Dawn and his associate, William Tuttle. He is best known for his work on horror movies of the 1950s in which he almost invariably had to make something out of nothing, but he has also worked more recently on such features as *Logan's Run* (1976) and *The Hand* (1981).

Did you have a fondness for horror or science fiction movies before you began your makeup career?

Yes. I especially enjoyed the Frankenstein films, and I was very thrilled when I later worked under Jack Pierce. He was a little, feisty man that I enjoyed knowing; I respected his genius. I used to visit him over at Universal in the 1940s.

Universal treated Pierce pretty shabbily during his last days at the studio. Was he ever bitter about that?

Yes, he was kind of bitter. Jack had a miraculous way of doing these horror makeups with Egyptian cotton, spirit gum, collodion, lens paper—very similar to the way I work. I believe his pride was hurt, and I don't know whether or not he resented the fact that Bud Westmore went in there and took his place. I believe that Universal mentioned that he was getting older, and they wanted somebody who would work faster, and do prosthetics; that was their excuse. I don't think anybody's ever compared with what he did. Universal was very, very ungrateful in doing this to a man whose pictures all made a lot of money. The makeup artist didn't get the recognition or the appreciation in those days—not like today.

I never like to work in a major studio. I did work in a lot of them; you did *all* the work and you got no credit. The man whose name does get up there on the screen never even came down on the set. It was very interesting, but the pay was low and the department heads never came to view your work. People who do nice work, or think they do, like to get some kind of appreciation. That's all we need, we human animals. Being independently working most of the time, I would get a little bit more for myself than I would if I worked under a department head. There was a couple of hundred dollars difference per day.

Previous page: Thomas applies final touches to the makeup of man-mountain Tor Johnson on the set of *Night of the Ghouls*. Thomas says he had to stand on a box to reach Johnson's face for these touch-ups.

One of Thomas' first Hollywood jobs was as an extra in films like Laurel and Hardy's *Pardon Us* (1931). Thomas is standing to the right of Oliver Hardy.

How did you become interested in working in the movies?

I was interested in *art*—I did some artwork during the Depression. That's when I had an opportunity to get into the motion picture business and do makeup and various other things. Early on I worked at Hal Roach; I did some atmosphere [extra] work, a little costuming, a little of this and a little of that. They had no unions to speak of in those days—you could do whatever you wanted to do, if you were willing, and nobody jumped on you. Today it takes five union people to move a makeup table, and they get after you if you try and do anything yourself.

Do you enjoy the many extra creative opportunities that come from working on a horror or sci-fi film?

Oh, I just love them. You know, I used to work here in my house, even when I didn't have a picture, and create things on my own. I used *my* face, because my friends wouldn't cooperate; they said, "I *eat* hamburgers, I don't want to *look* like one!" So I made myself up. For *The Neanderthal Man,* for instance, I didn't have anybody that would sit, and I worked on that by myself, on my own face.

Did you make up the Mole-Men for Superman and the Mole-Men?

Oh, I did the whole thing. The producers wanted to use children as the

Mole-Men at first, but I fought against that. Midgets are easier to work with, and their faces are older and more porous. I brought those midgets into my house and I took the size of their heads. I put bald caps on them and stuffed them with cotton to make them look a little larger than their faces. I crossed the eyebrows, and then, to make it a little different, I laid a little tuft of hair down near the mandible—the bone below the ear. Every one was different—they all had this to identify themselves. I wanted to make them look sympathetic—not horrible or scary, but lovable little creatures from another part of the planet.

And you later did the Adventures of Superman *TV series?*
Right. It was very nice work—I enjoyed it. I even did the first episode *[Superman on Earth],* and I made the parents progressively older while the kid grew up to be the Mighty Man of Steel.

What was George Reeves like to work with?
George was very pleasant; he sort of kept to himself, and wasn't a glib person. He had a sensitive personality. We got along very well; he told me that he was a nightclub singer at one time, so I'd go into his dressing room, say "Now, George, I like to sing, too," and we'd sing a little ditty together. So he *was* human, even if he did come from another planet.

How did the hectic pace of TV compare to that of the low-budget movies you worked on?
Television was a lot more hectic. They had budgets and schedules, and they don't want to go over—or *under*—because of the union demands for overtime, meal penalties, etc.

How did your makeup for The Neanderthal Man *evolve?*
To give it a little authentic touch, I went to the library and looked at several primitive people—the Cro-Magnon, the Neanderthal and a lot of others. I made up Robert Shayne. The Neanderthal Man was laid with cotton, spirit gum and stuff like that, the way Jack Pierce would do it. After I'd make Shayne up, I'd make a double up, because Bob didn't do all the running and chasing, or the tiger attack. When he died in bed, I think they reversed the process: Shayne had all the makeup on, and I took off the pieces so he'd look like he was changing back to normal.

The transformation scenes in that film are interestingly done and rather effective.
They could have spent more time, and photographed it a little better than they did, but everything is pressured on these low-budget pictures. Sometimes they'd say, "We've got to get this thing done today," and they'd start cutting pages out of the scripts. And this hurt me, because I figured that someday the

makeup was going to sell these pictures. It wasn't the hackneyed stories or the poor acting; it was the *makeup*.

You also made up the servant girl as a Neanderthal Woman for a series of still photographs seen in the film.
   The girl was very lovely; her eyebrows were fascinating, very heavy, as I recall. I left 'em that way; sunk her eyes; did the teeth, and all that sort of thing. She changed, but not as much as Shayne did. The minute we started that picture, it was makeup, makeup, makeup, all the way to the end. The Neanderthal Man worked a lot—it didn't just pop up once in a while to scare you. This thing they played to the hilt.

What can you tell us about the saber-tooth tiger sequences seen in the film?
   The tiger was very playful, just a big cat, like you'd have for a house pet. It weighed four or five hundred pounds—a beautiful animal—but it *wouldn't* get ferocious. I made the tiger's trainer up as the Neanderthal Man for the scene where the tiger jumps the monster. The cat wanted to lick his face and purr. In those days, I don't think they had the Humane Society or the restrictions they have today. They took a stick and poked the tiger from the back so he could look furious, but they never accomplished that.

What about the design of the alien eyes in Killers from Space?
   The producer-director W. Lee Wilder wanted to get ping-pong balls and cut them for the eyes of the aliens, because he didn't want to pay the price I asked, which wasn't very much. I made the eyes out of plastic and colored them, gave them a light film for the sclera and put a hole in the middle so the actor could see. Again, it was a hurry-up thing—what I wanted to do was punch the plastic eyes through cotton or lens paper, then seal all that to the face so it would look like they came out of the eye sockets themselves. They wouldn't give me that time, nor time to shade the sides of the eyes to give it some dimension and feeling.
   The main alien—did you notice his eyes *move?* What I did was put another pair of eyes over the first pair and pull them back and forth with strings. That was my own idea; I just couldn't see the picture without animation. I wanted to see those eyes move, and when it worked, that made my heart feel real good because *then* the audience believed it.

Throughout the '50s, you contributed to a number of Edward Wood's films. What was it like working on a Wood set?
   It was like a big, happy family. Eddie Wood was a happy-go-lucky type of person, really jovial, easy to get along with, rather good-looking. At that time, to me he looked pretty young for a producer-director. Eddie always used players who hadn't worked very much, or stars that were slipping. He would

Thomas manufactured a devil on the spot and then also appeared as an extra in the hallucination scene from Ed Wood's transvestite tract *Glen or Glenda*. Thomas can be seen in the center, between a blonde and a brunette; Wood is on the floor.

get these people and shoot hundreds of feet of film on them, like he did with Bela Lugosi. I'd say to Woody, "*What* are you going to do with all this film?" and he'd tell me, "I may make another Lugosi picture and not even use him." But it was kind of a sad thing: Lugosi, in two of the pictures I worked with him on, did not know what he was doing. One day Bela came to me and said, "Harry, vot am I doing?" I said, "Well—you're *acting!*" "But vot kind of acting? He tells me to look this vay, that vay, stare out this vay. I have no script, I don't know vot I'm doing!" Eddie would direct, at random, whatever came to his mind.

Did you make up the Devil for the hallucination scene in Glen or Glenda?

Yes. There was a fellow with a very strong accent who lived in an apartment next to Quality Studios. He'd come over to the set, and one day I said to Eddie, "Jeez, why don't I make him up to look like the Devil himself?" So I took his hair, lifted it up, took some of Max Factor's hair gel, wrapped it around and dried it so it looked like horns. I brought his eyes up, built his nose up in the middle, and I think I put a little chinpiece on him. And he looked like a devil!

So that bit wasn't even in the script until you suggested it to Wood?
   Oh, I helped him a *lot*. Woody'd come to me and whisper, "What do you think I ought to do?" I didn't tell him, honestly, what I thought he ought to do with these pictures *[laughs]*, but I'd make suggestions, like the one with the Devil. You know, I'm in that scene, too, when the Devil and all the people are pointing down at Eddie on the floor. I also made Eddie up as the girl—I put lashes on him, and *[lisping]* he was very *thweet*. I think Woody played that part real good—it was supposed to be a transvestite that led this closet life. *Glen or Glenda* was a little bit ahead of its time. Had there been more money in it, a little more quality and time, I think it would have been a successful picture.

How well did you get to know Tor Johnson?
   Tor and I were pretty good friends, and I got him a lot of work—whenever I'd get a job, I'd recommend Tor. I got him work in *The Unearthly*, and I got him other jobs with Wood. Tor was a big Swede—he was actually "The Super Swedish Angel" at one time in wrestling—and a wonderful character. A big, big, *big* baby! Tor was so big, I had to get a little box and stand up on it to touch him up. Otherwise I think I only came up to his navel *[laughs]*—really, he was a huge man! One day Tor said to me *[Thomas now doing an on-the-money Tor Johnson imitation]*, "Harry, I want you to come over to the house. The missus and I are going to have a little snack." I told him I'd be very glad to. I dared not let him sit in my car, because the seat would break—he weighed about four hundred and fifty pounds. We went over to his house and he brought out whole barbecued chickens. I said, "Gee, I just want a little piece." Tor looked at me and said, "You eat it all! You gotta! It's just a little snack, before we eat the big meal!" I said, *"What* big meal?" Next he brought out all these various cheeses—Tor's father had a farm in Sweden. And he *kept* bringing on food. So finally the main course was coming, and this I still can't believe: huge roasts of lamb and big roasts of pork. By the way, the forks and knives were extra big, and the spoon looked like a small shovel. *Everything* was made special! And when he'd walk across the apartment floor, the boards would sink, and you'd think there was a slight tremor!
   Tor said, "The little woman's coming home soon." I pictured her in my mind as some little dainty, transistorized woman. Then, down the hall, I heard *thump, thump, thump,* and then a knock at the door. And here's a big woman—not as big as him, but good-sized. Very pleasant, very sweet, nice-looking woman   but big! *Thump, thump, thump* down the aisle again, the knock at the door, and there was his "baby boy" Carl. These people were huge. The son was as big as Tor was!
   Outside, I heard dogs barking—Tor had three German shepherds. I said, "Oh, let 'em in, I wanna pet 'em!" They came bursting through the door, three big, beautiful dogs, and they got under the table. Every chance I got, I'd take a little food off my plate and slip it to these dogs. Otherwise, I wouldn't be here today speaking with you!

Tor was like a great big kewpie doll. After dinner, he took one of the bedsheets and made a diaper out of it for himself, with a huge pin. He said to me—he called me "Little Tor"—"You don't mind me being comfortable? You enjoying yourself, Little Tor?" These were *such* dear people—you've never seen such a happy family in your life.

One of your more elaborate makeups for Tor were the burns on his face for Night of the Ghouls.

All I used was some collodion and some Naturo Plasto—undertaker's wax, used by all the morticians to reconstruct cadavers. I used it quite frequently.

Tell us about making up Sally Todd for The Unearthly.

That was very simple; it took me about half an hour to do that. I put hair gel all over her face, then I took Egyptian cotton, wrinkled it up and put it over the gel. Next, I took some liquid makeup, dipped a brush in it and made highlight and shadow.

Certainly the best-remembered part of The Unearthly *is the closing scene where the two policemen find the cell full of monsters in the basement.*

I had all these things at home—rubber pieces, hair, eyes, pieces of leftover makeups from other pictures. I grabbed whatever I could, and stuck it on these people. Tor Johnson's son, Carl, was in there—he was the biggest, tallest fellow, and he had rubber on one side of his face, pulling it down. I just threw it together. If they had given me more time, I'd have done a lot better, really.

What's disappointing is that all these monsters are seen for only a few seconds in the film.

They should have stayed on a few of them. I worked on them, one by one, putting at least fifteen or twenty minutes into each, which is a lot of time when you're working on a budget and under strain. But I did all right. They looked good.

Did you contribute to the walking tree in From Hell It Came?

No, the tree was made, all I did was spray it. I don't know who made that tree; it could have been Paul Blaisdell. Whoever made it did a beautiful job. What I contributed to that film was the radiation burns on the natives. I used some egg seal that stretched the skin, Bosco chocolate for dried blood and so on.

It was also around this time that you did two makeup jobs which have received a good deal of criticism: the title characters in Voodoo Woman *and* Frankenstein's Daughter. *How did you become involved with* Voodoo Woman?

There was a man by the name of Les Cook, that I first answered to; he was supposed to produce the picture for American International. He had a different title for the picture, and I suggested *Voodoo Woman;* it was far better than the title he originally had, which I've forgotten. I told Les that *Voodoo Woman* would look a little better on the marquee, and it might attract people to the box office. Les and I sat around and talked about the movie — they didn't have a script yet. Les used to tell me what the story would be like, and Les said, "I want you on this picture." Well, *he* never did it; whatever happened to the poor guy, I don't know, I never heard from him again.

I made the skull-head, and laid the hair on it. When I took it over to Sam Arkoff, he liked it, and we made a deal right there. I asked Arkoff, "Now, what have you got for the body?" I suggested at that time that they should put a scary, Inner Sanctum shroud on it, and make the hands up, sort of skeletal. Then, they could put a bit under the mouth so that whoever was in the mask could bear down on the bit and the mouth would open. And leave the eyes free to animate. Arkoff said, "Oh, we've got something already made up." I had never seen it; I was never on the set. All I did was make the head and bring it to Arkoff. I was very surprised when I later saw pictures of it, with this hideous costume they had used in another movie *[The She-Creature]*. They had every opportunity *not* to put my name on the credits if they didn't like my mask; every opportunity not to *use* the mask — they could have gotten something that would have been more befitting to the horrible suit, which looked like a butcher who had meat cleavers all over his gown!

Some of the people who eventually worked on Voodoo Woman *charged that your mask did not become their monster suit.*
I believe that petty jealousy is the only vice that gives no pleasure. I think that's what it was. *They* didn't do the head.

What about Frankenstein's Daughter?
You know, a lot of times you get blamed for something that you tried hard to change, and nothing happened. I made up Harry Wilson as the Monster; I stretched cotton, used liquid plastic to make it stiff, painted over with liquid makeup and put it on him, partially with spirit gum. I didn't think *he* was Frankenstein's Daughter, I was only taking orders from the producer and the director. For some odd reason, these producers never gave me scripts; they cost two dollars, I think, and that could have bought a reel of film! When the scene started and the little man who played Donald Murphy's assistant said, "Look at that — *she's* alive!" I blew a gasket! I thought that Frankenstein's Daughter was Sandra Knight, 'cause I worked on her first. I wanted to change it right then and there.

So you wanted to do a new makeup on Wilson and then refilm those first monster scenes?

Oh, God, yes. Absolutely. I spoke to Richard Cunha, the director, and I said, "They won't buy this out there! I feel this is the wrong thing to do." Really, I'm not to blame for that. Being the producer and director, they could have done something about it then. They could have made the monster an *it* or a *he [laughs] — Frankenstein's Nephew!* I wanted to make Sally Todd up as the monster, but the producers didn't think she was big enough to fight and look menacing. If they had given me the time, I would have made up Sally Todd to play the monster. Or, I could have made this big fellow, Harry Wilson, look like Sally Todd. I could've put a wig on him, and put organdy over his eyes like Jack Pierce did on *Frankenstein*.

Richard Cunha told us that he wanted to hire Jack Pierce for Frankenstein's Daughter, *but he was unavailable.*
They would have *never* given Jack Pierce time to do that. Jack used to take an awfully long time to do something, but he'd do it really well. He wouldn't slop things together like that, and he wouldn't have worked as cheaply as I did. You know, I worked fast on those things, to get 'em out. I didn't get four or five hours, I'd get four or five *minutes!* I did all the makeup — there wasn't anybody else.

Mr. Cunha credited a Paul Stanhope for Harry Wilson's makeup, and for Donald Murphy's acid face.
Stanhope was never on the set, and there was no other makeup man but me. They couldn't afford it! They said they were going to throw the acid in Murphy's face, so just sprinkle a little blood on him and have him raise his hand to cover his face. I said, "Oh, no, no, let's make him look burned." You know, when you get on a low-budget picture, you *plead* with these people — you can see the future of it. So what I did — in less than five minutes — was, I put hair gel all over Murphy's face, then took large pieces of lens paper, wrinkled them up and pinched some little holes out, stuck them on him and painted chocolate into the holes. All this time they're yelling, "Hurry up! Hurry up! What are you doing now?!" I said, "It won't take a minute, let me do it. It'll be effective." Later on, they didn't even say thank you — they didn't say a damn thing. And now they've got the nerve to give the credit to somebody else! If they didn't like my work on *Frankenstein's Daughter,* why did they carry me over to *Missile to the Moon?* They should have shouldered some of the responsibility and accepted the blame for having a man do that female part. Now, don't let them blame *me* for that — I was not responsible!

Another filmmaker with whom you worked on several occasions was Roger Corman. How did you enjoy working for him?
Roger's a nice fellow; I did his first picture, *Monster from the Ocean Floor,* in 1954. He was very, very cooperative, and probably never realized that

Top: Thomas and actress Mamie Van Doren flank radiation-burn victim Charles Kramer on the set of 1966's *The Navy vs. the Night Monsters*. (Photo courtesy Robert Skotak.) *Bottom:* Harry Thomas (second from right) is still active on the Hollywood scene, teaching makeup and cosmetology as well as tackling the occasional film assignment.

someday he'd be a tycoon or a great movie mogul. He's a hard-working fellow and he's got a lot of foresight. Anybody who works as hard as that has my greatest admiration. On *The Little Shop of Horrors* Roger was very nice to me.

I like Corman a whole lot, and the more I could do to help him, the better.

What do you remember about The Bride and the Beast *and* Terror in the Haunted House?

For *The Bride and the Beast,* I laid some hair on the gorilla suit; a fellow by the name of Ray Corrigan was inside it. All I did was fix the eyes a little bit and spray the suit, which was already made. Ed Wood wrote that picture, but I never saw Ed on that set at all.

And Terror in the Haunted House?

I remember putting ax prints on people, and making some heads. You know, I've never seen that picture, and I would like to. There was some subliminal stuff in that, that I worked on, also. I just can't remember that picture!

What did you do for The Navy vs. the Night Monsters?

I made up the radiation-burn victim. He was not in the script, and it was a last-minute thing. An assistant director came to me and said, "I want this man burned to a crisp — and you've got a half hour or less. You think you can do it?" I told him, "I *know* I can do it" — there's always a way to improvise, if you just use your little head. Some men were packing fragile glasses and props in a barrel, and when I walked by it I saw all this excelsior. I took some out, went to a mirror and put it on myself — hair gel, the excelsior, liquid makeup, black pancake for highlight and shadow — and it looked like radiation burns! "I think I've got it!" I said to myself, as I smiled in the mirror. You know *[laughs],* this gives me aesthetic pleasure! When I was finished with the actor, by God, you've never seen anything so effective. They *loved* it! And, can you imagine, they didn't hold the camera on him long enough, but they used that one frame to blow up and put on the posters!

One of your more memorable makeups from the 1960s was seen in She Freak.

The actress playing the She Freak was a very pleasant girl, but she didn't want to be hurt. You get a lot of people who are very sensitive or allergic to makeup. I knew she was worried; when they start asking questions, you sort of back down on the hard chemicals and go with the simpler things. I guaranteed her that everything on her would be *edible.* I made her up as the She Freak out of kitchen stuff. The eyes were broken eggshells, pierced with a hot icepick. The hair was done with flour, water and food coloring. I took an orange peel, cut it into teeth and let it dehydrate for three or four days until it became solidified like rawhide. I put syrup on her arm. You've got to think of these things to use as substitutes. When we were finished, she asked me, "What shall I do with all this stuff?" I told her, "Peel it off and eat it!"

Do you have a favorite among your many horror makeups?

The acid-burn makeup in *Frankenstein's Daughter*, because I did that so fast, just minutes. I like that, and I also like the changes in *The Neanderthal Man*. That was a challenge to me.

What keeps you busy these days?

I'm teaching all kinds of makeup techniques at Joe Blasco's school, which is probably the best makeup school in the country. I also teach skin care and cosmetology at another school. Every day of my career has been a pleasure. It's the only job I've ever had where you get paid—*good* pay—for having fun.

*I've seen many producer friends go down the drain
because of what directors do to them. Because directors
are interested in getting something worthwhile. I don't
blame them for wishing to do that, but it doesn't fit into
the shoestring-type picture. It's the wrong chemistry.
My directing is what is adequate for
the type of films I wanted to put together.*

—————— *Jerry Warren* ——————

WITH ALL DUE RESPECT toward the man himself, it is hard to think of any horror filmmaker who made movies that were as cheap or as ridiculed as Jerry Warren's. Whether making shoestring quickies like *The Incredible Petrified World* or *Teenage Zombies,* or rehashing Mexican imports like *Face of the Screaming Werewolf,* Warren could be counted on through the late '50s and early '60s to deliver the lowest common, campy denominator in horror. Despite their low quality, or more likely because of it, these pictures have managed to consistently draw an audience through the years on late-night and early morning TV.

Like many quickie producer-directors, Warren proves to be more interesting than the movies he made. When speaking about his pictures, he doesn't entertain any delusions of adequacy, and he offers an intriguing look at the scruffy underbelly of Hollywood production.

Warren says that he grew up with the same natural inclination that every other kid growing up in Los Angeles had: He wanted to get into the movie business. He first pursued this ambition by playing small parts in such '40s films as *Ghost Catchers, Anchors Aweigh* and *Unconquered.* A producer once made a big impression on Warren when he said, "In this town, producers are the ones that have it all." Warren subsequently took the producer's plunge in 1956 with the horror film *Man Beast.* "At the time," says Warren, "the Abominable Snowman had gotten a lot of publicity, and there hadn't been many films on it. I had been a fan of it, I studied the phenomenon and it seemed like a natural for my first picture."

How did you go about getting Man Beast *into production?*

Some of my friends helped me somewhat; they told me things to watch out for on a first effort. Being very inexperienced and naive, it wasn't easy. *Man Beast* was made at a little tiny studio on Santa Monica Boulevard called Keywest Studio. I had to use actors who really had no film experience at all; as a matter of fact, I cast practically the whole thing out of the Pasadena Playhouse because I couldn't afford professional actors. I used 90 percent from there and 10 percent from other little theater groups.

Did you use clips from another picture in Man Beast?

Yes, there was a lot of mountain-climbing footage that we bought from Allied Artists Studios. I assume it was originally from a Monogram picture.

Where did you get your Yeti suit?

We got it from a Western Costume–type outfit on Highland Avenue. I can't say for sure, but I think it was the same suit that was used in *White Pongo,* which was a much earlier "white gorilla" picture. We changed the face, and had different people in it at different times.

Can you tell us your budget?

Let's just say it was about one-half of what the normal low-budget picture

Previous page: A behind-the-scenes glimpse of producer/director Warren from *The Wild World of Batwoman.* (Actresses unidentified.)

The mid–'50s fascination with the possibility of Abominable Snowmen sparked Warren's first production, *Man Beast*, in 1956.

cost in those days. This was very, *very* low-budget. I remember I needed a Mongolian village, because I had to establish where the characters were. We filmed around Bishop, California, which is a snowy ski area; we had ice and glaciers, that was no problem, but nothing to establish that it was Tibet. We couldn't possibly build a village, and naturally we couldn't go to Tibet. So I took my actors and we climbed over the fence into a major studio and shot our scene on *their* Mongolian set! We got our scene, and then climbed over the fence and out again. I was a good fence-climber in my younger days, and it really didn't seem weird to me, at that age, to do such things.

Who did Rock Madison play in Man Beast? *His name heads the cast list, but he doesn't seem to be in the movie.*

He was in the Yeti suit!

Did he appear in any other role?

Yeah, but we had to make some changes that cut what he did way down. Other than playing the Yeti, he may not even be in the picture anymore.

Like Roger Corman, you put together a small stock company of players who appeared in picture after picture.

Certain people I felt good about working with, and through the years some of them became my friends. In Hollywood, if you're known for making movies you get hounded by actors all the time, and a lot of them are very unreliable and present all kinds of troubles. I like to use the people that give me the least amount of problems; that's why I stuck with John Carradine for a lot of pictures.

A gal by the name Bri Murphy worked in different behind-the-scenes capacities on your various films, and even did some acting.
 Bri and I were *married* at the time! She worked with me on Man Beast, The Incredible Petrified World and Teenage Zombies. The only time she did any acting was in *Teenage Zombies.*

Was she any relation to G.B. Murphy, who was your production supervisor?
 That's *her* — Geraldine Brianne Murphy. G.B.M. Productions was one of our companies back then. I lost track of her, but she later directed a couple of pictures somewhere along the line.

How did you enjoy working with John Carradine in your various pictures?
 John Carradine is a grand old man. The first picture that I used Carradine in was *The Incredible Petrified World.* When I found I could get John, I spent the whole night expanding his part, because at that point his role was not a lead, it was just one of the scientists. The possibility of getting Carradine came about very suddenly, so I spent all night building up what I was going to shoot with him in the next few days. I wrote all kinds of crazy jargon to explain why a cable snapped and a diving bell was lost. I concocted dialogue where he explains what happened — it was immensely long and complicated, and made *no* sense at all — just because I was going to have Carradine!
 The funny thing is, when I was done I said to myself, "I hope he can learn this!" because the whole thing was full of ridiculous phraseology that made no sense whatsoever, and it was *l-o-n-g* and drawn out. I was thinking, "Nobody can remember all this stuff, but I gotta try." The first take, he does it *word-for-word,* absolutely perfect. Then, when he gets behind the camera and I get the reverse on the guy that he's talking to, he does it *again,* off-camera, and doesn't even look at the script! The guy has a photographic memory, and he is absolutely amazing. That was my first experience with him; he is such a marvelous actor that you can count on him for anything.

Have you appeared in any of these pictures?
 On *Petrified World,* I sat on the plane next to John Carradine. I thought I'd do a Hitchcock.

Petrified World *is probably the most accomplished of your early pictures, but what cripples that film is its tame survival-and-rescue story.*
 We had a monster who was supposed to play a very important role in that

picture—a real terrific-looking monster. We made the monster outfit in Hollywood, before we went to Arizona to shoot the picture. The base of the outfit was a black rubber scuba-diving suit; we painted it with bright colors, made a great big head, goggle eyes, big claws and all that. It was an earth monster, something that was supposed to be living down in the center of the earth.

The funny thing is, by the time we got to Arizona, the suit had shrunk, particularly the legs. Jack Haffner, the actor who was supposed to wear it, had big thick calves. The suit had been designed and fitted to him. When we got to Arizona and went down into Colossal Cave, he said, "I can't zip up the legs! This thing's *shrunk!* You're going to have to get somebody with small calves." So we started looking around amongst ourselves for someone that might have skinny legs. We had picked up a young black fellow named Willie from the unemployment office in Tucson to work as a laborer. Everybody was lifting up Willie's pantlegs and looking at his calves. And he was so *scared!* I told him, "Willie, I'll put your name on the screen! You can tell your friends, 'That's *me* in that monster suit!'" But he was terrified, and would not put it on! Finally we put it on Bri, she being so small. Her legs would go in because they were small enough, but she didn't fill out the top and it was too heavy for her. We shot the footage with Bri wearing the monster suit, but it looked so terrible that we had to cut that completely out of the movie.

Where was the rest of Petrified World *shot?*

We shot in Catalina, which is a little island twenty miles from L.A. We took our cameras underwater, and I directed underwater. We built a diving bell and sunk it off Catalina, so our people could swim up out of it. Then, when we were finished, we figured, "Let's just leave it there." I'm sure that in the years that have passed, that shiny half-dome way down on the bottom there has been spotted by many scuba divers who thought they were seeing a flying saucer! It looked exactly like a U.F.O., and we just left it there.

Robert Clarke was a good choice for leading man.

Bob Clarke is one of the nicer people in Hollywood. Actors are sort of a flakey bunch; Bob has a lot more intelligence than most and he's a very, very nice guy. And he's also a very adequate, dependable actor who can always come up with a good performance.

It certainly appears that you took more time and effort with Petrified World *than with most of your other early films.*

I probably did. I got a lot of flack on *Man Beast,* and some of the reviews were unmerciful—they really pounced on it. By the time I made the second picture, I thought that I ought to try and make it better. But in those days quickies were acceptable. You didn't have to go all-out and make a really good picture; you'd just make the kind of thing that was *weird.* But with *Petrified*

No, it's not a projectionist leaving the scene of a Jerry Warren triple bill; he's the victim of evil experiments in Warren's *Teenage Zombies*.

World I did try to make something that was a little better. I didn't with the third, though—not on *Teenage Zombies*, not at all. I just put together a picture that was long enough to play the lower half of my double bill.

How long does it take to put a film like Teenage Zombies *together?*
   I wrote the script in a week, sitting around a pool in Las Vegas, and I shot the movie in five days. Five days! And the budget was so low that it was preposterous. I remember sitting in a big screening room at RKO with the King Brothers. They were running *Teenage Zombies*, and Frank King said, "Tell me, how much did this picture cost you?" When I told him, he just fell over laughing! This huge bald man—all he could do was roll around roaring with laughter! He couldn't *conceive* of such a thing, because the price was so low that it was utterly, utterly preposterous. It was one-tenth of the lowest possible budget you could think of! I made it so cheap that it was really ridiculous; as a matter of fact, in one sequence, I ran out the whole magazine of film shooting the scene. There were no cuts—it was all the master shot, the whole thing going on for ten minutes. I just did it like a stageplay. I mean, you can't do it any cheaper than that—that's one-to-one shooting!

Katherine Victor is the only horror film "personality" that emerged from your pictures. Can you tell us about working with her?
   Katherine is a very sweet lady who's done a lot of these kinds of pictures,

Warren hoped to capitalize on the mid-'60s *Batman* craze with *The Wild World of Batwoman* with Katherine Victor.

for other people as well as for myself. She specialized in being "the spooky woman," and still does, as a matter of fact. She always was very, very dependable, and did a good job in everything that she and I were associated with. She's a good friend.

Would you agree that Teenage Zombies *is the film you're best remembered for?*
 I think it is. Wherever I go around the world, particularly Europe and places like that, they all know *Teenage Zombies*. If they're the right age, that's the picture that really clicked with them. They somehow liked it, but why they did I can't tell you *[laughs]!*

Was Invasion of the Animal People *your first sci-fi import?*

Animal People was really not an import; that was an American production that was shot in Northern Sweden and the Arctic Circle. Virgil Vogel directed the stuff over there, I directed extra scenes here. I did my scenes for *Animal People* in color, and I don't remember why. It was released in black-and-white. That was all done in English language.

The American dialogue and narration in your horror imports often tackle curious and abstract topics like man's conception of time, our image of the universe, things like that, which don't advance the plot at all. Were you trying to get points of your philosophy across, or was that all—

Gobbledegook. Definitely. I separate my private life entirely from the movies. I'm very, very serious about my researches and endeavors on the reality of the whole universe, and I would not try to inject my philosophy into a movie because I just don't think it can be done successfully. So anything I wrote was gobbledegook. Strictly ridiculous.

Why are so many of your imports from South America? Did you have a fondness for the films being made down there?

In Los Angeles there's a big Mexican movie market, because a lot of Mexicans live in L.A. There's a very, very big distributor called Azteca Films, and the president of that was a friend of mine. It was just a natural thing to get leads into possible Americanizing of those kinds of pictures. In other words, I, not being a great traveler, didn't want to go to various countries and try to put co-production deals together. Mexico is close, Azteca is right in L.A., the president was a friend, so it was just a natural, easy way to make movies without an exceptional amount of work.

Why didn't you simply dub these foreign films from beginning to end, and save yourself the bother of shooting additional scenes?

Those pictures that I imported were very low-budget to begin with. They did every cheat possible in their original versions—they wanted to build them up time-wise and they did it with dialogue scenes. Some of these Mexican films did that like mad; they're very, very budget-conscious down there. Therefore, I would have to delete an awful lot, for this reason or that. Sometimes their dialogue scenes were so lengthy, so bad and so impossible to dub that we had to cut big pieces out. And suddenly the character who was talking is somewhere else, and I was left with a big hole in the story! I'd bridge it—try to make it make sense—by sticking in something, like a shot of somebody who'd say, "He's gone down to the saloon," or wherever. When you see something that I shot stuck in there, it was probably done to try to take the curse off of something else. Mine was usually the lesser of two evils.

The people who poke fun at your movies—and there are lots of them!—sometimes judge your talents as a director by the static American scenes in these imports.

Those *l-o-n-g,* talky scenes you're speaking of now were never in the original theatrical versions. I had a television distributor who insisted on more length—that was the reason for those scenes. I didn't shoot that stuff until those pictures were ready to be released to television. The TV distributor said these things must run eighty-odd minutes, and most of them were down around sixty-five, seventy minutes, which was fine for theatrical showings in those days. But he insisted on fifteen, eighteen minutes *more.* So the only thing that I could do was to shoot lengthy dialogue scenes and stick 'em in. When these things were originally released, they were much faster moving, and they didn't have those long dialogue scenes at all.

It's apparent that more care went into pictures like Man Beast *and* Petrified World *than into the added scenes in the imports.*

Oh, yes. Absolutely. *No* care went into those! In those days, they were buying this kind of stuff for television a lot. Rather than get involved in a picture from start to finish, which takes a lot of work, I'd find something to use as a frame and hang my hat on it. I'd shoot one day on this stuff and throw it together. At that point I was in the business to make money. I never, ever tried in any way to compete, or to make something worthwhile. I did only enough to get by, so they would buy it, so it would play, and so I'd get the few dollars. It's not very fair to the public, I guess, but that was my attitude toward this.

People think that the Richard Webb who stars in your Attack of the Mayan Mummy *is the Richard "Captain Midnight" Webb.*

No, certainly not. Whoever this Richard Webb was, he couldn't have done very much in the picture, and I don't even remember the guy.

Probably the best-known actor to regularly appear in your Americanized imports was Bruno Ve Sota.

Aw-w, Bruno was a *great* guy. I just can't say enough good about Bruno; I wish he was still around today. He was very talented and a good actor. And I always liked to use Bruno because he could take over directing if necessary. He knew what shoestring budgets I was on, and he never gave me any fuss about money or anything. He knew the problems of directing, the pressure, what you're up against. He was not like actors who only think about their egos and their own selves, and have no concept of what it is to try to make movies, which is very, very hard work. He knew he had to wing it fast, do this and get that before the sun went down, and that there was no time to be a prima donna. That set Bruno apart.

Tell us about a picture you worked on without taking credit, House of the Black Death.

House of the Black Death was a movie produced by a friend of mine, Bill White. Bill had always wanted to make movies; he had worked for me as an actor, and had been around the business a long time. He finally got his opportunity and put *House of the Black Death* together. Then, apparently, they got into real trouble. They shot half a movie, with a pretty good cast — Lon Chaney, Jr., Carradine, Tom Drake, Andrea King — but they also had some production people who gave them a lot of problems. And it was one of those things where Bill wasn't experienced enough to put his finger on it and hold it together. Anyway, they had a terrible mishmash of a movie — it *wasn't* a movie, it was a bunch of film. Somebody took over the project, contacted me and asked if I could make a movie out of it. I looked at as much film as there was, told them I thought I could do it and made a deal with them to finish the picture. The whole thing was laid in my lap and I functioned as *everything* — as producer, as director, as editor, putting music in it, the whole works. It came out *bad* but it came out playable, too, and it did pull out some money for the people who backed it. That's what they were after.

Did you work with Lon Chaney on House of the Black Death?

I didn't have anything to do with him on *House of the Black Death* because all of his scenes were in the can by the time I got there. I did work with him on *Face of the Screaming Werewolf,* and he was a trouper. He didn't like doing this kind of film; he didn't like being classified as a werewolf at all. After he did such a fine job in *Of Mice and Men* [1939], he wanted to be Lon Chaney in pictures, not the sort of character whose face changed. But that's precisely what he had to do. Although he didn't have to do that in *House of the Black Death,* he did play the werewolf in *Face of the Screaming Werewolf,* and it was the same old thing with the slow dissolves and hair growing on his face. He did *not* like that, but in Hollywood people do the things that they have to.

Weren't you courting legal disaster doing a film like The Wild World of Batwoman *at the height of the* Batman *craze?*

No, I don't think so, not at all. It had nothing to do with Batman, it was Bat*woman.* But, yes, there was a big lawsuit, which I won. But it went on and on and on, so by the time I won it, the whole craze was over.

Was it you who changed the title to She Was a Hippy Vampire?

Well, yeah, but I didn't *have* to because when they finally made a settlement on the lawsuit, there was no demand that I change the title at all. But as I said, the craze was over, so to come out with a *Wild World of Batwoman* four years later would have been ridiculous.

Jerry Warren (right) and sculptor Jerry Syphers with the star of 1965's *Curse of the Stone Hand*.

What kept you busy between Batwoman *[1966] and* Frankenstein Island *[1981]?*

I was no longer interested in the movie business at all. I lived on my ranch ... a different kind of life.

So what brought you back for Frankenstein Island?

Frankenstein Island came about in a funny sort of way. I hadn't seen Katherine Victor in years, and she came down to see how we lived. She started talking about newer pictures, and how there were so many pictures out like the ones we used to do. I don't think I'd seen a movie, *any* movie, in almost fifteen years. I noticed that low-budget horror films were playing, and cleaning up. I figured that, since inflation was very tough, maybe I'd try and make a movie again.

The passage of time did not seem to affect your approach to picturemaking.

As I said, I don't think I'd seen a movie since maybe the mid-'60s. I didn't see what was happening, and I assumed that I could still make 'em like I used to. But they had changed an awful lot. I didn't update *Frankenstein Island* enough to really compete with what was out.

I changed *Frankenstein Island* a lot for the television version. I brought it up to date, shot new stuff, put in explosions and special effects and cut out an awful lot of bad stuff. It's not like the version that you see on prerecorded cassette; I really sharpened it up to make it more acceptable. It's never going to be anything like *Star Wars* or those big pictures, but it's much, much improved over the original theatrical version, which is the version that's on cassette now.

How would you describe your talents as a director—good, bad or indifferent?

I can only say that I have never gotten serious over such a thing. I only direct because it costs too much to *hire* a director. I do all my own editing as well, because directors have their own concepts and they fight with their editors. I don't want fights. To me, life is too short to be involved in hassles with egos. I feel that the easiest way is to control the whole thing, do as much as I can myself and hire as few people as possible. Even though I would *love* to sit back and let somebody else do all that work.

Most directors have aspirations—they figure, "People are gonna see this, and I wanna get another job through this." Before you know it, he's screwin' around, foolin' around, and the picture goes on and on. You can't survive on a shoestring budget with directors like that. If you want to eliminate all that and just make a vehicle designed to be merchandized and make a little bit of money, the easiest way is to control it yourself and not get involved in such things. I've seen many producer friends go down the drain because of what directors do to them. Because directors are interested in getting something *worthwhile*. I don't blame them for wishing to do that, but it doesn't fit into the shoestring-type picture. It's the wrong chemistry. My directing is what is adequate for the type of films I wanted to put together. I have never seriously wanted to be a director, or to do great things.

I was talking with Leon Blender and Sam Arkoff, friends of mine at American International Pictures, several years ago, and I was telling them how much flack I used to get on my pictures. And they told me how much they used to get on *theirs!* And their pictures, to my estimation, were really good stuff. Compared to mine, at any rate. I knew these guys for years, but they didn't reveal until recently that they were getting tremendous flack at the time they were making films, and people in the industry looked down upon them like they were the worst creeps that ever lived. *Now* their films are nostalgia, and acceptable. Theirs and, hopefully, mine.

I love toys, and in the movie business they give you a half a million dollars' worth of toys to play with on every picture. And they give you real live dolls to work with and splash blood on and shoot up — it's like playing cops and robbers all your life!

―――――― *Mel Welles* ――――――

AS PART OF the classic Roger Corman stock company, actor Mel Welles joined Dick Miller, Jonathan Haze, Ed Nelson, Bruno Ve Sota and others in lending his unique talents to such ten-day wonders as *The Undead, Attack of the Crab Monsters* and the famous Film That Was Shot in Two Days, the cult favorite *The Little Shop of Horrors*. His later experiences included overseas productions like *Island of the Doomed* and *Lady Frankenstein*.

Prior to his Hollywood acting career, the New York–born Welles held a variety of jobs, including clinical psychologist, writer and radio deejay. After some stage work he wound up in Hollywood, where he made his first film, *Appointment in Honduras*, in 1953. Other early credits included *Gun Fury, The Racers, The Silver Chalice, Abbott & Costello Meet the Mummy* and *The 27th Day*. In 1956 he teamed professionally with longtime acquaintance Roger Corman and played offbeat supporting roles in the maverick producer's *The Undead, Attack of the Crab Monsters* and *Rock All Night*. His best and favorite role, as Gravis Mushnick in *The Little Shop of Horrors*, was one of his last before leaving the U.S. in the early '60s and forging an acting-producing-directing career in Europe. Welles has racked up a total of fifty-eight features, three hundred and fifty TV appearances, twelve producer-director credits and an incredible *eight hundred* voice-over assignments during a career in which he has traveled two and a half million miles and worked in twenty-eight different countries.

Early on, was there any particular niche you were eager to fill in forging an acting career?

I kind of wanted to be a character *star*—my design was to do what Peter Ustinov wound up doing. The problem I had was lack of focus, in that after a while acting appeared very childish to me, and was not as provocative or as challenging as other parts of the business such as producing, getting the whole package together and directing. The other facets of the motion picture industry appeared much more enticing, so therefore I never really focused on my acting career.

Throughout my career, I have traditionally done many, many different things at the same time—in fact, that's kind of how I stay young, by learning a new skill every year. A few years ago I learned how to read, write, arrange and orchestrate music, and the last two years I spent becoming totally computer-literate. I'm in my sixties now, and in the last dozen or so years I've probably learned to master more things than I did in my formative years!

Do you remember how you first came in contact with Roger Corman?

I had known Roger Corman since his first picture because Jonathan Haze was a very good friend of mine, Dick Miller is still one of my best friends and Chuck Griffith, who wrote many of his early films, *is* my best and closest friend to this day. So I knew Roger and we were kind of friends, but I was just generally too busy to do his films or to join his "repertory company."

Previous page: A giant claw makes short work of Prof. Deveroux (Welles) in Roger Corman's *Attack of the Crab Monsters*.

How would you describe the professional relationship you had with him?

My professional relationship with him was always good, but ... at that time, he showed up as an entirely different person than he shows up as today. He was eager to try new things in those days and he was very, very decisive. That's what made him a great low-budget picturemaker: He could make a decision instantly if time was being wasted or money was flying out the window. Of course, with the kind of pictures he made, it wasn't a question of being very discerning or perceptive, or making an extraordinary comment on the human condition. The wonderful thing about horror films is that black is black and white is white, and there are very few grays that show up. Until *A Bucket of Blood* and *The Little Shop of Horrors,* the formula was basically pretty standard—kind of like making the same picture, with a few variations, over and over again.

Did you enjoy the offbeat character you played in your first film for Corman, The Undead?

The character I played, Smolkin, who sang evil nursery rhymes throughout the picture, was one of the best characters that I ever played. I played him kind of insane, and what was wonderful was that one of my reviews compared me to Stanley Holloway in one of his Shakespearean gravedigger roles!

Chuck Griffith wrote that script completely in rhyme, in *couplets,* the first time; it was a wonderful script and it probably would have been *the* cult film, rather than *Little Shop of Horrors,* had it been shot that way. But either Roger or someone at American International Pictures didn't think that it was commercially viable to do it that way, and at the last minute a decision was made to rewrite the script without that.

Where was The Undead *shot?*

We shot that picture in an empty supermarket on Sunset Boulevard, and we almost died of asphyxiation from all the creosote fog that was created in that place. We also shot at what we call The Witch House here in Beverly Hills. Some years ago, on the corner of Carmelita and Walden, someone who I would presume was a set designer or art director of some kind built a very nice house. But he built it like an absolutely authentic witch's house! We used that Witch House for exteriors, and we shot the beheading scene out in the back. The rest of the exteriors were actually all *in*teriors.

Did Corman give you creative freedom in shaping your characters?

Generally, yes—he was really busy with the actual filmmaking process, and he didn't have time to tell you much about them! That's why he kept a repertory company and always used the same group, because he could rely on them to do a competent or adequate job under any conditions. Since he made like ten, twelve pictures a year, an actor could always depend on Roger: If you called him up and you needed a job, you could count on a week's work. But

Welles (left) played the demented gravedigger opposite Dorothy Neumann (center) and Pamela Duncan in the Corman quickie *The Undead*.

that's *all* you could count on, because with the exception of only a few films, they took a week to write a script, a week to prepare the film, a week to shoot it and a week to finish it!

How did you enjoy working with the other members of the cast of The Undead?

Richard Garland was a nice chap, but he and I never got very close because I'm an intense investigator into the nature of one's being, and I live in questions a lot more than answers. Richard at the time was kind of a complacent guy that looked to escape the activity of living — to have it happen to him rather than to *make* it happen. I found Pamela Duncan very stiff and very affected, like she was very full of being a movie star — which probably is the reason she never really became one. Allison Hayes was a great person to work with because she was very loose — earthy and relaxed. She was a very pretty, attractive lady; I liked working with her because she had no pretenses or ostentation. She was just very real. What I really enjoyed on that picture was working with my colleagues like Dick Miller, Billy Barty, Val Dufour, Richard Devon, Bruno Ve Sota — Bruno and I were very close. I don't remember the name of the actor who played the knight on the horse, but he was like a Western actor and he had kind of a Western accent. And in medieval times it seemed kind of absurd and incongruous to hear that accent coming out of his mouth! I got kind of put off — I couldn't help but giggle whenever he talked to me — so instead I did the whole scene talking to the horse! Since I was supposed to be a nut anyway, I guess it was all right.

Would you agree that, even within the realm of monster pictures, Attack of the Crab Monsters *had a story that was just too farout?*
   That, in my opinion, is one of the worst pictures ever made. I think the only thing that saved that picture was the title — comedians all over the country began to crack jokes about it, and it really became a pop-art kind of cartoon. But aside from what the picture was, the making of *Attack of the Crab Monsters* was nothing but fun. Fun and absurdity. That picture was made about the time that pictures like *Them!* were being made. When they made *Them!*, I think they spent about twelve or fourteen thousand dollars for each of those giant ants. Roger spent a few *hundred* dollars building that crab. Chuck Griffith did the second unit underwater stuff on that picture, and when they went to Catalina to do that, they discovered that the crab was made out of Styrofoam, and so it wouldn't sink. They tried winching it under the water, and it exploded *[laughs]* — there were all kinds of fun things that happened. There were problems, but they were problems you could giggle about. Of course it was a farout story, but no more farout than some of the ones we're seeing today. Again, it took a week for most of those scripts to be written *[laughs]*, and nobody had time to fill the holes.

You also had a strong role in a non-horror Corman, Rock All Night *[1957] with Dick Miller and Abby Dalton.*
   Rock All Night was one of the more interesting pictures to me. There was an Emmy Award–winning television show called *The Little Guy* that starred Dane Clark; Roger bought the film rights, which I thought was very courageous of him, and had Chuck write it into a rock script to emulate the success that *Rock Around the Clock* [1956] and all those pictures were having. An interesting thing about the character I play in the picture, Sir Bop: Chuck, with my advice, wrote the part for a character *I* used to write for, Lord Buckley. He was a comedian who has a large cult following, even today. He was the first one to do "hip" talk — he did some very famous pieces like "The Nazz" and stuff like that, and I wrote some of that material for him. If you've seen a picture called *High School Confidential!* [1958], you'll remember that John Drew Barrymore does a routine about Columbus in front of the history class. I wrote that piece of material, and also the poetry and jazz piece that Phillipa Fallon does. Actually, I was the technical director on *High School Confidential!* for

the "pot" language on that picture; *[sotto voce]* I was an expert on grass, in my day. Anyway, that's the kind of stuff that Dick Buckley did, and Sir Bop was written for him. Then he disappeared somewhere, so I played it myself — dyed my hair silver and tried to do him the best that I could.

Because of the language in *Rock All Night,* Roger got really worried that nobody would understand the picture. So I wrote a dictionary called *Sir Bop's Unabridged Hiptionary: A Lexicography for Hipsters of All Ages.* A couple of million of them were distributed with *Rock All Night* so that people would not get confused when the characters talked about their short or their iron [their cars] or their kip [bed]. At that time, nobody knew anything except *groovy* and *dig,* and they only knew *those* because Steve Allen and Frank Sinatra had used them on television. The rest of hip talk nobody knew except musicians, carnies and subculture people.

I think people get the impression that you're a little like some of the characters you play — amiable; a little bit of a con man; aggressive but pleasantly so.

I'm not like them at all. I'm a very super-educated, professorial type, and a family man — I have five children, ranging in age from thirty-six to seventeen. I *am* amiable, and I have a terrific sense of humor, but I don't have any accent — in most of my pictures, I have an accent. Although I'm certainly not "a little bit of a con man," in a way I *am* a wheeler dealer. I can't sit idle waiting for the phone to ring, so I'm always creating some kind of action. And if there were no problems in my life, I would create a few so that I'd have some to solve!

Was it Roger Corman's success with low-budget pictures that inspired you to get into production in the '50s?

No, not at all. As I said before, I always found acting rather childish. In putting a creative jigsaw puzzle together, the producer has the provocation and the challenge in seeing that everybody gets what they need in order to be able to successfully translate the story to the screen. And the director gets a chance to play with *toys.* I love toys, and in the movie business they give you a half million dollars' worth of toys to play with on every picture. And they give you real live dolls to work with and splash blood on and shoot up — it's like playing cops and robbers all your life!

How many pictures did you produce in the '50s?

I made *Killers' Cage* [1958], and then Chuck Griffith and I started to work on a picture called *The Trouble Giants,* which we had to close down because we got involved in a jurisdictional dispute between the IATSE and NABET. *The Trouble Giants* was a film about Israel which we were making in the Imperial Desert near Indio. We tried to make it on a shoestring budget and so we didn't use the IATSE, we used NABET. But in the middle of it the IATSE spotted us and dropped a picket line in by helicopter! I also did a couple of pilots and things like that before leaving for Europe.

Mel Welles

Welles (right) gets serious with Jonathan Haze and Jackie Joseph in the classic *The Little Shop of Horrors*.

Weren't you originally slated to play the coffeehouse beatnik in A Bucket of Blood?

That role was written for me, but I just wasn't available for it—I was off in Mexico making my own picture, *Killers' Cage*, at the time. Chuck Griffith always wrote a role in every script for me; in fact, he's just recently written a picture called *Ghost of a Chance*, which is kind of a horror comedy, and there's a part in it for me. So I'm hoping that it'll be funded and done sometime in '88.

Is it true that Corman made The Little Shop of Horrors *in two days on a bet?*

No, not to my knowledge. A lot of stories have come out about *Little Shop of Horrors* that I was certainly not aware of, although I could not swear they were untrue since I was not privy to everything that happened. In actuality, the way it happened was this: Chuck wanted to write a comedy/horror script, and he wrote a *Dracula*-type comedy very much like *Love at First Bite*. It was called *Cardula*, and it was about a Dracula character who was really a music critic, and it kept him up at night going from club to club. It was a real funny script, but Roger didn't like that. Then Chuck wrote a script called *Gluttony*, about cannibalism, but Roger didn't like *that*. And then he wrote *Little Shop of Horrors*.

You know, one of Roger's ploys was to do pictures that he could shoot on sets that were already erected, and rent the sets before they were struck. By doing that, he saved oodles of money and got a lot of production value. Well, that shop was already constructed on the set at Kling Studios. Actually, what made Roger do the picture was that Chuck and everybody convinced him that we would be able to shoot it *tout de suite* because we would rehearse it, and do the exteriors ourselves. We made him a package that he couldn't really resist. But there was no bet about it that I know of; that's a nice story, but I don't think it's true.

Dick Miller told us that practically everything you and he did in Little Shop *was ad-libbed.*
Absolutely none of it was ad-libbed. Dick Miller and I used to talk to each other in accents all the time, and use Jewish expressions in conversation. But every word in *Little Shop* was written by Chuck Griffith, and I did ninety-eight pages of dialogue in two days.

Is it difficult to maintain a sense of humor when you're under pressure to make a movie in two days?
No, we weren't under pressure. We got together and rehearsed the lines for about three weeks before we got on the set, so we were all very well prepared and we did it like a play. Roger had two camera crews on the set — that's why the picture, from a filmic standpoint, really is not very well done. The two camera crews were pointed in opposite directions so that we got both angles, and then other shots were "picked up" to use in between, to make it flow. It was a pretty fixed set and it was done sort of like a sitcom is done today, so it wasn't very difficult. And sense of humor? Hell, that was a real love project — everybody on the film knew each other and was having a good time. Jackie Joseph, Jonathan Haze, Dick Miller, Chuck Griffith and myself were all very good friends; the first patient in the dentist's chair was Chuck Griffith's father, and Myrtle Vail, the woman that played the mother to Seymour Krelboined [Haze], was Chuck's grandmother. Chuck's mother was Marge and his grandmother Myrt of the first soap opera in the United States, radio's *Myrt and Marge*. Even the extras on *Little Shop* were friends! It was an exercise in love.

How involved was Roger Corman in all of this?
Roger, who gets a lot of accolades for having produced and directed this film, really didn't have a lot to do on *Little Shop* because we were so well rehearsed. As I said, it was a love project, and we "stole" a lot of time — we did fifteen minutes of exteriors for a total of $1,100. And Roger wasn't around at all for the whole chase sequence and things like that — that part of the picture was produced by me and directed by Chuck Griffith.

How were you able to produce all the exteriors so cheaply?
We paid the children who ran out of the tunnel five cents apiece, and all

those winos on Skid Row we paid ten cents a shot. The winos would get together, two or three of them, and buy pints of wine for themselves! We also had a couple of the winos act as ramrods—sort of like production assistants—and put them in charge of the other wino extras. We got a funeral home to donate the hearse that was in the picture—in fact, there was a real stiff *in* the hearse when we had it!

We shot all night in the Southern Pacific railway yard for two bottles of Scotch, presented to the guy who managed the yard that night. That was kind of a coup, because Twentieth Century–Fox had shot all day long in that same yard and it cost them something like ten or fifteen thousand dollars. We got a train with a crew, and had them back away from an actor; in the film we showed that footage in reverse, to make it look as though he was struck by the train. We cut it a little shorter than we could have, because they felt that seeing someone actually getting hit by a train was a little brutal for a comedy.

Didn't Little Shop *run into problems on its first release?*
We couldn't sell the picture for a year. The reason was that the exhibitors in the United States, who were largely Jewish at the time, thought the picture was anti-Semitic. They thought that, not only because I did it in a Jewish accent and because I was a little more worried about the cash register than about what was going on, but because we had a woman character in the picture whose relatives were always dying. We called her "Mrs. S. Shiva." And in the Jewish religion, when somebody dies in your family you *sit shiva*—sitting shiva is the mourning process. At the time the exhibitors thought that was kind of irreverent, so on the first swing around, with Filmgroup, the film got cold responses. The way *Little Shop of Horrors* finally got out was that Mario Bava, Italy's horror film director, had made his first picture with Barbara Steele, *Black Sunday*. American International bought it, mounted a sensational ad campaign for it and needed a companion feature—all those pictures went out in double bills in those days. So they agreed to put *Little Shop* out with *Black Sunday;* the ads didn't even mention the title of our film, just, "Plus Added Attraction." That's how *Little Shop* got out, and then of course word-of-mouth carried it.

Would you say that Roger Corman gave you your best acting opportunities?
No. I had a wonderful part in *Hemingway's Adventures of a Young Man* [1962], and *Soldier of Fortune* [1955] was a great character, although we don't see much of it these days in the television version. Of course, the best part I ever had was in *Little Shop of Horrors,* but it wasn't really because of Roger, it was because Chuck Griffith created the character based on things that I would say when I talked with an accent. The character was written for me, and there was no question about the fact that I was going to play it. And in playing the role I rose to the cause—it's always nice when you have a part written for

you. I'm kind of sorry I didn't get a shot at doing it in the new movie [the 1986 musical version of *Little Shop*].

You know, recently I did another role like it, in *Dr. Heckyl and Mr. Hype*. We tried to do the *Little Shop of Horrors* thing again, only this time with Chuck Griffith directing and Oliver Reed starring. It's kind of an arty, fun picture, but it isn't outrageous like *Little Shop*. And the reason it isn't is because of the way Oliver Reed played his character—we all had to tone down or we would have sounded crazy, because *[imitating Oliver Reed]* he plays everything very *intense* and *low* and *serious,* and everything is *whispered*. His sense of comedy wasn't real farcical, like in *Little Shop,* and so we didn't accomplish what we set out to do. And of course Cannon Films didn't really know how to distribute it, so it didn't go anywhere. But it remains one of Oliver's favorite pictures, and there's a very interesting look to the film because we shot it in all the French and Swiss Normandy-type locations in Los Angeles. There was a spate of that kind of architecture in L.A., and we picked all those locations so the picture has a weird look to it.

We enjoy talking to people who've worked with Roger Corman, but many of them have come away with less-than-fond memories.

Well, *I* have a lot of fond memories, but Roger himself is not an easy man to deal with. He's pretty self-indulgent, he's insensitive to other people's needs and wants—and he really doesn't care about it anyway. Somewhere along the line he sees his function as giving you an opportunity, so therefore I guess he considers that he has implicit permission to exploit you in any way that he wants to. I could go into a lot of stuff—he and I are not terribly friendly, although I just did a picture for Julie Corman called *Chopping Mall*. Roger and I are kind of friendly when we see each other, but we don't talk that much, and my experiences with him in recent years have been nil. You know, he *did* distribute my *Lady Frankenstein* picture [in 1972], and I've got to say this: In that particular instance he saved my ass. I had made a deal with a guy in New York to do that picture, and then some shenanigans with a letter of credit made the deal impossible. I had the sets built, the stage rented and about a hundred people employed in Italy, and I was suddenly without the necessary financing. So I got on a plane, came to California, went to see Roger and he rose to the cause. Now, I'm not saying that he didn't take everything that he could—in fact, I had to give him the picture in perpetuity and all of that—but nevertheless he did rise to the cause and work with me on it.

People windbag and gossip a lot about things, but in reality it's only their interpretation or their perception that we're getting. Everybody knew everything about Roger when they went to work for him—everybody went in with their eyes open, so they have nothing to complain about. And there are some things about Roger that are incomparable; he's a hard man to deal with, but he keeps his word down to the last letter. He provided, throughout those years, more work for actors than any other single producer around. He also gave people opportunities to play parts they would never otherwise have played, and to direct, and to write, and what-have-you. Like what a minor league is for professional baseball players, that category of picture was a place where you could sharpen your skills, and then go on. So that could still be considered a major contribution. Also, you could redefine all that to *opportunity* if you want to — you don't have to consider it burden and responsibility to work for Corman, you can redefine it to be opportunity and possibility. Look how many people have used it as a springboard.

What prompted your decision to relocate to Europe in the 1960s?
   Well, actually, television here; I created such polemics in the film industry that I found myself doing a lot of television and I didn't like it. A lot of *Rin Tin Tin, Circus Boy, Captain Midnight, Peter Gunn*, that sort of stuff. It was good work, but it wasn't my idea of anything. So I went to Europe to direct two pictures for a German producer: I had bought a short story from *Playboy* called *The Skin Diver and the Lady*, and they were going to finance that if I directed a picture for them called *Maid from Nymphenburg*. I went to Europe with my family, but those pictures never happened. On my way back I stopped in Italy, and got involved in the directing of a picture called *Le Teste Calde*. There we had a robbery in which everything we owned in life was stolen — we were left just with the clothes on our backs. I got very angry, and I said I was going to stay there until I got even. I stayed, and by the time I got even I loved it, so Europe was my headquarters for a long time.

What recollections do you have of acting in The She Beast?
   That was a wonderful experience, for several reasons. Michael Reeves, the young man that directed the picture, was only twenty-one years old. It was his first picture, he was very young and a couple of us were veterans, so he let us help him direct the picture. Michael was a wonderful boy, and Ian Ogilvy, who played the lead in *The She Beast* and also plays the son of *The Saint* in that English series, was a real nice boy, too. Chuck Griffith was in the picture — he's one of the "Keystone Cops" — and so was Amos Powell, another writer we know, and a longtime friend of mine, "Flash" Riley, who stars in the musical *Bubblin' Brown Sugar* all over the world now. He played the witch. It was a fun picture — we were all living and working in Rome and having a good time living the *dolce vita*. The producer of that picture was Paul Maslansky, who produced *Police Academy* [1984] and is now a very wealthy producer; that was his second film. I had done the looping on his first film, *Castle of the Living Dead*.

Some unwelcome comedy hurts The She Beast *a lot.*
   Paul couldn't make up his mind whether he wanted to do it as a comedy or not. It was a real farcical script, and by watering it down they kind of spoiled things. We made that entire picture in Italy and looped it there — in Italy you

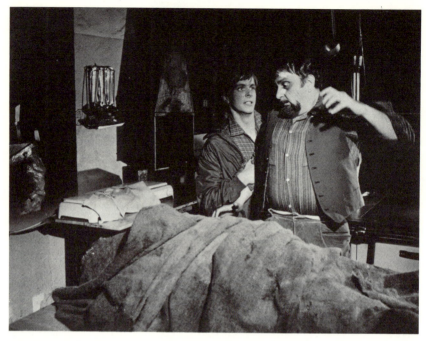

What's under that blanket? Ian Ogilvy can't get Mel Welles to tell him it's *The She Beast*.

don't make direct-sound pictures because you can't keep an Italian crew quiet long enough *[laughs]!* Like all Italian pictures, it was shot and then dubbed. In Italy they make pictures with three scripts—they make the deal on one script, they shoot another and loop another in the dubbing room!

How did Island of the Doomed *come about?*

A chap named Nick Alexander and I had a company called Compass Films in Rome, and we developed some properties. When nothing happened with that company and we divided up, I inherited the properties. One of them was called *Island of Death*. So I made a deal with a Spanish friend of mine and made it as a Spanish-German co-production in Spain, with Cameron Mitchell and with George Martin and Elisa Montes, who are Spanish actors. In all European countries, the industry is subsidized by the government, and each government has a ministry that controls that. If you make a Spanish-Italian or a Spanish-German co-production, your principal people are supposed to be from one or the other of the co-producing countries. I put co-productions like this together and directed the pictures, but could not go on record as being an American. I had to direct *Island of the Doomed* under the name of Ernst Von Theumer. Actually, he was the German co-producer, and I just used his name.

Does Island of the Doomed, *which is a movie about a monster plant, owe its inspiration to* The Little Shop of Horrors?

No, not at all. It's not about a carnivorous plant, it's about a *vampirical* plant. And it's a *tree*, not a plant. I didn't create the script anyway; it was done by a writer, independently of me.

Can you tell us a little about the film's special effects?

[Laughs.] We built a tree that was supposed to run electronically; it cost $30,000 in Spain to build it. And then it didn't work. So we wound up using the old-fashioned trick of pulling the branches with wires. The close-ups of the flowers opening and the pistil with the saliva on it attaching itself to the neck and sucking the blood were achieved on a special effects stage in Germany.

At the very end of the picture I wanted lightning to strike the tree and set it on fire, burning both the tree itself and the evil baron [Mitchell] who was trapped in its clutches. For a week I kept asking the special effects men—who had not accomplished *anything* correctly up till then—whether that effect was in place. And they kept telling me that, yes, it was, and explaining about the magnesium powder that would be used. On the night we were supposed to shoot it, they brought out the chemicals, and they had bought magnesium *salt* instead of magnesium *powder*. It was enough laxative for three movie companies *[laughs]*! We ended the picture without the fire because I didn't want to go an extra day, and there was no way to get magnesium powder late on a Sunday night.

After a promising start on stage and in legitimate pictures, Cameron Mitchell has wound up a top star of low-grade horror films. Can you describe working with him?

He wasn't terrific to work with in those days; he was an okay guy but at the time he was expatriated and he had some tax problems in the United States, and he was really unhappy about working in Europe. And when he did *Island of the Doomed* he was on an unusual health kick in which he ate twenty-six cloves of garlic every day—which kept everybody, especially the actors that he worked with, in misery! But I think he's a consummate actor and a real serious, wonderful worker. He's very interesting in the choices he makes as an actor, and he always brings something special to his roles.

Were you happy with the way Island of the Doomed *turned out?*

Oh, *very* happy—I can't tell you how happy! The film was made on a budget of like $4.23 *[laughs]*, and it sold very well all over the world.

What's the story on Lady Frankenstein?

I read a script called *Lady Dracula*, which was given to me by a guy who said, "If you want to make this picture, I'll give you the money." It was one of those dream things that can happen to a filmmaker—it's never happened

Welles (center) clowns with unidentified monster actor and screen veteran Joseph Cotten during a break in the shooting of the Italian-made *Lady Frankenstein*.

to me before or since. So I said, "Fine"—and then I questioned him a little bit and discovered that he didn't have the rights to the script but he was sure he could buy it. But in fact the fellow who owned the script didn't want to give it up, he wanted to make it himself. Because I was in the mood to make a Gothic horror picture, I went to England and got Eddie Di Lorenzo to write a script called *Lady Frankenstein*. The interesting thing about *Lady Frankenstein*, historically, is that it was the first Gothic horror film with an explicit sex scene in it. Another thing about it that I liked was Roger Corman's poster of it in this country. It said, *"Only the monster she made could satisfy her strange desires."* That was a very interesting campaign. *Lady Frankenstein* was shot at the oldest studio in Rome, Depaulus Studio. It was mouthed in English except for about four or five parts, but it was very well dubbed.

That was done about the time that Joseph Cotten seemed to be trying to make a name for himself in horror films.

Joseph Cotten's a great man, a dyed-in-the-wool professional. At the time he was traveling around, doing all those pictures in Europe, and enjoying his new entrance into the horror field. One of his best friends is Vincent Price, and Vincent always gave him hints on how to play those parts. In a horror film, regardless of whether it's a comedy, the guys in the film have to play it seriously. Cotten's wife Patricia Medina was there with him, too; she and I had worked together, years before, on a film called *Duel on the Mississippi* [1955] at Katzman Studios. Actually, the truth is that Joseph Cotten only worked a short time in *Lady Frankenstein*—his character was killed early in the piece. He was in it to get the name value.

You seemed to be out of the business for several years in the '70s.
Around 1972 I went from Europe to Southeast Asia, where I did get out of the film business and into the concert business—I became the Sol Hurok of Southeast Asia. I produced huge concerts all over Southeast Asia, with big orchestras and symphonies. I was very successful with that.

And back to the U.S. after that?
What happened was, my family and I came back to America for a visit—two of my kids had never *seen* America, and my wife, who is Australian, had never been here either. We came here and I fell in love with this place again. All the things that I kind of ran away from seemed to have been dealt with, and I was very impressed by everybody's energy—everybody was going to seminars and workshops, doing things and having classes. So I went back overseas, took half a year to close out all my obligations, and moved back here in 1976.

In what capacities are you working today?
I'm working mostly behind the camera—not directing, but doing post-production supervision. My passion and love right now is, I give effectiveness workshops to studio executives and key personnel in the entertainment industry. These are workshops on how you are when you're being effective and how you are when you're *not*. I've been giving these all over the U.S. and all over the world.

You've worn a lot of different hats in your career. Which facet of filmmaking have you found the most rewarding?
[Emphatically.] Producing. The ability to be able to give key people what they need to do their jobs properly is very provocative. Most people don't know how much goes into making a film. There are about four thousand steps, and if you blow any *one* of them, you could blow the film. It's so complex, and a fortune is spent in a very short period of time. Even on a low-budget picture today, you spend a couple of million dollars in four weeks or so. With that money you could open up several luxury restaurants, buy real estate or do a lot of other things. Instead you wind up with two small cans, which may or may not be worthless. They may also be worth $300,000,000—that's the thrill of it. But the interesting part about producing a film is to be able to creatively secure for your director, art director and so on, the things that they need in order to do their work. *That* I find very exciting and challenging, and I hope I can continue to do that and to help other people do that. That's really important to me.

Index

Every movie title is followed by year of release. Television series, stage plays, radio shows, etc., are identified as such in parentheses. The titles of novels, short stories, and magazines appear in quotation marks. Page numbers in bold indicate photographs.

A

The A-Team (TV) 41
Abbott and Costello Meet the Mummy (1955) 382
Ackerman, Forrest J 177, 207, 298
Acquanetta xi, 235-6, 240, **240**, 241, **246**
Adams, Neile 199
Adamson, Al 138, 139-140
Adler, Buddy 61, 98
The Adventures of Marshal O'Dell (TV) 106
The Adventures of Rin Tin Tin (TV) 391
Adventures of Superman (TV) 286, 288, 289, 358
Agar, John 1-15, **1, 4, 6, 7, 12**, 130, **281**, 337
Airplane! (1980) 210
Alda, Robert 305
Aldrich, Robert 151
Alexander, Nick 392
Alien (1979) 223-4
All About Eve (1950) 53
Allan, Elizabeth 174
Alland, William 5, 7, 8, 146
Allbritton, Louise **303**
Allen, Steve 386
The Alligator People (1959) 154, 164-6, **165**
Alperson, Edward L. 96
The Amazing Colossal Man (1957) 28, **29**
The Amazing Transparent Man (1960) 89
Amazzini, Bill xi
Amazzini, Roberta xi

Ambush Bay (1966) 263
Ament, Don 114
Ames, Ramsay 235, 236, 237, 240
The Amityville Horror (1979) 35
Anchors Aweigh (1945) 370
The Angry Red Planet (1960) 59, 262-5, **264**
Anguish, Toby 106
Ankers, Evelyn 238, **301**
Ankrum, Morris 108-9
Apache Woman (1955) 24
The Ape (1940) 299, 305
Apocalypse Now (1979) 45
The Appaloosa (1966) 184
Appointment in Honduras (1953) 382
Arabesque (1966) 194
Arden, Arianne 88
Arkin, Alan 344
Arkoff, Samuel Z. 17-36, **17**, 38, 88, 100-1, 267, 271, 363, 380
Arlen, Richard 170, 329
Arliss, George 172
Arnold, Jack 2, 5, 121, 144, 147, 148
Arnow, Max 66
Arsenic and Old Lace (stage, with Karloff) 76-7
Arsenic and Old Lace (stage, with Lugosi) 170
Arteida, Tony 44
Ashbrook, Donna 329
Ashcroft, Loraine xi
Ashcroft, Ron xi, 81, 82
Asher, William 40
Ashley, Jennifer 193
Ashley, John 37-46, **37, 41, 43**, 114
Askwith, Robin 192

Index

The Astonishing 12-Inch People (unmade) 282
The Astounding She-Monster (1958) **75**, 76, 81-2, 91
The Astro-Zombies (1968) 196, 203-4
The Atomic Submarine (1960) x
Attack of the Crab Monsters (1957) 85, 223, **381**, 382, 385
Attack of the Giant Leeches (1959) 94, 95, 98, 104, 222, 223, 224-7, **225**
Attack of the Mayan Mummy (1963) 377
Attack of the Puppet People (1958) **9**, 11
Avalon, Frankie 39-40
Axelrod, George 218

B

Baby Face Nelson (1957) 62
Baer, Buddy **105**, 107, 109
Bait (1954) 2
Balch, Antony 189, 191, 192
Banks, Harold 109, 116
Baretta (TV) 222
Barker, Lex 290
Barr, Tim 202-3, 206
Barrows, George 115
Barry, Gene 319
Barrymore, John 298
Barrymore, John Drew 385
Bartel, Paul 94, 262
Barthelmess, Richard 18
Barty, Billy 385
Batman (TV) 378
The Battle at Apache Pass (1952) 66
Battle Taxi (1955) 316
Bau, George **293**
Bava, Mario 31, 262, 271, 389
Baxt, George 191
Baxter, Les 215, 216
Beach Blanket Bingo (1965) 34
Beach Party (1963) 19, 25, 34, 35, 39
Beacham, Stephanie 194
Beast from Haunted Cave (1959) 94, 98, 99-100
Beast of Blood (1970) 42
The Beast of the Yellow Night (1971) 38, 42-3
The Beast with a Million Eyes (1955) 21
The Beast with Five Fingers (1946) 305
Beaumont, Charles 55, 103
Beckerman, Sid 150-1
Becwar, George 251
Bedlam (1946) 76, **77**, 78
Beery, Wallace 28, 114

Belafonte, Harry 95
Bellamy, Ralph 300
Benedek, Laslo 313
Benedict, Dirk **227**, 229
Benjamin, Richard 329
Bennett, Joan 55
Bergman, Ingrid 79, 104
Berle, Milton 170, 171
Bernds, Edward 47-64, **47**, **52**
Bester, Alfred 202
Beware! The Blob see *Son of Blob*
Beyond Atlantis (1973) 45
Beyond the Time Barrier (1960) 76, 82, 88-9, 90, 91, 92
Biberman, Abner 11
Bice, Robert **83**
The Big Bird Cage (1972) 43
The Big Doll House (1971) 43
Big House, U.S.A. (1955) 212
The Big Red One (1980) 94, 104
Bikini Beach (1964) 39
Birch, Paul **47**, **157**, 159-60
Bissell, Whit 321-2
Black, Noel 166, 167
Black Friday (1940) 298-9, 305
Black Mama, White Mama (1972) 43
The Black Pirates (1954) 81
The Black Room (1935) 48
The Black Scorpion (1957) 120-1, 127
The Black Sleep (1956) 210, 211-3, **211**, **212**, 214, 232, 241-4, 247, 248
Black Sunday (1961) 31, 389
Blackman, Honor 192
Blaisdell, Paul **25**, 362
Blakeley, Tom 187
Blasco, Joe 367
Blender, Leon 38, 380
The Blob (1958) 196-200, **197**, 201, 203, 205, 207
Blood of Dracula (1957) 30, 312, 320, 322, 324
The Blood Seekers see *Dracula vs. Frankenstein*
The Body Snatcher (1945) 76, 77-8
Bogdanovich, Peter 222
Boots and Saddles (TV) 222, 224
Boutross, Tom 82, 84
Boxcar Bertha (1972) 26
Boyd, William 170
The Boys (1961) 184
Bradbury, Ray 146-7, 149
Bradford, Bill 280
Bradford, Sue 280
Brady, Scott 136
The Brain (1962) 306

The Brain from Planet Arous (1958) 2, 10, 13
The Brain Snatchers see *Monstrosity*
Brando, Marlon 184
Braus, Mortimer 277, 278
Breckinridge, John 256
Breckinridge, John Cabell 256
Brent, Romney 170
The Bride and the Beast (1958) 366
Bride of Frankenstein (1935) 174
Bride of the Gorilla (1951) 307
Bride of the Monster (1956) 18, 250–4, 256, 259
Brides of Blood (1968) 40–2
Bridges, Jeff 14
Britton, Pamela 154
Broder, Jack 133–134
Brodie, Steve 91
Broidy, Steve 216
Bromfield, John 3, **161**, 162, 163
Bronson, Betty 288
Bronson, Charles 71, 73
Brooke, Ralph 107
Brooke, Sandy **195**
Brown, David 227, 228
Brown, Ewing xi
Brown, Vanessa 291
Browne, Robert Allen 137
Browning, Ricou 3, 4, 5, **6**
Bubblin' Brown Sugar (stage) 391
Buccola, Guy **225**, 226
Buchanan, James 256
Buchanan, Larry 2, 5, 13, 14, 38, 40
A Bucket of Blood (1959) 383, 387
Buckley, Dick 385, 386
Budrys, Algis 202
Bufman, Zev 344
Buñuel, Luis 305
Buried Alive (upcoming production) 18
Burn, Witch, Burn (1962) 191
Burr, Raymond 307
Burton, Richard 60

C

Cabot, Susan 65–74, **65, 69, 70, 71, 72**, 130–131, **131**
Cahn, Edward L. 11
Callan, Michael 192
Calling Dr. Death (1943) 232, 235, 237–8
Cameron, Rod 172, 177
Capra, Frank 237
Captain Bob Steele and the Border Patrol (TV) 106
Captain Midnight (TV) 377, 391
Captive Wild Woman (1943) 241
Captive Women (1952) 76, 80–1, **83**, 274, 278–9
Cardula (unmade) 387
Caribbean Adventure see *I Eat Your Skin*
Carlson, Richard 2, 5, 130, 148, 151, 307, 313, 314, 315, 317, 319
Carnival of Souls (1962) 348
Carnival Rock (1957) 66, 73
Carpenter, John 205, 206
Carradine, John 90–1, 137–138, 141, **211**, 212, **212**, 235, 236, 241, 242, 248, 372, 378
Carras, Nicholas 116
Carrie (1976) 91
The Cases of Eddie Drake (TV) 312
The Cask of Amontillado (TV) 170
Cassarino, Gianbattista see Cassarino, Richard
Cassarino, Richard 86, **87**
Castle, Peggie 171
Castle, William 38, 218
Castle of the Living Dead (1964) 391
The Cat and the Canary (1939) 192
The Cat and the Canary (1978) 192–3
Cat Women of the Moon (1953) 116, 356
Chambers, John 227, 229
Chandler, Jeff 7
Chaney, Lon, Jr. 32, 81, 138–9, **145**, 166, **211**, 212, 213, **231**, 233–5, **233, 234**, 237, 238, 239, **239**, 241, 242, 247–8, 274, 280, 281, 300, **301**, 303–4, **303**, 305, 309–10, 326, 334–5, 378
Chaney, Lon, Sr. 235, 247, 304
Chang, Wah 202–3
Chanslor, Roy 95
Cheyenne (TV) 210
A Chip Off the Old Blob see *Son of Blob*
Chopping Mall (1986) 390
Christie, Agatha 171
Christopher, Robert 91
"Chrysalis" 147
Circus Boy (TV) 391
Circus of Horrors (1960) 191
Clair, Richard 206
Clark, Dane 385
Clarke, Arthur C. 48
Clarke, Gary 323, **323**
Clarke, Robert 75–92, **75, 77, 83, 87**, 275, 278, 373
Clarke, Robin 193

The Climax (1944) 299
Coates, Phyllis 288
Cobra Woman (1944) 302
Coburn, James 344
Coffin, Tristram 329
Cohen, Herman 27, 30, 38, 39, 312, 319–21, 322, 323, 324
Cohen, Mickey 88
Cohen, Nat 33, 171
Cohn, Harry 61
The Colbys (TV) 194
The Comedy of Terrors (1964) 35
"Conjure Wife" 238
Conkling, Xandra 86
The Conqueror (1956) 38
Conqueror Worm (1968) 33
Conrad, Robert 132, 139
Conte, Richard 95
Conway, Gary **320**, 321–2, **323**
Cook, Les 363
Coppola, Francis Ford 36, 45, 222
Corday, Mara **1, 6**
Corman, Gene 69, 93–104, **93**, 222–3, 224, 225, 227
Corman, Julie 390
Corman, Roger xi, 21, 26–7, 31, 36, 38, 39, 42, 43, 44, 66–7, 68, 69–71, 72, 73, 85, 90, 94, 95, 96, 97, 98–9, 100, 101, **101**, 103, 104, 130, 131, 151–2, 154–5, 156, 158–9, 160, 222, 223, 224, 227, 245, 271, 272, 348, 356, 364–6, 371, 382–4, 385, 386, 387–8, 389–91, 394
Corridors of Blood (1963) 175, 176, 178, 179, 180–3, **181**
Corrigan, Ray 366
Corwin, Sherrill 277
Cotten, Joseph 394–5, **394**
Coulouris, George 173
The Counterfeit Plan (1957) 171
Court, Hazel **101**
Cowan, Will 121
Crabtree, Arthur 178
Craig, James **334**, 335, 337, 340
Crawford, Joan 95, 151
The Crawling Hand (1963) 312, 318, 327–9, **328**
Creature from the Black Lagoon (1954) 5, 86, 144, 148–9, **149**, 150, **150**, 151, 152
The Creeper (1948) ix
The Creeping Unknown (1956) 213
The Cremators (1972) 144, 148, 151–2
Crime Against Joe (1956) 293–4
Criswell 250, 256
Croydon, John 174–5, 180, 182, 189

Cunha, Richard E. 38, 39, 105–117, 356, 364
The Curse of the Fly (1965) 62
The Curse of the Living Corpse (1964) 343, 344, 347–9, **348**, 352, 353
Curse of the Stone Hand (1965) **379**
Curse of the Swamp Creature (1966) 14
Curse of the Voodoo (1964) 183, 184, 186
Curteis, Ian 188–9
Curtis, Alan 211
Curtis, Billy 316–7
Curtis, Tony 7, 66
Curucu, Beast of the Amazon (1956) **153**, 154, 160–4, **161**, 308
Cushing, Peter 187, 353
The Cyclops (1957) 332–6, **333, 334**, 337, 340

D

D.O.A. (1949) 154
Dalton, Abby 67, 68, 385
Damon, Mark 36
Daniell, Henry 77–8
Dark, Christopher 53
"Dark Dominion" 120
Dark of the Moon (stage) **155**
Dark Star (1972) 196, 205
A Date with Death (1959) 88
Daughter of Dr. Jekyll (1957) 2, 10, 277, 278, 281–2, **281**, 332, **333**, 336–7, **336**, 340
Davis, Bette 151
Davis, Nancy 306
Dawn, Jack 356
Dawson, Anthony (actor) 174
Dawson, Anthony (director) *see* Margheriti, Antonio
Day, Doris 352
Day, Robert 174, 175, 178
Day, Vera 173
The Day the Earth Stood Still (1951) ix
Day the World Ended (1956) 24, **25**, 28, 30
Dead Man's Eyes (1944) 239, **239**, 246
Dead of Night (1946) 185
Deadly Duo (1962) 245
Death Race 2000 (1975) 262, 271–2
Deathsport (1978) 272
Decoy (TV) 164, 168
Deep Space (1988) 141
Dein, Edward xi, 237
Dein, Mildred xi

Index

The Del-Aires 349
De Laurentiis, Dino 14
del Ruth, Roy 164, 165
Del Vecchio, Carl xi
Del Vecchio, Debbie xi
de Maupassant, Guy 245
De Mering, David 256
De Metz, Danielle 60
Denning, Richard 27, 177
The Desert Hawk (1950) 274
Desert Sands (1955) 212
The Desperate Hours (stage) 130
Destination Moon (1950) ix
The Devil at Four O'Clock (1961) 64
The Devil Bat (1941) 191
"Devil Doll" 184
Devil Doll (1964) 183–6, **183**, 194
The Devil's Messenger (1962) 309, 312, 326, 327
Devon, Richard xi, 68, 69, **69**, 385
Dhiegh, Khigh 219
The Diana Nellis Dancers 113
Diary of a Madman (1963) 232, 245–7, **245**, 248
Dietz, Jack 121
Dillman, Bradford 282
Dillman, Dean, Jr. 282
Dillon, Brendan **101**
Di Lorenzo, Eddie 394
Dinosaurus! (1960) 196, 199, 202–3, **204**, 206, 207
Ditky, Judy 151
Dix, Richard 39
Dix, Robert 39
Dr. Christian (TV) 319
Dr. Heckyl and Mr. Hype (1980) 390
"Dr. Jekyll and Mr. Hyde" 82, 282
Dr. Jekyll and Mr. Hyde (1931) 176
Dodge City (1939) 222
Domergue, Faith 247
Donahue, Troy 132
Donen, Stanley 194
Donovan, King 314
"Donovan's Brain" 306, 307
Donovan's Brain (1953) 298, 306–7, 312 3
Doomsday Machine (1972) 294–5
Dowling, Allan 306, 307, 312
Dowling, Constance 318
"Dracula" 176
Dracula (1931) 171
Dracula ('50s stage version) 170
Dracula vs. Frankenstein (1971) 138–140, **139, 140**
Dracula's Revenge (unmade) 176

Dragonslayer (1981) 210, 219
Dragstrip Girl (1957) 19, 38
Drake, Tom 332, 334, **334**, 335, 378
The Dream Machine see *The Electronic Monster*
Dressed to Kill (1980) 35
Driggs, Pearl 86
The Drunkard (stage) 344
The Duel at Silver Creek (1952) 66
Duel on the Mississippi (1955) 394
Dufour, Val 385
Duggan, Andrew 91
Dunaway, Faye 196, 206
Duncan, Charlie 329
Duncan, David 119–28, **119**
Duncan, Pamela 384, **384**
"The Dune Roller" 148, 151
Dunlap, Paul 215
Dunn, James 130
Dupont, E.A. 164, 275, 279–80, 281
During One Night (1961) 184

E

Earth vs. the Flying Saucers (1956) 298
Earth vs. the Spider (1958) 267
Eastwood, Clint 5
Edwards, Bill 179
Edwards, Cliff "Ukulele Ike" 196
Egan, Richard 315, 318
Eisley, Anthony 72, 129–142, **129, 131, 135, 139**
"The Electric Man" 144
The Electronic Monster (1960) 171–3
Elliott, Ross 329
Emergency Hospital (1956) 294
Emmet, Michael **97**, 224
Enemy Mine (1985) 268
Engstrom, Jean 215, 244
Equinox (1971) 196, 204, 207
"Escapement" 171
Escapement see *The Electronic Monster*
Essex, David 151
Essex, Harry J. 143–52, **143**
Everitt, David xi
The Eye Creatures (1965) 38, 40
An Eye for an Eye (1966) 341
The Eyes of Laura Mars (1978) 196, 206–7

F

"F.P.1 Antwortet Nicht" 298, 300
F.P.1 Antwortet Nicht (1933) 298

Index

The Face in the Water see *Bride of the Gorilla*
Face of the Screaming Werewolf (1965) 370, 378
Fallon, Phillipa 385
"Fangoria" x, 174, 180
"Fantastic Films" x
Fantastic Voyage (1966) 127
Farentino, James 346, 347, 348
Farrell, Henry 150
The Fast and the Furious (1954) 24
Faulkner, Ed 134
Favorite Story (TV) 319
Fearless Fagan (1952) 130
Fegté, Ernst 89
Feist, Felix 312
Fernback, Gerry 187, 188
Ferrante, Tim xi
Ferrari, William 318
Fetchit, Stepin **251**
Field, Margaret 78, 79, 275
Field, Sally 78, 275
Fielder, Pat 120
Fiend Without a Face (1958) 170, 173, 176–9, **177**, 182, 194
"Filmfax" x
First Man into Space (1959) 170, 178, 179–80
Fisher, Terence 187
F.I.S.T. (1978) 94, 223
Fitzgerald, Barry 336
Fitzgerald, Mike xi
Five (1951) ix
Fleming, Eric **47**, **55**, 56, **56**
The Flesh and the Spirit (unmade) 243
The Flight That Disappeared (1961) 244–5
Flight to Mars (1951) 48
Floating Platform 1 Does Not Answer see *F.P.1. Antwortet Nicht*
Florey, Robert 305
The Fly (1958) 59, 60, 61, 188
Fly by Night (1942) 302
Flynn, Errol 212, 216, 222
Follis, Stan 87
Fonda, Henry 2
Ford, John 2, 15
Fort Apache (1948) 2
Foster, Susanna 298
4D Man (1959) 188, 196, 199, 200–2, **201**, 203, 207
Fowler, Gene, Jr. 56, 338
Fox, Edward 192
Franciosa, Tony 199
Francis, Kay 170

Franken, Steve **270**
Frankenheimer, John 218–9
Frankenstein (1931) 171, 182, 364
Frankenstein Island (1981) 91–2, 379–80
Frankenstein Meets Dracula (unmade) 353
Frankenstein Meets the Spacemonster (1965) 352
Frankenstein Meets the Wolf Man (1943) 304
Frankenstein 1970 (1958) 174, **209**, 210, 216–7, **216**
Frankenstein's Daughter (1958) 38, 39, 106, 113–6, **115**, 117, 356, 362, 363–4, 367
Frankham, David 60
Franklin, Robert xi
Franz, Arthur 124
Fraser, Sally 108
Freaks (1932) 189
Frederic, Marc 113, 114
Frenke, Dr. Eugene 232
Friday the 13th (1980) 35
From Hell It Came (1957) ix, 362
Frontier (TV) 222
The Frozen Continent (unmade) 89
The Frozen Dead (1967) 177
Fuller, Dolores **251**
Fulton, John P. 298
Funicello, Annette 28
Furie, Sidney J. **183**, 184

G

Gabor, Zsa Zsa **47**, **54**, 55, 56, 57
A Game of Death (1945) 76
Garland, Beverly 2, 153–68, **153**, **155**, 157, 161, 165, 308
Garland, Richard 154, **155**, 384
Garner, James 352
Garr, Teri 329
Garrity, Karen xi
Garry, Robert 86
Gas-s-s (1970) 26
Gazzara, Ben 199
Geeson, Judy 194
Genius at Work (1946) 76
Gershenson, Joseph 124
Ghost Catchers (1944) 370
Ghost of a Chance (upcoming production) 387
Ghost Town (1956) 211
The Ghoul Goes West (unmade) 253
Giant from the Unknown (1958) **105**,

Index

106–111, 116, 117
Gibsone, Mary Whitlock 313, 321
Gilmore, Stuart 80–1, 278
Girard, Bernard 167
The Girl in Lovers Lane (1960) 99
The Girl in Room 13 (1961) 113
Glasser, Bernard 57, 58, 59
Glen or Glenda (1953) 18, 250, 253
Globus, Yoram 36
Gluttony (unmade) 387
Gog (1954) 312, 315–8, **316**, 360–1, **360**
Golan, Menahem 36
Gold (1934) 307, 312, 313
The Golden Mistress (1954) 2, 3
Goldwyn, Sam 19, 27
Goliath and the Barbarians (1960) 31
Golos, Len 144
Gone with the Wind (1939) 78
Gordon, Alex xi, 18, 27–8, 38, 170, 171, 177, 179, 180, 187, 188, 253, 259
Gordon, Bert I. 2, 11, 107, 332–3, 334, 336
Gordon, Flora M. 333
Gordon, Leo 95–6, 101
Gordon, Richard 169–94, **169, 183, 190**
Gough, Michael 192
Grave Robbers from Outer Space see *Plan 9 from Outer Space*
Graves, Peter x
Gray, Coleen xi, 340–1
The Great Gabbo (1929) 185
Gries, Tom 307, 312, 313
Griffith, Charles B. 382, 383, 385, 386, 387, 388, 389, 390, 391
Grip of the Strangler see *The Haunted Strangler*
Gross, Jack 301
Guild, Leo 308
Guillermin, John 14
Gun Fury (1953) 382
Gunslinger (1956) 154, 156–8, 160
Gunsmoke (1953) **65**, 66
Guthrie, Les 88, 89
Guthrie, "Pop" 89
Gwynne, Anne 238

H

Haas, Hugo 11
Haffner, Jack 373
Hagman, Larry 206
Hale, Alan, Jr. 329
Hale, Jean 346
Haliday, Bryant **183**, 184, 185, 186, **188**

Hall, Jon 293
Haller, Dan 223
Halsey, Brett 60
Hamilton, George 35
Hammett, Dashiell 306
The Hand (1981) 356
Hand of Death (1961) 2, 11–3, **12**
Harbor Command (TV) 319
Hard, Fast and Beautiful (1951) 76
Hardy, Oliver **357**
Harris, Anthony 205–6
Harris, Jack H. 195–207, **195**
Harris, Robert H. 322, 323–4
Harrison, Sandra 322
Hartford, Kenneth 141; see also Herts, Kenneth
Hartman, Margot **343**, 345–6, 347
Harvey, Cy 184
Harvey, Laurence 219
Harvey, Marilyn **75**
Harvey, William Fryer 305
Haskin, Byron 262, 268, 272
A Hatful of Rain (stage) 199
Hatton, Raymond 28
The Haunted Strangler (1958) 170, 173–6, **175**, 177, 178, 181, 182, 194
Hawaiian Eye (TV) 130, 132, 139, 210
Hawks, Howard 96, 223
Hawthorne, Nathaniel 101
Hayden, Sterling 53
Hayes, Allison 155, **384**
Hayes, Helen 31
Hays, Bill 159
Haze, Jonathan xi, 158, 382, **387**, 388
Hecht, Ben 55
"Hector Servadac, Or, Career of a Comet" 62
Heermance, Richard 48, 49, 51, 53, 55, 64
Heflin, Van 66
Hell Raiders (1968) 14
Hell's Angels on Wheels (1967) 191
Hemingway's Adventures of a Young Man (1962) 389
Hemsley, Estelle **340**
Henley, Hobart 290
Henreid, Paul 305
Hepburn, Audrey 341
Herts, Kenneth 308–9, 325, 327; see also Hartford, Kenneth
Hewitt, David L. 136, 268
Hewitt, Heather 352
The Hideous Sun Demon (1959) 76, 82–8, **85, 87,** 89–90, 92
Higgins, John C. 243, 267

Index

High School Caesar (1960) 38
High School Confidential! (1958) 385–6
Highway Patrol (TV) 319
Hiller, Arthur 96
Hiller, Wendy 192
Hilliard, Richard 346
Hilligoss, Candace 348
Hiner, Phil 82
Hit Man (1972) 94
Hitler, Adolf 298, 302
Hoag, Doane 83
Hockman, Ned 166
Hoey, Michael 132, 134
Holloway, Stanley 383
Holton, Scot xi
Homeier, Skip 166
Hope, Bob 192
Hopkins, Anthony 185
"The Horla" 245
Horror Hospital (1973) 191–2
Horror Hotel (1960) 191
Horror of Dracula (1958) 176
The Horror of Party Beach (1964) 344, 347, 348, 349–52, **351**
Horror Planet see *Inseminoid*
Horrors of the Black Museum (1959) 27
Hot Car Girl (1958) 94, 95, 222
Hot Rod Gang (1958) 38
Hot Rod Girl (1956) 19
House of Frankenstein (1944) 298, 304
House of the Black Death (1965) 378
How to Make a Monster (1958) 38–9, 312, 320, 322–4, **323**
Howard, Moe 59, 262
Howlin, Olin **197**
Hud (1963) 38
Hudson, Rock 7, 8
Hughes, Howard 80, 278
Hussey, Olivia 192
Huston, John 146, 306
Hyde-White, Wilfrid 192, 193

I

I Eat Your Skin (1970) 344, 348, 352, 353
I Escaped from Devil's Island (1973) 104
"I, Gabriel" 300
I Led Three Lives (TV) 84, 315, 319
I Married a Communist (1949) 2
I Married a Monster from Outer Space (1958) **331**, 332, 337–40, **339**
I, Mobster (1958) 96–8
I, The Jury (1953) 150

I Walked with a Zombie (1943) 298, 299, 305–6
I Was a Teenage Frankenstein (1957) **20**, 27, 30, 312, 319–22, **320**, 324
I Was a Teenage Werewolf (1957) ix, **20**, 27, 30, 39, 322, 338
Illing, Peter 172
In the Heat of the Night (1967) 52
The Incredible Petrified World (1960) 76, 90–1, 370, 372–4, 377
Indestructible Man (1956) 274, 278, 280–1
Indiana Jones and the Temple of Doom (1984) 204
Inseminoid (1981) 193–4
The Intruder (1961) 103
Invasion from Mars see *The Angry Red Planet*
Invasion of the Animal People (1962) 376
Invasion of the Body Snatchers (1956) 308
Invasion of the Saucer-Men (1957) 40
Invasion of the Zombies see *The Horror of Party Beach*
Invasion, U.S.A. (1952) 279
Invisible Agent (1942) 298
Invisible Invaders (1959) 2, 11
The Invisible Man Returns (1940) 298, **299**
The Invisible Woman (1941) 298
Ireland, John 158, 325
Iselin, Alan 347, 348, 349, 352
Island of Death see *Island of the Doomed*
"The Island of Dr. Moreau" 44
Island of Terror (1967) 187–8, 189
Island of the Doomed (1966) 382, 392–3
It! (1967) 177
It Came from Hollywood (1982) 86
It Came from Outer Space (1953) 144, 146–8, **147**, 150
It Conquered the World (1956) 21, **157**, 158, 223
It Happened One Night (1934) 48
It! The Terror from Beyond Space (1958) 223

J

Jacobs, Arthur A. 105–117
James, Chic **201**
Jet Attack (1958) 11
Joan of Arc (1948) 79, 276
Jochsberger, Steve 4, 6, 12, 56, 211, 234

"Johnny Guitar" 95
Johnny Guitar (1954) 95
Johnson, Carl 257, 361, 362
Johnson, George Clayton 103
Johnson, Russell **147**
Johnson, Tom xi
Johnson, Tor **211, 212,** 250, **251,** 257, 259, **355,** 356, 361-2
The Joker Is Wild (1957) 164
Jones, Carolyn 308
Jones, L.Q. 138
Jones-Moreland, Betsy 67
Jory, Victor 319
Joseph, Jackie **387,** 388
Journey to the Center of Time (1967) **129,** 136
Journey to the Seventh Planet (1961) 13, 262, 265, 267
Joyce, William 352
Judge, Arline 329
Jungle Woman (1944) 232, 240-1, **240,** 246

K

Karloff, Boris 32, 33, 39, 48, 76-7, **77,** 78, 170, 171, 173-5, **175,** 176, 178, 180, 181, **181,** 182, 192, **209,** 212, 215, 216, **216,** 217, 218, 244, 247, 298, 299, 300, 305, 309, 324-5
Katch, Kurt **214**
Katzman, Sam 2
Kay, Richard 308
Kaylis, Al 34
Keene, Tom **255,** 256
Kelly, Paul 239
Kemmer, Ed 108
Kent, Carl 77
Kent, Jean 174
Kent, Robert E. 245
Kevan, Jack 86
The Keys of the Kingdom (1944) 210
Khigh Dhiegh 219
The Killers (1946) 298
Killers' Cage (1958) 386, 387
Killers from Space (1954) 356, 359
Kilpatrick, Shirley **75,** 81
King, Andrea 378
King, Donna 86
King, Frank 374
King, Marilyn 86
King, Maurice 374
King Kong (1933) 136
King Kong (1976) 14

King of the Monsters (unmade) 217-8
The King Sisters 86
Kinnoch, Ronald 178
Kirkman, Robin 82-3, 85
Kiss of Death (1947) 66
Knight, Sandra 39, 114, 363
Koch, Howard W. 209-220, **209,** 241, 267, 293-4
Kovack, Nancy **245**
Kowalski, Bernard L. 104, 221-9
Krakatoa, East of Java (1969) 222
Kramer, Charles **365**

L

LaBarre, James xi
The Lady and the Monster (1944) 306
Lady Frankenstein (1972) 382, 390, 393-5, **394**
Lady in the Lake (1946) 238
Landis, John 204
Landon, Michael 39, 322-3
Lang, Fritz 298
Langan, Glenn **29**
Lange, Jessica 14
Lansing, Robert 201, **201**
Lapenieks, Vilis 82, 87
Lassie (TV) 113
Laurel, Stan **357**
Lauren, Rod 327
LeBorg, Reginald 211, 215, 217, 218, 231-48, **231, 246**
Leder, Herbert J. 177
Lee, Christopher 176, 353
The Leech Woman (1960) 124, 332, 340-1, **340**
The Legend of Hillbilly John (1973) 196
Lehmann, Beatrix 192
Leiber, Fritz 238
Leigh, Nelson 53
Leonard, Sheldon 113
Lesser, Sol 286, 289, 291
Levine, Joseph E. 21, 31
Lewis, Louise 322
Lewton, Val ix, 76, 78, 241, 298, 305-6
Life Returns (1934) 232
Lightning Bolt (1966) 134-135, **135**
The Linden Tree (stage) 170
"The Lion Man" 186
Lippert, Robert L. 19, 57, 59, 61, 94-5, 322
The Little Shop of Horrors (1960) 356, 365, 382, 383, 387-90, **387,** 393
The Little Shop of Horrors (1986) 390

Littman, Bill xi
The Lizard Man (unmade) 213
Lloyd, Harold, Jr. 39
Lockhart, Gene 319
Logan's Run (1976) 356
"London Mystery Magazine" 184, 185
The Lone Ranger (TV) 106
Long, Amelia Reynolds 177
Lorre, Peter 32, 39, 243, 305
The Losers (1970) 191
Lost Horizon (1937) 48, 237
The Lost World (unmade remake) 2
Love at First Bite (1979) 35, 36, 387
Love from a Stranger (1937) 171
Love Me Forever (1934) 232
Love Slaves of the Amazon (1957) 308
Lovejoy, Frank 53
Lubin, Arthur xi
Lucas, George 21
Luce, Greg xi
Lucisano, Fulvio 271
Ludwig, Edward 121
Lugones, Alex xi
Lugosi, Bela 18, 31, 77, **169**, 170–1, 176, 182, 191, 196, 212, **212**, 213, 241, 242, 248, 250, 251–5, 256, 259, 298, 299, 300, 360
Lugosi, Bela, Jr. **251**, 253
Lugosi, Hope 254
Lund, John 66
Lundigan, William 315
Lundin, Vic **266**
Lupino, Ida 76, 91
Lynley, Carol 192

M

M (1931) 32
M Squad (TV) 226
Macabre (1958) 218
"Macbeth" 101
McCalla, Irish 112
McCarty, Norma 256
McCoy, Tony 253
McDonnell, Dave xi
McDowall, Roddy 346
McEnery, Peter 192
McGee, Mark xi
Machine-Gun Kelly (1958) 67, **70**, 71, 73, 100
Macho Callahan (1970) 222
McKinnon, Mona **255**, 257
McLendon, Gordon 14, 40
MacMurray, Fred 95

MacQueen, Scott xi
McQueen, Steve 199, 340–1
Mad Doctor of Blood Island (1969) 38, 42, **43**
The Mad Room (1969) 59, 154, 167
Madison, Rock 371
Magic (1978) 185, 194
The Magic Carpet (1951) 2
The Magnetic Monster (1953) 307, 312, 313–5, 316, 318, 321
The Magnificent Seven (1960) 52
Maid from Nymphenburg (unmade) 391
Maine, Charles Eric 171
Mainwaring, Dan 57, 58
Maley, Gloria 193
Maley, Nick 193
"The Maltese Falcon" 306
The Maltese Falcon (1941) 306
Man Beast (1956) 370–1, **371**, 372, 373, 377
The Man from Planet X (1951) ix, 76, 78–9, 80, **80**, 81, 88, 91, 92, **273**, 274–7, **276**, 278, 281, 283
Man Made Monster (1941) 144, **145**, 280
The Manchurian Candidate (1962) 210, 218–9
Mank, Greg xi
Mankiewicz, Joseph 53
Manlove, Dudley 256
Mann of Action (TV pilot) 325
Manning, Patricia 85
Mantee, Paul **266**
Maraschal, Launce **177**
The March of Medicine (TV) 262
Marco, Paul 249–59, **249, 251, 255, 258**
Margheriti, Antonio 135
Marlowe, Hugh 53
Marquette, Jacques xi
Mars, Lani **71**
Marshall, Herbert 60–1, 318
Martin, George 392
Martin, Skip 192
Martin, Strother 227, 229
Marton, Andrew 313, 314
Martucci, Mark v, xi
Mascelli, Joseph 282
Maslansky, Paul 391
Mason, Tom **255**, 256
Massey, Daniel 192
Master of Horror (1966) 196
Matinee Theater (TV) 338
Maurer, Norman 59, 262–3, 265
Maverick (TV) 210
Maxwell, Robert 286
May, Joe 298

Maytime (1937) 332
Medina, Patricia 394
Meet Corliss Archer (TV) 319
Megowan, Don **309**
Meisner, Sanford 66, 71
Melchior, Ib J. 261–72, **261, 270**
Melchior, Lauritz 262
Men in Space (TV) 272
Men of Annapolis (TV) 38, 319
Menzies, Heather 229
Menzies, William Cameron 286, 289–90
Mesa of Lost Women (1953) ix
Metropolis (1926) 298
Metzger, Radley 192
Meyer, Lloyd **155**
Miami Undercover (TV) 210
Midnight Movie Massacre (1988) 92
The Mighty Gorga (1969) 130, 136, 140
Miles, Sylvia 346
Milland, Ray 95, 100
Miller, Dick 68, **69**, 158, 382, 385, 388
Miller, John 88
Miller, Mike 88
Miller, Robin 346
Millgate, Irvine 198
Milli, Robert **348**
Milner, Dan 24
Milner, Jack 24
Milton, Dave 57
Miner, Allen 211
Mirisch, Walter **52**, 53, 199
Missile to the Moon (1958) 106, 113–4, 116–7, 364
Mission: Impossible (TV) 222
Mr. Deeds Goes to Town (1936) 48
Mr. Roberts (stage) 130
Mr. Smith Goes to Washington (1939) 48
Mitchell, Cameron 91, 392, 393
Mitchell, Laurie 55, 56, **56**
Mitchum, Jim 326
Moby Dick (1956) 146
A Modern Marriage (1950) 78
Mohr, Gerald 88
The Mole People (1956) 2, 5, 7–8, **7**
The Molten Meteor see *The Blob*
Monroe, Marilyn 291
The Monroes (TV) 222
Monster from the Ocean Floor (1954) 94–5, 364
Monster on the Campus (1958) 120, 122, 123–4, **123**
The Monster That Challenged the World (1957) 120, **121**, 127
Monstroid (1978) 130, 141, 326–7
Monstrosity (1964) 278, 282, 283

Montes, Elisa 392
Montgomery, Robert 238
Moore, Alvy 138
Moore, "Duke" **255**, 256
Moore, Grace 232
Moorhead, Jean **37**
Moreno, Antonio 84
Morgan, Cody xi
Moritz, Milt 38
Morrill, John 87
Morris, Barboura 68, 130–1
Morris, Chester 170
Morris, Wayne 177, **311**
Morrow, Jeff xi
Morrow, Jo 141
Moses, Chuck 213
Mother Goose a Gogo (1966) 203
Mother Riley Meets the Vampire (1952) 18, **169**, 171, 196
Motorcycle Gang (1957) 38
Move Over, Darling (1963) 351–2
Mowbray, Alan 286
The Mummy and the Curse of the Jackals (1969) 136–7, 141
The Mummy's Ghost (1944) **231**, 232–7, **233, 234**, 240
The Mummy's Tomb (1942) 236
Muren, Dennis 204
Murphy, Audie 66
Murphy, Bri 372, 373
Murphy, Donald 114, 363, 364
Murphy, Mary 172
Muscle Beach Party (1964) 39
My Science Project (1985) 22
My Son, the Vampire see *Mother Riley Meets the Vampire*
Myrt and Marge (radio) 388

N

N.Y.P.D. (TV) 222
Nader, George 7, 45
Nagel, Anne **145**
Naish, J. Carrol 138, 238
Naked Evil (1966) 186–7
Naked Paradise (1957) 27, 154, 160
Napier, Alan **101**
The Navy vs. the Night Monsters (1966) 130, 132–134, **133, 365**, 366
The Neanderthal Man (1953) 154, 164, 274, 275, 278, 279–80, 356, 357, 358–9, 367
Nelson, Ed x, 68, 98, 224, 382
Nelson, Gene 11

Nelson, Lori xi, 3, **6, 25**
Neumann, Dorothy **384**
Neumann, Kurt 59
Never Love a Stranger (1957) 199
Newland, John 196
Newman, Paul 199
Nicholson, James H. 18, 19, 27, 33, 34–5, 38, 88, 100–1, 271
Nicholson, Meredith 111
Night Crawlers (upcoming production) 36
Night of the Blood Beast (1958) 94, 96, **97, 221**, 222, 223–4, 226
Night of the Ghouls (1959) 250, 256, 257–9, **355**, 362
The Night the Silicates Came see *Island of Terror*
Nixon, Allan **251**
Nolan, William 103
Non-Stop New York (1937) 298
Norma Rae (1979) 275
Nosferatu (1922) 176
Not of This Earth (1957) ix, 154, **157**, 158, 159–60
No. 13 Demon Street (TV) 308–10, 312, 325–6

O

O'Bannon, Dan 205
"The Obi" 186
O'Brian, Hugh 346
O'Brien, Edmond 11, 154
O'Brien, Willis 202
O'Connolly, Jim 191
Octaman (1971) 144, 151
The Odd Couple (1968) 210
O'Donnell, Bob 30
Of Mice and Men (1939) 242–3, 378
Ogilvy, Ian 391, **392**
Old English (1930) 172
On the Isle of Samoa (1950) 66
1,000,000 A.D. (1973) 140–1
One Million B.C. (1940) 62, 63
One Night of Love (1934) 232
Operation Pacific (1951) 130
Ordung, Wyott 180
The Other (1972) 338
Ottoson, Carl 265
Our Town (1940) 289
Ouspenskaya, Maria 300, 304
The Outlaw (1943) 80
Outrage (1950) 76

P

Paige, Robert 305
Pal, George 21, 120, 121, 124, 125–6, 127, 203
Pallos, Steven 186
Pardon Us (1931) **357**
Paris, Jerry 132
Parla, Paul xi
Payne, Tom 163
Payton, Barbara 307
Peckinpah, Sam 52
Perkins, Gil xi
The Perry Como Show (TV) 262
Peter Gunn (TV) 391
Peter Pan (1924) 288
Peterson, Nan 85
The Phantom from 10,000 Leagues (1956) 24
Phantom Lady (1944) 298
Pharaoh's Curse (1957) 210, 213–5, **214**, 286, 293–4, **293**
Philips, Lee 346, 348
Phillips, Kate 198–9
Philo Vance's Secret Mission (1947) 211
Phobia (upcoming production) 18
Picnic (stage) 130
Pierce, Arthur C. 88, 89, 91, 134
Pierce, Jack P. 109, 114, **145, 233**, 356, 358, 364
Pine, Howard 122
Pine, William H. 122
Pink, Sidney 13, 33–4, 262, 263, 265
Pit and the Pendulum (1961) **32**, 35
Pivar, Ben 124, 233, 236, 237, 238
Places in the Heart (1984) 275
Plan 9 from Outer Space (1959) 250, 253, 255–7, **255**, 259
Planet of the Apes (1968) 49, 227
Planet of the Vampires (1965) 262, 271
"Playboy" 226, 391
Poe, Edgar Allan 31, 33, 35, 101, 170, 196, 245, 348
Police Academy (1984) 391
Pollexfen, Jack 78, 80, 273–83, **273**
Pollock, Ellen 192
Port Sinister (1953) 278, 279, 356
Powell, Amos 391
Pratt, Jim 8
The Premature Burial (1962) 94, 100–1, **101**, 348
Presley, Elvis 63
Pretty Poison (1968) 154, 166–7, 168
Price, Stanley 194
Price, Vincent 31, 32, **32**, 33, 39, 60,

101, **102**, 103, 154, 166, 245–6, **245**, 248, 298, **299**, 394
Private Parts (1972) 94, 104
The Projected Man (1967) 184, 187, 188–9, **188**
Psycho (1960) 166, 227, 347
Psychomania (1964) 344, 345–7, **345**, 348, 353
PT-109 (1963) 352

Q

Quattrocchi, Frank 188
Queen of Outer Space (1958) **47**, 51, **54**, 55–7, **56**, 58, 117
"Queen of the Universe" 55
The Quest (TV) 41

R

"The Racer" 262, 271
The Racers (1955) 382
Racket Squad (TV) 130
Raid on Rommel (1971) 60
The Rainmaker (stage) 346
Rains, Claude 300
Ralston, Vera Hruba 306
Randall, Meg **249**
Rathbone, Basil 31, 33, 171–2, 212, 241, 242, 243, 247
Rathbone, Ouida 247
Rawhide (TV) 56
Ray, Aldo 332
Ray, Fred Olen 141
Ray, Nicholas 95
Read, Jan 173, 176
Reagan, Ronald 317
Real Genius (1985) 22
Reason, Rex xi
The Rebel Set (1959) 338
Rebel Without a Cause (1955) 95
Redgrave, Michael 185
Redlin, William 268
Redmond, Harry 313, 317
Reed, Oliver 390
Reeves, George 286, **287**, 288, 358
Reeves, Michael 33, 391
Reeves, Steve 31
Reicher, Frank 234, 235
Reinhardt, Max 274
Renay, Liz 88
Reptilicus (1962) 13, 33–4, 262, 265–7

Return of the Fly (1959) 48, 59–62, 64
Revenge of the Creature (1955) 2–5, **4**, **6**, 8
Rey, Alvino 86
Reynolds, Burt 329
Reynolds, J. Edward 256, 257
Rice, Milt 215
Richard, Cliff 184
Richard Diamond (TV) 222
"Richard III" 101
Ride Clear of Diablo (1954) 66
Riders to the Stars (1954) 307, 315, 316, 317, 318
Ridges, Stanley 298–9
Riley, "Flash" 391
Rive, Kenneth **183**, 184
Rivkin, Allen 306
Roach, Hal, Jr. 325
Robards, Jason, Jr. 201
Robards, Jason, Sr. **77**
Robbins, Harold 66
Roberts, Byron 62, 63, 64
Roberts, Kenneth 122
Robertson, Cliff 352
Robertson, Joseph F. 327
Robinson, Ann 92
Robinson, Chris 99
Robinson Crusoe on Mars (1964) 262, **266**, 267–8, 272
Robson, Mark 78
Rock All Night (1957) 382, 385–6
Rock Around the Clock (1956) 385
The Rocket Man (1954) 2, 154
Rodan (1957) 120, 122, 127
Rogers, Jean Scott 180
Rogers, Lorraine 347
Rogers, Wayne 203
Rohauer, Raymond 192
Romero, Eddie 41, 42, 43, 44
Rosemary's Baby (1968) 218
Rosenberg, Aaron 5
Roth, Gene **110**
Rudley, Herbert 243
Run Angel Run (1969) 191
Runaway Daughters (1956) 27
Runser, Mary xi
Ruppel, K.L. 178
Rusoff, Lou 24–5, 38
Russell, Jack 280
Russell, Vy 280
Ryan, Sheila 211
Rybnick, Harry 308

S

The Saga of the Viking Women and Their Voyage to the Waters of the Great Sea Serpent (1957) 66, 67–8
The Saint (TV) 391
Sands of Iwo Jima (1949) 2
Sangaree (1953) 122
Sarino, Ben *see* Cassarino, Richard
Satan in High Heels (1962) 345
"Satellite of Blood" 180
Savage Sisters (1974) 42, 45
Sawaya, George **211**
Sawyer, Joe **147**
Saylor, Syd 329
Scared to Death (1947) ix
Schallert, William 81, 275
Scheider, Roy 348, 349
Schenck, Aubrey 210, 217, 218, 241, 243, 267, 293
Schenck, Joseph M. 217
Schlock (1972) 204–5, 207
Schwalb, Ben 49, 55, 56, 57
Schwartz, Fred 183
Schwartz, Sidney 144
Science Fiction Theatre (TV) **311**, 319
"The Scientific American" 316, 317
Scott, Gordon 290–1
Scott, Zachary 171, 177
Secret File: Hollywood (1962) 91
The Secret Invasion (1964) 100
The Secret Man (1958) 178
Secret of the Purple Reef (1960) 98
Secrets of Sex (1970) 189–91
Seeley, E.S. 83
Selander, Lesley 294
Selznick, David O. 2, 19, 315
Serling, Rod 49
Shadow of the Cat (1961) 191
Shakespeare, William 101
Shayne, Robert 358, 359
The She-Beast (1965) 391–2, **392**
The She-Creature (1956) 363
She Demons (1958) 106, **110**, 111–3, 115
She Freak (1966) 366
She Was a Hippy Vampire see *The Wild World of Batwoman*
She-Wolf of London (1946) 277–8
She Wore a Yellow Ribbon (1949) 2
Sheena, Queen of the Jungle (TV) 112
Sherman, Sam xi, 187
She's for Me (1943) 233
Shields, Arthur **281**, 282, 336
Sholem, Lee 214, 285–95, **285**, **293**
Shonteff, Lindsay **183**, 184

The Shop at Sly Corner (stage) 170
Shorr, Richard 329–30
"Siblings" 298
Siegel, Don 62
The Sign of Rome see *Sign of the Gladiator*
Sign of the Gladiator (1959) 31
The Silver Chalice (1954) 382
Similuk, Peter 86
Simms, Ginny 298
Simonson, Theodore 198
Sinatra, Frank 164, 218, 219, 386
Siodmak, Curt 154, 160–1, 162, 163, 297–310, **297**, **309**, 312–3, 314–5, 325, 326
Siodmak, Robert 298, 302–3, 307, 313
Sirk, Douglas 336
Skillin, John xi
"The Skin Diver and the Lady" 391
Skotak, Robert xi, 83, 87, 270, 274, 365
The Slams (1973) 94
A Slight Case of Murder (stage) 130
Small, Edward 102–3, 245, 246, 247
Smith, Maxwell 317
So Evil, My Sister (1973) 232, 247
Soldier of Fortune (1955) 389
Solomon, Joe 191
Somebody Up There Likes Me (1956) 199
Something for Nothing (stage) 144
Son of Ali Baba (1952) 66
Son of Blob (1972) 196, 205–6, 207
The Son of Dr. Jekyll (1951) 277–8, 281
Son of Dracula (1943) 242, 298, 302–4, **303**, 305
Sondergaard, Gale 237
Song of Frankenstein (stage) 305
The Sorcerers (1967) 174
The Sorceress (unmade) 91
Sorority Girl (1957) 66, 67, 73
Space Master X-7 (1958) 48, 57–9, 63, 64
Space Patrol see *Midnight Movie Massacre*
Space Station, U.S.A. see *Gog*
Spacek, Sissy 91
Spalding, Harry 59, 61, 62
Spelling, Aaron 113
Spielberg, Steven 21
The Spiral Staircase (1946) 298
SSSSSS (1973) 222, 227–9, **227**
Stalag 17 (1953) 344
Stanhope, Paul 114, 115, 364
Star in the Dust (1956) 7
Star Slammer (1986) **195**
Star Wars (1977) 22

Stark Fear (1962) 166
"Starlog" x
Steele, Barbara **32**, 389
Steele, Bob 108
Steffen, Sirry 328, **328**
Stein, Michael xi
Sten, Anna 27–8
Stevens, Connie 132
Stevenson, Robert Louis 82, 282
Stewart, David J. 73
Stokey, Susan **195**
Stone, Lewis 19
A Stone for Danny Fisher (stage) 66
Stover, George xi
"Stranglehold" 173
Strasberg, Susan 247
Streisand, Barbra 206
Striepeke, Dan 227, 228, 229
Strock, Herbert L. 141, 247, 309, 311–30, **311, 328**
Strudwick, Pete 271
Strudwick, Shepperd 346
Studio One (TV) 199
Sturlin, Ross **221, 225**, 226
Sullivan, Jim 14
Superman and the Mole-Men (1951) 286–7, **287**, 288, 357–8
Sutton, John 60, **299**
Svengali (1931) 185
Swamp Women (1956) 154, 156
Sweet and Lowdown (1943) 332
Sword of Venus (1953) 76, 278
Syphers, Jerry **379**

T

T-Bird Gang (1959) 99
Talbot, Lyle 256
Talbott, Gloria 10, **281**, 331–41, **331, 334, 336, 339, 340**
Tales of Frankenstein (TV pilot) 308, **309**
Tales of Robin Hood (1951) 76
Tales of the Bizarre see *Secrets of Sex*
Tamiroff, Akim 242, 243
Tana, Leni 112–3
Tarantula (1955) **1**, 2, 5, **6**, 8
Tarzan and the Slave Girl (1950) 291
Tarzan's Magic Fountain (1949) 286, 290
Taussig, Frank 107
Taylor, Eric 302
Taylor, Kent 329
Taylor, Richard 316
Taylor, Rod 49, 53, **126**

Teenage Caveman (1958) 224
Teenage Monster (1957) ix
Teenage Zombies (1958) 370, 372, 374–5, **374**
Temple, Shirley 2
Tennant, Victoria 194
Tenney, Del 343–53, **343**
Terenzio, Maurice xi
Terrell, Ken 282
Terrell, Steven 40
Terror in the Haunted House (1958) 366
Terror Is a Man (1959) 44
Terror of the Bloodhunters (1962) 92
Terry, Phillip 340
Them! (1954) 120–1, 385
They're Here (upcoming production) 18
The Thing from Another World (1951) ix, 96, 223
The Thing That Couldn't Die (1958) 120, 122–3, 124
Thomas, Danny 113
Thomas, Harry 114, 115, 251, 355–67, **355, 357, 360, 365**
Thomas, Hugh, Jr. 257
Thomas, Larri 162, 163
Thomas, William C. 122
Thompson, Marshall 177–8
"The Thought Monster" 177
The Three Stooges in Orbit (1962) 59
The Three Stooges Meet Hercules (1962) 52, 59
3000 A.D. see *Captive Women*
Thriller (TV) 309
Tickle Me (1965) 63
"The Time Machine" 49, 124–5, 128
The Time Machine (1960) 49, 120, 124–7, **126**, 128, 203
The Time Travelers (1964) 262, 267, 268–71, **268, 270**, 272
Timpone, Tony xi
Tobey, Kenneth 2, 130
Tobor the Great (1954) 286, 291–3, **292**
Tobruk (1967) 94, 96, 223
Todd, Sally 114, 117, 362, 364
Tomahawk (1951) 66
Too Much, Too Soon (1958) 216
Tors, Ivan 307, 312, 313, 314, 315–6, 317, 319
Totter, Audrey 11
Tower of Evil (1971) 184, **190**, 191
Tower of London (1962) 95, 101–3, **102**
The Trail of the Lonesome Pine (1936) 111
Trans-Atlantic Tunnel (1935) 298
Treasure of Monte Cristo (1948) 274

Index

The Treasure of the Sierra Madre (1948) 45
A Tree Grows in Brooklyn (1945) 332
Tremayne, Les 263
The Trouble Giants (unmade) 386
Tryon, Tom **331**, 338, 339
"Der Tunnel" 298
Turner, Lana 329–30
Tuttle, William 356
The 27th Day (1957) 382
Twice Told Tales (1963) 154, 166
The Twilight People (1972) 44
The Twilight Zone (TV) 49
Tyler, Beverly 244

U

Ullman, Elwood 55, 63
Ulmer, Edgar G. 79, 88, 89, **273**, 274, 275, 277, 279, 280, 281, 336
Ulmer, Shirley 88
Unconquered (1947) 370
The Undead (1957) 382, 383–5, **384**
The Unearthly (1957) 361, 362
Untamed Women (1952) ix
Untamed Youth (1957) 216
The Untouchables (TV) 210
Usher, Marge 250, 253
Ustinov, Peter 332, 382

V

Vail, Myrtle 388
Valley of the Dragons (1962) 51, 60, 62–4
Valley of the Redwoods (1960) 98
Vampira **249, 251**, 253, 255–6
The Vampire's Tomb (unmade) 253, 255
Van Doren, Mamie 134, **365**
Van Eyck, Peter 306
Van Patten, Dick 346
Variety (1925) 275
Vaughn, Robert 344
The Veil (TV) 324–5
Velia, Tania 56–7
Verberkmoes, Robert 350
Verne, Jules 62, 63, 263
Ve Sota, Bruno 377, 382, 385
Vetter, Charles 179, 180
Vickers, Yvette 226
Victor, Katherine xi, 90, 374–5, **375**, 379
Victoria Regina (stage) 31

Violent Midnight see *Psychomania*
Virginia City (1940) 222
The Virginian (TV) 227
Vittes, Louis 338–9
Vogel, Virgil xi, 5, 376
Volpe 213
von Nordhoff, Baron Florenz 178
von Stroheim, Erich 185, 306
Von Theumer, Ernst 392
Von Zell, Harry 107
Voodoo Blood Bath see *I Eat Your Skin*
Voodoo Island (1957) 174, 215, 217, 218, 244
Voodoo Woman (1957) 362–3
Vosper, Frank 171

W

Waggner, George 300–1, 302, 304
Wah Chang 202–3
Walcott, Gregory **255**, 256
Wald, Malvin 78, 82
Wanger, Walter 55
Wanted: Dead or Alive (TV) 341
War of the Satellites (1958) 66, 69, **69**
War Paint (1953) 210, 214
Warner, Jack L. 216, 305
Warren, Bill xi
Warren, Gene 202–3
Warren, Jerry 81, 90, 91, 92, 369–80, **369, 379**
Warren, Norman 193
The Wasp Woman (1959) 66, 71–4, **71**, 100, 130–131, **131**
"The Water Witch" 122
Watson, Alan 191–2
Watson, Bobs 344
Watz, Ed xi, 286
Wayne, John 2, 15, 38
Wayne, Pat 45
Weary River (1929) 18
Weaver, Jon xi
Webb, Gordon 228
Webb, Richard 377
Weird Science (1985) 22
"Weird Tales" 177
Weird Woman (1944) 238
Weisburd, Dan 202
Weissmuller, Johnny 290
Weld, Tuesday 166, 168
Welles, Mel 381–95, **381, 384, 387, 392, 394**
Wells, H.G. 49, 124, 125, 128, 263
Wengraf, John **316**

We're No Angels (1955) 332
Werewolf (TV) 41
Werewolf in a Girls' Dormitory (1963) 183
West Point Widow (1941) 302
West Side Story (1961) 52
Westmore, Bud 356
"What Ever Happened to Baby Jane?" 150
What Ever Happened to Baby Jane? (1962) 144, 150-1
When Hell Broke Loose (1958) 263
When Worlds Collide (1951) ix
White, Bill 378
White, Jon Manchip 186
White Pongo (1945) 370
Whitney, John Hay 19
Who Was That Lady? (stage) 132
The Wild One (1953) 344
The Wild Ride (1960) 99
The Wild World of Batwoman (1966) **369, 375**, 378, 379
Wilder, W. Lee 359
William, Warren 300
Williams, Bill 77
Williams, Grant 132, 340
Williams, Wade xi, 92
Willock, Dave **56**
Wilson, Harry 114-5, **115**, 363
The Winds of War (TV) 194
Windsor, Marie 156
Wisberg, Aubrey 78, 80, **273**, 274, 277, 278, 280
Wise, Robert 77-8
Witches' Brew (1980) 329-30
Witchfinder General see *Conqueror Worm*
The Witchmaker (1969) 138
The Wolf Man (unmade Karloff film) 300
The Wolf Man (1941) 298, 300-2, **301**, 307, 310
Wolff, Ed 61
A Woman Called Golda (1982 TV movie) 104
Womaneater (1959) 173
The Womanhunt (1972) 43

Women for Sale see *The Womanhunt*
Women of the Prehistoric Planet (1966) 134
Wood, Edward D., Jr. 18, 171, **249**, 250, 251, 252, 253, 254, 255-6, 257-9, 356, 359-61, **360**, 366
Woods, Jack 204
Woolner, Larry 39, 44, 45
World Without End (1956) 48-55, **50**, 64
Worth, Lothrop 315, 324
Wrather, Jack 113
Wray, Ardel 306
Wrixon, Maris 299
Wurtzel, Paul **293**
Wynn, Ed 325

Y

Yarnell, Sally 211
Yates, George Worthing 58
Yates, Herbert J. 94, 306
Yeaworth, Irvin S., Jr. 196, 198, 199, 203
Yeaworth, Jean 203
The Yellow Tomahawk (1954) 216
Young, Gig 318
The Young Racers (1963) 36
Young Sherlock Holmes (1985) 22
Youngstein, Max 218

Z

Zabel, Edwin 210, 216, 218, 267
Zanuck, Dick 227, 228-9
Zimbalist, Al 62, 63-4
Zimbalist, Donald 62, 63
Ziv, Frederic W. 319
Zombie see *I Eat Your Skin*
Zombies see *I Eat Your Skin*
Zombies on Broadway (1945) 76
Zontar, the Thing from Venus (1966) 13-4
Zucco, George 236
Zugsmith, Albert 278, 279

You have reached...

The End

But wait...

There's More

"There's *another* book in there?" Bela Lugosi and Richard Gordon, *Mother Riley Meets the Vampire.*

Science Fiction Stars and Horror Heroes

Interviews with Actors, Directors, Producers and Writers of the 1940s through 1960s

by Tom Weaver

RESEARCH ASSOCIATES:
JOHN BRUNAS
MICHAEL BRUNAS

McFarland & Company, Inc., Publishers
Jefferson, North Carolina, and London

Library of Congress Cataloguing-in-Publication Data

Weaver, Tom, 1958–
  Science fiction stars and horror heroes : interviews with actors, directors, producers and writers of the 1940s through 1960s / by Tom Weaver
    p.   cm.
  Includes index.
  1. Science fiction films — History and criticism.   2. Horror films — History and criticism.   3. Motion picture actors and actresses — Interviews.   4. Motion picture producers and directors — Interviews.   5. Screenwriters — Interviews.   I. Title.
PN1995.9.S26W46   1991   791.43'656 — dc20   90-53528
                                                    CIP

ISBN 0-7864-0755-7 (paperback : 50# alkaline paper) ∞

British Library Cataloguing-in-Publication data are available

©1991 Tom Weaver. All rights reserved

No part of this book may be reproduced or transmitted in any form or by any means, electronic or mechanical, including photocopying or recording, or by any information storage and retrieval system, without permission in writing from the publisher.

Manufactured in the United States of America

*McFarland & Company, Inc., Publishers
  Box 611, Jefferson, North Carolina 28640
  www.mcfarlandpub.com*

This book is
dedicated
to the fifty.

Table of Contents

Introduction ix
Acknowledgments xiii

Acquanetta 1
Phyllis Coates 19
Hazel Court 39
Richard Devon 53
Gene Fowler, Jr. 69
Arthur Gardner/Arnold Laven/Paul Landres/Pat Fielder 81
Albert Glasser 95
Bernard Glasser 109
Herk Harvey 127
Gordon Hessler 141
Louis M. Heyward 155
John Howard 185
Kim Hunter 205
Robert Hutton 225
Nancy Kovack 243
Anna Lee 253
Janet Leigh 275
Richard Matheson 289
Gregg Palmer 321
Mala Powers 339
Robert Shayne 355
Yvette Vickers 369
Katherine Victor 385
Virgil W. Vogel 401
Robb White 413

Index 433

Introduction

I'd like to think that someday I'll interview somebody who can solve a few of these vexing riddles: Why do the older science fiction and horror movies still have the audience that they do today? Why have many bigger (and often better) "prestige" pictures fallen by the wayside while hordes of fans still gobble up B films like *The Return of Dracula, The Creeping Unknown, Tarantula* and *Horror Hotel*? Why, in this modern age of ultra-slick moviemaking and state-of-the-art special effects, when the complete budget of *Carnival of Souls* (1962) wouldn't pay for six seconds of *Batman* (1989), do people still lionize the low-budget likes of Roger Corman, Jack Arnold and Edgar G. Ulmer? Why did the natives in *King Kong* build a wall to keep Kong out with a giant door to let him in?

These are not easy questions.

The fact is that these vintage SF/horrors do retain a following while many "better" films do not. This probably isn't fair, but it sure works to that following's advantage: The pictures still play on television, come out on video cassette and turn up in revival houses, and magazines partially or entirely devoted to them abound. (Except for horror and sci-fi, what other genres have a whole slew of current magazines exclusively dedicated to them? Or even *one* magazine?) Or whole books of interviews with luminaries of the genre?

Most of the interview subjects in this book were denizens of the Hollywood B movie mills of '50s vintage, but the '40s and '60s are also represented. British sci-fi/horror also comes under scrutiny. Performers, producers, writers, directors, a composer, a one-shot filmmaker . . . all are included. There are even a couple of participants you wouldn't call B people.

Sad to say, as we head into the 1990s, efforts to locate and interview the older filmmakers are becoming more of a race against time than ever. It's not a pleasant thought, but there are horror films from the '30s and '40s that have no notable survivors today. There are even some '50s flicks (*The Four Skulls of Jonathan Drake; The Alligator People*) well on their way down that same dismal road. The history of these pictures has to be written soon because these people are not going to be around forever, as three of the subjects from my previous book, *Interviews with B Science Fiction and Horror Movie Makers,* have already gone *way* out beyond the call of duty to demonstrate:

On March 25, 1989, Reginald LeBorg, 86, suffered a heart attack one block from the Norris Cinema Theatre, where the Academy of Family Films and Family Television was waiting to present him with its Life Career Award. LeBorg accepted his status as a horror movie director with a grain of salt, but he was unfailingly charming and enthusiastic, and he'd often call me long-distance just to chew the fat (I could never get him to call me anything except Mr. Weaver). People just don't come any nicer than Reggie LeBorg.

Jerry Warren, king of the rock-bottom filmmakers, died of lung cancer on August 21, 1988, in his Escondido, California, home. He lied about his age like an overripe starlet, but he was somewhere in his sixties when he died. Warren never really had a handle on what people wanted or expected from a film, and this was only too well reflected in his awful movies. But he was forthright enough to come out and admit that he really didn't *care*, that he was in it strictly for the bucks. You just have to take your hat off to that kind of honesty.

And on December 10, 1986, Susan Cabot, 59, was bashed to death with a weight-lifting bar by her own son Timothy in the bedroom of her Encino home. In typical modern-courtroom style, the victim became the accused: The defense said that Tim was an emotional wreck because Cabot was an overprotective, disturbed mother, and because their home was filled with such "massive filth and decay" that the conditions constituted child abuse. ("Child" Timothy was 22 when he caved in his mom's head.) None of the above was even faintly evident to this frequent visitor to the Cabot home, but there was also some legalese double-talk about steroids and an experimental hormone the kid was taking (he was born dwarfed), defense arguments that conjured up images of Cabot as *Sunset Boulevard*'s Norma Desmond, and even published accounts which made Tim the love child of Cabot and either actor Christopher Jones or Jordan's King Hussein. By the time all the hot air cleared from the courtroom, Timothy Scott Roman received a three-year suspended sentence and was placed on probation.

On a far brighter note, all of our other favorites from the earlier book are still with us and some of them are continuing to make news (not all of it good). John Agar had a co-starring role in the end-of-the-world suspenser *Miracle Mile* (1989), and to the surprise of cynical fans, he actually got a number of good reviews. He also had a small part in director Clive Barker's *Nightbreed* (1990), playing a hermit who'd like to be a monster and who is killed off by lead heavy David Cronenberg. John Ashley produced two genre-related television series in a row, the Fox Network's *Werewolf* and NBC's *Something Is Out There*, both of which were flops; he's vowed never to produce this type of show again. Robert Clarke joined the long list of veteran players that have done time in films by Fred Olen Ray, the indefatigable king of modern exploitation; Clarke is in Ray's *Alienator* (1989), a sci-fi send-up of *The Astounding She-Monster*, and *Haunting Fear* (1990), based on Poe's "The Premature Burial." Anthony Eisley turned up in a small part in *Evil Spirits* (1990), which featured a great who's-who/who's-through cast (Karen Black, Arte Johnson, Virginia Mayo,

The late Susan Cabot with son Timothy in a 1985 pose.

Martine Beswick, Yvette Vickers [q.v.], Robert Quarry). Jack H. Harris's remake of *The Blob* was a good, crowd-pleasing action/horror thriller, even though it didn't set the 1988 summer box office on fire. And Howard W. Koch, another of the all-time great guys, accepted the Jean Hersholt Humanitarian Award at the 1990 Oscarcast, receiving a standing ovation as 70,000,000 Americans watched on television. Koch also exec-produced *Ghost,* the sleeper-hit of the 1990 summer movie sweepstakes.

Scads of people aided and abetted on this book, most notably repeat offenders like Mark Martucci, always Johnny-on-the-spot with video cassettes of hard-to-find movies (and never resenting the fact that I always needed them a.s.a.p.); Dave McDonnell (*Starlog*) and Tony Timpone (*Fangoria*), two of the best editors and nicest fellas you'd ever want to run across; John Cocchi, film historian/raconteur/bon vivant; Paul and Donna Parla, the Sherlock Holmes and Dr. Watson of celebrity-hunters; and Bob Skotak, Mr. Rare Behind-the-Scenes Stills (and a good guy).

Also, for their cooperation, tapes, stills, leads, advice, lip service, and whatever, yet more thanks go to Bill and Roberta Amazzini, Merry Anders, Richard Anderson, Mon Ayash, everyone's friend and co-worker Bandit, Edward Bernds, Bill Brent (J & J Video), Hugh and Abigail Crain, Robert Day, Carl and Debbie Del Vecchio, Richard Denning, Squeamy Ellis, Tim Ferrante, Michael Fitzgerald, Flippy the Educated Porpoise, John Foster, Katie Gohdé, Bruce Goldstein, Alex and Richard Gordon, Rose Hobart, Allan Hoos, Donna Hope, Joe Jaworsky (noted scientist), the late Steve Jochsberger, Tom Johnson, James LaBarre, Richard Lamparski, Greg Luce (Sinister Cinema), Alex Lugones, Mark McGee, Gilbert McKenna, Greg Mank, Kevin Marrazzo, Dick

Miller, Cameron Mitchell, Ed Nelson, Michael Pate, Vincent Price, Fred Olen Ray, Max Rosenberg, Mary (Bunky) Runser, Elizabeth Selwyn, John Skillin, Jonas Slydes and his wife, Steamroller Smith, Michael Stein (*Filmfax*), Venetia Stevenson, Herb Strock, Vladimir Strowski, Gary Svehla and the whole gang down at FANEX, Ed Watz, Jon Weaver, John Wooley, Xerxes the Cat, and all the other good people at *Fangoria* and *Starlog*.

Neither last nor least, my research associates (and best friends) Mike and John Brunas, two more terrific guys. This can be one hell of a hobby when you have friends like them sharing your enthusiasm.

And finally, the biggest thank-yous are saved for my 28 interviewees. They are, for all intents and purposes, the true authors of this book. I just take the credit and get paid. It's a great arrangement.

Tom Weaver

Acknowledgments

Abridged versions of the interviews featured in *Science Fiction Stars and Horror Heroes* originally appeared in the following magazines:

Acquanetta: "Where the Wild Woman Runs Free," *Fangoria* #94, July, 1990
Phyllis Coates: "Phyllis Coates, Superman's Girl Friend," *Starlog* #138, January, 1989, and "Phyllis Coates—Byline: Lois Lane," *Starlog* #139, February, 1989
Hazel Court: "Queen of '60s Horror," *Fangoria* #91, April, 1990
Richard Devon: "I Survived Roger Corman," *Fangoria* #76, August, 1988
Gene Fowler, Jr.: "'I Was a Middle-Aged Blackballed Director from Tinseltown' or 'How to Make a Terribly-Tilted Exploitation Monster Movie with Class,'" *Filmfax* #22, September, 1990
Arthur Gardner/Arnold Laven/Paul Landres/Pat Fielder: "Monster Interlude," *Fangoria* #47, August, 1985
Bernard Glasser: "The Care and Breeding of Triffids," *Starlog Yearbook* #7, 1990
Herk Harvey: "Death Comes to Kansas," *Fangoria* #86, September, 1989
Gordon Hessler: "An AIP Director Screams Again," *Fangoria* #53, May, 1986
Louis M. Heyward: "Going AIP," *Fangoria* #96, September, 1990, and "Heyward's Heyday," *Fangoria* #97, October, 1990
John Howard: "Beyond the Lost Horizon," *Starlog Yearbook* #5, 1989
Kim Hunter: "Chimp Life," *Starlog* #160, November, 1990
Robert Hutton: "Slimebuster!" *Fangoria* #87, October, 1989
Nancy Kovack: "Lady and the Argonauts," *Starlog* #151, February, 1990
Anna Lee: "Member of the Stock Company," *Starlog Yearbook* #6, 1990
Janet Leigh: "Mistress of Menace," *Starlog* #132, July, 1988
Richard Matheson: "Richard Matheson and the House of Poe," *Fangoria* #89, December, 1989, "Quoth Matheson, 'Nevermore!'" *Fangoria* #90, February, 1990, "Master of Shrinking Men," *Starlog* #150, January, 1990, and "Master of the Last Men on Earth," *Starlog* #151, February, 1990
Gregg Palmer: "The Creature Walked Beside Him," *Fangoria* #93, June, 1990
Mala Powers: "Maiden of Yesterday," *Starlog* #153, April, 1990
Robert Shayne: "Inspector Henderson Reports," *Starlog* #129, April, 1988
Yvette Vickers: "Vamp! Vixen! Vickers!" *Fangoria* #83, June, 1989
Katherine Victor: "Talking Turkeys," *The Bloody Best of Fangoria* #10, 1991
Virgil W. Vogel: "Terror on the Low-Budget Express," *Fangoria* #73, May, 1988
Robb White: "An Outspoken Conversation with Robb White," *Filmfax* #18, January, 1990

*I don't criticize anything that I ever did [in films],
except that I would have liked to have done it my way....
I'm a good actress, I know that I'm a good actress,
but I feel that I have never really achieved my acting potential,
or had the right opportunities.*

Acquanetta

LANDING A BLOW for feminism long before the days of women's rights, Paula the Ape Woman stood proud in the male-dominated monster world of the 1940s. Her stamping grounds were the sound stages at Universal Studios, her films included *Captive Wild Woman* and *Jungle Woman,* and the actress who portrayed her, exotic in name and appearance, was the beautiful Acquanetta. Trapped in a horror/jungle film rut, Acquanetta also appeared in such movies as *Dead Man's Eyes, Tarzan and the Leopard Woman* and *Lost Continent* before retiring from the business, although the Arizona-based actress is currently eyeing the possibility of a screen return.

The story of your early life is a little different every time you tell it.

I think many people who interview personalities add their own concepts to it, and they all write it their own way. I'm not certain *what* people have written about me; every time I picked up a paper I found things that I never said. My mother was Arapaho, and I was born on the Arapaho Reservation in Wyoming, near the Wind River. Of course I have no recollection of that, because I was given away to my father when I was approximately three years old. My father took me to Pennsylvania and gave me to his then-wife, and I grew up in Norristown, Pennsylvania, where I went to school.

And after high school you started out on your modeling career.

Right. After high school, I went to New York and became a model, and lived at the Barbizon Women's Hotel. I became a model first for Harry Conover, and then I met Arthur William Brown, who did illustrations for various magazines, while I was with Conover. We were at the Stork Club in the Cub Room one night, and John Powers was there. The following morning Powers called Brown, who then called *me* and said, "The big man wants to see you." I went to see John Powers, and he pulled open a drawer of his desk, threw a contract at me and said, "Sign!" *[Laughs.]* He said, "Harry Conover used to work for me. He's a good model, but he's never been very bright and he doesn't put anybody under contract. You are now a John Powers model." This was all really neat. I was thrown into an entirely new atmosphere, from a small town to the Big Town. And I went from a small amount of money a week, in a small town, to $100 an hour on some jobs, which in those days was incredible. This was during the war years, the early '40s, and things were moving very fast.

By the way, when I was in New York, Louis Sobol and Walter Winchell and all the scribes were writing about me in their columns. At first, when they found out that I was an Indian in New York, they said, "Oh, nobody cares about Indians." But Roosevelt was president and the big South American Hands Across the Border policy was on, and it was decided that I was now going

Previous page: Priceless publicity pose from Acquanetta's *Captive Wild Woman.* **The man in the monkey suit is Ray "Crash" Corrigan.**

to be a South American. It was almost like Pygmalion—they fabricated for me this story that I came from Venezuela. I looked the part—I was dark and exotic, and I wore these big scarfs and a big gardenia, flowered skirts, collars and capes and those kinds of things *[laughs]!* I became "The Venezuelan Volcano"— William Randolph Hearst dubbed me that. I had met Mr. Hearst and his wife Marion, they were my friends, and W.R. pushed me, he wanted me to succeed so tremendously. He was so impressed with my background *[laughs],* and he called me the Little Princess.

Somehow a bit of my background came out, that my father was a descendant of the Royal House of England—be it legitimate or not! My dad was English and French, and from what I'm told, his grandmother, who was French-Jewish, was a lady-in-waiting or something in the Royal House and she became pregnant, and out of that union eventually came my father! That's why the background was shaded in mystery—in days gone by, illegitimacy was very taboo. They actually called illegitimate children bastards, which is a horrible thing, but today it's a badge of honor—now women announce that they're going to have a baby by this married man or that married man. Everything is so changed today! But as I was saying, this business about being descended from the Royal House was true, and so of course that always impressed people like Hearst. And J. Edgar Hoover knew it—he was a personal friend of mine. As a matter of fact, because I had no birth certificate, I couldn't get a visa or a passport to get out of the country, and so Hoover arranged for that. He was a curious man. Although he had interesting stories around him, because he was never married, he still was attracted to certain types of women, he liked to photograph them. And he would come to New York and photograph us.

Your publicity also says that you were a paid escort back then.
In those days, men liked to have attractive women to escort them places. So it was almost like a job. Now, with me, I was a very innocent young girl from a small town, and I never got involved in what they called "the fast set." People were attracted to me because of that—they called me Miss Innocent. When I left Hollywood, they still called me Miss Innocent!

So how did you finally wind up in Hollywood?
I met some people from Rio de Janeiro, and they wanted me to come to South America and perform at the Copacabana in Rio. I was a natural performer and a dancer, and that's what they wanted me to do at the Copa. So I packed my things, I left the Barbizon and got on the train. We stopped in Hollywood and we went out to the Mocambo. The head of casting at Metro-Goldwyn-Mayer was there, the head of Warner Bros., Dan Kelly from Universal Studios and so on. And Walter Wanger—he was the one that really went wild over me. He tried to get me for the lead in *Arabian Nights* [1942], but unfortunately they had already signed Maria Montez. That started the big

Her original name was Burnuacquanetta (translation: Burning Fire, Deep Water), and she was an exotic presence in several Universal B films of the 1940s.

so-called "feud" between the two of us. She said, no, she would not *geev* up *thees* role—it was to be her first starring role, in Technicolor and all that. She later drowned in her bathtub, but before her demise we became friendly—never really *friends,* because there was a tremendous jealousy on her part. That is something I have never known in my entire life; I do not know what envy is, I do not know what jealousy is.

You made a test at MGM, didn't you?

 I was tested by both Metro-Goldwyn-Mayer and Universal. And before Universal even saw the rushes of my test, when they heard that I had tested the day before at Metro, they immediately signed me because they thought Metro would use me as a threat to Montez, who Universal was building then as their number one star. Dan Kelly was the one who said that my full name, Burnuacquanetta, was too long for any marquee, so I could either be Burnu or I could be Acquanetta. I chose Acquanetta.

And you ended up with a bit in Montez's Arabian Nights.
   That's right—I had a small speaking part, as one of the harem girls. Universal found there was so much reaction to my appearance, my presence, whatever, that they threw me into the so-called B & B pictures.

The bread-and-butter pictures.
   Yes. Those were the films that they spent less money on, but made the most money off of. And the prestige pictures were called the A's, because those were what they used to promote their studio. My films, each and every one of them, within the first few weeks of release made over a million dollars. People stood in line to see them, and somehow I caught on. However, because of the kinds of films that I was doing, I was not very happy. Of course, being the sort of person I was, I never got really close to any of those directors or producers; they were always trying to get young girls into an amorous situation. That never happened with me—that's why I never did any of these big Technicolor extravaganzas!

How exactly did you get involved on Captive Wild Woman?
   I know that they were testing various actresses at the studio; I think Yvonne de Carlo was one under consideration. Yvonne de Carlo was at Universal, and in her autobiography she says I took several films from her. I think that's not the case, I think it was the opposite *[laughs]!* They were always threatening *me* with *her,* and again, like with Maria Montez, she got the big Technicolors. I think she was tested for *Captive Wild Woman,* but I'm not absolutely certain. But in any event I tested, and they said I was perfect for the role.

How did you feel, going into a picture where you would be playing a mute ape woman?
   Whatever I was given, I did my best. I became a character actress. I am a natural actress—they tell me that when I was a little girl I used to gather the children of the neighborhood and put on shows! I did write a play when I was in junior high school, and I was in a play when I was in grammar school—I played an angel! So apparently acting was to be part of my life. I believe that our lives are somewhat—not pre-programmed, because we do have free choice—but I believe those choices are known. People here in Arizona call me a medium, because I do sometimes see the future—don't ask me how, it's like a waking dream. I was at a party the other night where people were standing

Mad scientist John Carradine transforms an ape into a beautiful woman (Acquanetta) in Universal's way-out *Captive Wild Woman*.

in line to ask me, "Acquanetta, what's in store for me?" I can touch their hands, and sometimes I can see what's going to happen. For some people I do not say what I see; others, I tell them. It's like channeling.

Was it exciting to be handed a leading role so early in your Hollywood career?
    You know something very curious? Nothing I ever did in Hollywood was exciting to the degree where I felt, "This is going to be my life." It was wonderful and surprising, but I just seem to have taken everything in stride. It was just another part of my destiny, and I somehow knew that, always. I did my very best, but it wasn't something that was so meaningful to me that I would give up something else for it. That's why I ended up walking away from Universal.

How did you prepare for your role as the Ape Woman?
    [Laughs.] There was no preparation on my part, but I sat sometimes for two and a half hours being made up by a makeup artist. They used rubber and clay, and you sat in that chair while all this stuff was put on. You could hardly breathe — it was kind of scary! I think I had more emotional feeling, being

Acquanetta in full Jack P. Pierce makeup for *Captive Wild Woman*.

made up for that, than anything that I ever did, because it was exhausting sitting being made up for those kinds of things.

What memories do you have of Edward Dmytryk, who directed Captive Wild Woman?

We had great rapport—in fact, we dated briefly. What a career he should have had—what a talent! He was my favorite director. Actually, I had *two* favorites, Eddie and Reginald LeBorg; they were the two that I really liked the best. But Eddie and I used to talk—oh, God, we could sit and talk for hours! I thought he was tremendous. Many directors seem to want to step into your skin and to tell you everything to do; they never allowed me the freedom to interpret a role the way I wanted to do it. And I resent it to this day. Eddie gave me more freedom than other directors. Nevertheless, I've always felt that I was never "me" in movies—do you know there was never a film where I was allowed to smile? And that's curious, because my personality is very exuberant. I was a happy nymph of a person in those years, and that's why people were attracted to me. I was like a butterfly *[laughs]*—I wanted to spread my wings! And I had to stifle all of that. I thought that that was an injustice at the time. But I have to say "que sera sera"—had things been different, had I soared and become the star which I could have been, my life would have been totally different. And God knows what it might have been. My people say that, for the good as well as for what we think of at the time as *not* being good, we must be thankful, because that is why we are in the place that we are in now.

Did you enjoy working with John Carradine on Captive Wild Woman?
Oh, very much so. I think of him a lot. He was great—he was always acting, you know *[laughs]!* Even when we were off the set, there was John being John! I always think of him as Dracula, always picture him in my mind's eye wearing that cloak! I wonder what he was in his past life....

That was about the time that he cared more about his Shakespearean stage company than the pictures he was doing just for the bucks.
He was always doing something away from filmdom. He had it in his soul—he was an *"ac-tor."* And he lived it in his private life! He was a character in his day, and I loved people like that. Milburn Stone was a gentleman, a real nice person, and Evelyn Ankers, too. Evelyn and I were never really close, like close girlfriends, but that could have been partly because of me. I was somewhat withdrawn in a sense; even to this day I do not have a lot of very *close* close friends. People think that they are close friends of mine, but I don't think that. I walk among, but I am not of.

Who were your close friends during your acting days?
I think Eddie Dmytryk was a friend. I don't think of Walter Wanger as a friend, because he was more like someone who thought that he could exert power over you. And when he couldn't, then he was vindictive! So, because I was not what he wanted me to be, he denied me the roles that I could have had. It was not because they were not available, it was a simple matter of exchanging a role for what I was willing to give. I wasn't willing to do that, and I never will be willing to do that! I maintained my self-respect. I had it then, I have it now—that's a very important thing. It's not what other people feel about you, but what you know about yourself.

Were you pleased with your performance in Captive Wild Woman?
Yes. You know, I don't criticize anything that I ever did, except that I would have liked to have done it *my* way. But the director's in charge. And

as I look back on those films, they were effective. I'm a good actress, I *know* that I'm a good actress, but I feel that I have never really achieved my acting potential, or had the right opportunities.

You also were scheduled to star in The Mummy's Ghost, *and in fact worked on the picture for one day.*
  On *The Mummy's Ghost* I remember that we had scabs [non-union workers] on the set. We were shooting a scene where I had to walk along a path and then fall, and these scabs had put real rocks down on the path. They were supposed to put down papier-mâché rocks but they didn't — these scabs painted real rocks white! I fell and struck my head, and that's all I remember — I woke up in Cedars of Lebanon Hospital! I have the effects of that to this day: I also struck my arm when I fell, and when I had my second son, my elbow swelled up like a ball. They said that was still from that accident, because it crushed a little bone in my elbow.

What other mishaps have you had in films?
  I remember that on one of the Ape Woman pictures my costume was too tight, around the neck. The blouse part went up around my neck and was tied with a string, it started choking me, and they couldn't get it off. I'm not sure how it happened, but I fainted. Then there was another film, *Flesh and Fantasy,* which they wanted me for, but I became ill. That was a tremendous disappointment. I was supposed to be in the Barbara Stanwyck-Charles Boyer episode — Charles and I were friends always. He later came to Arizona, and died here.

How did you get involved on Dead Man's Eyes?
  I was assigned to all my films. I refused quite a number, I simply wouldn't do them. I was never handed a script and asked, "Would you like to do this?" I never reached that pinnacle of stardom.

How well did you get along with Lon Chaney on Dead Man's Eyes?
  Beautifully. He was a good friend.

LeBorg told me he was a drunk and a pain in the neck.
  Yes, but I did not see that. During *Dead Man's Eyes,* I never saw that.

You finally had some dramatic scenes in Dead Man's Eyes.
  Yes, but they still would not allow me to "come out." Everything was kind of capped; they wanted me to hold it to a low key. Emotions inside that were building, I had to hold down.

Why did you enjoy working with Reginald LeBorg?
  Because he was a gentleman — with an accent on the *gentle*. I don't like

people who are harsh, and some directors are, you know—I've seen them screaming at people on sets! But Eddie Dmytryk was my very favorite, because it was just as if I had known him forever. What a nice man. You know, when I saw him at the [1987] Universal reunion, his wife [actress Jean Porter] would not allow me to talk to him? We had very little time to visit, because she pulled him away!

Were you happy with the job you did in Dead Man's Eyes?

Pleased, let's say. As I say, the directors were always in control. When you become a big star, *then* you have freedom; then you take charge, you're in control to a great degree, and you can do your own interpretation of roles. But when you're new and you haven't had the experience, as they call it, the directors are in charge. And they like that, because they project themselves through you.

You ended up in a horror film rut at Universal. What kinds of roles would you have preferred?

Drama. Playing a woman, a *real* woman—a loving, sharing, caring person. Really, almost anything except what I did *[laughs]*! Not that I hated what I did, but I came to dislike the roles.

So you saw the rut getting deeper when they asked you to repeat your Ape Woman role in Jungle Woman?

I just did it because I was assigned to it. But once I accepted it, I did it to the best of my abilities.

Jungle Woman *really is a disappointing sequel—cheap and badly written.*

Yes, but they made money on it because Acquanetta was in it. I came to realize that I was the property, not the film. That's why I left Universal. I wanted to be a part of a film—add to it. I didn't want to be used. And I felt that I was being used.

Were you glad to get dialogue in Jungle Woman?

I thought it was really interesting to work without speaking in *Captive Wild Woman*; it was more difficult, a challenge. But, you know, I read an article once that said that I was not an actress at all, and that in fact I couldn't even talk. They didn't understand that this was deliberate, and that I had to project more—because I had to do it with my body language, my eyes, my face. Every movement had to mean something!

Did you enjoy working with J. Carrol Naish on Jungle Woman?

He helped me more than any actor or actress that I ever worked with, because he was a fabulous actor, I think one of the greatest. Why he didn't achieve stardom, other than being a character actor, I don't know. They

The popularity of the first Ape Woman film prompted a perfunctory sequel with three of the original stars.

missed the boat. But he was always offering suggestions and being very helpful and kind and gentle. What a nice man!

Naish was nominated for two Supporting Actor Oscars around that time [Sahara, 1943, and A Medal for Benny, *1945]; it's curious to find him in a stinker like* Jungle Woman.

You know, I think that he accepted *Jungle Woman* in order to work with me. He always had visions of the two of us working together in something fabulous, because he really liked me as a person and as a friend. I had met him at Universal prior to *Jungle Woman,* and we became friends—he was kind of like a mentor.

Putting the pictures themselves aside in your mind, did you enjoy working at Universal?

Oh, yes. The people that I worked with there, they were just beautiful. I never had a problem—in fact, we were just one big, wonderful, happy family. Universal was like that, but I understand that a lot of the other studios really were not. At Metro they had people working together that didn't speak to each other off the set *[laughs]!* At Universal we never had that, we had a family.

Not long after Jungle Woman *you wound up quitting the studio.*

What happened was that I went to Mexico at the instigation of the president, Mr. Roosevelt, as one of the emissaries from Hollywood. Somehow during that trip to Mexico I made lots of contacts with really important people there, plus some of the producers, and they wanted me to come to Mexico and do films. I did not speak Spanish at the time, but they said, "If you live here, we'll get you tutors." And while I was there, I met Jorge Pascal, who immediately showered me with jewels and proposed to me. Of course we had press people with us, and so it hit the newspapers in Hollywood that I was going to marry the wealthiest man in Mexico, who had proposed to me on my first night there. But I really didn't care for the man. Pascal later lured into Mexico some of our big baseball players that were jumping their contracts, and he started his own big team in Mexico. He was killed in a big air crash, on his way to Acapulco. So had I been married to him, I wouldn't be here right now!

By the time I got back to Hollywood, I was so fascinated with Mexico that I asked for a release from my contract—I wanted to go to Mexico and make films. Well, Universal wouldn't allow it. So I went to my friend Joe Schenck, who was the head of 20th Century–Fox. I told him my problem, and he said, "We'd better get this contract." He called Dan Kelly at Universal and Dan arranged for my contract release. Universal never forgave me for that. They had this *Jungle* series on the boards and they tried desperately to find someone else, and in fact they did get a girl who did one film [Vicky Lane in *The Jungle Captive*]. It bombed, and that was the end of that series.

People asked me, "You walked out on a contract, when they were ready to extend it?" and I said, "Not only that, but they offered me more money to stay." I couldn't—I had to go. It was like something drawing me, pulling me away. And I now know that my spirit guides had charge of my life, without my awareness of it. I ran into Dan Kelly at the Farmer's Market, years after I left Universal, and we sat and chatted, and he said, "Oh, if we could relive it." And I said, "This is the profound statement down through centuries. But it is for those who have wisdom to be able to perceive what is to come. Those are the ones who grasp the opportunities now." We talked like that—sat there philosophizing and just having a great time. Dan was getting old and tired, and he said, "If I could relive it, we would never have let you go."

You soon ended up under contract to Monogram.

That's right. At Monogram I had approval of my scripts because I had been so unhappy about my pictures at Universal. And I disapproved of every one! The scripts they submitted to me were mostly cowboy things. Had I done them, I probably would have gone on to be a Western star *[laughs]*! Of course they did not renew my contract, because they thought I was difficult. Again, I must say that I guess it wasn't meant to be.

Did you like working with Johnny Weissmuller on Tarzan and the Leopard Woman?

Oh, yes, very much so—he was a nice man. He'd sit and tell jokes a lot,

Acquanetta strikes a beguiling pose on the set of RKO's *Tarzan and the Leopard Woman.*

One of Acquanetta's last film roles was a minor part as a native girl in Lippert's *Lost Continent*, a *Lost World*-style sci-fi adventure.

and also episodes from his life and memories of his past. A few years after we did *Tarzan and the Leopard Woman,* Johnny was about to start the *Jungle Jim* series and he wanted me to play opposite him in the series, but I declined to do that, because it was to be shot on the backlot somewhere. And, you know, it was a very curious thing: just ten days before Johnny Weissmuller's demise, he came to my mind, and I tried to reach him in Hollywood and Acapulco, but I couldn't locate him. I felt that I needed to talk to him, and I also wanted to meet him and to be photographed together again—I had that desire. And then I read, a week later, of his passing. It was so incredible.

A few years later you popped up in the sci-fi Lost Continent, *again as a jungle character.*

[*Laughs.*] Once you're cast, or *mis*cast, you become *that*—that was the sad part in those days.

You dropped out of pictures in the early '50s.

The last film I did back then must have been *Take the High Ground* [1953]. You know, I never saw it? What happened was, after we finished a scene one day, the director [Richard Brooks] said, "You're through," and what he meant was with that particular scene. I thought he meant I was *through*! I went home and packed and went off somewhere, and I never did the whole part that they wrote for me [*laughs*]! They used the little bit I did, from what everybody tells me, but I never saw it. And they were very unhappy with me because they said I walked out, but it wasn't quite like that.

After leaving films you became a local television celebrity in Arizona.

That was through my husband Jack Ross. My first husband, by the way, was Luciano Baschuk, a Russian, very, very wealthy, and we had one son, Sergei. We were divorced because I found out after our marriage that he was somewhat sadistic. Our son died of cancer—five years old. In the meantime, I married one of my mentors, Henry Clive. He had painted seven covers of me for *The American Weekly,* which was the most that any star had ever done. Marion Davies was on the cover three times, Sonja Henie and Simone Simon twice. No other star was ever on more than once. Then, after I separated from Henry, I met Jack Ross, who was working at a Lincoln-Mercury store in Culver City.

Jack and I were married; I bore a son, Lance, in California; we moved to Arizona and we bought the Lincoln-Mercury dealership in Mesa, Arizona. I immediately went on television here—that's like some 30 years ago. I was on live for almost ten years, five days a week for an hour and a half, and what I did was introduce movies. It was the first program of this sort in the nation—every 15 minutes I had five minutes to come on and talk [*laughs*]! So instead of doing commercials, I started to talk about community events and to interview people. My commercials became totally different than anything anyone had ever done. I would also say, "By the way, we *also* sell automobiles!" Time marches on—I had all of my next three children "on television." I would be on the week before they were born and the week after. I was the first person to appear on television pregnant! I would give ongoing bulletins on what was happening, and when I was in the hospital they showed pictures of me and the babies, those kinds of things. It was just incredible. My four sons now have all graduated from the university, gotten their M.B.A.s and so forth, and are doing fabulous. I couldn't ask for more—God has been very good to me.

I intend never to marry again, I have taken that vow. I am very happy where I am; feel super-great; I'm 5'7", weigh 127 pounds, and everybody in Arizona tells me I look fabulous. Whenever I hear that, it's really flattering and it makes me feel good.

I am very well known here and I'm very involved in the community, and I have been involved in the eleemosynary, fund-raising charities for all of the thirty years-plus that I have been here.

I live in a home that I was drawn to. This is a strange place where I live; this home is inhabited by the unseen. And people *know* that. People who have never had an experience have strange experiences here. I cannot tell you all of the things that have happened, because the press here would just go nuts—they have asked me not to divulge many of the things, they've said, "Acquanetta, please don't tell people about your miracles." But here is one thing which they could not cap: we had fourteen hundred people at our home for a party some years ago, and the biggest storm in the history of Arizona struck. The water was several feet deep within a couple of blocks of my home, but not one drop of water fell on our home or our garden. That was in the newspaper, of course, but they didn't spread the story beyond Arizona because they didn't want the "religious nuts" to converge here. But, oh, I have had many such experiences.

I have had a fountain spring up in my garden, for six hours, out of the earth; it watered a rose bush, which then burst into the blooms of 20 different roses. It was photographed and documented, and viewed by different people, including the clergy. All kinds of things like that.

No real regrets, then, about the way Hollywood treated you.
Had I been a big star in those days I wouldn't have my four sons, and I'll tell you, there's nothing in this world, no amount of jewels, money or love, that I would have exchanged for my life in Arizona. My four sons are worth more than anything precious that you could think of in the material sense. No way would I exchange them. Barbara Stanwyck said to me, some years ago, "I would give up my career and everything I have for your life, and what you have." Because she could see how happy I am. I am on Cloud Nine.

The actress that '40s audiences went ape for (and vice versa) recently acted in the direct-to-home video release *Grizzly Adams—The Legend Never Dies* (1989).

ACQUANETTA FILMOGRAPHY

Arabian Nights (Universal, 1942)
Rhythm of the Islands (Universal, 1943)
Captive Wild Woman (Universal, 1943)
Jungle Woman (Universal, 1944)
Dead Man's Eyes (Universal, 1944)
The Jungle Captive (Universal, 1945) (filmclip from *Jungle Woman*)
Tarzan and the Leopard Woman (RKO, 1946)
Lost Continent (Lippert, 1951)
Callaway Went Thataway (MGM, 1951)
The Sword of Monte Cristo (20th Century–Fox, 1951)
Take the High Ground (MGM, 1953)

I do take pride in Superman *because it was one of the most
loving relationships that I ever experienced....
We worked like gangbusters, we did it and did it well,
and there were never any beefs or arguments within our group.
I'd have the crew come in my dressing room and have a drink
and prop their feet up — nobody drew lines in those days,
and that was a good feeling. I don't think that'll ever be again,
that kind of closeness between crew and cast.*

Phyllis Coates

SHE'S KNOWN to her friends by her real name and to countless thousands of fans by her professional name, but for untold millions of television viewers she'll always be Lois Lane, ace reporter for the Metropolis *Daily Planet*. "That's only one facet of me," Phyllis Coates stresses, but whatever other acting challenges this veteran performer has met (either in her formidable '50s career or in her current comeback), they can only be icing on the cake; her niche in entertainment history is already established. The popularity and permanence of TV's *Adventures of Superman* seem in no danger of fading, and the series' first and feistiest Lois still remains the fans' favorite after nearly four decades.

Born in Wichita Falls, Texas, the future movie and television actress (real name: Gypsie Ann Evarts Stell) moved to Hollywood as a teenager with intentions of enrolling at U.C.L.A. A chance encounter with Ken Murray in a Hollywood and Vine restaurant landed her in the comedian's vaudeville show. She started out as a chorus girl and worked her way up to doing skits before moving on to work for veteran showman Earl Carroll and later touring with the U.S.O. Coates got some of her first motion picture experience in comedy short subjects at Warner Bros. and then graduated to roles in early '50s films like *Blues Busters*, *Outlaws of Texas* and *Superman and the Mole-Men* (the feature that led to the long-running *Superman* teleseries). After a one-season stint with the Man of Steel, Coates began to divide her time between TV, B-movie assignments and serials at Republic.

How did you become involved on Superman and the Mole-Men?

I had an agent at that time who sent me out to the old Selznick Studios, where they were interviewing gals for the part of Lois Lane. I met Bob Maxwell, who was then one of the producers. I read for him and he said, "I think you're perfect for the part." It was that simple: I didn't even get a call-back on it, they just decided that I was it. And there were a *lot* of good gals up for it.

So working on Mole-Men *was when you met George Reeves for the first time?*

I met George in pre-production, and, yes, that was the first time we worked together. I thought George was a great guy, and I never did change my feelings about him. We were very good friends, and we socialized off the set. I also knew the lady he was involved with, Toni Mannix. Toni was the wife of Eddie Mannix, who used to be the production manager at MGM when the studio was in full swing. He was Toni's husband, and Toni was George's girlfriend.

And Eddie Mannix didn't mind this?

Apparently not—Eddie was very sick at that time. In their house in Bel-Air there was an elevator for him, in the home—I mean, he was really, really ill. But Eddie was the one I think was later responsible for getting George into the Screen Directors Guild.

Both George and Toni were very good to my oldest daughter. At that time she had a hip problem, and Toni Mannix used to pick her up and we'd all get

---

Previous page: Too-long missing from the acting scene, Phyllis Coates—TV's first and best Lois Lane—is now on the comeback trail.

Phyllis Coates (during her cheesecake days) helps to usher in a new year.

together for dinner after work. We also saw each other sometimes on the weekends. We were all very good friends, and I had a marvelous working relationship with George.

How quickly did you make Superman and the Mole-Men?

Very fast. Oh, man, we went lickety-split on that movie, and that whole series. You never knew which episode you were shooting! Sometimes we'd be shooting four or five episodes at one time — that's why I had one hat and one suit, and that was it! I didn't even dare change earrings!

Lee Sholem, who directed Mole-Men, *told me the picture took four weeks.*

I don't think we shot four weeks — my God, that would have been extravagant! Lee might've *liked* it to go four weeks, but I think we wrapped it up a lot more quickly than that. We shot in Culver City, around in that area. The studio was out there, and we couldn't venture too far away from it because of time.

Did you think that the midget actors playing the mole-men were effective?

I guess at the time they were. It was all hysterical to me—George and I laughed through the whole thing! Somebody recently sent me a still of George and the mole-men, and one of the midgets is holding an Electrolux vacuum cleaner, which was their weapon *[laughs]*! It really was funny.

Were you pleased with the final results on Mole-Men*?*

Well, how *could* you be? You know *[laughs]*, I took my money and went home! It was nice working together and everybody liked everybody, but in the final analysis it was a crock of crap! But I guess when you're involved in something like that, you take yourself a little more seriously. Probably if I saw it now I'd enjoy it, and maybe laugh my head off. One thing I do remember especially was that Jeff Corey, who played the leader of the mob that chases the mole-men, was very good in it. He got caught up in those damn McCarthy investigations, but Jeff has always been a good actor, and the proof of the pudding is that he went on to become one of the best acting coaches in Hollywood. Another thing I remember is that, not long after we finished it up, I was over in Scotland, visiting Edinburgh, and it was playing over there. There was this big billboard advertising the picture, and I just roared with laughter. We went directly from that *Mole-Men* feature right into the *Superman* series.

Had you been aware of the Superman *comics as a kid growing up?*

Yeah, but strangely enough I was never a comic book reader when I was a kid. I got sort of soured by *Little Orphan Annie,* who never did change, and *[laughs]* I put 'em all down!

Do you remember what Reeves's initial feelings were about the Superman *role?*

Yeah, he was not happy about it. The first time we ever got together, we toasted each other and he said, "Well, babe, this is it: the bottom of the barrel," and I felt the same way myself! George had had quite a good career going at one point, then he went into the service and it was a whole different ballgame when he came back. And he never, ever was happy. For one thing, in the beginning both of us were getting low dough—I mean, we were working for *very* little money, and George was really teed off about that. Later on, though, he really was able to get it up.

Jack Larson [Jimmy Olsen] made $350 an episode and Noel Neill [the later Lois Lane], $225.

Did they really say they worked for *that?* Jeez, then I got more than *they* did! I got $350, $375 an episode. And when I was preparing to leave the show, Whit Ellsworth [producer of *Superman* after the first season], who was trying to get me to stay, made me all kinds of offers!

What kind of money was George Reeves making?

George "Superman" Reeves is about to knock that smug look off of baddie James Craven's face, as Phyllis "Lois Lane" Coates watches approvingly. From the *Adventures of Superman*, episode "Riddle of the Chinese Jade."

As best as I can remember, George may have been getting around $1,000, maybe a little less. But we complained about it all the time.

Rumor has it that Reeves owned a piece of the show.
No, George did not. That syndicate, National Periodical Publications [now DC Comics], was very tight.

In working on the show, did you feel that your only audience would be kids?
Yes, definitely. And that was discouraging, particularly for George.

For an early TV show Superman *had very good special effects.*
The special effects were some of the best things in the old series — in fact, I don't know why Jack Larson and I stood for as much as we did. We were nearly blown up, beaten up, exploded, *exploited* — I guess it was because we were young and dumb, but we put up with a lot of stuff. Not too long ago I saw an episode *[Night of Terror]* where I got knocked out! The heavies on that show were so mean and so tough, but in real life they were the sweetest guys in the world — I worked with 'em on *Superman*, on Westerns, in gangster stuff, just all the time. The one that knocked me out, an actor named Frank Richards,

certainly was not responsible, I was. In an action show like *Superman* you had to hit your marks exactly. I missed my mark by about three or four inches, I moved too close to him, and he decked me! I was knocked out cold, and they sent me home—that left me a little black-and-blue, but I was back at work the next day. The funny thing to me is that Lee Sholem, who was directing, left that shot in! So if you watch that episode you can see that I really took a punch.

People have said that when Bob Maxwell produced *Superman* it was a more violent series, but I think it was just more action. Maxwell was, for my money, more imaginative that Whitney Ellsworth, and I thought it reflected Bob's tastes more than Whit's. As the series went on, after Bob was gone and Whit had taken over, it got a little sugary and sweet. It got cutesy-cutesy whereas before the episodes had a little bit of bite.

Do you remember anybody else getting hurt on the show?

George. He was about to do one of his famous takeoffs when the wires broke. And I thought he was going to kill me, because I couldn't help but laugh—it was just too funny! He could've been hurt and he knew it, and he grabbed me by the throat—kiddingly—and he said, "God damn it, don't you laugh, I could have been killed!" But it was just too funny for me to contain myself!

Did you have any inkling, early on, that the show was going to be a hit?

George and I had no idea, none whatsoever, that this kind of thing would develop. In fact, I wonder what it is—what is the magic about *Superman*? Is it that the good guys and the bad guys are so clearly defined?

For fans of that first season it's the dark, violent tone of the show, plus the excitement and suspense.

Well, that was Bob Maxwell—that reflects his taste. I can't tell you how many people have written me and said exactly the same thing that you just did. Maxwell was a more daring and more interesting guy than Whit Ellsworth; Maxwell just had that zip. He left *Superman* about the time that I did, and he died [in 1971] after he worked on *Lassie*. Bob had some fire and imagination—maybe that's the conflict he had with National Comics.

I guess I can see why the first season appealed to a more adult audience: I've had people write me to say that as kids they watched those early shows where the heroes were clear, the bad guys got it, Superman was really Superman and so on. I've got doctors and lawyers writing to me—really, it's amazing, the people who grew up on the series. And they all say the same thing: that that first season was the best one for them, the most meaningful in their lives.

National Comics apparently got fed up with the violence on the show, and wanted something entirely different from what Maxwell was delivering.

Well, they got it, didn't they? The new gang came in and turned it all to pudding!

I've heard people tell anecdotes that don't speak too well for Maxwell; in fact, one of the Superman *directors calls him a shit!*
Bob could be a shit, but I think anybody who has definite likes and dislikes, who's not afraid to let you know what he thinks and who shoots from the hip, is going to be a shit in somebody's eyes. I've been called that myself! I think Maxwell was tough, but I liked him — George and I socialized with Maxwell, and we *both* liked him. I just think that anybody who's definite is a bit of a shit.

Didn't Maxwell's wife also work the show?
Oh, God, did she! Jessica didn't really work the show but she was always there, hanging around on the set all the time. I can play comedy and I was always trying to slip some extra little touches in here and there, but she'd report me *[laughs]*! The directors, Lee Sholem and Tommy Carr and George Blair, were shooting and working so fast that I could have gotten away with a little — a look here, a look there — but Jessica always had her eagle eye out. I always got the feeling she was "the spy"! And she's the one who picked out that bloody suit and hat that I wore.

Did you ever tag along with Reeves on any of his frequent promotional tours?
No. He had asked me to do some, even when everybody was trying to get me to come back on the series. George wanted me back on *Superman,* and he spent some time talking to me about doing some of these personal appearances. I got talking to him about the p.a.'s he did, and let me tell you *[laughs],* he hated 'em! It always appeared that George liked kids, but he told me some of the worst stories. Kids were always poking him, jabbing his rubber muscles — oh, God! But he did what was expected of him — George was one of those dear, sweet guys, and first and foremost he was an actor. So he would always rise to the occasion, but he said some terrible things happened on his personal appearances.

I know from several people that he had a short fuse. Did he ever lose his patience with you?
Never. But I did see him lose it a couple of times with other people, and of course he was always bitching about money. Barney Sarecky, who was head of production, used to come down and raise hell with us because George would whip out the bottle every day on the set about four o'clock. In those days we worked six days a week, from very early in the morning until six, seven o'clock at night, and we were working for short money. And so at four we drank — George and I became good drinking buddies *[laughs]*! This drove the production office crazy, and George would say to them, "Go shit in your hat!" That

was really one of the reasons why I wanted out of the series: After George and I had set up this pattern, it was getting hard to break it.

George had a photographic mind, and he was such a fast study—it was great to work with him. I'm a fast study, too, but not as fast as he was. We averaged 24 pages of dialogue a day, and that's a *lot* of dialogue. And that involved only two people, not 12, 13, 15. We shot fast, we were seldom into two takes. And George was the kind of guy who, if you had a close-up, didn't let the script girl read his off-camera dialogue, he would be there—at least, he was that way for me. We just had a great working relationship as well as a good friendship.

Was he one to clown around?

Yeah, George was always telling stories. And he used a cigarette holder, and that gave him a very foppish look—George in his Superman suit, with a cigarette holder! He and John Hamilton [Perry White], they were always telling stories, and George was always pulling jokes and gags. He was a dear, sweet guy.

Have you ever seen any other actors who have played Superman?

I never did see Kirk Alyn play Superman. Christopher Reeve, the new Superman, is a wonderful actor and a good-looking guy, and really is the Superman for the 1980s. In 1988 Margot Kidder [Lois Lane in the new Superman movies] was here in Carmel, California, stumping for Jesse Jackson, and I was invited through some publicity people to attend that luncheon. And I thought it was kind of cute to be able to meet there with her. She really is my favorite Lois Lane—I think the two of them make a great team, and their relationship in these new movies is the way it should have been. But times have changed; when we did it, it was the '50s—sex was taboo. In those days, if Lois even *smiled* at Clark, they'd say *[wagging her finger]*, "No, no, no—none of that!" I felt like a horse with a bit in its mouth! But, again, I do like Christopher Reeve, I think he's a very good actor, and I like Margot Kidder better than anybody who's ever played the role. And that includes myself.

Have you ever met Noel Neill?

In 1957 I was working at the old Eagle-Lion studio in Hollywood on a picture called *I Was a Teenage Frankenstein*, and the *Superman* people had moved their operation over there and were working there at that time. I ran into George one morning, about eight o'clock, and he said, "C'mon, let's have a drink." I said to myself, "Jesus!" George's face was like a baby's butt—he never did show it when he would drink, but I couldn't do it anymore. But anyway, I went over to his dressing room with him and he started pouring me a brandy, he was talking about the series then and he said, oh, God, he was so sick of it all. Then he took me over to meet Noel Neill. He knocked on her door and she said, "Come in." He opened the door and said, "I want you two to meet—

Phyllis, this is Noel." I said *[exuberantly]*, "Hi!" and she said, "I *hate* you!" And George reached in and closed the door!

I thought she was kidding *[laughs]*—I still to this day can't fathom this! This is the only time I ever met the lady—she can't stand me, I hear! We have never been able to appear together, have any fun together, laugh about it or anything. I did an interview on KGO-TV—Jim Eason's talk show, in San Francisco—and he told me that Noel never could call me by name, she always says "the other lady." Noel and I could have had fun and laughs, and had some cute things happen, but we've never been able to share anything. It's as though her whole life revolves around being identified with Lois Lane. I mean, if you had the suit and hat, you were Lois Lane—this is a comic strip, it's not a way of life, it was not all that serious!

People tend to say that I'm the original Lois Lane, and I *was* the first to play her in the *Mole-Men* movie and the TV series, but they forget that she did do the *Superman* serials with Kirk Alyn in the late '40s before I came on the scene. Maybe that's part of it. Noel travels and lectures at colleges and so on, and she's really milked this for whatever she could. I can understand that, but Lois Lane is not what I'm all about—that's only one facet. I really would like a career other than *Superman*.

What were your impressions of Jack Larson?

Jack is a swell guy, and we got along great together. The last time I saw him we were in Brentwood, which is where he lives; he keeps busy writing these days. The guy he lives with, Jim Bridges, is a very fine writer-director; Jim at the time was doing *Bright Lights, Big City* [1988], and Jack got cut in on that somehow as associate producer. Jack is a very sweet guy, and we always had a lot of fun with him.

Was he "the third musketeer" during that first season—you and George Reeves and Larson?

No, Jack didn't socialize too much with us then. I think later on maybe he got closer to George; early on, no.

Any memories of John Hamilton?

John was great. John liked everybody, he was a big b.s.er—he just told stories and laughed and roared and carried on. Very sweet—everybody liked John. He was a bit older than most of the other players, and we certainly all honored that. Everybody was very considerate of John.

How about "Inspector Henderson," Robert Shayne [q.v.]?

I got along great with Bob; in fact, I'm still a very, very close friend of his daughter Stephanie, who's a good actress, by the way. Whenever I have an interview that takes me to L.A. I go down and stay with Steph and her husband. And Bob is still alive and kicking—he's in his nineties, you know.

Like Jeff Corey, Bob Shayne, too, got caught up in those McCarthy investigations.

I remember the day they busted Bob—the day the Feds took him off the set. It was early in the morning, seven-thirty or eight o'clock, George and I were walking along and George looked down and said, "Those two guys with Bob are *heat*." I said, "How can you tell?" and he said, "I just know." So we went right down to the set, where everybody was in a state of shock, and we found out what it was all about: An ex-wife of Shayne's turned him in. Well, this was one time when I really saw George with his dander up. We immediately went to Maxwell, and George raised hell. And Maxwell, who was a bleeding heart liberal, New York Jew, got right on it—I mean, everybody moved as fast as they could. We wrote letters, we did everything. Bob Shayne *had* been, I think, a card-carrying Communist, but a lot of people in Hollywood were then. I was involved with the Actors' Lab, and they were thick down there! But this wrecked Bob's career—he had to go into insurance, so on and so forth, and there were some rough years there for Bob.

That was the only time I had ever seen production stopped on *Superman*, the only time that anybody ever slowed down for anything. We didn't get going until late in the morning, and ordinarily we'd have been in front of those cameras by eight o'clock, sometimes a little bit before. But this stopped production dead.

Was there ever any danger of Shayne being bumped from Superman?

No, everybody hung on: George, myself, Bob Maxwell, we all took a strong stand.

Shayne feels very hurt that Jack Larson downplays his contribution to the show, and that he tells people Shayne wasn't part of the Superman *"family."*

Yes, he was! Number one, George liked Bob, very much, and they were always telling stories. Bob was from New York, where he had done a lot of work on the stage; he had even worked with Ethel Barrymore. Bob had a lot of strong credits behind him, and George always liked Bob. And on occasion we saw Bob and his wife Bette socially. George was a rapper *[laughs]*—you know what I mean?—and he got along with anybody who could sit around and rap. So Bob was definitely a part of the "family," and George took a very strong stand when Bob was busted. If George hadn't really cared about Bob, he wouldn't have said, "Come on, we're going to get some action." You wouldn't have stuck your neck out like that for somebody you didn't care about, particularly during that period—remember, that was a hot time. And George didn't hesitate for one second—I never saw anybody move so fast. Jack Larson wasn't even on the set that morning, he doesn't even know what happened. And in those days, George was not enamored of Jack—maybe later on they became closer friends, but I don't know because I was no longer there. George always considered Jack a kid.

When you talk about the *Superman* "family," it was not just the cast, it was the crew and everybody. My daughter was in a cast then because she was born without a right hip socket, and the grips would take her around on their bicycles and they would sit with her in my dressing room—they were just great with her. It was this kind of atmosphere. I would see George move things for grips—pick up something and carry it from one stage or one set to the next. Today you don't dare touch anything, but in those days we just were one big family and we moved like a house afire. George was very good, very fast, I was fast, it was frantic and hectic, but we all liked the pace. And that's why, at four o'clock, we all had a cocktail!

Was Superman *that much more hectic than most other TV shows?*
The reason that we did so much and did so well was that we all liked each other. I think this was part of the problem with Noel Neill: I had some of the crew people tell me that the reason that Noel grew to dislike me was because the directors would say, "Oh, do it like Phyllis did it." So hearing that constantly would get to be a drag, for anybody.

Don't you think that your Lois was maybe a little too *hard on Clark Kent?*
That was the way they wanted it. But I always felt that, too—that she came down a little heavy on him. In fact, I talked to George and Bob Maxwell about this, and I said, "It's almost as if she's really jealous, too much so, of him," and Maxwell said, "Yes, yes, but that's what it's supposed to be—to give him something to play off of." In other words, to really set Clark up as a softie, he had to have something hard to play against. I said, "Gee, what a ballsy broad!" and Maxwell said, "You got it!"

Did you enjoy playing tough, sassy broads?
Well, they're a hell of a lot more interesting than those sweet, saccharine types—at least they're roles you can get your teeth into *[laughs]*!

Do actors appreciate lightning-fast directors like Lee Sholem, Tommy Carr and George Blair, or do they feel like nothing good can come of something slung together so quickly?
We were all in the same boat—with one oar *[laughs]*—so it was row together or sink! These guys are known as action directors, and you had to bring to the roles what you could. That's why I say, if it hadn't been for Jessica Maxwell on the set, I could have gotten some *stuff* in there for Lois! They were not about to re-shoot scenes, so Jessica stood around with that sharp eye of hers and watched us, because I could have gotten away with a little bit with Lee and Blair and Tommy Carr. They were very easy to work with, sweet guys all of them, and I don't think an actor can blame them for shorting him.

Did you or Reeves ever try to pitch in creatively—suggest changes in dialogue or share ideas with directors?

Yes, George would, he was always contributing, and if there was any time he would get in there and pitch. Time was a great factor.

Your Lois is a feisty and aggressive girl. Is that you?
I'd like to be more aggressive—I'm not as aggressive as I might appear! Sometimes I am feisty, and I have got definite likes and dislikes, and that kind of thing.

Why did you leave Superman?
There were a number of reasons; one of them was that I didn't want to become typecast in that kind of thing. The minute we stopped shooting I'd bleach my hair and do other things, but for George this was it—he became typecast, and he was very unhappy about that. When I left the series and didn't renew my option, they offered me the moon. Whitney Ellsworth offered me about four or five times what I was getting if I'd come back. But I really wanted to get out of *Superman*.

A few months before he died, George came to my house. One Sunday after church he and Toni came by for brunch, and he told me that he had joined the Screen Directors Guild. He had a project he was going to do, and he wanted to know if I would play the lead. I said, "Why, if you've got the project and the money, of course." So he was preparing a picture which he really wanted to direct. It was a sci-fi—I can't remember the name of it, it was so long ago. Then the next thing I know Toni Mannix is calling me and telling me that George had been shot—you know, bullet holes around the bedroom and all this other stuff. She wanted me to go over to George's house with her and I couldn't at the time, and so she got Jack Larson to go with her.

What's your opinion about George Reeves's death?
I don't think we'll ever know. I do know that my friend Bill Cassara, who is with the sheriff's department here in Carmel, told me that he had seen a photograph of George Reeves, showing the bullet hole. They had examined that photograph and took into account the angle at which the bullet had entered the head, and they definitely determined that it was self-inflicted, that he was not murdered.

You once told an interviewer that the only TV appearance you're proud of is an episode of The Untouchables. *Does that mean you take no pride whatsoever in* Superman?
Yes, I *do* take pride in it because it was one of the most loving relationships that I ever experienced. The closeness with George, the crew—God, it was just such a great crew, I'll never forget those guys. I do take pride in it, and in the fact that we worked like gangbusters, we did it and did it well, and that there were never any beefs or arguments within our group. I'd have the crew come in my dressing room and have a drink and prop their feet up—

During the declining days of the serials, Coates made a great no-nonsense heroine in Republic's *Panther Girl of the Kongo*.

nobody drew lines in those days, and that was a good feeling. I don't think that'll ever be again, that kind of closeness between crew and cast.

I just did a picture here, after being away from the cameras for so many, many years. Larry Buchanan, who has Chaparral Productions, did a film on Marilyn Monroe called *Good Night, Sweet Marilyn* [1987] and I played her

mother, who was insane. I walked back in front of the camera and did my stuff in one take, after being away for so long—the crew couldn't believe I hadn't been in front of a camera in that long. So I'm starting back up again, and it feels good.

Early on, before you got mired in all those low-budget Westerns and then Superman, *what sort of niche were you hoping to fill as an actress?*
  I really felt I could play comedy, after I'd worked vaudeville. I'd done some shows overseas with the U.S.O. and I played "straight man" to stand-up comics, and I found that I could play comedy. I did a comedy series called *This is Alice* [1958] for Desilu, I worked with Bob Cummings and Abbott and Costello and so on. In fact, another reason why I left *Superman* was because I thought Jack Carson and Allen Jenkins were headed for a comedy series, and I committed myself to a role in that. I also did a pilot film with Bert Lahr [*Thompson's Ghost*, 1966] which never got off the ground even though it was a cute idea. So I wanted to play comedy, and I hope still, even at this late date, to get into something with some comedic value.

Superman *took an unfortunate turn toward silly comedy soon after you left.*
  And none of 'em can *play* comedy! That's why it turned into what it did.

I get the impression that you're not one to sit around watching your old pictures.
  No, as a matter of fact, I really have never seen anything! I don't even know whether or not, if I *had* done some great things, I would sit down again to see them. Once something is done, it's done, and I never look back because you can always say, "God, I could have done that so much better." There's always that element.

Your serials for Republic, Jungle Drums of Africa *and* Panther Girl of the Kongo—*were they a hectic grind, too?*
  Whew! Let me tell you, they were tough to make. In *Panther Girl* I wore a short costume in order to match stock footage from some older jungle serial [*Jungle Girl*, 1941], and I had to ride an elephant all day. And my legs were raw from the hair on the elephant—I never knew 'til then that an elephant even *had* hair! Then one of the natives fired a gun near my ear, and I was deaf for a couple of days! We'd go in this terrible lake at Republic, this water pond where the alligators would be snapping at your ass, and the minute we'd climb out of this awful, stagnant water we'd have to get a shot of penicillin so we would survive and not die of some sort of disease! I guess it was my sense of humor that kept me going through the thing. A fellow said to me one time,

Opposite: **Coates ground out Republic serials such as** *Panther Girl* **after leaving the** *Superman* **teleseries.**

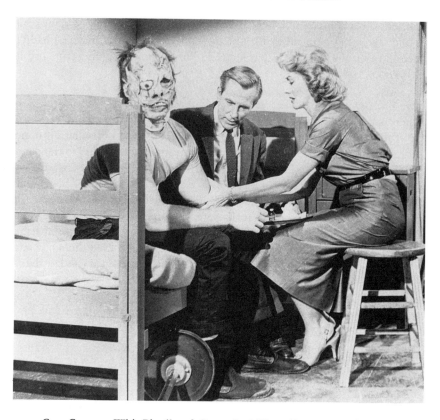

Gary Conway, Whit Bissell and Coates in *I Was a Teenage Frankenstein*.

"You were sort of the last-ditch effort at a serial queen, weren't you?" and, to be honest, I guess I was! I don't mind telling you I never read the scripts on those things—in fact, I never read the scripts on *Superman*, if you want to get right down to it. I knew the character, it became one-dimensional for me and I would just go in and wing it with George. And when I did Westerns, you either played the whore with heart, or you played the sweet mother, or you played the ingenue. In Westerns they lit the horse and the cowboy, and to hell with the leading lady! And it was the same way on *Superman*.

How did you become mixed up on I Was a Teenage Frankenstein?

I just went on an interview, I guess, and got the job. I don't really remember too much about that picture except that the star, Whit Bissell, was very nice to work with. I also remember that they had live alligators there, and they were throwing some bones to 'em—they were supposed to be *my* bones, as a matter of fact *[laughs]*!

Your worst film has to be The Incredible Petrified World.

A friend of mine from my teenage days, a fellow by the name of Jerry Warren, called me and said, "Gypsie, you have to do me a favor, I've got to get started in the business. I've got this script, Robert Clarke is gonna do it, John Carradine's gonna be in it," so on and so forth. After I read the script I said, "Jerry, I'll never work again if I do this picture!" and he said, "I promise you this picture will never show on the West Coast. I just gotta get started!" I knew Bob Clarke, who was a doll of a guy, and so I let Jerry twist my arm. And I did not take a salary, I did it as a favor.

You shot that in Colossal Cave, New Mexico.
What an awful experience! That place was full of bat guano—it was hideous! Jerry's father-in-law played the monster, and his wife was the production head.

We did have a lot of laughs over there, though; Bob Clarke's wife, Alyce, was trying to get pregnant, and I was telling them all about Vitamin E. So they started taking Vitamin E like crazy—eating it, drinking it, rubbing it on 'em and everything else *[laughs]*—and finally they did have a baby, a gorgeous son named Cameron. And it was fun working with Carradine, who was a wonderful nut—John would get drunk, and carry on with Shakespeare *[laughs]*! He was dating Della Jacques, the girl who stood in for me on *Superman,* and one time they were over at my house for dinner. I finally went to bed, I got up again about three in the morning and there he was, stark naked, "to-be-or-not-to-be"-ing in my living room! John was absolutely, marvelously insane—a brilliant, funny actor.

And then, of course, the film did play in California.
Oh, I could have *killed* Jerry *[laughs]*! He lost me more jobs with that film, because it did show out here. That was the biggest mistake of my life, and I never spoke to him after that.

If you could turn back the clock, what would you do differently in your career?
I would not do *The Incredible Petrified World* with Jerry Warren, that's for sure *[laughs]*! But, seriously, I don't know what I could do differently: I was in a bind, I had a child who had a physical handicap and I had to work. My mother was in and out of mental institutions, and I had a lot of heavy stuff in my life. People in Hollywood remember that I had an alcoholic grandmother who lived with me for awhile—in fact, I can remember that I was on the set of *Teenage Frankenstein* when I got a call from the police, that my grandmother was sprawled out on somebody's lawn! I had all this crap in my life, trying to handle an alcoholic grandmother who would be selling my clothes to neighbors to get money for booze, and a mother who almost drove me insane with *her* problems...! So there were great limitations on me in those days, and I had to work. And to try to work and handle this and keep it all under wraps was tough. Evidently I had some dues to pay and, man, I paid 'em!

Thanks to Superman *you're a cult actress with a large, loyal and loving fan following. Is that adequate compensation for never having broken into the big time?*

It sure is—it means a lot. The hundreds of letters I get and the requests for autographs, it's all very heartwarming. I was happy to be in *Superman;* I was also happy to be in *This Is Alice,* although the director Sidney Salkow was not very imaginative, he was one of those crank-'em-out guys. I adored working with Ida Lupino [on *The Untouchables*], she was a charge; and I loved working with Larry Buchanan in '87 on *Good Night, Sweet Marilyn.* This guy is an action guy—he's from Hollywood, he's made a lot of low-budget films and he's a very talented man. He is going to form a stock company, and I'll be a part of it. I liked the cameo role I did in *Good Night, Sweet Marilyn,* and maybe I'll do things in the future that I'm going to like even better.

PHYLLIS COATES FILMOGRAPHY

So You Want to Be in Politics (Warners short, 1948)
Smart Girls Don't Talk (Warners, 1948)
So You Want to Be a Muscleman (Warners short, 1949)
So You're Having In-Law Trouble (Warners short, 1949)
The House Across the Street (Warners, 1949)
A Kiss in the Dark (Warners, 1949)
My Foolish Heart (RKO, 1949)
So You Want to Hold Your Husband (Warners short, 1950)
Blues Busters (Monogram, 1950)
My Blue Heaven (20th Century–Fox, 1950)
Outlaws of Texas (Monogram, 1950)
Man from Sonora (Monogram, 1951)
Canyon Raiders (Monogram, 1951)
So You Want to Be a Cowboy (Warners short, 1951)
Nevada Badmen (Monogram, 1951)
Oklahoma Justice (Monogram, 1951)
The Longhorn (Monogram, 1951)
So You Want to Be a Bachelor (Warners short, 1951)
So You Want to Be a Plumber (Warners short, 1951)
Superman and the Mole-Men (Lippert, 1951)
Stage to Blue River (Monogram, 1951)
Flat Top (Monogram, 1952)
So You Want to Get It Wholesale (Warners short, 1952)
So You're Going to a Convention (Warners short, 1952)
Invasion U.S.A. (Columbia, 1952)
Fargo (Monogram, 1952)
Guns Along the Border (Monogram, 1952)
Hired Gun (Monogram, 1952)
The Gunman (Monogram, 1952)
Canyon Ambush (Monogram, 1952)
The Maverick (Allied Artists, 1952)
So You Want to Wear the Pants (Warners short, 1952)

Wyoming Roundup (Monogram, 1952)
Marshal of Cedar Rock (Republic, 1953)
So You Want a Television Set (Warners short, 1953)
So You Love Your Dog (Warners short, 1953)
So You Think You Can't Sleep (Warners short, 1953)
So You Want to Be an Heir (Warners short, 1953)
She's Back on Broadway (Warners, 1953)
Topeka (Monogram, 1953)
Perils of the Jungle (Lippert, 1953)
El Paso Stampede (Republic, 1953)
Here Come the Girls (Paramount, 1953)
Jungle Drums of Africa (Republic serial, 1953)
So You're Having Neighbor Trouble (Warners short, 1954)
Panther Girl of the Kongo (Republic serial, 1955)
Girls in Prison (AIP, 1956)
So Your Wife Wants to Work (Warners short, 1956)
I Was a Teenage Frankenstein (AIP, 1957)
Chicago Confidential (United Artists, 1957)
Cattle Empire (20th Century–Fox, 1958)
Blood Arrow (20th Century–Fox, 1958)
The Incredible Petrified World (Governor Films, 1960)
The Baby Maker (National General, 1970)
Good Night, Sweet Marilyn (Chaparral Productions, 1987)

It was on The Masque of the Red Death
that I got the review from Time *magazine that read,
"The sexy, lusty redhead is played by the English actress
Miss Hazel Court, in whose cleavage you could sink
the entire works of Edgar Allan Poe
and a bottle of his favorite booze
at the same time." I* [laughs] —
I rather liked that one!

Hazel Court

IN THE ROYAL TRADITION of Fay Wray (the 1930s), Evelyn Ankers (the '40s) and Beverly Garland (the '50s), voluptuous Hazel Court was the undisputed queen of '60s horror. Her reign spanned two continents; her regal consorts included horror kings Karloff, Price, Lorre, Cushing and Lee; and her loyal subjects were the legions of Hammer and AIP fans. In 1964 the flame-haired scream queen relinquished her throne to attend to the more pressing responsibilities of being a wife and mother, but she continues to look back with affection on a remarkable career in horror and science fiction.

Born in Birmingham, England, Court carried on a love affair with the world of movies and make-believe that made her a leading student at her hometown's School of Drama and later helped her land a contract with the J. Arthur Rank Organisation. Graduating from bits to supporting roles to leads, she made her fantasy film debut in 1953's *The Ghost Ship* and later reinforced her genre rep in British-based productions like *Devil Girl from Mars, Doctor Blood's Coffin* and Hammer's landmark *The Curse of Frankenstein*. Relocating to Hollywood, she also became a regular in Roger Corman's Poe series, acting opposite the grand old men of horror in such chiller classics as *The Masque of the Red Death* and the comedic *The Raven*.

Your first horror film was a minor picture called The Ghost Ship. *Do you remember that film at all?*

Yes, I do. That was with Dermot Walsh, who was my husband at the time—he and I made several films together. I remember the wonderful old teak sailing ship we worked on in *The Ghost Ship*. It belonged to the director of the film, Vernon Sewell, who was marvelous; he had a certain "throwaway" technique that worked *[laughs]*, and he did lots of wonderful early English films. *The Ghost Ship* was a very quick film, a low-budget picture, and to be honest with you I really don't recall much about it except that beautiful yacht. We shot everything, including the interiors, on her.

Over the years your Devil Girl from Mars *has acquired a campy,* Worst Films *kind of reputation.*

Devil Girl from Mars! That one really has become a "classic," hasn't it *[laughs]*? But, you know, I ran my tape of that film just the other day and I really thought it was amazing—for the time, and for what it cost. And the photography wasn't bad, for a three-week picture. And I recognized a lot of old friends that I'd forgotten: Adrienne Corri was in it, and Hugh McDermott, and others. I was just fascinated.

How about Patricia Laffan, who played the Devil Girl?

I don't remember her much. Hugh McDermott was the one with the great sense of humor—with that lovely Scottish accent, he'd seem to be sending everything up.

Previous page: The undisputed queen of '60s horror, Hazel Court is all pigtails and sunny smiles in this candid shot from *The Masque of the Red Death.*

Court *(left)* and space invader Patricia Laffan in the schlocky British SF film *Devil Girl from Mars*.

What about the Devil Girl's robot?
  [*Laughs.*] It kept breaking down! It was mechanical, and it kept breaking down!

So you enjoyed working on Devil Girl from Mars?
  I remember great fun on the set. It was like a repertory company acting that film: We were all friends and got on well, we rehearsed and acted and it was great fun. We kind of giggled and laughed about it all, but we were aware we were doing something different.

What do you recall about some of the behind-the-scenes people?
  I remember the director, David MacDonald, he was sweet. And the producers [Edward and Harry Lee Danziger] made a lot of money out of the films they made in England. They really were very tight on budget, tight on everything—they'd even write the next script on the back of the old one! And they'd give you *a* Kleenex if you asked for a box *[laughs]*! They became very rich and I'm told they own half of Paris today.

How rushed and low-budget were these minor SF films?

Very. I wouldn't know the exact budgets on any of those things, but they were staggeringly small. We shot for like three weeks, working into the night. And you never got a chance for a retake unless the film was damaged. But they were organized, though, I must say that.

As a kid growing up, did you enjoy going to the movies?
Oh, yes. I used to go with my mother and father and we'd stand in line at the local cinema. And then on the way home I would act out the film—I walked about ten paces behind them, and do absolutely the whole film *[laughs]*! It's fun now, looking back on that time and on coming to Hollywood, seeing Sunset Boulevard for the first time and so on. I never lost my awe for it.

Is it true that, early on, your parents disapproved of your interest in acting?
They weren't that keen on it, really, but they didn't stop me. My father was a sportsman, a well-known English cricketer, and there was no theatrical background at all. At fourteen I was at the Birmingham Repertory Theater and the Alexander Theater in Birmingham. I had had my London Academy of Dramatic Art prior to that. I must have been about sixteen when Sir Anthony Asquith, who directed many wonderful British films, saw some pictures of me that my sister Audrey had, and he said, "She should be in pictures!" And Audrey said, "Well, she *is* an actress." So I was sent to London to meet him, and then he sent me to Sir Michael Balcon at Ealing Studios, where I made my first film, *Champagne Charlie* [1944]. I only had one line: It was an Edwardian film, I was up in a balcony and I'm watching the gaiety people, and I say, "I never had champagne before," as I'm giggling and laughing. That was my introduction to it.

If you had had your druthers, what types of roles would you have wanted to play?
I did love the theater and I enjoyed doing comedy—it was comedy that actually brought me to America, through doing the TV series *Dick and the Duchess* [1957–1958] with Patrick O'Neal. And then of course I ended up going back into the horror films *[laughs]*—*The Premature Burial*, *The Raven* and *The Masque of the Red Death*.

Did you see horror films as a kid?
No—never! Fred Astaire, Ginger Rogers, yes. Horror films? I wanted nothing to do with them *[laughs]*!

In making films for Hammer, did you get to meet the people who ran the company?
Oh, yes, I knew Jimmy Carreras and his son Michael very well indeed. They took over the Manor House at Bray, and the grounds became the studios.

It was all on a shoestring, but the amazing thing is that I remember incredibly beautiful sets. And I never had cheap costumes there, I had the best of everything. We didn't get much money for working in Hammer pictures, and they didn't cost a great deal, but they made a fortune.

Did the Carrerases enjoy making horror films, or did they make them only because they saw the future in them?
I think they had a feel for horror films *and* they saw the future. They were both wonderful men.

Had you seen any of the old Frankenstein films before making The Curse of Frankenstein *for Hammer?*
No. But we ran the original film with Boris Karloff—and little did I think that I would act with Boris Karloff years later, in *The Raven*. We didn't really know what we were doing, but Terence Fisher had a wonderful eye for all that and he would get it all on film without any fuss. He was marvelous in that way. We were always at great ease and we were never pressured; with Terence Fisher you had all the time you wanted.

A screenwriter named Chris Wicking, who wrote some films for Hammer, says that Fisher looked upon his horror films as "a bit of a joke."
Terence Fisher may have thought of them as a lark, but he had such a good technique that he did a good job. He was excellent—a good, solid, well-informed and knowledgeable director.

Were these Hammer films one-take pictures?
No, we'd go two and three takes on those.

How did you like working with Peter Cushing on The Curse of Frankenstein?
He was a wonderful man, a trained actor from the Old Vic. Peter Cushing was born a century too late—he really comes from the nineteenth century. A lovely man. I don't remember too much about Christopher Lee, to be honest with you, even though I worked with him twice, in *The Curse of Frankenstein* and *The Man Who Could Cheat Death*. He was a very funny man, a great raconteur with lots of stories

Your daughter is also in Curse of Frankenstein.
That's right—she's a little girl of three or four. They wanted someone who looked like me to play me as a little girl, in one of the flashback scenes, so I suggested Sally. She hated it—*hated* being in it! I think it was all very foreign to her, and she didn't understand it. She still remembers it today, and still doesn't like it!

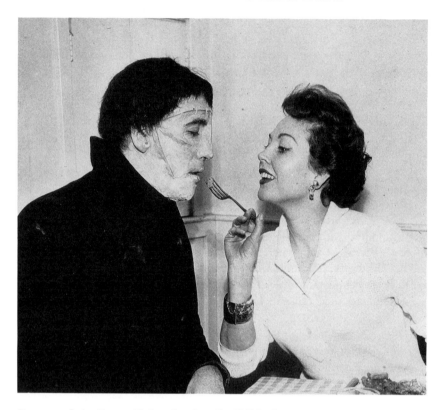

Beauty and the Beast: Christopher Lee (in Phil Leakey monster makeup) accepts a morsel from Hazel Court, behind the scenes on Hammer's landmark *The Curse of Frankenstein*.

The gory and sexy scenes in The Curse of Frankenstein *were groundbreakers in 1957. What did you think of them at the time?*

You know, we took it lightly, and kind of almost tongue-in-cheek, even though we always played it seriously. But it was fun. The [slasher] films they make today are horrible—I think they're awful! So many fans write to me and say that it's not the "true" horror anymore. They're just nasty films, whereas the Frankenstein films and all the other ones we made there were tongue-in-cheek—played for real, but kind of tongue-in-cheek, and fun. Today's films have different connotations. I honestly believe that the films which I appeared in are among the last of the really well-done horror films.

The Curse of Frankenstein had its opening night at the Metro-Goldwyn-Mayer Theater in Leicester Square. If you remember the picture, after Peter Cushing has participated in some particularly bloody scene, the film cuts to me having breakfast with Peter the next morning, and he says, "Pass the marmalade, please." The whole house roared with laughter—and now it's become a line that's quoted!

Hazel Court

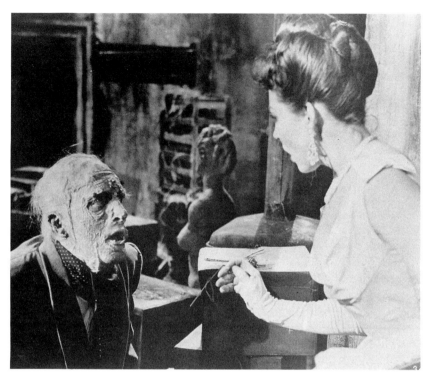

Hazel Court went nose-to-nose with a record number of movie monsters, including a withered Anton Diffring in *The Man Who Could Cheat Death*.

Your other film for Hammer was The Man Who Could Cheat Death *with Anton Diffring.*

That was a lovely movie. It seemed to me that they took greater pains with *The Man Who Could Cheat Death* than with *The Curse of Frankenstein,* and that it was a more elaborate movie. I remember there was a nude scene in there, too—that was one of the first! In the domestic version you see only my head and shoulders, in the scene where Anton Diffring is sculpting me, but we also shot a European version and there I am—front and back *[laughs]*! Somewhere in Europe there must be a print of that floating around.

Were you comfortable doing that?

[Hesitantly.] Y-e-s. It was new in those days, but it was a beautiful setting and supposedly I was being sculpted, so ... it didn't worry me. Actually, to make that bust, a plaster cast was taken of my body, including my face; I remember having the straws out of my nose and my mouth, for breathing. It's a terrifying thing, and they ask you to keep it on for as long as possible. (I didn't keep it on very long!) I'm sure that bust is still somewhere in the property department at Pinewood Studios!

Anton Diffring always gives such icy performances. Was he any "looser" off-camera?

He was just the same off-camera as on film. He was from the old Berlin school of acting, and he was a very good actor, very renowned as a stage actor in Germany. Anton Diffring was charming, a very educated man. He died just a while back [May 1989].

In preparing for this film did you get to watch the older version, The Man in Half Moon Street?

No, but I remembered it, from seeing it as a young girl growing up. I loved it, thought it was wonderful, and it had been very prominent in my mind always.

When you started getting roles in horror films, one after another, did this suit you or did you feel they did you no good?

No, I was looking for something more, much more serious roles. But that didn't happen. It almost started to happen with *Carnival* [1946] which I won a British Critics Award for playing a crippled girl. But it never really came about.

What memories do you have of Doctor Blood's Coffin?

That it was shot in Cornwall, England—I love Cornwall, it's a wonderful part of the world. *Doctor Blood's Coffin* was one of the first films of Sidney Furie, who went on to direct lots more films. He was always interesting; he was always trying to find ways to shoot something differently. I saw his future potential, absolutely—it was right there for all of us to see.

What can you remember about the rest of the cast?

Kieron Moore, who played Dr. Blood, seems to have dropped out of movies. He was a beautiful Irish actor and I don't know what happened to him—I would like to know! He was lovely to work with and a very attractive man. And Ian Hunter was a lovely man, too, he was very good.

Were the cave scenes shot on a set?

No, in a cave—the real thing, at Cornwall. And very wet!

Throughout this late '50s–early '60s period you were back and forth to Hollywood a number of times.

I did the TV series *Dick and the Duchess,* which we did in England, and then CBS brought me to America, where I did several episodes of the Alfred Hitchcock TV series. I did four of those—in fact, my present husband, Don Taylor, was the director of the first episode I did, which was called "The Crocodile Case." So I was doing a lot of going back and forth.

Hazel Court is less than pleased to find her husband (Paul Stockman) has been revived from the dead in the climax of *Doctor Blood's Coffin*.

Did you get to know Hitchcock at all?
　　Yes, I knew him well, and I am also great friends with Pat Hitchcock, who is his daughter. Of course Hitch never cared much about actors, it was always the camera, you know. So you were always fighting that. But he was fun — he was a great storyteller and a very funny man.

One of your Hitchcock *episodes,* Arthur, *was directed by Hitchcock himself.*
　　Oh, yes, with Larry Harvey. Two thousand chickens and me and Laurence Harvey! I remember Harvey saying to me, "Are you as nervous as I am?" and I said, "Yes, I am!" I remember us both saying, "This is *not* going to be our best day" — we were very nervous.

Did Hitchcock put you at ease?
　　[Laughs.] Halfway!

Then in the early '60s you moved here permanently.
　　That's when I also did *The Premature Burial* and *The Raven* . . . my God, I did do a lot of horror films *[laughs]*! No wonder they call me a scream queen! But I had fun, I must say that — lots of fun. It was sheer delight to be working

with Peter Lorre and Karloff and Vincent Price, who I became a lifelong friend of. He was instrumental in getting me started in my art—he thought I had great talent—and which I've gone on to do ever since. He's a wonderfully interesting man, and still my mentor today. He's written quotations for me, on my brochure about my painting, and now he's going to do one about my sculpting. He, like Peter Cushing, was born in the wrong century.

Your first horror film over here was Roger Corman's The Premature Burial.

That's one of my favorites. There was a mood to it, a strangeness and a mood. And working with Ray Milland was lovely—when I was asked to do the film, I thought it would be wonderful to work with him, and in a Poe story at that. Roger Corman was fun, he and I got on well—we all got on well. I enjoyed working with Roger very much; he was efficient, never went over budget, never went over time. He was quite marvelous.

Corman's stepped on a lot of actors' toes, and some have come away bitter.

On the pictures I did with him, if you wanted more time, you'd just say, "I've got to do it again." He did rush, there was no question about that, but you had to rush with him *[laughs]*—you had to stay right alongside Roger! I never had rows or anything with him, it was always fun.

Did he really direct you, or was he a camera director?

He directed a little—mostly he was camera in those days.

Did you enjoy making so many period pictures?

Even as a kid I always did—I was always dressing up with crinolines and shawls and things. So it was kind of a natural follow-up for me—I dwelled in the past a lot! So I enjoyed all the costumes and so on.

What about your Premature Burial *co-stars?*

Well, I discovered that Ray Milland was a marvelous poet, which I didn't know—he used to write beautiful things. He was Welsh, and the Welsh do write poetry. He was charming. *The Premature Burial* was Richard Ney's last film. He was involved in the stock market, and he was more interested in that than in the acting at that point; then I think he really went into it in a big way, became a broker or something. He made a lot of money at it. And Alan Napier was sweet, it was nice to work with him. There's a song that's called "The Grand Old English Gentleman," and that's what Alan Napier truly was.

You must have a story about the scene where you're buried alive.

Yeah, I was really in there—I did it. They actually did bury me! On rehearsals I had a straw in my mouth, and in covering me up they didn't cover the top of the straw. But on the actual take I had to hold my breath for a minute—a full 60 seconds—covered up with cork. It was horrible!

You appeared with a trio of top horror stars in The Raven.

That was a fun one. Boris Karloff was a great gentleman, but the raconteur, of course, was Peter Lorre, who had great sex appeal, and great charm for the ladies. You always felt that you were the only one in the world he was talking to. He used to make me laugh—a highly intelligent man. Peter Lorre was not well at all on that picture, I think his heart was bad—he perspired all the time, and his eyes were always teary. But nothing would hold him back, he was a wonderful pro. And I remember, too, that Karloff's leg was hurting him, very badly.

They say Peter Lorre ad-libbed a lot on The Raven.

Yes, he never quite got the lines right *[laughs]*—he'd just do his version, and the rest of us would just muddle along! But then there were three of them at it—Vincent and all of them! It was wonderful to be with them, because one would tell a story, then that would spark another one, and then that would spark Vincent, and on and on. This round robin of stories would keep going, and you'd just sit there fascinated and your eyes would go from side to side...!

Would Corman crack the whip on these oldtimers like he did most of his other actors?

Oh, no—there was no problem at all, he never did that. We used to make him laugh a lot—I was always giggling. He never told me off!

Did you see any spark of stardom in Jack Nicholson?

You would look at him and you never would think that this little Jackie Nicholson would turn out to be this big star! He was so young, and so much fun—like a little stuffed elf popping around!

Did you ever encounter James Nicholson or Sam Arkoff?

Oh, yes, I knew them quite well and they were nice people, and great to work for. I'll always remember Sam Arkoff—he didn't like "dark" pictures, he said, and it was funny because on these pictures it was *always* dark!

In your Corman films you played scheming vixens to perfection. Did you enjoy these roles?

I loved doing them—I liked sacrificing myself to the Devil and branding myself in *The Masque of the Red Death* and all that. But that's not me at all! It was on *The Masque of the Red Death* that I got the review from *Time* magazine that read, "The sexy, lusty redhead is played by the English actress Miss Hazel Court, in whose cleavage you could sink the entire works of Edgar Allan Poe and a bottle of his favorite booze at the same time." I *[laughs]*—I rather liked that one!

Much more money was spent on *The Masque of the Red Death*—it was a more opulent production. It was a big production, lots of costumes and a wonderful cameraman, Nicolas Roeg, who photographed me beautifully in that. I think I was like two or three months' pregnant when I was doing the film!

What else do you remember about the picture?
Working with Jane Asher. She was in love with Paul McCartney, they were seeing each other at the time and she wanted to marry him—I kept telling her she was too young *[laughs]*! And of course she didn't marry him. And she was knitting balaclava helmets—the kind of knitted helmet they wore in the war, in cold climates, with the face showing. These balaclava helmets were for the Beatles, so they could go out at night and they wouldn't be recognized. I liked Jane Asher, she was talented, and she still is a good actress today.

Many fans think Red Death *is the best of the Poe films.*
I think *The Raven* is.

Why did you turn your back on acting after The Masque of the Red Death?
I had my son Jonathan, and I firmly believe that you cannot have a marriage, a career *and* bring up a child in Hollywood. It was a decision I had to make. By the way, right now Jonathan is managing a marvelous rock-and-roll band called The Rotters, and I think they're going to break out—I think their sound is going to be known very soon.

In 1981 you surprised everyone by turning up in the third Omen *film,* The Final Conflict.
I was on vacation in Cornwall with Harvey Bernhard and his wife. Harvey was the producer of all three of the *Omen* films: *The Omen, Damien—Omen II*, which my husband directed, and *The Final Conflict*, which was then shooting. And Harvey said, "Would you mind just popping in and doing this?" I giggled and laughed and accepted, never thinking that anybody would see me. Well, I tell you *[laughs]*, *everybody* saw me! They all asked me, "What were you doing there?" and I'd say, "Well, that's supposed not to be seen." It's a foxhunt scene, and I'm handing around a stirrup cup.

And today sculpting is your new passion.
Oh, sure. I study in Italy part of the year every year, I'm in many big collections and I've had shows in Los Angeles, in La Jolla and in Pisa, Italy. I'm in the Dupont collection in New York, I'm in Vincent's collection—many prominent people. That's my life now, and I'm becoming very prominent.

What favorites, among your horror films?
The Premature Burial I loved doing; I don't know why, but I did. If it isn't that, then it's *The Raven*, because it was so much fun working with "the boys."

What would it take to lure you back to acting?

Hmmmm ... a small role, one that had some substance to it. But I have no great desire to do that, I'm well and truly wedded to my art. It's a whole new dimension, a whole new direction, and it's very exciting. New people, a new career—it's wonderful.

HAZEL COURT FILMOGRAPHY

Champagne Charlie (Ealing, 1944)
Dreaming (Ealing, 1944)
Carnival (General Films Distributors, 1946)
Dear Murderer (Gainsborough/General Films Distributors, 1947)
Holiday Camp (Universal, 1947)
Meet Me at Dawn (The Gay Duelist) (Fox, 1947)
The Root of All Evil (Gainsborough/General Films Distributors, 1947)
It's Not Cricket (Gainsborough/General Films Distributors, 1948)
My Sister and I (General Films Distributors, 1948)
Showtime (Gaiety George) (Warners British, 1948)
Forbidden (British Lion, 1949)
Bond Street (Stratford, 1950)
The Ghost Ship (Lippert, 1953)
Undercover Agent (Counterspy) (Lippert, 1953)
The Scarlet Web (Eros Films, 1954)
A Tale of Three Women (Paramount, 1954)
Devil Girl from Mars (Spartan, 1955)
Behind the Headlines (Kenilworth/R.F.D. Productions, 1956)
The Narrowing Circle (Eros Films, 1956)
The Curse of Frankenstein (Warners, 1957)
Hour of Decision (Eros Films, 1957)
A Woman of Mystery (United Artists, 1957)
The Man Who Could Cheat Death (Paramount, 1959)
The Man Who Was Nobody (Anglo Amalgamated, 1960)
Model for Murder (Cinema Associates, 1960)
The Shakedown (Universal, 1960)
Breakout (Continental Distributing, 1961)
Doctor Blood's Coffin (United Artists, 1961)
Mary Had a Little ... (Lopert Pictures, 1961)
The Premature Burial (AIP, 1962)
The Raven (AIP, 1963)
The Masque of the Red Death (AIP, 1964)
Madhouse (AIP, 1974) (filmclips from *The Masque of the Red Death*)
The Final Conflict (20th Century-Fox, 1981)

Anything that costs a penny over his minuscule budgets turns Roger Corman into a monster. He is a dual personality: You meet him in his office and he's absolutely charming. That boyish face of his, he digs his toe in the carpet, all of that jazz. You get him on the set, and he's Attila the Hun.

Richard Devon

YET ANOTHER talented member of Roger Corman's early stock company, actor Richard Devon provided consummate villainy in such B productions as *The Undead, Machine-Gun Kelly* (1958), *War of the Satellites* and the cumbersomely titled *The Saga of the Viking Women and Their Voyage to the Waters of the Great Sea Serpent.*

Devon wanted to be an actor from the time he played a small part in a first grade grammar school production. After finishing high school he answered a small ad in a Los Angeles newspaper which offered training to the novice. This drama school, "Stage Eight," allowed him to work his way through as he hadn't money for tuition. He painted walls, built sets, waxed floors and strung lights. It was during this time that he made his first live television appearance for the experimental TV station W6XAO, atop Mt. Lee in the Hollywood Hills.

Amidst much additional work in television, radio and little theater, Devon also played a recurring character on the kiddie-oriented teleseries *Space Patrol* (when Devon asked for a pay hike, his character was put into permanent suspended animation!). He made his major motion picture debut in Metro's Biblical spectacle *The Prodigal* (1955) with Lana Turner, appeared in his first film for Corman two years later, and picks up his own story from here....

How did you first become acquainted with Roger Corman?

I became acquainted with this boy wonder on a film called *The Undead.* There was an interview, I got the role and I appeared in the film as the Devil. As far as my part was concerned, *The Undead* was shot entirely in an abandoned market on Santa Monica Boulevard. Roger got ahold of some phony boulders and he filled the place with dead shrubbery and all of that. They had a bee-smoker to create the dreadful-smelling fog, and a camera, and the whole thing was shot there. As you know, Roger was not great on budgets and he was extremely tight on schedules.

What else do you remember about working with Corman?

His temper was really quite awesome. On *The Undead,* someone had left one of my speeches out of the script, and naturally I couldn't learn what wasn't there. And he was not just upset, he was *maniacal.* Anything that costs a penny over his minuscule budgets turns Roger Corman into a monster. He is a dual personality: You meet him in his office and he's absolutely charming. That boyish face of his, he digs his toe in the carpet, all of that jazz. You get him on the set, and he's Attila the Hun. With Roger, if anything costs more than what he has figured, it's a disaster for everybody that's around him.

So what exactly happened when you skipped that Undead *speech?*

He was just screaming his head off. Everybody was telling him that it could be rectified, and I said, "Roger, it's all right, don't worry about it. We'll

Previous page: **Richard Devon is still active in Hollywood doing occasional acting and voiceover jobs.**

get somebody to write it out on a card or something and I'll read it." So one of the prop guys wrote it out on a little cardboard box of some sort and I read it—we did it in one take—and that was it. Roger never did another take unless it was absolutely impossible to get around it. If something went wrong or if a take was blown or something like that, what he would do was give it to the editor, and use some footage to cut around.

Did Corman give you enough creative freedom as an actor?
Roger's direction didn't consist of too much beyond, "Let's get fifteen pages in the can"—I mean *[laughs]*, Roger was a quick-buck boy. Roger was great for saying, "Let's try the rehearsal on film"—that kind of thing. I didn't know very much of his background; I understood that he took a course at one of the colleges in cinematography, he finished the course and that was it—he was on his way. He did a picture called *Monster from the Ocean Floor,* which he made for about twenty cents, and he sold it for something like 250 grand! He bootlegged most of the footage—this is Roger. You're talkin' about Roger, you're talkin' about bootleg.

And he never got away from working that way, even when it seemed like he could have.
He did have chances at really getting up there and being a good producer and a good director of big films. As a matter of fact, at one point he was given a film at Columbia [*A Time for Killing,* 1967] to direct. He was given a fine budget and stars and everything else. But what happened was, he started shooting the film and he just couldn't get out of his old ways. He was pushing the actors, they were upset, the crew was upset, so on and so forth. The Columbia brass looked at the rushes and called him in and said, "You know, Roger, we want something to be on the *film*—we don't need this fast kind of attitude that you've had in the past. There's a talent there, there's an ability—stretch it out." But he couldn't hack it. And he was replaced on the film.

Do you think you were chosen for the Devil role in The Undead *because you "looked" the part?*
I think so. My agent was good, and I'm sure he sold me well to Roger. And the fact that I was able to cope with the hectic pace impressed Roger very much. Anybody that could save Roger a buck impresses him tremendously.

How did you get along with the other Undead *cast members?*
I got along with the people fine—everybody knew what they were supposed to do, so we just delivered.
One thing that Roger did look for was people that were going to deliver; that was extremely important, because his budgets were like twenty cents. Every time you worked for Roger it was up-and-go, quickly.

Richard Devon in full costume and makeup for his role as the Devil in Corman's *The Undead.*

Anybody that blew a line, it was like the kiss of death—really and truly. But Roger had a penchant for getting together people who could get along. The problem was getting along with Roger *[laughs]*!

Did you find it difficult trying to keep the dialogue in The Undead *from sounding too awkward?*

I didn't, but a number of the other people did. It was stilted, and there was just no way to get a flow into it. Mel Welles just played everything off the top of his head and he came out all right, but it was difficult to keep from looking foolish. Pamela Duncan pressed very hard and Dick Garland worked hard, too, but everything was against them as far as the dialogue was concerned. It was just coming down around their ears. But as I recall everybody that was on the show was quite professional and they really tried—they really put forth an effort.

The Undead always struck me as a film that was just a little too bizarre, and that probably left a lot of young audiences very cold.
Very definitely. I took friends to see it, when they had the preview in Redondo Beach, and *[laughs]* I don't think they've ever forgiven me! It's a film where you keep trying to figure out what exactly is going on. This was a problem which I tried to distance myself from; I knew what my character was and what I was doing. But some of the other things in there just didn't work—they just didn't go together.

Weren't you next scheduled to appear in Corman's Attack of the Crab Monsters?
Yes, I was. However, I was slated to do another film at the same time, and there was just no way at all to work out the scheduling. Richard Cutting did the part that I was supposed to do in *Crab Monsters*. Later I turned down a part in Roger's *Teenage Caveman*. I looked at the script, and I just didn't believe it. I simply walked away from that picture, and *[laughs]* I was delighted to be able to do so! Bob Vaughn said it was the worst picture ever made.

I guess he never saw Saga of the Viking Women.
[Laughs.] You're probably right! Frank de Kova got stuck with that *Teenage Caveman* part. I ran into him some time after that and asked about it, and he said, it was ... *okay*. Whatever that means.

Did you enjoy playing the Grimault chief in Viking Women?
That was a disastrous film to work on. It was as if Roger were really trying to short his skimpy shooting schedules, even *more* than what he had done. He was trying to beat his own record. He didn't waste a frame, nor did he spare anyone's feelings on the set. He was an absolute demon. As I said before, in his office he would purr like some wide-eyed kitten—but he could be dangerous. I remember some jokes on the set where the people freely discussed him as the sea serpent's brother. On the sets of my six Corman films there were several "Roger-isms," whispered softly among cast and crew alike. I don't know if he ever heard any of them, but it would be difficult to believe that he had not heard at least a few. "The Sultan of Trash," "The Doge of the Dreadful," "The Lord of Film Litter," and this one, which seemed quite popular: "The Robin Hood of Rubbish."

In one sequence in *Viking Women* I had to ride this horse through a small cave. It was like seventeen and a half hands tall, and that's a tall horse. I was leading the other Grimaults through the cave on this huge horse, and the

sucker hung me up on a wall and damn near tore my kneecap off. As I recall, there was never any nurse or any first aid people on the set; Roger said "uh huh" to my problem, and, "Let's get on with it." You can see the bruises on my right knee in the film; I doctored it up with makeup the best I could, but it's still there. And there was a lot of pain connected with it.

What do you remember about working with the other members of that cast?
Abby Dalton was a delight — Abby you could kid around with and she'd kid back. Lynn Bernay was a lot of fun, and Betsy Jones-Moreland also, in a quiet sort of way. Susan Cabot was a *bit* standoffish; I think she and Roger were close friends at the time. She never really got involved with any of the cast members or anything like that, but she was pleasant and she knew her work, and that was swell.

Where was Viking Women *shot?*
We shot up at Iverson's Ranch, which was out in the San Fernando Valley — that's where all the exteriors were done, and some of the cave stuff. We also shot in the caves in Bronson Canyon, which is off Bronson Boulevard. And the interiors were done at the old Ziv Studios on Santa Monica Boulevard. They're long gone now.

What about the scenes on the beach?
That was a condemned beach at Cabrillo. Nobody bothered to tell us it was condemned. They used to post signs when they condemned a beach; somebody had picked up the sign and threw it in the bushes, but I found it. And then we saw the water, and there was a tremendous undertow — it was sort of scary. We were all down there on the day when Roger shot the scene where the Viking women launch their ship. If you recall the film, the rudder falls off the boat. Needless to say, that was not supposed to occur, but Roger is undaunted — nothing stops Roger. They just kept going. The girl who swam after the boat was swimming to save her life, because of the undertow. She got to the boat, and they pulled her in. Then when we got on the stage, to shoot dialogue scenes in front of a process screen, they did a bit of a rewrite. The girls are in the boat, and one of them is hanging onto an oar which she's presumably using as a ruddder. She has a line to Abby, something to the effect that they can't make this long journey using an oar for a rudder. And Abby has to reply — straight-faced — "We *must!*" So *[laughs]*, they go on this tremendous voyage with no rudder on that boat! But to Roger it didn't make any difference; with Roger you just drove ahead. Period. If something went wrong — give it to

Opposite: Rare behind-the-scenes still from Corman's *Saga of the Viking Women*. Brad Jackson is tied to the stake; prop man Karl Brainard (face partially hidden by stake) watches the action. Moving right from Brainard are Jay Sayer, key grip Chuck Hanawalt, Richard Devon and Lynn Bernay. Abby Dalton is at far right.

the cutter. If you could pick it up in another shot—that's fine, too. But there was no backtracking.

There's a scene in there where we're chasing the Vikings—me as Stark and my men, the Grimaults. We dismount from our horses and jump into these canoes—

You used the same beach for the Viking and Grimault *coastlines?*

Oh, sure—the beach worked for everything! We climbed into the boat, and I asked the guy behind me what Roger had told him to do. He said Roger told the guys to keep rowing out to sea until they heard him yell *cut*—and not to stop until they heard it. Now, what Roger had told me was that these guys would row out a very short distance, and he would cut the scene. Quickly I became aware of the fact that Roger had no intention of yelling *cut*—and we were going into some dangerous water. I was furious. I turned around, I screamed an obscenity at Roger and I bailed out of the boat. The water was about waist-high, but the waves were coming in. So I spewed out a couple more expletives at Roger—and if I could have gotten to him...!

The wardrobe I was wearing consisted of Indian moccasins; heavy sheepskin leggings; East Indian rompers; some sort of velvet shirt you wouldn't want to be buried in; a ridiculous belt; upper torso armor over which was flung this huge, heavy sheepskin; and a fur-trimmed hat with earflaps and some kind of point on the top. I looked like Genghis Jerk *[laughs]*—I mean, it was unbelievable! Just then a huge wave hit me from behind, the sheepskin and the armor filled with water, and I went down and under. I couldn't get up; I was struggling, I was furious, and I thought I was going to drown, right there, on this ridiculous seashore. Somehow, through anger I guess, I got to my feet, I tried to move toward the shore—shouting everything at Roger that I could think of—and I remember screaming, "If I ever get my hands on you I'll strangle you!" But I was constantly being knocked down by waves—every time I'd get up, the damn things would hit me again. I struggled and struggled and I finally got to shore. Roger, very tactfully, moved offshore—when I got to the shoreline he wasn't around. People on the shore said they could see me shaking my fists and arms but they couldn't hear me, because of the surf. Anyway, Roger had disappeared for a while, so I cooled off.

Did you enjoy being typecast as a villain in Corman pictures and in other productions as well?

Not really. I had a penchant for comedy, and I've rarely been given an opportunity to play it. I did a series called *Yancy Derringer* [1958–1959] where I was a recurring character called Jody Barker, and that was a delight. The first time I did the show, I was a heavy on the street—I was a pickpocket, but I held up somebody with a gun. After that first show we talked and decided that it would be a good idea if, the next time he appeared, there was a change in the character—to make him cowardly, and to get away from the gun entirely.

Devon as the barbaric Stark in *Saga of the Viking Women:* "I looked like Genghis Jerk!" (Photo courtesy Robert Skotak.)

So then Jody became the Jody that you see in the shows: He's fussy, he's funny, he's upset and nervous all the time, and *hates* violence. It was a lot of fun to play.

You toiled briefly on the right side of the law in Blood of Dracula.
    I really don't have a lot of memories on that one. Herb Strock directed it, and Herb was from the Corman school: Get the footage in the can; push it; shoot the rehearsals; and don't fiddle around with everything. Never mind *creativity;* if you've got something in mind, don't discuss it with me. If you had something that you wanted to do character-wise or something that you

thought should be done, just keep your mouth shut about it and do it, because nine chances out of ten it was going to be printed. So if you had a good solid idea where you wanted to go with the character, just hang loose and go with it.

By the time of Corman's War of the Satellites *you had worked your way up to star.*

What had been happening was that I had become progressively more impressive to Roger, as a performer, through the things that I had done. It was apparently a logical chain of events, and he felt that I would be the right person for this film. I always knew my lines and I could handle any situation that came up unexpectedly, which was paradise for Roger. Anything that would not get in the way of his budget or cost him extra bucks was wonderful—Eden.

You really did have a good part in Satellites *playing that dual role, one sympathetic and one villainous. Did you enjoy the opportunity?*

Very much so, yeah—that's one of the few I really did like.

What do you remember about those satellite sets?

They were practically non-existent; I think if Roger could have gotten orange crates and made them work, he'd have done it *[laughs]*! They built two corridors, and they made them work for about twelve dozen in the picture. Our sets were basically just flats, more along the lines of what you'd have in a stage show. And that was it! They were endlessly re-dressing them, to make them look like different parts of the satellite. Most of Roger's sets consisted of two walls, and you played the third like it was really there.

Now, the punchline to this story is that a few years ago I got a very strange phone call from someone who wanted to know whatever happened to the sets from *War of the Satellites!* I mean *[laughs]*, how should I know, and why should I care? He took me completely off-guard, I didn't know what to say to this fellow. As far as I know, they perished—you could fold them up and put 'em in a cigarette pack!

Satellites *is really a study in corner-cutting: the same sets used over and over, some actors playing multiple parts, and even Corman himself turning up in two parts. Did you resent all of this economy and wish you were working in bigger-budgeted films?*

A thing that I learned a long, long time ago is, "Pay close attention to your own garden." I'm the one that's ending up on the film, and what I want to occur is up to me. And if I start letting these things bother me, I can start nitpicking and destroy whatever I might have in mind or what I might be trying to do. I was fully cognizant of the fact that this was not a big-budget picture, and that anything that I could bring to it would be a plus factor for me. But I couldn't get into the area of being worried about cheap-here and cheap-there.

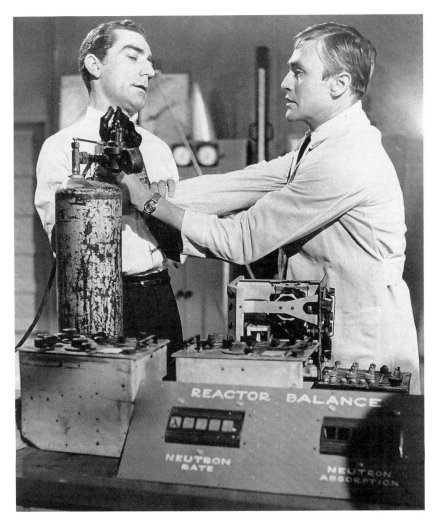

Devon grapples with Jerry Barclay in a tense scene from Roger Corman's *War of the Satellites*.

The silliest scene in Satellites, *the one that really torpedoes the picture, is at the end, when you create a heart for yourself and start making love speeches to Susan Cabot.*

[*Laughs.*] The direction on that was, "Do something, Richard." What do you do when somebody says to you, "We need you to create a heart"? I grabbed at whatever I could, trying to figure out who this person was, which was difficult because his background was totally splintered. So whatever I built into it I built in step-by-step. I figured if I played it the way that I did play it, that it would work, at least for me, under the circumstances.

The climax of *War of the Satellites* finds Devon duking it out with Corman perennial Dick Miller.

You also had a good supporting role in one of Corman's best pictures, Machine-Gun Kelly.

We were beginning to grate on each other, Roger and I, by the time of *Machine-Gun Kelly*. We weren't getting along too well and so on, but work is work and you try to smooth things over and keep going. The wardrobe on that film was a nightmare; on all of Roger's pictures you sort of did it yourself, and you can see on the film how it turned out. Somebody handling the wardrobe said, "It's near something like the 1930s" — so you did whatever you could with that kind of a situation. Charlie Bronson and I got along just fine; we've also worked together on *Kid Galahad* [1962] and in his *Man with a Camera* TV series. But for Roger nothing had changed. In his office he was Peter Pan and on the set he was an ogre. Without any discussions we kept our distance from each other, and that was it.

Corman's "war movie" Battle of Blood Island *[1961] gave you your most sizable film role.*

It was a two-character film, and several parts of the film worked very well for me. Unfortunately you can do a great job in a rotten film, and — you're in a rotten film. It doesn't make any difference; none of the nuances are watched or anything. I've got a drunk scene in that picture that I *loved* — it played well and it worked well, but we were in some stupid cave in Puerto Rico doing this damn thing.

That was your last film for Corman, wasn't it?

Yes, it was; I had pretty much had it at that point. When this film came up I asked my agent, "Where did this film come from?" and he said, "Well, Roger is in the background on it, but he's not involved in it at all." I asked him if he was sure about that and he said that, yes, he was. *Battle of Blood Island* was directed by a fellow named Joel Rapp; Stan Bickman was the producer; and it was based on a short story called "The Forgotten Ones," which was also our shooting title, by the way.

After being reassured by the agent that Roger really didn't have anything to do with this film, I flew down with the cameraman, Jack Marquette, to the airport in Puerto Rico. And who's there to greet us but *Roger*. And the first words out of his mouth are, "Why don't we all have a strawberry daiquiri?" So I looked at Jack, Jack looked at me — we both knew Roger — and we were wondering what was going to be happening next. He took us to the baggage area and we had the daiquiris and we were chatting, and I finally said, "Roger, where are we staying?" Roger was very exuberant when he said, "We're all staying at a villa." Now, *that* gets you a little shaky. So they put us in a little dinky car and they took us to this *house*. I mean, it's a house — and a small one! And everybody who's concerned with this film, or with the other films that they were doing back-to-back with it, is chucked into this place. Robert Towne, who ended up writing *Chinatown* [1974], was there — he was involved with Roger, and he was writing a script, in longhand. It was the script for the next film they did down there *[Last Woman on Earth]*, and Roger wanted to know if I would play the lead. I turned it down because I had three shows waiting for me in Hollywood; Tony Carbone flew in and played the part.

Anyway, Towne was writing in longhand and people were cooking their own meals in the kitchen—it was a disaster, the whole thing. Jack and I got together and we said there was no way we were going to go along with this. We wanted some decent accommodations. So we talked to the rest of the people there and we said, "C'mon, let's move out of here, let's do it all at one time." They said it was a good idea, but when the chips were down and it came time for all of us to talk, it was only me and Jack. But Jack and I were very smart in one way: We had round-trip air tickets in our pockets. I was doing the lead in the film and Jack was the cameraman; if they lost us, they lost everything. There was a lot of dialogue, back and forth—we didn't want anything out of bounds or fabulous or anything like that, just clean—and they finally put us up in the Caribe Hilton, which was delightful. And then everybody was mad at us, because we didn't have to live in the villa! But that got smoothed over after a while.

Blood Island *was entirely shot in Puerto Rico, right?*

Yes, and all exteriors. There were a lot of problems on the show in that we were working in rain forests and jungle, and several of the crew guys were eaten so badly by the bugs that they just had to be shipped back. We were all a mass of welts. Of course, no doctor, no nurse.

One of the sequences in the film was done with a guy who was the house detective at the Caribe Hilton. They hired him to play a Japanese that I was supposed to fight in a scene on the beach. The guy was not an actor, he was a detective. I gave him a crash course in "picture-fighting" and we started shooting. While we're going through this, the tide's coming in, more and more—nobody bothered to check the tides in this area. The detective got so involved in the scene and in the fact that he was doing a movie that he ran straight at me during a take where I'm holding a bayonet—he scared me to death, because I damn near ran him through. I dropped the bayonet, off to the side, I spun him around and threw the punch. He took the punch and threw himself back into the water—and hits a coral reef! He hit it on his chest, and it just shredded him. And by that time the water had come in completely, and the sand crabs were jumping in and out of our jackets! But this was typical of a Corman film: he was in the background this time, but you had the feel, you knew that he was there...!

Was that what finally tore it for you and Corman?

No, it was one day when we were out on location, and Roger came out bringing lunch. There's a large group of us out there, and he brought dry sandwiches with some indeterminate kind of meat on them, and two quarts of milk. For the *whole crew.* I had gone through this whole picture, I'm eaten alive by bugs, and we're all tired, just wiped out. So I just blew my stack—I said, "Get him off the set. If he doesn't go, I go." People were trying to settle me down, but I said, "Get him off. *Now.*" Boom. And that was the kiss of death—that was the end for Roger and I. Roger had just cut every corner in the world where

I was concerned and where everybody else in the film was concerned. I mean, the fulcrum of Roger's life is a dollar bill, and not in a singular sense. And anything in the world that gets in the way of that monetary move—forget it. You're in deadly, deadly trouble.

Have you seen Corman at all in recent years?
 I haven't seen him in many, many years. I don't know whether he's changed—I don't really believe that people basically change. Maybe he has, I don't know—I read things about him in the trades and that kind of thing. But that's pretty much my adventure with Roger.

In 1988 you returned to the horror genre with the supernatural suspenser The Seventh Sign.
 When I first met the casting director on *The Seventh Sign,* the only hitch was that she thought I was too young to play the cardinal. I told her that I work all different ways, that I could do the part with gray hair and all, and it should work out just fine. As usual with films, the role was much larger when I first read it; it was trimmed down and trimmed down and so forth. But we worked out the deal and I did it. The entire sequence in the film that is supposed to take place in the Vatican was shot at the Wilshire Ebell Theater on Wilshire Boulevard.

How active are you in the business today?
 I'm living up here in San Francisco now, but I do go back to Los Angeles for various things. I also do TV voiceovers and radio spots up here in San Francisco.
 I don't know whether this belongs in the interview or not, but it is very important to my wife, Patricia, and me: This winter [1989] we are going back to Paris (the one in France, thank goodness, not the one in Texas) to celebrate our 30th wedding anniversary—it seems like barely 30 minutes! It'll be cold and blustery, but when you're in love, who cares?

Do you enjoy or resent being permanently associated in the minds of many fans with the Corman stock company?
 I don't resent it, not at all. When you're starting out and you're trying to be an actor, you just go after whatever you can get. You hope you can get some decent breaks, but you still go after whatever you can and do your damnedest to make it the best that you possibly can.
 And I have no regrets whatsoever for any of the things that I did with Roger; I did the best job that I knew how and I worked hard, and that was it. When films are finished and you get to see them, of course you re-evaluate and find things in there that you would like to re-do. But you say, "Hey—move on." And that's what I did.

RICHARD DEVON FILMOGRAPHY

The Prodigal (MGM, 1955)
The Racers (20th Century–Fox, 1955)
Escape from San Quentin (Columbia, 1957)
The Undead (AIP, 1957)
The Saga of the Viking Women and Their Voyage to the Waters of the Great Sea Serpent (AIP, 1957)
Blood of Dracula (AIP, 1957)
3:10 to Yuma (Columbia, 1957)
The Buckskin Lady (United Artists, 1957)
Teenage Doll (Allied Artists, 1957)
The Badlanders (MGM, 1958)
Machine-Gun Kelly (AIP, 1958)
Badman's Country (Warners, 1958)
Money, Women and Guns (Universal, 1958)
War of the Satellites (Allied Artists, 1958)
Gunfighters of Abilene (United Artists, 1960)
Battle of Blood Island (Filmgroup, 1960)
The Comancheros (20th Century–Fox, 1961)
Kid Galahad (United Artists, 1962)
Cattle King (MGM, 1963)
The Three Stooges Go Around the World in a Daze (Columbia, 1963)
The Silencers (Columbia, 1966)
Three Guns for Texas (Universal, 1968)
Magnum Force (Warners, 1973)
The Seventh Sign (Tri-Star, 1988)

*There were a bunch of these exploitation pictures
being made ... [in the '50s], but at that time there didn't
seem to be a very big market for them. I guess the other producers
must have been spending just about the same amount of money that we were,
but their pictures were such shit. I did not try to make
just an exploitation picture. I was trying to do
something with a little substance to it.*

Gene Fowler, Jr.

BEFORE 1957, who would have suspected that horror movies and true confessions would have combined forces to produce one of the most successful exploitation film phenomena of the '50s? Certainly not Gene Fowler, Jr., and he directed the movie that kicked off the trend, *I Was a Teenage Werewolf,* as well as *I Married a Monster from Outer Space* one year later. In a decade filled with spectacular film titles, these names stood in the forefront of no-holds-barred '50s sensationalism and earned a notoriety that has lasted to this day. Much of the credit for their box office (as well as dramatic) success is due to the professionalism and dedication of the doubting director Fowler, who was so surprised by the popularity of a werewolf in a high school jacket.

After years in the cutting room, you made your directorial feature debut with I Was a Teenage Werewolf *in 1957.*

I was working in a cutting room next door to a fellow named Herman Cohen. Herman kept dropping into my cutting room and we talked pictures, naturally, and one day he came in and said, "How would you like to direct a feature?" I said I would. He said, "It's got the worst title in the world, but it's a very good script." He gave it to me to read, and it was a thing called *I Was a Teenage Werewolf.* I remember I read the thing as I was lying in the bathtub one night, and after I read it I said to my wife, "I can't do this god-damned thing!" She said, "How was the script?" and I said, "Fair." She said, "Look, why don't you do it anyway? You'd like to do a feature, and nobody will ever see it." There were a bunch of these exploitation pictures being made (I know Roger Corman was making the damn things), but at that time there didn't seem to be a very big market for them—they were very specialized showings. I guess the other producers must have been spending just about the same amount of money that we were, but their pictures were such shit. I did not try to make just an exploitation picture. I was trying to do something with a little substance to it.

What kind of a producer was Herman Cohen?

I enjoyed working with him. We had our normal fights and so on, and there was a lot of rewriting of the script to be done. It was the usual kind of mad scientist picture, which I disagreed with. In the script, after the first interview with Michael Landon, a maniacal gleam comes into the scientist's eyes and he rubs his hands together. I always figured that a villain, in his own eyes, was a very good, very nice fellow. So I tried to make the villain that—he was actually trying to do good for the world. I tried to get some sympathy for him, or at least some understanding. I remember talking to Whit Bissell, who played the doctor, and telling him, "Keep in mind you're *not* a bad man."

Previous page: Son of the famous author/scenarist Gene Fowler, Sr., Gene, Jr., turned his hand to directing after years as a film editor.

I'm surprised that Cohen let you rewrite. Herbert Strock told me Cohen was touchy about things like that.

He didn't know it, while I was doing it! Otherwise he'd have fought me every step of the way. Actually, Herman wasn't too bad. He generally came on the set in the morning and was there for about an hour and left. He was busy promoting other stuff, and he left me alone pretty much.

There's a scene in *Teenage Werewolf* where Michael Landon argues with his father, Michael gets mad and the old man leaves. And Michael is left standing there, boiling. I said, "The scene needs a capper, to show that the kid is a little unstable." So I figured that, since Michael had in his hand a big bottle of milk, I'd have him throw it at the wall. I told Herman and he was against it, but finally I figured I was going to do it anyway—I was all set up, and I might as well do it. And Herman liked it after he saw it. In the dialogue I wrote, I tried to give the characters dimension, to show where they came from, instead of just moving them around and having them say the obligatory lines. I tried to give them a reason for these things. For instance, the milk bottle was not a big production thing; the only thing I was trying to do was give a demonstration of how screwed up this kid was.

Is that a mask on Landon, or applied makeup?

It was applied—it took about two hours to put on the damn thing. We had to do an awful lot of shooting around him while that was going on. I think he did an incredible job.

Teenage Werewolf *was shot by Joseph LaShelle, who was a superb photographer.*

Joe LaShelle was an old friend of mine. When I was over at Fox, he was the operating cameraman for Artie Miller, who was one of the premier cameramen in Hollywood. He and Gregg Toland, in my opinion, were the two best. I became a very good friend of Artie, who was an amateur still cameraman as well; I used to go up to his house all the time and we'd make stills together. To me he was a genius. He asked me one time if I would like to become a cameraman; maybe I was a fool to say no, but I did. Anyway, Joe LaShelle was his operator and I got to know Joe very well. He was one of the sweetest men in the world. So when I got this assignment to do *I Was a Teenage Werewolf,* I called Joe and said, "How 'bout it?" He said, "What's the title?" I told him and he said, "You're kidding! I don't want to do something like that!" I said, "Well, I didn't, either *[laughs],* but this is my first feature and I could sure use some help." So he said all right, and he did it with me, strictly as a friend.

Did he pitch in creatively on Teenage Werewolf?

We worked together. I worked with the art director, the cameraman and the head of pre-production, and tried to lay out everything in the most

Years before he co-starred in TV's *Bonanza*, Michael Landon frothed and foamed as the "I" in the Fowler-directed *I Was a Teenage Werewolf*.

economical way we could. (The theory being, if you know what you're doing, you can do it faster!) Joe did contribute, there's no question about that. And so did the art director, Les Thomas — there was another sweet guy. I've always claimed that all art directors must have to take a course in being a nice guy before they can get the job, because I have yet to find an art director who is a shit! They're marvelous people. On *Teenage Werewolf* Les and I really cheated on sets — we were building them out of spit and polish.

So it was all this planning that helped you bring the picture in so quickly.
  Well, I had no choice, it had to be done quickly, and that's how we did

it, by planning. We made the picture in six days—no, five and a half days, because we got rained out one day. Our budget was $82,000—not very much *[laughs]*!

Who cast the movie?
   Oh, we all did that. Herman Cohen brought a bunch of kids in and we worked together picking them. I think *I Was a Teenage Werewolf* may have been Michael Landon's first picture. I loved Michael—he was a very young kid at that time, maybe twenty years old, but he was good, a hard-working guy, always knew his lines. You could ask him to do anything and he'd do it. It became kind of "family," the way everybody was working together on it. All of these guys were tremendously cooperative; we treated the picture as though it were *Gone with the Wind* and we didn't make fun of it. I told the crew, before we started, "Look, anybody who can give me a suggestion, I'll consider it." That is, anybody except the producer—I won't even listen to him! *[Laughs.]* That's a general rule of mine!

The screenplay of Teenage Werewolf *is credited to someone named Ralph Thornton. Was there really such a person, or did Cohen write it himself?*
   No, no. *Teenage Werewolf* was written by a novelist named Abe Kandel. He wrote a lot of novels and he wrote a lot of pictures, including some very famous ones. He was a very nice fellow.

Why the pseudonym?
   'Cause he probably didn't want his name on a thing called *I Was a Teenage Werewolf [laughs]*!

Any other Teenage Werewolf *anecdotes that you can recall?*
   Because of the half day that was rained out, we had to go back and pick up a couple of shots. We had already used a police dog in a scene, but we couldn't afford the dog anymore so we were going to do without that scene. But I owned a police dog and it matched the first one pretty well, so I said, what the hell, why not use my own damn dog? We were up there at Bronson Canyon, and my dog Anna was having a hell of a time running in the forest while Michael was getting his werewolf makeup on. Finally he came on the set, Anna turned and took one look at him and ran like hell *[laughs]*! What eventually happened, I guess, was she figured that since Michael *smelled* like a human being he must *be* a human being, and we got some very close and very quick shots of her loving him to death! That seemed to work all right.

What do you think of I Was a Teenage Werewolf *today?*
   I guess it's all right. Looking back at it, I can think of many things that I wish I had done, but to be realistic there wasn't time to do them anyway!

Did you have an opportunity to meet with AIP heads Nicholson and Arkoff?

Only on the wrap party. The last shot I shot was the destruction of the lab, and everybody came down to look at it. I think I went about a half-hour over schedule, and everybody was trying to hurry me up so they could open the bar! So, no, I didn't know Nicholson or Arkoff that well, all I know is that *I Was a Teenage Werewolf* was the picture that put 'em in the black.

Were you surprised by the film's success?

Indeed I was. I think the thing, when it was first released, grossed something like $6,000,000, maybe even $8,000,000. Which, for a picture that cost $82,000, is a hell of a profit! And apparently that put them on the map.

Did you work for a salary, or a percentage?

A salary. I was *offered* a percentage, and I turned it down because I didn't believe it would make any money *[laughs]*!

Cohen himself turns up in one short scene in Teenage Werewolf.

He very well might have. I remember we used to do those "in" things all the time. Even I would do it occasionally — I remember having my shoes shined by the producer on some picture, I don't recall which one.

Are you in either Teenage Werewolf *or* I Married a Monster?

No — only my hands. I always did my own inserts, in all my pictures. That I got from Fritz Lang — Fritz and I were very, very close friends, and Fritz always put his hands in the picture.

What were some of the things you learned from Lang that came in handy on movies like Teenage Werewolf *and* I Married a Monster?

Firstly, prepare. I remember one time when I was going up to San Francisco to do the *China Smith* shows for TV [1952], he asked me, "Have you prepared?" and I said, "Heck, I haven't even seen the sets yet." He said, "Look, a window's a window, a door's a door. Prepare your show and just adapt yourself to what the set is, and you'll have no problem." Which I did. So he taught me preparation, and he taught me use of the crane; this man really knew how to move the camera and so on. I used to work very closely with Fritz. As a matter of fact, I would lay out the following day's work, then Fritz would come over and say, "Well, why do you want to do it this way?" and I'd tell him. And he'd say, "I think it'd be better *this* way, don't you?"—and we'd work together. That's a unique situation. He didn't teach me much about acting, because *[laughs]* he and I always differed on what actors should do. He was probably righter than I was, but we both were very stubborn people. And, my God, he was a master of suspense!

How were you able to break into the movie business?

I got into the business by being introduced to Allen McNeil, who was a fellow that my father had interviewed while writing a book called *Father Goose*. *Father Goose* was the story of Mack Sennett, and Allen McNeil was the chief editor for Sennett at the time. McNeil asked me, "Would you like to get into the cutting department?" and I—not even knowing what the cutting department was—said yes. So I started working there at night, and going to U.S.C. in the daytime. The first picture I ever worked on was a Fox picture called *Thanks a Million* [1935], which was directed by Roy Del Ruth and written by my future father-in-law, Nunnally Johnson. I remember the first time I walked into the place—I never saw so much film in my life! It was all off-reels and trimmed ends and so on, and I was just stunned, and couldn't figure out how the hell anybody kept track of anything. But he taught me the business, and I was cutting there until 1941.

At what point did you decide that you wanted to become a director?

Around 1950, or maybe a bit earlier than that. I thought at the time that my experience in the editing room was a helluva good background, and it turned out to be true. I worked at first in TV, on *China Smith,* a very popular show in those years. It was a half-hour show—it starred Dan Duryea, we made it in San Francisco, and shot it on 16mm. We started out by making two of those a week. Dan was on salary, $250 a week, guaranteeing that he wouldn't make more than two shows a week. But, as time went on, we suddenly started making three shows a week—that translates to two days per show *[laughs]*! We made a lot of those things, and then when I finished with that I did a lot of other television stuff.

Why didn't you stay on with Herman Cohen and AIP?

I don't remember exactly but, to be honest, I don't think I wanted to. Anytime you wanted something a little special for your picture, you'd have to fight like a dog for it. I remember directing pictures for Bob Lippert, a man whose eye was on the budget at all times. One thing I always wanted to do, particularly in these low-budget pictures, was have one day with a crane. Well, the crane cost maybe $250 a day and $250 for the operator. I remember shooting *The Oregon Trail* [1959] for Lippert, and I traded 25 Indians for the crane *[laughs]*! It sounds stupid, but that's the way you had to work. Lippert was releasing pictures through 20th Century–Fox; he had a deal whereby he'd make pictures for $125,000, and if the picture came in for less than that, he'd steal from the top. That was Lippert, not me—I didn't get *any* of that *[laughs]*!

That Lippert experience was wonderful in a way because we had the run of the Fox lot; whatever sets happened to be still standing, we'd use those sets. My partner, Lou Vittes, and I would walk through these sets that'd already been used for much more expensive pictures than we could make, and we would pretty much write out scripts around the sets! I did a number of pictures for Lippert: *Showdown at Boot Hill, Gang War* [1958], *Here Come the Jets*

[1959] and *The Oregon Trail*. *The Oregon Trail,* that was a son of a bitch—Lippert really screwed that one up. He made a bet with Spyros Skouras [president of 20th Century-Fox] that he could make a big outdoor Western without ever leaving the Fox lot, and like an idiot I agreed to direct it!

As a former editor, did you supervise the editing of your films?

I have a theory about that. I think you should allow the editor to put the picture together without any kind of supervision whatsoever. Because he sometimes can find things that you don't even know you shot. So I stayed out of his way, and I only came in after the whole thing was assembled. Directors shouldn't be allowed to edit their own movies, unless they have a helluva lot of training. Directors have an awful habit of remembering how difficult the scene was that they shot. And the thing is just crying to be cut in half or thrown out *[laughs]*! Just the other night I saw Sam Peckinpah's *The Wild Bunch* [1969] on TV, and it was advertised as his cut, as opposed to the one that was released. I looked at the thing and I said, "I am sure that the studio was more correct than he was"—it was a very self-indulgent thing. I hope I was never guilty of that.

George Gittens edited I Was a Teenage Werewolf *and George Tomasini did* I Married a Monster from Outer Space.

Tomasini was Hitchcock's cutter; I was in the army with him. And George Gittens was a funny guy—he was deaf as a post. When we'd run *Teenage Werewolf* with Herman Cohen, Herman would say something to George and I had to write it down. George couldn't hear and I didn't want Herman to know he was deaf *[laughs]*! So afterward I would have to transcribe all my notes, go up to his cutting room and show him what had to be done. George was Louis Loeffler's assistant at one time; Louie was the man who cut most of Otto Preminger's pictures. Louie's eyesight was going and George's hearing was going, and they'd both collaborate on cuts. One could see and the other could hear *[laughs]*!

How did I Married a Monster from Outer Space *come about?*

Lou Vittes and I had worked together over at Lippert's, and Lippert would always work from a title. He'd say, "Oh, I've got a great title, here it is, now write a story about it," and that's what we'd do! So both of us were trying to break away from that, and try and find a subject we could write about. So I said, "Let's do what they did on *Teenage Werewolf*. Let's find some absurd title and write a good script for it." And actually the script, for what it is, is all right. But I looked at *I Married a Monster from Outer Space* just the other night and, boy, all I can say is that there are an awful lot of things I would have done differently.

Such as?

In the first place, I hated the main title—it really looked like the cover of a comic magazine. And then within the picture I would have done a lot of things differently. Just little things.

What extra responsibilities did you have as producer?
Oh, pretty much all of it except where sometimes the studio heads would come in and insist on something. I remember they were the ones that wanted the glowing effect on the monsters. I didn't want that; I think that without the glow it would have been a little more subtle. But I guess it worked out all right. I designed those monsters, and I designed them with only one thing in mind: so I could get rid of the god-damned things *[laughs]*! I gave them a vulnerable spot, those tubes on the outside of their bodies, which gave the dogs something to grab hold of. That was the only reason for that! We had two costumes, which we used over and over to make it seem like there were a bunch of them.

Is that your dog in I Married a Monster *as well?*
Oh, yes. Having dogs kill off the aliens was probably the cheapest thing we could think of *[laughs]*!

Tom Tryon gives a wooden performance that doesn't do much for the picture.
You're right, he *was* wooden. He did not want to do this picture—there was no *way* he wanted to do this picture. But this was at the time when the studios had all the power, and they'd say to an actor, "You do this picture or you're put on the blacklist." So he did it, much to his chagrin. But then about halfway through we became good friends, he eased up a bit and started doing things. And Gloria Talbott I love. She's another person who'll do just about anything you ask her to do.

How much of a spaceship did you actually build?
Almost nothing. I think it was just a door, and the rest was foliage. Then the interior was just some plain curved flats, that's all. We suspended the actors inside with harnesses and piano wire.

Did you shoot the whole picture at Paramount?
No. We did some shooting up in Bronson Canyon, and then also out on the streets. That was the dumbest damn thing in the world. We had to shoot a scene on a public street and I was told, "Make it very convenient, find a location near the studio." So I picked a spot about two blocks away. Well, when I went to that location to shoot that scene, I saw more god-damned trucks than I ever saw in my life! They had honey wagons, they had grip trucks—we must have had fifteen or twenty trucks to shoot that simple silent scene! When I was on location on *China Smith* in San Francisco years before, we had two trucks and a station wagon. One little truck carried the camera equipment and the sound, and then we had a regular two-and-a-half-ton truck to carry whatever

Posse members, led by Steve London (holding dog), examine the body of a slain alien in *I Married a Monster from Outer Space*.

other crap we needed. The station wagon was for us, and we had cardboard inserts that we would put up against the windows so that Dan Duryea could change his clothes while we were driving to the next location! And we would shoot all over San Francisco. I'd see a good location, we'd come screeching to a stop and within five minutes we were shooting.

Did you learn your lesson and work for a percentage this time?

I did work for a percentage, yes—I owned 25 percent of *I Married a Monster*. But they "bookkeeped" me out of everything they could—they told me the picture never made any money. And yet I'd go out and see kids lined up around the block to see the picture on a Saturday, and I'd say, "You mean to say this picture isn't making any money *yet*?" Our budget was $125,000.

I Married a Monster is so well-done that nearly every reviewer at some point apologizes for the title.

Well, that was the purpose of that title, the exact purpose. I mean *[laughs]*, we were certainly capable of coming up with a decent title! This was strictly an exploitation picture. But there again I tried to put characterization into the monsters. The so-called monsters, the aliens, were very sad people. One of the things I've always found is that you've got to accept the premise, regardless of how ridiculous it is. If you accept the thing as very realistic and very honest, then you can come up with very honest performances and make a fairly honest picture out of it. And this premise was kind of sad; these aliens, all of their women had died off, and they were searching the galaxy for women to propagate their race. They were desperate. What they were doing, as far as they were concerned, was very honest and very necessary. The fact that they were kicking the shit out of Earthmen made no difference!

Why did you turn your back on directing after only seven pictures?

I didn't turn my back on it, it was the result of something I didn't even know was happening. My father-in-law had written a script called *Flaming Lance** and a producer, whose name I won't divulge, heard about it and he wanted me to get my father-in-law to give it to me, for him to produce and me to direct. I said I wouldn't do it, that he should be paid for his script. And the producer got very upset about the thing. Suddenly I stopped working, and I didn't know why. For a year. Then a friend of mine stopped by my house at seven o'clock one morning, and he said that he had been in a poker game with the producer who was upset with me. He told me that there was someone at the poker game who was about to make a picture and this producer asked him who he was going to hire to direct. The fellow said, "I was thinking of getting Fowler," and the producer said, "You can't hire him — he's a *Communist.*" Well, that was his way of getting back at me for not giving him a free script. I went back into editing some time after that.

Aside from Fritz Lang, some of the other name directors you edited for were Stanley Kramer and Sam Fuller.

Stanley's very nice. He used to say after he finished a picture that we should run it and then take all the gags out. Stanley did not have a very good sense of humor *[laughs]*! And Sam Fuller? Christ, he's a maniac! I remember he was doing a picture called *Run of the Arrow* [1957] up in St. George, Utah, and I kept getting film back from him — I got twenty reels of film, all silent, and I had to run this god-damned stuff. What they were, were shots of a wagon train; you'd see the wagon train in the distance, it would move slowly across the frame, kept *going* and *going,* and then it would disappear over the other horizon. A thousand feet *[laughs]*! And every so often the picture would jump or jerk around. So I went up to St. George and I told Sam about this jerking action and said, "Sam, there's something wrong with the camera or the film." Finally I found out what was happening: Sam always used to cue actors with guns, and he'd shoot this .45 right next to the camera operator's ear! And the operator would jump every time *[laughs]*!

Sam did a picture called *Park Row* [1952], about the newspaper business, and he wore a green eyeshade; when he did *Run of the Arrow* he wore a cowboy

---

*Later made into *Flaming Star* (20th Century–Fox, 1960), an Elvis Presley Western.

hat; and on *The Big Red One* [1980] he wore a helmet! Whatever picture he was doing, he wore the hat that went with it!

You've worked with a lot of filmland's top talents in your long career. Are you pleased with what you've done in Hollywood?

I guess more or less; Lord knows, I don't think *any*body's ever achieved *all* the things they set out to do. But I must say I've had a lot of fun doing it. I think back to the days of working with Fritz Lang; my wife worked with me on those, she was my assistant. We were young, and to work with Fritz you had to be young, because he'd work you into the ground. But I learned a helluva lot from him, and Margie did, too. And directing I loved — I'm just sorry that I didn't do more. There was a certain sense of achievement in it — you seemingly expressed yourself a little more fully than you do in any other field, with the possible exception of writing. What I did do was a lot of fun.

We thought we could take our sense of good picturemaking, apply it to science fiction, and in so doing enable our company [Gramercy Pictures] to keep the momentum going, pay the rent.... It was in that spirit that we started to develop some ideas and brought them to UA. They went along with our thinking, and we were in the science fiction business.... — Arnold Laven

Arthur Gardner
Arnold Laven
Paul Landres
and *Pat Fielder*

UNDER THE DIRECTION of Jules V. Levy, Arthur Gardner and Arnold Laven, Levy-Gardner-Laven Productions has been a consistent supplier of well-crafted entertainment, from such films as *Vice Squad* (1953), *Geronimo* (1962) and *The McKenzie Break* (1970), to TV series like *The Rifleman, The Detectives Starring Robert Taylor* and *The Big Valley*. During the 1950s, the company (then calling itself Gramercy Pictures) applied their professionalism to the science fiction and horror genres in four films, three of which rank with the best of that decade's independently produced thrillers: *The Monster That Challenged the World, The Vampire* and *The Return of Dracula*.

Levy, Gardner and Laven met while serving in the Air Force's motion picture unit during World War II (the same unit that included Capt. Ronald Reagan, Capt. Clark Gable and Lt. William Holden). The ambition to create a Levy-Gardner-Laven production company was born during the war but was not realized until 1951, after each of them had accumulated some film industry experience at already existing studios. With Levy and Gardner producing, and Laven directing, the newly formed company made several successful, modestly budgeted pictures released by United Artists. In 1956, they entered the currently popular field of sci-fi/horror. Their first venture, *The Monster That Challenged the World*, was written by Pat Fielder, a woman promoted from Gramercy's production assistant, and was directed by Laven; the directing chores for the next three Fielder-scripted horror films were then handled by Paul Landres. We are fortunate to have here a four-way interview with Gardner, Laven, Fielder and Landres.

What prompted Gramercy Pictures to enter the horror/sci-fi field in 1956?

Laven: We really were not successful at certain periods of time in getting some of our story ideas and scripts into the kind of shape where our parent organization, United Artists, was willing to finance them. It occurred to us that the field of science fiction was one which we could enter and, if we used the knowhow which we believed we had, make better films for lesser money. We thought we could take our sense of good picturemaking, apply it to science fiction, and in so doing enable our company to keep the momentum going—pay the rent, keep up production activity and maintain an ongoing relationship with UA. It was in that spirit that we started to develop some ideas and brought them to UA. They went along with our thinking, and we were in the science fiction business for a couple of years making those four films.

Did your production unit have complete creative freedom making these films for UA?

Gardner: We had a reputation for bringing our pictures in on budget and on schedule, so we really had complete creative freedom. We only showed the pictures to UA after they were completely finished.

Laven: They were the ideal company to work with. The earlier films we had made all showed profits—really very good profits, based on the cost of the

Previous page: Using a little business savvy and a lot of production knowhow, Jules V. Levy, Arthur Gardner and Arnold Laven parlayed their minor production company into a major purveyor of motion pictures and television series.

pictures. They showed a profit of 50 to 75 percent of each investment. UA trusted us: They knew that we were scrupulously careful and tremendously devoted to putting every dollar on the screen. With that assurance, they really let us do pretty much anything we wanted.

Fielder: That was the good thing about UA in those days—they put up the money but they really didn't inhibit their filmmakers from doing what they thought was best.

What sort of budgets and shooting schedules were these films allotted?

Gardner: *The Vampire,* I believe, was $115,000, *The Return of Dracula* around $125,000, and *The Monster That Challenged the World* was the most expensive of the four—that was $254,000. *The Flame Barrier* was the cheapest; I think that cost $100,000. I would say that the average science fiction film being made at that time probably had a cost of anywhere between $25,000 and possibly $200,000.

While most of the sci-fi films of that era were geared toward teenage tastes, your added production values and use of respectable actors seem to indicate that you aimed for a broader audience.

Laven: Part of our sales pitch to United Artists was that we could make these films look as though they were more expensive, to look richer, to have a greater market presentation than the competitive science fiction films, because of our knowhow and our design in writing scripts that would allow us to *use* our knowhow.

Fielder: We had a limited area that we could travel to in order to make a picture; we really had to deal with the elements that we had close at hand, and find a story that would fit into those parameters. We also had certain titles that we could work with, and often we would start with a title and construct a story around it. We would discuss the type of film that we were going to make, and then I would prepare some kind of an outline for the story and talk it through with Arthur and Jules.

How did The Monster That Challenged the World *come about?*

Fielder: There was an article in *Life* magazine, a true story about ancient shrimp eggs being discovered and reconstituted after millions of years buried in a salty pond. We transposed it all to the Salton Sea. There was an earlier draft on the screenplay [by David Duncan] which was not used at all—UA had decided that they wanted a rewrite on that script. So because of my strong desire to write and the fact that I was right on the scene, I convinced Levy-Gardner-Laven to give me an opportunity to rewrite it, to see whether I could do the necessary work. I plunged into it, and found that it was great fun and I loved doing it. We even made a survey research trip down to the Salton Sea prior to the shooting—Arnold Laven and I took a trip down to the unit where they did the parachute jumping, which was in El Centro, and around the area of the Salton Sea.

Did you pattern parts of your screenplay after Them? *The two films seem quite alike.*
   Fielder: I had seen *Them!* and so had Arthur and Jules. It was a fine picture, and I'm sure that it was the inspiration in some ways for *Monster*. I think it inspired a whole bunch of pictures of that era, but our independent research had allowed us to develop an awful lot of other material, too. Once we had gone down into the Imperial Valley, there was so much that was exciting and interesting about the area, and it only took a skip of the mind into fantasy to see how such an incident could have really happened. But we did try to keep within the realm of reality, because the best science fiction is something that you can strongly believe could have happened.
   Gardner: *The Jagged Edge* was our original title for *Monster,* and we thought at the time that it was a very good one. In retrospect, we all feel that *The Monster That Challenged the World* was not a very good title. We may have been better off releasing the picture as *The Jagged Edge*.

Western hero Tim Holt and eccentric character actor Hans Conried seem odd choices for the top male slots in Monster.
   Laven: I suppose in a way they were, except that we knew both those gentlemen to be marvelous actors. I had been a fan of Tim Holt's from the time that he did *The Magnificent Ambersons* [1942] and *The Treasure of the Sierra Madre* [1948]. When I was a script supervisor, some years before I became a director, I had worked on a low-budget Western that Holt did, and I remember having a very nice relationship with him and finding him to be a fine quality kind of person. There's no star temperament or that kind of thing in Tim Holt's makeup. And the same goes for Hans Conried; I can't remember exactly how we cast him, except that I know that either I or all three of us were aware of the fact that there was a very rich acting background in Conried's past. He was noted more for comedy and for slightly cliched or stereotypical parts like in *The Five Thousand Fingers of Dr. T,* and some of the other things that he did. But we knew better—we knew that, beneath some of the lighter things he did, he did have a background in classic theater, and it would be an interesting, maybe slightly offbeat performer for *The Monster*. We always looked to find those actors who could bring something special to a part, and who might be just a little different so there's a freshness to the films.

Where exactly was The Monster That Challenged the World *shot?*
   Laven: In and around the L.A. area. We went down to the Salton Sea and to Barstow, where the water irrigation system had little locks—a very visual atmosphere that fitted in with the whole development of *The Monster*. The underwater sequences were shot outside Catalina, with "Scotty" Welborn,

who is a very well-known underwater cameraman, and Paul Stader, who was the underwater director. He has since gone on to be quite a well-known and highly praised second unit director. The nice thing is, whenever I see Paul, he comes up and shakes my hand, because *The Monster* was the picture that got him a director's card. Prior to that, he had just been a highly acceptable stuntman, especially around water sequences.

Gardner: The underwater scenes were shot after the bulk of the film was finished. We then went back to the sound stage for underwater inserts, shooting through water-filled tanks that had artificial seaweed in them, for closeups of the actors peering at the camera from behind the tanks.

Were you involved at all in the underwater scenes, Mr. Laven?

Laven: I tried to go down a couple times—I found that I was not a very good scuba diver. But I did view the sets and review what was to be photographed underwater, with Paul, before it was shot.

Talk about your giant mollusk prop.

Gardner: The mollusk monster was conceived by us and executed by a very good special effects man named Augie Lohman. Augie went on from that picture to do many, many famous special effects films. The monster stood around ten feet high, and the exterior was made of fiberglas. All the movements were controlled by Augie and two assistants—it took three men to operate it. It worked with a series of air pressure valves. I believe it cost around $15,000 to build, and weighed about 1,500 pounds.

What became of it after you finished the picture?

Gardner: We sold it to the Ocean Park Pier, where it was a children's attraction for several years afterwards.

Were you pleased with the way Monster *turned out?*

Laven: Through the years, people who have a rapport with science fiction films have made me aware that *The Monster That Challenged the World* has made a mark of some kind in the catalogue of SF films, and that's very pleasing to me. I remember when I finished it, I felt that I had done a good job, and thought it came out pretty well. It wasn't meant to be an elaborate, overwhelming film at that time, but just good, strong, effective entertainment.

Then why is Monster That Challenged the World *your only sci-fi credit?*

Laven: Partly because of the damn snobbishness that existed, especially around that time. Thank God, since then George Lucas, Steven Spielberg and others have broken that barrier down. But at that time sci-fi was, overall, regarded as a lesser credit for directors. I can give you a very specific example: I had directed, before *Monster That Challenged the World,* a film called *The Rack* [1956] that launched Paul Newman's career. It was made at MGM and

Barbara Darrow struggles with the giant mollusk in this publicity shot for Levy-Gardner-Laven's *The Monster That Challenged the World.*

critically it was a highly regarded film — a character study of a man who became a collaborator in Korea. It was from a Rod Serling teleplay, adapted by Stewart Stern, who wrote *Rebel Without a Cause* [1955]. Wendell Corey, Walter Pidgeon, Eddie O'Brien and Lee Marvin were some of the other people in the cast. It was a really fine screenplay, a pretty damn good movie, and I did get some interesting attention after *The Rack*. Subsequent to *The Rack,* Art, Jules and I were trying to find a script of some significance — something that maybe we could look to get an Academy Award for, or something like that. But, as I explained earlier, we went into the business of making sci-fi films. I almost didn't direct *Monster,* but I felt I owed it to the company — to Art and Jules, for their confidence in me, and to UA—to do the first one. But I knew at the same time that it was not going to enhance or advance my career as a director.

The specific situation came up after *The Monster That Challenged the World*, when I was in contention to do a picture called *The Dark at the Top of the Stairs* [1960], which came from a highly acclaimed play by William Inge. It was going to be a very important film on the Warner Bros. schedule. As I understood it, they were debating between hiring me and another director. I went on an interview with a man who was then in charge, under Jack Warner, of production at Warners. I thought it was a very good interview—we talked about *The Rack* and my relationship with Paul Newman, who had subsequently become a star. I felt that I was making some points. Then he looked at a memo on his desk and said, "I see here that you also did a film called *The Monster That Challenged the World*." I realized when he started to talk about that, that I was going to be put into a slightly embarrassing position because the actors who were scheduled to be in *The Dark at the Top of the Stairs* would not necessarily be impressed with a man who just recently directed a monster snail. I realized that the interview had taken a downturn. I didn't get the picture. Maybe I wouldn't have gotten it even if I had *not* directed *The Monster That Challenged the World*. But I do know that the idea of directors doing low-budget science fiction didn't fit in with their concept of the kind of director they wanted for the pictures that I truthfully would like to have done. I love pictures that are rich in human characterizations, and where the story has maybe some social or psychological significance—the kind of film that, if you were to make a broad generalization, could be nominated for the Academy Award. I've come close, but never quite achieved the identity that would get me those assignments.

So Paul Landres stepped in and directed the remaining three SF/horror films.

Landres: I first met Art Gardner when I was doing a film at Allied Artists in 1952. At that time he was production manager for an independent company releasing through AA. He suggested to his producer that I read and give a critique on a script they had. I gave the producer a comprehensive critique with positive suggestions to correct and help the script. The producer was so impressed that he offered me the picture to direct when and if it was made. Unfortunately the picture was *not* made, but Art Gardner was also impressed with what I had done and he suggested that I meet his partner Jules Levy. Together they had an option on a property called *Invaders from Mars*. They asked me to come in with them as director of that property if it was made. We worked long and hard on that story, but they lost the option on it.

Was that the Invaders from Mars *that Edward Alperson later made?*

Gardner: That's right. A writer named John Tucker Battle brought the story to me, we optioned it, and then Jules Levy and I worked with Battle on the screenplay. Jules worked for Eddie Alperson at the time, and Alperson became involved in the picture, too. Through a series of circumstances, our option expired, and Alperson picked it up and went on to make the film.

Extensive outdoor photography is a major highlight of The Monster That Challenged the World, The Vampire *and* The Return of Dracula.

Landres: Shooting in a studio is and was very costly. Not only did a company renting studio space pay top dollar, but there was an additional overhead charge that I believe was about 25 percent. This doesn't mean that we never shot in the studio—we did when we had small sets and it was convenient to do so. But when we wanted scope and realism from a location, we went outside if it was at all possible. Also, the less shot in a studio, the longer the shooting schedule was.

Laven: We learned from the earlier pictures that we did that the richest, most visual, effective sequences, production-wise, were those that were shot outdoors, where even a low-budget film is in a sense on equal standing with the most high-budgeted pictures. When you shoot the Pacific Ocean, or meadows, or city streets, those are the same visual backgrounds that the highest budgeted picture will shoot; they can't change or alter them any more than we can. We would look for things such as the Salton Sea locations; the ability to shoot the underwater sequences, by planning, with a minimal camera unit and almost no overhead. The fact that our company operated with as small an overhead as probably any company in town was again one of the reasons we were able to put whatever dollars were spent right on the screen.

Miss Fielder, did the films of Val Lewton influence your writing?

Fielder: I was very much influenced by Lewton. I thought *Cat People* was one of the great masterpieces. But I also have always loved horror films, and horror in general. I loved Poe; the darker side of storytelling has always been appealing to me, putting it in terms of American life.

Jack Mackenzie, who photographed several of your pictures, had also worked for Lewton.

Fielder: Certainly he was responsible very much for creation of mood, but of course you can't get there without first having it indicated in the script. Suggesting the frightening aspect of any film is probably more effective than actually showing it in detail. I suppose you finally get to the point where you feel that you must satisfy the audience's curiosity as to what "it" really is, although there've been a few great films where you have never seen the monster other than by suggestion. On *The Vampire,* the theme of the father potentially destroying the thing he cared about most—the ultimate victim being his daughter—seemed to me a classic theme around which to build a story. It seemed to have a particular kind of horror, going back to the Greeks, to Oedipus and Medea, all the great classics.

While The Vampire *and* The Return of Dracula *stand with the better horror films of the '50s, surely they must have represented a comedown for actors like John Beal and Francis Lederer.*

Gardner: John Beal and Francis Lederer did not consider it a comedown to appear in these films. Even in those days actors were actors, and if the film had any sign of being anywhere near a quality production, they would agree to appear in them.

Landres: I had no feeling whatsoever that they were in any way condescending to play these parts. As a matter of fact, it was just the opposite—they were both most cooperative. And because of their cooperation and friendliness, the feeling of camaraderie on the set was wonderful and affected not only the cast but the crew as well. This is the feeling I believe you sense when you see each of these films.

What was John Beal's reaction to the grisly makeup he had to wear in The Vampire?

Gardner: John Beal is a real trouper. He loved playing the vampire, and he did everything—he played the monster in the long shots, and in most all the action scenes.

Fielder: He thought it was one of his best jobs. He also liked the chance to come back to Hollywood—he had been living somewhere on the East Coast, and had really not been in Hollywood that much.

The Return of Dracula *was certainly the eeriest of these four films.*

Fielder: For the *Dracula* picture, I was influenced by the original Bram Stoker story, of course—the angle about the friendship of the two girls. Also, I'm sure that Thornton Wilder's film for Hitchcock, *Shadow of a Doubt* [1943], had an influence on my thinking. It was fun to create a character that was so suave, so evil—so far from Transylvania, and right on our own back doorstep.

Francis Lederer gives an outstanding performance.

Fielder: Francis Lederer had not been in that many recent films at that point; he was conducting a theater school, I think, at the time. And certainly he couldn't have been a more handsome, suave, marvelous Dracula. Both Francis Lederer and John Beal were a delight to work with, and they brought a tremendous professionalism to the sets and to their parts.

How was the effect of the gushing blood achieved in the female vampire's staking scene?

Gardner: We accomplished the effect by getting a goat bladder, filling it with makeup blood and taking it down to the stage with an insert crew. I remember that I held the goat bladder full of the makeup blood while Jules Levy, off-camera, plunged the sharpened stake into the bladder. We had to do

Top: Stage and screen star John Beal played his most offbeat role in the 1957 horror thriller *The Vampire* (with Coleen Gray). *Bottom:* Francis Lederer, a Continental leading man in the 1930s, made a fine Count Dracula in 1958's *The Return of Dracula*.

Count Dracula (Francis Lederer) meets a grisly fate in the climax of *The Return of Dracula*. Notice the movie light by the Count's left foot.

it three or four times, and when we finished I had makeup blood all over my clothes.

What prompted the decision to film this scene in color?
Landres: Obviously it was done for shock value. Color was not in common use at that time, so what could be more shocking than to suddenly have the rich red color of blood practically come popping off the screen? The decision to do this part of the film in color was the producers', and a very good one it was. However, it entailed a considerable amount of effort and money to do this. The original cost of the color film and the camera was the least of it. It

got involved in negative cutting, the number of color prints that were made and, most important, cutting the color footage into all of the theatrical prints. All I can say is that it was not inexpensive. Art and Jules deserve a great deal of credit for doing this.

The Flame Barrier is indisputably the least of the four sci-fi/horror Gramercys.
Gardner: It really was the most inferior of the four, and the only reason I can give for it coming out the way it did is that the screenplay, obviously, wasn't as good as the others. Without a good screenplay, you just can't make a good film.
Fielder: I think we were kind of following a pattern of other jungle movies of the time—but there *had* been the event of a Sputnik going up with a monkey on board. We had fun making *The Flame Barrier,* but we shot it entirely on a sound stage, and we had a very limited budget and schedule.
Gardner: I think that three of the four films turned out as well as we hoped. We were disappointed in *The Flame Barrier.* And if we were doing them again today we would, of course, try to make them better. But at the time we did the best that we could with the budgets we had, and with the screenplays and casts that we had.

If you were remaking these films today, what elements would you change?
Landres: If we were shooting these films today, I would shoot *The Vampire* and *The Return of Dracula* without change. As for *The Flame Barrier,* I would not do it!

Considering the high quality of The Monster That Challenged the World, The Vampire *and* The Return of Dracula, *why has Levy-Gardner-Laven neglected this genre in recent years?*
Gardner: To be honest with you, the four films we did make were not very profitable. That may sound strange because of the low cost, but I don't believe United Artists really knew how to release this type of film at the time. We'd have been far better off if we had made them for a distributor like American International or one of the other, smaller releasing companies.
Laven: UA didn't have too much experience releasing science fiction films, and I think for that reason the maximum probably was not gained from the films. Columbia, which made the Sam Katzman sci-fi films, and some of the smaller companies that dealt in sci-fi, probably had a better knowledge in where and how to release them. But UA did their best, and we in no way complained about the fact that maybe they didn't do as well as some other studio because they did give us their backing and they did invest their money and show confidence in us. That whole company now has changed around considerably, but they were indeed a marvelous organization to work for.

Which is your personal favorite of the four films, and for what reason?

Arthur Franz and Robert Brown battle an extraterrestrial blob in the last (and least) of the Levy-Gardner-Laven science-fictioners, *The Flame Barrier*.

Laven: It's always one's own work which one tends to most admire, so — *The Monster That Challenged the World*. It's funny, I do a certain amount of television work these days — *The A-Team, Hill Street Blues, Mike Hammer* — and, in truth, I hardly look at any of those shows except when mine are on, and then I look with great fascination! Such is the nature of this particular director and, I suspect, of most all directors.

Gardner: My personal favorite is *The Vampire*. I think that we got the most out of that screenplay, and the most for our money. Of the four, it really did the best at the box office.

Fielder: It's gotta be *The Monster That Challenged the World*, because it was really a super picture. It was a bigger production and a great experience for me because it was my first picture. It was very, very special.

Landres: Of the three shows that I did, *The Vampire* was my favorite. It was a very successful combination of all of the elements necessary to make a successful show — producing, writing, directing, acting, editing, camera, etc. And the feeling on the set, from top to bottom, was one of great camaraderie, one of every person involved trying to do his best. It was a wonderful feeling and doesn't happen very often.

*[I was told] many times that my music was better than the picture.
Years back, in the '40s and even into the '50s, the reviewers in town
would never even mention the composer. Once in a while they would mention
a top guy like Steiner or Korngold. But us little guys in the Bs, never.
All of a sudden you would see, "Al Glasser did an outstanding job."
They would never say that about anyone else.*

Albert Glasser

A CONVERSATION with Albert Glasser reminds one of Sydney Greenstreet's classic line to Humphrey Bogart in *The Maltese Falcon*: "I like talking to a man who likes to talk." Glasser has had a long and lucrative career and certainly has a lot to talk about. One of the most prolific Hollywood composers, he started off as a copyist in the music department at Warner Bros. in the late 1930s, learning the art of film scoring from scratch while working under such big guns as Max Steiner and Erich Wolfgang Korngold. He graduated to orchestrating and by the mid-'40s was composing and directing his own scores.

A hard, fast worker, Glasser found his musical skills were put to the test in the frantic, down-to-the-wire world of B-picture making. He can certainly boast of a voluminous filmography, having scored a staggering 135 movies between 1944 and 1962, not counting at least 35 features for which he received no official credit. In addition to scoring 300 television shows and 450 radio programs, he arranged and conducted for the noted American operetta composer Rudolf Friml and orchestrated for Ferde Grofe (with whom he first collaborated on the science fiction classic *Rocketship X-M*).

Glasser probably holds the record for composing more sci-fi music than anyone else in the 1950s; he scored practically all of Bert I. Gordon's special effects epics and even worked for Roger Corman and William Castle. Glasser's style was unmistakable: pounding, hard-driving rhythms and crashing crescendos which set the pace for the lurid, action-packed quickies they accompanied.

How did you become interested in music?

It started when I was in high school here in Los Angeles. I fell in love with medicine because I had two broken noses in two fistfights. The guy who fixed my nose was a great plastic surgeon, so whenever I had the spare time I would run down to his office and hang around for an hour or two watching him work. I was just fascinated and decided to become a doctor. I started to take all of this pre-med stuff in high school. About halfway through, around eleventh grade, I started to hear music in my head that you couldn't believe. I was playing the flute and my sister was a fine concert pianist. I wanted to switch courses, but they said I couldn't do that. Well, screw *them [laughs]*! There was a lot of yelling and screaming, but finally they said, go ahead. From there I graduated and went to a junior college and started taking harmony classes. Finally I got a scholarship at U.S.C. for a violin concerto in 1934.

How did you break into the movies?

When I finished up at U.S.C., a lot of my friends were saying, "Hey, Glasser, as long as you're so inventive in your god-damned music, why don't you get a job at the studios? They need musicians." This was a period when the studios were getting guys from New York and Europe, anyone who could come here and conduct, play a fiddle, blow a trumpet, any damned thing. The soundtrack had only just come in in 1929–30 and they were always looking for

Previous page: Al Glasser at home, 1987. Glasser is today happily retired. He maintains a full schedule of writing and is an ardent photography and ham radio buff.

good people to work in the music department. But the next question is, how do you get into the movies? It's *still* a good question *[laughs]*! I went to the movies two or three times a week just so I could write down who the musical directors were for all of the studios. For Warner Bros. at that time it was Leo Forbstein. I called up the Warner Bros. music department. "This is Mr. Forbstein's office," the secretary would say. "This is Mr. Glasser. I'm a composer." "Sorry! We've got plenty of composers. Goodbye!"

And the same result for each of the other studios?
Exactly the same. So I figured, there's got to be a way of finding these guys—I had to go to them directly. So I figured out a little pattern and it worked like a charm. I hiked to Warner Bros. and went to the head cop at the gate. "Hi, officer. Has Mr. Forbstein come out yet?" "Oh, no. Around five o'clock, usually. Did you see his new car?" I said, "What new car?" and he said, "He's got a gorgeous new red Packard." Now I walked across the street and sat on the curb and waited and waited. Finally the cars started coming out and here's this great big red Packard. I *got* him! That's *him*! He's the man sitting in the back seat with the chauffeur in the front. I got the license number, that's all I wanted.

The next morning I hitchhiked to the license bureau and got his address. By now I had been orchestrating all kinds of stuff: Bach, piano sonatas, the *Toccata and Fugue* like Stokowski made, my own personal stuff. I had a mountain of music. So I got dressed up one Sunday morning and brought this whole bundle along. I rang his doorbell. I was all ready to put my foot in the door in case the butler would tell me to get the hell out of there. The door opened and here's a short fat man in a bathrobe who hadn't shaved in a couple of days. I said, "Mr. Forbstein?" and he said, "That's me. What do you want, kid?"

I told him who I was. He said, "I'm making breakfast. Come in." We went into the kitchen and I'm jabbering away a mile a minute. He said, "Just a second, kid. Let me see what you got here," and he was looking and looking at my stuff. And I'm so happy. Here's the guy who runs the whole goddamned music department for the studio, he's looking at my music. Later on, I found out that this was bullshit. He couldn't even read music. He was a fiddle player from St. Louis. He was a good musician, and a good, sharp cookie, a good businessman. He became the musical director in the theater in St. Louis and then when Warner Bros. was looking for people, he talked them into giving him a job. But he couldn't read an orchestration, not a god-damned thing!

Did he like your music?
He said, "Hey, your writing is very good. Better then we have. Tomorrow morning call my librarian, Vito Centroni, and you come and work for us." Holy shit! The door is opening up! I ran home, I was flying! The next morning, first thing, I called up the music department. "Vito Centroni, please. Hello,

I'm Al Glasser. I talked to Mr. Forbstein." He said, "Oh, yes, he just told me about you. I'm so busy I can't talk now. Goodbye!" Boom! He hangs up.

So that was the end of Warner Bros. for you?

Temporarily. I tried the same trick on all of the others, found out where they lived, tracked them down one way or another. Some were very nice like Forbstein, others were sons of bitches. *Get out of here, don't bother me, you little snot!* Finally I call up again this Centroni guy. He says, "All right, kid. Come in tomorrow morning. I could use you." So I go hitchhiking the next morning, a car stops and I jump in. The guy says, "Where are you going?" I say, "Warner Brothers." "Do you work there?" "Sure. In the music department." So, he dumps me off at the front gate. When I finally walk into the music department, who's sitting in the front desk? The guy who picked me up, Centroni himself *[laughs]*!

What was your first job at Warner Bros.?

I was a copyist. From there on, I just took off. I corrected things I wasn't supposed to at times. All of the other copyists wouldn't bother correcting obvious mistakes, they couldn't have cared less. But I could tell a mistake in two seconds. I was good, so to speak. Soon, other studios like Paramount and Universal called. I went from studio to studio. (Except Universal. Very cheap!) So, in a hurry I was making money and moving up! I learned the ropes. I watched Max Steiner. I used to pull out his original sketches, take them home and stayed up to three, four and five o'clock just analyzing every god-damned thing that Max Steiner was doing. The transpositions, the resolutions, the whole bit, the mechanics of it. The best school in the world for pictures was right there. [Erich Wolfgang] Korngold came along right after that. I started to study his sketches. He was unbelievable, a great genius. I decided to get out of the copying racket because you could be locked in forever. I saw others who tried to get out, but they waited too long.

When did you finally quit?

I quit in 1943 when I was working with Dimitri Tiomkin. I started working on orchestrations exclusively at MGM. Composing was something else, where they would ask me to write something because they knew I could, and I would knock out whatever they wanted. In 1946 Johnny Green called me to write the overture for the Academy Award show. When they got through playing it, the whole audience stood up, cheering and clapping for Johnny Green. Green said, "Ladies and gentlemen, thank you so much, but it's not for me, it's for Mr. Albert Glasser who did the show." So, I was on the way up and starting to get credit.

What was your first movie as composer?

I did *The Monster Maker* for PRC—for $250 I composed, orchestrated,

Glasser received $250 for writing the score of *The Monster Maker,* the 1944 horror cheapie starring J. Carrol Naish and Ralph Morgan.

copied, conducted, worked with the music cutter. What the hell? If I didn't want it, they had ten guys waiting. I wanted credit. I did about three or four of them for [Glasser's agent] David Chudnow—for $300, then $325, then $350. I did a picture called *In Old New Mexico* [1945] and the producers were so impressed that they called me in for another one. They said, "What did we pay you last time?" I said I got $350. They said, "Wait a minute! We paid $3,000 for that!" I said, "You paid Chudnow $3,000! He gave me $350." They said, "Oh, that son of a bitch! From now on, forget about Chudnow, you come straight to us and we'll hire you for $3,000."

How much time did they give you to score The Monster Maker?
   One week. Luckily there was very little for me to do. Mostly piano work for that. It was the story of a pianist who gets acromegaly; his hands get big and he cannot play anymore. I had to find a concert pianist to record all of the piano stuff and write a couple of cues here and there. Nine times out of ten, all I had was a week. Occasionally two weeks.

What size orchestra would you use for a typical PRC film?
   About 20, 22. It was way too small.

The studios have their own orchestras?
That came later, in the '50s. In the '40s, all of the best musicians in Hollywood were drafted. I was working with Dimitri Tiomkin at the time, orchestrating the scores he was writing for the War Department. We got all the stuff recorded with the Army bands. They had the best damned orchestras in the world.

How did your collaboration with Ferde Grofe during Rocketship X-M *come about?*
That was a helluva situation. I was with Lippert Productions at that time. I was the head honcho, which worked out very well. They fell in love with my stuff, and you couldn't blame them. I gave them some very good scores—*I Shot Jesse James* [1949], *The Return of Wildfire* [1948]...

Lippert, the boss, called me in one day. Short, fat guy. He said, "Look, Al, we're going to do a big one, a science fiction thing called *Rocketship X-M* and we've got to work very fast. The guy who wrote the script tried to peddle it all around town for a couple of years, no one wanted it. Why? It's science fiction, who gives a shit about science fiction? But now, that big idiot, that asshole George Pal is making one about going to the moon. He's been making it for a year and a half, and there's trouble, trouble, trouble—all of those special shots, the photographic tricks and whatnot. He even took out a five-page ad in *Life* magazine, announcing that *Destination Moon* is on the way and will be out in about three or four months."

So, Lippert said, "We're going to knock *Rocketship X-M* out in three or four weeks. We'll do it real cheap, and get ahead of him. George Pal is making everyone conscious about moon pictures. *We'll* give 'em moon pictures!" So he did. We worked day and night, like sons of bitches.

How did Ferde Grofe become involved?
Lippert said, "We have to have a high-class name, we're going for class now. We know you're good, and don't get me wrong, but I had a long talk with a guy named Ferde Grofe last night. He's going to compose the music, but he wanted so much more money for the orchestration and the conducting! Holy cow! Half the budget would go to him! So I made a deal for him to compose and I want you to orchestrate and conduct it. Which means we'll save a big chunk of money." I think they paid him $5,000 for the composing only.

Were you looking forward to working with Grofe?
To work with Grofe! What an honor! What a *privilege!* So, I went out and met the old guy. We had a ball. First they had to finish the movie. It took about two or three weeks. They worked every day and half the night, two crews going, just to push it through. Grofe started writing, and I started orchestrating for him.

Glasser *(left)* conducts alfresco on *The Return of Wildfire*. The comely cowgirl is leading lady Patricia Morison.

Rocketship X-M *had an innovative score for its day.*
 We wanted some different sounds, something unusual, once they got out into outer space. The theremin at that time was really hot, since Miklos Rozsa's score for *Spellbound* [1945]. So I met the guy who invented it, he was a foot doctor. He followed my orchestrations as closely as he could and it worked like a charm. Grofe was a doll to work with, a wonderful man. He was enormous, fat as a pig! An old beer-drinker from way back.

Did you visit the set of Rocketship X-M?
 Oh, yes. Many times. Kurt Neumann, the director, was very nice, very gentle, very intelligent. A good, hard worker. He wrote his own scripts.

Preparing to soar through space to the sound of music orchestrated by Albert Glasser are Noah Beery, Jr., Hugh O'Brian, Lloyd Bridges, Osa Massen and John Emery — the crew of *Rocketship X-M*.

What's your opinion of the movie?

I loved it. I'm an old science fiction fan from way back. When I was in junior high school, I wrote two science fiction stories.

You worked on a few SF films with the production team of Jack Pollexfen and Aubrey Wisberg. How well did you work with them?

Aubrey Wisberg was a helluva nice guy; in fact, we got very close with him. A very fine gentleman, very direct and honest. But in the last picture I made with them, I got screwed. They wanted me to sign an agreement that

I'd take 10 percent now and the balance when the movie was released. This is an old trick that I heard about many years ago. But I took a chance.

Do you remember scoring Invasion U.S.A.?

Oh, yes. That was for Albert Zugsmith. He's a wild man! I thought I wrote a pretty good score for it; there were some good scenes in it. I tried to imitate the Russian national anthem. I turned it around, upside down, to give some flavor. That's one picture I don't have the tape on. In most cases, I saved everything I had. From the very beginning, I would get copies of what I was doing. Most of them now are in the University of Wyoming. Sixteen crates! I'm living in a fire zone here. We had a big fire in 1961 and it burned up half of the area; about four hundred homes went in two hours. If my music got burned up, I'd shoot myself!

Sci-fi fans probably remember you best for your long association with Bert I. Gordon. Did you and he get along all right?

Wonderful guy. We had more fun with him! He got me into ham radio for which I am very grateful. I met him right after I finished *Huk* [1956]. That was the biggest job I ever had, the biggest orchestra, forty men! It paid off just beautifully and almost came into the last runoff for the Academy Awards. Anyway, I was laying the tracks in with a film cutter. Suddenly the door opens and Bert Gordon comes in and says, "Who wrote that stuff? It's marvelous. I'm working next door finishing up a picture I just made and I'm looking for a composer." He wanted to hear some more of my stuff and so he came over to the house. He said, "I want *you*! I've done two pictures so far but I'm not very happy with the music, it didn't give me the lift that I wanted. Your kind of stuff has *balls*!"

Which brings me to another story. During the war, when I was working with Dimitri Tiomkin, we used to record all of his stuff at the army camp and one of the things we had to do was *Battle of Britain* or *Battle of Russia,* one or the other. We were running out of time, and Tiomkin asked me to write one section for it. So I knocked out one big number, about four or five minutes. Later on, when he went to conduct it for the recording, the whole orchestra, a hundred musicians, got up *[clapping]*—"Bravo, Dimi, bravo! That's the best thing you ever wrote!" I cringed! Tiomkin said, "Gentlemen, thank you very much but I can't accept that. Mr. Glasser, come up here. Here's the man who wrote the music: Mr. Albert Glasser, my assistant."

Later, when I drove him home (I was his chauffeur), we pulled up in front of his house, he got out and started yelling! "You son of a bitch! I hate you! You lousy bum! You piece of shit! I worked two weeks on that music, day and night, you do one lousy number and for you, they clap and for me, I get nothing!" The next morning when I came to pick him up I was trembling. I see him walking towards me, laughing and happy. Tiomkin got in the car and said to me, "Do you know what's wrong, why I got so god-damned mad

A 1952 Manhattan shattered by enemy bombers (and still cleaner and safer than modern Manhattan) was the setting of *Invasion U.S.A.*, scored by Glasser. Pictured here are Gerald Mohr and Peggie Castle.

yesterday? The difference between you and me is that the music you write, it has balls! Mine doesn't!"

What was the first film you scored for Bert Gordon?

  The Cyclops. He paid me $4,000 for the whole thing, including the orchestra. I had fun with it—it was a cute little picture, well done. From then on, I was his boy. The next one was *The Amazing Colossal Man* and then *War of the Colossal Beast.* I was fascinated. I used to watch on the set as much as I could while he was doing the effects. He used to work a lot out of his garage, where he had his equipment. The funny one, of course, was *Attack of the Puppet People.* On the set, they made chairs ten feet high so when the actors would sit on them, they would look little. It was cute, a lot of fun. In fact, we wrote a song for that for which they're still paying me—*[singing]* "You're a dolly, you're a dolly." I can't believe it.

So you got to know Gordon well.
    Oh, yes, we had a lot of fun. He even gave me the ham radio test to get my license. I still hear from him but not too often. He keeps to himself a lot. His father used to manufacture a certain part for the old Studebaker, the door handles or something, and so they lived very well. When he was growing up, Bert had a fascination with movies. When he was ten or eleven years old, he made a movie by himself. He would take pictures one at a time, and when he played it back real quick, it started to move — the basic element of movie technique. He made a movie, it wasn't very long, of about two or three hundred pictures. He showed it at his birthday party and the kids loved it. His parents almost had an orgasm. *Look at what our son did! He's a genius!*
    When he got out of college, he wanted to get into making movies. He borrowed some equipment and figured out a gimmick how to make commercials — television was just getting started. Eventually he started making a lot of money in this little city outside of Detroit. Then he got married and came out here. In the meantime, his family started raising money for him to make a movie. He had all of these gimmicks and tricks of moving animals, of animals getting big. He developed a system and it wasn't bad. You've got to hand it to him, he did it all by himself. He sold these pictures, made a profit, paid back his family. It was a good investment for the family, but eventually they started to lose money — the science fiction thing was disappearing. I worked on four or five of his pictures.

You worked with Roger Corman, also.
    He walked into the cutting room where I was doing this science fiction stuff. He said, "Hey, I need you. I did a little picture recently and it's so bad that nobody wants it. Even the music was terrible. Can you give me a good score on this?" We went down to the projection room and put it on and ran it for about an hour *[groans]* — *Viking Women and the Sea Serpent!* That was a weird one, *very* bad! I said I'd try. He said, "Give it all you have!" When it got wild, I gave it wild music. When they were on the boat in the middle of a storm, I gave it storm music. That's easy, any asshole can write that kind of music. When we got through, he said, "You saved my picture! You saved my *life!* I just sold it and it's all set. The music did it!"
    That I heard many times, that my music was better than the picture. Years back, in the '40s and even into the '50s, the reviewers in town would never even mention the composer. Once in a while they would mention a top guy like Steiner or Korngold. But us little guys in the Bs, never. All of a sudden you would see, "Al Glasser did an outstanding job." They would *never* say that about anyone else. I cut them all out for my scrapbook.

Did the B directors have any input or suggestions on these scores?
    Very seldom. Only Sam Fuller, when I did *I Shot Jesse James*. He was a wild character, very dramatic, but he got good results. There was one scene

when Jesse James [Reed Hadley] was talking to his wife, he's saying that one of these days he's going to buy a farm out in Oklahoma. And it's getting sadder and sadder. Reed Hadley was a marvelous actor. I started to cry while I was watching it, so did the electrician and the cameraman. The whole god-damned company was sitting there crying!

Memories of Giant from the Unknown?

You mean *The Giant from Devil's Crag?* They changed the name, the crooks! That was a little cheapie that I never paid much attention to. We had to record it in a lousy, half-assed recording studio because they were broke.

How would you rate some of your colleagues who worked in B movies? Like Ronald Stein and Gerald Fried?

I knew Ronald Stein quite well, we used to work together on the science fiction stuff. Nice guy. I didn't care for his *music* too much, but he was adequate, a good musician. Gerald Fried was one of the top oboe players in New York. He came out here in the mid-'50s because he wanted to compose. He did good work. Never great, but good.

Raoul Kraushaar?

Kraushaar was a nice person, but his work was never worthwhile. He was good for a cheap Republic Western.

Leith Stevens?

Leith Stevens was a good man, very good. When work started to slow down in the late '60s–early '70s because the B movies were out, I couldn't get a god-damned thing to do. So I went out to talk to Stevens. He said, "Bring along some of your stuff. I like your work." So I brought along the record of *Huk*. I put the record on and he started to listen to it and all of a sudden he said, "Jesus Christ!" I knew I was dead because he didn't want any competition. If I had done anything with him, I might supersede him, so I had cut my own throat. He said, "I'll be in touch," but he never was.

Did you have much contact with Bernard Herrmann?

I met him once or twice. He scored *Jane Eyre* [1944], which I happened to catch on TV. What struck me was the music. *There* was a fine composer; I was just thrilled! So I stopped what I was doing and watched the whole god-damned movie just to listen to the score and it was marvelous. When I got through, I got him on the telephone. I said, "I want to congratulate you. I just saw *Jane Eyre* and your score was so god-damned beautiful, so fantastic, I still have goose pimples!" There was a long pause. He finally said, "So what do you want?" I said, "I'm congratulating you for the marvelous job you did. All of your stuff is great but this is the best score you ever wrote. I'm *proud* of you!" He said, "Well, what do you *want?*" I said, "Oh, fuck you!" and I hung up *[laughs]*!

Was there much rivalry between the top Hollywood composers?
I'll tell you a story. When I was working with Tiomkin at the War Department, the telephone rang. It was Miklos Rozsa. He said, "I just got my draft notice from the Army. I want Dimi to call Washington to have me transferred to your place. I'll do anything—I'll orchestrate, I'll conduct, I'll clean the toilets! As long as I can stay here in town." Later, when Tiomkin walked in, I said, "Dimi, you got a phone call from Rozsa. He wants you to call Washington 'cause he has to go for a draft call, and he wants you to transfer him over here. We can use him." We were scoring Frank Capra's war shorts at the time. Tiomkin blew up: "Hell, no! The dirty bastard. Let him suffer like all of the other boys are suffering!" As it turned out, when Rozsa went for the draft, he was kicked out anyway. He had a bad foot or something and he was too old.

What was Tiomkin's problem?
Tiomkin was making big money for his scores, but the problem was that he was charging too much. His price was going up and up. He had scored a big musical show, an extravaganza over at MGM, and he wanted the violin section to sound so rich and so warm that he rented about 25 Stradivarius violins, at about $5,000 to $6,000 apiece. It was an enormous bill and MGM was paying for it. The next picture he made for Capra the orchestra bill was so steep, the studio said, "Get this guy out of here and *keep* him out of here!" By 1940, all of the studios said, "Hands off Tiomkin. He's too expensive, he's a crazy Russian!" Tiomkin couldn't get another feature for about a year. Here comes Rozsa, moving up fast, getting all of the biggest and best pictures. Tiomkin hated him! He said, "The son of a bitch is taking all of my pictures away from me!"

How about contemporary composers like Jerry Goldsmith?
Excellent! I wrote him a fan letter years ago. Whenever I hear good work, I drop off a note or phone. Including Johnny Williams. I even wrote a letter to John Barry. Marvelous writer, one of the top group.

Of the more than 100 film scores you've written, which is your favorite?
I like 'em all!

The production of motion pictures, especially overseas, was an exciting way of earning a livelihood. It was a method of providing the necessities of life for one's family and having a great time in the process. Oddly enough, I didn't consider it a career.

Bernard Glasser

ONE SCHOOL of film criticism holds that the director is the one and only true author of a motion picture, while others consider the writer's contribution the most vital. The only time these two camps seem to fully agree is in ignoring the role of the producer, without whose participation no movies would exist at all. During the '50s and '60s Bernard Glasser worked as a producer in both TV and films, sometimes turning his talents toward directing and writing as well. His list of credits range from a Three Stooges Western (*Gold Raiders*, 1951) to the Cinerama war epic *Battle of the Bulge* (1965), and also include frequent detours into science fiction via such well-remembered genre titles as *Return of the Fly*, *The Day of the Triffids* and *Crack in the World*. Glasser left the business after twenty industrious years of squeezing dollars, stretching budgets and making successful pictures, and now looks back without regret at his Adventures in Filmland.

The Chicago-born Glasser grew up in what he calls "the movie generation" and fell in love with pictures at the ripe old age of four. In the late '40s, while working as a teacher at Beverly Hills High School, he got his feet wet in the film industry by working as a production assistant. In 1950 he invested in an old motion picture studio and turned it into a rental lot. Glasser leased his Keywest Studio out to producers like Roger Corman *(The Fast and the Furious)*, Burt Lancaster *(Apache)* and others as well as using the facilities to make a five-day, $50,000 film of his own *(Gold Raiders)*, directed by his friend Edward Bernds. When Glasser's studio lease expired in 1955, Glasser and Bernds combined forces on a series of budget features for Robert Lippert's Regal Films, with the pair making their joint SF debut on 1958's *Space Master X-7*.

How did you hook up with Robert Lippert's organization?

While shopping for a release for *Gold Raiders*, I was introduced to Bob Lippert, and he invited me to his house to screen the film for some of his associates. Lippert was pleasant, but the deal he offered for distribution was not. A few years later I purchased a Western novel entitled *Long Rider Jones*. The property was submitted to David Brown, then the story editor at 20th Century–Fox, and Brown indicated that the studio was interested in the property. After a meeting with Brown and [Fox production chief] Buddy Adler, I was told that they would buy the story but I could not produce the picture for Fox. I thanked Brown for his interest, but told him that my goal was to produce *Long Rider Jones*. Several weeks later I received a call from Brown. He said that Bob Lippert had just signed a multiple picture contract with the studio for the production of second features, and that if I was interested in making a budget Western, he would recommend my project to Lippert. I accepted his offer. *Long Rider Jones* was retitled *The Storm Rider* [1957], and it was one of the first productions made under Lippert's Regal banner for 20th Century–Fox distribution.

What were your impressions of Lippert and his organization?

Bob Lippert knew how to choose capable employees to supervise his

Previous page: **Long retired from the hassles of the picture business, Glasser (seen here in a shot from a 1989 trip to Malaysia) and his wife now travel extensively.**

Years before his producing career veered off into science fiction, Glasser *(center)* turned out the low-budget Three Stooges Western *Gold Raiders* (1951), co-starring George O'Brien (in cowboy hat).

company. Harry Spalding was one of these capable men. He had been a newspaperman in Seattle when Lippert hired him as the chief booker for Lippert theaters. When Lippert entered production, he sent his scripts to Harry for comment. Harry had a good story sense and a tactful way of making criticism. Bill Magginetti was another capable Lippert employee. Magginetti was originally a bookkeeper in Lippert's office, but as production activities expanded he became proficient in analyzing budgets and supervising the Regal operation.

My relationship with Bob Lippert was always friendly and productive. On occasion he asked me for advice regarding pictures that were experiencing difficulties.

What are your recollections of Space Master X-7?

After Ed Bernds and I had made several Westerns for Regal we decided to widen our horizons. One of us mentioned outer space as about as wide as a horizon could get. That afternoon I called my agent and asked him if he knew of an inexpensive idea for a space film, and he described a property involving trains and a submarine. The script had been turned down by several producers as being too expensive to produce. Ed and I read the script and agreed that we could make it work, but the writers, Dan Mainwaring and George Yates, wanted more money than we could afford. I told Harry Spalding that I would find the extra money somewhere in the budget, and he approved the purchase. Ed rewrote the script gratis because we were already over budget in the story department. We had seen some exciting stock footage of an airliner "wheels-up" landing and decided to utilize it for a "big," inexpensive ending for the picture.

What were your budget and shooting schedule?

$125,000. But we had to pay Mainwaring and Yates $25,000 for their script — $15,000 that had been set aside for it, and then an extra $10,000 that they insisted on. That left us an even $100,000 to lavish on our production. Bill Magginetti's approval of the budget of *Space Master* was necessary before we could start shooting, but he rejected the budget because it was too low. He was correct, but what he didn't know was how we planned to shoot the inserts, special effects and "documentary" footage. At a luncheon meeting in Lippert's office, the conversation went something like this:

Lippert: "Bill tells me your script calls for a lot of location shots as well as special effects, planes, trains and I don't know what else. Are you sure you can make it for $100,000?"

"$90,000," Magginetti corrected. "He paid $20,000 for the script."

"We're going to do the special effects at Mercer's [an old-time special effects house in Hollywood]. Ray Mercer has given us a flat deal which includes everything, even the titles. Our principal photography is about eight days. I don't know how long the second unit will take, we're handling it ourselves. John Link, the editor, has made a flat deal which includes everything — sound effects, music, even negative cutting. I've 'locked in' most of our costs," I replied.

"What about the creeping fungus?" Magginetti asked.

"We're going to do that ourselves," I answered.

Magginetti shook his head "no way."

"Well, Bill, what do you say?" Lippert asked.

"It's his ass if he goes over," Magginetti said.

That ended the budget discussion. We were subsequently given the green light.

Ed Bernds told me Norman Maurer helped out quite a bit on Space Master. *How did he get involved?*

Moe Howard of the Three Stooges had asked us if there was a place on our production team for his son-in-law, a comic book illustrator. Moe said that Norman would work without a salary in order to learn the film business. Norman

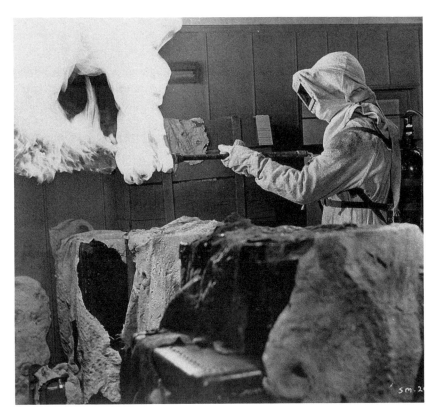

With today's high-priced, high-tech special effects, it's hard to believe that the alien threat in *Space Master X-7* cost "less than $1,000."

invited me to his house to show me his artwork. He was an enthusiastic person brimming with suggestions for the special effects in the script. We became fast friends, and he went to work the next day. Upon the completion of *Space Master,* my friend Sid Pink asked me if I wanted to help him produce a science fiction film *[The Angry Red Planet].* I suggested Norman for the producer position and described his abilities as a conceptual artist as well as a practical executive. Sid Pink hired Norman for the picture.

Who devised the fungus effects in Space Master?
   Norman Maurer did. This effect was composed of a foam rubber rug about a yard square. Several different models were made at a latex factory in Hollywood. Norman and I supervised this operation while Ed rewrote the script. These latex "rugs" looked like miniature volcanoes. In the vortex of each volcano, Norman inserted a plastic tube. Compressed air forced a red powder through the tube and out of the vortex. Compressed air was also utilized to make the rug sections undulate. The entire effect cost us less than $1,000.

According to Space Master's *publicity, you rushed it into production ahead of schedule to capitalize on publicity surrounding the Explorer liftoff.*

Yes, we did, a bit. Most of the publicity surrounding *Space Master* was generated by Marty Weiser, Lippert's staff publicity man. Marty gave *Space Master* special treatment, and the trade papers assumed that Ed and I were making a big-budgeted science fiction picture. This didn't hurt our feelings. We had no money in the budget for anything except production. Marty also suggested the title change from *Missile into Space* [the film's shooting title] to *Space Master X-7*. He claimed that his title was more imaginative and less "on the nose," and we agreed with him.

What were some of the cost-cutting measures you used?

We tried to lock in most production expenditures: music, editing, transportation, set construction, electrical, set dressings and props, etc. Most of the companies we dealt with were willing to give us a flat deal because we had a continuity of production. If the companies lost money on a particular production, they knew that we would try to make it up to them on the next show. We photographed the second unit with a handheld Eymo 35mm camera. We shot police car run-bys, inserts, airport scenes, etc., at all hours of the day and night, and without compensation. Our team consisted of Norman Maurer, [stuntman] Joe Becker and myself. For our studio facilities we returned to Keywest. That place went back to the days of silent serials, according to what people told me; it's still standing, but it's deserted now. It's at the corner of Santa Monica Boulevard and Van Ness in Hollywood.

In order to make a picture "for a price," you have to be acquainted with all elements of production. As an example of "hands-on": Most of our set construction was done at night, and I would have the construction foreman call when the sets were completed. Sometimes this would occur at three or four in the morning; I would go to the studio and approve the sets, whatever the time. We couldn't risk any surprises the next morning.

Have you appeared in any of your own films?

Space Master was my only screen appearance. Ed Bernds suggested that I appear; he wanted an extra "extra" to fill the camera frame in the bunker scene. My wife [Joan Barry] was also in *Space Master;* she had been an actress prior to our marriage, and it was practical to call her, especially when an actress did not report on time. With four children in her care she didn't appear as frequently as she would have liked. Our oldest son and daughter obtained their Social Security cards at a very early age—they were the children seen in *Space Master* and *Return of the Fly.*

The finale to Space Master *is a slight letdown. Was the climax of the original script utilized?*

For the most part, we followed the script. In editing we deleted an office tag scene by the government official who opened the film. We felt that once the plane landed, the movie was over.

Was the film a moneymaker?
Space Master did very well for Lippert and Regal. Fox billed *Space Master* with *The Fly,* and this combination outgrossed many of the more expensive Fox productions. Lippert became a celebrity on the Fox lot, and the Regal low budget films were the main topic of conversation in the Fox commissary. The Fox distribution department then pulled *Space Master* from the bill and replaced it with an expensive Fox picture that was not getting good grosses. The revised bill did not do well. The chemistry of two science fiction pictures on the same bill was the key.

How exactly did Return of the Fly *come about?*
The Fly was the sleeper everyone had hoped it would be. It was Harry Spalding's idea to make a sequel. He suggested that Ed and I be given the project. *Return of the Fly* was supposed to be just another Regal project. Perhaps it was the quality of Ed's script or revised thinking on Lippert's part that upgraded the project.

Robert Lippert was originally supposed to produce the original Fly.
The Fly was an "in-house" project; Regal purchased the short story by George Langelaan that appeared in *Playboy* magazine. Lippert felt that he had something special with this project, and he requested and received additional funds to produce the picture. If Bob relinquished producer credit, it must have been for a good reason; I'm sure that he could've had producer credit if he felt it was important.

You did have a better budget and shooting schedule on Return of the Fly.
Our budget was increased to $275,000. The production department of the Fox studio asked Lippert to move *Return of the Fly* to the studio instead of our shooting it at an independent lot. Of course this meant an increase in production costs and no controls. Because of the inefficiency of the slower Fox crews and the added charges and surcharges for set operation and construction, it was impossible for me to lock in any expenditures. Most of our money was being spent unproductively. The net result was that Lippert had to obtain additional production funds. I had been reluctant to make the move to Fox and had predicted problems. Bill Magginetti backed me in this opinion, but Lippert didn't want to antagonize the Fox big brass. But shooting on the Fox lot greatly enhanced the production values of the picture.

What about your shooting schedule?
Still tight, because of the slower Fox production pace.

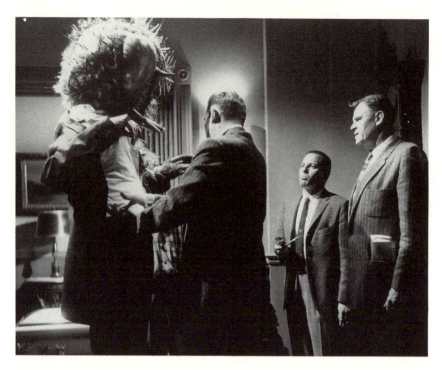

Glasser (with pipe) and director Ed Bernds watch as Ed Wolff is prepared for the cameras, on the mortuary set from *Return of the Fly*.

What can you tell me about working with Vincent Price?

We were surprised when Lippert approved Price and his salary. Perhaps Price had been a good luck omen for Lippert. It began with Price appearing in Lippert's *The Baron of Arizona* [1950]. Or perhaps Lippert was playing a hunch. At any rate he approved the additional expenditure for Price, $25,000. Price was always a gentleman, always ready and prepared, but as I recall he was not overly enthusiastic about the screenplay!

What do you recall about your Fly portrayer, Ed Wolff ("Hollywood's Tallest Actor")?

Just that he couldn't stand on his feet for long periods of time, and he had great difficulty breathing while wearing the Fly head. Our friend Joe Becker, the stuntman, did most of the closeups wearing the Fly's head. Joe did all the action sequences for Wolff.

How did Return of the Fly *do at the box office?*

One afternoon Lippert took out his tally sheet from Fox and pointed to *Return of the Fly;* our grosses were just a tad lower than some very large Fox productions. I have to assume that the film did very well.

You split with Lippert around 1960.

When I informed Lippert that I was leaving Regal to pursue other film ventures, he was disappointed. He said he was ready to commit for a budget war film if Ed and I could satisfy Harry Spalding with a storyline. (Gene Corman got this project.) I thanked Bob for giving me the opportunity to make films for him, and we exchanged a warm goodbye. I recall walking down the stairs of Regal headquarters, knowing it was the last time I would visit the office. It was time to close the chapter and move on.

You worked with Philip Yordan several times in the '60s. How did you hook up with him?

Yordan was represented by attorney Herbert Silverberg. Silverberg, who was also *my* attorney, had knowledge of my attempts to sell my television series idea. He calculated, and correctly, that with Yordan's name associated with the project he might possibly make a sale. Yordan and I were partnered in Liberty Enterprises and we produced 39 episodes of *Assignment: Underwater* for NTA.

Did you enjoy the experience of working with Yordan?

Yordan was primarily a deal maker, more concerned with the next deal than with the current production. It was a fascinating and educational experience working for, and with, Yordan. He was an original character. He made a study of each person whom he dealt with, and knew the exact buttons to push to further his objectives. He had a charm about him that was most compelling. Yordan could also be vindictive when someone did not go along with his plans. He extended to me complete autonomy and support during our association. Also, the basis of my business relationship with Yordan was cash — I didn't want any promises or percentages of pictures. I was paid a handsome salary plus a living allowance for my efforts. I have no regrets concerning my association with him.

As a result of my long production association with the Bank of America, the Yordan pictures were financed by the Bank of America. Our pictures were negative pick-up deals with the various distributors. We set the "pick-up" low enough so that the distributors were not concerned about recoupment.

How did you become involved on The Day of the Triffids?

During a visit with Yordan in Paris, he handed me a script of *Triffids* and asked me to read it. The next morning, after a discussion, he offered the project to me to produce. I also was the financial liaison between the Bank of America and the production company.

Why does the producer credit go to George Pitcher?

In order to qualify as a British production and receive a film subsidy, Yordan formed a British company and *Triffids* became a British production. In

Top: Behind the scenes on *The Day of the Triffids* are *(left–right)* co-director Freddie Francis, actress Janette Scott, producer Bernard Glasser, troubleshooter Lester Sansom and actor Kieron Moore. *Bottom:* A tree monster accosts Janette Scott in *Triffids*.

order to effect this qualification, two-thirds of the above-the-line elements had to be British. The producer was considered one of those elements. The screenplay and star artists were also elements of the one-third above the line. It was obvious that with the script and two foreign stars [Howard Keel and Nicole Maurey] we had reached our quota. By employing a British producer — in name only — the quota would be maintained. George Pitcher, who had been in retirement, was a pleasant older gentleman happy to be back at a studio with the title of "producer."

You could have taken producer credit on non–U.K. prints of Triffids, *couldn't you?*

[*Laughs.*] That's one of my pet peeves. My contracts on *Triffids* stipulated that I would receive credit as producer on all U.S. prints, and I didn't see one until I came back to the States. When I finally did get a chance to see it, and saw Pitcher's name on the credits, I was just burned up. My kids asked me, "How could you have produced this picture when your name's not in the credits?"

What recollections do you have of director Steve Sekely?

Sekely brought the project to Yordan with the understanding that he would direct. He was a gentleman of the old European tradition, a tall, thin man with a large head, closely cut gray hair and well-trimmed gray military mustache. These features accentuated a somewhat bulbous nose. Sekely spoke English with a slight accent that was part French, part Hungarian. He was a capable director who worked well with the cast and was always understanding and cooperative.

Who was responsible for the Triffid effects?

Wally Veevers was the special effects supervisor at Shepperton Studios. He was a rolypoly kind of a man, turned-up nose, sparkling eyes and an easy smile. He reminded me of an Irish gnome from nursery rhymes. His appearance was deceiving; Wally was a brilliant special effects technician. He enjoyed problem-solving: If he was at a loss about how an effect could be done, he would think about it for several days, recommend a technique and generally it would work.

Was all of the work on the Triffids done in pre-production?

No, *during* production — Veevers had a backlog because of the volume of production requiring special effects at Shepperton. The design of the Triffids had constituted another production delay. We experimented with various designs: When we had a Triffid that looked exciting, we could not get it to move properly. We settled for a motor-driven model designed by an artist named Hugh Skillen. Every step of the way was experimentation and exasperation. We had three motor models which were also articulated with compressed

Despite difficulties encountered in production, *The Day of the Triffids* remains the best—and best-remembered—of Glasser's SF forays.

air. For the most part our Triffids were engineered and built by a theatrical prop company in London. The Triffid sound effect was another challenge. Most of the sound effects didn't work with the appearance of the Triffids. The least objectionable sound appeared to be a clicking noise.

Did you have to contend with effects problems during shooting?

Yes, we did. Many effects had to be deleted because they were too difficult or too expensive. We had a lot of mechanical troubles; some sequences were working, others were not. It was a most frustrating experience. Several times a week I would call Yordan in Madrid and during our long conversations I would tell him what scenes were not working. The main difficulty was getting the Triffids to perform action called for in the script. [Screenwriter] Bernard Gordon was in Madrid working with Yordan on Samuel Bronston projects. Yordan kept assuring me that all the script problems would be remedied by Gordon, that there was nothing to be concerned about. But the script revisions were not forthcoming, and the delays forced schedule changes.

Some prints of Triffids *give screenplay credit to Yordan, others to Gordon.*

As the producer and as a faithful employee, I always saw to it that Yordan had screen credit on any picture that I was associated with, when most of the time we had a team of writers that did the work. Phil did very little writing. He wore very thick glasses and he suffered from cataracts, so writing for any length of time was a great strain on his eyesight. He never told anyone that he had cataracts, and he was also color-blind — these cataracts seemed to show everything in sepia.

Reportedly, Howard Keel rewrote his own dialogue, either because he was displeased with it or because there wasn't enough of it.

In one of the sequences Keel and the women were escaping in a van. The scene didn't play for one reason or another and Sekely asked me what I could do about it. I wrote some additional dialogue that seemed to fit the mood. As I recall, Keel was unhappy that I had written this material. I suggested that he rework it. He did and was pleased with his efforts. The changes were minor.

Did you ever meet John Wyndham, who wrote the Triffids *novel?*

Yes, on the second day of production he came by, and we chatted briefly.

Sekely's version of Triffids *came out disastrously short.*

Sekely wasn't to blame. After completion of principal photography, he asked me if I wanted him to stay for the second unit work. Because of the delay by the studio in completing our effects, I informed him that he could leave and perhaps return at some future time to see the rough cut. He was pleased to return to sunny California. Once we had deleted the special effects sequences that did not play, the picture was short. Steve Broidy, the head of Allied Artists, was on his way to see this short version which I knew was not satisfactory. Yordan kept advising me that he would come over with Gordon and solve the problems, and he told me to screen the picture for Broidy. Broidy was unhappy after seeing *Triffids,* and he suggested that he would send his editor and troubleshooter Lester Sansom to view the film and make suggestions. When Yordan received Broidy's reaction, that the film was too short, the alarm bells sounded for the first time and he came to London with Gordon. Gordon, Yordan, Les Sansom and I spent several days looking over the outtakes, looking for ways of stretching the picture. Some of the footage played very well but did not have a climax. We had to find a way of cutting away from the action and then returning to the scene after the chaos was resolved. I was too close to the film to see the very obvious solution.

The lighthouse scenes that were added, you mean.

Right. The lighthouse sequences were written in conjunction with the existing footage and directed by Freddie Francis at MGM Elstree. Freddie was a former lighting cameraman, and he understood the difficulties inherent in lighting the Triffid sequences. He was a marvelous person to work with, a fine cameraman and a good director, too.

Did Francis mind working without credit?
  No, not at all. People that have talent and ability really don't mind, it's just another job.

After Sekely left, you also shot some second unit scenes in Spain.
  Right, all of the carnival van scenes, using Spanish doubles for Keel, Nicole Maurey and Janina Faye. We also did a sequence in which the Triffids walk into the sea. In the original script, the van had loudspeakers and the Triffids were following the music, so when the van drove into the Mediterranean the Triffids followed. We hired 150 or 200 Spanish extras for the scene and had Triffid wardrobe made for them. I was on a platform out in the Mediterranean with two cameras, and it just wasn't working — the poor Spanish men and women felt so ridiculous dressed as these Triffids that they were embarrassed, and because they were embarrassed they started to joke, and sashay to the music...! The whole thing was just a fiasco. So we had to go back to the drawing board.

Where in Spain was this scene shot?
  At a place called Sitges. The cathedral at the end of the picture is the Cathedral of Sitges. Bill Lewthwaite, who was one of our editors, directed those scenes as well as some retakes that were shot in London.

What was your budget on Triffids?
  As I recall, the total budget, including special effects, was $750,000. Rank Film Distributors guaranteed a portion of the budget in return for U.K. distribution rights and Allied Artists guaranteed a portion for the U.S. and Canada distribution rights.

Was Triffids *a moneymaker?*
  The picture did very well for Allied Artists, so well that Steve Broidy asked Yordan to make two more pictures for AA, *The Thin Red Line* [1964] and *Bikini Paradise* [1967].

Any final comments on Triffids? *What do you wish you had done differently?*
  In retrospect, the original shooting script for *Triffids* was deficient because it assumed that the Triffids could perform action just like an actor. We were terribly limited in what the models could do and how much it would cost to get them to do it. It was surprising that the production did not exceed the funds available. As for doing anything differently, the services of a good special effects specialist, like a Eugene Lourie, would certainly have been a must.

How did Crack in the World *come about?*

While I was in London completing *The Thin Red Line,* Yordan and Gordon arrived. In a meeting Yordan suggested that we look for a science fiction subject for our next production. He suggested a visit to Foyles, a large London bookshop, and a search of the racks for an idea. In the meantime he was going to contact a few literary agents and see if they had any suggestions. One of the agents suggested that Yordan meet with the novelist Jon Manchip White, who currently was teaching at a university. Jon was a bit austere and standoffish at first, but Yordan with his usual charm put him at ease and before long we were bouncing ideas back and forth. Jon came up with the basic premise for *Crack in the World,* Yordan liked it at once and made a deal with Jon to write the story. Gordon wrote the screenplay with a dialogue polish by his friend Julian Halevy. Gordon did an excellent job on the screenplay. (Yordan on more than one occasion jokingly asked, "Why should I write when Bernie does it better? If Gordon could make deals for pictures, I would let him do it, and I would write the scripts.") Our shooting script for *Crack in the World* was technically authentic thanks to the work of my neighbor Dr. Tom Slowdowski, a geologist working for a major oil company in Spain.

What prompted the decision to make this film, and several of your other films, in Spain?

During the production of *Triffids,* Phil Yordan was developing projects for Samuel Bronston Productions in Madrid. He observed the lower production costs and the ease with which pictures were shot in Madrid. Above all, he felt that having his unit in Madrid would be more convenient. On *Crack in the World,* we utilized the Bronston Studio in Madrid and the C.E.A. Studio, near the Madrid airport, for all the interior shots, special effects and some of the exteriors. The underground complex required a large stage that had to be integrated with the hanging miniature that Eugene Lourie created. We took space at C.E.A. for this set. The United Nations meeting hall was shot in a museum in Madrid. The main unit shooting schedule was about seven weeks.

Where were the exteriors shot?

The opening sequence was filmed in a mountainous region not far from Madrid. The company traveled to the coast to do the island sequence. The exterior of the bunker was constructed at the Bronston Studio "ranch" at Las Matas.

The scene in the volcanic shaft?

The exterior of the shaft was shot at the Bronston Studio just outside the stage. The interior was a combination of interior set and special effects.

What can you tell me about working with the celebrated Eugene Lourie?

Lourie was what I would term a "team" art director. This is said not to denigrate Lourie's abilities. He was an artist and thoroughly understood the

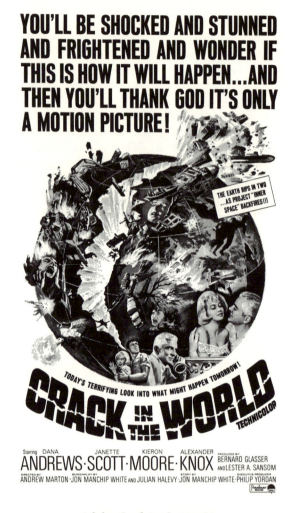

Ad for *Crack in the World*.

special effects process. Much of his knowledge of special effects came about when he directed and supervised a monster picture called *Gorgo* for the King Brothers. On *Crack in the World*, Gene had the good fortune of working with the Bronston Studio special effects chief Alex Weldon. Weldon constructed and supervised the physical effects, explosions, etc. For the construction of miniatures, Gene contacted and brought to Madrid a team of three French special effects men that he had known. All of these people were supervised by Lourie. The special effects costs accounted for about 40 percent of the budget.

Lourie told me Crack in the World *was "a tremendously cheap picture."*

Lourie didn't have any accurate knowledge concerning our productions in Spain. He probably was not familiar with the much lower production costs in Madrid (we worked a five-day week). He did, however, realize that his department was functioning efficiently with rather stringent cost controls. The special effects (without principals) was not bound to a schedule, but rather to a limit of expenditure.

Was it Lourie who designed and built your miniatures?
Lourie designed the miniatures and they were constructed by the French special effects crew under the supervision of Henri Assola, one of the crew members.

The train wreck scene is a highpoint of the picture. How large a miniature was involved?
The individual train cars were about three feet in length. The special effects set including the backdrop was about 100 feet wide.

Dana Andrews had a good, dramatic part. Did he seem to enjoy himself?
Andrews felt an identification with the role of the older scientist, and he had an immediate rapport with Janette Scott. The music for their love scene, which we jokingly referred to as "I Want a Baby," was beautifully written and scored by the English musical talent Johnny Douglas.

Why do Janette Scott and Kieron Moore turn up in so many of your films?
Kieron and Janette were sensible actors, always prepared for the day's shooting, cooperative even when the locations were difficult. Hiring them made casting in Spain simpler for us. We were never disappointed with their work.

Were you happy with the finished film?
I considered *Crack in the World* a good picture of its type. [Director] "Bundy" Marton and Gene Lourie worked well together and were responsible for the look of the picture. Lester Sansom and a competent editorial staff supervised the many details of editing and sound effects. As with all our Spanish productions, we worked with a distributor's guarantee. All our films were financed by the Bank of America, without a bond of completion. It was my personal relationship with the vice-president of the bank, Al Howe, which made this working arrangement possible. As I recall, the pick-up for *Crack in the World* was about $875,000.

Why did you retire from the picture business?
After directing *Todd* [1967], my enthusiasm for production was greatly dampened. Ted Sewell, the vice-president of Four Star Television, proposed that I join him in developing a program of budget features. Only one film was

produced [*Madron,* 1970]—Four Star experienced severe financial difficulties and I thought it was a good time to retire. Which I did.

What keeps you busy these days?
Over the years, between assignments, I involved myself in commercial real estate development. What started out as a method of providing activity and income during the lean times has evolved into a going business.

Are you pleased with your movie career?
The production of motion pictures, especially overseas, was an exciting way of earning a livelihood. It was a method of providing the necessities of life for one's family and having a great time in the process. Oddly enough, I didn't consider it a career.

Which of your films is your personal favorite?
Ed Bernds and I did a Western called *Escape from Red Rock* [1958]. We made it for $100,000, starring Brian Donlevy and a cast of unknowns. The script had all the elements of an A picture. It was a warm personal story and also contained the action necessary for the genre.

How do the sci-fi films stack up, in your estimation?
I was surprised and not unhappy to learn that *Return of the Fly, Day of the Triffids* and *Crack in the World* are considered cult films. The films were well done, especially when you consider the economical production and that they were produced independently outside of the Hollywood system.

Any Famous Last Words?
They say that hindsight is 20/20 vision. I have tried to avoid the "should have, could have" syndrome. A production executive should consider all the alternatives and make a decision based upon the facts at hand. I made the best calls that I could. I have no regrets.

I remember one night ... I was sitting outside by myself putting makeup on. I have no idea where they came from or where they were going, but these two little boys came walking by and saw me. I didn't have a chance to talk to them, I just turned around and looked at them. And they didn't say a thing, didn't scream or yell or anything, but, boy, did they take off— they ran like hell!

Herk Harvey

It isn't every day that a low-budget, Kansas-made indie captures the fancy of an entire generation of horror fans—in fact, it's happened only once. The story of a church organist (Candace Hilligoss) who survives a near-death experience only to be stalked by the cadaverous embodiment of death, *Carnival of Souls* has been raising goosebumps on late-night TV viewers for nearly a quarter-century. And now the man behind 1962's spookiest shoestringer steps out of retirement to reminisce about the near-legendary cult favorite he crafted.

Colorado-born Herk Harvey majored in theater at Kansas University, directing and acting in stage productions and later returning to the school in a teaching capacity. Harvey broke into the film business as an actor in some of the films being made by Centron Corporation of Lawrence, Kansas, an educational and industrial production company for which he subsequently went to work as a director. In 1961 he took a working vacation from Centron to try his hand at feature filmmaking: producing, directing, co-starring (as *Carnival*'s footloose phantom) and writing a new page of horror film history.

How did you come up with the idea to make Carnival of Souls?

I was on location in California shooting an industrial film for Centron, and decided to travel home by car. Driving back, I was passing Salt Lake, and I saw for the first time an abandoned amusement park called Saltair. Saltair was an amusement park that was built probably at some time in the '30s, a terrific park in its day, built right on the edge of the lake. Its attraction was that people could go there and bathe, and because of the salt content in the lake they could float very easily; supposedly it was also medicinal to a certain degree. They had all of the amusement park facilities there also—a roller coaster, games and a big pavilion.

Well, with the sun setting and with the lake in the background, this was the weirdest-looking place I'd ever seen *[laughs]*! I stopped the car and walked about a half or three-quarters of a mile to the place, and it was spooky indeed. And I thought, "Gee, what a tremendous location!"—because it's completely isolated from everything and everybody, and at that time it was completely defunct. But most of the things were still standing—the only thing that wasn't was the roller coaster. I came back and talked to John Clifford, who was a writer at Centron and a co-worker, and told him that I needed a horror script that would revolve around Saltair. So basically in talking we came up with some of the general plot, and he wrote the script in a matter of a couple weeks.

How did you go about raising money to go into production?

A man here in town named Joe Traylor had told me that if I ever had an idea for a feature film, he would be interested in getting some local businessmen to help out. I told him about our idea on a Friday night, and by Monday morning he had raised $17,000. I figured we could defer $13,000 and

Previous page: **Abandoning his plan to devise an elaborate makeup for his own character, Harvey emoted from beneath a simple coat of greasepaint in** *Carnival of Souls.*

do the film on a budget of $30,000, and so we started production. John and I made up the name Harcourt Productions just for that show, I took three weeks' vacation and we shot the film.

Did you do any "ad-lib"-style shooting?

Oh, sure. Often it was a case of find-what-you-can-on-the-streets, as in the scenes where Candace Hilligoss goes out of touch with reality. That also happened when we got to Saltair—some of the scenes there, how the dance was staged and so on. That sort of situation, it's not something that you plan in detail.

Where did you shoot all those street scenes?

All of those we shot in Salt Lake City. The department store, all the scenes in the street and in the bus station, all of those are "grab" shots. For instance, we just walked into that department store and asked, "Can we film here?" Everything in Salt Lake City was shot in a day.

For the most part, did you shoot on sets or in actual locations?

Just about everything was location. The organ factory scene was shot at the Reuter Organ Factory here in Lawrence; we knew it to be a fine location, and so the idea of making the lead character an organist came about because of that! What we were basically trying to do was to get everything we could out of Lawrence and Salt Lake City, so that we wouldn't have more locations to go to. The church was here in town, and still is; the rooming house was a house that was vacant at the time. Joe Traylor was in the real estate business, and this was a house they had not rented for that month. I asked if we could just rent it for a week, he said sure and so that's what happened. Some of the interior car scenes we filmed at Centron, using a projected background. Only one scene, the doctor's office, was a set, built at Centron.

The psychiatrist's office, you mean.

Well *[laughs]*, he really isn't supposed to be a psychiatrist. I've always felt that that doctor character just didn't come across, mainly because of the situations we put him in. The actor who played it was fine, but everything was too pat in his character. Both the doctor and the minister have the sort of stereotypic character that doesn't add anything to the film. There are quite a few things like that in *Carnival of Souls [laughs]*, and as we look at it now we hope that people can realize that we knew better! But when you write a script in two weeks or three weeks, and you shoot it in that same amount of time, you just make it happen rather than sitting and fine-tuning it.

What can you tell me about some of the other creative people involved on Carnival of Souls?

[Director of photography] Maurice Prather was, again, in the educational and industrial film business. At that time, Calvin Company in Kansas City and Centron here in Lawrence made this area one of the hubs of educational and industrial production in the Midwest, and Prather worked for a number of different companies of this type. [Assistant director] Reza Badiyi, who was also working in this field, worked with Bob Altman a lot in Kansas City. Then when Bob went to California, Reza went with him, and later became a successful television director — as a matter of fact, I got a call from him just the other day and he has just finished his 350th television show. Almost any adventure show you could name, he's directed; in fact, I would imagine he is now as prolific a director as exists in Hollywood.

How large — or small — a crew were you working with?
I think we had a crew of about six — me, a sound man, a cameraman, an assistant cameraman, an assistant director, and then a gaffer or two. In those days we were using the old blimped Arri camera, which weighed about 75 pounds, and the sound man was using the Magnasync tape unit for 16mm magnetic sound, which also weighed like 35, 40 pounds. In comparison to the way you go now, it was a real giant operation.

How did you happen to select Candace Hilligoss for the lead?
The fellow that played the part of John Linden, Sidney Berger, was a theater major here at Kansas University and had acted for me in some of the shows I did. He was going back to New York on vacation and I said, "We've got to have a lead for this show in a hurry. Could you find me a good actress from New York?" So he talked to an agent he knew there and came back with Candace.

When I first saw Candace at the airport, she just didn't look like what I thought a Candace Hilligoss would look like, and I thought, "I don't think it'll work out." She looked very dowdy, very "hippie" and this sort of thing, and I asked myself, "How am I going to tell her tomorrow that we can't use her?" But the next morning when she walked in, she was gussied up and looked exactly like what I wanted in the show, and that took care of that. We paid her $2,500 for three weeks' work.

How did you enjoy working with her?
Very much, as a matter of fact. Most of the time she was very eager to do the best she could. She was a method actress, though, and that made for problems a couple of times. For instance, in a scene where she was to walk across the street to the doctor's office, she said, "What is my *motivation?*" It was noontime in Salt Lake City and the street was very busy, and I told her, "Your motivation right now is to get across that street without getting killed!" Well *[laughs]*, she understood that, and she did it! But at other times I really did appreciate her attitude because, being an actor myself, I do respect actors and actresses and their desire to do a good job and to get into the part. And she

"So far out—it races ahead of time!" Pressbook cover for *Carnival of Souls*.

was really attempting to do that in a logical and professional manner. But with this kind of a budget and shooting off the cuff in many instances, a director really doesn't have time to say, "Do it because of this and this and this."

But overall you were happy with her work?

I was very, very pleased with Candace, yes. She had the look and the ability to do what I wanted. There was a scene at the end where she was in the car, dead, with the other two girls; this was shot in late September [1961] and the Kaw River here in Lawrence is very cold at that time of year. We put the car in the water and the other two girls climbed in and shook and shivered, and Candace put her foot in the water and said, "I'm not gonna do it." I tried to reason with her, to convince her that the show had to have that scene; she understood that and put her foot a little further in the water and, once again, "It's too cold, there's no way I can do it." And so finally *[laughs]* I just had to grab her and *throw* her in the car and get her underwater. There was an officer from the sheriff's department standing there, and he just turned around and left, because he knew he was either going to have to arrest me or do something if he stuck around. He must have said to himself, "Let *them* take care of it!"

Did any one scene present a particularly interesting challenge?
   The opening sequence at the bridge [where a car topples into the river] was an interesting one for me; I just wasn't that sure of myself, I hadn't done that many action scenes. We had no people here to do stunts for us, so we had to do it all ourselves. The bridge was between two counties, Douglas and Jefferson, and I had to talk to both of them about my plan to shoot on the bridge — to run a car through the railing and into the river. Douglas County said they didn't think they would be interested, but if I could get permission from Jefferson, they would go along. So I went to Jefferson and told them that I *had* Douglas's permission, and they said, "Then, fine, it's okay with us!"
   One stipulation they placed on me was that I had to get the car out and I had to pay for damages to the bridge. So I crossed my fingers and hoped things worked. I got two old cars and painted them the same color; if it didn't work the first time, at least we'd have another car. Luckily it did work the first time — we put mannequins in the car and used cables to drag it off the bridge.

So everything went smoothly shooting that scene?
   In dredging the river for the car, they managed to grapple it and get it out of there in a matter of about a half-hour, which was great, and when I left they were repairing the bridge. And when I got a bill for it, it was for twelve dollars *[laughs]*!

Why is Candace Hilligoss's Mary Henry such an uptight, standoffish character?
   What we had in mind was, here is a woman who had never really lived. She played an organ and she lived by herself, and nothing had really happened in her life. And so the fact that she was passive in her life before the accident gave more credence to the fact that she now really *wanted* to live. When faced with death, she refused it and came back as a poltergeist or what-have-you. I'm not sure, though, that we got all this across in the show; the way we developed it, you really didn't get much indication of this. We tried to point it out by showing her character as being very passive, but I think there were other things that would have been good to play up in order to get this point across.

I wonder if that didn't hurt the picture. A leading character who was a little more real might have gotten more audience sympathy.

This surrealistic collage of images captures the spooky flavor of *Carnival of Souls*.

It probably would have. As I say, Candace kept wanting to know how to get into her role, and for the most part I didn't want her to get into *any*thing—I just wanted her to sort of walk through it. Basically this is how we explained it to her, but in some of the scenes she still wanted to know, "Am I warm? Am I this? Am I that?" And we had to explain *again* that she was nothing, neutral, very passive. That is very hard for someone to do—they say, "If I'm passive, how am I going to interest anybody in this character?" As an actor I can certainly understand that.

Some of the neatest moments in the film are when she goes "out of touch" with reality.
    I'd probably have to give John Clifford the credit for coming up with that, because I think most of the ideas in the developing of the show were his.

What can you remember about some of the other people in your cast?
    Frances Feist [Miss Thomas, the landlady], who is now dead, was an actress at K.U. and had been in the Broadway production of *Harvey*, in the female lead. Stan Levitt [Dr. Samuels] is an actor from Kansas City, and he's done several industrial films for me; Art Ellison [the minister], the same. Art Ellison has probably done more industrial and educational films than any other actor in the country— a huge number of them.

There's a long castlist at the beginning of Carnival of Souls, *but no one seems to know what roles any of these minor actors play.*

[Looking over castlist.] Tom McGinnis was the man in the organ factory; Forbes Caldwell was a carpenter in that same scene. That organ factory scene originally went on longer and those two discuss Candace's character, that she's a very strange girl, and bring out the fact that she's never lived; the distributor, Herts-Lion, cut that out. Dan Palmquist played a service station attendant in another scene which was cut; he was the assistant editor on the film. Bill De Jarnette, who also did some editing, played a different service station attendant, the one who puts Candace's car up on the hydraulic lift. Steve Boozer was Sidney Berger's friend in the dance club; Sharon Scoville and Mary Ann Harris were the other girls in the car in the opening scene; [production manager] Larry Sneegas was one of the guys in the other car. The other names in the opening castlist must have been the people who played the ghouls; we used a dance class from Utah University for the scene where the ghouls are dancing. Reza Badiyi, who doesn't get a screen credit, plays the little guy in the bus station who's trying to buy a ticket as Candace comes up.

What prompted your decision to play the head ghoul in the film?

Economics *[laughs]*! Also, the fact that there were no lines, and I didn't have to memorize anything. We had to go fast and furious, and in playing the ghoul I had nothing to do except to stand around.

If you had had a few extra bucks in the budget, would you have still played the ghoul?

[After a pause.] I probably would have. Call me an egoist! However, I did not take a screen credit for appearing in the film; it just seemed a little much, producing, directing *and* starring, I mean.

What kind of makeup sessions were involved?

Very short ones! That again was a compromise, because originally I had intended to use egg white and make it so it would flake off, and I really was going to work on the makeup to quite an extensive degree. But I realized that between getting into the water and some of the other things I had to do, that that type of makeup would not be feasible, and I finally got down to using just greasepaint because the other just wouldn't have worked. I put the makeup on myself.

I remember one night out at Saltair, the crew was inside setting up lights and so forth and I was sitting outside by myself putting makeup on. I have no idea where they came from or where they were going, but these two little boys came walking by and saw me. I didn't have a chance to talk to them, I just turned around and looked at them. And they didn't say a thing, didn't scream or yell or anything, but, boy, did they take off *[laughs]* — they ran like hell!

Did you feel any concern as you were making Carnival *that perhaps it would be too weird, too dreamlike a movie for mass consumption?*

Very much so. Not so much during the time we were making it as when we started putting it together in the editing stage. I thought it was kind of far-out for its time; most horror films, even then, really weren't that far-out as far as inter-dimension, the character of Death coming back to reap his just reward and things like that.

As with many other films of this type, the music really helps do the trick.

Gene Moore, who did the music for us, was in charge of music at Calvin Company in Kansas City. I gave him a 16mm print of the movie and he looked at it a very short time and said, "Okay, I'm ready." So we went over to an organ sales company that had a big Thomas organ, and he simply sat down and started in. Most of it he had scored, but some of the music, just for general effects, he just sat and ad-libbed. We started around eight o'clock in the morning and probably by two o'clock in the afternoon we were done.

Did you get a positive reaction from audiences when you first showed Carnival of Souls?

No, I didn't. The reaction was very neutral. When we had the opening here in Lawrence, we had a big premiere and a full house—the Granada Theater brought out searchlights and that sort of thing and we really did it up. The audience was very nice but they just didn't know how to react to the film.

What was your own initial reaction to the finished film?

I shared their skepticism. Also, some of the things I let go because of budgetary restraints have haunted me forever—footsteps being out of sync and a lot of other stuff. I should have taken time and said, "No, I am not going to let this film go out this way," and waited until I got more money and done it right. But when I told the investors that I would have it done by a certain date, that became the foremost thing in my mind, rather than the quality of the film.

If you could turn back the clock, what would you do differently?

I would sound-effect it completely different. Also, we lost a roll of film through the lab—General Labs in California did the processing, and there was one roll of film that was lost. That was the ghouls coming out of Salt Lake. We had a scene of them coming out from behind pilings, out of the lake itself, white hands coming up and grasping the railings, black silhouettes coming in, getting ready for the Danse Macabre. It should have been very effective, but I never saw it.

How did you get mixed up with the Herts-Lion company?

A friend of mine, the president of General Labs, turned me on to Herts-

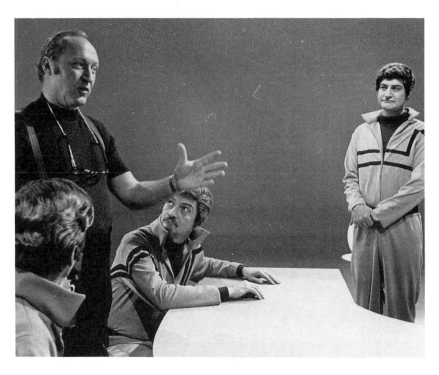

Harvey returned to directing for Centron after completing *Carnival of Souls*. Here he directs actors Jim Claussen, Ross Copeland and William Kuhlke in a futuristic skit for AC Spark Plugs.

Lion because they were a newly formed distribution company. He didn't know Ken Herts, the president of Herts-Lion, but he said it was a public-held company and that they did need product. I had already had the experience of taking the film to New York and showing it to people like United Artists—they looked at it and their reaction, too, was very neutral. At that time independents were kind of a new thing, and I really don't think the majors wanted independents in the business—at least that's the excuse I made to myself, rather than blame the film!

So I took *Carnival of Souls* to Herts-Lion in Hollywood and showed it to them, and they said, yes, they would be interested. I guess they already had *The Devil's Messenger,* which was a Lon Chaney, Jr., film, and they thought that that film and *Carnival of Souls* would make a good double feature. There was no money up front but they offered a good percentage on the distribution. Then I took off on a trip to South America to shoot seven films down there, for Centron. When I got back I saw all these reports—the film had shown primarily in the Southeast, in drive-in theaters—and these were glowing reports, that the film had been doing well, and that they owed me so-much money. Well, pretty soon I started realizing that they *owed* me money but I wasn't *gettin'* any. I called Herts up and said, "I'm going to get some money or I'm coming out there," so he sent me a check and it *bounced*. Then I knew we really had trouble. By the time I got ahold of Herts again, he was in Europe and the company had folded. Con men are con men and he was a good one. I'd sure like to meet him again — I would *love* that.

Why did Herts-Lion cut your film prior to release?

Basically, I think Herts-Lion wanted it cut because it was going to be part of a double feature and they wanted a certain length. Then, too, they just thought artistically it was better that way. Herbert Strock, who was the director of *The Devil's Messenger,* did the final cut on *Carnival* — he edited it down about nine minutes.

If we had simply shown *Carnival of Souls* in theaters here in Lawrence and in Kansas City and in Salt Lake City, the film would have made the money back. I'd have just hand-carried it around and made arrangements with the theater owners and explained that it was filmed in the area. Our receipts here in Lawrence were very good, and I think that would have worked.

Are there deeper meanings in Carnival of Souls, *as some of the artsy-fartsies claim, or is it simply an exercise in weirdness?*

It's an exercise in weirdness. Some of the "deeper" meanings in there, like the call of death and that sort of thing, John Clifford and I intended, but a lot of the things that have been read into it have happened because of audiences. Shortly after the film was released, a teacher here at the Spooner Thayer Museum went on a vacation in Sweden and brought me back a review. And the Swedes were really, really reading things into it — the dimensions of death and so on — because they're much more preoccupied with death than we are. They were also comparing it to Bergman and that sort of thing — not so much the story as the *look* of the film.

Given the fact that the film lost money for all its investors, do you regret having made it?

No, because basically what we did was right, and what we intended to do was righter. John Clifford had also written another show called *Flannigan's Smoke,* a kind of experimental comedy and a much better script than *Carnival.* We did *Carnival* because we thought that the horror genre at the time was much more apt to be bought by a studio than something that was very experimental in comedy. We thought we would do *Carnival of Souls* first and then, if we could make any money on it at all, that would give us an avenue to make *Flannigan's Smoke.*

I assume you had no desire to dabble in features again after Carnival *went bust.*

It was one of those things where you're too busy with your own job to start over again. And by that time, of course, Mr. Traylor and all his investors knew

Herk Harvey still remembers how to turn on The Look.

that they had been burned by Ken Herts, and nobody was really all that interested. But I want you to know that all of the people who put money into *Carnival of Souls* were very understanding. I was never hassled by anybody — not by a soul — and I think that's fantastic. Nobody told me they were sorry they did it, I think everybody just kind of got a kick out of taking their shot at making a movie. But I never would have had the guts to go back and say to 'em, "Well, we're gonna try it again, you want to put up some more?" So that was basically what happened.

Looking back on the film today, are you proud of Carnival, *and happy that it's your claim to fame?*

A 1989 reunion of the makers of *Carnival of Souls* brought together production designer Larry Sneegas, actor Sidney Berger, writer John Clifford, actors Candace Hilligoss, Stan Levitt and Art Ellison, and director/star Harvey (left to right).

I have to say yes and no. When you work someplace for thirty-five years making educational and industrial films, and the one feature that you make is really what you're known for *[laughs]* — a film on which you spent a total of maybe five weeks — that to me doesn't seem right. Some of the things I'm much more proud of, we did in the industrial area. We shot hour-long films in two days, musicals with people like Eddie Albert and Ed Ames and so on. Some of those with skits and original music and all that, are really kind of interesting. And I think that many of the other films that we made in the educational and industrial area really had something to say. Yet, as you say, I'm known for *Carnival of Souls*.

John Clifford and I are both surprised that *Carnival* "came back" the way it did because there was a long period there where it was just plain dead. Ken Herts had left and the movie had stopped and there was nothing. Then the TV rights were sold to Walter Manley, and through his efforts the film started showing on late night TV and I started getting letters from people all over. And that was kind of interesting.

But you must be pleased by the film's ongoing popularity.

Of course. At that time in our lives *Carnival of Souls* was an expression of our desire to get into moviemaking. It was an exciting time for all of us that worked on it, a very enjoyable time. Even though we worked long hours, it was a feature film where we were expressing ourselves, doing new things, trying to make do with little money. All of that adds a great deal to the general excitement of doing and moving and making things happen. *Carnival of Souls* was certainly an enjoyable experience.

*I think Hitchcock's early films
were the great, great films that he did....
But later on he lived in some kind of an ivory castle —
he was like an emperor at Universal Studios, he became less and less
accessible to people, and he moved in and out of the studio
rather mysteriously. I felt he seemed to lose
that common bond he had with people.*

Gordon Hessler

PROVING THAT there is indeed Life After Corman, director Gordon Hessler took the reins on AIP's Poe series in the late 1960s and helmed the English-based productions of *The Oblong Box, Cry of the Banshee* (both starring Vincent Price) and the Spanish-made *Murders in the Rue Morgue*. While these films have not attained the following that Roger Corman's trendsetters enjoy, Hessler's Poe adaptations were unique and intricately plotted productions which reaped handsome profits for AIP and typed Hessler as a horror/suspense "specialist" who continues to work in the genre to this day.

Gordon Hessler was born in Germany, the son of a Danish mother and an English father. Educated in England, he moved to the United States while in his late teens and spent several years working in documentaries. At Universal Studios, "I guess because I had an English accent," Hessler was placed under contract to Alfred Hitchcock and went to work on the master director's video series *Alfred Hitchcock Presents* and *The Alfred Hitchcock Hour*, climbing the ladder from story reader to associate producer and finally to producer in the series' final year. A novelette rejected for the show became the basis for *The Woman Who Wouldn't Die* (1965), Hessler's first feature film as director.

When production of the AIP Poe series was shifted to Britain, Hessler collaborated with producer Louis M. Heyward (q.v.) and horror enthusiast/screenwriter Christopher Wicking on the aforementioned Poe films and on the science fiction shocker *Scream and Scream Again*. Carrying on in the fantasy field, he also directed the Ray Harryhausen stop-motion swashbuckler *The Golden Voyage of Sinbad* and additional small-screen suspensers like the *Psycho*-inspired *Scream, Pretty Peggy* with Bette Davis and *The Strange Possession of Mrs. Oliver* with Karen Black.

Apart from directing a handful of episodes, what input did Alfred Hitchcock have on Alfred Hitchcock Presents *and* The Alfred Hitchcock Hour?

He approved all the stories before they were shot, but really it was an entity of its own. Hitch looked at all the scripts, and if he didn't like something we had to change it. And he did all the introductions, but you know of course that they were all done in one day. Joan Harrison, who wrote some of the scripts and was Hitchcock's personal assistant, was the actual producer of the show. Norman Lloyd, who was an actor in his own right — he was in Hitch's *Saboteur* [1942] — was also a producer, and was sort of my boss. When he moved up from associate producer to producer, I became the associate, then when he moved to executive producer I became producer. He was always one step ahead of me *[laughs]*!

Early on, what did your duties as story reader entail?

To locate stories, work with writers, develop new stories and then present them to the management — that would be Joan Harrison and Hitchcock. Hitch was very, very tough on stories; there were some stories you'd be angry that he wouldn't use, but he was adamant. It was a very tough job.

Previous page: **Gordon Hessler, who worked on the *Hitchcock* teleseries early in his Hollywood career, and has since become a frequent presence in the horror and suspense genres.**

The great thing was that all the scripts were finished before any of the shows were shot, so you could really get the best actors in town and give the scripts to them long before they were booked. If you look at the roll call of that *Hitchcock* era of television, you'll see that many of those people turned into big, big film stars.

Were you at Universal when Hitchcock was making Psycho?

Oh, yes. It was made with the same television crew that made the show, so he made that in a very short space of time. Bob Bloch, who is a very famous short story writer, came up with this very pasty, B-picture story, but Joseph Stefano, who wrote the screenplay, did a wonderful job. It was a very modern and dangerous kind of film, far away from any of Hitch's concepts, which were kind of fairy-tale suspense stories.

Later in your career, pressbooks for the films you directed labeled you a Hitchcock protégé.

[*Laughs.*] I don't know how that got in there. I was under contract to him — to Shamley Productions — but that's really not a fair thing to say. Obviously, since he was my employer, I watched his films more closely than I would otherwise.

What do you remember best about working with him?

The extraordinary thing was how well he prepared everything. When he directed an episode, he would finish it up much more quickly than any of the young hotshot directors; he "cut in the camera" as he was shooting, so there was no waste of film. He would only put on film what was going to be in the finished episode. He was able to use very little film and he used little time because he knew exactly what he wanted — it was all pictured and storyboarded in his mind very, very carefully beforehand.

Is it true that Hitchcock was mistrustful of writers?

Well, he liked to work with them very closely, and he had a very good relationship with Ernie Lehman [*North by Northwest* (1959), *Family Plot* (1976)] for many, many years. But he had a problem when the new writers were introduced because they were posing *their* ideas and he was very authoritative in *his* picture-making ideas. He had very, very clear visual images of what constituted suspense and what didn't. I think Hitchcock's early films were the great, great films that he did — some of those silents were absolutely brilliant, way ahead of their time. But later on he lived in some kind of an ivory castle — he was like an emperor at Universal Studios, he became less and less accessible to people, and he moved in and out of the studio rather mysteriously. I felt he seemed to lose that common bond he had with people. You know his father was a poulterer in England and he came from a sort of middle-class background. It's a shame, but in later years he didn't make his films as magical as the early ones were. But still, Hitch was one of the great masters; if there *are* any great picture-makers, he certainly was one of the greatest.

Why was production of AIP's Poe series shunted to England in the mid-'60s?
   Samuel Arkoff, who was the head of AIP, saw the great advantage of shooting in England because the dollar was very high and the pound was very low, and you could shoot there very, very cheaply. You also got the advantage of all the backlots that were full of wonderful sets that we could "steal" for our pictures, plus the very talented art directors and cameramen and the classical actors that this kind of film needed. Louis "Deke" Heyward, who executive-produced these films, was an extraordinary character, an American who I had first met at Universal Studios. He got a job with Arkoff as his right-hand man, and then he opened up AIP offices in London. He ran the whole company in a marvelous and very creative way, and we had a wonderful time there. It was then that the whole of America was making movies in England—Fox, Columbia and Warner Bros. were all shooting pictures in Europe like mad.

How did you get involved on The Oblong Box?
   I was producing a film called *De Sade* for AIP. *De Sade* was a film that was going to be the biggest production that they had ever made; they had asked me to produce it and Michael Reeves was going to direct it. Michael was an American, living in England, who was having severe mental problems at the time. He was a wonderful man and he would have been one of our most brilliant directors. I flew to England to talk with Michael about *De Sade,* but he was sick at the time. Michael was not able to do *De Sade* because he was getting mental treatments—electric shock and all those horrible things. They put another director, Cy Endfield, on it.
   I got fired, virtually, on that picture, and I thought my career was over. But they came to me and said, "Look, there's another film *[The Oblong Box]* which we'd like you to produce in Ireland." Michael Reeves was going to direct it but, again, he was not up to it, so I took the film from Ireland, put it into Shepperton Studios and directed it myself. AIP was so worried about their "big" production in *De Sade* that they didn't pay any attention to us. We just made the film we wanted to make, they were very happy with it and we got a contract to make another three pictures after that: *Scream and Scream Again,* which I think was our best; *Cry of the Banshee,* which none of us liked particularly, but we weren't really allowed to change it; and *Murders in the Rue Morgue,* which I think *would* have been my best picture.

Would you agree that The Oblong Box *had a story that was hard to follow?*
   I would, yes. The story was sent to us from America—written by an American—and we had to try to re-adapt and save it. Chris Wicking, who is an absolute horror buff, rewrote the script. We only had three weeks to shoot it, and the budget was very small—we're talking about $175,000, maybe a little bit more. An incredibly small amount.

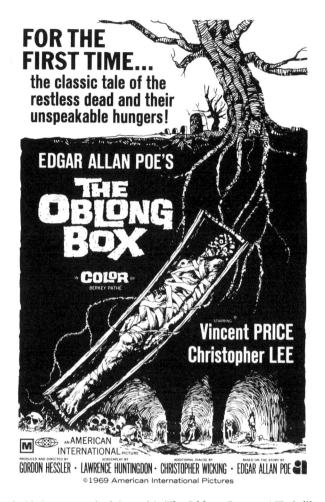

Hessler made his horror movie debut with *The Oblong Box,* an AIP thriller from the tail end of the studio's Poe cycle.

How did you enjoy working with Vincent Price and Christopher Lee on The Oblong Box?

Vincent Price is an extraordinary man. We had a prince from Nigeria come to lunch with us at the Shepperton Studios; we were showing him around the place and we asked Vincent if he wouldn't mind coming along. Many actors have to talk about themselves or their careers and so on, but not one word of that from Vincent. All he talked about was African art, by region and in such detail that this prince was absolutely amazed! Vincent Price is a wonderful personality. Christopher Lee is made of much sterner stuff: very exacting, very correct. But he was very well educated and has a great deal of charm. I enjoyed working with him as well.

As you mentioned before, Scream and Scream Again *probably is your best film from this period.*

We got a pulp magazine–type story [*The Disoriented Man* by Peter Saxon], which if you read you know was just trash, but the ingenuity that Chris Wicking brought to it made it a film of a much grander scale. He showed his potential talent on that because it really was just pulp—he really uplifted it, made it something very, very different.

Sort of like the difference between Robert Bloch's book Psycho *and the Hitchcock movie.*

Robert Bloch is a wonderful short story writer but he's not really that good at scripts. The fellow who did the screenplay for *Psycho,* Joseph Stefano, really whipped it into shape. I thought he did a marvelous job.

Did you get to know Max Rosenberg and Milton Subotsky, the heads of Amicus Films, while making Scream and Scream Again *with them?*

I had not that much contact with Max Rosenberg; Milton Subotsky was a kind of line producer on *Scream and Scream Again.* They had sold the whole project to AIP. Early on Subotsky wrote a script for *Scream and Scream Again* and it was pretty bad—that was when we put Chris on it.

Fans' complaint with Scream and Scream Again *is that, except for one short moment with Price and Lee, none of the horror stars have scenes together.*

That was an unfortunate thing but it just worked out that way. It was a last-minute Deke Heyward decision to try and get all three stars together in one picture, and we hadn't designed *Scream and Scream Again* for anything like that. But I enjoyed working with Vincent Price and Christopher Lee again, and then of course Peter Cushing, too. Peter Cushing is just a wonderful individual to work with; you couldn't have a better professional than that man.

And you remain happy with the film?

It was ahead of its time, I thought, and we tried to figure out some kind of stylistic approach. But again, these films were made in three and four weeks.

Cry of the Banshee *turned out to be a pretty unpleasant and kinky movie, and it isn't well-liked by the fans.*

I agree. Again, we were sent the script from Hollywood, we read it and we were all unhappy with it. It was a dreadful script—what we got from AIP was something unbelievable—and so I asked if I would be allowed to change it. Chris Wicking and I went to Scotland and we were planning to do a completely different, very, very interesting movie. We wanted to shoot *Cry of the Banshee* there; all the witchcraft seemed to emanate from Scotland, "The

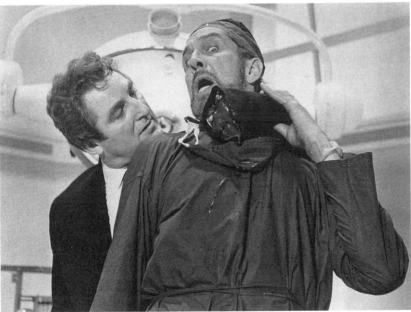

Top: Hessler *(right)* directed horror icon Peter Cushing in the AIP/Amicus thriller *Scream and Scream Again. Bottom:* Vincent Price, on the receiving end for once, is manhandled by Marshall Jones in the climax of *Scream and Scream Again.*

Land of Witches," and we thought that would be a wonderful place to film it. As a matter of fact *[laughs]*, we *met* a number of witches, Chris and I, while we were doing the research in Scotland! We were trying to get inspiration to do something very different, but as it turned out we were never really given the power to do that. We would have had to change the script so much that the AIP people in London got worried. They felt that the original script had been approved and pre-sold, and if we changed it very drastically we might be cutting our own throats. They said, "Ten percent is the maximum amount you can change," so that was about all we could do.

What sort of changes did you plan to make?
  What Chris wanted to add into it was that those of the "old religion," the people that everybody thought were so terrible, were actually the *good* witches. But as I said, we rewrote it so far away from the original script that Hollywood had sent us, that Deke got a little worried and said, "Look, this is not the story that everybody's bought. You're going to have to go back to the original concept."

What is there in The Oblong Box *and* Banshee *that makes them Edgar Allan Poe films?*
  There isn't anything; that was a pure and absolute lie.

Banshee *was Elisabeth Bergner's first film in 29 years. It wasn't much of a comeback picture.*
  No, it wasn't. I really can't say why she agreed to do that part, except maybe because there was very little film work in London at the time. Deke Heyward had an amazing ability to persuade actors to go into pictures.

Were you happy with the demon makeup in Banshee?
  Not really, we just didn't have the money to do it. *Banshee* cost maybe $450,000, $500,000 maximum, with perhaps four weeks' shooting. We had an incredible English musician named Wilfred Joseph do the music for that, and the music was on the first print. Wilfred Joseph gave the picture another level with the music—it was really marvelous. But when it went back to Hollywood AIP took that music off and put a very lame piece of music on in its place. The new score was by Les Baxter and it was totally inappropriate, it was just *so* bad, especially when you know what a fantastic score Wilfred Joseph did. It was such a pity. There is at least one print floating around somewhere with the original music on it, and I wish I could get hold of it. It would have made a tremendous amount of difference. *Cry of the Banshee* did all right for AIP but it was, I think, the least interesting of all the films I did for them.

Did you encounter Sam Arkoff and James Nicholson while making these pictures?

Yes, I knew them both pretty well. They would come over when a film was finished, look at it and then take us out for dinner, that kind of thing. I liked them both very much—in the way that you like executives *[laughs]*! They were characters, they had their own niche in the film world and they made pictures that were highly successful. They dissociated around this time, but they were necessary to each other. I haven't been in contact with Arkoff for some time now—he's not really that much involved in the film business. He's got his new company [Arkoff International Pictures] but I think that Arkoff by himself is probably a little bit lost.

Cry of the Banshee *had a wrap party honoring Vincent Price, didn't it?*

We had an incredible party, everybody dressed in costume. After-picture parties are always so boring and so uninteresting, so I said, "Anybody who wants to come to this party, executives included, has to wear a costume." We got all the costumes from the Richard Burton movie *Anne of the Thousand Days* [1969]—we had rented them from Berman's—and they were marvelous costumes. (We used them in *Cry of the Banshee*.) Everybody had to wear one of those costumes, including Arkoff and Nicholson. Vincent was very upset at the time for some reason to do with his contract, and he was having a fight with Arkoff—I don't really know what the details were. And Vincent didn't want to come to the party. I said, "Vincent, you've got to come, this is a party in your honor." He refused and refused, but finally I persuaded him to come. But by the time he arrived, he had drunk too much.

What happened next?

What we had done, we'd got a big cake and there was a naked girl supposed to pop out of it. And Vincent was supposed to cut the cake. I had told Arkoff he had to make a speech, to present the cake and all that sort of thing, but when Vincent found out that Arkoff was going to make the speech, he said, "If he does, I won't be there to cut the cake!" So, we had to rush back to Arkoff and tell him *not* to make the speech! I remember also that we couldn't find a knife to cut the cake, and Vincent, who was roaring drunk, said, "Use the knife that's in my back!" *[Laughs.]* I thought, "God, this is going to be disastrous!" but everything turned out all right—the party was great fun, a lot of liquor was flowing, we had a band and dancing and I think everybody enjoyed themselves.

Murders in the Rue Morgue *owes a lot more to* Phantom of the Opera *than it does to anything Poe ever wrote.*

The problem was that the Poe story, which is a mystery where the *monkey* did it, was not the kind of story you could do anymore. So we used *Murders in the Rue Morgue* as a play-within-a-play; the Poe story was being done on the stage, and we developed a mystery that was going on around the Poe play.

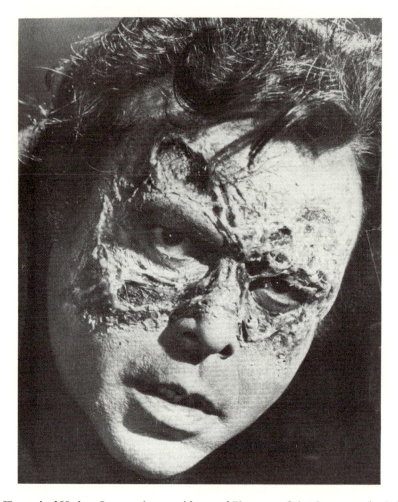

AIP recruited Herbert Lom to play an acid-scarred Phantom-of-the-Opera type in their made-in-Spain *Murders in the Rue Morgue*.

This time around you shot in Spain.

 Murders in the Rue Morgue was made in Spain, on a budget of maybe $700,000. I was very disappointed when that was sort of re-edited in Hollywood. When James Nicholson came to Spain and looked at the final cut, he was very, very excited about it. But apparently when it went back to California they didn't like it. Now I must say that it was a very different film from anything they'd ever done, and to me it was one of the best films I had ever made. But they took out a whole end sequence and made the film unintelligible! I almost begged them just to put back that end sequence, but they never did it. Our original finish was a wonderful twist ending, but they took it all out and I was very unhappy.

Can you speculate on why they did that?
England was where practically all the AIP pictures were being done at that time; literally, the Americans were doing little or nothing. There was a great rivalry there, and I suspect that's probably one of the reasons why *Rue Morgue* was re-edited, so all the editors in America could re-assert themselves. Lilli Palmer had a marvelous role in the picture—she was the catalyst for the film to shift into a new gear, and her role made the whole story make sense—but it was almost all cut out! *Incredible!* They cut it down so she was almost like an extra. I don't know what she must have thought when she saw the film.

Any anecdotes about working with Jason Robards?
Jason realized after we started that he had taken the wrong role—he suddenly realized he should have been playing Herbert Lom's role. But he realized that a little bit too late *[laughs]*! He was great fun to work with, though.

Your Poe films never gained the following that Roger Corman's have. Can you guess at the reason for that?
I don't know; I never really thought about that. That's a good question *[laughs]*! Well, maybe Roger's are better!

Nobody's really liked my films that much in Hollywood, for some reason or other. Roger Corman, who's a wonderful director, is a great hero in Europe—the French just love him—but over here they just think he's a bum director because he was working on low-budget films and he took short cuts and so on. But he was a great cinema-maker, and he *taught* Hollywood how to make low-budget pictures, which they didn't know.

What was it like working on a stop-motion film like The Golden Voyage of Sinbad?
That film is all Ray Harryhausen's; as you certainly know, he's a marvelous effects man, an American living in London. It was a great education for me to make a film like that. *Golden Voyage* was filmed in Spain, in Palma de Mallorca and in Madrid.

What were your impressions of Harryhausen and producer Charles Schneer?
I got along well with both of them. Ray Harryhausen is a real sort of Victorian Anglophile, a super guy, just wonderful. I learned a lot from him, because I knew nothing about that area of special effects picture-making— knowledge which he supplied. He was marvelous. I pressed him to do more and more things special effects-wise, and he would do anything you asked him—he said, "There's nothing you can't do on film if you've got the time and the money."

Charles Schneer is a real character in every way. He can be very difficult, and very hard to get to know. (Somehow I got on well with him.) He's enormously hard-working, works harder than anybody else; he sees every single play that comes to London. His taste hasn't come along with the same depth as the amount of work that he does, to see all these plays, but I must say he's a wonderful producer, really. He's one of those producers who goes all the way through with a picture and is involved in every phase; everything that is being done in the picture, all the way through to the very end, he's absolutely, totally involved in it. And he's very tough with a buck, but anything he says he'll give you, he gives you. While we were making *Golden Voyage of Sinbad* there was a young fellow who was running Columbia Pictures, Peter Guber, and actually that was the only picture that was being made by Columbia at that time — Columbia was in a very bad way. And the way Charles Schneer treated Guber — if Guber didn't return Schneer's phone call in a few seconds, Schneer would treat him like a nobody! I think Charles must have had an enormous number of shares of Columbia, to have such power there. Now he's retired, and enormously wealthy.

Golden Voyage of Sinbad was a very tough picture because we were only allowed eight weeks on it — formerly you'd get about fourteen weeks. By the skin of my teeth I managed to finish it on time *[laughs]*! And I know the film did well.

Was it difficult directing a film of that sort?

No, it was surprisingly easy because we had Ray, a man who had done so many of those, on the set with us all throughout shooting. What was great was that I kept asking him if we could do more and more difficult things — "Couldn't we do this, and this, and *this*?" — and he had no problem accomplishing any of them.

Did you stick with the film throughout the months of post-production effects work?

No, I didn't. I made another film, *Embassy* [1972], in between there, and when I came back we did the final editing.

What hurts Golden Voyage *is that John Phillip Law's performance lacks the necessary dash.*

He was the best we were able to get on the budget that was made available to us. He did lack the style that made stars of an Errol Flynn or a Douglas Fairbanks.

One of your newer films, Pray for Death *[1985], ran into trouble with the censors, didn't it?*

You know, there's a double standard in the Motion Picture Association. If you're working for a major, they really let you show heads being blown off and all of that sort of thing. If you're not a major — *Pray for Death* was made for Trans World Enterprises — they just come down on you. They took out a sort of rape scene — it was not a voyeur scene, it was a necessary story point to

John Phillip Law battles to rescue Caroline Munro from the Centaur's lair in the stop-motion adventure *The Golden Voyage of Sinbad*.

show the villainy of one character and make the hero's revenge so much more satisfying. It's the same sort of rape scene that you can see at the opening of *Jagged Edge* [1985], but they arbitrarily took *ours* out. You've got five old women making these decisions, and you cannot argue with them, you can't discuss it or use logic, you're finally blackmailed into accepting their wishes and cutting down, because a small company has just got to get the film released. The people here would not give it an R rating and we had to cut some very, very good sequences out of it.

Pray for Death was a horror film as well as being an action film; there are great horror overtones in it. It's a very good picture and I think it's very different from any martial-arts film that you've ever seen.

You recently made another film that's being described as Hitchcockian.

Yes, and I'm very, very happy with it. It's called *The Girl on a Swing* and it's from a novel by Richard Adams—you may know him from *Watership Down*. It's a love story that goes awry, the story of an Englishman who meets a German girl in Denmark and falls hopelessly in love with her. He gets involved with this girl, and she has something terrible in her past—*we* know it, and *he* begins to sense it. And then everything awful begins to happen. There's suspense in it; it's a kind of love/suspense story, and a very unusual picture. We shot it in England, Denmark and here in America, in Florida.

After many years of working extensively in TV, you seem to finally be back in features again.

I did a tremendous amount of TV, but now I *am* going back more to features; I've sort of almost lost touch with television. What I'm involved in now is very interesting: Trans World asked me to do two films and I am preparing them. One is a kind of remake of *The Mummy;* it's being written by Nelson Gidding, a wonderful writer who wrote *The Haunting* and got an Academy Award nomination for *I Want to Live!* [1958]. And then the other picture is an H. Rider Haggard novel called *Ayesha.* So I'm preparing those two projects, and those will probably be the next pictures I'll be directing.

*[My AIP experience] . . . was a period
that had never existed before and will never exist again.
My first cousin was Irving Thalberg; he existed at a time and in a place
where things were just right for him. Things were just right for
the American producer in England when I was there for AIP.
It was the right time, the right place,
and a great opportunity
to learn and grow.*

Louis M. Heyward

THERE'S JUST A (very!) thin line separating horror from humor in low-budget thrillers, and no one knows this better than Louis M. Heyward. A specialist in both categories, Heyward honed his comedy craft while working in TV with such small-screen comic luminaries as Ernie Kovacs and Milton Berle, and later learned the fine points of horror filmmaking during his long stint at AIP. Merging the two divergent genres, Heyward helped to create the most popular AIP horror character, Dr. Anton Phibes, in the campy classic *The Abominable Dr. Phibes*.

Born in New York City, Louis Heyward ("Deke" to his friends) was headed for a career as a lawyer while at the same time moonlighting as a writer of scripts for various radio series. After a six-year Air Force hitch, he landed a job with the Associated Press but continued to dabble with radio scripts, and later found an eight-year home as a comedy writer on daytime TV's *The Garry Moore Show*. Other jobs in New York TV included writing comedy material and skits for *The Ernie Kovacs Show* (the program was Emmy-nominated in 1956, the same year Heyward won the Sylvania Award as its top comedy writer) and developing *The Dick Clark Show*.

Migrating to Hollywood, he held executive posts at 20th Century–Fox and MCA before joining forces with AIP, first as a writer, then as their director of motion picture and TV development and ultimately as head of the company's London-based foreign arm. During his years with AIP, Heyward worked alongside many of its top stars and directors on a wide assortment of exploitation films, from froth like *Pajama Party* and *Sergeant Deadhead* to the horror thrillers *The Crimson Cult* and *The Oblong Box* and cult favorites like *Dr. Phibes, Dr. Phibes Rises Again* and *Conqueror Worm*. Now the vice-president of development at Barry & Enright (producers of game shows, features and TV movies), the funny, feisty Heyward looks back with affection (and frustration) on the glory days of AIP.

How did you initially hook up with American International Pictures?

I heard about The Jolly Green Giant, which is what AIP was known as in those days, and I went up to see Jim Nicholson, who was a wonderful man. Strangely enough, he knew me as a writer, I don't know why or how, and he'd heard of my association with Ernie Kovacs—he was a Kovacs fan. Of the two, Nicholson and Sam Arkoff, I felt that Jim was the more literate. There was Arkoff, puffing his big brown cigar and pontificating on the lack of art in the business, but really not doing anything *but* business, and Jim, really being involved in film. Jim truly loved film, and he also loved horror—he was the one who came up with the idea of doing the Edgar Allan Poe films. He was doing all these pictures with no money; we were doing things with spit and pennies, and nothing more.

So it was Nicholson that initially got you aboard.

He said, "Look, I'd like to ease you into the company, but horror is a very involved thing and you don't know that much about it. But you're funny. Can you write a funny script?" I said, "Of course I can." He said, "In two weeks?"

Previous page: Louis M. Heyward, who made the switch from TV comedy to AIP fright films, proving that the line between comedy and horror was often thin indeed.

The first one I did for him was called *Pajama Party*. I tried to write this particular thing as a cartoon and indeed, if you look at it, it's done almost in cartoon cuts, in four-strips. That was a large part of it.

Did you know in advance, on a picture like Pajama Party, *who would be playing the various parts?*
You could never be sure. It was dependent on the budget, and the budgets were sometimes virtually non-existent. If an actor was out of work and hungry enough, you were going to get him—that's substantially what we fed on at AIP. I knew that I wanted Buster Keaton; I had used him when I was doing *The Faye Emerson Show* way back when, and he and I became friendly. I regarded him as a wild genius that nobody really appreciated. (They've rediscovered him since.) I sat down with him and we worked out gags.

Were these beach pictures as much fun to make as they seemed to be on the screen?
It was the old "Hey, kids, let's put on a show!" atmosphere. It was great, because everybody contributed. It wasn't you standing there alone and naked with your two weeks' or three weeks' worth of script; everybody pitched in and came by with ideas. This was wonderful, it was "the old college try."

Pajama Party *is sort of like the* Mork and Mindy *of the '60s.*
Yes, it pretty much was. At the time, I was very pleased with the way the picture turned out, and it did well financially, for its price and for its time.

Both of the beach pictures you wrote incorporated SF or horror elements.
I also did *Sergeant Deadhead*, which had a lot of science fiction to it. I grew up on horror and science fiction films; as a matter of fact, as a high school kid I was adapting Edgar Allan Poe to radio. I sold the same *Tell-Tale Heart* three times, to three different buyers *[laughs]*!

In writing The Ghost in the Invisible Bikini, *did you anticipate that Basil Rathbone and Boris Karloff would be in the cast?*
That I knew, and I knew that Susan Hart would be in it. She was Jim Nicholson's girlfriend. I had met her at a party: I sidled up to her and I said, "Whose girl are you?" She pointed with her eyes, I turned around and there was Nicholson, and he said, "Mine. Lay off. She's in the next picture."
I want to jump ahead. Jim said to me one day, "We're doing *Dr. Goldfoot and the Bikini Machine*," and I said, "What's the story?" He said, "You're the writer, I want *you* to tell *me* the story! But I got an idea. Vincent Price is a crazy scientist, and he's got a machine that turns out rowboats." I waited a proper period, because I'm not about to contradict the president of the company, but finally I said, "Rowboats?" and he said, "Yeah." And I waited again *[laughs]*! "Jim, I don't mean to be disrespectful, I think it's a great idea, but I've never

Torn between two lovers (Aron Kincaid, *left,* and unidentified ghoul, *right*), Nancy Sinatra doesn't know whether to laugh or cry. An amazingly bad posed shot from the even-worse *The Ghost in the Invisible Bikini.*

seen a rowboat machine." He said, "Not rowboats! *Rowboats!*" I said, "Jim. Help me." He spelled it out: "R-o-b-o-t-s. Rowboats!"

Susan's acting talents at that time were limited. I later discovered that the reason that he wanted "rowboats" in the picture was ... the ... way ... she ... moved ... her ... arms ... and ... the ... way ... she ... walked ... and ... turned—she *needed* to play a rowboat!

Where were these AIP pictures shot?

We shot them at Producers Studio for the most part, where we had what we used to refer to as a leftover deal. Any sets that people had used in prior shooting, that were not hauled away or destroyed, we had the right to use. It was a grungy studio—oh, God, you couldn't walk there barefoot, because the floors were wood and splintery. A lot was lacking, but the spirit was there, and I think that was a large key to AIP's success. There were times when Jim would say, "Hey, come down with me and let's look at the sets that are left over," and two or three weeks later, we'd have a script.

What kind of input did Sam Arkoff have?

During those years, precious little; he stayed in the background and let Jim carry the ball. Remember, it was initially Jim's company, and then Sam came into it as Jim's lawyer and then as Jim's partner. During the period when I joined them, Jim had the big office and Sam had the ancillary office nearby. It wasn't until Jim left the company that Sam took over command functions.

Did you meet Basil Rathbone on Invisible Bikini?

Of course. I had a horrible experience with him, because I have a penchant for twisting names in my mind; I am aware of it and I don't want it to happen, and I said to myself, "I must *not* say Mr. Nosebone." So when we were introduced, I said, "I'm so pleased to meet you, Mr. Nosebone," and he glared along that bony nose of his and said, "Are you making jest of me, sir?" And relationships were strained for the first few weeks thereafter!

How about Boris Karloff?

The Boris Karloff I knew was a studious, delightful, funny funny *funny* fellow, and I don't think anybody has talked about him being funny! He had a wry sense of humor, and he would say sly, funny things. By "sly," I don't mean "naughty," they were just cute, they were words within words, totally encapsuled. If you understood it, great, and if you didn't, also great. When he found that I understood almost half of his little secret jokes, he would nod his head and his eyes would twinkle, which was a kind of precious thing to have with him. Now, skip a number of years. When I used him in England, on *The Crimson Cult,* he was confined to a wheelchair and I was told we could not get insurance. I've been told that with a number of people. I said, "Screw it. Here is one of the greats of our time. He goes on." And no one came in as well prepared as Boris. He was the consummate, thorough professional, with respect for his craft and respect for his fellow workers. He was just a total delight to be with.

Your first encounter with Karloff was on Invisible Bikini, *right?*

No, I had written a script where he was a babysitter for radio, and he played the part of the babysitter with his lisp. He was cute and he was funny. He wanted to do comedy.

He got chances on TV, but almost never in movies.

The comedy that he did in TV was at his own expense, it wasn't with "precious words." He poked fun at what he had become, and that to me is sad comedy.

What kind of shape were Rathbone and Karloff in on Invisible Bikini?

They both moved well. Rathbone moved almost like an aging athlete, he did have a grace and style to him. He had tremendous panache.

What do you think of Invisible Bikini *today?*

I just saw it again very recently and it was bad—*unbelievably* bad! It left me in a state of shock.

What kind of money went into these movies?

Pajama Party I'd say we did for about $200,000, *Invisible Bikini* about the same, maybe a bit less. I wasn't really happy with *Invisible Bikini,* it was a "created" picture. There was no reason for it to be made, other than Jim's trying to prove that he could make Susan Hart into a star.

How did you get involved on War-Gods of the Deep?

I was here in the United States, doing whatever nonsense I was doing for AIP. *War-Gods* was being shot in England and they ran into problems with the then-producer. I don't remember his name, but he was English and he was causing some sort of problem. I called, and he said, "Dear lad, the script's impossible." I said, "*Most* of our scripts are impossible!" (And the ones that weren't impossible were improbable!) He said, "I cannot possibly shoot." So I went to Sam Arkoff and I said, "Sam, we are having genuine trouble." Sam clutched his breast and said, "It's gonna cost money!" *[laughs]*, and I said, "Yes. They don't like the script." He said, "Well, dictate something over the phone."

I said, "Sam, that isn't the way you do scripts. I've got to see what they've shot, see how I can blend whatever it is that I'm going to write into it, find out what's lacking." So I went to England, and found there was a war between [co-producer] Dan Haller and the English producer, which is always very, very destructive. And they were getting nowhere. Dan Haller had been a scenic designer prior to this, and a protege of Jim Nicholson's. Dan was an extremely good scenic designer, and he came up with some awfully good sets on *War-Gods.*

Did you end up reworking the screenplay?

Yes, I did. The one thing that I felt was missing was humor, and that's where the chicken appeared. There was no chicken in the script, so I wrote it in along with the David Tomlinson character. Tomlinson was enjoying great vogue at that time because he had just done *Mary Poppins* [1964] for Disney. At the point when the English producer saw that I had written in a chicken, and knew that whatever I wrote was going in, he quit—he said, "I don't do chicken pictures!" And Dan Haller took over the reins.

Did things go smoothly after that?

No, there were continuous problems there, because Dan at that time did not really know how to do what Sam used to refer to as "take over the power." I called Sam and said, "Okay, I've completed the rewrite, but I think I better stay here 'til the picture is finished." Again, I had a mental picture of him clutching his breast and thinking in terms of dollars, but I did stay, because there had to be someone backing up Dan. Dan turned into a very good producer later, but he couldn't do it alone in the face of an English crew who probably resented the fact that the other producer had walked off.

Where does Jacques Tourneur fit into all of this?

Poor Jacques! Jacques was, again, at the nadir of his career, but he wanted to direct another picture or two. He was overly agreeable, and there was a sadness to that. At AIP, it was the same with directors as with actors. If you were a young director, AIP was giving you a chance; if you were an old director, your career was on its way down when we inherited you. You were usually afraid to fight because it would influence the next picture. But face Jacques with a technical problem and he would come up with answers. He knew his craft and he knew his media.

What was the point in continuing to stick Poe's name on all these movies that had absolutely nothing to do with him?

As I recall it, Jim Nicholson had a vision. He believed in television, and thought that if he could get together enough Edgar Allan Poe movies, he'd have a television series. I admired him for being a visionary, which he very much was. There'd be times when he'd come into my office with advertising for a picture, magnificent advertising. But the picture didn't exist, the script didn't exist, we hadn't cast it! He sold on the basis of advertising. He was enough to inspire you with his own enthusiasm for things.

War-Gods of the Deep *has a Jules Verne flavor.*

It felt *very* Jules Verne, and *to* whom did we attribute it? Poe. This was Jim. Give him any script — *Broadway Melody of 1938 [laughs]* — and he'd derive the title from an obscure Edgar Allan Poe sonnet! And you could always find something to validate it — if you're easily satisfied!

Did you know the original War-Gods *screenwriter, Charles Bennett?*

Oh, yes. The screenwriters out here, most of us know one another, and it's senseless to attempt to work with someone unless you get along. I had a number of meetings with Charlie, and in fact I worked with him on another picture shortly thereafter. He did as good a job as he could. I remember that Charles's credits were very heavy and he was used to working for the majors, so when I said to Charles, "You've got two and a half weeks to do this script," a little question mark lit up in the middle of each eyeball *[laughs]*! He said, "You mean for corrections?" and I said, "Not for corrections — to do the *script!*" So we worked on that one together, and he did as good a job as any man could do under the circumstances and for the money.

Did anyone actually sit down and read any of these Poe stories or poems for ideas?

No. *No. No-ooo-ooo [laughs]*!

What do you think of War-Gods of the Deep?
   There was a lot that was satisfying. The worst thing in it was my own contribution. The chicken didn't belong there in a diver's helmet, not really *[laughs]*. It was insanity. But that's the way we were doing things. There never was any time, there always was a crisis.

Did you enjoy working with Vincent Price throughout this period?
   We had a thing. I collect art, have collected since I was 14. I bought my first Paul Klee, my first Henry Moore when I was a kid, and paid for 'em five dollars a week. Vincent of course is famed as an art collector, and so we started talking art. I also enjoy cooking, and Vincent is well known for that. So Vincent and I had a community of interests to keep us busy talking between takes. Occasionally he would read a line, then look at me and say, "Deke—dear, sweet Deke—you are screwing my career into the ground!" And indeed I may have *[laughs]*! But I appreciated his frankness about it. He was a delight to work with.

That was about the time you started getting involved in AIP's overseas production.
   It was just the beginning of co-productions and films acquiring their own nationalities and having a life of their own. If you were an Italian picture, great, they could show you in Italy and derive benefits therefrom. If you were a German picture, they could show you in Germany, and so on and so forth through the countries of Europe. But then someone said, "Hey, what if a picture is both German *and* Italian?" And then somehow laws were passed there that allowed you to say, "With American participation." So if an American production company came in with, say, one-quarter of the money and sold off bits and pieces to various countries, it could walk back and get the entire western hemisphere. Put down 25 percent of a picture and bring along a star with whom you have a contract, and you were in business!

And the picture would play in all those other countries, too.
   That's right. The advantages in shooting there were, one, prices were lower; two, very little union problem; and, three, the fact that you could give the picture a series of nationalities that would lower the cost of a picture below what we could do here.

What was the story on Planet of the Vampires?
   Planet of the Vampires was Mario Bava, shot at Cinecitta in Rome. Again,

Opposite: AIP's *War-Gods of the Deep* was Jules Verne-ish in flavor, but AIP prexy Jim Nicholson insisted on marketing it as a Poe film.

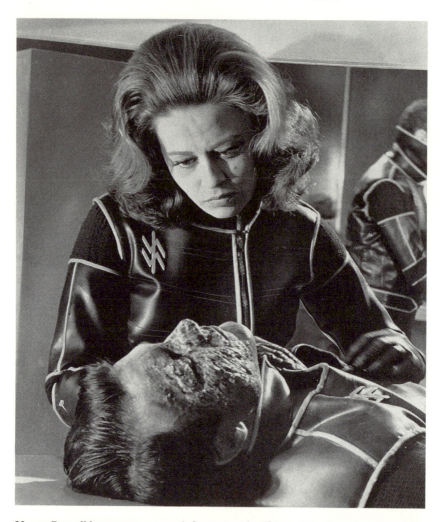

Norma Bengell hovers over a mangled astronaut in *Planet of the Vampires*. According to Heyward, Mario Bava's "hots" for Bengell may have caused trouble on the *Vampires* set.

I think there were a lot of strange things going on. At that time Mario, genius that he was, was undergoing a number of problems, one a typical Italian mental dichotomy between girlfriend and wife. It bothered him during this period; he was a mass of guilts and he wasn't even Jewish. I think that may have interfered with the tempo of his shooting. On *Planet of the Vampires* we had Norma Bengell, a Brazilian lady with enormous boobs—which I think were a testimonial to her talent *[laughs]*. She could only speak Portuguese. And I think Mario fancied *her,* too! It turned into a real mishmash, a disaster. I was rewriting the Italian script day by day, virtually line by line. As an executive of a company you do a helluva lot of rewriting and you do producing; you fill in in all ways. I would go to the Italian producer, Fulvio Lucisano, and say, "Look, the lady is standing behind the man naked. What is the sense, what is the motivation?" And Fulvio would look at me sagely, rub the side of his nose and say, "She's a-wanna have something to do with him!" Well, *that* I could have figured out, I think, given time *[laughs]*! But it was not good writing. So we had to get rid of these extraneous things which appealed then to the Italian market and the Japanese market, where they wanted to see as many naked ladies as they could at one time. I was busy taking naked ladies out and he was putting naked ladies in!

You also had Ib Melchior over there helping out.
　　Ib was wonderful. Ib is a very competent, very good writer, and he was an enormous help. When we originally got that script in, it was a typical Italian script on long sheets of paper, larger than legal, divided into audio on one side and video on the other, and an Italian student's translation into English. Nothing ever made any sense, and Ib was forced to try and make sense out of the first draft. And he did as good a job as he was capable of. We had not worked together before, but he was a delight and we became close personal friends.

That was an AIP co-production, of course.
　　AIP, American participation; Fulvio Lucisano, for Italian International; there was a German company involved; and somehow I think there was a South American company involved. It was a Tower of Babel, because we were shooting virtually silent at the time, everything to be dubbed into English. There'd be one voice talking in Portuguese, another in Italian, another in German, and there was no communication, just a lot of facial writhings. Barry Sullivan was the star of the American version; each company star-billed the player that was important to their country. In fact, we had to try for line balancing: "Your star has got more lines than my star!" "Okay, I'll trade you two of my star's lines for one of yours." Which ain't the way pictures should be made. And they ain't never gonna be made that way again *[laughs]*!

Was Mario Bava better to work with on Dr. Goldfoot and the Girl Bombs?
　　Emotionally, yes; craft-wise, sometimes superb, like on his glass shots. He was great, he would paint them himself. But then there were periods of extreme forgetfulness—he'd forget what he had shot the night before, and so how do we match it the next day? There would be fights, and you had to wait until the dailies came back and you could match it.

You worked without credit on Dr. Goldfoot and the Bikini Machine.
　　I did. Robert Kaufman's name was on that as writer; I brought in [director] Norman Taurog, who was a personal friend, and we screwed *his* career into

the ground! In Italy I did the rewrite on Kaufman's script, but I didn't take a credit on that one.

You don't know the number of pictures I've done. I've been on over 80 films. But you don't always get credit. You do a tremendous rewrite, and I would say under the Writers Guild here you would be entitled to credit. But Sam Arkoff would say, "What do you want credit for? I *pay* you, don't I?"

Was that first Goldfoot *film really successful enough to warrant a sequel?*
It didn't take that much. Remember, we were grinding these things out. That may have cost $300,000, and if we grossed $2,000,000, there was a lot of profit in it. Also remember that we were grinding out a lot of them a year.

You also did some borderline horror and SF films like The Glass Sphinx *and* House of a Thousand Dolls.
I remember a lot about *The Glass Sphinx.* I loved the adventure of going to Egypt, and I loved working with Robert Taylor and Anita Ekberg. While I was in Egypt I had (with the government's permission) entered two or three tombs that had been sealed. I was also given handfuls of scarabs, with hieroglyphics on them! *Glass Sphinx* was with Fulvio Lucisano and, again, there were day-to-day rewrites. But my compensation was in looking at what to me was a living legend, namely Robert Taylor.

House of a Thousand Dolls we shot in Madrid, in a palace that had belonged to a Spanish prince who was a member of the House of Hapsburg. The palace had later turned into a whorehouse, which was kind of setting the pattern for what the picture was about. And I remember the casting of the B-girls, at various of the gin mills in Madrid *[laughs]*! Vincent Price approached me when we had about five girls there and he whispered, "Deke, please, give 'em some garlic. They *stink!*" Which is beautifully anomalous to me! *Thousand Dolls* was done in partnership with Harry Alan Towers. We had some horny scenes in there, and I wondered how we got away with it—there was a lot of nudity in *Thousand Dolls* that was excised for the American version.

One day I come onto the set, which is a jail set, and I see a guy with a stovepipe hat ... a beard ... a wart on the left side of his face ... and a frock coat. And I'm struggling to think of the scene to be shot, because standing before me is Abraham Lincoln! I go over to Harry and I say, "Harry, what are we shooting?" and he says, "Just be calm." What had happened was, he had a copy of the script of *Abe Lincoln in Illinois* that he had submitted to the Spanish censors to get permission to shoot. And whenever the censor came by, there was this fucking Abe Lincoln walking back and forth *[laughs]*!

Your most famous AIP film is probably Conqueror Worm.
I had just gone over to England on a permanent deal as a result of a conversation I had with Sam Arkoff. I told him, "Look, I'm running around like

Behind the scenes on *Conqueror Worm*. *Top:* Vincent Price consults with the "real" witch hired by Heyward as a technical advisor for the film. *Bottom, left–right:* Heyward, Price and Sam Arkoff huddle between takes.

a doctor, fixing things that shouldn't have to be fixed, they should be right in the first place. I'm putting Band-Aids where 35mm film should be. And this is wrong. Why don't we open an English office?" Sam was very wise, and he saw the possibilities of this. And he had a strong ally in Fulvio Lucisano in Italy. To show how close they were as friends, Sam went on Fulvio's honeymoon with him *[laughs]*, which I never really understood! So we opened an office in London, right opposite the American Embassy—a gorgeous townhouse.

Now this is how *Conqueror Worm* came about. There was an English producer named Tony Tenser. Tony had [director] Michael Reeves, about whom I really had not heard anything except just a few whisperings; he had a script called *Witchfinder General,* which was in some sort of condition but not completely correct; and he had some good locations scouted. What he *didn't* have was the full amount of money for total production, and he didn't have a star. We had a contract with Vincent Price, so what we did was make a trade: We gave 'em Vincent Price and a few dollars, and in exchange we got western hemisphere distribution rights.

Did you have confidence that a director as young as Reeves could pull it off?

Not initially, but a very strange thing happened in our relationship. I was very dubious of him, and I exerted a lot of controls. But little by little we developed a relationship that to me was a very touching thing. He virtually became my son. After the picture was completed, he'd come to my office in the penthouse there, and just sit on the floor. He'd say, "I just like being here. I like being with you. I like to be around. Is it all right? Am I bothering you?" It was sad.

Ian Ogilvy was in all three of Reeves's pictures. Do you remember knowing him?

I thought Ian was tremendous, and that he deserved a much bigger career than he's enjoyed. I thought he would become the ultimate Bond, that he had the capacity of being the next Olivier. And yet somehow his agents did not guide his career correctly, in my opinion.

What other memories do you have of Conqueror Worm?

We had a girl named Hilary Dwyer on *Conqueror Worm,* the typical English rose, and Tony Tenser was fighting for a nude scene. I have spent a large part of my career concealing nipples, and with this particular English rose I did *not* want to shoot her nipples. Michael also did not want to do the nude scene, there was no necessity for it. At a point where Vincent was supposed to be plucking at some child's breasts, I could see Michael getting very tense and very tight, and I became conscious that there was a problem of some kind. That required my going over to him and giving him a nip in the back of the neck and saying, "Hey, everything's all right, you're doing a beautiful job. If it bothers you to shoot this, we'll change it. Let me know, let me be the bad guy." I think that was what solidified our friendship.

Did anyone worry during production that the film might not get past the censors?
　　The English did; we didn't. The English censorship was very heavy at that time, violence more than nudity. Poor Tony Tenser would run with edited clips to the English censor, daily—"Hey, can I do this? Can I do that?" Yes, there was a lot of worry.

Was Conqueror Worm *a success right away?*
　　In the United States, yes; in England, after all of the horrified letters came in to *The London Times,* yes. In Germany it was so successful that, two weeks after we delivered the prints to the distributor, a bootleg company came out with *Conqueror Worm II [laughs]*!

It's become fashionable to say that Reeves would have gone on to become a major talent.
　　I couldn't agree more. He was wonderful. He saw pictures in his head, which is what good directors do; he knew what the pictures would be before he shot them. *Conqueror Worm* was made for $175,000 and it didn't look it; at the time, it looked rich and full and complete to me. That was thanks to the genius of Michael Reeves. I think *Conqueror Worm* is a good film for that genre and that time, and it may be one of the better things that Vincent Price has done.
　　Michael and I started talking, post–*Conqueror Worm,* about doing *De Sade.* I had a vision on *De Sade* and I wanted to do the picture desperately, to accommodate the vision. I described scenes that I would like to have written and scenes I'd liked to have shot, and I could get very enthusiastic about them. *De Sade* started with a dream of mine—it may have been an erotic, self-pleasuring dream. I had an idea of a marble floor with a number of naked female bodies on it, and a pair of boots walking amongst the naked bodies. That's as far as I went. It tied into the Marquis De Sade because I was interested not in what he had done, but why he had done it. Also, I was interested in experimenting on a number of time levels. I broached it to Nicholson, and when you say Marquis De Sade to an exploitation king, he has got to respond. And I felt there was only one person who could write it, and that was Richard Matheson [q.v.]. Matheson did not want to write horror, which suited my purposes entirely. I've got to tell you that of every script I've held in my hands, his script for *De Sade* has got to be one of the best; if there are any fuck-ups in it, it's my fault, and in no way do they reflect on the writer, who in my opinion did a beautiful job in handling time. I recently reread the script and it's a good script, fine writing.

Once Michael Reeves died, Cy Endfield got the picture.

Reeves really was never in the picture 'cause there was no script when Reeves was alive. Just my concept of naked bodies and boots behind the opening titles — that's all that existed. Endfield had directed *Zulu* [1964], which was a brilliant piece of picturemaking. I should have wondered why he agreed so readily to do *De Sade* — apparently he had been having difficulty getting work, and I do not know the reason. Also, a mistake on my part: I should have examined more carefully the content of his other films, to see if he could handle the sexual aspects and if he could handle things of moderate delicacy in terms of time. I did not.

Move ahead. We are shooting in Germany (West Berlin for the most part, but other locations as well), and running fairly much on schedule, which is the one thing I always prided myself on. Then, as we approached the sexual scenes, there was a slowing-down. I came on the set one cold morning and there were about twenty naked girls sitting around doing nothing. And Endfield was there playing a recorder. I said to myself, "Oh, dear God, we're in trouble." We lost almost a day's shooting. I got on the phone and told Arkoff, "Sam, I think we're facing a problem." Next day I come on the set and we're falling *further* behind. And I suddenly realize that Endfield, for whatever reason, either did not want to do the orgies, or was incapable of handling them, or distressed at being faced with them. Or perhaps he felt then as I feel now: that they were out of place. But he wasn't working, and every day you don't work, you're losing money. Then Endfield caught the flu, and he was sent to the hospital. All we had left to do were the orgy scenes. I told Sam I would do the setups on them, and that he should send over Roger Corman to finish directing. That's eventually what happened. We sent Endfield the rushes, at the hospital, every day.

How much contact did you have with Corman throughout those AIP years?

We were old buddies from AIP from the West Coast and it was my request that he come out to Germany. I respect Roger totally. He is a fast craftsman. You go to McDonald's and you get the masterpiece of hamburgers, the best one of which they're capable. Roger does that with pictures. We had talks before this on *The Wild Angels* [1966], which was an initial concept of Jim Nicholson's. I went out to do the research on it and came back with tons and tons of it. I also did research on *The Trip* [1967], which was an original concept of mine that Corman changed totally because he was working with Jack Nicholson at the time. Which is fine — I get no credit on it, and I don't deserve any. Roger Corman was charming and wonderful, and good to be with.

De Sade was another of your international co-productions.

We had a partner named Arthur Brauner who put up half the money, and he was co-executive producer or co-producer, I don't remember. (I don't remember what *I* was!) Arthur Brauner was a wonderful partner and a good fellow. A Jew who had escaped from a concentration camp, he was owner of the CCC Studios in Berlin, which is where they made the gas which killed the Jews. It was kind of an ironic thing: Arthur, escaping from the concentration camp, came out with hundreds of pairs of shoes that he had taken off dead bodies, went to Berlin, sold them and parlayed that into the studios and a real estate fortune.

You could always josh or jolly Arthur into going along with you, with a little bit of caviar and German champagne, which is about the foulest thing known to man or God. He would cry into the caviar, which Heaven knows was salty enough, then agree to another $25,000, $50,000, a few more days of shooting or whatever. Remember the pin that De Sade wore, shaped like a figure-eight—the snake swallowing its own tail? I had drawn a sketch of it which Arthur took to a local jeweler, and he was going to have it cast in *[laughs]* some kind of cheap tin compound, and then dip it to make it look like gold. I said, "Arthur, it has to be gold." He said, "For a movie it doesn't have to be gold!" I said, "It *does*. Think of the actor's psyche." A little question mark lit up in the middle of each eyeball—"What's a psyche? I'm not gonna argue with this guy." He said, "All right, it can be gold." Then I said, "And I want real rubies, too." He cried out, "You're meshugana!" but I got my way. 'Cause in the back of my little head was the idea, I was either gonna steal it or buy it back for my then-wife, whoever she may have been *[laughs]*!

Speaking of your star's psyche, how did you like Keir Dullea?

Keir Dullea had a problem on this picture in that he had just gotten engaged, and had brought along his fiancée. I could not bar her from the set, but for her to sit there through the nude scenes was very hard. She would always go over to Keir at the end of a take and say, "Keir, you don't have to be so *close!*" or "Keir, you're *touching* her!" It got to be a bit of a problem. Keir was good to work with, he came in prepared, but I always had the feeling he felt he was above the picture.

And how about John Huston?

John Huston was wonderful. He and I would sit in a gin mill at night, pouring down the wee drops. He was an Egyptologist. Remember those Egyptian scarabs I told you about before, when we were talking about *The Glass Sphinx?* I would take them down to the gin mill at the Berlin Hilton, and with his Irish charm Huston would read me the hieroglyphics, which always knocked me for a loop. Here is a drinking Irishman, reading hieroglyphics *[laughs]*! As an actor, he handled himself well. I went to him when I was having the problem with Endfield and I said, "John, how do I handle this?" He looked at me with some love, because he had a sense of humor and we knew the same Irish drinking songs and we had a very strong rapport. He said, "Dear Deke, you hired me as an *ac-tor*." That last word was in italics and underlined; the meaning was, "Hey, don't ask me about directors—we have our own fellowship." I had to respect that.

Richard Matheson told me that Huston later said to Jim Nicholson, "Why didn't you ask me to direct De Sade?"

I wonder if he would have. If he had, he would have done a superb job, I think.

Was De Sade *a moneymaker?*

It was a moneymaker, but not as much as it could have been. Most of the things we did were moneymakers, because we brought 'em in for such low budgets. Is it the picture I wanted it to be? No. Is it the picture it *could* have been? No. A lot of mistakes were made, but with my name on it as producer, I've got to accept the brunt of it. Those orgies didn't belong in there and that irks me to this day. They lessened the quality of the picture.

Although they weren't released here until 1970, you also did The Crimson Cult *and* Horror House *around this same time.*

That was Tony Tenser again—Tigon Productions. My involvement on *The Crimson Cult* was the rewrite of the script; the bringing-in of the American elements; sitting on it to the degree that we controlled the budget, and AIP could not be penalized if it *did* go over-budget. But creatively, not that much. Tony Tenser didn't do that much, either. Vernon Sewell was an extremely capable director whom you trusted to run with the ball.

What do you recall about Christopher Lee and Barbara Steele?

Christopher Lee was a personal friend, and still is. He's a dear, sweet man of many talents, easy to work with, has a charming wife and I love him. Barbara Steele I really don't remember, I just know that there were mutterings about someone who was modestly notorious. But what she was notorious *for* I never could quite figure out *[laughs]*!

The Crimson Cult *is the picture where Karloff had to shoot scenes outdoors in cold weather, and caught the cold that killed him.*

If it was so, I was not aware of it. I am strongly disinclined to believe it. However, Karloff was a good enough person and a strong enough actor that if he were told to sit outside, he would sit outside. Like a good soldier, he would not abandon his post, so it is within the realm of possibility. I never heard that before, but if it is so, it's sad.

And Horror House?

I have no recollection of it; a merciful Heaven has struck me amnesiac with regard to it.

Boris Karloff's death resulted from the cold he caught on the set of *The Crimson Cult*, prompting AIP publicists to (falsely) play up the film as the actor's final role.

The Oblong Box was originally supposed to be shot in Ireland, with Michael Reeves directing, so it was Reeves's death—that got Gordon Hessler [q.v.] the picture. And he stepped in with maybe two days' notice, and we did it in England, on location. Gordon always turns in a workmanlike job. In *Scream and Scream Again* he did shots that are impossible—you would swear Hitchcock had done them. The pull-backs and the follow-throughs in the police station—shots like that are destructive to a director's stomach, and he *did* 'em! I had known Gordon from my days at Universal, when he was

Hitchcock's protégé. I realized how good Gordon was, and I had a script called *The Oblong Box*—again, nothing to do with Edgar Allan Poe *[laughs]*! In trying to get this picture in on budget and on schedule, knowing Gordon as a quick director, I propositioned him to do it for an infinitely small sum. He accepted it. But Gordon is a little more than a director, he also happens to be a tremendous producer and a tremendous respecter of budgets. Once you tell him a budget, he will keep it inviolate. Gordon saved my ass on that picture, because we didn't have the money to do it. Gordon pulled that picture through.

Price was pretty disgruntled about the quality of some of the later AIP scripts, and in fact he feuded with Arkoff about it.
   This is very possible. Arkoff at times was difficult to get along with, and so was Vincent, in his own way. There is an alternative, however. If Vincent did not like the scripts, he either had to tell me, "I would like a rewrite on it," and I would have obliged him; or, he could have told Arkoff, "I don't want to do it." You can't bitch about a script after it's made.

Arkoff told me that he was bummed by how frugal Price could be.
   What we would do is pay Vincent X-number of dollars, whatever the fee was—not great, but considerable. Vincent would breeze into London, not spend a penny on lunches or dinners, expecting you to take him out. That's fine. I remember one day when I was picking him up at this little hotel near the railroad terminal in London. I was up in the room waiting for him. I said, "Vincent, where's the lavatory?" and he said, "It's down the hall, dear chap." I said *[reprovingly]*, "Vincent...!" and he said, "Have you considered how little time you spend in the toilet? There's no sense in paying for it." That was his attitude. But what he would do—and he would very proudly recount it to anyone who would listen—was save as much money as he could, and then go on an art-buying spree at the end of the picture.

What do you remember about Cry of the Banshee?
   That was Gordon again, Gordon with his wild, wild enthusiasm. We had Essy Persson in *Cry of the Banshee*, and she had just come off *I Am Curious—Yellow* [1968]. We had a rape scene in *Banshee*, it was in the script and she knew it beforehand, and I told her we had to have a nude scene there. But after having done *I Am Curious—Yellow* in Scandinavia, she wouldn't take her clothes off for Gordon so the guy could rape her! And I'll tell you, it made Gordon into a total nervous wreck. So in that scene there are some very goofy camera angles concealing the fact that she is not exposed at all.

Was she difficult in general?
   In that we had a language barrier. She spoke some English but it was difficult to understand. We also had Elisabeth Bergner in there, making her

first picture in like 30 years. Why she would do a picture like *Cry of the Banshee,* I don't know. Actually, as I remember it, I don't think the picture was that bad—it could have been worse. Which is about the best you can say for most of the AIP pictures *[laughs]*!

Where in the world did all these half-assed scripts come from?

[Laughs.] Most of 'em came from Hollywood. They would send us scripts that couldn't be shot, *shouldn't* be shot, and yet we had to fill a schedule for the distribution arm.

Is it tough to care about the quality of your pictures, when your own bosses have this sort of hit-and-run attitude?

Not for me it wasn't. I prided myself on doing the best I could with whatever I did. When I did *Ernie Kovacs,* it was the best show of its kind; when I did *Garry Moore,* it was the best show of *its* kind; the same thing when I produced *The Dick Clark Show.* I busted my ass to do the best job of which I was capable, whether or not the people involved were concerned with quality. AIP was an atypical case in that they had to feed that enormous distribution machine, and I think that was their prime concern.

Hessler and Chris Wicking did an extensive rewrite on Banshee, *but said that you couldn't allow him to shoot that version.*

I can tell you that whatever Gordon tried to put together was probably infinitely better than what we went with. But there was a problem with Nicholson at that time—he wanted, "No more changes! No more changes!"

AIP tried to promote two of Price's movies as his 100th, Abominable Dr. Phibes *and* Cry of the Banshee.

This is most probably one of Jim's promotions, and I'm surprised he didn't do it several more times. And let me also add that I'm sure *neither* picture was Vincent's 100th *[laughs]*!

How much contact did you have with Milton Subotsky and Max Rosenberg (Amicus Pictures) in making Scream and Scream Again?

A lot. They brought in the project, which was a paperback, and they were two guys full of enthusiasm. If I recall correctly, I had Subotsky thrown off the set, and Rosenberg allowed to come on. I felt there was too much interference going on. They were earnest, they were well-meaning, but they got in the way of production. I didn't have that much traffic with them, but it was very difficult. I don't bar people from sets too frequently, but when you're trying to protect time and a budget, you have no recourse. You can't fight about the little things.

Gordon Hessler says Subotsky's initial script was so bad it was unusable.

Chris Wicking was brought in and together with Gordon they fixed it. Because it was a script that had not come from Hollywood, we could get away with tinkering with it. I was protecting the future I hoped to have when I left AIP *[laughs]*!

It was your idea to put all three of the horror kings — Price, Lee and Cushing — into Scream and Scream Again. *Did it work well?*
Not as well as it could have. It was interesting to have them all in the same film, but they should have had contretemps between them, utilizing all three in one scene in a face-to-face showdown. But there was no way of doing it. We just brought them in to take advantage of the names, for marquee value.

Cushing was the one that got the short end of the stick.
He really did. I played that film just the other night and I asked myself, "Why did he accept it?" I think the reason is, the British are so damn nice as actors — again, they're good soldiers and they'll do what they're told. They're dear sweet people and they're professionals.

Any other Scream and Scream Again *anecdotes?*
I felt Michael Gothard was going to be the biggest thing that ever happened. He had that insane look and that drive, and he was wonderful. Here is a kid who really threw himself into the picture wholeheartedly. Do you remember the scene where he appears to be walking up the cliff? That's a stunt that, as an actor, I would not have agreed to; I'd say, "Hey, get a double or get a dummy. I ain't either one." But the kid agreed to do it, without a double — he was that driven. He had a lot of class and a lot of style. Gordon came up with the idea of using an overhead cable to give that illusion of his walking up the cliff.

What did you contribute to The Vampire Lovers?
Vampire Lovers was done with Hammer — Jimmy Carreras. I was allowed first look at the girls who were to be nude, as a courtesy, and I think that was the limit of my involvement with it *[laughs]*! Hammer was like a ship without a rudder; they were reduced to, "The script doesn't mean anything, the picture doesn't mean anything, it's the deal." It was a question of, "Can we crank out *one* more picture? *Two* more pictures?" I don't think anybody really cared. And that's a pity, because it was a good house at one time. We kind of stumbled through that picture; I had precious little to do with it other than playing floor monitor, protecting the money again.

Why was Murders in the Rue Morgue *shot in Spain?*
Budget. That was a Spanish-Italian-German co-production, and we shot in Spain because Spain was the signatory country. Lilli Palmer and Jason

Heyward felt that the Hammer Film company was on its last legs by the time he got around to collaborating on *The Vampire Lovers*. (Peter Cushing and Ingrid Pitt are pictured.)

Robards would sit down in a gin mill and they would talk fine points of acting to a degree that was well beyond my knowledge or ken. They both knew more about acting than I, a poor, lowly, self-appointed producer, did, and there were impassioned discussions. I think Herbert Lom was having wife problems at the time; he was married to an English lady agent, and he was more concerned with his domestic life than with his craft. Gordon Hessler filled the opera house (I believe it was in Seville) with a group of gypsy-extras, and he got them all to work for free by giving away a refrigerator. He called me and said, "I'm giving away a refrigerator," and I said, "But there's no electricity in the gypsy caves!" He said, "It makes no difference. This one has no motor!" *[Laughs.]*

This was another of those slapdash Hollywood scripts.

Right. It arrived in the mail in one form and Chris Wicking did a job on it. He was a good rewrite man.

AIP Hessler says re-edited that picture, making it incomprehensible.
That's correct. They didn't understand what Gordon was trying for. Gordon had a lot of dream sequence effects in there that were integral to the story, and once they cut out the background they destroyed the story.

Sounds like De Sade *all over again.*
You betcha.

Most of these later AIPs have quite a nasty edge, and probably could have used a bit of humor.
You're totally correct. As I said, they would find a script in America and send it to us in England, and they would not look kindly upon rewrites. I think it was Jim, protecting what he considered his sense of integrity. And he did have it—I'm not demeaning Jim in any way. Jim was a guy who came out of nowhere and started making pictures instead of talking about making pictures, and you gotta give credit to the guys who really make them. I think he felt each script was like a personal possession—"This is my script. Even though I didn't write it, I found it and I'm sending it to you to make." Now, they could not interfere in a thing like *Conqueror Worm,* on which I'd say I did a 50 percent rewrite, because that was a script that was in existence over here. They had no idea what the script was, they only had an idea of what the deal was. This was during the period when the deal was as important as the script, which is a fairly interesting concept. "We need a film, 90 minutes of screen time—whatcha got?" That's the way things were working.

However, I am now in England a couple years, there's a feeling of power that is growing within me, and I had to say to myself, "I do not like particularly the script I am about to shoot, and I am going to try and change it." And then you start pulling rewrites. Like on *The Abominable Dr. Phibes.* A fellow by the name of Ron Dunas found the script by James Whiton and William Goldstein and brought it to Jim. Ron was a real estate developer who always wanted to be a producer. Whiton and Goldstein were good writers, very competent, but the script had that edge of nastiness to which you refer. Here is a man [Dr. Phibes] on a vendetta, killing people. It could have been a gross piece of nastiness. It was changed by doing slight rewrites here and there.

But not changing the plot.
Right. The plot was even intellectual in spots, when it went off into the Talmudic background of the killings. But here's what I thought up. You know that I was head writer for Ernie Kovacs for four years. Ernie did a little schtick where he minced and pranced and did imitations of Vincent Price. It occurred to me, if Vincent were to do an imitation of Kovacs-doing-Vincent Price, we

might have something strange here! And indeed it could be a *black* black comedy. That was the hope I had for it. So there were a lot of funny little things that were inserted into the script, to take advantage of this concept. To the point that, when Sam came to London to see the film, he clutched his breast, rolled his eyes upward and said, "I am undone!" *[Laughs.]* He said, "You got a cockamamie comedy here! Take my name off it!" So I took his name off it. Then we won some film festival award, and he said, "Put my name on!"

Do you remember specifically any of the things you added?
No. They were nuances, they were moues, they were stage directions.

Did Price enjoy playing what was essentially a non-acting part?
I think it *is* an acting part. Remember the scene [in *Dr. Phibes Rises Again*] when he's in the tent, eating fish with Vulnavia [Valli Kemp]? He seems to swallow a fish bone, and he takes it out of the little vent in the side of his neck. He does it with such delicacy that it's great acting, and funny funny *funny*. That's the way Kovacs would have done it. I would say that Vincent enjoyed himself as Dr. Phibes.

The "look" of the film attracted a lot of favorable comment.
We had a guy named Brian Eatwell do the scenery, which I think was superb for a budget show. He did it for pennies—pennies and brains. He did a number of pictures for me, and he eventually ended up here in Hollywood. And I'd welcome an opportunity to work with him at any time, because here is a scenic designer who puts in a helluva lot more than he gets.

Robert Fuest, who directed, has gotten most of the credit for the way the film turned out. Is this fair?
For the most part, I would say yes. Bob Fuest had a great sense of style and flair. He struck up a very good rapport with all of the actors; being an ex-scenic designer himself, he knew how to guide Eatwell, and I think that was a very strong key to the picture. He conceptualized a lot, and he also had a very sly English sense of humor. I would say, "Hey, wouldn't it be funny if...," and he'd ponder; he was a very serious young man. I was always expecting him to say no, and he'd say, "Yes, but I think it would be *funnier* if...," and he extrapolated upon any thought I had. And he was a working director; when we did the River Styx scene [in *Dr. Phibes Rises Again*] he went in the water up to his waist—he didn't have to. (Maybe he had to pee!) Also, he was very conscious of budget, which I'm sure doesn't mean diddly-squat to your readers, but it means a lot to a producer.

Ron Dunas gets a co-producer credit. What did he contribute?
Ron was a very wealthy guy who fancied himself a patron of the arts. He

Vincent Price had one of his best roles...

may or may not have put some money into *Dr. Phibes;* they shipped him over to England and told me to treat him nicely. I found him a source of difficulty on the set.

Did you like Joseph Cotten and Hugh Griffith on Dr. Phibes?

Cotten was just like Boris Karloff, the original gentleman. He also was not in good health at that time, but he went home and he studied, and came in the next day knowing his lines letter-perfect, attempting to contribute, using every one of the tricks that he had acquired over years in the business to enhance the picture. He was a big plus.

...as the vengeful two-faced killer in Heyward's *The Abominable Dr. Phibes*.

It was around this time that Cotten seemed to be trying to establish himself as a horror star.

I don't think that's quite right. Bette Davis, poor thing, discovered that when your career is on the way down, you will do a horror picture, just as you will when your career is starting. You don't do them in the middle of your career, you do them on the way up and the way down. Cotten was on the way down, and the job was available. People really don't want to do horror pictures, they are driven into them.

And Hugh Griffith?

When I got to England, Hugh could not be employed, he had a reputation as an alcoholic. But I desperately wanted to use him, and I knew he could use the work. I told him, "I will accept the fact that you are uninsurable. You've got to accord me the same respect I give you." He said, "I give you all the respect in the world, guv'nor." I said, "That ain't it. The respect I want is a promise. From the moment you come on the set, you don't touch a drop. When we yell *cut* and it's a wrap for the day, do whatever you want, I don't care. But you give me your hand-to-God promise that you're not going to touch a drop while we're shooting." He held out his hand and said, "Lad, you've got it." Well, I did five, six pictures with him, and he adhered to that promise.

You came up with a sequel to Dr. Phibes *in fairly short order.*

I don't know if you saw the reviews, but the reviews on the first *Phibes* were great and, strangely enough, the English reviews on the second one, *Dr. Phibes Rises Again,* were even better. I brought out from L.A. a writer named Bob Blees, a dear friend; he did what was for me one of the best emotion-laden pictures ever made, *Magnificent Obsession* [1954]. And he also had a sly sense of humor which I felt would fit in with *Phibes*. Now, Bob Fuest wanted to write this second film, and the two of 'em did not see eye-to-eye on *anything*. They were two men with great senses of integrity, but one protecting director's viewpoint and the other protecting writer's viewpoint. The visions that Fuest enjoyed were in his head; the visions that Blees had were on paper, and easier to handle. So suddenly you were referee, placed in a position you did not want to be in because they were both right. It was a question of allowing them to go as far as they could, and then saying to yourself, "Don't worry, there'll be a rewrite at the end and we'll straighten out whatever doesn't seem to work." That's of course what followed.

Was Rises Again *as good as the first movie?*

In some ways better, in some ways worse. It did not hit some of the beautiful, beautiful highs that I felt we had in the first, but there was a steadiness to it that I liked. Because after all the fighting was done, it turned into a very good script, one that I think could be used in writing classes. Indeed, if I ever get around to teaching again, I will use that as one and *De Sade* as the other.

Where were your desert scenes shot?

Ibiza, off the coast of Spain. It's a little bit of a desert and rosemary grows wild all over and the air is scented with it. And the sheep shit that beautiful smell of rosemary *[laughs]*! The rest was shot in England.

Do you remember your impressions of Robert Quarry?

I enjoyed working with him. I felt he was misunderstood, he was being given short shrift by AIP. He had a decent role in *Rises Again* but I felt that his career was being mangled. He deserved more, I felt. He was a delight to work with.

AIP was supposedly grooming him as a replacement for Price.
They were. Those were my instructions. But I was not privy to any fights or discussions or animus between them.

There was talk about a third Phibes, *which never happened.*
This was such a personal venture, I felt Phibes was mine. AIP made attempts to get scripts — they even went back to Whiton and Goldstein — and apparently they couldn't lick the script problem. Because again there's a philosophical approach to making a picture of this kind. You're treading a funny middle ground between humor and murder. Precious few pictures have stayed on that tightrope.

What's the story on Who Slew Auntie Roo?
Curtis Harrington brought in a script by Jimmy Sangster; Bob Blees was brought in to rewrite it. Harrington directed, and all we had at the time was Shelley Winters and a very nervous Jim Nicholson, who said, "Don't say no to her on anything." 'Cause Shelley Winters was a big name for AIP. Then I also got Ralph Richardson, which as I said before is the wonderful thing about the English: They will say yes to a small part if it's a good part. We got Richardson, Hugh Griffith, Lionel Jeffries — a lovely, very good cast. The picture was a delight to make, and it did good business — not great, but good.

Curtis Harrington has a good reputation as a creative director.
I thought he was wonderful. Over and above being a creative director, he was a pleasure to be with. He was never demanding, he was always smiling and suggesting rather than insisting.

And, on the flip side perhaps, how about Shelley Winters?
No comment — except to say that *is* the flip side *[laughs]*!

Gordon Hessler told me there was great enmity between "American AIP" and "English AIP." Sam Arkoff told me that was bullshit.
There wasn't great enmity; Sam Arkoff was best man at whatever wedding it was I had at that time, so there was a fondness between Sam and me. But beyond Sam, they had gotten in a new head of production who did not want there to *be* a European AIP, who wanted all the pictures to originate in America. Now, I can't blame the man for wanting to do that. We were doing nothing but making money with our pictures and we were helping to keep AIP going, but for me to fight a battle 3,000 miles away, I gotta lose.

And you did lose.

What happened is that somehow Sam and I got into a tangle, and I don't remember what it could have been—we were very, very close friends. And we mutually decided to part. I remember a party in Cannes (we always had the best parties in Cannes) and Sam Arkoff making an announcement that we were going to do a sequel to *Wuthering Heights* [1970] and we were going to do *Camille*. The BBC covered it, and it was a very tearful thing, Sam and I both knowing we were going our separate ways but putting on a show for the BBC, to allow them to believe there was going to be continuity. Now, after I left, they had three other people in rapid succession take my place in England, and I don't think any of them made a picture, over a period of two or three years. It was a sad break-up.

Can you sum up your AIP experience?

What it was, was a period that had never existed before and will never exist again. My first cousin was Irving Thalberg; he existed at a time and in a place where things were just right for him. Things were just right for the American producer in England when I was there for AIP. It was the right time, the right place, and a great opportunity to learn and grow.

*I've always been disappointed
that movies have not done the job
they* could *do with science fiction....
I've done a lot of science fiction movies,
but I never was satisfied with them —
they always looked dumb to me.
Unimaginative. Not poetic.
Not done the way they
ought to be done.*

John Howard

ALTHOUGH BEST KNOWN to film buffs as the dapper star of Paramount's *Bulldog Drummond* series and as the rich and stuffy fiance of Katharine Hepburn in *The Philadelphia Story* (1940), actor John Howard is no stranger to fantasy and science fiction films. In the 1937 *Lost Horizon,* Howard starred with Ronald Colman and Jane Wyatt in the timeless James Hilton tale of survivors of a Tibetan plane wreck spirited away to the gleaming monasteries of Shangri-La. He later added to his list of credits such horror and sci-fi titles as *The Mad Doctor, The Invisible Woman, The Undying Monster, The Unknown Terror* and *Destination Inner Space.*

A native Ohioan, John Howard (born John R. Cox, Jr.) had no interest in working in theater until schoolmates at Cleveland's Western Reserve University turned him on to acting. After some work on his college stage, he made his movie debut in a bit part in Paramount's *One Hour Late* (1934) before moving up the Hollywood ladder to featured parts and ultimately landing his own series (the *Bulldog Drummond* mysteries). An avid lifelong reader of science fiction books and stories, John Howard can boast a career in fantasy, horror and sci-fi films that has spanned a full five decades.

Your first fantasy film was Lost Horizon *with Ronald Colman. Do you remember how you became involved on this film?*

Frank Capra was making tests of lots of people for this particular part. I was under contract at Paramount and Frank was working for Columbia, so I thought it was kind of peculiar when Paramount phoned me and said, "Frank Capra wants to test you for a part in *Lost Horizon.*" At that moment I didn't know what *Lost Horizon* was, but I said yes—naturally! After all, Capra was a big name at that time, after *It Happened One Night* [1934]. So I went out, grabbed a copy of *Lost Horizon* and read it. But as yet no one had said which part I was going to play. When they told me I was going to play Mallory, I said, "Wait a minute! That's a terrible part—the guy is an absolute jerk!" But Paramount said this was going to be a big picture and that I should do it. So I made the test, and afterwards Frank told me that I was going to play the part. Then he asked me if I would mind acting opposite some girls who were testing to play the part of Maria. Naturally I couldn't say no. Strangely enough, I didn't make a test with Margo, who got the part eventually, although I had worked with her many times previously—she was a real close friend of mine. You might be interested to know that one of the girls I did make a test with was named Rita Cansino. She just didn't work out as far as Frank was concerned, but later on she turned out to be Rita Hayworth!

This whole experience, of course, was a pivotal moment in my career. Without *Lost Horizon,* I doubt very much whether I would have survived in Hollywood.

What made Capra think of you?

Previous page: **John Howard puckers up for a peck from** *The Invisible Woman* **(who, unaccountably, isn't making a hole in the water). Of this experience Howard says, "My feeling was, 'Jeez, I'm going to look like an absolute idiot here!'"**

I asked him that. I said, "Frank, this character ought to be British, right? He's the brother of a man who's going to be the prime minister of Britain if he ever gets back to England. How in the world did you think of me?" And he had a rather equivocal answer; he said, "It's just something that I saw in you in a picture which was about the Naval Academy." That was a picture I'd made for Paramount, *Annapolis Farewell* [1935]. How in the hell he figured out from *that* that I had the kind of quality he wanted for *his* picture, I don't know. Bless his heart, I'm glad he did, but I'm not quite sure still to this day that I was right for that part. And a lot of British actors, including David Niven, Richard Greene and a number of others, had also made tests for it. Of course I couldn't object to the fact that Frank picked me, but I also couldn't understand why!

We talked about this as the picture went on, and of course we had some different opinions about how this character ought to be played. And even though I was a dumb kid, I was brash enough to occasionally say to Frank, "I don't think this guy would do such-and-such a thing." And then Frank would explain to me why he thought I should do whatever it was. It was a nice relationship.

There were some changes between the character in the book and the character you ended up playing.

Mallory is a very important character in the book because he's the guy that louses up everything. They changed it in the picture into a different kind of character, but he still does the same job of messing things up. I guess [screenwriters] Capra and Robert Riskin also felt that it would be a good idea to make this character the brother of the leading character, Conway [played by Ronald Colman], and I think they were right about that. In fact, the author of *Lost Horizon,* James Hilton, actually *said* that — he said, "My gosh, if I would have thought of this, I would have made him Conway's brother to begin with!"

So you got to meet Hilton?

Yes, he was on the set quite a lot. He was a very interesting fellow — really, the first major author that I had ever met in my life. Such a shy little man — he just didn't want to talk at all, he sat in corners of the stage and it was very difficult to get him to talk. But when he did, he spoke like a Cambridge don: with great understanding, and a delicious sense of what was wrong with people and with the world. He had a great love for humanity, and a strong feeling that humanity was doomed to some kind of horrible fate unless they picked themselves up. I think all of his novels kind of reflected that.

On the other end of the spectrum, possibly: Was Harry Cohn on the set very much?

No, not at all. I had a good relationship with Harry, personally. I was just

Margo and John Howard in a publicity photo for Frank Capra's *Lost Horizon*.

a little jerk, so I don't want to make this thing into a big deal, but I did several pictures for Harry and he was always very nice to me. I never found him to be the awful ogre that other people made him out to be. On the other hand, I didn't give him any trouble *[laughs]*! But, no, he seldom came on the set of *Lost Horizon;* I think when Frank made the deal with Harry, he must have said, "Look, you stay off the set!"

Because Lost Horizon *was being made by Columbia, which was then a Poverty Row studio, Ronald Colman initially had misgivings about the project. What were your feelings about having to work at Columbia?*

In those days everybody was a slave; "sold down the river" was a real term then. We couldn't control our lives. If you were under contract at MGM or Paramount or Warners, you belonged to them, and they just sold you. It wasn't an awful thing, usually, although I did a couple of pictures under these conditions that I didn't like at all. But in this particular case I realized that this was a real chance, because *Lost Horizon* was going to be one of the big pictures of the year—or, for that matter, of the century! My feeling about Capra, of course, was a matter of worship; I thought this guy was the greatest director to come along in a long time. To have a chance to work with him was great.

Howard *(left)*, Margo and Ronald Colman in *Lost Horizon*. Howard's role in this hall-of-famer ensured his niche in Hollywood history, but 50 years later he remains unhappy with his performance.

How did you like working with Colman?

I enjoyed it tremendously. He was a difficult man to know—a man who had a kind of "shutter" on his personal relationships. He would close the shutter and you just couldn't get any further with him. On the other hand, a couple of times I was privileged to have him open up about his past life, and that was fascinating. I thought, and still think, that Ronald Colman was the acme of film actors. He had this amazing ability to do *nothing,* and let you look into his eyes and imagine everything that *you* thought he was thinking. I wasn't ever convinced that *he* was thinking the things that the audience thought, but at least he gave them the chance to put their thoughts into those big brown eyes.

Where was Lost Horizon *shot?*

The exterior Shangri-La sets were built on the Columbia ranch. They raised doves and pigeons there, from eggs, so that they would never leave—they were always floating around in the air there. They also planted all the trees and plants, so that they grew there. The first time we walked onto this set, we couldn't believe our eyes. It was paradise! Everything was blooming, the birds were flying around making cooing noises—it was very exciting. Personally, I thought at the time the design of the temple was wrong, because it looked too art-deco; I thought it ought to mirror the actual temples in Tibet. But I must say that I think maybe they were right and I was wrong; it made people in the movie audience sit up and take notice, because they'd never seen anything like it. Maybe that's what made it exciting.

The scenes at the airport were shot out in the San Fernando Valley. The scene where we land our plane in the desert was done out in what's now called Antelope Valley—in those days it was complete desert. Some of the aerial stuff, flying over the Himalayas, was done over the state of Washington; some of it was clips of the actual Himalayas. The rescue scenes after the plane crash were done in an ice house in downtown L.A. They had several machines that chopped up ice and they blew it around, and it looked like snow. The temperature in there was *just* below 32°, just enough to keep everything frozen, and we worked there for two or three weeks.

At that particular time—1936, '37—somebody discovered that you could take a film can cover and flip it through the air, and make it glide. Does that sound familiar? During our lunch break, all of us went out into the street outside the ice house and we had great games flipping this film can cover around. But none of us had brains enough to realize that we could develop this into something that would be commercial—

The Frisbee!

Right! Every day we'd get out there and play this game. It was in July, I think, and the temperature was around 100°. We got all boiled up, sweated like mad, and then we went back into the ice house, where it was like 28°. We all thought we'd die of pneumonia. Well, nobody got even a cold—nobody had any problems at all, which I always thought ought to have been investigated by scientists.

It was in this same area of downtown L.A. that Frank found the old woman who stood in for Margo as the ancient crone. They found her on the street! They had tested all kinds of people—they even put old-age makeup on Margo—before they finally noticed this old Mexican woman whom Frank found while he was wandering around during the lunch hour. They signed her for like $50 a week and put her on Ronnie Colman's back for that final scene, and she played the part. She didn't have to do anything, of course, except look incredibly old—and she did! It was not makeup, she was just an ancient, *ancient* crone.

Looking at the reconstructed Lost Horizon *recently, it struck me that a few of the cuts made over the years may have been for the better.*

I've got to disagree with that. As far as I'm concerned, the reconstruction is marvelous, but then *[laughs]*, I have a reason! They put back two scenes that I was in that had been lost for years. When I used to see the cut version on television, I always felt that my character didn't make any sense, because they had taken out those two very valuable scenes which explain why this idiot kid did all these dumb things. So I appreciate the reconstruction from that standpoint: I still think that I did a bad job of *playing* the character, but the motivation for what he did now makes more sense.

You don't think you did a good job in Lost Horizon?

No. I began to feel this way the first time I saw the film, at a preview! Damn it, I thought I was too brash, too uncontrolled, too unbelievable. And I've wished always that I could go back and do it again.

Did you ever see the Ross Hunter remake [1973]?

[Groans.] Oh, God! I didn't—I didn't want to. People told me, "Don't watch it—please! Don't go and see it!" And I have not seen it yet.

How did you become interested in becoming an actor?

I actually wasn't. My father studied drama at Carnegie Tech, and as a little tiny kid I remember going to see productions that he was in. But I never thought anything about doing it myself until I was in high school. They suddenly put me into the senior play, much against my will *[laughs]*, and as I think back on it I must have been absolutely awful—*ghastly!* Then when I got into college [Western Reserve University, Cleveland, Ohio], through my fraternity I met a couple of guys who were really fascinated with the theater and knew a lot about it, and they educated me. I began to see that this was something worth doing. I'd always been interested in doing something artistically—playing some instrument, perhaps. And at that point I thought, "Well, this is something I can do, and I don't have to compete with trombonists and pianists. I can just do this on my own." So I got fascinated with the idea of theater, and the more I got involved, the more excited I got about it.

And then how did you break into pictures?

A talent scout from Paramount came to Cleveland to see a local stock company, but they had a dark house that night—the leading lady was sick or something, and they closed down. The talent scout called William McDermott, who was the drama editor of *The Cleveland Plain Dealer,* and said, "I've got a free evening, where can I go?" And McDermott said, "Go out to the university and see the show." Our show, incidentally, happened to be the first production ever made of Stephen Vincent Benét's *John Brown's Body.* The talent scout picked out me and a girl in the show and said, "How would you two like to come to New York and make a test for films?" I wasn't quite sure—I thought he was nuts *[laughs]*! I didn't really believe that he was a talent scout. I thought he was one of these guys that wanted to pick up little people and milk them for their money. But of course he was legitimate. I called McDermott and he said, "No, no, this guy is a big wheel!"

So I went to New York and made the test, and they said, "Would $75 a week get you through your New York experience?" Seventy-five dollars in 1934 was a fortune—it was like a *thousand* dollars today! I swallowed a bit and said, "I *guess* I can get by on that." Actually, I'd been living on three dollars a week! So that's how I got into the business—completely by accident.

How did you get involved on The Mad Doctor?

I was in a funny kind of state at Paramount at that time: I was right at the end of my contract, and they didn't know quite what to do with me. I had done the *Bulldog Drummond* pictures and several other things like *Disputed Passage* [1939], which was one of my favorite pictures but didn't make any money. So Paramount came and said that *The Mad Doctor* was going to be a good picture for me because Basil Rathbone was going to play the title role and I'd be playing the hero who defeats him in the long run. Also, I was secretly in love with [co-star] Ellen Drew; we'd sort of grown up together at Paramount, and I thought she was great. So I felt that *The Mad Doctor* was going to be a marvelous opportunity.

How did you like working with Rathbone?

I think he was a superlative actor. That's the first time I'd ever really met him personally, and I didn't realize he was such a robust conservative. He was trying to sell everybody on the idea that America could not survive unless we had some kind of a really strong, conservative government—and, of course, at that time I couldn't have disagreed more with that kind of philosophy! So we had a lovely running argument for the six or seven weeks it took to make the picture. Also, we were both stamp collectors, and we got into a situation where he was trying to sell me his stamps and I was trying to sell him mine. And nothing happened, because I thought he was a crook *[laughs]*! And I still think so!

The Mad Doctor *was a B picture with A picture length and A picture pretensions. Strange as it sounds, I think with a little* less *effort it might have been better!*

I'd go along with that, they tried to make too much out of it. But *The Mad Doctor* was a real experience for me because I actually learned a lot from Basil Rathbone. Not in the sense of copying what he did, but in seeing the kind of timing that he had in his readings. I really did appreciate working with him. I also loved the director, Tim Whelan. He was a great, marvelous guy, and I just couldn't understand why he didn't go on to become really famous.

Did you enjoy yourself when you made Universal's The Invisible Woman?

Yes, I did. That movie was absolute hilarious fun. I'd worked with John

Howard remembers his illustrious *Mad Doctor* co-star Basil Rathbone as a superlative actor, but he wouldn't buy a used stamp from this man.

Barrymore before, several times, and I just loved the guy — I adored him! After all, how many people have achieved the stature of John Barrymore in the theater? I thought it was fantastic just to be able to sit in the same room with him. We had a good relationship. Barrymore was an ordinary fellow; he wasn't stuffy, no pretense whatsoever. He kept saying, "I never wanted to be in the theater. I wanted to be a cartoonist." He wanted to be an artist, actually, but couldn't do it that well, so he decided he wanted to be a cartoonist — at which he was very good.

Even in pictures that you felt weren't up to snuff, I don't think he showed any disdain. We knew perfectly well that *The Invisible Woman* wasn't going to be an award-winner, but it was fun to do and interesting to those of us who never did one of those invisible things before. Which included the whole cast, I guess.

Curt Siodmak, the writer of The Invisible Woman, *told me that Barrymore was at the point where he couldn't memorize dialogue anymore.*

That was true even before *The Invisible Woman*. When we did the *Bulldog Drummond* pictures at Paramount, the first few starred Barrymore and I was second-billed as Drummond. And he had great problems. It wasn't that he couldn't memorize lines, he did fine with that; the problem was that he got so petrified that he couldn't remember the first line. For instance, if he and I happened to be walking together into a scene already established, he would grab my arm with a vicious grip — he was very strong for a small fellow — and he would say *[frantically]*, "What's my line? What's my line?" I'd tell him, we'd go in and he would be brilliant from that point on. But later on, in the second picture, he began to develop a kind of aphasia: he would get going well, but then he would lose lines during the scene, which wasn't true in the first picture. So he developed, with my help, a system of cutting up the script and putting it down on the set: behind vases, behind phones, in drawers, on the backs of other actors, whatever! They were like cue cards, although this was long before television. This way he could just look around and find the lines. And of course he was such a superlative actor that it looked as though this was an inspirational way to *say* the lines! It worked very well, but it must have driven him nuts — he must have realized what was happening to him, and I felt terribly sorry about that.

Did you get along well with the rest of the cast?

I loved everybody in that picture. It was a ball from start to finish. Working at Universal was fun. Not as much fun as Paramount, but still a relaxed kind of atmosphere. I never really had any contact with the front office at Universal; we worked for a producer and that was it. In fact, most of the time I didn't even know who was running the place! But it was fun to work there in the sense Universal was kind of at the second level — it wasn't really a major studio, but it had a history of making good pictures.

Were any of the "invisible" effects achieved before your eyes on the stage?

Yes, some of them were achieved right there. You know of course how they made a person "invisible" on film — dressing them in black garments and then shooting them against a black background. But there were other things, like footprints on the carpet, which could not be done that way. They were achieved in a very strange way that involved putting springs and wires under the carpet, to get the imprint to go down. The same thing when an invisible person sits in a chair: How can you indicate that they're sitting there except to show the padding in the chair become concave? That, too, was done mechanically.

The thing that was difficult for me was that I had to work opposite *nobody* — to talk to a non-existent person. The first time I mentioned this to a reporter he said, "Well, that's no different from doing a scene with anybody who's not there, and *that* happens all the time in pictures." But it's not the same, it really isn't. There is a difference between trying to deal with somebody "invisible" compared to somebody who had played a scene with you before, and now just doesn't happen to be there physically. There's a kind of funny transition that you have to make, and I think it's a different technique in a sense. I'm not sure we did it well, but we tried.

I always wondered whether actors working in Invisible Man films felt silly going through all these bizarre motions.

That's exactly what I'm talking about. My feeling was, "Jeez, I'm going to look like an absolute idiot here!" For instance, how can I kiss an "invisible" hand? Am I going to look as though I am *pretending* to kiss an invisible hand? That would throw the whole picture out of kilter. As an actor, I have a responsibility — I have to make this thing look believable. But how can I do it? I have no experience in my life that deals with this kind of thing *[laughs]*! This is pretty frustrating! Of course the director's no help, 'cause he doesn't know, either!

How do you feel about science fiction, fantasy and horror films in general?

I guess I was one of the original science fiction buffs of all time. In the '20s I used to smuggle science fiction books and magazines into classrooms, and put them inside of history books. Science fiction I love, and always have. Horror movies I always loved to go and see, just for the fun of it, but I don't think they really fall in the same category. I still read a lot of science fiction, more science fiction than fantasy; I make a great distinction between the two. I think *real* science fiction is the only remaining area where imagination can really work — the imagination of authors or poets or dreamers. So I'm still very devoted to it; I still read *Omni* and *Discover* and everything else I can find.

I've always been disappointed that movies have not done the job they *could* do with science fiction. Movies are the real medium for this kind of thing, but it's never really come about as far as I'm concerned. I've done a lot of science fiction movies, but I never was satisfied with them — they always looked dumb to me. Unimaginative. Not poetic. Not done the way they ought to be done.

The Undying Monster *was one of your last films before going into the service during World War II.*

It was *the* last film. Here's the story on that: Instead of waiting to be drafted into the army, I decided that I wanted to be in the navy. So the navy picked me up and put me "on hold," so to speak. My agent said, "The navy says you won't be called up for six or eight months. Wouldn't it be a good idea if we got a contract with some studio? That way, when the war is over, you'll

Ultra-rare closeup shot of Howard in full werewolf makeup, from the climax of *The Undying Monster*. (Photo courtesy Steve Jochsberger.)

have something to come back to." I thought that made sense, and so, months later, he got me a contract with 20th Century-Fox. Fox didn't do a damn thing about it for a couple of months, and then suddenly they came up with this picture, *The Undying Monster*. I couldn't refuse it, and yet I didn't really feel I belonged in the thing. It had a British setting, and I thought I was out of place.

What about James Ellison? He was a cowboy star, and he played a Scotland Yard sleuth in it!

[Laughs.] To have Jimmy in that picture was absolutely stupid. It wasn't his fault, he did a good job, but again, why in the world put this guy in that

particular part? It didn't make any sense at all. To be honest, until I finally saw the film, very recently, on television, I had forgotten that Jimmy was even in it! When I saw him in there, I was just shocked.

The leading lady, Heather Angel, was the only star who seemed to belong, but her character is so high-handed and standoffish that you just don't care about her.

I don't think they thought much about what they were doing. I didn't really care, though, because about three weeks after the darn thing was over I was already on my way to Casablanca. So I was not really concerned with it; I was only concerned with the idea that I'd have some place to come back to.

The director, John Brahm, now has something of a reputation as a horror specialist.

[*Laughs.*] John and I had an adversary relationship going way back to a picture that we made together at Columbia, *Penitentiary* [1938], with Jean Parker. I got sold again by Paramount for that particular picture; Brahm was the director, and we had some difficulties. He's a German, after all, and he expected people to listen to the director and to *obey* the director. I didn't really feel that way; I thought I could listen, but that I didn't have to obey. He wanted me to do a lot of things that I thought were just hammy and stupid. We had quite a long to-do during that picture, and neither one of us wound up liking the other much. So when I found him also directing *The Undying Monster* I was not too happy about that [*laughs*]! But everything went okay — he wasn't worried about my performing like a German actor. Maybe he had changed — maybe *I* had changed! — but we got along fine. I respected him for being a technically good director, but I just didn't like his Germanic attitude.

That whole movie was done indoors, even the scenes on the moors, right?

Yep. Really, the only thing I remember about *The Undying Monster* — with great pain! — is the scene in which I changed from a werewolf to a human being. I was clamped down in some kind of vise while they put this makeup on, and this was not fun at all. It took about four hours, and in the picture it only lasts about thirty seconds. As I said, I had never seen the picture until recently, and I was astounded. I remembered this thing as being a long, long transformation, but from what I see in the film now, it's *nothing*. And I thought, God, I spent all those hours in agony there, with no real result!

The camerawork and art direction were the best things about Undying Monster. *Despite its classic rep, it's pretty poky and drawn-out.*

I couldn't agree more about that. I thought it was dull. The intention was good and the whole ambience was good, but I don't think that it held up, or that it had any great appeal. It certainly didn't keep *my* interest [*laughs*]!

After World War II your feature film career never really seemed to get back into gear.

I got out of the service early because I got a medal, and according to the rules if you get certain medals you get out early. I thought that was a good opportunity to get a jump on all the other actors who were coming out later on. So I wired my agent and said I was being released, and that I could be in Hollywood in a week. "Call Fox and see what they've got going," I told him. He did, and he wired me back to tell me that they didn't have anything for me. Most of the people who were under contract to Fox were not out of the service yet; how could this be possible? I got the feeling that they just didn't give a damn.

A man named Leland Hayward, who had been an agent in Hollywood and became a producer in New York during the war, called my agent and said, "I want to talk to John about doing a play in New York." I read the script, thought it was very exciting, called my agent and said, "I love this thing, but how can I get out of my contract with Fox?" Eventually what happened was that I flew back to the Coast, we went to Fox and talked them into letting me out of the contract. This accomplished, I went back to New York and we tried to make this play work — and it just didn't work. We opened it in New Haven, we went to Boston, we went to Pittsburgh and we closed in Pittsburgh because everybody realized it wasn't going to work. The New York critics would have killed it; it just had something missing. I went back to Hollywood, but really I had nothing to go back to. I was an actor who had not worked in five years, coming back from a flopped show. How could they sell me? I had to scrounge around and do lousy little pictures until television raised its ugly head, when finally I got a chance to start again. But it was a long, long period of absolute dearth.

How did you land your part in The Unknown Terror?

The director, Charles Marquis Warren, was a guy who had a great reputation: He created *Gunsmoke, Rawhide* and several other TV series, and he was a good director. I don't know where he glommed onto the idea that I should play in this picture, but I was approached. I had just finished doing my TV series *Dr. Hudson's Secret Journal* [1955-1957], and I was delighted to get a chance to work with him.

It was a good script, basically; as far as science fiction was concerned, it was all right. I had seen Mala Powers [q.v.] in *Cyrano de Bergerac* [1950] and thought that she was absolutely delightful, so I also looked forward to working with her. She turned out to be a fascinating person. And since the film was shot at the Producers Studio, which is where I'd made *Dr. Hudson's Secret Journal* and several pictures, it was like old home week.

So you enjoyed the experience?

It was a delightful picture to work on. I thought everybody involved was

Howard played his last film lead in the science fiction quickie *The Unknown Terror*.

very good at his craft; in my opinion, [co-star] Paul Richards was one of the best actors I've ever run across. He was just superb. Mala was good and so were all the other people. It was fun to do.

Where were all the cave scenes shot?
 All of them were done right on the set. I had never heard of the word "spelunking" before; to have to climb down those damn rope ladders and swing across crevasses was a challenge, and made it kind of exciting. There were no stuntmen involved, and these were not easy things to do. I will tell you, in case you have to run down a rope ladder someday, that you had better learn how to do it first. The thing sways around like mad, and you've only got a little

four-inch place to plant your foot—it's hard to find where those rungs are. And swinging on a rope across a 12-foot gap was no fun, either. That chasm was about twenty feet deep! They had tried desperately to find a way to film us swinging across from above; they wanted to have a rolling stream down there, and to show us swinging across the chasm from that high angle. That didn't work out, but it was still a 20-foot drop! We couldn't miss—to drop off in the middle would have been a disaster.

I never could figure out where your character in that film was coming from.
   I couldn't figure that out, either, and that was one of the things I talked to Charles about! I was just a set-up *[laughs]*—obviously Paul was the hero and Mala was in love with him, so why was I there at all? I didn't understand, and he couldn't figure it out, either!

Were you around when they shot the cave scenes with the fungus?
   I was out of there by the time they got around to those scenes; I wasn't involved with that at all. In viewing the movie, I thought that it looked like soap bubbles coming down the cave walls. I didn't see how this could frighten anybody, but it sure frightened the hell out of my kids—they were scared to death! So if all the movie set out to do was to scare young people, I guess it worked!

How about the fungus people—did you find them effective?
   Nah, that was just nonsense. I didn't think *The Unknown Terror* was a very good film at all. But I thought what they did with the Indian ritual angle was good—I thought those scenes gave you a pretty eerie feeling that strange things do go on, that modern people don't really know about. I liked that part, and thought they should have made more of that and less of the monster stuff.

The Unknown Terror *was your last sizable film role. Why? Because you went into teaching?*
   Not quite. The actual fact is that no one gave me any decent offers for a couple of years. I did many, many appearances on television shows, so I was making a living, but nobody came to me with a picture. I did go into teaching, but it was several years after that. I went into teaching with the provision that I could do a picture or a television show whenever I got a chance, and I did. But gradually I began to be aware of the fact that every time I took off from school and had fun on a set and made a lot of money out of it, I was having to ask some fellow teacher to take over my class. I began to feel pretty bad about that *[laughs]*—I felt like saying, "I made $400 today and *you* ought to get $385 of it for doing my job!" Also, the longer I was with the school, the more involved I got in the operation of it, and I finally became a kind of principal there. At that point I just didn't feel that I had time enough to go and do little movie jobs, one-day bits and things anymore. So my acting career petered out

Flanked by the Fabulous Brunas Boys (Michael and John), Howard smiles for the birdie in the backyard of his Los Angeles home. (Photo: Jon Weaver.)

because I was working twelve hours a day at school and feeling that it was worth it. And since I retired from the school, I haven't even attempted to get back in the business because I just don't like what I *see* about the business. I think it looks like a crock of shit! I probably shouldn't say that, but it's true—I just don't like what I see.

Your last genre assignments were smallish roles in Destination Inner Space, The Destructors *and* So Evil, My Sister.

There was a fish-man in *Destination Inner Space,* I was some kind of an engineer, and I just don't remember anything else about that picture! I've also completely forgotten everything about *The Destructors* except that it involved laser. *So Evil, My Sister* was a real under-the-rug production, a very strange picture, made on a shoestring. We didn't have any sets at all; we worked inside of little houses in Pasadena and on sidewalks in Burbank and so on. Very weird—it's the only picture I ever made like that. It was a good attempt with good people in it, but it was made for no money at all, just buttons.

Lost Horizon *is unquestionably the film you'll best be remembered for. Why does it hold up so well after so many years?*

Jane Wyatt and I did a lot of tours with this new reconstructed version, since we're the only players left, and that question always came up. It's so easy to say that it's a dream that people have of a world where there is no danger;

it's a dream that we could establish a place on Earth where there is absolute peace and love and happiness—which, of course, we all would like to see. I think it's more than that; I don't think people like the film only because of that. I think they like it because the people involved are led into this world at peace sort of against their will. All the characters, even Conway, are originally repelled by this idea. This is kind of a reflection of the way most people think about the world: They love the *idea* of a world at peace, and yet they tend to question what this would be like. We are a contentious bunch of people, aren't we? We are basically still animalistically fighting to survive and trying to make ourselves interesting and better. Maybe that's part of it.

JOHN HOWARD FILMOGRAPHY

As John Cox, Jr.:

One Hour Late (Paramount, 1934)
Car 99 (Paramount, 1935)
Four Hours to Kill! (Paramount, 1935)

As John Howard:

Annapolis Farewell (Paramount, 1935)
Millions in the Air (Paramount, 1935)
Soak the Rich (Paramount, 1936)
Thirteen Hours by Air (Paramount, 1936)
Border Flight (Paramount, 1936)
Valiant Is the Word for Carrie (Paramount, 1936)
Easy to Take (Paramount, 1936)
Lost Horizon (Columbia, 1937)
Let Them Live (Universal, 1937)
Mountain Music (Paramount, 1937)
Bulldog Drummond Comes Back (Paramount, 1937)
Hold 'Em Navy! (Paramount, 1937)
Bulldog Drummond's Revenge (Paramount, 1937)
Hitting a New High (RKO, 1937)
Penitentiary (Columbia, 1938)
Bulldog Drummond in Africa (Paramount, 1938)
Bulldog Drummond's Peril (Paramount, 1938)
Touchdown, Army (Paramount, 1938)
Prison Farm (Paramount, 1938)
Arrest Bulldog Drummond (Paramount, 1939)
Bulldog Drummond's Secret Police (Paramount, 1939)
Grand Jury Secrets (Paramount, 1939)
Bulldog Drummond's Bride (Paramount, 1939)
What a Life (Paramount, 1939)
Disputed Passage (Paramount, 1939)
Green Hell (Universal, 1940)
The Man from Dakota (MGM, 1940)

The Philadelphia Story (MGM, 1940)
Texas Rangers Ride Again (Paramount, 1940)
The Invisible Woman (Universal, 1940)
The Mad Doctor (Paramount, 1941)
Tight Shoes (Universal, 1941)
Father Takes a Wife (RKO, 1941)
Three Girls About Town (Columbia, 1941)
A Tragedy at Midnight (Republic, 1942)
The Man Who Returned to Life (Columbia, 1942)
Submarine Raider (Columbia, 1942)
Isle of Missing Men (Monogram, 1942)
The Undying Monster (20th Century-Fox, 1942)
Love from a Stranger (Eagle-Lion, 1947)
I, Jane Doe (Republic, 1948)
Motion Picture Mothers, Inc. (Columbia short, 1949)
The Fighting Kentuckian (Republic, 1949)
Radar Secret Service (Lippert, 1950)
Experiment Alcatraz (RKO, 1950)
Models, Inc. (Mutual, 1952)
Make Haste to Live (Republic, 1954)
The High and the Mighty (Warners, 1954)
The Unknown Terror (20th Century-Fox, 1957)
Destination Inner Space (Magna, 1966)
The Destructors (Feature Film Corporation of America, 1968)
So Evil, My Sister (Psycho Sisters) (Zenith International, 1972)
Capone (20th Century-Fox, 1975)

*Becoming a star wouldn't have bothered me,
but what is a star? A star isn't anything.
An actor acts. That's the important thing.*

Kim Hunter

BY HOLLYWOOD'S skewed standards of normal behavior, Kim Hunter probably qualifies as "the eccentric type": She lives in a Manhattan apartment and not in L.A.'s smoggy climes, her Oscar statuette is tarnished and inconspicuously displayed, and she doesn't give two hoots in a barn about owning any of her films on videotape. But in Hunter's case, "eccentric" also translates into warm, intelligent and charming. On a bleak spring afternoon, an electrician is rummaging through her Greenwich Village digs as rain spatters the windows and lights flicker off and on, but Hunter is unruffled and unfailingly pleasant, giving her full attention to an interviewer whom any "normal" Hollywood actress would have gladly kicked down the stairs on such a trying day.

Née Janet Cole, the future stage, screen and television actress began her acting career fresh out of high school, first as a member of a Florida stock company and later with the Pasadena Playhouse. A talent scout for Hollywood mogul David O. Selznick spotted her in one of the Playhouse productions, and Selznick quickly placed the young actress under contract. Hunter film-debuted in the Val Lewton chiller *The Seventh Victim* and has since gone on to appear in more than twenty films and close to a hundred stage roles. One of her finest and most challenging roles was as Stella Kowalski in Broadway's *A Streetcar Named Desire* (she later reprised the role in the 1951 film version, copping a Best Supporting Actress Oscar), but by her own admission she is best remembered today for playing the chimpanzee psychologist Dr. Zira in the '60s classic *Planet of the Apes* and two sequels. Truly a class act, Kim Hunter has more than made her mark in the annals of fantastic filmdom.

How did you get involved on Val Lewton's The Seventh Victim?

Val Lewton knew me because he had been in charge of the screen test that got me my contract with David O. Selznick, and Jacques Tourneur had directed it. In fact, Tourneur and Val were around when Selznick said my name had to be changed. Val had worked for David during the time of *Gone with the Wind* [1939], and Val was assigned to get audience comments during the intermission. He didn't want to do it, and what he finally ended up doing was making up a list of comments and inventing names to go with them. David later found out what Val had done, and when he sent me over to see Val at RKO, he said, "I'm sending you to a man who's very good at making up names!" *[Laughs.]* Anyway, the three of us sat in Val's office — Val Lewton, Tourneur and me — thinking up first names, and Val's secretary was writing down a whole list of last names. *Hunter* was among them. And in our list of first names I suggested Kim, only because I remembered it from *Showboat* — I sort of liked it, thought it was kind of fun. And Selznick put the two together — I had nothing to do with that. He called me and asked, "*Kim Hunter* — do you like it?" *[Laughs.]*

What were your impressions of Val Lewton?

Previous page: Petite (5' 3½"), brown-haired, hazel-eyed Kim Hunter, Oscar-winning actress of *A Streetcar Named Desire* fame and a frequent visitor to the SF and horror genres.

"Terrified to move a muscle," Hunter had a classic case of first-picture nerves on the set of RKO's *The Seventh Victim*. The bookworm is Erford Gage.

A darling, gentle man—so wrong to be known as the king of the horror films *[laughs]*! Just a sweet human being.

Was he on the set of Seventh Victim *much?*
I don't remember his being on the set all that much, I really don't. He saw all the dailies, I know that, and he insisted that I not! He had brought me in to look at my tests, and I damn near burst into tears, and so he said, "Oh, no, no, keep her out! She's one of those that has no objectivity about her own work." Actors do that, they just sit there and criticize everything.

Did you have first-picture jitters?
It was just all so new. I remember them telling me to be very, very careful because the camera exaggerates everything, and what an actor might do on stage is not necessarily a good idea on film because it looks five times as large. Which meant that I found myself terrified to move a muscle *[laughs]*! Every now and then Val would say, "Would you relax, please? You look like you're embalmed!" So I had to find a way, somehow, and I concentrated on trying to understand the medium. Camera marks, those were hard to get used to, and the silence drove me absolutely crazy. There is nothing quite as silent as the

silence during the shooting of a film in a studio. It was [director] Mark Robson's first picture, too, so we were hangin' onto each other for dear life *[laughs]*!

What do you think of the film today?

Oh, I don't know—it's very hard for me ever to see myself. I keep seeing things I wished I'd done, or not done, or what-have-you. I just know from what I'm told and what I read that it was considered one of the best of the whole lot of horror films that Val Lewton did. But Lewton's way of dealing with horror films, I thought, was so marvelous, letting the audience use its imagination rather than showing all the blood and guts and all of that.

Another one of your early pictures was When Strangers Marry *[1944], once called the best-ever B movie, directed by William Castle.*

I liked working with Castle very much, but *When Strangers Marry* was a very peculiar experience. In a way, it was a horror film of its own type *[laughs]*! The King Brothers produced it, and they had quite a reputation in Hollywood for having notches on their guns—little things like that! Mama kind of ran the gang, but it *was* a gang, those guys! They slapped a ten-day schedule on the film, and Bill Castle said *[whispering]*, "Would you all mind if we sneaked a rehearsal period for about a week in my apartment?" And we said *[still whispering]*, "Yes, we'd love to do that!" So we had an illegitimate week's rehearsal, Dean Jagger, Bob Mitchum and I. That saved our lives, in order to do that film in ten days.

The King Brothers were absolutely fascinated with Mitchum, and Bob was very glad when the ten days were over. Because frequently, while Bob was waiting to do a scene, two of the King Brothers' "henchmen" would come over to him, one guy would stand on one side of him and the second guy on the other, and he swears they had guns in their pockets. They would say to him, "You really oughta leave MGM and move over to the King Brothers. They really want you under contract." Bob said, "No, I don't think I can get out of my MGM contract," and they said, "We'll manage it, we'll get you out of it!" They were at him the whole time, and he was glad when he was able to get out!

How did you land your role in A Matter of Life and Death?

While I was under contract to Selznick, I got a call asking if I would mind coming into the studio and substituting for Ingrid Bergman in tests that Hitchcock wanted to make for *Spellbound* [1945]. I said hell, yes, because I wanted to go and watch the guy work. He would shoot the back of my head, testing various male minor roles, and it was very exciting—I worked with him for about three days doing that, and we had lunch together each day. And that was the end of that. A year later, Michael Powell and Emeric Pressburger came to this country looking for somebody to play the WAC in *A Matter of Life and Death*. They saw people in New York, then they came to California and had dinner with Hitch. And Hitch said, "Well, there *is* a girl you might see..."

That's how I got brought to them, and we just sort of talked. I had just finished making a film with Lizabeth Scott, *You Came Along* [1945], and they asked to see snippets of that. I didn't know anything more until some time later, when my agent got a call saying that I should go to London, etc., etc. — I was *in*. Later, talking to Mickey [Powell], I found out that he had hired me on a hunch and it was not *You Came Along* — in fact, seeing that film almost turned him against me, because he didn't like the hairdo!

You liked Powell?

God, what a gorgeous man! I was so sorry when he died, but he had been quite ill so it was probably a relief. He was on morphine almost 24 hours a day toward the end. I saw him just before he went back to England, where he died — he was dear, but he wasn't "in" the conversation, because he couldn't hear, couldn't relate. So sad. I had much more contact with Mickey than I did with Emeric during the making of *Life and Death* because Emeric didn't come around the set all that much. His work was basically done when they had decided on the finished script. The two of them worked pretty closely together in writing it — the first draft would always be Emeric's, then Mickey would get his hands in it, and then Emeric would tidy it up! So as I said, Emeric didn't really come to the set that much, but I got to know him because of various little gatherings. Another dear, sweet man.

Where was Life and Death *shot?*

In Denham Studios in London — I believe the whole film was shot there except for one scene at Saunton Sands, where they did the opening shots on the beach. But most of it was in the studio. I liked England very much; the work was very good, very exciting, particularly after Hollywood. The attitude was so much more concentrated on the work — that was the important thing. How you lived, what kind of car you drove and what-have-you didn't mean a damn thing; it was each to his own taste over there. I'll never forget when I bought my first car in California, a Ford business coupe, and I drove it up to my agent's office and I said very proudly, "Look!" And he said, "You're crazy — take it back!" He said, "When you're well-known, you can be eccentric and drive a Ford business coupe, but until you get to be a star you need a Cadillac!" To impress. And that's insane. It was such a relief to find that that attitude just didn't exist in England.

Life and Death *was a fairly prestigious picture for England, wasn't it?*

Yes, it was. And it was the first Royal Command Film Performance — it took place at the Empire Theatre in Leicester Square. It was quite a show that night, because there were so many of us involved. There was a stage show as well as the film, and actors from all over the world were there. From Sweden, from Greece, from France and the States, and of course all the top English people. After the show we went upstairs to the Royal Lounge and they had us all

Congregated on the *Stairway to Heaven,* Marius Goring, Kathleen Byron, Robert Coote, Roger Livesey, unidentified players, Joan Maude, Abraham Sofaer and Raymond Massey look on as Kim Hunter reaches out to David Niven.

lined up in a semi-circle and the Royal Family came around us. Mickey said later that when King George got to him, he was very complimentary, and then he said, "*I* know what you did! *I* know how you got the film to go from black-and-white to color and back!" What Mickey had done was shoot the black-and-white scenes on color film and then print only one of three color matrices—you had to print all three to make it color. The King said, "That's how you slid back and forth, isn't it?" He was right, and he was terribly pleased with himself that he had figured it out!

Then when the film was released, all the critics laced into it, calling it an anti–British film! In the trial scene, Raymond Massey had all these marvelous things to say about America and terrible things to say about England, and Roger Livesey just sort of sat there quietly and once in a while said, "But you're wrong..." Roger won the battle, but because he didn't say enough, the critics all thought ultimately that Massey's character had won! It was crazy.

Why did they change the title to Stairway to Heaven *for U.S. release?*

Jock Lawrence [head of the Rank Organisation in the U.S.] said, "You've

Hunter's finest hour on the screen was Elia Kazan's 1951 production of *A Streetcar Named Desire*. From bottom in this photo are Vivien Leigh, Marlon Brando, Hunter and Karl Malden.

got to change the title because nobody in the United States will come to a film with *Death* in its title." So it became *Stairway to Heaven* — this is the only country in the world where it's called that. Also we're the only country in the world that had various little cuts, like the little goatherd boy on the beach. He was perfectly decent *[laughs]* — the way he was sitting, you couldn't see his parts! — but no, no, you couldn't have any nudity in the United States.

The color in Life and Death *is very striking.*

Powell was relentless, he kept sending prints back to the lab until he got it exactly the way he wanted it. He was marvelous.

You also appeared in scenes for Powell & Pressburger's A Canterbury Tale.

They had already made that film, and they wanted to shoot a few new scenes and bring it up to date for release in the States. So they brought back [actor] John Sweet and they used me in those scenes as well. Mickey knew he was going to do it before he got me to London, because he had me shopping in New York for a hat and clothes and what-have-you for *Canterbury Tale*. I was just in the prologue and epilogue for American audiences.

In 1951 you starred with Claude Rains in an acclaimed play called Darkness at Noon.

That was fascinating, because Claude was a dear to work with, absolutely marvelous. He was so generous to the entire company of *Darkness at Noon,* because [writer/director] Sidney Kingsley—bless his heart—was a beast *[laughs]*! Sidney was terribly insecure about that particular play of his; I talked to him before we started rehearsals, and he was a perfectly reasonable, intelligent, gentle, nice man. Then we got into rehearsals! Because of the McCarthy idiocy during that period, he was terrified that people might think the play was slightly pro-Communist, so this beautiful play that he'd written he damn near ruined by insisting that everything be either black or white—no grays. And he'd written a lot of lovely grays, but didn't allow any of them to be on stage for fear that people would get the wrong impression. So he was very difficult during rehearsals. I think Claude and he had a lot of controversies and disagreements, but Claude kept them absolutely private so that the rest of the company was not involved in their fights. Whatever Sidney said during rehearsal, Claude just went ahead and did, and then had his fight with him afterwards, away from the company. Which was very generous of him, believe me, because everybody was so on edge.

Sidney was almost going to fire Claude—he was trying to find someone to replace him while we were in Philadelphia, but fortunately all the agents in town were on Claude's side and nobody that Sidney suggested was available at all! Claude finally opened, and Sidney was there every performance. Finally after one matinee Sidney came backstage to Claude's room and said, "You were marvelous this afternoon, Claude! Very, very good! What happened?" And Claude said, "Well, I just said to myself, 'Fuck Sidney Kingsley!'" Sidney's jaw dropped, and he didn't come back after that *[laughs]*!

You also had Jack Palance in Darkness at Noon.

Claude and Jack worked quite differently, and one time Claude asked Jack if he couldn't sort of do something like the same thing each performance, so that Claude at least would have some notion as to what to expect from him! Well, Jack was one of those people who on one side of his nature was the sweetest, gentlest person in the world and on the other side was really terrifying! He got into one of those moods, and after the curtain call he went after Claude. Claude was in his dressing room with the door locked, and Jack was pounding on it and screaming. Claude wouldn't leave until Jack finally gave up and left, because he thought Jack was going to kill him! Jack and I were in *Requiem for a Heavyweight* [on live TV] and the people there were really scared to death, because one scene called for him to hit Ed Wynn. Well, Jack was absolutely marvelous on that one—he faked it beautifully. But going into it *[shaking with terror],* everybody was like *this!*

You once said that you got into the business to be an actress and not to be a star.
  That's fully accurate, I think for a great number of us. Becoming a star wouldn't have bothered me, but what *is* a star? A star isn't anything. An actor *acts.* That's the important thing.

Why don't you collect your own films on video?
  Generally I've seen my pictures once, and *[laughs]* I'm not a big one for repeating the experience! So why save them? They just take up space!

Do you even own A Streetcar Named Desire?
  No. I've seen it enough *[laughs]*!

Do you remember what your initial reaction was when you were asked to play a chimpanzee in Planet of the Apes?
  I was sent the script by my agent in California, and he wanted to know whether I'd be interested in his following through on it. I read it, I thought it was a damn good script and I said sure. But from reading the script I knew that we were all supposed to look like real apes, and I asked my agent how they were going to deal with this. He said, "Don't worry about that, 20th Century–Fox is a reputable firm. They'll find some way—put little bits of fur here and there." I didn't hear anything more for a while, and then I got a phone call from Fox, from somebody in casting, and he asked, "Miss Hunter, how tall are you?"—which I thought was a very peculiar question. I said, "Five-three and a half, why?" He said, "No, that's fine, thank you very much," and he hung up *[laughs]*! Then later I heard from my agent that the role was mine. Well, of course, I hadn't realized that all the apes had to be short and all the astronauts over six feet, and they wanted to make sure I wasn't going to be too tall!
  Then came the shocker. The first call was to go out for a fitting, and all I could think of was costumes, right? *Wrong!* First they stuck me into a death mask or a life mask or whatever the hell it is, which was quite different from most of them. Usually you had straws in your nostrils, but we had a block of wood between our teeth. We had to breathe through our mouths because

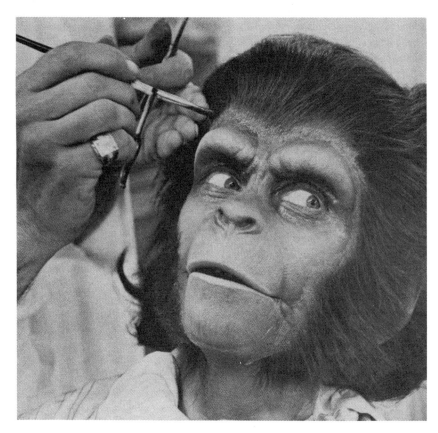

The price of movie stardom: a four-hour morning makeup session (and an hour and a half to remove it at night) to transform Hunter into Dr. Zira for *Planet of the Apes*.

everything else was covered—you'll notice in the film and in photographs that the lips of the apes never come together, because that was the only way we could breathe. The noses above were purely aesthetic, they had nothing to do with reality. Then [makeup man] John Chambers showed me some photographs of some of the testing they'd been doing, and what it would look like eventually. I thought to myself, "Oh, boy, what am I getting into?" But I came back again, and the next session was to do full testing with the appliances. The first time it took four and a half hours just to get the face on.

Did it take that long to put on the makeup every day you worked?

During the filming they brought it down to three, three and a half, but that initial time took four and a half. Roddy McDowall and I were there and they found out our voices weren't coming through properly, so we were sent off to a sound studio and we worked on that until we finally figured out just where to place the voice so it wouldn't be nasal and fuzzy. Anyway, a short time later I came back here to New York and I went to my doctor right away, and I said, "I need some help for this one, because this is going to be terrible. I need some kind of a tranquilizer for the makeup period, and then I have to be sharp as a tack once we start working." He gave me Valium, and that really was the only way I could get through it.

Did other ape actors have that problem?

It was just insane, for all of us. Psychological problems for everybody—everybody, without exception. We went through hell. I remember on the third one, *Escape from the Planet of the Apes,* Roddy and I were hugging dear Sal Mineo like crazy. Fortunately his character got killed right off so he wasn't in it all that long, but we'd hug him 'cause *[shaking violently]* he was like *this*! Just crazy, the whole time! Roddy and I both kept saying to the other apes, "Everything's fine, don't worry about it, you'll get used to it"—*nobody* got used to it, but we kept trying to reassure 'em. One of the gorillas came to me once and said, "My wife tells me that I've started talking in my sleep, and I've never done that before in my life!" One of the gorillas *[laughs]*!

Who was your day-to-day makeup artist?

We each had our own, and mine was Leo Lotito. After about three weeks I thought to myself, "Oh, come on, I don't need the Valium anymore," so this day I didn't take it before I sat in the makeup chair. And when we got to the set, Leo said, "You bloody well better take that pill from now on, or you get somebody else to do your makeup!" He practically had to hold me in the chair that morning, and he was a wreck!

How uncomfortable were you in that makeup, in that heat?

That was odd. In the heat we damn near died, and in the cold we nearly froze to death. It was no insulation one way or the other, which was very strange.

Did you really faint a number of times because of the makeup?

No, that was publicity. They had fans for us all over the place and they did their damnedest to help us all survive, but it was very hard, very difficult. We had to use straws for drinking, there was no other way, and for eating they brought in makeup tables and mirrors for everybody. [Producer] Art Jacobs provided us with lunch every day because we had to look into a mirror to eat, in order not to mess up the appliance. If you ruined it in any way, that was hours out of the shooting schedule to replace it! My mouth was a good inch or more behind the mouth of the makeup appliance.

And how long to take the makeup off at night?

Four hours to get it on in the morning and an hour and a half to take it off at night. Nobody said lightly, "You're through for the day"; they made

Taking a break between set-ups, Hunter monkeys with the camera on the set of *Beneath the Planet of the Apes*. Note the cigarette holder, required for smoking while in makeup.

damn sure you were through *[laughs]*! Our days were very long — mine started at four A.M. and I'd be lucky to get home by 9:30 at night. Leo and I had a little routine: He had his Scotch and I had my gin, through a straw, while he took off the makeup! One time Roddy pulled at the makeup to take it off — and it took his whole eyebrow off. But just to get it *off*...!

But you came back sequel after sequel.

The second one *[Beneath the Planet of the Apes]* they had to talk me into — I mean, they *really* had to talk me into. They said, "Look, it's only ten days' work and it's continuity. Please!" Roddy didn't do the second one because the timing was bad for him, he was making a film in England and couldn't, so somebody else [David Watson] took over for him. But I said all right, and I came back. And *Escape*, the story was good enough for me to want to come back, even though I still had my reservations about the makeup! And I was very glad I got killed on the third one! Roddy went on and did the last two, playing his own son, but for me three was enough, thanks a lot.

Did you get a chance to rest at all during the day?

Yes, but that was dangerous, too. You had to lie on your back, absolutely flat, and one time I did fall asleep and I had the nightmare of my life. "It's happened," I said to myself. "I have *become* one!" I couldn't see down below, but I was sure that my legs and everything had become like an ape's! I told myself, "No more sleeping! None of that foolishness!" *[Laughs.]* I gave up eating, too, I didn't like looking at it anymore.

Were there discussions about how you would move and act playing an ape?
No, but Roddy and I both did our own research, he in the L.A. Zoo and me at the Bronx Zoo. I found a chimpanzee up at the Bronx Zoo who was the only chimp up there—they had orangutans and gorillas, but only the one chimp. Which was unfortunate, because he saw me watching him and it got him very angry! I kept trying to hide, I'd get behind groups of people that came into the ape building, but he'd spot me and turn his back *[laughs]*! I really felt badly, and, believe me, I understood exactly how he felt while we were shooting. We felt like *we* were in a zoo! We finally got Fox to stop bringing around visitors, because they'd come up and poke our faces with their fingers—they literally did that to us. I couldn't believe it!

What happened was that Roddy and I got together before we started shooting and exchanged our observances, and we kind of mushed around and figured out the best way to move and all of that. We were basing it on what we had seen real chimps do, but we also knew that we were playing *evolved* chimpanzees, which made it kind of crazy! We brought all of our thoughts to the director, Frank Schaffner, and he said, "Great, it's up to you, you guys figure it out." So we taught everybody else what to do. The one thing that Frank did tell us, something he found out after a few days of dailies, was that we had to keep those appliances moving. He said, "The minute you hold absolutely still, it looks like a mask." So that's why Roddy and I ended up twitching our noses a lot *[laughs]*, to keep them moving!

If audiences had found Planet of the Apes *funny, it would have been the Hollywood embarrassment of all time.*
John Chambers said, "We're either gonna be real or it's gonna be Mickey Mouse. And we won't know until it gets on the screen."

What do you remember about Apes *producer Arthur P. Jacobs?*
I had known Art for a long time because he was a publicity agent for years before he went into producing films—he was my publicity agent when I won my Oscar! So we'd known each other for a long time. Art was a good producer, very sweet and very generous to us—he brought all the straws on the set so we could drink, cigarette holders so we could smoke, food and so on. I think one of the reasons why we weren't allowed to go to the commissary was that they were afraid that no one else would go *[laughs]*—that no one could look at us and eat, too. It would have killed their appetite!

Did Rod Serling ever show up on the set?

Rod came by once, yes, and I even remember the scene—it was the courtroom scene. Of course it wasn't his script anymore; he had done the original script, and then they reworked it into what we ended up with. I knew Rod from *Requiem for a Heavyweight* and from other television things I had done with him. I liked him.

What role was Edward G. Robinson supposed to play in Planet?

Dr. Zaius, the role Maurice Evans ended up playing. Robinson tested and then told his doctor what he had to do, and the doctor told him not to do it, that it would be very bad for his heart. But he would have been right for the role. There were others who were asked to be in *Planet of the Apes,* and then they got a load of the makeup and said no—I think Mickey Rooney was one. I think all the short people in Hollywood were approached *[laughs]*!

What kind of an army of makeup people did you have on that film?

At one point when we were out on the Fox Ranch, I think we had just about every makeup artist in Hollywood—there were something like 65 of them working for a few days. If the camera was far enough away, actors could wear overhead masks, but if it got at all close you could see the difference *[snap of the fingers]* like *that.* There was one section where the camera had to see a lot of different people—chimps and orangs and gorillas and such—and an incredible number of makeup artists had to come in. But even with just the few of us, our regular group, we not only had makeup trailers but the lab had an awful lot of people working because each day we had to have a new set of appliances. I suppose if they had used acetone to take the appliances off, they might have been able to save them from day to day, but acetone would have killed us so they had to use alcohol. So every day the appliances were new.

Where did you shoot Planet of the Apes?

At the Fox studio itself; the Fox Ranch; and Lake Powell, which is on the Arizona/Utah border. We were also at Point Dume, up above Malibu.

Any special memories of Charlton Heston?

Chuck was very dear—Roddy called him Charlie Hero. I remember we were up at Point Dume, which is where we shot the ending—the Statue of Liberty, the caves, all that stuff. We were out there quite a while, a good week or more; the first day we met at Fox, we were made up and then driven all the way out to Dume (over an hour driving). Then that night we had to be driven all the way back to Fox and the makeup taken off. That first day was just insane. Chuck was the one who said, "Look, you've got to do something for Roddy and Maurice and Kim," and so they got us a helicopter and took us back and forth that way from then on. That cut the time down considerably.

The picture of wedded bliss, time-travelers Hunter and Roddy McDowall are (temporarily) attuned to 20th century life in *Escape from the Planet of the Apes*.

Linda Harrison? Maurice Evans?

Linda Harrison later married Richard Zanuck, she was his first wife. She was a contract player at Fox at the time, I believe, and Zanuck was very interested in her, so we saw a lot of him — he wasn't part of the picture, but he'd hang around because of Linda. She was very pretty and very bright. And Maurice Evans *[laughs]*, I remember they had to keep taking his wig off all the time because he perspired so! They'd take it off and *[fanning the top of her head]* try to cool his head down! Fortunately, as an orangutan, he had a little less makeup than the rest of us, but he survived absolutely marvelously. We were a little worried, because of his age and everything else, but except for the heat he had no problems.

A lot of actors would probably insist on a stand-in whenever they could get away with it on a picture like that.

The only time I insisted on it was when we were all on horses, waiting for the blowing-up of the cave. I'm not that good a rider—I'm not an expert at all!—and I was terribly afraid I wouldn't be able to control the horse if it were bugged by the sound of the explosion. I said, "It's dumb to take a chance on that, since I don't know what I'm doing on a horse!" I just didn't think it made any sense for me to tackle that one, since we still had a few more scenes to do and they couldn't write me off. They got a guy to put on my makeup.

But that's you in the other riding scenes?

Yes, and it was tough. Our "ape feet" were much longer than our real feet, and they had "thumbs" jutting out to one side. So to put your foot in a stirrup was really silly. You could put the whole foot through, including the thumb, and then you could never get your foot out; or you could put only the toes in, and then it was floppy. There was no control at all.

How long were you on Planet of the Apes?

About three months. *Beneath* I was on longer than I expected because the weather was cockeyed and most of my stuff was outdoors. *Escape* was then cut short, of course—budgets change when you're making sequels, don't they *[laughs]*? That one only took a month or six weeks.

It posed a few heavy questions, but Escape *was the most light-hearted and charming of the* Apes *pictures.*

I liked that one. I mean, it wasn't any easier in terms of the makeup—in fact, it was very peculiar, because Roddy and I were the only chimps. Although the atmosphere on the set was very friendly and fun and all of that, Roddy and I both felt sort of out of it. John Randolph, an old, old friend of mine, was in it, and I grabbed him and asked, "Am I being paranoid or something?" He said, "The problem, Kim, is that I know in my head that underneath all that makeup it's you, but I can't keep that in my mind all the time!" For some reason the [human] actors tended to keep us at arm's length on that one *[laughs]*, because they couldn't quite ignore the barrier of the difference!

Did you think Beneath *and* Escape *were worthy sequels?*

I didn't think *Beneath* was, particularly; *Escape* I do, that was interesting. Then I saw the fourth one, *Conquest of the Planet of the Apes*, and I was *mezzo e mezzo* about it, so I never did see the fifth [*Battle for the Planet of the Apes*].

Would you have kept going with the series if you had been asked?

They asked me if I would do a guest shot on the TV series. And I said no, thank you. I was very glad I was killed off in the third!

Do you mind the fact that many fans remember you primarily for the Apes *series?*

No, I don't. The fan mail I get today, nine times out of ten relates to the *Apes* pictures.

You did a film called Dark August, *about a witch, that got little or no release.*

I think they tried to release it but couldn't—I heard that they released it in South America or someplace, and then I haven't the foggiest notion what ever happened to it. I don't think I ever saw it. It was about a guy who accidentally killed a child that ran out in front of his car. He was exonerated as far as the courts were concerned because of the nature of the accident, but the child's father never forgave him and put a curse on him. And the curse was working, so he had to find a "good" witch that would take the curse off of him. I was the witch and we had a séance to get rid of the curse. Well, we got rid of the curse all right, but I got killed in the process *[laughs]*!

Where was Dark August *made?*

We shot it all in Stowe, Vermont, and I do remember one thing about the shooting that was fascinating. Before they went up to Stowe, the director, Martin Goldman, had a pre-production meeting with a chap who was very knowledgeable about that sort of witchcraft business. Goldman said, "Let me tape-record this conversation that we're having, and the words that you use in describing the séance I can use in the script." Well, he had a whole tape from this man explaining the meanings of all the words and the whole rigmarole, Martin said goodbye to him, he went back to play the tape—and everything had been *erased!* So he brought him in again, and me at the same time, and had him go through it all a second time. This chap was very interesting—he said, "I do not know your schedule, but I suggest that you do not shoot this scene during the dark of the moon. Arrange your schedule so that you don't do that, because all the words that you'll be using are absolutely right—and you don't muck about with them!"

Well, the day that we went to shoot it, we were in an old barn that had been transformed into a house. It was a gorgeous day, absolutely beautiful when we started. We rehearsed and rehearsed because they were going to do the entire scene in a long shot before they came in for closeups. As the director called *action* for the take, there was *thunder* like you have never heard in your life, pouring-down *rain*—it went on throughout the entire scene! They did not say *cut*, fortunately, we went on and did the entire scene, and when the scene was over with, it all stopped! And there were some other little incidents that they mentioned—I wasn't involved in any of the others—when some very weird things happened. And then the film never got released. Well, maybe *it* had a curse on it, too *[laughs]*!

How about The Kindred, *with Rod Steiger?*

I know nothing about that, I've never seen it. I went out to L.A. for two days' shooting — I played a woman in a hospital bed — and left. Rod Steiger seemed to enjoy doing the picture, but it got such a bad review I wasn't eager to see it.

And your newest film is Two Evil Eyes, *a two-in-one Poe thriller.*

It's funny, but our director on that, Dario Argento, has a daughter who's living in this apartment building now — she just moved in a short while ago. The two directors, the Two Evil Eyes, are Argento and George Romero — Romero lives in Pittsburgh, but they brought Dario over from Italy and made the film in Pittsburgh. The segment I was in, along with Martin Balsam and Harvey Keitel, was *The Black Cat,* and I don't know how it turned out. All I know about Dario Argento is what I've been told, that the kinds of films that he makes are very bloody *[laughs]*! He brought his own cinematographer, and various others in the crew were his — some of them spoke English, some didn't. He speaks English a bit, but when he's working all the English words leave his head, so he has somebody around all the time to interpret. He would try to say what he wanted, but the way he worked you could tell that the camera angles and all of that were much more important to him than scenes.

So how did you get enticed into doing this one?

Oh, I just got asked if I would do it, and I said, "What the hell, yes." I think the reason Dario wanted me in particular was because he was a fan of Val Lewton, and he was very excited that I had been in *The Seventh Victim [laughs]*! That, I think, was the only reason he knew who the hell I was! All of it was done on location, and Martin Balsam and I play next-door neighbors who have a feeling something odd is going on in that house.

What do you think of newer horror films?

I don't go — I'm not sure I'm going to go see *Two Evil Eyes!* I don't like them that much, I don't really enjoy them. I get very nervous! I don't like gore particularly, and I don't like "scary."

Plans for the future?

Oh, I haven't the foggiest what they are. At this age, there aren't really that many roles, unless *Driving Miss Daisy* [1989] changes everything around *[laughs]* and they start writing for us again. But right now there aren't that many roles in films or television in general, although there still are bloody good roles in theater every now and then. When it comes to films, sometimes I do them simply because I want to work — I think that's true with *Two Evil Eyes,* 'cause I certainly had very little to do in it. I'm not retired, if that's what you're asking — not on purpose, anyway. I'm just unemployed *[laughs]*! I take it day by day.

KIM HUNTER FILMOGRAPHY

The Seventh Victim (RKO, 1943)
Tender Comrade (RKO, 1943)
When Strangers Marry (Betrayed) (Monogram, 1944)
You Came Along (Paramount, 1945)
Stairway to Heaven (A Matter of Life and Death) (Universal, 1946)
A Canterbury Tale (Eagle-Lion, 1949)
A Streetcar Named Desire (Warners, 1951)
Deadline U.S.A. (20th Century-Fox, 1952)
Anything Can Happen (Paramount, 1952)
Storm Center (Columbia, 1956)
The Young Stranger (Universal, 1957)
Bermuda Affair (DCA, 1957)
Money, Women and Guns (Universal, 1958)
Lilith (Columbia, 1964)
Planet of the Apes (20th Century-Fox, 1968)
The Swimmer (Columbia, 1968)
Beneath the Planet of the Apes (20th Century-Fox, 1970)
Escape from the Planet of the Apes (20th Century-Fox, 1971)
The Kindred (F/M Entertainment, 1987)
Two Evil Eyes (Taurus Entertainment, 1991)

Hunter's scenes were cut from *Jennifer on My Mind* (1971), although she can be spotted in some long shots. *Dark August* (1976) received no theatrical release in the U.S. Her 1979 TV movie *The Golden Gate Murders* received some theatrical play under the new title *Specter on the Bridge*.

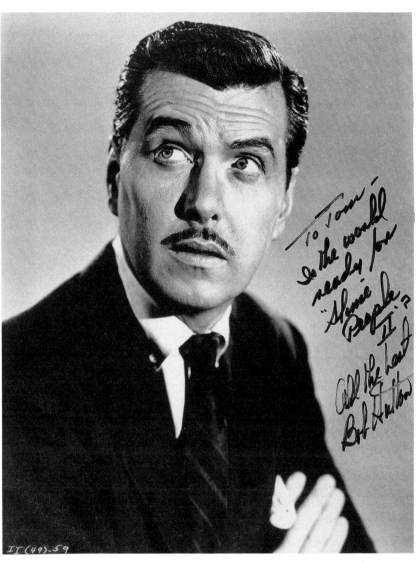

When I went out to Hollywood
with a seven-year contract in my pocket
I never dreamed things would turn out the way they did.
The people I've met. The superstars I've worked with.
The friends I call true friends. My memories
of the Hollywood I knew are wonderful memories.

Robert Hutton

B FILMS SOMETIMES serve as a stepping stone for actors on their way up, but too often they're a refuge for players whose stars have slipped. A contract player at Warner Bros. in the declining days of the studio star system, Robert Hutton appeared in a string of Warners' 1940s productions and acted opposite many of the Burbank lot's top stars, but by the 1950s the B-movie mills had become his new stomping grounds. Bitterness, however, doesn't seem to be part of the Hutton vocabulary: Now a permanent resident at an upstate New York health facility, Hutton remains a man of enthusiastic perspectives and great personal charm, and he looks back with affection and candor on a film career that ran the gamut from A to Z, from *Destination Tokyo* and *Hollywood Canteen* to *Invisible Invaders* and *The Slime People*.

How did you become involved on The Man Without a Body?

I suppose, for money! W. Lee Wilder was Billy Wilder's older brother, and he was an interesting guy. I remember that we were in his office in Hollywood, and he told me about this picture *The Man Without a Body* that he was preparing to make in England. Willie offered me the lead by saying, "If you don't take the job, the hell with you, I'll get somebody else. It's as simple as that!" And he told me to make up my mind by six o'clock that night. He wasn't at all delicate about it; I was just another actor as far as he was concerned and I guess he felt we were a dime a dozen. A very cold-blooded type, but a nice guy; we had worked together previously on a picture called *The Big Bluff* [1955] with Martha Vickers, so *[laughs]* I guess he didn't hate me all that much! Well, I wanted to go to England, and there wasn't that much work going on in Hollywood, so I took the job. He gave me very little to live on in England, but he arranged for a beautiful London apartment for my wife, Bridget, and myself. And we saw England and had a lot of fun.

You had an illustrious co-star in George Coulouris.

He was a fine actor, and very nice to work with. I think he had been blacklisted in Hollywood, which is why he left and went to England. I knew him from Warner Bros., but of course his first really important picture was *Citizen Kane* [1941] with Orson Welles.

Did Coulouris seem pleased to be in a movie called The Man Without a Body?

Now, you see, over there in England it is completely different from Hollywood. Over here if you made a movie like that, they'd say, "The guy's washed up, he's finished." But over there the main thing is to *work*. They couldn't care less if the movie has a fifty-cent budget or a fifty-million-dollar budget, as long as you worked. That's why I enjoyed living there so much: You could play a lead one day and a cameo role the next, it made no difference whatsoever. There are dozens of English actors who worked that way.

Previous page: A contract player at Warner Bros. in the 1940s, Robert Hutton went on to star in no-frills SF flicks like *The Slime People, The Man Without a Body* and *Invisible Invaders* (pictured).

(Left-right): George Coulouris, Sheldon Lawrence, Robert Hutton and Julia Arnall manage to look quite serious in this scene from the risible *The Man Without a Body.* Poking up through a hole in the table is The Man (Michael Golden).

Why does The Man Without a Body *have a second director, Charles Saunders?*
  In order to fulfill the quota requirements in England, there was a limit on the number of non-British resident personnel that could be employed on the picture. Charles was "in name only"; I remember him being on the set all the time, and not doing anything. To satisfy the union, they had to hire an English director because of the rules.

What did you think of the story of The Man Without a Body?
  It was ridiculous — it was stupid, really stupid. And we felt stupid talking to that head — we would almost break up! The actor was underneath the table, with his head stuck up through a hole in the tabletop, and you felt like a damn fool talking to him.

What memories of The Colossus of New York?
  To be quite honest with you, I had completely forgotten that I even made that movie until I saw it just recently on television. It was wonderful working with Otto Kruger — he was great, a fine actor. Except for that, it was not a very memorable experience *[laughs]*! I recall that Eugene Lourie was the director, but other than the simple fact that he was there, I don't have any recollections of him, either.

You're the third person I've interviewed that worked on The Colossus of New York, *and none of them remember the picture at all.*

On a movie like that, if you say the dialogue that they've written for you, or something rather close, they don't even care. The same thing, unfortunately, is also true of *Invisible Invaders;* that's another picture I really can't remember too much about. The thing I do remember about *Invaders* was a Jeep ride with John Agar—he damn near turned the thing over. We were doing a scene where we were driving up to the cave entrance in Bronson Canyon, and he made one turn where we went up on two wheels—he was a madman! But he was a very nice guy to work with, very quiet and very serious.

What do you think of horror and science fiction films in general?

I think there's a place for them, but not the ones they make today. They're well-made—my gosh, I can't believe the special effects—but they're too bloody, too gory, too much violence and killing. The kids, it must be so bad for them. As a kid, I went to see all the classics: *Frankenstein, Dracula, The Invisible Man,* all that stuff, and they were wonderful. They scared the daylights out of us *[laughs]* but they didn't give us nightmares or plant any crazy thoughts in our heads.

How did you become interested in being an actor?

Truthfully, I wanted to get away from my home town, Kingston, New York. It was a very quiet little town, and I was supposed to go into business with my father, who had a rather good business here. But one day I told him that I wanted to be an actor, and asked him if I could go to dramatic school.

Had you ever done anything in the way of acting?

No, nothing whatsoever. But I was a movie buff; I went to see every single movie that ever played in the area. And the life appealed to me. Beautiful girls, wine, women and song—I liked the whole idea! And my father said "Fine!" because he, too, was a big movie buff. I went to the Feagin School, in Rockefeller Center in New York. Some of their students were Angela Lansbury, Jeff Chandler, Susan Hayward—some pretty good names. I went there for two years, and after that I ended up at the Woodstock Playhouse, and did a season of stock. And during the summer I met two gals who kind of changed my life: They were Gloria Vanderbilt, Sr., and her twin sister, Thelma Furness. *Lady* Thelma Furness—she was married to Lord Furness, who owned the Furness Line, and she had been the mistress of the Prince of Wales [the future King Edward VIII]. They befriended me, and every free moment I had I would spend with them and listen to stories about another lifestyle, one that completely fascinated me. They suggested that I go to Hollywood, that I couldn't miss. My father agreed to sponsor me out there for one year, and so I drove to Hollywood to "knock 'em dead." I spent a year, and nothing happened. So I came back, and did another season of stock.

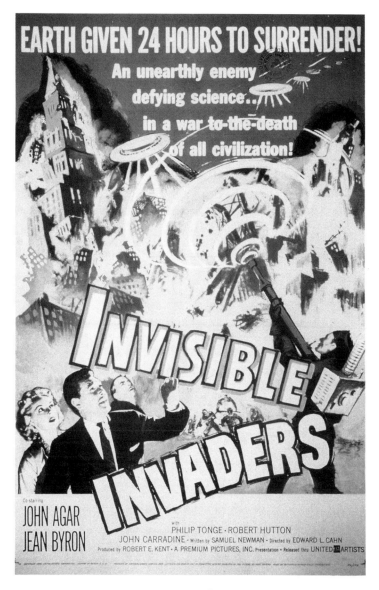

Hutton remembers little about *Invisible Invaders* except that John Agar nearly turned a Jeep over during a wild ride.

So how did you end up back in Hollywood?

My mother and father divorced, and I went from being a rich kid to a kid without a nickel to call his own. It was do-or-die, so I went to Manhattan and walked into the Louis Shurr Agency, which was the biggest at the time. They asked me, "What the hell do you want?" and I said, "I want to go to Hollywood, to get into the movies." And they said, "Give us two weeks." They got me a test with Paramount in New York, and I made what I'm sure had to be the worst test ever filmed. But Paramount wanted to sign me, for $200 a week, which to me was a magnificent sum. I wanted it, but the agent turned it down—which convinced me that he was crazy. Then, out on the Coast, they took the test over from Paramount to Warner Bros., and Warners gave me a contract for $250 a week. I went out with the contract, and that was that.

You were gone from Warner Bros. by the end of the '40s.

Warner Bros. actually got rid of all their contract people; people like Errol Flynn left, and so did Bette Davis. By the way, when Bette Davis left, nobody said goodbye to her, not a soul—that's a well-known story. I felt that the time for me to leave was then. Also, I had been offered a starring role with Franchot Tone and Charles Laughton and Burgess Meredith in *The Man on the Eiffel Tower* [1949]. I accepted it for less money than I should have got, but I wanted to go to Paris, which is where the film was made.

In the '50s, after you left Warners and got into a low-budget rut, you put the blame on an agent who stuck too high a price on you.

That's when television was coming in, and everybody was scared to death. All I wanted to do was work; I thought that was the most important thing. And, yes, after I got back from doing *The Man on the Eiffel Tower,* my agent was asking way too much money for me. Consequently I didn't work. Something else that hurt was the fact that I was very outspoken about my politics. I'm a Republican, and a very conservative one—always have been— and there was a period when I had a hell of a time getting a job because of that. The leftists had made real inroads into Hollywood, I was very anti–Communist, they knew about my feelings and I didn't work for quite a while.

Sort of a reverse blacklist.

Yes, it *was* a reverse blacklist. Those were bad days—they were terrible. I remember I was at a party one night at Ann Rutherford's, I was playing gin rummy, and directly in back of me, talking the way we're talking now, were two guys talking to Larry Parks, saying, "Larry, come on, join the party, it's the thing to do." And he joined the Communist party that night.

Did you like working with Jerry Lewis in the fantasy CinderFella?

CinderFella was a great experience from beginning to end. I got the part because I happened to go over to Paramount as a visitor to see Bobby Darin make a test. He was doing "Mack the Knife," and I was on the stage with some friends. Jerry came on with a pair of scissors, and he went around cutting everybody's necktie off *[laughs]*! He saw me—we had known one another since the Dean Martin days—and he didn't cut my tie; instead he took me by the arm and said, "You're just the guy I want to see." He took me back to his office,

Taking five at Bronson Canyon, Hutton, Philip Tonge and Jean Byron get ready for their next clash with the *Invisible Invaders*.

set me down and said that he was going to make the story of *CinderFella* — Cinderella in reverse. He had Dame Judith Anderson, Anna Maria Alberghetti, Ed Wynn, and he wanted me to play one of the stepbrothers. He said, "No agent involved, you just decide here and now, you don't read the script." Then, as far as money was concerned, he said, "You write down what you want — ten-week guarantee — and I'll write down what I'm going to give you. It could be more, maybe it could be less." I wrote down what I thought was a very fair amount, we exchanged these little pieces of paper, and his figure was double what I had written down! So we shook hands and that was it, right then and there. But that's what it was like to work with him, it was wonderful.

How did The Slime People *come about?*

A promoter by the name of Joe Robertson found some people who ran a string of launderettes, and got them to put up some money to make *The Slime People*. Joe and his wife had written the screenplay, but they wrote under made-up names ["Blair Robertson and Vance Skarstedt"] because they didn't want the credit — and I don't blame them! They needed a director and he knew that I was very anxious to direct — so anxious that I would do it for practically nothing.

The Slime People was a lot of fun to make — oh, we had a *ball*! We had a very, very low budget, but I'd always wanted to direct a movie and they gave me the opportunity. We only could afford to have two outfits made for the

Bob Miles, Hutton's stunt double, gets tossed around by Slime Person Robert Herron. The ultra-cheap *Slime People* was Hutton's first fling at directing.

Slime People, and they were supposed to take over the world in the movie! We had a drunk in the slime outfit, we had anything that could move! But it was fun, and it made money, so that's all that really mattered.

Were you satisfied with the job you did as director?

I found out that directing was not that simple a job. There were a lot of things I didn't know, and I don't think I'd ever want to do it again. But I did it, and I had fun. And I did, I suppose, as much as anybody could do with the amount of money we had—which was nothing!

How much is nothing?

I think our budget was $56,000, which *was* nothing, even back then! I knew that I was in way over my head and I tried to fake it. In making the movie I went to all my friends, because we couldn't afford to pay any kind of salaries. We borrowed an office on Hollywood Boulevard to cast the female lead, and the first girl who came in was Susan Hart. She had a sweater on and she looked good, and I didn't ask her to read or anything; I said, "You've got the part!" And that was it! She was attractive, and I knew she was going to photograph well. Susan Hart did all right for us, and she went on to do some pretty good work; she later married one of the heads of AIP, Jim Nicholson. I got Les Tremayne because he was a friend—I said, "Please help me, this is my first chance as a director"—and we paid him scale. He helped me a lot.

Richard Arlen was originally going to play the professor. He was an old friend, and he had been having a real tough time—I think he had a drinking problem, and he hadn't worked regular for quite a while. He was doing this as sort of a favor to me, and I very badly wanted him to do it because he was a big star of yesteryear and that would have been good for the picture. At eleven o'clock the night before we started shooting, as I was going to bed, the phone rang, and it was a nurse from the hospital saying, "Mr. Hutton, we've got Mr. Arlen here and he's a very sick man. He wanted me to call and say he can't do your picture." So I got on the phone and called Robert Burton, asked him if he could take over the role and start work in the morning, and he said, yes, he could. He was a fine actor, too; he worked like a dog on the thing. He died shortly thereafter of a heart attack, and I felt very bad about that; he was a nice man. So we had good actors, even if it wasn't a very good movie.

Where did you dig up William Boyce, who played the young marine?

He didn't know anything about motion pictures. I think Joe Robertson found him walking down the street one day, asked him if he wanted to be in movies, the guy said yeah and that was it.

The film is listed as a Hutton—Robertson Production. Does that mean you had money in the movie?

Oh, no. Joe and I simply formed our own company to make it. We had great plans—we were going to go on, and make a lot of movies, but [laughs] it didn't pan out that way! And Robertson was completely crazy, like a little boy. He was producing a movie and he was as happy as I was directing. I remember driving down with him to pick up the monster costumes—the wolf's head masks and also the Slime People's outfits—which had been made in New York. He had them in his car and I was driving mine. And on the way back I stopped at a stoplight and looked over, and the damn fool had the head of the wolf on, and he was growling at me from his car [laughs]!

What's this about wolf's head masks?

That was something that they cut out of the movie. It was really the mask of a vole, which is some sort of burrowing rodent. I think the voles belonged to the Slime People, and they were brought along by them—for what reason, I don't know! We didn't do too much research on that movie; the only research involved was what manhole could these Slime Men come up out of without any traffic around?

Right around this time they had one of their yearly fires in Bel-Air, and some very beautiful mansions were destroyed—Burt Lancaster lost his home, Zsa Zsa Gabor, people like that. Joe called me and said, "Listen, I'll get a police pass and a 'wild' camera, we'll go up there, shoot the whole thing and use the scene in the movie." And we did. Thank God for that fire *[laughs]*!

Where else did you go on Slime People?

The airport scenes were shot at Van Nuys Airport. The TV station was KTTV—we got in because we knew somebody there. The butcher's shop was up in Lancaster, California, and *[laughs]* it belonged to my father-in-law! He said, sure, we could use the place, but he refused to shut off the refrigeration and we nearly froze to death in that scene in the meat locker. Man, that was cold! That was the scene where the voles came in—we hired a couple of midgets to put on these vole costumes, and had them jumping down from the ceiling onto people in the market. And my father-in-law didn't want to close the shop! We had paid him, but he didn't see the sense in closing up and losing business. So he didn't stop customers from coming in, and we frightened the daylights out of them for a while!

Were your Slime People costumes expensive?

Yes, they cost a lot of money; they ran us three or four thousand dollars, and that was a big chunk out of $56,000. I think we had two complete outfits, and then also those vole heads. Those costumes were pretty good—I mean, they were as good as any you'd find in that type of movie. I think they used too much fog in a lot of scenes, but on the other hand, that fog covered up a lot of sins, a lot of mistakes. We had fog machines going all the time and, like I said, a few times they laid it on a little too thick and you couldn't see anything—no scenery, no actors, nothing but fog.

Why does the second unit director, William Martin, get such a prominent credit?

After I had finished with the picture, Joe said they had to go back to do some added scenes and that William Martin was going to direct them, and would I share billing with him? I had a contract with Joe which stated that I was to get sole director's credit, and I insisted upon it. So that must be why he gets such a prominent credit.

I was told that you were never paid for directing and starring in The Slime People.

I didn't even get the first week's salary.

I talked to two of the stuntmen who played Slime Men [Robert Herron and Fred Stromsoe], and if it makes you feel any better, they weren't paid, either.

It does—makes me feel a *lot* better *[laughs]*! The man who played the monster the most often was a friend of Joe Robertson's, and he was drunk the whole time. And he was very good as a Slime Man, because he stumbled around and it looked real good! He also had a couple of bucks in the picture.

The Slime People *came out through a small outfit called Hansen Enterprises.*

Donald Hansen was the man who owned the launderettes. I think I brought that film in for $51,000 or $52,000, and what little money was left I would imagine they used for advertising. It took three weeks to shoot.

When did you move to England, and why?

My brother-in-law and I were together one night playing cards, and then all of a sudden, late at night, we started talking about making a movie and wouldn't-it-be-fun? And slowly it all came together and we co-produced this picture [*The Secret Door,* 1964]. We shot in Lisbon—I had already made one movie in Portugal, I liked the country and the people very much, and so I chose Portugal as our location. After shooting the picture we had to go up to London to do the scoring and editing and so forth, and while I was there I was offered quite a bit of work. And so I stayed on.

How did you get involved on The Vulture?

Jack Lamont was a producer I knew from Hollywood, and he asked me if I'd like to play the lead in *The Vulture*—it was that simple. English agents didn't make the rounds of the studios like American agents did. They waited for the phone to ring and for the producer to call them, rather than going out and seeking jobs for the actor, as I was used to. So most of the negotiating was done by me, with Jack Lamont—salary and all that. Also, I wanted to work with Akim Tamiroff, and Brod Crawford was an old friend of mine—we'd had the same agent in Hollywood and I'd known him for years and years.

In the movie Brod had a cane with a wolf's head on it, very highly polished. And I remember I had a long speech by a fireplace and he had to just sit there and listen to me go on and on. During rehearsal he played with that wolf's head and twisted it around and made it reflect the light. Stealing the scene. And I thought, "Now, that's not right, not while I'm talking—I've got a long speech here!" So just before we got to the actual take, I said, "Brod, are you going to play with that wolf's head, like you did in rehearsal?" And he said *[laughs]*, "No, I was just trying you out." He was a wonderful guy.

And how about Tamiroff?

He was just beautiful—such a fabulous actor! To be working with people like that was an honor. This may sound stupid, but sometimes I didn't think about money or anything like that; it was just fun to work and to know those people.

How did Akim Tamiroff feel dressing up in a vulture costume?
Stupid *[laughs]*! But he never argued, never complained. Again, you see—he was *working*. And he was really into the thing.

The Vulture really is the pits, probably the worst sci-fi thing you did.
The idea wasn't bad, but I think this was one film where they needed more horror. They talked about the Vulture all the time but you hardly ever saw the damn thing. It called for less talk and more horror. But, of course, that would cost money, and talk doesn't cost as much. I think *The Vulture* took five or six weeks; we even went out on location, down to Devon and Cornwall.

Were the people who made films like these open to suggestions, or were they only interested in getting the thing in the can?
I can tell you a story that I think will answer your question. In *The Vulture* there was a left-to-right move that I had to do that didn't make any sense to me. I asked the director, Lawrence Huntington, "Laurie, why do you want me to do this?" and he got all flustered! I said, "I don't want motivation or anything like that, just why do you want me to move there?" And he took me aside and said, "Bobby, please just do it. I don't care if it doesn't make sense, just do it." Laurie didn't care and Jack Lamont, who was also on the set, *he* didn't care, so I did it. And that's it. Why? Because it said in the script that the character moves from left to right at that point, and they just wanted to get the thing on film and forget it.

About this time you landed a small part in You Only Live Twice.
That was fun. [Producer] "Cubby" Broccoli and I kind of grew up together in Hollywood; there was a point where Cubby wasn't doing very much of anything, and he bought all of Ian Fleming's works. He got on the phone and called a whole bunch of people one day, just to say, "Hey, listen, you know what I did?"—and people in Hollywood laughed at him! Later, of course, the James Bond films caught on, which was wonderful for Cubby. And when I was over in England, I used to visit the sets a lot—they would take over the biggest stage at Pinewood and do miraculous things. One day I was there talking to some of the production people when I happened to say, "Boy, I'd love to be in a James Bond sometime," and they said, "You're in it right now!" They sent me to wardrobe, put me in a general's outfit and there I was! It was as simple as that.

Your next science fiction film was They Came from Beyond Space.
What I remember best about that picture was Freddie Francis, one of the nicest guys in the whole world, and a good director. He came to me, out to

Hutton *(second from left)* pals around with fellow cast members Jennifer Jayne and Michael Gough between takes of *They Came from Beyond Space.*

my home, said he was going to make the movie, gave me the script and asked me if I'd like to do it. We got along fine and became very good friends. We shot at Pinewood in Twickingham, that magnificent studio where some of the Bonds were done.

Sounds like you enjoyed the experience.

Yes, and also the film itself. A lot of the *Movies on TV*-style books call it a bomb, but I don't think it was bad. I know that it was selected by some group of scientists in America as one of the better science fiction movies, and they said this *could* happen. I also enjoyed working with Michael Gough, who was a good actor and a fine guy.

The picture reminded me quite a bit of Invisible Invaders.

That's right—aliens coming down from the moon, and dead bodies coming back to life. But *They Came from Beyond Space* was done a bit better; in fact, I thought it was done very well. One thing I could never understand was why my character drove that old car. I know I asked Freddie why, and he gave me an answer and it seemed reasonable at the time, but looking back now I still don't understand how I ended up with that miserable heap!

You worked with Freddie Francis again on Torture Garden.

Yes, that was Freddie again. Amicus made a specialty out of that sort of anthology horror film, but I think they're confusing, and I didn't care for them. You become involved in one story, and suddenly it's over and you're into another. And it takes a bit of time to build up interest again. Now, *Dead of Night* was a classic, just great, especially the episode with Michael Redgrave as the ventriloquist—that was scary. That apparently was the film Amicus was copying, but they didn't do as good a job. I later did another horror anthology film called *Tales from the Crypt,* but it was a very small part and I just don't remember it at all.

Most of your Torture Garden *scenes were with Beverly Adams.*

She was very nice, but she was a terrible actress. I know that when we did the scene where we disclose the fact that I'm made of steel, she had an awful time—she couldn't hit me or do any of the things she was supposed to do. But she was very, very beautiful, and a delightful person.

You got special "and" billing in Cry of the Banshee *but not a very good part.*

I had known Vincent Price for years and years but I had never worked with him*, so that's why I did it. It was shot at Grim's Dyke, which was the house that belonged to W.S. Gilbert of Gilbert and Sullivan fame. We were there in the dead of winter, and it was cold because they didn't have any heating! *Cry of the Banshee* was Vincent's 100th movie, and after shooting they gave a big party for him in the house. And they had a girl come out of a cake—a nude girl. This was another first for me, I had never seen that before. The poor thing was freezing to death, naked as a jaybird, and Vincent was very embarrassed because that isn't his cup of tea. A nude coming out of a cake, that isn't Vincent Price, not at all.

How about working with Joan Crawford on Trog?

I did that film because she asked me to; I lived right around the corner from Bray Studio, which is where *Trog* was shot. Joan and I were old, old friends from Warners, and to see her working on a picture like *Trog* was very, very sad. But, by golly, she worked hard and she gave it her all.

Joan couldn't stand the heat, and they didn't have air conditioning at Bray. So she had electric fans all over her dressing room, and she carried a little hand fan when she went on the set. I wasn't working one day, and I went over just to see her and talk about old times. I was in her dressing room waiting for

---

*Hutton and Price both appeared in *Casanova's Big Night* (1954), but not together.

her, because she was on the stage. She came in and she had a flowing dress on, a full skirt, and she sat down and complained about the heat. And she lifted up her skirt so that the fans could blow some fresh air, and a moth flew out. She roared with laughter, looked at me and said, "My God, it's been so long it's got moths in it!" *[Laughs.]*

Did you ever get to see Trog?

No. I don't think I'd want to see her in something like that; I'd rather remember her for *Mildred Pierce* [1945] and *What Ever Happened to Baby Jane?* and pictures like that.

A few years later you wrote a horror film called Persecution. *How did you come up with the idea for that?*

I don't like cats, and I came up with this idea about a cat that could destroy a family. The original title was *I Hate You, Cat,* which I thought was a much better title than *Persecution*. Everyone who read the script thought it was good. I sent it to Bette Davis, who complimented me on it, but she said that the lead character was *so* bad, *such* a horrible woman that she didn't dare play it, although she would like to. And she suggested other people.

I gave Freddie Francis a copy of the script. And from what I understand his son Kevin came over one night, picked it up, took it home and decided it was a good movie to break into the motion picture business with, as a producer. I must admit he did it—he went out and raised the money—but still I say he received the money on the basis of the script.

Did you like Kevin Francis?

I liked him, yes, but he was kind of a devious little fellow and I like him less now because of what he did, or what he allowed to be done. I wish you could see the original script. It was a great script, and they changed the whole thing. I figure if Lana Turner decided to do it, and Trevor Howard, who was a damn good actor, if the people who are in it decided to do it on the basis of my original script, it must have been pretty good. But then, you know what happens, "I want to change this" and "I want to change that," and all of a sudden they changed everything. I have both scripts, my original and the shooting script, and it's like day and night. What they did to it broke my heart.

The one thing the movie has going for it is the Lana Turner name.

Lana and I used to go together, but once we broke up we didn't see or speak to each other from about 1946 'til when they made *Persecution*. I didn't know that they hired her, I had nothing to do with that; by the time they got around to shooting *Persecution,* I was making a movie down in Madrid. I thought the thing to do was to phone Lana at the Dorchester in London, to wish her well on the movie, and so I made the call. I got through to her suite and I heard them say, "Miss Turner, Mr. Hutton's calling from Madrid." And she wouldn't speak to me. Maybe because of what was happening—I know that she didn't like Kevin Francis at all, and she didn't like the fact that he had never done anything before. I didn't hear from her until 1985, when she found out I was here and sent me a lovely letter—but never mentioned anything about *Persecution!*

In 1975 she publicly called it a bomb.
I don't blame her!

Have you ever seen the movie?
No. Some friends of mine saw it down in Sarasota, Florida, and they said it was all they could do not to walk out. Because they were friends, they stayed. It opened and closed the same night in that theater.

Reviewing Persecution, *Rex Reed wrote about director Don Chaffey, "Lock that name in a steel box, drop it overboard 200 miles out to sea and never mention it again."*
I wish that Freddie Francis had directed *I Hate You, Cat*—he wanted to, he thought it was an excellent script, but his son got involved. Why Kevin didn't hire his father to direct it, I'll never know. Freddie would have made a doggone good movie out of it, I guarantee you—he would have shot what I wrote. And Lana Turner wouldn't be ashamed of it. And the whole world would be a different place today *[laughs]*!

What made you decide to come home to the United States?
In 1972 I thought it was about time to come back to Hollywood, and on the way back I wanted to stop off in Kingston because I knew my mother and my aunt were not well. And I found out that they were much more *un*-well than I realized, or had been told. I figured that I just couldn't leave, and so I stayed on here. And then I broke my back. I was in the hospital here in Kingston for nine months, on my back, couldn't move—and had a *ball*!

Really!
I did, I had a ball—it was a great experience! Everybody was so kind to me. And then they sent me to New York to have a real delicate operation which would allow me to sit up, and I was down there for five months. After that I needed complete rehabilitation and therapy, and they told me, "You can go to the Helen Hayes Institute, or a place up by Schenectady, or, there's a brand new place up in Kingston called the Health Related." I said, "The Health Related!"

What do you do to pass the time here?
I wrote a book since I've been here, about Hollywood, about what it was like. I think every publishing house in New York has read it, and every one

turned it down with the same comment. That it was charming, delightful, wonderful reading. But nobody would buy it. And when I asked why, they said, "Because you *liked* everybody." Because I don't have anything rotten to say about anybody! I do know "provocative" stories about people that haven't been told—stories that involve big names that I was fortunate enough to call my friends—but I don't think it's right to divulge stories like that, and I'm not going to rewrite the book. Unh-uh. No way.

Y'know, it's strange. When I went out to Hollywood with a seven-year contract in my pocket I never dreamed things would turn out the way they did. The people I've met. The superstars I've worked with. The friends I call true friends. My memories of the Hollywood I knew are wonderful memories.

ROBERT HUTTON FILMOGRAPHY

Northern Pursuit (Warners, 1943)
Destination Tokyo (Warners, 1943)
Janie (Warners, 1944)
Hollywood Canteen (Warners, 1944)
Roughly Speaking (Warners, 1945)
Too Young to Know (Warners, 1945)
One More Tomorrow (Warners, 1946)
Janie Gets Married (Warners, 1946)
Time Out of Mind (Universal, 1947)
So You Want to Be in Pictures (Warners short, 1947)
Love and Learn (Warners, 1947)
Always Together (Warners, 1948)
Wallflower (Warners, 1948)
Smart Girls Don't Talk (Warners, 1948)
The Younger Brothers (Warners, 1949)
The Man on the Eiffel Tower (RKO, 1949)
And Baby Makes Three (Columbia, 1949)
Beauty on Parade (Columbia, 1950)
Slaughter Trail (RKO, 1951)
New Mexico (United Artists, 1951)
The Racket (RKO, 1951)
The Steel Helmet (Lippert, 1951)
Tropical Heat Wave (Republic, 1952)
Gobs and Gals (Republic, 1952)
Paris Model (Columbia, 1953)
Three Chairs for Betty (RKO short, 1953)
Half-Dressed for Dinner (RKO short, 1953)
Casanova's Big Night (Paramount, 1954)
The Big Bluff (United Artists, 1955)
Yaqui Drums (Allied Artists, 1956)
Scandal, Inc. (Republic, 1956)
Thunder Over Tangier (Man from Tangier) (Republic, 1957)
Showdown at Boot Hill (20th Century-Fox, 1958)
The Colossus of New York (Paramount, 1958)

Outcasts of the City (Republic, 1958)
The Man Without a Body (Budd Rogers, 1959)
It Started with a Kiss (MGM, 1959)
Invisible Invaders (United Artists, 1959)
Jailbreakers (AIP, 1960)
CinderFella (Paramount, 1960)
Wild Youth (Naked Youth) (Cinema Associates, 1961)
The Slime People (Hansen Enterprises, 1963) Also directed
The Secret Door (Now It Can Be Told) (Allied Artists, 1964) Also Associate Producer
The Sicilians (Butcher's Films, 1964)
Los Novios de Marisol (Marisol's Boy Friends) (Spanish, 1965)
Busqueme A Esa Chica (Find Me That Girl) (Spanish, 1965)
Finders Keepers (United Artists, 1967)
Carnaby, M.D. (Doctor in Clover) (Continental Distributing, Inc., 1967)
The Vulture (Paramount, 1967)
You Only Live Twice (United Artists, 1967)
They Came from Beyond Space (Embassy, 1967)
Torture Garden (Columbia, 1968)
Can Heironymus Merkin Ever Forget Mercy Humppe and Find True Happiness? (Regional Film Distributors, 1969)
Cry of the Banshee (AIP, 1970)
Trog (Warners, 1970)
Tales from the Crypt (CRC, 1972)
Persecution (Fanfare, 1974) Co-wrote story and screenplay
It Came from Hollywood (Paramount, 1982) Clips from *The Slime People*

... I don't think there's one film that I can point to that really represents what I might have done. And consequently there's not one film or role that I look at of which I'm proud, nor one which I would recommend to anyone to see. It's a very sad statement, isn't it?

Nancy Kovack

THE CALENDAR says it's been more than 20 years since she worked in pictures, but—impossibly—Nancy Mehta looks every bit as chic and lovely as she did when (as Nancy Kovack) she stepped off the set of her last film, *Marooned,* in 1969.

A native of Flint, Michigan, Kovack was a student at the University of Michigan at fifteen, a radio deejay at sixteen, a college graduate at nineteen and the holder of eight beauty titles by twenty. Her professional acting career began on TV in New York, first as one of Jackie Gleason's Glea Girls and then, more prominently, on *The Dave Garroway Show, The Today Show* and *Beat the Clock.* A stage role opened Hollywood doors for Kovack, who signed with Columbia Pictures and played in such studio films as *Strangers When We Meet* (1960), *Cry for Happy* (1961) and *The Great Sioux Massacre* (1965) as well as in Paramount's *Sylvia* (1965), UA's *Frankie and Johnny* (1966) and an imposing list of episodic TV credits (she was Emmy-nominated for a 1969 guest shot on *Mannix*). Her best-remembered role came early on in her career, however, as the alluring high priestess Medea in Columbia's landmark stop-motion adventure *Jason and the Argonauts* in 1962. Now she's the first lady of music, happily and busily married to world-renowned maestro Zubin Mehta of New York Philharmonic fame.

Do you recall how you became involved on Jason and the Argonauts?

Being a Columbia contractee, we just did what we were told. But I was very happy to go abroad at that time—I was very young. *Jason and the Argonauts* was shot at the exact place in Italy where the legend was set. For instance, when our *Argonaut* sailed around a certain cape, the real one had in fact sailed around that very same cape.

Did you enjoy working in Italy?

Oh, I loved it. We were there a long time, as I recall, longer than we expected to be, and I've had a very warm place in my heart for that part of Italy. It's like a second home. We were there for something like four months.

Do you remember meeting the producers, Charles Schneer and Ray Harryhausen?

Charles Schneer, yes, I knew him well and I thought he was wonderful. He was a civil man, congenial and humorous. I enjoyed his wife—she was there—and I think his children were there, too. It was a very family-like situation. And Ray Harryhausen was on the set constantly. A very dignified, noble, quiet, "still" man—I appreciated that, and had a great respect for him. A very gentle man as well. And the special effects which he added to the film were phenomenal—I don't even have to say that. For that period, they were unique, were they not?

How did you prepare for your dance scene in Jason?

Previous page: One of Nancy Kovack's better roles during her five-year stint at Columbia was as the high priestess in the fantasy adventure *Jason and the Argonauts.*

In *Jason and the Argonauts,* Kovack (as Medea) joined flash-in-the-pan actor Todd Armstrong in his quest for the Golden Fleece.

Charles Schneer sent me to Rome a week ahead of time to learn this so-called dance. But it wasn't structured very well; in other words, I wasn't given much instruction in it, and I thought it was a little weak. And I also thought, at the time and in retrospect, that it was meant to be suggestive and erotic, etc., and *[disapprovingly]* I find that's a great form of titillation in films. And that's all I have to say about that...!

Any other Jason *anecdotes?*
It used to be very cold in the morning, and we'd have to get up at four A.M. sometimes in order to be ready for a six A.M. sunrise. We were in the village of Palinuro, in the shin of Italy. It was freezing, and I had a purple sweater that was very warm. And I was told that I couldn't wear the sweater, because the color purple was offensive to the people of the village! Purple meant death, and I was asked not to wear it. I said, "But I love this sweater!" It was all I had, and we had no access to other clothing, etc. I also remember staying long times on that ship, because the shooting was very difficult. I can't say why particularly, but shooting took a long time. But in general I just remember a great deal of warmth from everyone involved and from the Palinuro people.

Any recollections of Todd Armstrong [Jason]?

He was a nice boy, the son of someone who was a friend of someone at Columbia—as I understand it, that's how he was given this part. He found it phenomenal that I learned a little Italian before I went there. He was always frustrated and seemed sometimes disturbed, I don't know why. He was reactionary. And subsequent to that I understand he left the business, and I don't know what he's doing now.

What do you think of the picture?

I think it's a fine record for the legend, and I think that is important. I also feel that it's important for young people to see these things as opposed to other things that we may be seeing today. I do feel that society is deteriorating because of many of the effects of films.

How did you get interested in becoming an actress?

I came to New York City for the wedding of a friend. I was to be here for two days, and a girlfriend asked me if I wanted to go on a cattle call. I didn't know what that was. She explained that Jackie Gleason was having a cattle call, and that I should go. So I went, and I became one of the Glea Girls. And that's how it began. Also I did Broadway—*The Disenchanted*, with Jason Robards, Jr. From the Broadway show I was signed by Columbia Pictures.

Early on, what kind of roles did you think you were going to play in films?

Harry Cohn, who was the head of Columbia when I was signed, felt that I was a replacement for Rita Hayworth—my hair at that time was darker and slightly red. But he died, even before I got to Columbia. So those areas never came about. I had really, desperately hoped to play some serious roles. They never came my way. That was before this feminism crept into the industry. There are many roles now for women that are serious and very realistic, instead of paper doll cutouts. I'm sorry to have missed this period.

You next appeared in a Vincent Price picture, Diary of a Madman, *for United Artists.*

I must have been loaned out for that, because I couldn't do anything other than what Columbia agreed to. I enjoyed working with Vincent Price on *Diary of a Madman;* he was very respectful and I found that unusual. I knew that I wasn't known, and yet he was very respectful of me and kindly—he didn't have to be. He was professional, and I appreciated that. I remember that just before the scene where he kills me with the knife, Vincent Price was tickling me and I was laughing, and I couldn't stop laughing after that!

Did you pose for the painting, sketches and bust of you that are seen in the film?

No, I think they took a photograph and used that to do the painting and

Sculptor Vincent Price wants just the right look from model Kovack in the dismal *Diary of a Madman*.

the bust. I still have the painting; I think the busts were broken in the picture.

You had a director from the old school in Reginald LeBorg.
I had great empathy for him and sympathy for him. He was a good director, a fine director, and I respected him highly. Subsequent to that he didn't do much in the way of films and he wanted to, and I felt very badly about that.

Diary of a Madman *really wasn't much of a picture.*
I think these are all kind of "light" pictures, and they didn't get heavier with time *[laughs]*! I was very happy to be working. I don't know if you know the debilitating feeling of being under contract and not working. You're not permitted to work anywhere else, and you're really their puppet. And if you're not working, it's so debilitating, mentally and emotionally. So I was just very grateful to work.

Do you spend much time looking at your own movies?
No, I never see them, never. I'm a little embarrassed—in fact, a *lot* embarrassed. And sometimes I can't bear to see them!

You worked alongside the Three Stooges and Adam (Batman) *West in Columbia's* The Outlaws Is Coming *(1965).*

I was stunned that I was working with the Three Stooges, because they were a household word. I really didn't know they were still working—and neither did they *[laughs]*! That's why they were grateful for this film, I suppose. I was pleased to watch them, because after many years of seeing them on film, then all of a sudden you're sitting around drinking coffee and talking with them ... it was quite extraordinary for a young person. And I liked Adam West very much. I thought he was a very whole person, his feet on the ground, and very likable.

Why such a small role in The Silencers?

It was also Columbia Pictures. One's career could go right down the tube, being signed during that period when there was no studio head like a Harry Cohn. This was during the segue from "big studio-dom" into what we have today, where there's nothing. And it was kind of a deterioration. I'm not here to tell you that it was the studio's fault, but it is a fact, analytically, that at that time the studio was moving away from what it was known as. So I just did what I was told. But I had a lot of fun for the short time I worked on *The Silencers*. Dean Martin was a nice, funny guy.

You also did plenty of "fantastic" TV, including The Man from U.N.C.L.E., Batman, *many episodes of* Bewitched *and also* Star Trek.

I had a lot of fun on the *U.N.C.L.E.*s, I enjoyed doing them; it was quick work, and I love to be quick in my work. I was capable of doing that, so it worked nicely. What stands out in my mind regarding *Batman* is that the episodes I did came at the beginning of the series, and it was very difficult for many of the guest actors to understand in what ilk to play. We had not been used to playing farce, and we didn't quite know what farce was—but we didn't want to admit that we didn't know! And when asking what form this was taking, we were told to play it straight. So we played it straight, although with what I know now of farce I would surely have played it differently. I was in the *Bewitched* pilot, playing Samantha's [Elizabeth Montgomery] girlfriend, and this pilot was so popular that they kept bringing me back as the girlfriend. And on *Star Trek*, I remember that William Shatner was a very warm actor, and it was easy to act with him. I enjoyed doing it.

What do you recall about Tarzan and the Valley of Gold?

That I wanted desperately to work in the jungle, and I begged them to let me swing on a vine. Which they promised they'd let me do, lying about it, of course. I remember that I felt that there was great discrimination against the Mexican workers, and that was very disturbing to me. I also remember a helicopter nearly crashing, and that scared me because I had just gotten out of it *[laughs]*! Robert Day was the director—a little worried because he was behind schedule, a little nervous. A nice man. But I loved more than anything the animals—I loved so much that lion, and the snake that worked with us. I feel that I really became fast friends with them. When they couldn't find me or call me to the set, they'd say, "Oh, she must be with the lion." The lion used to put its head in my lap, and we would just sit quietly under a tree.

You shot part of that film in the ancient city of Teotihuacan, which caused a furor.

There were armed soldiers watching over us, making sure that we did only what we had announced we were going to do. Once we got our scenes shot, we had to slip out of the country with the film underneath jackets, just to get home! The Mexican government felt that we were desecrating in some way the image of their monuments.

Did you get along well with Tarzan *Mike Henry?*

Mike Henry was an extremely handsome man, and I felt one of the finest Tarzans physically, but I found him very cold and always disgruntled. He was always unhappy about something, and I didn't know why. He always seemed as though he were someplace else. Mike was angry with the chimp always, very angry, and hurt him—treated him very roughly. That very much disturbed me, and so I took the side of the animal! We didn't have any contention, Mike Henry and I, I don't wish to say that, but in all sets there's tremendous

Kovack in full wardrobe for Columbia's *The Silencers.*

Kovack poses with the Lord of the Apes (Mike Henry) and the King of Beasts during production of *Tarzan and the Valley of Gold.*

warmth and camaraderie, and there wasn't with him. It was my first experience like that.

On the next Tarzan *picture, the chimp ripped open Mike Henry's jaw.*
I remember that—that happened in Brazil *[Tarzan and the Great River]*. That's because he worried the chimp, because he treated it so badly.

Around this time you also made several films in, of all places, Iran.
I lived in Iran for nearly three years. I used Iran as a base for seeing all of the world east of there—Afghanistan, India, Cambodia, Japan, all those sorts of places. Then I'd come back, do another little film in three weeks, and went west to Kuwait, Israel, Turkey, etc. Another little Iranian film in two weeks, and then I went into Russia through Samarkand and Tashkent, and saw Russia from that view, which was very special.

What kind of country was *Iran in those days?*
Just magnificent. I cannot tell people enough, how magnificent the people were, and still are, in my view, regardless of how we see what's going on

now. How beautiful I thought the country was, what expectations I had for the country. And I felt that the Shah and his politics, at that time, and given the development of the country, were correct for the moment.

Stateside you turned up in a small role in the borderline SF Marooned.

What I remember about *Marooned* is that I had severely damaged my leg and could hardly stand, and [producer] Mike Frankovich saying, "If you weren't an actress, you'd be in a hospital!" It was a very small part. *Marooned* was my last film. I met Zubin Mehta, and we were married.

Whose decision was it that you curtail your acting career?

My husband's. I do sometimes miss the camaraderie of show business, but I am so busy that there seems not to be any space. I love my marriage, I just try to be a good wife and do the best that I can in my marriage. That's all.

Throughout the ten years you were an actress, you kept busy and worked opposite a number of top stars. Are you happy with your career?

Oh, no—absolutely not! I feel it was very shallow, and that I never was able to play a real person. I was perceived as a girl with combed hair and lipstick, and no matter what I would do, they would not give me the role of a real woman. I wanted that, and I could have done that—easily, and well. But I don't think there's one film that I can point to that really represents what I might have done. And consequently there's not one film or role that I look at of which I'm proud, nor one which I would recommend to anyone to see. *[Smirks.]* It's a very sad statement, isn't it?

NANCY KOVACK FILMOGRAPHY

Strangers When We Meet (Columbia, 1960)
Cry for Happy (Columbia, 1961)
The Wild Westerners (Columbia, 1962)
Diary of a Madman (United Artists, 1963)
Jason and the Argonauts (Columbia, 1963)
The Great Sioux Massacre (Columbia, 1965)
The Outlaws Is Coming (Columbia, 1965)
Sylvia (Paramount, 1965)
Frankie and Johnny (United Artists, 1966)
The Silencers (Columbia, 1966)
Tarzan and the Valley of Gold (AIP, 1966)
Enter Laughing (Columbia, 1967)
Marooned (Columbia, 1969)

*... At first I thought
I was going to be very intimidated
by [Boris Karloff], because I'd only
known him as the Frankenstein Monster. But he was
the kindest, sweetest, nicest, quietest man
I think I've ever worked with.*

Anna Lee

ANNA LEE HAS far too much poise and class to be hung with the label of "scream queen," but the petite blond leading lady *has* appeared in horror, fantasy and science fiction films with some regularity since she first broke the ice in the genre in the mid-'30s. Her first fantastic film credit was the Christ allegory *The Passing of the Third Floor Back,* made on her native English soil in 1935, and in the half-century since she has not only established herself as one of Hollywood's great character actresses but also reinforced her genre status in many other fantasy and SF titles, including *The Man Who Lived Again, King Solomon's Mines, Flesh and Fantasy, The Ghost and Mrs. Muir, Jack the Giant Killer, Picture Mommy Dead, In Like Flint* and more. Horror film fans will remember her best as the spirited Nell Bowen, running afoul of sadist Boris Karloff in Val Lewton's classic historical thriller *Bedlam.*

The daughter of a clergyman, Anna Lee was born Joan Boniface Winnifrith and encouraged to pursue an acting career by her father. After training at London's Royal Albert Hall, she took to the boards and later began appearing in English films, first as an extra, then working her way up to featured parts and finally earning the unofficial title "Queen of the Quota Quickies." Lee and her husband, director Robert Stevenson, relocated to Hollywood in the late '30s, and Lee began starring in stateside productions as well as becoming a fixture of the John Ford stock company (she appeared in *How Green Was My Valley, Fort Apache* and a half-dozen others). In 1970 she became the seventh wife of novelist, poet and playwright Robert Nathan *(Portrait of Jennie, The Bishop's Wife),* and she remains active today, still radiantly charming and strikingly attractive, regularly playing wealthy Lila Quartermaine on TV's hottest soap opera, *General Hospital.*

I was born in England, in a very small village called Ightham. My father was rector of Ightham for about 25 years; I was born in the rectory and I grew up there until he died when I was ten. My real name is Joan Boniface Winnifrith but for obvious reasons I had to change it, because the moment I started doing a play they said, "We can't put that on a marquee, we can't even put it in the program!" And they told me to choose a name that was short and easy to remember. I was reading Tolstoy at the time and I thought Anna — from *Anna Karenina*—was very romantic, a lovely name. Then I was also reading American history and I thought Robert E. Lee was a rather good chap, so I decided to take the name Lee. The story that goes with that is, when they put in the paper that I had changed my name to Anna Lee, I had a telephone call from a writer friend of mine — he did all the Hitchcock pictures, his name was Charles Bennett. And he said, "Joan, if you had to change your name, why did you choose something that sounds like a Chinese laundry?" Of course it hadn't dawned on me *[laughs],* but Anna Lee *does* have a certain Chinese feeling. When I was making *Seven Women* [1966] for John Ford, we all had our dressing rooms on the stage and our names on the doors. One day I came back from lunch and I saw this little old Chinese lady gazing up at my name — we had a lot of Chinese extras in that picture. I came up to her and said, "Good

Previous page: Anna Lee and horror great Boris Karloff in a moody two-shot from *The Man Who Lived Again.*

After a series of glamorous leads in British and American films, Anna Lee matured into one of Hollywood's finest character actresses.

afternoon," and her face fell. She said, "*Yoooo* are Ah-na Lee?" I said I was, and she said, "Ooooh, I t'ought it was a *Chinese* actress!" *[Laughs.]*

So how did a rector's daughter end up in show biz?

I believe it was really my father's fault. I think most clergymen, at least in England, are frustrated actors—Laurence Olivier's father was a clergyman, so was Matheson Lang's and, oh, about five or six others at the time. My father wanted one of his five children to be an actor, and I think because I was the one who showed off a lot, a very extroverted child, he decided, "Joan is going to be an actress." And so it never occurred to me that I was to do anything else!

When I was about 15 I couldn't wait to start, and my mother, who was a widow by that time, was a little worried because she'd heard all these wild stories about what happened to actresses. So she took me to see my godmother, who was Sybil Thorndike, quite a famous actress in her own right. I was in boarding school then, and I went up to the Old Vic to see her in my gym tunic and blue serge bloomers. I recited "There Are Fairies at the Bottom of Our Garden" and I don't know how she kept a straight face *[laughs]*! Anyway, she said, "I think you should go back to school, and once you've been properly educated I want you to go to the Central School of Speech Training and Dramatic Arts at the Royal Albert Hall in London." Laurence Olivier and John Gielgud and Ralph Richardson had all been students there, but before my time — about three years before I arrived. So I spent the rest of my school term just swatting away, trying to pass the exam, which I did. And so my mother had to let me go to the Albert Hall.

How long were you there?
About three and a half years, until I left in disgrace. I had heard that you could get a job as an extra at Elstree in a movie they were making, I went down there and I got a part — it was probably *Ebb Tide* [1932]. This got back to Elsie Fogarty, who was the head of the school. I was dragged in front of everybody and she said, "I regret to tell the class that one of our most promising pupils has prostituted her art by playing in the cinema!" In those days for a stage actor to work in the cinema was really considered rather demeaning. I was forced to leave the Albert Hall, but then I went to the London Repertory Company and stayed for quite a while. My leading man there was a man named Bernard Lee, whom years later I found in the 007 movies, playing James Bond's boss, M! He and I worked in two or three plays together. Then I went on tour in things like *The Barretts of Wimpole Street* and so on.

This was about the time that your film career was starting as well.
I did lots and lots of extra parts in what were called quota pictures. Quota pictures — "quota quickies" — were made to conform with some kind of law, and so they were all exceedingly low budget and very, very fast. Of course in those days we had no union in England, so we had to sit up all night many, many times in order to finish them. But they were good training. I must have done seven or eight of those.
I did a film called *Rolling in Money* [1934] for an American man, an agent at that time, Al Parker. Whilst I was doing that he wanted me to sign a contract and come to America as an actress. About a week before that, I had been sent for to go down to Gaumont-British to test for a part in a picture called *The Camels Are Coming* [1934], and they *also* wanted me to sign a contract. So, without thinking, I signed both contracts *[laughs]*! Well, fortunately, I was under 18 at the time so they were null and void, and I chose to stay in England. I was with Gaumont-British for five or six years.

Your early publicity is full of far-out stories about your running away to join a circus, and encounters with Chinese bandits.
Well, the circus story is more or less correct: I did fall in love with a lion tamer and I did run away to the circus. I thought I could get a job there, and

the only job they could give me was as the girl who had knives thrown at her! So I was very briefly the girl who had knives thrown at her, until my father soon found out about it and I was dragged home in disgrace. That was my circus career. Chinese bandits? Again, they're on the right track. I had a rather wealthy godmother who decided that she didn't want me to go on the stage (it wasn't respectable) so she thought she'd take me out to China, where British mothers sent their daughters to find suitable beaux—there were a lot of soldiers and sailors stationed there at the time. We went to China, and whilst we were in Hong Kong we took a trip to Macao. And on the way there the boat that we were on was boarded by Chinese pirates. I was thrilled *[laughs]*—I wanted to go meet the pirates—but a British gunboat came by very fast and chased them away!

It was after you were in pictures a few years that you married director Robert Stevenson.

I was making *The Camels Are Coming* with Jack Hulbert—we made it out very near the Suez Canal, out around where the Sphinx is. We were supposed to drink Evian water, but the Egyptians who took care of us, all they did was go down to the Nile and fill up the empty bottles with Nile water *[laughs]*! So everybody came down with awful attacks of dysentery—except me, because I didn't drink the water. But at any rate they were all sick, and the production was almost at a total standstill. So Gaumont-British sent Bob Stevenson out as a troubleshooter. I remember I was riding across the desert on the little Arab pony which they had given me, and I saw this man who looked like something out of a Noel Coward movie. Everybody who was already there was looking so dirty by this time—they were unshaven, they were living in tents and everybody was half-sick. And this character came out wearing a white shirt and white shorts and white socks and white everything. We met and fell in love, and when we got back to England, I married him. We worked together quite a lot—actually, there were usually three of us on the team, Bob and myself and Ronald Neame, who was our cameraman. And now Ronnie is doing so well here as a director.

What memories do you have of the making of the fantasy The Passing of the Third Floor Back?

It was the first time I had worked with Conrad Veidt, and of course like all young girls I was madly in love with him. He was a big, very ... *[laughs]* strange man. He was a very egotistical man, I think—he was always admiring himself in a mirror, he had mirrors all the way around, rather like Marlene Dietrich. But he was very nice, and he had a great sense of humor. My mother was played by Cathleen Nesbitt, who of course at one time was the great love of Rupert Brooke, the poet. I had always wanted to meet her but I was a little shy at that time about asking her questions. But years later when I was out in Hollywood, about '72 or '73, I did a play here at the Westwood Playhouse and playing with me was Cathleen Nesbitt, who was then in her eighties. We had a wonderful time together, and remembered back to when she played my mother in *The Passing of the Third Floor Back*.

The film got some good writeups when it opened, but it really seems to have fallen through the cracks.
   It's a strange picture, a little hard, almost impossible to describe. It was directed by Berthold Viertel, whom I also met again in America — he came out here when war broke out. He was married to Salka Viertel, who was Garbo's great love. Conrad Veidt played a Christ-like character who has an impact on the lives of the tenants of a London boarding house and *[laughs]* of course it always made people smile to think of Conrad Veidt, who always played such evil characters, playing Christ!

He once described it as his most difficult role.
   I'm sure it was — quite sure. But he was good in it.

What do you remember about working with Boris Karloff on The Man Who Lived Again?
   Of course at first I thought I was going to be very intimidated by him, because I'd only known him as the Frankenstein Monster. But he was the kindest, sweetest, nicest, quietest man I think I've ever worked with. He had a great love for poetry, and I did, too, and so we used to have a sort of jam session: He would start a poem, like, "Between the dark and the daylight, when the night is beginning to lower," and I'd go on, "Comes a pause in the day's occupation, which is called the Children's Hour." We went on for hours and hours doing this, seeing if we could stump each other! He was a very, very nice man.

Did Karloff enjoy his return to England?
   Yes and no. He was very, very perturbed and frustrated to find out that there was no union. He said, "You've got to have a union! We have a union in California, and an actor should have a union." And I thought to myself, "Well — why?" I worked Saturdays and Sundays and everything else, and we'd never heard of anything like double time; we even did our own stunts. In a film called *Young Man's Fancy* [1939], I played Miss Ada, the Human Cannonball, and I was fired out of a cannon! Here in Hollywood they'd get an extra for that, but back then I was fired out of a cannon. Well, Karloff thought this was all wrong, and I remember that he lectured us all quite firmly on the fact that we must have a union.

Did he clash with the higher-ups on that picture?
   I think they wanted us to work on a Saturday, and he said that, no, he would not work on a Saturday unless he was paid more for it. We all listened to him, because English actors had never heard of a union at that time.

What other recollections of the film?

We made that at Gainsborough, I remember that distinctly because the dressing rooms were rather small. And right next door to me, practically sharing my dressing room, were the monkeys—the chimpanzees that you see in the film. And they smelled awful! I remember holding my nose whenever I had to go into my dressing room!

How long did shooting take?

We took quite a long time, I think probably about eight to ten weeks—we very seldom got more than three sequences a day on that. I saw the picture again recently and I loved it, because it was so long since I'd seen it—I saw old faces like Frank Cellier, whom I played with several times after that, and Donald Calthrop and Cecil Parker. And I thought it was very well done, that it stood up remarkably well. I think it was one of Karloff's better pictures.

Certainly one of your best-respected films from this English period is King Solomon's Mines.

Everybody agrees that that was by far the best of all the versions they made. They made a second version [1950] with Deborah Kerr and Stewart Granger which was not as good as ours—and I wasn't the only person to say that, I heard that all around. And the third one [1985], with Richard Chamberlain, I think was a disaster. Ours was really very, very well done, in my opinion, and I love watching it again now.

Location photography was done in Africa.

But *we* never moved outside the studio! They had a second unit in Africa, but we had *our* desert in the studio. We had two of the largest stages at Gaumont-British, and we built that huge cavern you see in the film. All done in the studio! And I skinned my knees on those rocks—it was really a tough picture to do. I remember when we did that scene in the desert, where we're all dying of thirst, they wanted realism so they filled my mouth, and I think most of the other people's, too, with alum. And you could hardly open your mouth by the end of the day!

Non-Stop New York *was another highly entertaining film with fantasy elements.*

That film depicted the first trans-Atlantic passenger flight, which of course was still a few years in the future in real life. I remember that John Loder and I did a love scene which was supposedly set on a sort of veranda, built outside the plane. They had a wind machine blowing our hair, but the idea that this plane, which is supposedly going six hundred miles an hour, should have an open deck for passengers to stroll out onto...! But it was fun, that film, and there was a wonderful cast: We had Francis L. Sullivan and Athene Seyler, Desmond Tester and Frank Cellier.

Is it just coincidence that you made so many films [The Man Who Lived Again, King Solomon's Mines, Non-Stop New York *and others] with John Loder?*

No, I think Gaumont-British thought we made a good pair, Anna Lee and John Loder. He died only recently, at 90.

He was one of those actors that, when he died, everybody thought he had *been dead!*

I know, a lot of people did, it was such a shame. I did myself at one time! I last ran into him in London, about 20 years ago, and he was pretty old then. He had just gotten married again — he was always marrying rather expensive ladies *[laughs]*! My sister sent me a clipping out of an English paper, his obituary, which read, "Anna Lee, the actress, said, 'He was the most beautiful man I ever worked with.'" And he *was*, he was very beautiful at the time. He was the very youngest British Army officer in World War I.

Did you enjoy working so often with him?

I was madly in love with him before I met him, but he was rather heavily involved with a lady in London, and whenever I met him he was always married. He married four or five times at least! He was a very nice, sweet guy.

What made you decide to come to America?

I didn't decide to come to America. I had already turned down two Hollywood contracts, maybe three, because I was doing very well at Gaumont-British and I had a wonderful contract with them. I was very happy because my family was there, and I had no desire to go to Hollywood. But I was married to Bob Stevenson, and he had signed a contract with David Selznick to do the first American Ingrid Bergman picture.

Intermezzo *[1939]?*

I believe it was *Intermezzo*. Selznick took Bob to see (I think it was) the Swedish version of *Intermezzo* [1936], and Bob said, "Oh, she's got no sex appeal, she's just a fat Nordic broad." And I wanted to kill him *[laughs]* because I adored Ingrid Bergman, and I still do! But he wasn't really that interested in directing her. Anyway, before we left England he was trying to talk me into coming and he said, "Well, why don't you come with me just for the trip, and we'll bring the baby?" — our daughter Venetia was just 18 months old then. So I thought, "Well, maybe if I go over for three weeks..." So I took Venetia and my English nanny with me.

In those days you did things in such style (with Selznick). We went across on the *Normandie*, we were wined and dined in New York by Selznick's people and then put on the train to California. And they didn't let you disembark at Los Angeles; you had to get out of the train at Pasadena, because it was more beautiful. They didn't want you to see downtown Los Angeles *[laughs]*! All you saw when you disembarked were these beautiful orange groves and the snow-capped mountains in the distance. It was really a beautiful, beautiful place. Then they took you by limousine down to Los Angeles, to Hollywood. We arrived there and they put us up at the Garden of Allah, which was a sort of chic place in those days. It was lovely—it wasn't all that comfortable, but it was very exciting because Bob Benchley and Scott Fitzgerald and a lot of other interesting people lived there.

The night we arrived at the Garden of Allah, I remember I was very tired and we were unpacking when suddenly the telephone rang and it was Selznick. He told Bob, "I want you both to come to dinner tonight, I'm going to run a movie and I want you to see it." I said to Bob that I didn't want to go, I was so tired and I had all the unpacking to do, but he said it was a command because it's David Selznick and you mustn't say no to him. So very wearily I decided to go, and we went. The only other guests there were Clark Gable and Carole Lombard, and the film that we were to see was the rough cut of *Gone with the Wind* [1939]. So *[laughs]* it was worth staying up that late!

How long did you reside at the Garden of Allah?

The bungalow they gave us at the Garden of Allah was a little too small, so we moved over to a bungalow at the Beverly Hills Hotel. Next door was Marlene Dietrich and Erich Maria Remarque, and across the way was Edna Best and Herbert Marshall and their babies. It was a pleasant life; I was getting homesick, but I thought, well, I'll stay on a bit longer. This was August 1939. In September, war broke out in England, so I said, "Well, now I *am* going home." I went down to the British Consul and asked for a visa to get back, and he said, "I'm afraid we can't give you a visa because you're a married woman with an infant child." They had strict instructions that no married woman with infant children were to go across, because of the submarines and so on. I was very angry, and I went up to Canada to try to join the Red Cross, but they wouldn't take me, for the same reason! So I had to wait. Eventually I joined up with the U.S.O. and I thought, "This time I really *will* get back to England." Instead of that, they sent me with Jack Benny to the Persian Gulf *[laughs]*! Anyway, that was how I came to Hollywood—very reluctantly!

And after all this, your husband never did direct anything for Selznick, did he?

He was under contract to Selznick, but I think Selznick just sold him out. He never made a picture for Selznick, but Selznick loaned him to other studios. And Selznick got all the money!

You made your American starring debut in My Life with Caroline *[1941], then made your first of eight films for John Ford.*

How Green Was My Valley [1941]; there's a curious story about that, too. William Wyler was supposed to direct that picture, and I went to interview him at 20th. He was very nice, very polite, and he said, "I would love to have had

Anna Lee first worked with the John Ford stock company of character players in *How Green Was My Valley* (1941). The film and its director remain her favorites to this day.

you as Bronwyn, but I'm afraid I've just promised the part to Greer Garson." I thought, "Well, that's that." He did take me around, told me about this wonderful young English boy that he'd got, Roddy McDowall, and showed me some of the sets. But I went home and forgot all about it for six months. Then I got a call to say I was to go and interview John Ford for *How Green Was My Valley.* Somebody told me I wouldn't have a chance—Ford only liked Irish actresses and wouldn't work with anybody who was English—so thereupon I made up a purely fictitious Irish grandfather, and it was years before I told Ford the truth about it! I went in, and evidently he liked me. The only thing he'd seen me in was *My Life with Caroline,* and you can't imagine two roles more entirely different, Bronwyn and Caroline. But at any rate he hired me; I made a test with Roddy and the next thing I knew, I was playing Bronwyn.

Roddy McDowall, Maureen O'Hara, Patric Knowles and I are the only survivors of *How Green Was My Valley* — Patric called me the other day, to assure me that he *was* alive! I think everybody else is gone and, frankly, I'm starting to get a little bit worried *[laughs]*!

When people think of the John Ford stock players, they think of John Wayne and Ward Bond, Victor McLaglen, people like that. It's so funny to find you lumped in there!

They were all such dear friends, it was just like being in a repertory company again. I loved it. But then of course I learned the lesson that you must never, never refuse any part that you are offered by John Ford. He never lets you see a script; you might have three lines, or you might be playing the star part. *The Man Who Shot Liberty Valance* [1962], I was in there less than two minutes. I was attacked by Lee Marvin, right in the beginning of the picture, and you never saw me again! But you must never say no. Arthur Shields turned down a part, and he never worked for Ford again.

You seem more like the type that would turn up in, say, the occasional Hitchcock film.

I never worked for Hitch; I knew him quite well, and in fact he gave me away when I married my second husband in 1944, but I never particularly *wanted* to work with Hitch. I'd heard a lot of stories about him in England which had rather frightened me *[laughs]*; his humor was somewhat sadistic. Apparently he was much nicer when he came over here!

What about the horror stories that are told about Ford?

He was wonderful to me, I loved him from the moment I met him. But God forbid that you want to be a star with Ford, because he hated the very idea of a star — nobody is a star but John Ford. He said one day that the only three women he liked working with were Maureen O'Hara, Katharine Hepburn and Anna Lee. And to the people who say, "That was why you never became a star in Hollywood, because you joined the John Ford stock company," I say, "I would much rather have been a member of the John Ford stock company than the biggest star in Hollywood," and I really mean that. It was wonderful, really wonderful; I loved Ford, and he's godfather to all three of my sons.

Getting back to your fantasy films, you had a good supporting role in the best segment of Flesh and Fantasy.

That was at Universal, directed by Julien Duvivier. It was a little odd working with him, as all his directions were in French and had to be translated by somebody else. Edward G. Robinson played my suitor in that, and he was a

Their lives darkened by a fortune-teller's prediction of murder, Lee and Edward G. Robinson face a doubtful future in the anthology *Flesh and Fantasy*.

charming, delightful man. He may have been a bit miscast in that, because you always imagined him as a sort of typical gangster character, but he was exceedingly well read and he loved paintings, and we had a lot to talk about in the way of art and so on. And I remember wearing a lovely green and silver gown which I took with me overseas when I was entertaining the troops — and it was stolen by the Arabs *[laughs]*!

How did you get involved on Bedlam?

After *How Green Was My Valley*, I think *Bedlam* is my favorite picture. I loved it. I knew Val Lewton quite well, because I had been close friends with Val and his wife Ruth — I used to go have dinner with them all the time. Val told me he was writing this story, this historical picture about St. Mary's of Bethlehem, but I forget exactly how I became involved; I suppose it would have to have been Val who wanted me to do it. I know Mark Robson, the director, had other ideas; he rather wanted Jane Greer for the part and Val wanted me. And finally I did it, on the condition that I change my hair from blond to dark, which is nothing unusual. Ford always said the same thing; anytime I went down there I had to be dipped into dye.

Lewton is rightly famous for these brilliance-on-a-budget horror thrillers.
   Boris used to get quite annoyed when people referred to *Bedlam* as a horror picture. He said, "It's not a horror picture, it's a *historical* picture," and he was right, absolutely dead right. There was never any thought of making it into a so-called horror picture; it was exactly what happened at St. Mary's of Bethlehem, so much so that it was not allowed to be shown in England for a long, long time. In fact, only very recently have they permitted it to be shown over there. They felt it was a true but rather melancholy description of St. Mary's of Bethlehem.

But once a Karloff becomes involved in a picture like that, it automatically becomes "horror."
   He used to get so annoyed about that—*[imitating Karloff]* "I'm not playing a horror part!" And he was so good in that, he was wonderful.
   Bedlam was done on a very low budget, but I don't think it ever really showed because it was (*I* thought) so beautifully done. I remember I had very, very bad strep throat halfway through it, and we didn't dare stop because I had no insurance. There's one part, during the game of paroli, where you can hear my voice getting huskier and huskier *[laughs]*!

The film's publicists built it up as though it were a big-budgeter.
   I always thought it was a low-budget film because of not having proper insurance and various other things. I know that my costumes were not made for me; the green velvet riding habit that I wore was Vivien Leigh's dress, the one she makes out of curtains in *Gone with the Wind*. I was always very happy about that *[laughs]*! And the lovely ball gown that I wore in the gardens was Hedy Lamarr's. So I wore all hand-me-downs from various actresses!

Can you tell me a little more about Lewton?
   Val Lewton was a sweet, very kind, lovely man and I liked him very much. I don't think Val really thought of these pictures so much in terms of "horror," either. He started out with *Cat People,* of course, and that's still doing well today, and I think I did get the impression that he enjoyed doing these horror films. I know *Bedlam* was the favorite film that he did—he told me that again and again. It was based on the Hogarth paintings and it was all done so beautifully authentically, with the background of the Hogarth pictures and so on.

What can you recall about director Mark Robson?
   I had never worked with him before. I had only known Val Lewton very well, but I was sure that if Val thought he was good, then he *was* good. Val had done such a fabulous piece of work on the script and the dialogue that it would have been tough for anyone to do a bad job, but I thought Mark did an excellent job of directing. As of the time that we made *Bedlam* Mark hadn't

Lee had one of her best and favorite roles in the Val Lewton thriller *Bedlam*, with Boris Karloff. The abused inmate on the floor is B-star-to-be Robert Clarke. (Photo courtesy Robert Skotak.)

yet done anything really in a big way, but I know that David Selznick saw the picture and immediately wanted to sign him. And I know that Robson's next picture was *Champion* [1949], which of course is very good. He went directly from so-called B pictures, right up to the top.

What do you remember about some of the other people in the cast?

Ian Wolfe, well, of course I loved him; I also remember dear Billy House, and Jason Robards, Sr. Richard Fraser, who played the young Quaker, I never heard of him again after *Bedlam!* We had a sweet little script girl on the picture who was dying to be an actress, and Mark Robson had sort of talked about it and we were all encouraging it. It was Ellen Corby — remember her? They gave her the part of "Betty, Queen of the Artichokes." She had this very bad stroke several years ago and she can't really talk very well, but I keep running into her and she always comes up and puts her arms around me. I also remember Robert Clarke, the actor who played "Dan the Dog," and also the man in the cage, "Tom the Tiger" [Victor Holbrook]. He wasn't an actor, I think he was a professional wrestler, but he was a very nice man. We had a great, wonderful cast.

You were at the Academy's "Centenary Tribute" to Karloff in 1988.
The Academy invited me. Mrs. Karloff was there — I had met her once before. Vincent Price was there, and Peter Bogdanovich and Mae Clarke, whom I hadn't seen since we made *Flying Tigers* [1942] — she lives out at the Motion Picture Country Home. The Academy was packed, and I think Mrs. Karloff was very pleased about it.

You certainly did have one of your best roles in Bedlam.
I really think it was one of the better parts that I had here, and I loved the film.

Did Bedlam *do well for RKO?*
No, unfortunately. RKO didn't put as much p.r. behind it as they should have done; they didn't promote the picture at all, maybe because they didn't like historical pictures. That was certainly true of RKO after Howard Hughes came in. Howard Hughes hated anything that was historical, he hated anything that was British.

You had a small but memorable role in The Ghost and Mrs. Muir.
I did have a very, very small part in that. The only condition under which my agent would let me do it was if they gave me twice my usual salary, because the part should probably have only run three days at the outside. I reported to work on the first morning and I was just getting my makeup on when a message came down that Gene Tierney had fallen down stairs and broken her toe, and therefore there could be no shooting that day. I was held on salary, which was quite a lot, for six weeks, so I made more on that picture than I'd made on a lot of pictures before that —

You sure you weren't behind Gene Tierney *on those stairs?*
[Laughs.] And all for this part which literally is just two or three minutes on the screen! But it's amazing how many people remember me in it, and recognize me in it. I played the wife of George Sanders — a *nasty* idea! — and he is running around with Gene Tierney. And apparently it is what is now called a "cameo"!

What did you dislike about George Sanders?

I disliked him because he was so supercilious and condescending in his attitude, particularly toward women. As a matter of fact, my friend Brian Aherne wrote a book about Sanders and he called it *A Dreadful Man [laughs]*, so evidently I wasn't entirely alone in my opinions! But my real dislike of him didn't come until after he died, because when I read that he had committed suicide because he was bored with life, I thought, my God, what an excuse! What a ridiculous, ridiculous thing to say!

Looks like you had another "cameo" in What Ever Happened to Baby Jane?

I've got mixed memories about that. I really enjoyed the experience because I've always adored Bette Davis; when I was offered the part, I told them that I would love to work with her. Who wouldn't? My dressing room was sort of "center stage"—Joan Crawford's was on the right and Bette's was on the left—so I got all the vibes that came across *[laughs]*! Of course Bette did everything in her power to antagonize Crawford, but in a very quiet way. She would put little notes on her dressing room door—"Of all my relations, I prefer sex the most"—and she thought that Joan would be shocked at that.

But it still sounds as though you preferred Davis.

It was a wonderful experience working with them both, because they were both big actresses, but I was particularly in awe of Davis. I remember my very first scene, where I come to the door with the flowers and it's opened by Bette, who is in her cups, very blowsy. Afterward the director, Robert Aldrich, came to me and he said, "Well, you passed muster. Bette came up to me and said, 'It's good to be working with a pro.'" I was very pleased with that.

Your daughter in that film was Bette Davis's real-life daughter, B.D.

That's right. And B.D. was very, very tall, much taller than I was, so we had to have all my scenes sitting down because if I had stood with her she would have towered over me!

That's the daughter that later wrote the tell-all book about Davis.

Yes, I know, and that's very sad because they seemed to be so close at that time.

What impressions of Joan Crawford?

She was very, very gracious, and she always had this big box of Pepsis outside of her dressing room door. And when my sons came to visit me on the set they made a horrible *faux pas:* They asked if they could have a *Coke.* And Joan, who was on the Pepsi board of directors, growled, "It's not Coke, it's Pepsi!" *[Laughs.]*

When I was sent the script of *What Ever Happened to Baby Jane?* I remember that when I got to the point where the rat is on the plate, I was shocked — oh, how horrible! But then there was nothing really offensive about my part, except I played a rather stupid woman. I was always out in the garden and poor Joan Crawford was throwing bits of paper down at me and I completely ignored it *[laughs]*! So I don't know that I liked my role, but it is a film that I am very glad that I was in.

Around that same time you also made a fantasy costumer, Jack the Giant Killer.

You know, I had never seen *Jack the Giant Killer* until just a few weeks ago? *Jack the Giant Killer* I remember for two reasons: First, I had a very nasty encounter with a raven. Do you remember the scene where I carry the raven to the window, and let it fly off? Well, this bird came into the studio one morning with its trainer, and the first thing I noticed was that the trainer had long rubber gauntlets on, and he had little marks all over his face. And I said, "Are you sure this bird is quite safe?" "Oh, yes," he said, "birds never hurt anyone. This is a perfectly trained bird." Well, I looked at him with a great suspicion *[laughs]*, because this was a nasty-looking creature. And I had to perch it on my wrist! I had no gloves on, but I did have this big emerald ring, and as it perched on my wrist of course before we even started the take, it had pounced on my ring and pulled the emerald out. Then later, right in the middle of dialogue, I was holding my hand up (with the bird perched on my wrist) and looking at the actor I was playing to, and suddenly this bird pounced down and bit my lip open! Blood was streaming down my face — and *[laughs]* I think the camera went on cranking! They rushed me off to the hospital and I had a tetanus shot and everything else. Normally I don't mind working with animals, but I think that was the only bird I ever did work with. Never again *[laughs]*!

The other thing that I recall was that, for the scenes where I turn into the witch, I had to be fitted with contact lenses. They weren't like the usual, they were opaque, great big things. When I went to the optometrist to be fitted with these things, he said, "Don't you wear reading glasses?" and I said, "No, I don't need them," and I showed him how well I could read. He said, "Well, at your age, in six months' time you will be back here asking for reading glasses." Well, maybe it was because the thought had been planted in my mind, but in six months' time I was back and I've worn reading glasses ever since *[laughs]*!

How did you like having to wear those contact lenses?

They were hideously uncomfortable, very painful. They were green and yellow, as far as I remember, and they didn't even allow little pinholes for me to see through. I was completely blind all the time I had those things in, and I was led from one part of the set to the other.

What do you think of the film now that you've seen it?

I was fascinated because I didn't realize in making it that it was going to be a special effects movie. The effects were not all that well done, but they were there!

How about Picture Mommy Dead?

[Groans.] Well, again, there's a story about that! I forget how I got involved; I think it was [casting director] Marvin Paige who got me to do that picture. He told me that Hedy Lamarr was starring and that my part would be a cameo and that Signe Hasso was doing a cameo and that it was going to be a great picture. The moment I heard the title, I thought, "Oh, no!" but I had to go along with it. I played my scene, and I can't even remember what I did except that I was at some kind of auction with a crowd of people behind me — eight or ten extras. The next thing I knew was, they called me up and told me that Hedy Lamarr was going to be unable to do the film, and they had an idea that they would like to replace her with me. I said, "Well, I've already shot two days on it," and they said, "Yes, that's the problem. We're going to have to count how many extras are involved, because it may be too expensive to reshoot that scene." And *[laughs]* they literally counted the heads that I'd worked with and decided that it would cost too much to reshoot that scene with somebody else!

Lamarr was replaced by Zsa Zsa Gabor.

And of course Zsa Zsa Gabor at that time weighed at least twenty pounds more than Hedy Lamarr, and they had to squeeze her into the wardrobe *[laughs]*!

You next turned up in a science fiction spy adventure, In Like Flint.

In Like Flint was a favorite and again, it has a weird story attached to it. I was cast in that and I'd been fitted for all my wardrobe, and four days before we were due to leave for Jamaica I was involved in quite a bad car accident. I had thirteen stitches in my thigh, I had ribs cracked, and I was taken off to a hospital in Canoga Park. I told them, "I can't stay in the hospital because I've got to go to Jamaica in four days' time." And the doctor said, "Oh, don't be ridiculous, you can't possibly go." I persisted, and he said, "Well, if you can walk down the corridor outside your room in three days, I will say you can go." So somehow or other I did, I walked down that corridor, and the next day I was on that plane. I had so much codeine in me — and then of course I drank on the plane, too *[laughs]* — that when I arrived in Montego Bay, we were met by the producer, Saul David, and I didn't know who he was!

Did you tell anyone that you had been in an accident?

No, I knew I couldn't tell anybody because the insurance people would have immediately sent me home. I had all these stitches in my leg but fortunately I knew that my wardrobe consisted of all pants and clothes that would

Lee in a 1950s pose.

keep me well-covered—I was black-and-blue from my head to my feet! The only person who knew was the wardrobe girl, who screamed when she saw me. I told her, "Don't you dare say anything to anybody!"

I managed to get along but later on I found that I couldn't turn the handle of a door or take a cap off a Coke bottle, things like that, so I knew there was something wrong. The doctor in Los Angeles had told me that, whatever happened, I must go and have the stitches out before 13 days went by, otherwise they'd turn ... gangrenous or something *[laughs]*! I waited and bore the pain until they had enough footage in the can that I knew they wouldn't replace me, and then I very cautiously approached the assistant director and asked for the loan of a car, that I had to go and see a doctor in Montego Bay. So I went in, had the stitches out, and the doctor said, "I don't like the look of your arm, there's something wrong with it." Two days later I get a cable from the United States saying, SEE A DOCTOR IMMEDIATELY, YOUR WRIST IS BROKEN. And it was! So they gave me a sort of movable cast that could come off, and when I was working I took the cast off. If you watch the film again you'll notice the awkward way my hand goes up and down because I couldn't bend it! But at any rate I did the picture and I loved it.

In 1970 you married the well-known author and poet Robert Nathan.
That was when my life really started, because I always thought that the other two marriages were no good, but this was really a perfect marriage. The only sad thing was that we had so short a time; I was 55 when I married him and he was 75. I met him when I was rather down on my beam ends; I had three young boys to raise without benefit of any child support and I couldn't make enough money as an actress, so I was working as a sales clerk in a Beverly Hills silver shop as their expert on Georgian silver. I used to get terribly embarrassed when friends of mine came in. I remember Angela Lansbury came in one day and I practically burst into tears! Then another friend of mine, Joanne Dru, came in and she said, "Oh, Anna dear, we've got to find you a husband!" Joanne was giving a party for Barbara Ford's birthday—Barbara was John Ford's daughter—and she told me she wanted me to come because she had somebody in mind. So very reluctantly I went—I was so tired after doing a day's work, but I did take a change in clothes and I did go. And I never met the man that she had in mind for me, but I met Robert. He had been widowed fairly recently. We had dinner together and we discovered that we both had the same birthday, the second of January. The party was continuing, but we sat in a little room off the main room and talked and talked until around two o'clock in the morning, when the host and hostess came in to clean out the ashtrays or whatever *[laughs]*, and there we were! We were married three months later, and I always have said he was the one love of my life. I really feel we were soulmates in a way, because it was as though I had known him all my life and yet never had.

What can we look forward to in the near future?
First, I'm working on editing my husband's autobiography. I want to get that published, and also the last poems he wrote that were never published, a collection entitled *An Old Poet Speaks to His Wife*. Then next I'm off on my autobiography, which I want to write—I keep on getting pestered about it, but I want to do Robert's first and then, God willing, I'll get around to mine. And then of course *General Hospital*—they've re-signed me for the next two years and built up for me a very nice, funny storyline, so they must have faith in my longevity!

ANNA LEE FILMOGRAPHY

Ebb Tide (Paramount, 1932)
Say It with Music (British and Dominion Productions, 1932)
Chelsea Life (Paramount, 1933)
The King's Cup (British and Dominion Productions, 1933)
Mannequin (RKO, 1933)
Mayfair Girl (Warners, 1933)
Yes, Mr. Brown (British and Dominion Productions, 1933)
The Bermondsey Kid (Warners, 1933)
Faces (Paramount, 1934)
Rolling in Money (Fox, 1934)
The Camels Are Coming (Gaumont-British, 1934)
Lucky Loser (Paramount, 1934)
First a Girl (Gaumont-British, 1935)
Heat Wave (Gaumont-British, 1935)
The Passing of the Third Floor Back (Gaumont-British, 1936)
The Man Who Lived Again (The Man Who Changed His Mind) (Gaumont-British, 1936)
King Solomon's Mines (Gaumont-British, 1937)
Non-Stop New York (Lisbon Clipper Mystery) (Gaumont-British, 1937)
You're in the Army Now (O.H.M.S.) (Gaumont-British, 1937)
Young Man's Fancy (Associated British Films, 1939)
Return to Yesterday (Associated British Films, 1940)
The Secret Four (The Four Just Men) (Monogram, 1940)
Seven Sinners (Universal, 1940)
My Life with Caroline (RKO, 1941)
How Green Was My Valley (20th Century-Fox, 1941)
Commandos Strike at Dawn (Columbia, 1942)
Flying Tigers (Republic, 1942)
Flesh and Fantasy (Universal, 1943)
Forever and a Day (RKO, 1943)
Hangmen Also Die! (United Artists, 1943)
Summer Storm (United Artists, 1944)
Bedlam (RKO, 1946)
G.I. War Brides (Republic, 1946)
High Conquest (Monogram, 1947)
The Ghost and Mrs. Muir (20th Century-Fox, 1947)
Best Man Wins (Columbia, 1948)
Fort Apache (RKO, 1948)
Prison Warden (Columbia, 1949)
The Last Hurrah (Columbia, 1958)
Gideon of Scotland Yard (Gideon's Day) (Columbia, 1958)
The Crimson Kimono (Columbia, 1959)
The Horse Soldiers (United Artists, 1959)
This Earth Is Mine (Universal, 1959)
The Big Night (Paramount, 1960)
Jet Over the Atlantic (Inter-Continent Films, 1960)
Two Rode Together (Columbia, 1961)
Jack the Giant Killer (United Artists, 1962)
The Man Who Shot Liberty Valance (Paramount, 1962)
What Ever Happened to Baby Jane? (Warners, 1962)

The Prize (MGM, 1963)
The Unsinkable Molly Brown (MGM, 1964)
For Those Who Think Young (United Artists, 1964)
Bearheart of the Great Northwest (Pathe-Alpha/Medallion, 1964)
The Sound of Music (20th Century-Fox, 1965)
Picture Mommy Dead (Embassy, 1966)
Seven Women (MGM, 1966)
In Like Flint (20th Century-Fox, 1967)
Star! (Those Were the Happy Times) (20th Century-Fox, 1968)

... Hitch was trying to determine which dummy of Mother to use in Psycho, *and so periodically when I would walk into my trailer on the set, there would be this apparition there — a dummy of Mother. There were various forms of Mother; I don't know whether he was gauging the volume of my screams or what, but I'm sure I had something to do with the decision as to which Mother was used in the climax!*

Janet Leigh

A GENERATION AGO it wasn't entirely fashionable for a mainstream actress to lend her name and her talents to horror and fantasy film subjects, but through those years Janet Leigh brought her blend of charm and screen acting skill to a number of genre productions. She played the wife of the world's celebrated Master of Escape (portrayed by her then-husband Tony Curtis) in George Pal's production of *Houdini;* added a touch of romantic sophistication to John Frankenheimer's *The Manchurian Candidate;* played opposite her real-life daughter Jamie Lee Curtis in John Carpenter's *The Fog;* and took on the mantel of monster fighter in the hare-brained ecological thriller *Night of the Lepus.* Her best-remembered role, however, was and will always remain Marion Crane, the most grossly inconvenienced guest in motel history, in Alfred Hitchcock's landmark *Psycho.*

California-born, Jeanette Helen Morrison spent a movie-crazy youth in darkened theaters before being "discovered" by former MGM top-liner Norma Shearer. Signed to a Metro contract, the wholesome ingenue, now rechristened Janet Leigh, appeared in a succession of popular films (including *The Romance of Rosy Ridge, If Winter Comes* [1947], *Act of Violence* [1948], *Little Women* [1949] and *The Naked Spur* [1953]) which quickly propelled her into the front ranks of '50s stars. (The veteran actress recounted her experiences in these and other film classics in her 1984 autobiography *There Really Was a Hollywood.*) Leigh took a break from her current writing activities to reminisce about Pal and Hitchcock, escape artists, shower scenes and bloodthirsty bunnies in this interview.

How did the film Houdini *come about?*

As I understand it, the producer, George Pal, had wanted to make *Houdini* for a long time. He was the man who had done all those wonderful Puppetoons, as well as several features prior to *Houdini*—he was a brilliant man. George was very interested in having Tony [Curtis] play Houdini; Tony and I had just been married and so they wanted *me* to play Mrs. Houdini. My studio, Metro, was not very happy about the idea of loaning me to Paramount, but I was so excited at the thought of doing it. Eventually they made their deal, so that we could do it. George hired [mentalist] Joe Dunninger to do the illusions, and he also had [magician] George Boston to be on the set and to teach us some of the magic and escape tricks. It was fascinating to do. *Houdini* was the first picture either of us did for Paramount.

Did you enjoy working there?

Yes, it was a wonderful lot. It was like Universal—it was small, and very family-oriented. It was fun because you rode bicycles all over, everybody knew everybody and so on. I liked it a lot.

George Pal has a large following among fans of science fiction and fantasy films. What more can you recall about working with him?

He was just the sweetest, nicest, gentlest man—and, obviously, brilliant.

Previous page: A star in four dozen films, Janet Leigh is destined to be best remembered for her role as Marion Crane in the opening reels of Hitchcock's *Psycho.*

Very meticulous, very caring, always wanting everything to be *right*. He was just an extraordinary person, to be that brilliant and to be that gentle.

Was he a hands-on producer?
Yes, he was there on the set a lot. He was not an interfering type—he was there to make sure that everything went smoothly and that everything was right.

Wasn't Houdini *originally scheduled for black-and-white?*
That's right, it *was* scheduled for black-and-white. I remember that Edith Head, who did the wardrobe, and I were going through the first fitting together, and the costumes were just so beautiful and so colorful. Edith called George over to the fitting room and said, "You just look at these costumes. I mean, if these are not just wasted in black-and-white! It's ridiculous." And George, in his quiet way, said, "I know ... I just came from the front office, and it's going to be in color." Of course it wasn't just the costumes that prompted that, he had also been thinking about the whole atmosphere of the picture—the magic and the sideshow settings and all the rest. If *Houdini* had been done in black-and-white, it *would* have been a waste.

What kind of shooting schedule was Houdini *made on?*
It was a fairly long one. *Houdini* didn't have a blockbuster-type budget, but it did take time to shoot some of the sequences. I don't remember the exact amount of time, but I imagine it was somewhere between six and eight weeks.

What was the necessity for you and Tony Curtis to learn actual illusionists' tricks when they could have been easily faked with camera trickery?
Oh, but that was the point, so that it *wouldn't* have to be done with camera trickery. When Tony "levitated" me, there were no cuts, and there were no cuts during some of the other tricks—they were done "legit." Now, when it came to the escape scenes, the roping and chaining and all, those scenes had to be fixed because Tony wasn't Houdini; he didn't have the ability to contort his body or to manipulate the locks like Houdini did. Houdini had tremendous spiritual energy; he could get his body into positions that were just *[laughs]*—not human, almost!

How closely did the film follow Houdini's life?
As much as it could; I mean, there was obviously some dramatic license. You have to be true as much as you can, but you still are making a picture that is supposed to be entertaining. Bess Houdini *was* a little "off" in reality, evidently—a little strange *[laughs]!*—and you don't want to depict that. But they did the best they could, trying to make an accurate yet still an enjoyable motion picture.

Leigh and husband Tony Curtis in producer George Pal's *Houdini*.

In preparing for your roles, did you meet and discuss Harry and Bess Houdini with people who actually knew the couple?

Yes, with Dunninger, and with a couple of other people. We also read a lot of books about the life history of Houdini.

Orson Welles, who knew Houdini when he [Welles] was a kid, really used to put down Houdini, *especially the fabricated ending. Did he ever say anything to you?*

No, he never did mention that to us. I guess he felt it wasn't what it should have been—maybe he would have made *Citizen Kane* out of it [*laughs*]! Obviously he would have done it differently, which is fine—

everybody has a different approach. We couldn't depict what really happened to Harry Houdini [a college student suckerpunched Houdini, rupturing his appendix] because some of the heirs to the guy who did it were still alive, and they would have sued. That's why in the movie we had to have Houdini bump into a table! We *knew* that the guy had hit Houdini and ruptured his appendix — Houdini wasn't ready, he hadn't tightened his stomach muscles so that he could "take" the punch — but legally that was something we couldn't do.

Were there any dangers or risks connected with the film's stunt and escape scenes?
   Not really. I do recall that there's a scene where Tony, in preparing to go into the Detroit River, sits in a bathtub filled with ice so that his body would get used to that temperature. Well, he got ice burn, and he broke out all over his body — that wasn't very pleasant. Also, there's an early scene where Tony and I are on a stage and everything starts going haywire, and a fishbowl falls and shatters. We actually slipped and fell on some glass — it was supposed to be a fiasco, and it was! But the scene itself really turned out well.

The first two-thirds of Houdini *is fun and colorful, but once the picture takes that turn toward spiritualism and heavy drama, it becomes a turnoff.*
   There's where their strangeness came in; as I understand from what I read, Houdini spent the last part of his life trying to find out if he could reach his dead mother. Toward the end the film began to depict that part of their lives rather than his wonderful ability and the love between the two of them. It was very strong, and I agree with you; I feel that the last part of *Houdini* was much harder to pull off. Houdini was exposing the falsity of these charlatans [spiritualists], and I think it was more difficult for audiences to accept that phase of the picture, especially at that time — that was before Shirley MacLaine's book came out *[laughs]*! It was a little far-fetched for the audiences of that era. Of course, *now*, maybe not.

Supposedly Houdini left a secret message to his wife; the idea was that if a spiritualist could repeat that message after Houdini was dead, she would know that he was legit.
   And she went to dozens and dozens of spiritualists, and apparently none of them knew that message. *They* hadn't read Shirley's book, either!

Exactly how did you become involved on Psycho?
   Mr. Hitchcock sent me the book and said that he would like me to play Marion Crane. He said that the script was not quite finished, and there would be some changes — they would not change the fact that Marion got killed, but there would be changes in the character. The movie Marion would not be quite as mousy; in the book she was really quite plain, and Hitchcock didn't intend

Top: Vera Miles, John Gavin and Janet Leigh in a publicity photo for *Psycho*. *Bottom:* Leigh consults with the Master of Suspense during a break in the shooting of *Psycho*, as costumer Rita Riggs makes an adjustment to her wardrobe.

to do that. He wanted the love scenes between the characters of Marion and Sam to be very realistic. I read the book and I could see what was there, and just the idea of working with Hitchcock was enough for me.

How did you enjoy working with Hitchcock?
    I loved him—just adored him. He was obviously the most prepared director. After I did get the script and I was signed, I went to meet him and he showed me how every shot in the picture was already worked out.

Psycho was made quickly and inexpensively with TV technicians. How did you adjust to the more rapid pace?
    I loved it. The sophistication of the equipment had progressed by that time, so things didn't take so long. It's very difficult to "sustain" a character when you're waiting, forever it seems, between shots. So I absolutely adored it.

In your book you wrote that Hitchcock promised to let you alone and allow you to shape your own performance. Did he provide you with much in the way of direction or guidance?
    If I needed it. But as long as what I did fit into his camera and fulfilled the piece of his picture I was supposed to fulfill, he let me pretty much alone. If I didn't come up to it—in other words, if there was more he needed—or if I went beyond it and should do less, he would tell me. But otherwise I was on my own.

Much has been recently written about the "dark side" of Hitchcock's personality, but you never seemed to be on the receiving end of any of this.
    Nope. I assume that that is true, I can't say yes or no, I can only talk about what was with me. He couldn't have been better with me. One funny thing I recall is that Hitch was trying to determine which dummy of Mother to use in the film, and so periodically when I would come back from lunch and I'd walk into my trailer on the set, there would be this apparition there—a dummy of Mother. There were various forms of Mother; I don't know whether he was gauging the volume of my screams or what *[laughs]*, but I'm sure I had something to do with the decision as to which Mother was used in the climax!

Both Vera Miles and John Gavin got a dose of Hitchcock's displeasure.
    I never worked with Vera Miles, I was done by the time that she started, and I only had that one opening scene with John Gavin. I remember John had a little trouble in the love scenes—it just wasn't as passionate as Hitchcock wanted—but I don't know first-hand whether or not John and Hitchcock had any subsequent run-ins.

The bathroom and shower scenes were well ahead of their time. Were you pleased with the history-making opportunity, or did you go in with misgivings?

I had no misgivings whatsoever. None. I knew how hard Hitchcock had worked and how he had manipulated the censor office to get certain things into the picture. He would put outrageous things in the script, knowing that the censors would tell him there was no way that he'd be allowed to do them; and then Hitchcock would say, "Okay, then I'll give *that* up, but I *have* to have *this*" — the things he had actually wanted all along.

Is it really true that Psycho *has turned you off on taking showers?*

[*Ingenuously.*] Uh huh — it is absolutely true. I'm a scairdy-cat [*laughs*]! I won't even take a bath in a hotel unless I can face out, even if I have to have my back to the faucets. It just scares me — I never thought about it before *Psycho,* but you are absolutely defenseless in that situation.

Did Hitchcock actually try to inveigle you into doing that shower scene in the nude?

That is b.s. There have been so many myths about that shower scene, and I've tried to put them to rest every time they've come up. What some people forget is that we had the Hays Office in those days. There was censorship. There was no *way* we could do it in the nude — no possible way! There *couldn't* have been a nude model, because it would not have been allowed in the picture. The only time that they used a stand-in for me was when Tony Perkins pulled the body out of the bathroom. Hitchcock said there was no sense in my doing that; no one could see who was wrapped up in that shower curtain, so there would be no purpose served by me getting dragged and bumped around in that scene. But getting back to what I was saying, those people don't realize what the censorship restrictions were like at that time, as compared to today. Today, of course, there'd be no fuss at all about a person doing a scene like that in the nude. But at that time we couldn't. The fact that I had a bra and a half-slip in that opening scene with John Gavin caused such consternation at the Hays Office, you wouldn't believe; Hitchcock had to fight like hell to get that into the picture. And you never see *anything* in the shower scene. That was the genius of Hitchcock. People swear they saw the knife go in, but they never showed that — it was not allowed. You saw a belly button, and even *that* was something that was very difficult, and was almost not allowed. But that's all you saw — you *thought* you saw more, but you didn't.

You received a death threat after Psycho *was released.*

Oh, yeah — several. Some of them were so bad that we had to turn them over to the F.B.I. There were several they wouldn't even let me look at. One really explicit one came from Chicago, just as we were leaving to go on a publicity tour to Chicago! And I was terrified. The F.B.I. traced it down and found the guy—he was sort of a "listed" nut—and they made sure that he was not loose while I was there!

The influence of Psycho *changed the face of horror films. What do you think of the new breed of gore-spattered horror films* Psycho *helped spawn?*
   The brilliance of *Psycho* was that your imagination was allowed to flourish. Today, you don't have to use your imagination, they show you everything. I think the new horror films are not as good. Your imagination is much stronger than anything that they could graphically depict.

Do you see many new horror films?
   No.

Did you see the Psycho *sequels?*
   I saw *Psycho II* but I haven't see *III* yet—I should see *III,* because Tony Perkins directed it, but so far I just haven't. I didn't think very highly of *Psycho II;* it left nothing to the imagination. As I said earlier, what your mind conjures up is so vivid that nothing can match it.

In your opinion, what would Hitchcock have thought of these sequels?
   [Looking heavenward.] Hitch, I hope I'm saying it right—here goes: I think he would have just been revolted. That type of film is just so contrary to what he believed in, which was suspense and mystery, imagination and titillation. And there's none of that in *Psycho II.*

Was there ever any talk of working with Hitchcock again after Psycho?
   No. After the impact that *Psycho* had, you couldn't have Marion Crane in another Hitchcock picture—you just couldn't! Because no matter what role I played, it still would have been Marion Crane. So it just couldn't be.

If by some stretch of the imagination you had been offered a role in a new Psycho *film, would you have accepted it?*
   No—and my daughter Jamie [Lee Curtis] didn't, either. She was offered a part in *Psycho II* [the Meg Tilly role].

What prompted her decision to turn it down?
   [Laughs.] Wisdom!

In preparing for your role in The Manchurian Candidate, *did you read the original novel by Richard Condon?*
   You want to hear something really weird? Before there was any talk at all about making *Manchurian Candidate* into a movie, I read the book on a chartered plane on the way to President Kennedy's inauguration ball. It bothered me so—I got so *mad*—that I threw the book across the plane! I had

that same reaction reading *From Here to Eternity* — when Prew got killed in that book I was so upset that I threw the book. And as I said, that happened again with *Manchurian Candidate*. And Frank Sinatra was on the plane! I had no idea that Frank was going to do the picture or that I was going to be in it! All I knew was that I had a very strong reaction to that novel.

You did another especially good job of acting in that film.

I loved that part; it was a very difficult one. One of my most difficult roles, in fact — not in its length, but in its *brevity,* almost! The book had the luxury of being able to relate all of the characters' thoughts and what was happening within them, whereas in the movie everything is conveyed either through the visuals or through the dialogue. My character, Rosie, comes in around the middle of the film; all of a sudden there's this lady on the train! It was really difficult because I had to make an impact right away; the audience had to know, when I'm making these ridiculous non sequitur remarks, what I was trying to do. It was a very hard thing to do, and I was very pleased. For the kind of role that it was, I was very happy with it.

And it really is one of John Frankenheimer's best pictures.

He was such a strong, dynamic director — I really enjoyed working with him. We had lunch before we did the train scene, because that scene had to be so "on" and it had to have that impact. He was wonderful, and I liked him a lot.

In growing up, did you have a fondness for fantasy, horror and science fiction films?

I've always liked *all* movies, horror movies included. I remember there was one picture we saw, my girlfriend and I — we weren't supposed to go — and it was about a house, almost like the *Psycho* house in a way, and there was a crazy person on the third floor [probably Universal's *The Old Dark House*]. I'll never forget that one — we were scared out of our wits! And I remember *Dracula* and *Frankenstein,* and the other classics. I saw everything — I lived at the movie theaters.

What possessed MGM to make a film like Night of the Lepus?

[*Shaking her head.*] Don't ask me [*laughs*]! No, I take that back. I read the script, and I have to tell you that it read very well. *Night of the Lepus* was made at the time of science fiction pictures like *Willard* and *Ben* and *Frogs,* and I must repeat that the script read very well. No one twisted my arm and said I had to do it. What no one realized was that, no matter what you do, a bunny rabbit is a bunny rabbit! A rat, *that* can be menacing — so can a frog. Spiders or scorpions or alligators — they could all work in that situation, and they have. But — a *bunny rabbit?* How can you make a bunny rabbit menacing, what can you do? It just didn't work.

Leigh took on killer bunny rabbits in the infamous *Night of the Lepus*.

Wasn't a man in a bunny suit used in several scenes?
 Yes, there was somebody they put a bunny suit on, to achieve some of the effects—I've forgotten as much as I could about that picture.

Did the rest of the cast and crew go in with good intentions and high hopes, or did everyone else know from Day One that it was a losing battle?
 Oh, no—it didn't dawn on anyone until—

Day Two?
 [Laughs.] It took about four or five days before we realized that perhaps we didn't have the ideal director. That was disheartening. And then it was not

until the first scene with the big bunnies that we all realized that it was hopeless.

How did you land your part in The Fog?
I saw *Halloween,* Jamie's first picture and I thought that for $300,000 or whatever it cost, there was so much value on the screen that it was wonderful. I was anxious to meet [director] John Carpenter after seeing the picture; we met and talked, and became friends. He asked me if I would ever want to work in one of his pictures and I said I would love to do it. And that's when he wrote a part for me in *The Fog*. We shot *The Fog* outside of San Francisco, by Point Reyes, where the Sir Francis Drake Bay is.

How did you enjoy acting alongside your daughter?
Oh, it was fun — we didn't have enough scenes together, though.

Is Jamie Lee glad to have shed her "Queen of the Horror Films" image?
Jamie was very grateful for those pictures — *very* grateful! — but then after a period of time she felt that she didn't want to just do those. And she was fortunate enough to go another step, into another genre — the "body" pictures. Then, when it seemed like every picture had to have a nude scene in it, she realized that she didn't want to move from Horror Queen to Body Queen. That's when she started doing pictures like *Amazing Grace and Chuck, A Man in Love* [1987] and *Dominick and Eugene* [1988]. It's a legitimate kind of progression, and she's been fortunate enough to take these steps. She really wants to keep growing, because in this business that's what you hope you do, as a person and as an actress.

The Fog *is a very slick and good-looking film, but it really didn't come off very well.*
No, not as well as it should have. I, too, thought it was *done* well; I agree with you, but I don't know just what's wrong. The special effects came across and everything. Maybe it was just a little too farfetched. *Halloween* had a more understandable, basic kind of menace, whereas in *The Fog* they were really reaching. That probably was the reason that it didn't quite make it.

If you had to be remembered for just one film, would you want it to be Psycho?
[*Laughs.*] I don't know if I have a choice!

But isn't it unflattering for a star to be best remembered for a supporting part?
If you think about it, the rest of the picture, after Marion's been killed, is about trying to find Marion. So Marion is really there the whole time, even though you only saw her for X-number of minutes. Also, one picture does not

Movie-making is a family affair on the set of *The Fog*. From right to left are Janet Leigh, daughter Jamie Lee Curtis, writer/director John Carpenter and Carpenter's then-actress wife, Adrienne Barbeau.

a star make, and one picture does not a career make. For an actress to be remembered at all is very flattering.

JANET LEIGH FILMOGRAPHY

The Romance of Rosy Ridge (MGM, 1947)
If Winter Comes (MGM, 1947)
Hills of Home (MGM, 1948)
Words and Music (MGM, 1948)
Act of Violence (MGM, 1948)
Little Women (MGM, 1949)
That Forsyte Woman (MGM, 1949)
The Doctor and the Girl (MGM, 1949)
The Red Danube (MGM, 1949)
Holiday Affair (RKO, 1949)
Strictly Dishonorable (MGM, 1951)
Angels in the Outfield (MGM, 1951)

Two Tickets to Broadway (RKO, 1951)
It's a Big Country (MGM, 1951)
Just This Once (MGM, 1952)
Scaramouche (MGM, 1952)
Fearless Fagan (MGM, 1952)
The Naked Spur (MGM, 1953)
Confidentially Connie (MGM, 1953)
Houdini (Paramount, 1953)
Walking My Baby Back Home (Universal, 1953)
Prince Valiant (20th Century-Fox, 1954)
Living It Up (Paramount, 1954)
The Black Shield of Falworth (Universal, 1954)
Rogue Cop (MGM, 1954)
Pete Kelly's Blues (Warners, 1955)
My Sister Eileen (Columbia, 1955)
Safari (Columbia, 1956)
Jet Pilot (Universal, 1957)
Touch of Evil (Universal, 1958)
The Vikings (United Artists, 1958)
The Perfect Furlough (Universal, 1958)
Who Was That Lady? (Columbia, 1960)
Psycho (Paramount, 1960)
Pepe (Columbia, 1960)
The Manchurian Candidate (United Artists, 1962)
Bye Bye Birdie (Columbia, 1963)
Wives and Lovers (Paramount, 1963)
Three on a Couch (Columbia, 1966)
Harper (Warners, 1966)
Kid Rodelo (Paramount, 1966)
An American Dream (Warners, 1966)
Grand Slam (Paramount, 1968)
Hello Down There (Paramount, 1969)
Night of the Lepus (MGM, 1972)
One Is a Lonely Number (MGM, 1972)
Boardwalk (Atlantic Releasing, 1979)
The Fog (Avco Embassy, 1980)
Psycho II (Universal, 1983) clips from *Psycho*

*I realize that ... it's
almost impossible [to break away
from my image of being a "horror writer"].
I wrote that TV movie called* The Morning After ...
*about an alcoholic, and it worked out well—it's a beautiful film
and they use it in hospitals. And one of the critics wrote
a review and said, "This situation is a real horror. And
who better to write the script than Richard Matheson."
And so I figured, "To hell with it!"
I'll never get away from it!*

Richard Matheson

LONG RECOGNIZED as one of the deans of modern-day fantasy writers, Richard Matheson has been screenwriting many of his tales of terror for a third of a century—from the cobweb-festooned mansions of Edgar Allan Poe to the subconscious world of the Marquis De Sade, from the dark dens of ghosts and vampires to the submicroscopic haunts of the Shrinking Man. Still active within the genre, Matheson shows himself in this interview to be as personable as he is prolific and popular.

Born in New Jersey and raised in Brooklyn, Richard Burton Matheson first became a published author while still a child, when his stories and poems ran in the old *Brooklyn Eagle*. A lifelong reader of fantasy tales, he made his professional writing bow in 1950 when his short story "Born of Man and Woman" appeared in *The Magazine of Fantasy and Science Fiction*, and he continued to turn out a number of highly regarded horror, fantasy and mystery stories throughout that decade. Matheson broke into films in 1956, adapting his novel *The Shrinking Man* for the big-screen *The Incredible Shrinking Man*, and has gone on to write dozens of movies, TV movies and series episodes.

Where did you come up with the idea for your book The Shrinking Man?

I was in Redondo Beach, California, in a theater, and I was seeing a picture called *Let's Do It Again* [1953] with Jane Wyman and Ray Milland. There was a scene where Ray Milland is leaving this apartment in a huff, and by mistake he grabs Aldo Ray's hat, sticks it on his head and it comes right down over his ears. And I wondered, what if a man put on his *own* hat, and that happened? That was the genesis of it.

Did you peddle the story around to studios, or did Universal come to you?

I believed then, and still do pretty much, that the best way to break into the movies is to write something that the studios would want to buy and then say, "I want to adapt it." So, after the book was written, I had it submitted by my sometimes-agent out here, a man named Al Manuel, who had never sold anything of mine before. And Universal made an offer on it.

Was Universal the only studio to show interest?

I don't know. They were the first to make an offer, and it was all so stunning to me that I never even asked Al whether he had submitted it elsewhere! That was when I broke into screenwriting, when I told them that I wanted to do the script.

What were your impressions of producer Albert Zugsmith?

I ended up writing a couple of pictures for him *[Shrinking Man* and 1959's *The Beat Generation]*. He seemed typical of the ten-inch-cigar-smoking executive of the time. He came out of the newspaper field, and he always used

Previous page: Renowned for his continued presence at the leading edge of innovation in SF and fantasy literature, Richard Matheson has many times turned his hand to the writing of screenplays.

to say to me, "I'm gonna give ya a scriptwriting lesson, kiddie!" At that time I assumed that I would be using the structure of my book.

Why did Universal insist on dropping your book's flashback story structure?
That was not the way they handled things in those days. I mean, they couldn't do *Last Year at Marienbad* back then; the story had to be in chronological order, to begin at the beginning and progress from there. As a result of which, I think the first part of the film is the weaker part. I wrote it that way in my novel originally and it got tedious, so I decided I would structure it the way I had structured *I Am Legend:* start smack-dab in the middle and then, in flashbacks, bring the story up to date.

What changes did writer Richard Alan Simmons make when he came along?
Gosh, it's been so long that I can't really recall—I don't think I had the paint can sequence in my script, and there must have been other things as well. I remember that Universal asked me to share a writing co-credit with him, and I wrote some enraged précis of all the changes he had made, and insisted that he had done really nothing to it. I realized in later years that, since it was my first picture, and because he was a very nice man, he may well have just backed off and let me have the solo credit. I did meet him; as a matter of fact, he's the one that got me to join the Writers Guild. He came into my office at Universal, representing them, and since I was working then as a professional he said I should plan on joining the Writers Guild. He's a very talented writer.

Did you get to meet Jack Arnold at that same time?
Oh, yeah, sure. A little on the picture—not too much—but later on through the years we really met. As a matter of fact, I believe it was his wife that showed us the house where we're now living; she was doing some realty work at the time, and in fact they lived right around the corner from here. So we got to know them here and at conventions.

Did Zugsmith have anything to do with the picture? Arnold's always insisting that the man did nothing.
Well, if Jack says that, I believe it; I'm sure the film was Jack's "vision." Actually, it took me a long time to appreciate what the picture was. I have a tendency always to have in my mind an image of what a picture should be, and of course the picture almost never matches the image. So I'm always disappointed, and sometimes it takes me a long time before I look at it for what it is. *The Incredible Shrinking Man,* it took me forever! My son Richard finally got me to come around by pointing out to me how unusual it was for that time and how wonderfully visual it was. I had never compared it to the pictures that were being made at that time, especially by Universal. And that ending was not a typical Universal ending.

Another day, another dollar: Grant Williams punches in at Universal in a gag shot for *The Incredible Shrinking Man*. (Photo courtesy Mark McGee.)

Technically, was the film everything you hoped it would be?
    Oh, yeah, you couldn't fault that, it was remarkable what they did. Visually it was a feast, and Jack Arnold did a very good job.
    I went on from there and wrote a sequel because Universal wanted to use all those sets and giant props. It was called *The Fantastic Little Girl,* and it had his wife shrinking and joining him in the submicroscopic world. But Universal never made it.

You ended up writing a few scripts for Zugsmith that never reached the screen.

Zugsmith wanted to do *Gulliver's Travels,* and I did an entire screenplay in which a little boy played the part of Gulliver. Then after that, because this was about the time of *Around the World in 80 Days* [1956], Zugsmith wanted to get David Niven and Cantinflas to star in it, so I wrote another screenplay in which David Niven was Gulliver and Cantinflas was some little Lilliputian soldier. Needless to say, these were not made.

How did your Fantastic Little Girl *script end?*
Oh, that one had a Universal ending. Something happened where the process was reversed and they ended up back in hearth and home, happy as a couple bugs in a rug *[laughs]*! I don't know why the sequel wasn't made; at that time they told me that only *To Hell and Back* [1955] and *Away All Boats* [1956] had made more money for that studio than *The Incredible Shrinking Man* did. It made a ton of money! The picture cost $800,000, which for that time I guess was quite a bit, but it made a lot of money and I have no idea why they didn't shoot the sequel. They had all those big sets, Grant Williams and Randy Stuart were available and Jack Arnold was available. They were crazy, they should have done it, because it would have made a bundle of money. They use some of those giant props on the Universal tour—or at least they did, a few years ago.

Did you visit those oversized sets?
Oh, yeah. I was watching them the day they shot the flood scene, with the giant pencil and the water heater breaking and (Jack's famous anecdote) the prophylactics filled with water to get the effect of giant water droplets. Poor Grant Williams, that guy looked beat! He nearly killed himself; he was almost blinded by an arc light, he was nearly electrocuted, he was half-drowned...! Boy, did he work hard!
In later years, when my agent told me they were going to do a remake of *The Incredible Shrinking Man,* in my naivete I said, "Well, I want to do the structure of the book now." And it turned out they were going to do *The Incredible Shrinking Woman* and make it into a comedy, so that was the end of that *[laughs]*!

What did you think of Shrinking Woman?
I thought it was terrible. The fact that they were doing a parody, that was okay, that didn't bother me, but I just thought it was bad—not funny. I think *I* could have written a funnier comedy!

Who approached you to write the screenplay for House of Usher?
American International—James Nicholson. Nicholson was my contact; we really got along very well and he liked what I did. I saw Sam Arkoff, of course, but Nicholson was my friend in court, my compadre. Nicholson had the desire to do better and better things. In the beginning I didn't know

An overworked Grant Williams catches his breath between shots on *The Incredible Shrinking Man*. (Photo courtesy Robert Skotak.)

American International; I didn't really know anything about these people. When I met Roger Corman, I assumed that *House of Usher* was his project. I didn't know that he was working for AIP, and he had this deal where he would be producer and director. I don't even remember exactly when I met Nicholson and Arkoff — probably during the shooting of the picture.

House of Usher was AIP's first stab at a reasonably respectable picture.

    I don't think they planned to make a "respectable picture"; it just turned out that way because I wrote a very good script. Maybe they wanted to go classy with Edgar Allan Poe, but if it had turned out like *Attack of the Crab Monsters* [*laughs*] I don't think they would have cared that much! As a matter of fact, from what I understood they were totally thrown off by the fact that *House of Usher* did so well. It was running all summer — it ran in a double-bill with *Psycho* in many places. The very fact that American International could make something that had some semblance of quality, and still make a lot of money, I don't think that had ever occurred to them.

At that point Corman had only a history of low-budget SF/action films. Were you aware of his rush-rush, fast-buck reputation?

I didn't really know his background, I was no fan of that kind of picture, so I had no idea where he came from. When I met him through *House of Usher,* I would say that to all effects it was the first time I had met him or even knew of him.

So you were never a follower of the kind of SF films that came out during the '50s?
  No, I wasn't—I never cared for those "monster" movies, atomic radiation things or giant insects. There were a few good ones, like *Them!,* but it got very repetitious. I always preferred fantasy movies; when I was a teenager I was a big fan of Val Lewton's. Subtle types of horror pictures, not the smash-you-over-the-head-with-a-club type. To me the ideal fantasy film was *Rosemary's Baby,* which is just so realistic that it sneaks up on you.

So what's your verdict on today's horror films?
  [Groans.] Oh, I don't even go see them! I don't write this stuff anymore; I have opportunities all the time, but I literally don't want to have anything to do with them. I mean, they're revolting—axes in heads and people's stomachs splitting open...!

What are some of the ins and outs of adapting a Poe story like House of Usher *to the screen?*
  Except for maybe some of the short Poe stories I adapted for *Tales of Terror, House of Usher* probably came the closest to the original. I tried to stay close, but even at that I added a romance to it. Other people have made it exactly the way Poe wrote it, and it's a pretty moody piece. I really worked on it, I tried very hard to get the whole flavor. I did a long, complex outline, and American International was very pleased with it. Vincent Price was delighted, because he hadn't done anything good in quite a while. I think he really outdid himself in *House of Usher.* I had seen him so many times with a mustache that when I saw him for the first time on the set and he was clean-shaven, I was startled *[laughs]*!

Price really did have enthusiasm for House of Usher?
  He had enthusiasm about a number of those films—or, at least, I spoke to him and he sounded enthusiastic. (Of course, he's a very genial man.) I think he was impressed by the scripts and he felt inspired, elevated to give an outstanding performance. When you're handed a potboiler script, your tendency is not to do an outstanding Shakespearean performance. I think he enjoyed *Master of the World,* and that he also enjoyed *House of Usher* because it gave him something to work with. Then later on I gave him comedy to do, which he was very good at. So I think he was very pleased with them; at least he has said so.

Sibling tensions flare as Myrna Fahey and Vincent Price lock horns in *House of Usher*.

The books say that House of Usher *cost $300,000, with $100,000 of that going to Price.*

As far as I know, they made it for $125,000 exclusive of salaries. I had the usual 5 percent of the net profit, and every time I got a statement from AIP the price of the picture had gone up. It was ludicrous. And I know they made millions and millions of dollars!

Corman used to threaten to take AIP to court all the time.

I should have done that, because I had the same thing happen on all their pictures. Finally I got tired of it and I let them buy my little 5 percents, on all my pictures, for a total of $10,000. I would have gotten back a lot more just out of TV residuals and video cassettes. Arkoff was a . . . shark. Someone told me that if while they were making a picture they went out to lunch, and on the way back Arkoff bought a pack of gum, the pack of gum became part of the budget *[laughs]*!

Did you ever see Arkoff on the sets of these movies?

No, he was strictly business. Although I do remember that on one of the cast parties (it may have been *House of Usher*), his wife cooked up all the food! AIP was still on that level. Arkoff's a strange man; he would go to New York, so I was told, rush from the airplane to Broadway, grab a hot dog and go to the theater. Which seems out of keeping with the image that he presents: all business, no taste. But it turns out that's not the case.

The story that goes around is that Arkoff was down on the idea of doing House of Usher *because there was no monster, no real selling point.*

I never heard that, but I wouldn't be surprised. I'm sure it was Nicholson's notion. I mean, anytime that anything of an artistic nature came up, and it was going to cost more than ten dollars, I'm sure Arkoff tried to veto it. They were a strange combination.

The punchline is that Arkoff had to be convinced that the house itself was the monster.

I remember writing lines like, "The house itself is evil" and stuff like that. That's probably what got Arkoff to get off the dime.

Did you have any say in casting?

No, I think Roger did that. Outside of Price, he had a little coterie of people that he kept using. As they got more into the oldtimers, the casts got better and better; in the early pictures the casting was not that good. But they tried—God knows they were sincere about it.

What were your impressions of Corman?

My impression of him was that he was a camera director. I never saw him talk to actors, he would just let the people determine their own performances. The only thing I ever heard him say repeatedly was, after he'd do a shot, he'd spin on his heel and say, "We're on the wrong set." Once he's done, he just wants his crew to get where the hell they're going *[laughs]*! That's how he saves so much money. I've known him for years and he's a funny guy. You'd think he just got off the ferryboat—he's got that sheepish smile, and he acts as though he just came out of the cornfield or something! But, Jesus, what a mind—a very smart man!

Charles B. Griffith, Corman's regular scriptwriter, was put out that he didn't get to write House of Usher. *Corman told him that no screenwriter who gets less than $50,000 a script is any good.*

[Laughs.] Well, they sure didn't pay me $50,000—they paid me $5,000!

Did you visit the sets this time around?

Hanging around sets can get extremely boring. You figure, the picture's going to be 80, 85 minutes long, and they had two-week shooting schedules. So 14 days, at eight to nine hours a day, to end up with 80 minutes means that there's a lot of time spent just setting up lights and moving sets and dressing people—and that's very boring. And then when they actually do a scene, it's very brief, half a page or something. But I was on the *House of Usher* set a little bit; I remember that they shot it at the old Chaplin studio. Mark Damon was playing, I guess, at being a method actor, and before he went on the set he would run in place and huff and puff *[laughs]*! Then he'd walk in on a scene where Price would be chatting with somebody, and Price would out-act the hell out of him!

Then there was the only time that I ever saw Vincent Price angry. Mark Damon comes in and he's about to strike Price with an axe, he flings the axe down, and it bounces right off Price's shin! Price uttered the only profanity I ever heard him say, he left the stage, walked around the whole thing. And then when he came back, he was himself again. Really, he's an incredibly nice man—you never met a nicer man than Vincent.

What changes would you make in House of Usher *if you could?*

I would like to have seen (let's say) Joseph Losey direct it *[laughs]*, and some of the performances were a little limited, I think.

It was a hit nevertheless.

It made millions of dollars, and AIP was totally bowled over by it. It opened in June, I think, and it just kept running all through July and August and made millions. I don't think they had any plan to make a whole series of Poe pictures; if it had done the usual, they would have just moved on to something else.

Who came up with the idea to do Master of the World *at this point?*
They did. I didn't realize until just recently that in writing my screenplay for that I had combined two Jules Verne books, *Master of the World* and *Robur the Conqueror;* I didn't know I had done that.

And came up with a picture that most resembles the movie 20,000 Leagues Under the Sea.
The similarities were in the books: a man who has this enormous image of creating peace in the world. Incidentally, I thought *20,000 Leagues Under the Sea* was a marvelous picture. I was so impressed when I found out that the guy who wrote the screenplay for that picture [Earl Felton] had been with it, not only all through the writing but all through the shooting, under contract. Which, to me, is the obvious way to do a picture, but which they almost never do.

Isn't it frustrating to write a screenplay like Master of the World, *one that requires a champagne budget, for a Kool-Aid company like AIP?*
Oh, sure. AIP spent like a half a million dollars on it, which for them was just incredible, but it still had a limited look to it.

Charles Bronson was certainly miscast.
He was miscast, and he knew it; he was very unhappy. Testy is more the word. I remember a real strange day on the set: The first day I went in to watch them shoot, I walked up to him and said, "Hello, Mr. Bronson. I'm the writer of this picture—" And he said, "Oh, don't talk to me," and he walked away! Which, of course, really pissed me off. Later on he came back, I guess feeling a little guilty about it, and said, "Hey, I hear you're a very good writer." I said, "I am," then walked away from *him [laughs]*! Then after lunch, I went back to him and said, "Can we start all over again?" We chatted awhile; he said, "I hope you don't mind my playing it like a coal miner." And then the next morning he walked by me and never said a word. Vincent Price, who could make friends with a dead man—and very often *has*, in his movies *[laughs]*—said, "I can't get through to this guy. I cannot make friends with him." I guess Bronson's always been that way. Very strange.
Anytime I found actors to be unpleasant at all, they were always the younger actors. Either they were uptight, or they felt arrogant, or whatever. But the oldtimers, I never met one who wasn't really pleasant, congenial, very friendly.

Did you think that Price did a good job in Master of the World?
Yeah, I think he did a very good job. I only wish that they had had the budget of *20,000 Leagues Under the Sea.* What annoyed me most was all that damn stock footage that they rented from *The Four Feathers* [1939], for God's sake, and from *Henry V* [1945]—I mean *[laughs]*, history periods were jumping all over the place!

David Frankham, Mary Webster and Vincent Price don't care what composer Les Baxter is pointing at on the set of *Master of the World*. (Photo courtesy Robert Skotak.)

Do you remember encountering Henry Hull on Master of the World?

I think maybe very briefly. Now there was a real ham. Henry Hull was a very nice man, but I think he always had the tendency to overact; he came from the stage, and I guess he just never really was able to shed that.

How about William Witney, the director?

Yeah, sure—I had an argument with him in our first meeting! I have had so few arguments down through the years—I've been at it since '55—and we were at each other's throats in seconds! He had a demeaning attitude about the whole project—"Well, if you really want to do this stupid thing, I'll see if I can pull it together"—and I really got ticked off about it. Nicholson had to act as an arbiter. Witney had done gangster movies and serials, he was not suited to direct *Master of the World*. (I don't know who *was*, that AIP could have afforded, but he was not the one.) I'm sure that didn't do the picture any good.

Nicholson was the one who really got behind Master of the World *and pushed to make it, and Arkoff was very much against it.*

At that kind of cost, I'm sure he was.

Going by the box office receipts, which of them was right?
  Oh, I think *Master of the World* made money — I don't think I ever wrote a picture for them that didn't turn a profit. Even *The Comedy of Terrors,* where it turned out that the title was self-defeating, it still made a profit. And most of the Poe pictures made a really good profit.

I always had the feeling that Nicholson had more of an affinity for this type of picture than Arkoff did.
  As I said, Nicholson was my connection there, a very nice man, very genial, very appreciative. Again, on *Master of the World* and *Pit and the Pendulum,* they paid me $5,000 each on them. There was a writers' strike at the time, so actually I was doing pretty well — everybody else was starving. And Nicholson liked both those scripts so much that he gave me a bonus, which he didn't have to do. That was a nice gesture.

Many fans don't realize that you also wrote a lot of Western TV shows back in this era.
  I love Westerns, and some of my nicest experiences, I think, were on a show called *The Lawman* — more than *The Twilight Zone!* There was a producer named Jules Schermer, and he would do my scripts word for word and he would get good actors — I mean, the guy who played the marshal, John Russell, was sort of like a monolith, but Peter Brown, who played his deputy, was good. Schermer got this good director who used to work with John Ford and he'd get good actors, and, really, there were some nice — *very* nice — pieces. I got a Writers Guild of America Award for the first one I ever wrote. Ray Danton played sort of a tired gunman who literally committed suicide, which you couldn't do on television! He just intimidated this marshal, insisted he was going to gun him down. And in the end the marshal shot him down, and Danton's gun was empty. He just wanted to die, but he didn't want to kill himself. The last one I did was with John Carradine, it was called "The Actor," and it was a charming piece. Carradine was this actor who finally ended up doing some noble thing and saving somebody's life, and he got shot. It's in a barroom, he's on a table, he does a death scene, he dies, the camera pulls back and a curtain comes down. That wasn't in my script, it was the director's idea, Richard Sarafian's — he was a very good director. I had never seen anything like that on television — what a wonderful little touch! And Schermer let it happen. So, yes, I've always loved Westerns; as a matter of fact, I'm submitting a Western novel right now to Spielberg, because he's said he wants to do films of every genre.

Pit and the Pendulum, *unlike* House of Usher, *was a totally original screenplay.*
  Pit and the Pendulum was a lot more of a challenge — Poe's story was just one scene of a guy lashed to a table with a blade that's going to cut him in half.

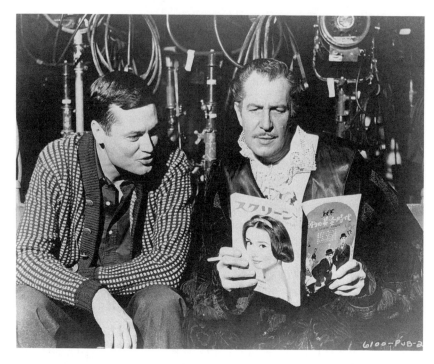

Roger Corman and Vincent Price are probably just looking at the pictures behind the scenes on *Pit and the Pendulum*.

And now most people ascribe what I wrote to Edgar Allan Poe! I mean, first there's Poe's short story; then I do the screenplay; then somebody writes a novel called *Pit and the Pendulum* which is based on my script. And so anybody who reads it thinks, "Hmmm, that Poe was a hell of a good writer...!"

Sounds like you were never a big fan of Poe's.
   Obviously I read his books, early on in life, but, no, I was not a big fan.

How about H.P. Lovecraft, whose stories formed the basis for some of the later "Poe" films?
   I never read Lovecraft until later on, after people told me about him, and then I didn't like him. His stories were just so thick and turgid; he would write about some abomination that was just too awful to describe, and then fifty pages later he'd take a crack at describing it anyway *[laughs]*! Stephen King says that he sort of grew up on Lovecraft and he assumed that that was the kind of stuff you had to write—full of crypts, that sort of stuff. And then when he read *I Am Legend*, he realized that you can set that type of story in a tract neighborhood, and then send it off in a different direction.

Did you meet Barbara Steele on Pit and the Pendulum?

No, I never met her. People in the business told me that her part had been dubbed in—they said her voice was not good enough for it. Whether this is true or not I don't know, but that's what I was told a number of times. And I was thoroughly astonished when I recently saw her name as producer on the mini-series *The Winds of War* and *War and Remembrance*.

Were you a visitor to this set as well?

I think I was there for the pendulum scene—that was a huge set, very impressive. That was a very well executed and well edited and very effective scene.

Was that all laid out, shot by shot, in your script?

It could very well have been. Years ago I learned that directors who have an ego problem don't pay any attention to shooting scripts, but right from the start I've always written them.

Now that he's attained some station in life, Corman insists that he liked his horror films Freudian—long scenes of people walking down corridors and that type of thing. But somehow I can't imagine him dictating to you, or to anybody else, to put that stuff in there.

Corman got his reputation in France because he had these constant shots of Jesus' mother holding the baby, and so they thought, "Ah, there's some religious significance here!" *[Laughs.]* I know for a fact that he had never used a boom shot until I wrote one into one of my pictures.

Did he have any input at all on your scripts?

Oh, yeah, sure, I would work with him on the scripts. I remember that American International always had me cutting; I went along with it, didn't argue. Then when they went to shoot it, it was too short! It used to happen all the time.

Even as early as Pendulum, *you were already reusing elements from* Usher. *Were these Gothic melodramas really your cup of tea?*

No, not at all, I was just trying to earn a living off of them. I was raising four children and the first film, *House of Usher,* did well, and so we went on from there. But as you can see, by the time I got to the third one, *Tales of Terror,* I couldn't take it seriously anymore and I started adding comedy to it.

So you prefer your more contemporary stories, then, like the ones you did for The Twilight Zone.

Oh, yeah. I have never written science fiction about the year 9000 or some distant galaxy, I just couldn't visualize that. I had to do it here and today, living in your tract house and there's a ghost next door, something like that.

Rise and shine! Vincent Price levitates from his deathbed in the Matheson-scripted Poe anthology *Tales of Terror*.

How much time would they give you to write one of these Poe scripts?

It probably wasn't long—they didn't take me that long! Maybe a month, month and a half. I mean, they shot 'em so fast they were practically standing outside my door waiting for new material so they could take it and run to the cameraman *[laughs]*! They always shot them word for word. And I stand by those scripts; what makes me wince is some of the performances!

Did you ever regret anything in a script written in haste?

In *Pit and the Pendulum* Vincent Price played Sebastian Medina, and I had all the characters calling him "Don Medina," which you don't do—it's "Don" and then the *first* name, so he should have been "Don Sebastian." And I made a terrible mistake on *The Incredible Shrinking Man*. In the film, and even in the book, I had him worrying about jumping from great heights, and then someone pointed out to me that at his size he would have just sort of floated down like an insect. I don't know why these little things stay with me, but I just hate to make mistakes like that!

When I asked Sam Arkoff what his favorite AIP movies were, the first one he named was Pit and the Pendulum.

Really? Well, I guess it *was* pretty clever, pretty intricately plotted. I guess he liked that.

Do you remember how you became involved on Burn, Witch, Burn?

Chuck Beaumont and I were friends, we went out one night to have a drink and we said, "Hey, let's write a movie together." We both loved the novel *Conjure Wife* by Fritz Leiber, and even though we knew that Universal owned the rights to it and had made a very poor picture [*Weird Woman*], we did it anyway. I took the first half, he took the second half, we got together and did a polish, and then we showed the script to Nicholson. He liked it, but because they had to get the rights from Universal to do it, we got very little money for it—I think we split $10,000. Then it went over to England, and it was made by a group of people who had made some very good pictures. And Chuck and I were delighted, we thought it was really well done.

Who came up with the British title, Night of the Eagle?

They did—I mean, either AIP or the people in England. Our title was *Conjure Wife*. And when the American release title ended up as *Burn, Witch, Burn,* we thought, "Hey, that's a little odd. What will Abraham E. Merritt's family think of this?"

In a TV interview, a writer named George Baxt talked about Burn, Witch, Burn *as though he was the sole writer.*

Obviously he's full of you-know-what. Stefanie Powers said the same sort of thing on *Die! Die! My Darling!,* that they had to rewrite the thing while they were doing it. And yet when I look at the movie, I see my script. I don't know why people do that.

And are you still happy with Burn, Witch, Burn?

I like it, I think it's excellent. Janet Blair, she's not bad. And the actor who played her husband, Peter Wyngarde, was the guy who played the ghost in *The Innocents;* his pants were a little too tight *[laughs]*, but he was okay, too. The director, Sidney Hayers, did a great job.

Fritz Leiber had reservations about the film because you transposed the action to England.

That was necessary. But we followed his structure and his story very closely; I mean, that was the whole idea! You have a wonderful book, you try to follow it as closely as you can. That's what I did with *The Devil Rides Out [The Devil's Bride]*—so much so that Dennis Wheatley, the fellow who wrote the book, wrote me a letter thanking me for staying so close. There are so many wonderful books that have never been filmed the way they were written, it defies the senses.

Armed with stake and mallet, Vincent Price addresses the homeless problem in *The Last Man on Earth*.

Did you ever go over to England while any of the films you had written were being filmed?

No. I did go over to England, and I was there for about six weeks, adapting *I Am Legend* into a screenplay for Hammer Films, around 1957. I was working for Tony Hinds, who was going to be the producer. It turned out very well, then later he told me that the censor wouldn't pass it, and they finally ended up selling it to some guy in the United States, Robert Lippert.

I remember going to Lippert's house and having him tell me, "We're gonna get *Fritz Lang* to direct this thing *[The Last Man on Earth]*." And I thought to myself, "Oh, Jesus — how wonderful!" Then later I got a call, and they told me, "Now we're going with Sidney Salkow." And I thought *[in a sarcastic tone]*, "Well, *there's* a bit of a drop!" The last I heard of him, Salkow was teaching at some college in the Valley, and he regards *The Last Man on Earth* as one of his masterpieces.

Why was that film shot in Italy?

It was cheaper, I guess. I'm sure it was a matter of price — financial, not Vincent. The film was released by AIP.

What's wrong with all the versions of I Am Legend, *that you're never happy with them?*

They never followed the book! *The Last Man on Earth* followed most closely, but it was inept — in fact, I put my pen name, Logan Swanson, on it. And that was one part that Price was not right for. I mean, they should do it today with, say, George Miller directing it and Harrison Ford playing the lead; it would make a wonderful movie. Of course George Romero has done it so many times now; the first time was *Night of the Living Dead*. I caught that on television, and I said to myself, "Wait a minute — did they make another version of *I Am Legend* that they didn't tell me about?" Later on they told me he did it as an homage to *I Am Legend*, which means, "He gets it for nothin'." *[Laughs.]* Dan Curtis is trying to get the rights, he's tried several times, since he'd like to do it.

What did you think of Night of the Living Dead?

It was . . . kind of cornball. At one point Roman Polanski had a contract at Warners, and my son Richard said, "Why don't you try and get him to do it?" Now, if Polanski did it, it would be wonderful; it should be done the way *Rosemary's Baby* was done, with a really outstanding actor as the star. But I don't think they'll do it. Why they keep making vampire movies, I don't know; if any monster has been "used up," it's the vampire.

Where did you get the idea for I Am Legend?

I think I got it before I came to California. I was watching *Dracula*, the old Universal film, and I thought, "If one vampire is frightening, what if the whole *world* was vampires?" That was the beginning of it.

How about the second "official" version of I Am Legend, *Warner Bros.'s* The Omega Man?

That one made me feel less bad because it was so far removed from the book that I believe it was almost unrecognizable. Too many cooks always spoil the broth.

Who now owns the rights to I Am Legend?

It's very complicated. What I was told was that Orion, being the ultimate offshoot of American International, owns the book rights whereas Warner Bros. owns the film rights. So whoever wanted to make it would have to offer both Orion and Warner Bros. something. It's not likely to happen.

Peter Lorre, who co-starred in your Tales of Terror *and* The Comedy of Terrors, *reportedly ad-libbed his way through these pictures.*

The rest of the actors in those pictures read my lines word for word; that dialogue was very well written, and they relished the way it fell trippingly off their tongues. Lorre just sort of gave the basic essence. Usually that kind of thing really bugs me, but he was such a nice man I couldn't really get fired up. He used to tell me that he drove Sydney Greenstreet out of his mind like that. Greenstreet came from the theater and would do every line down to the last semi-colon, and then Lorre would just sort of spew out some general reaction to it and Greenstreet would get all bent out of shape! And they were in a lot of pictures together.

People tell me that Lorre was on drugs throughout this period.
He may have been, for physical pain. I think he had some serious physical problems. If he took drugs, it certainly wasn't just for the sake of taking drugs. Lorre was really a charming man.

The three-in-one Poe film Tales of Terror *gave you an opportunity to be more faithful than usual.*
I must sound like I'm an egomaniac, but once again I thought that was a very good script. But on that first segment [*Morella*] the casting really bugged me—I always refer to that first segment as *Shirley Temple in the Haunted House.* In my script it was a really great character relationship between the two of them: Price was up to it, and I was visualizing someone like Nina Foch playing the dying daughter. But this girl that they got [Maggie Pierce] was terrible. And they also cut a lot out of it, so it just didn't work. The middle one [*The Black Cat*] had Lorre and Price and Joyce Jameson, who was marvelous. I enjoyed that middle one, I thought Price was wonderful and that the wine-tasting sequence was just delightful. And the last one [*The Facts in the Case of M. Valdemar*]—except for the lousy special effect at the end—I thought was very good, one of my favorites. They did a really nice job on that, very intelligent.

The omnibus approach was whose idea?
American International's, I guess, I don't remember. I think I picked the stories that went into it.

In writing The Raven, *did you know which actors would be playing each role?*
Sure, I wrote with them in mind, and I deliberately tailored the dialogue to fit their ways of speaking. In writing *The Raven* I didn't even have an original story to work with, they gave me a poem *[laughs]*, and I really had to start from scratch there! I couldn't take it seriously anymore and I did it as a comedy.

Lorre's ad-libbing threw Karloff for a loop.
I'm sure that it threw everybody for a loop who was disciplined and followed the script. Short of firing him, though, there was nothing you could do about it—you couldn't talk him out of it. Of course I think his memory was failing anyway.

(Left-right) Sam Arkoff, Vincent Price, Jim Nicholson and Peter Lorre confab on the set of *The Raven*.

Karloff and Lorre appeared together on a New York talk show where Lorre said they had the time of their lives on The Raven. *But it was obvious from Karloff's reaction that* he *didn't think so!*

Karloff was always the essence of politeness, a very charming man. He was in great pain from some physical condition; I remember that he had to walk down these really precipitous steps in *The Raven* and he was in such pain. In most of his pictures after that, he just sat down most of the time. I really never did get much of a chance to know Karloff too well; I think he stayed to himself, he didn't just hang around the sets.

You gave Karloff opportunities to play comedy, which was something rare in his films.

You're right, comedy was something he almost never got to do in movies, and I thought he was very adept at it. He had a wonderful droll sense of humor that I thought came across very well in those pictures. It was delightful to watch him doing it.

Was the special effects duel at the end of The Raven *up to your expectations?*

No, no — I was very disappointed in that duel, it seemed very laborious to me. The effects were what I had written, it was just the way they were presented. Everything seemed too slow, it should have been a lot faster. People seem to enjoy it, but for a "duel of the titans" it seemed very, very heavy. With today's techniques, they could really do that right.

Was The Raven *a big moneymaker for AIP?*
    I believe so. AIP was smart, they didn't reveal that it was a comedy, they let the word-of-mouth get around and so it made a lot of money.

Did you like the music Les Baxter wrote for these pictures?
    Yes. It was very lush and very effective. He was great at big orchestral effects and melodies that were easily remembered.

Are your Poe pictures withstanding the test of time?
    I think that there are a number of people who feel that they are. The fact that they are such period pictures helps; they don't age as noticeably as the contemporary pictures made back in the '50s and '60s, which became very archaic very quickly. If the Poe films have dated at all, it's just because of the way they do films today, more extravagantly and with more know-how.

Your screenplays; Floyd Crosby's camerawork; Dan Haller's art direction; Vincent Price's performances. Can you articulate exactly what Roger Corman's contribution was to these movies?
    Traffic cop. I think he was good with the camera, he knew how to move with it, but as I said I don't think I ever saw him work with actors. He just cast them and assumed that they knew what they were doing. He was good at making pictures quickly and on a budget, and he gave an interesting look to his films. They were always crisp and fast-moving.

How did you get involved on The Comedy of Terrors?
    I think I just told Jim Nicholson my idea about a couple of rascally undertakers who, when business is too slow, begin to murder people to get customers. That was enough to sell him.

Karloff was originally supposed to play the part Rathbone eventually got.
    And Rathbone was going to play the father. They were approximately the same age, but Rathbone was really sprightly whereas Karloff by that time was really having pains. So Karloff requested that they switch parts, which was fine.

Did your continued leanings toward comedy sit well with AIP?
    I think Nicholson liked it. Nicholson liked change, he liked variety. Arkoff probably would have done *Return to the House of Usher, Son of the House of Usher* and so on.

What extra responsibilities were entailed in your associate producer credit on The Comedy of Terrors?

Probably very little, except that I was the one that got them to hire Jacques Tourneur to direct. "Associate producer" is probably one of the most meaningless titles in the motion picture business.

What turned you on to Tourneur?

I was a fan of his from way back—I wrote letters to Val Lewton when I was 17, about *Cat People*. I'd always been a tremendous fan of Tourneur's; as a matter of fact, even before *The Comedy of Terrors*, I had talked to Bert Granet about hiring him to do one of my *Twilight Zones* ["Night Call"]. They said the one reason they didn't want him was because he was a movie director, and it would take him too long. Well, they hired him anyway, and Tourneur was so organized that he shot the shortest *Twilight Zone* shooting schedule ever—I think he had it done in like 28 hours. The man was a master, and he had great taste, too.

The Comedy of Terrors *is also known as* Graveside Story. *Was that your original title?*

[Laughs.] No, it was probably Nicholson. He had a penchant for very bad titles. *West Side Story* [1961] had been a hit not long before that, so he might have come up with it. I remember I was having a meeting once, I was going to begin work on a screenplay based on my story "Being," and I said, "Well, you know, you could call this picture *Galactic Octopoidal Ooze — G.O.O.* for short." Next thing I know I'm looking through a trade paper and I see that *G.O.O.* is the next picture they're going to be doing! I was just joking, but you must never do that in this business because it'll backfire on you almost every time.

People who knew Basil Rathbone toward the end say he was bitter over the fact that he had become too closely associated with horror films.

It's possible. I mean, look at the background of the man, the things he'd done; he probably should have retired sooner if he didn't want to do 'em. I always wonder at these stars who, just for the sake of continuing, will appear in dreadful movies. They should retire, they should get out of the business.

Rathbone couldn't afford to retire.

Well, that's obviously the reason for his continuing on the way he did. He didn't have to, he had made a lot of money, but he and his wife Ouida lived awfully high on the hog and threw enormous parties and everything. But he was very happy, I think, with both *Tales of Terror* and especially *The Comedy of Terrors*, because it was a great part. We had a luncheon before production began on *The Comedy of Terrors*, all the stars were there and they were all really "high," Basil Rathbone especially, because they loved the script.

It's obvious that Peter Lorre has a stunt double throughout much of the film.

Oh, Lorre could do nothing. There were scenes calling for him to climb up on the roof and run around and drive the carriage, and he could do none of it. So they got this famous old stuntman, Harvey Parry, to stand in for him because he couldn't do any of this stuff. Rathbone did virtually all his own stunts.

You mentioned before that the title hurt the picture.

The public apparently did not like the juxtaposition of the words "comedy" and "terrors" (I think it's a great title), and that apparently hurt the box office. But it was the best of the lot, of course, because Tourneur directed.

In my last years with AIP I wrote some marvelous scripts—Nicholson had me really going for ambitious stuff—but none of them ever came to fruition. One that I kept turning down, and Nicholson kept wanting me to do, was about the pornography business in England. It was called *Public Parts and Private Places,* and it was just so black that I made this sort of *Dr. Strangelove* comedy out of it, really bizarre. And they never made it. Then there was another one, based on a novel called *Implosion.* It took place in England—I guess, because they were going to shoot it in England, I set it there, too—and it was about what happened when something got into the water and the majority of the women became sterile. Those who could have children were put into breeding camps, and one of the big ministers in the government has a wife who is one of the women that had to go to the breeding camp. It was such a good script that they gave me a three-picture deal after I wrote it—none of which I wrote. (Or maybe one, from my story "Being.")

Your script Sweethearts and Horrors, *which AIP never got around to filming, seems like it would have been a hoot.*

Yeah, that was very disappointing. It was going to follow up *The Comedy of Terrors,* and it had all of them—Karloff, Price, Lorre and Rathbone, plus Tallulah Bankhead. It was about a family called the Sweethearts. Boris Karloff was the host of a kiddie show, a very irascible host—always muttering curses under his breath; Basil Rathbone was an aging musical comedy star; Peter Lorre was a very inept magician whose specialty was a fire act, and every theater he worked in he burned down; Tallulah Bankhead was an aging Hollywood actress; and Vincent Price was a ventriloquist. They're all called back to their father's home, after he dies, for the reading of the will; the father manufactured gags, and the whole house is booby-trapped with gags. Then they start getting murdered off, one by one. It would have been a ball, because it was a very funny script; I was very happy with that script, and it would still make a very cute picture. As a matter of fact, I just recently sent a copy to my agent, because there are still a few of the oldtimers around—Price and Peter Cushing and Christopher Lee.

You worked for AIP one last time several years later, on De Sade.

I was very happy when I learned that *De Sade* would be directed by the man [Cy Endfield] who directed *Zulu* [1964], which to my mind is the best action movie ever made. But he was having a mental breakdown at the time—at least, that's what they told me. He was putting red crosses through script pages, which meant that they had been shot—but they hadn't been! So there was a lot of stuff that he literally hadn't shot. In my script, everything you saw was very inscrutable and had an interesting kind of texture, and it turned out ultimately to be what was going on in De Sade's brain as he was dying. And [Endfield] decided that, no, he wasn't going to do that, he wasn't going to make it a fantasy, he wanted a straight chronology. And yet he kept shooting scenes that I wrote, scenes that (except in a fantasy context) made no sense at all! Roger Corman ended up going over to Berlin and shooting some cheap orgy scenes.

The punchline to this story is that Jim Nicholson told me that he was talking to John Huston one day [Huston co-starred in *De Sade*], and Huston said, "Why didn't you ask me to direct it? I'd have been glad to direct it." That *[groans]*—that really made my day!

What do you recall about writing Die! Die! My Darling! *for Hammer?*

Tony Hinds sent me this book called *Fanatic*, and asked me if I wanted to adapt it. And I did. They were lucky enough to get the director who did *Georgy Girl* [1966], Silvio Narizzano, who did a very nice job. It got a little heavily melodramatic toward the end, but I thought it worked very well.

Early on there are scenes which at times are very funny.

Oh, sure. When something strange happens to people, if they have a sense of humor, they're going to try to respond to it; I thought Stefanie Powers did an excellent job of that. The situations were amusing to her character; only later did it gradually begin to dawn on her what the hell was going on.

Stefanie Powers's one complaint was that, in the scenes where Tallulah Bankhead beats her up, Bankhead didn't bother pulling her punches.

Oh, I can believe that; Tallulah Bankhead was a tough old broad. What that *Sweethearts and Horrors* would have been like on the set, with smiling Roger contending with her, would have been a picture in itself!

The business in Die! Die! My Darling! *about Bankhead having once been an oldtime actress is not well developed.*

That's not in the book at all, and I think they must have added that themselves. I didn't know Tallulah Bankhead was going to be starring in it, so I didn't make the lead character an actress; in the book she's like a little dumpy old lady who's just fanatical about her son. After they cast Tallulah Bankhead they might have just thrown in those other scenes.

Bankhead sued Columbia when they changed the title from Fanatic *to* Die! Die! My Darling! *for U.S. release.*

Well, I suppose they were looking to cash in on *Hush, Hush ... Sweet Charlotte.* They're always so imitative, so slavishly imitative. *Fanatic* was the title of the book and the title I wrote my script under.

Hammer Films tend to be lionized by some fans but it's always struck me as being just a British AIP.

Yeah, I think they were pretty much alike, and that there are a lot of similarities between them. Maybe because their actors have an English accent, it just sounds nicer *[laughs].* I was just talking recently to Michael Carreras, who is the son of the man who started the studio, and he is trying to get *I Am Legend* to make, the way I wrote it.

You worked for Hammer again on The Devil's Bride, *adapting Dennis Wheatley's book* The Devil Rides Out. *Was Wheatley offered an opportunity to adapt it himself?*

I have no idea. I thought I wrote a very good adaptation—I used the major sequences of the book, and it flowed together very well. Again, I thought the casting had some flaws in it, although I just saw it again recently and it wasn't as bad as I remembered it. Charles Gray was good, but I don't think I'd ever heard of a lot of the other people who were in it—maybe they chose them because they looked like they came out of the 1920s or something!

Did you write the screenplay knowing that Christopher Lee would be playing the hero?

No, I don't think so, but he did a fine job. It was the three leads who I found lacking—Tanith [Nike Arrighi] and Rex [Leon Greene] and Simon [Patrick Mower]. And that whole sequence where they're under attack was much more complete and much longer and much more interesting in my script than it turned out to be, because they didn't have the money to spend on special effects. They went for the big spider *[laughs]*—they always go for the goddamned big spider! That wasn't in my script. And the scene where they're in the attic and the great big black guy shows up, that wasn't that frightening— really good special effects would have added some more fright to it. But the picture had a nice period look to it, and the plot certainly zipped along. One of my favorite scenes in the film, probably *the* favorite, is where Charles Gray is reassuring the wife [Sarah Lawson] and gradually segues into getting control of her.

Variety *pointed out that two character names in* The Devil's Bride, Mocata *and* Tanith, *were "lifted" from* Rosemary's Baby.

Those names were in the original book, and it must have been *Rosemary's Baby* that lifted them. Wheatley wrote *The Devil Rides Out* in the '30s, long before *Rosemary's Baby.*

It's odd, after all those Gothic Poe pictures you wrote, that Hammer never approached you to write one of their Dracula or Frankenstein films.
No, they never did. But I wouldn't have done it anyway.

Who approached you to adapt your own book Hell House, *for* The Legend of Hell House?
Jim Nicholson again. He was starting his own company, and he wanted to do that as his first project.

Did you ever ask him why he had left AIP?
I think it was financial. He got divorced and he had to give half of his shares in AIP to his ex-wife, and I think he lost control. Previously he'd had enough control so he could fight off Arkoff, but when Arkoff had total control, I think he just knew he was going to be too unhappy. So he started his own company. He died shortly thereafter.

Were you happy with The Legend of Hell House?
It was made by some of the same people who were involved with *Burn, Witch, Burn*. When I first saw it, I didn't like it—as usual—because I had an image of it in my mind. Pamela Franklin seemed too young, and Roddy McDowall wasn't quite right, either; I thought the guy who played the doctor, Clive Revill, was good. The score I found a little inappropriate at first; it doesn't bother me now. When you see something over and over, you forget what you originally planned for it and how you saw it.

None of the "residents" of Hell House *are on display in the film the way they are in your book.*
I guess the filmmakers made up their minds that they weren't going to show anything—for instance, I had in the script what Pamela Franklin saw when the ghost makes love to her, and I had also described it very vividly in my novel. They chose not to show it in the movie, you just see the look on her face. But that was their choice, that was okay. It was intelligently done.

The Haunting *is probably the best haunted house film ever to use that "unseen" approach.*
I liked *The Haunting* a lot. What I didn't like was the way it copped out, the way it turned out to be in the mind of one of the characters who was there. I was so tired of that; that was part of the reason I wrote *Hell House*. But *The Haunting* was well-done and it was scary as hell—I mean, how about that scene where the wife's [Lois Maxwell] face appears through the trap door and the camera zooms in! That was one of the three moments in my moviegoing career where I actually recoiled in my seat. Another was when the shark appeared behind Roy Scheider while he's chumming in *Jaws,* and the third was in *Diabolique,* when the dead husband came up out of the bathtub.

Matheson got less than the dream cast he had envisioned when *The Legend of Hell House* went before the cameras.

Reportedly, Jim Nicholson had you dilute your Legend of Hell House *screenplay in order to get a PG rating.*

I cut out some of the sexual stuff; there was quite a bit left, but there had been a lot more. Originally I was going to do the picture with Stanley Chase, who produced that very good science fiction picture *Colossus: The Forbin Project*. He and I were going to do it and it was going to be really explicit—the book is extremely explicit. At one time I had in my mind a dream cast of Richard Burton and his wife Elizabeth Taylor to play the two mediums, Rod Steiger and his wife Claire Bloom to play the professor and his wife. Just after they made *The Legend of Hell House* people began making the really classy, A-picture-type horror films, starting with *The Exorcist,* so if I had held onto *Hell House* a few more years, it might have gotten that kind of treatment, too. It's a B-plus *[laughs],* but it didn't make A!

Have you given any thought to trying your hand at directing?
   Sometimes, when it's something that I've written or something that I know particularly well. But, as I've mentioned to other people in the past, I would probably get walked all over or I would turn into a Nazi. And I wouldn't want to do either one.

Did you have any misgivings when Christopher (Superman) *Reeve was cast in the lead of* Somewhere in Time?
   No; as a matter of fact I thought at the time that he was probably the only actor around that could have pulled it off. Not because of his acting ability, although I liked what he had done in *Superman,* but because of his looks. In my mind it was essential to the story that the attraction between Richard [Reeve] and Elise [Jane Seymour] be a love-at-first-sight thing. I had breakfast once with Dustin Hoffman, who was interested in doing it, and I remember thinking, "Well, he would end up fascinating the girl but it would take like five *days"* — I mean, his personality would have to overcome his looks, so it would hardly be love at first sight! In that respect Chris Reeve was ideal, although my attitude toward his acting has sort of diminished through the years. But it was a nice experience; I spent more time on that shoot than on any other picture, over two weeks on Mackinaw Island, Michigan, where the Grand Hotel is. It was a lovely experience.

Did you adapt your own novel (Bid Time Return) *faithfully?*
   In the novel, Richard's dying, because he has a brain tumor, and at the end his brother, who has analyzed the whole story, realizes that this type of hallucination was perfectly within the bounds of what Richard was going through — although the brother hopes that it had actually happened. Universal didn't want to do that. Also, to present Reeve, who had just played Superman, as somebody who was dying would have been kind of ludicrous.

Somewhere in Time *was the sort of gentle fantasy that's tough to "sell" to the public.*
   And it *was.* They made a mistake in the way it opened; it should have opened in a few little theaters all over the country and got word-of-mouth working for it. Once word-of-mouth started working, it did very well. On the Z Channel out here, it was like the most popular picture; they would show it

two times a day, it would be shown at Christmastime and so on. And the video cassette sales have been great. But the original box office was not that hot— maybe $15,000,000. But since it was made for five and a half, I guess it was still all right.

What can you tell us about Universal's Jaws *3-D?*
Once again, I wrote an outline which was really very interesting—and I found out later, when the picture was done and I saw the credits, that they gave the credit for the story to some other writer! And I had never read anything by him!

I wrote a very interesting script. I would much prefer to write the second sequel to a popular film than the first sequel; when you're writing the first sequel, you're bound to directly follow what happened in the original film, but when you do a second sequel you can make a deviation. Universal made me put the two sons of Chief Brody [Roy Scheider] in the film, which I thought was dumb, but not only that, they wanted it to be the same shark that got electrocuted in *Jaws 2 [laughs]*!

Were you happy at all with the finished film?
No, not at all. I'm a good storyteller and I wrote a good outline and a good script. And if they had done it right and if it had been directed by somebody who knew how to direct, I think it would have been an excellent movie. *Jaws 3-D* was the only thing Joe Alves ever directed; the man is a very skilled production designer, but as a director, no. And the so-called 3-D just made the film murky-looking—it had no effect whatsoever. It was a waste of time.

You seem to be happier with your work in television than you are with most of the movies you've been associated with.
Oh, I've gotten much more satisfaction out of television. I did *Duel* for television, *The Night Stalker, The Night Strangler, Dracula, The Morning After* [1974] with Dick Van Dyke, *Dying Room Only* [1973] with Cloris Leachman—*Dying Room Only* is the one I always tell people was better than it deserved to be. It was just a simple, well-done suspense story, but the producer Allen Epstein put so much effort into it...!

Were you one of the instigators of Twilight Zone—The Movie?
No. I had lunch with Steven Spielberg and John Landis and Joe Dante, and they said they were going to make this movie. Landis was going to write his own segment and Joe was going to do "It's a Good Life" and Spielberg was going to do "Kick the Can." It seems to me that their initial plan was to use "Nightmare at 20,000 Feet" just as like a filler—I remember them talking about doing it in ten minutes, and I couldn't understand how they were going to do it. At one point they were going to get Gregory Peck for the "Nightmare" episode in the movie—they told me once that Gregory Peck was going to be

in *Duel!* So I wrote a whole script in which Peck was like the character he played in *Twelve O'Clock High* [1949] — he's familiar with the idea of "gremlins," he's heard pilots talking about 'em, and now he finally sees one for himself. Then, suddenly, it wasn't going to be Gregory Peck in the role. And then they hired George Miller to direct it — he's a wonderful director — but he decided to go back to scratch.

The movie version of "Nightmare" is slightly different from the TV version, and not nearly as good.

In my story, and in the original *Twilight Zone* episode, the guy had had a mental breakdown, but George Miller thought to make it just a guy who was afraid of flying. I can't say that I liked the characterization, but I must admit that John Lithgow was marvelous — I mean, to start out at 99 percent of hysteria and build from that is a little difficult, but he somehow managed to do it! Visually that episode was marvelous, although a lot of it I didn't care for. And I thought the monster in the movie was much better than in the television show.

How would you rate the other episodes on which you worked?

"Kick the Can," the one that Steven did, I thought was too treacly; "It's a Good Life," the one directed by Joe Dante, I liked the best. I was called to task by a lot of the fans on that one; they cannot stand happy endings, they love to have stories end on a bleak, dark, fatalistic note so that they can all shudder and go, "Ooo-oo-ooh, wasn't that *wonderful?*" I decided, "Oh, screw it" *[laughs]* — I wanted to see if I could put a positive ending on it. It didn't work too well, the way it was done, but I still stand by it; up 'til that point, I thought that Joe did a marvelous job.

Twilight Zone — The Movie struck me as a yuppified, hotshot-director's movie that didn't suit the tone of the old TV series.

They started the movie out with that little backroads bit with [Albert] Brooks and [Dan] Aykroyd that set a tone, which they never followed. And it was not a success.

It's amazing what can be done without millions of dollars or big special effects, but don't try telling that to most of today's filmmakers.

When I was a teenager, as I have told you, I wrote a letter to Val Lewton and I told him I thought I had discovered their secrets of scaring people. One of them was a long period of absolute dead silence, suddenly broken by a noise. It could be anything — I remember a scene in *The Body Snatcher* where the hero is in a stable and suddenly this horse sticks its head into the shot and snorts, and everybody in the theater jumped out of their skin! Another way is to lead the viewer's eye across the screen and then all of a sudden something pounces in from the other side — they did that in *Wait Until Dark* [1967], which was another time that I jumped. It's so easy! I mean, you have to have the situation first and it has to be well done, but once you've got that, it's very simple. And yet they never do it.

Do you like to scare people?
I used to; I don't now, because I have a different attitude. They say that horror films allow you to get things out of your system and help you deal with your own private terrors. I don't believe that anymore. I think that everything that's created on the screen, and that kids see, becomes rooted in their minds, it never leaves. And then it builds itself up. I think in the long run it does nothing but create a negative effect.

And that's why you sometimes appear to be trying to distance yourself from the image of being a "horror writer"?
I realize that, out here anyway, it's almost impossible. I wrote that TV movie *The Morning After* for David Wolper, about an alcoholic, and it worked out well—it's a beautiful film and they use it in hospitals. It's probably the truest presentation of an alcoholic that they've ever done. And one of the critics wrote a review and said, "This situation is a real horror. And who better to write the script than..." *[Points to himself and laughs.]* And so I figured, "To hell with it!" I'll never get away from it!

The producers hired a bunch of wrestlers to play the zombies, and they caught me a couple of times within the film. They would grab me and literally pick me up and throw me against a palm tree! And I could hear my vertebrae just cracking, going down! ... That's what I remember about Zombies of Mora Tau!

Gregg Palmer

EVERY WAR has its unsung heroes, and in the great 1950s onslaught of sci-fi beasties upon the world, many Hollywood actors risked life and limb (not to mention their professional reputations!) to preserve the human race. Another in the long line of classic monster fighters, Gregg Palmer took on the Creature from the Black Lagoon, the Zombies of Mora Tau and, perhaps most perilously, the Most Dangerous Man Alive, and has survived to tell the story of his heroic on-screen exploits.

Norwegian by heritage and a San Franciscan by birth (January 25, 1927), brown-haired, brown-eyed Gregg Palmer (born Palmer Lee) broke into show biz as a radio announcer. After an early '50s stint as a contract player at Universal, he turned to freelancing, closing out the decade by starring and co-starring in a number of detective, Western and science fiction adventures. In the '60s, Palmer drifted into supporting roles and much TV work, and reinforced his growing reputation with Western fans by becoming a regular member of John Wayne's latter-day stock company in *The Undefeated* (1969), *Chisum*, *Rio Lobo* (1970), *Big Jake* (1971) and *The Shootist* (1976). Big (6' 2"), beefy and robust in his sixties, this gentle giant kicked back to reminisce about his filmland skirmishes with Old West marauders and Atom Age monsters.

I was discharged out of the Air Force in 1946 and undecided about what to do, and I went back to college. One day my friend Frank called me up and he said that he had attended a radio announcer school, that he wanted to become a radio announcer, and would I tell him where [radio station] KGO was located in San Francisco? I told him, and he said, "Listen, why don't you join me, and afterwards we'll go to lunch?" So we went down to KGO, and they asked him to fill out some forms. And since I had asked a question or two, they handed me a form and asked me to fill it out, too. The following week when Frank came down he said, "I'm going for my interview. Why don't you join me, and we'll have lunch again?" So we went down there, he went in for his interview and he was in and out within four minutes or less. I asked him how he did, and he said, "I don't know, but they said they'd call me." Whereupon I heard *my* name called. Frank said, "Go 'head, see if they tell you the same thing they told me." I went in, and I was in there for an hour and a half *[laughs]* — reading all kinds of copy off the teletype and whatever. And as I was leaving, Noel Francis, who was a lady producer at KGO, said, "I would suggest you stay in the field of radio. I think that there's a future there for you." I thanked her for that and I went home, and one day when I came home from playing golf my mother told me that KGO had called, and they wanted to know if I would be interested in going to work as a radio announcer. I said, "Well, I don't have the experience for that"—I immediately thought of the millions of people out there listening to me fouling up and mispronouncing words and whatever. But I went in and told them, "I tell you what: I'll go to school, and after six months I'll interview again. And if you still feel that

Previous page: Palmer's knife-in-the-throat attack doesn't even slow down the walking corpse—played by "Killer" Karl Davis—in Columbia's *Zombies of Mora Tau*.

I have a future in the business, so be it." So I went to radio school and soon after got my first job in radio at Radio KEEN in San Jose — *[mellifluously]* "1370 on your dial, San Jose, California." I did shows emanating out of the studio and I would go out on remotes. I worked there for a period of about a year.

And shortly afterwards you tried your luck in the movies.
There was a columnist who worked in San Francisco by the name of Dwight Newton, and he and Noel Francis suggested that I try for the movies. I put that off for about eight months until finally one day they *drove* me on down to Los Angeles! I kept hanging around, hanging around — I drove a truck, bounced at the Palladium, did all the things that struggling actors in those days would do, and then went on my interviews. I can recall Paramount in the old days, they had what they call the fishbowl. You would go in there and bright lights would be on you. You wouldn't know who was sitting outside — a voice would say, "All right, go ahead," and you'd do your scene. And when you were finished, the voice would say, "Thank you, we'll be in contact." Now, that could be the janitor sitting out there *[laughs]* — you didn't know who it was — and off you would go! But these interviews were not too frequent; you might wait for four months, five months.

In 1949, before I got into the picture business, while I was still trying to find my way, I had an interview with two people at NBC Studios. One of them was Busby Berkeley, who was the choreographer for those big 1930s musical extravaganzas, and the other gentleman was Al Capp, who created the *Li'l Abner* comic strip. They told me that they were looking for someone to play Li'l Abner on TV, and they thought I had possibilities. I was introduced to a young lady, we rehearsed for a couple of days, then we went to a sound stage and we made the test, which I'll never forget. I was dressed as Li'l Abner, sitting on a log, she as Daisy Mae. She came up to me and she said, "Li'l Abner, I just inherited $24. Will you kiss me?" And I looked at her and I said, "I cain't. If'n I kissed you for money, I couldn't face myself in the mornin'." She threw the $24 off-camera and she snuggled up, as Daisy Mae would, and she said, "Then kiss me without money." And I said, "I cain't. 'Cause without money, you ain't *worth* kissin'!" Now, as you laugh, do you know who the young lady was? She became Marilyn Monroe. And I've often wondered where that filmclip went to!

Finally one day I was about to chuck it and go back to San Francisco, and I was approached by an agent. He said, "Why don't we go over to Warner Bros.? I think there's a future here for you, Palmer." (I was still called Palmer Lee in those early days.) So we went to Warner Bros. and they said they had a war story coming up and I could play a navigator, and I said fine. And then they said, "Yeah, but it's about eight months away." I said, "Forget it!" Now, as we're going back over the hill, we pass by Universal Studios, and I went in there and there was some interest; they said, "Well, how 'bout coming back next week and reading for us?" I said, "No. If you promised to give me the *studios* next week, I wouldn't come back. I'm leaving Friday evening and I'm going back to San Francisco, go back to college and plan my future in another direction." So I was called in on Friday afternoon to read and Friday evening my agent called me up and he said, "Palmer, the studio would like to give you a seven-year contract." And I said *[disappointedly]*, "Seven *years?* I don't know if I'd want that." Having just been out of the service a few years prior, I knew that would be like being tied up. But I sat with my cousin out on a curb in front of his house, we talked it over and finally I figured, well, all right.

It was a nice experience at Universal Studios. I met a lot of nice people and I enjoyed the time there. This was in 1951 that I signed there. Those were the days when they had a stable of people that they would train. We had training in voice, training in diction, training in tap dancing and ballet — if you can picture me doing ballet! Me with my size thirteen *[laughs]*! We were all submitted to these classes — Rock Hudson, Audie Murphy, Jeff Chandler, Clint Eastwood, Anita Ekberg, Piper Laurie, all of us. Many happy hours were spent there. We would maybe have a featured role in a picture, maybe we would star, maybe we would do a little cameo, but we were working. They were good and happy days.

You had your first role in a fantasy film when you appeared in Universal's Francis Goes to West Point.

There's a story that goes with that film, a story that begins about a year earlier when I had a bit part in an army comedy called *Up Front* [1951]. I was to play a binocular M.P. in a reconnaissance vehicle in *Up Front* and I really studied my one line, because I wanted to be good, to make a career in this business. The line was, "I think I see the truck up ahead, sir." I would sit at home in front of a mirror, as many of us actors do, pretending to be holding binoculars, reading the line different ways and so on. Finally the day came when I was going to do that line. I went over to the recon and I started to get in when the assistant director came over and he said, "No, wait a minute, Palmer, I want Alex to get in there." I said, "But I'm the binocular M.P., and — ." "Don't worry about it," he said, "just get into this motorcycle sidecar here. Alex is going to do the line." Well, Alex was a friend of the assistant director. So I climbed into the sidecar and Alex did the line.

Three or four months later I signed the contract with Universal Studios, and I was assigned to *Francis Goes to West Point*. Arthur Lubin was directing it, Donald O'Connor and Lori Nelson were starring, and I was fourth-billed, as the football player. We went out to a local college stadium and we're standing out there in the early morning hours and Lubin was explaining to me the scenes that they were going to shoot that morning. All of a sudden he interrupted himself and said, "Gee, it's awfully chilly here, would you like a cup of coffee?" And he turned to the assistant director, the same one that took me out of the recon, and said, "Would you please go get Mr. Lee a cup of coffee?"

First a radio announcer, then a Universal contract player, Gregg Palmer turned freelancer in the mid-'50s and appeared in horror-action flicks like *Zombies of Mora Tau*.

So he walked *all-l-l* the way out of the stadium and came back with the cup of coffee for me. And now Lubin said, "Gee, it's gonna be a while before we start, you should sit down." And he turned to the assistant director again and said, "Would you please get Mr. Lee a chair?" So *[laughs]* out he walks again, *all-l-l* the way out, and he came back with this chair. When he put it down, I looked at him—I bore no animosity towards him—and I said, "Nice seeing you again. Remember me?" And he said, "Yeah . . . you never know, do you?" *[Laughs.]* And it's true, you never do.

Do you remember much about the scenes you shared with Francis the Talking Mule?

Yes, and that was interesting. I was quite taken by the way the mule would talk—that was done with wires. The wires, which were attached to the mouth of the mule, would be pulled and that would kind of irritate the mule, and he'd move his lips around. To which Chill Wills, who was the voice of Francis, would add the voice. We had personnel on the set at all times protecting the animals, making sure that they were not injured or mistreated. Even in Westerns, when we did horse falls, they want the ground dug up, softened up first, for the horse. *Not* for the rider *[laughs]*!

Why did you leave Universal?

I left 'em because they dropped my contract *[laughs]*! I was supposedly on my way, the next in line for the "big buildup" that they'd given to Rock Hudson and Jeff Chandler, Tony Curtis and Audie Murphy. I was told that, "Now the big push is on you, Palmer." But then, long about 1954 or '55, the policy changed. Instead of having the stable of talent there that would try to build, they brought in name stars—give them a piece of the picture or whatever. So I left, and within three months after I left they called me up and I went back to do another film for them at Universal: *The Creature Walks Among Us*.

Did you enjoy appearing in The Creature Walks Among Us?

I was fascinated by the Gillman, that costume that Bud Westmore had designed, and I often thought, "Gee, wouldn't it be nice to have a beach party some night and be sitting out there, and hire this guy to come out of the waves?" I had a young lady in for lunch one day and we were in the makeup room and I was showing her around, and in walked Don Megowan, who wore the costume in the film. He walked up behind my lady-friend and started breathing heavily, to give the effects of the gills working. She turned around, shook like an $18 television set, screamed and took off *[laughs]*!

Any memories of your Creature Walks *co-stars?*

Good memories. I saw Jeff Morrow not too long ago and we discussed *The Creature Walks Among Us* as one of the films we enjoyed making. Rex Reason, speaking of voices, is one person who really has a resonant voice—a wonderful guy. A few years down the road after the *Creature* movie, Rex left the business—took another avenue, and did well in real estate. He was a good actor, considerate and helpful. Both Rex and Jeff Morrow were professionals. They would stand off-camera and read the lines to you, and not let the assistant director or the dialogue director read them. I think that's a professional way to do it—I've always done it. You get more of a motivation out of looking at the person that you're doing the story with than you could with a person reading it out of a script.

Palmer first turned monster-fighter for Universal's third Gillman adventure, *The Creature Walks Among Us.*

How about the men who played the Creature, Megowan and Ricou Browning?

Ricou I don't remember too well, but Don Megowan was a very dear friend of mine. We would always kid one another about size and weight and all that sort of thing. I used to ask him, "Don, what do you weigh?" and he would say, "194 pounds." And I'd say, "No, no—with *both* feet on the scale!" *[Laughs.]* I remember that Don and I played brothers on an episode of *Gunsmoke,* there was a shootout at Dodge City and Don was hit. "Ma" told me, "Go git your brother," and I had to go out into the street, grab Don Megowan, pick him up, put him over my shoulder and carry him off. Well, when I draped him over my shoulder, his head was dragging and his feet were dragging, and it was a full day's work to make that ten steps off-camera with Don Megowan *[laughs]*! Don was a super guy. He died young.

One of the best scenes in Creature Walks *is when your party stalks the Gillman down that narrow channel in your motorboat.*

Yeah, that was kind of an ominous scene. At times you get "into" a scene—you know that this animal, this Creature, is out there, and all of a sudden the water breaks and this head pops out and reaches in for you—! It was a frightening moment, an exciting scene, and I remember it well. That was all done on a sound stage at Universal Studios.

I liked *The Creature Walks Among Us,* I thought it was well-done, well-presented. And they still talk about it today. I travel around quite a bit and I have fans come up to me and talk about science fiction, and they always bring up *The Creature Walks Among Us* as opposed to some of the other sci-fi things that I did.

Were you a fan of science fiction films?

Oh, yes, I enjoyed them. I used to think of science fiction as being something that was different from being up in the hills — my claim to fame was a lot of Westerns and cavalry things. John Agar made a lot of these science fiction pictures, he would sit with me in the Universal commissary and we would talk about it and I'd think, "Gee, they're on a sound stage, they don't have to get up there in the wind and the blizzards or whatever!"

Zombies of Mora Tau I'll never forget, that's the one where I played a diver and we were diving for jewels that were protected by these zombies. The producers hired a bunch of wrestlers to play the zombies and they caught me a couple of times within the film. They would grab me and literally pick me up and throw me against a palm tree! And I could hear my vertebrae just cracking, going down! Then one of the wrestlers would say, "Come here, Gregg." I'd walk over to him, he'd turn me around and lift me up and pop my back for me, and put it back into place *[laughs]*! That's what I remember about *Zombies of Mora Tau!*

Do you remember how you got involved on Zombies of Mora Tau?

Sam Katzman was the producer on that, and the director was Edward L. Cahn. My agent set up an interview and I went over there to read. There were four or five other actors there, too, waiting to go in and try out. I went in and I read with Mr. Cahn — he was reading the other parts — and he said, "Now read this scene." And then, "Now, *this* scene." And pretty soon we're going through the whole script! Lenny Katzman, who was the nephew of Sam Katzman, came in and asked Cahn, "How long are you going to be? There's four or five more people out here." To which Mr. Cahn replied, "Send 'em home, I got the party right here. Palmer's gonna play it!"

Do you recall if Allison Hayes liked her role? She plays a zombie throughout much of the film.

I think she enjoyed it. We remained friends after the show for a period of time, then when I heard of her passing I was deeply moved by that. She was just wonderful, a really talented and beautiful person. And Morris Ankrum was in *Zombies of Mora Tau,* too — he was a great pro, was around a long time. That was shot out at the Baldwin Ranch, near Santa Ana Racetrack — Baldwin was an old pioneer and they used that ranch in many movies. We did the interiors at Columbia, on sound stages.

Another funny thing about *Zombies of Mora Tau,* which involves a fellow called Joel Ashley, who played the fortune-hunter in the film. When you're working in a movie you get call sheets handed to you at the end of each day. Each actor would have a number—I would be #4, you would be #14, the leading lady would be #6—and you would match that number up against the scenes that they would be shooting the next day, to know when or if you'd be needed. So this one day on *Zombies of Mora Tau*, as we were leaving, Harry, who was the assistant director, handed out the call sheets; we accepted them and departed and came back the next day. Early that morning we're sitting in the dressing room when Harry came in and said, "All right, Scene #22 today, let's go." And Joel said, "*What?*" (That was his big scene.) "You didn't give me that, it wasn't on the call sheet!" And Harry said, "It sure was. Look at your call sheet." So Joel went over and took it out of his script and handed it to Harry, and said, "Do you see my number on there?" Harry looked at it and said, "No. But this is *Zombies of Mora Tau*. What's the title on *that* call sheet?" And Joel looked at it and cried out, "*The Man Who Turned to Stone*—!" Well *[laughs]*, with that, sweat started to come out of Joel's forehead: Everybody was now waiting, the director was there, the scene was lit and so forth. Joel had to go in there and really work hard, and he's never to this day forgiven Harry for that!

Edward Cahn has a reputation as a lightning-fast director.
Edward Cahn was quick—in those days you had to be! But he knew what he wanted and he always had his shots all lined up. He was once a film cutter, and directors who have had film cutting experience know in their heads as they go in just how they're going to cut it and what they need. Those kind of directors are not around anymore. I remember doing *Death Valley Days* [on TV]—I made a bunch of those—and I would shoot one episode in two and a half days. We'd do 18 pages a day! When I started out we would make a movie in three weeks, five weeks, and they were good features. Today they go months.

How'd you end up with such a small part in From Hell It Came?
That was done at the request of my agent, Jack Pomeroy. We went over to the studio and the producers, the Milner Bros., told me about the part, and I said, "You want me to lay down and be staked out and have chickens around me? And then I turn into a tree?? Come *on*—!" But as I walked down the hallway Jack said to me, "Gregg, *do* this. A lot of people are going to see this—science fiction is coming around. I'll make it up to you." You always hear that in the business, "*Do* this, I'll make it up to you." So he kept chewin' on my ear, and the next thing I know, I was staked out on the ground and the chickens were all around me! I believe that was one day's work.

Did you get to see the tree monster prop while you were there?
Oh, yes, I saw the tree monster. I saw it in makeup and I saw it when it

Sacrificially slain and buried inside a hollow tree, Palmer returned to seek revenge in *From Hell It Came*.

came out to be viewed by the director. I didn't play the tree monster— that was a "wrap" that day!

Was it a whole new ballgame, now that you were gone from Universal and freelancing?

It's different, yeah. The money changes; you get more as a freelancer, considerably more. And some of the offers you get are interesting. I remember, after I left Universal Studios, I was offered Tarzan. I was on my way out to Culver City one morning to meet with the producers and sign a contract for Tarzan, and it was a cold, chilly morning. And I got to thinking, "I'm gonna have to stand out in weather like this and go *a-woooo-a-woooo-a-woooo* in a loincloth? No, that's not for me!" So I went up there and I told them, no, I don't think I want to be Tarzan. Then there was also an interest in me for *The Lone Ranger*. Clayton Moore had left and they needed another Lone Ranger, my agent had me over there and I made the test on it. And after the test, he told them, "After the shows are shot, we'd like to go out and hit the rodeo circuit"—I would ride around and say "Hiyo, Silver!" and so forth. But they told us we couldn't do that, so we passed on *The Lone Ranger* and John Hart was the one that got the part.

You worked with a real "name" director on Most Dangerous Man Alive, *Allan Dwan.*

Allan Dwan went back to the days of silent pictures. I'll never forget the day when I came up on the set and I was introduced to Allan

Ad for *From Hell It Came*.

Dwan. We were in a lava canyon down in Mexico, he was sitting there, and I was introduced to him—"Mr. Dwan, this is Mr. Palmer. He's playing the police lieutenant." Dwan looked at me and then he turned to the wardrobe man, and he said *[out of the corner of his mouth]*, "Where's his hat? Who ever heard of a detective without his hat?" I had never met Mr. Dwan, but I knew he had a reputation for being very firm. I said, "There's no problem, Mr. Dwan," and he said, "What d'ya mean, no problem? You gotta have a hat, Cowboy!" Where he got "cowboy" from, I don't know, but he hung that sobriquet on me *[laughs]*! I said, "Well, I'll use *your* hat." "My hat? No, no, no, no—you see all this stuff here?" and he took off his hat and revealed to me little sun spots on his forehead, from too much sun. So I called for property, they came over and I said, "Do you have an umbrella? A big beach umbrella?" They went off and they came back with a beach umbrella, and I remember struggling to jam this thing into the ground. Now there was shade covering Dwan, and I held my hand out and I said "Gimme the hat." So—reluctantly—he handed me the hat, he looked at me and he said, "Cowboy, this is my favorite hat. You damage this hat, and you got big troubles."

As I looked off in the distance I could see a car scurrying down the canyon, toward Mexico City, to find a hat—and they came back with maybe a dozen! Dwan picked one up and said, "This one here, Cowboy, this is your hat. Gimme my hat." And I looked at him and I said, "I'm afraid I can't do that, Mr. Dwan. This one's already established. *You* wear that hat." He again looked at me and he put it on and he said, "I'm telling you again, Cowboy. Injure that hat and you got big problems!" Well, the upshot of this story is that we became very good friends, and even after the show I was invited up to his house for dinner and so forth!

So you enjoyed working with Dwan.

Oh, yeah. He was a great man, a legend, just a super person. I enjoyed working with him and just being in his presence. We had a little gag going on *Most Dangerous Man Alive:* He would do closeups on me, which you would have to do in shooting a film. And after he'd get through with each closeup, I'd walk over and I'd give him a five-dollar peso. And he'd laugh, because that got people to thinking that I was paying Dwan to give me these closeups *[laughs]*! He was a great joker himself and he liked to kid around.

I'll never forget one scene in there where they used a bomb—it was supposed to be a tear gas bomb, in the scene where the police have the bad guys trapped in a power house. We were all concerned about our clothes and everything, but Ben Bogeaus, who was the producer of the show, said, "Don't worry about it, no problem." Well, cameras rolled, the bomb went off, and that liquid got on Tony Caruso's suit and my suit, and we had nothing but holes left in 'em! Another thing I remember is Morris Ankrum, who played my boss in the picture, he took ill, I guess from drinking the water. (We shot *Most Dangerous Man* down in Mexico City, at Churubusco Studios.) A lot of

Although he plays a machete-wielding sadist in *Big Jake*, Big Gregg looks jovial enough in this posed shot.

people fail to realize that in Mexico, even if you ask for bottled water, the ice they put in it is made from water that is not pure. And when you get the turistas, it brings you right on down to the ground—you couldn't be thrown faster, and you don't want to get up! It's an experience you'll never forget. And Morris Ankrum had that. Anyway, there was a scene that went for about a page and a half and it was decided that I would take all of Morrie's dialogue. They gave me the lines, and 15 minutes later I was before the camera. They were very appreciative about it, especially Mr. Dwan and Ben Bogeaus. But I'll never forget Morrie, so ill down there with that.

Fed up with L.A.'s smog and traffic, Palmer (seen here in a recent shot) is planning to head for the tall timber.

Just a few years ago you popped up in a Friday the 13th–*style film alternately called* The Outing *and* Scream.

What ever happened to that film, I'd like to know; I don't know where it went, but my guess is that it didn't go too far *[laughs]*! Some friends of mine approached me to do the picture and I said, "Well, why not?" Ethan Wayne was the star of it; Ethan was also in *Big Jake,* as the little tyke that Richard Boone and I kidnaped. A handsome young man — he's still in pictures today as an actor and doing very well. *The Outing* was about a bunch of campers turning up in a town where people are getting killed by various means. I played one of the campers, and I end up getting axed, I think *[laughs]*! We shot it at the Paramount Ranch here in the Valley. I read that it was released in New York and the first week, from what I read in the trades, it made a lot of money. But where it is now I don't know.

What would you say was the highlight of your career?

I would say that working with John Wayne was one of the highlights of my career. It was a pleasure working with this man—he was a legend. He was a person that gave you the bottom line, you knew where you stood with him. I can recall as a kid watching him in the movies, never realizing that someday I would be in his presence ... acting with him ... having him give me a nickname. "Grizzly" *[laughs]*—he hung that one on me! Six pictures I worked with him in. And I guess what I admired about that man most of all is his love for our country. He stood for the best in America and he always spoke very highly of it. He had that strength, and I'll never forget him for that.

Are you retired today?

Around the beginning of '89 I was taking the 405 freeway up over the hill, back into the San Fernando Valley where I live. I looked down at the bumper-to-bumper traffic and the smog and everything, and I just said to my wife, "Honey, that's a wrap." I called up the [Screen Actors] Guild and took my pension. Which doesn't mean that I can't go out and do other shows. My plans now are to go up into Oregon, or maybe Montana or Wyoming, and hunt and fish a little bit. But I still intend to do some more work; even though you draw your pension, you can still work seven days out of the month.

Overall, are you happy with your career?

I think that I had a very exciting career. I was able to meet a lot of nice people and I was fortunate enough to travel quite a bit. I made a few films in Durango, Mexico, a couple down in Mexico City and I've made films throughout the United States. I also went to Europe, and made a couple of spaghetti Westerns! I still have recognition, still have people that write to me. I've just recently gotten mail from Switzerland, Germany, England—even one from the outlands of Australia! When I look back now I think of some 50, 60-odd movies and close to a thousand television shows, and so, yes, I would say that I've been very lucky to have done as much as I have. I've had an exciting life.

GREGG PALMER FILMOGRAPHY

As Palmer Lee:

My Friend Irma Goes West (Paramount, 1950)
That's My Boy (Paramount, 1951)
Up Front (Universal, 1951)

The Cimarron Kid (Universal, 1951)
The Battle at Apache Pass (Universal, 1952)
Willie and Joe Back at the Front (Universal, 1952)
Son of Ali Baba (Universal, 1952)
Red Ball Express (Universal, 1952)
Francis Goes to West Point (Universal, 1952)
Meet Danny Wilson (Universal, 1952)
Sally and Saint Anne (Universal, 1952)
The Raiders (Universal, 1952)
The Redhead from Wyoming (Universal, 1952)
Abbott & Costello Go to Mars (voice only; Universal, 1953)
It Happens Every Thursday (Universal, 1953)
Column South (Universal, 1953)
The Veils of Bagdad (Universal, 1953)

As Gregg Palmer:

All American (Universal, 1953)
Francis Joins the Wacs (voice only; Universal, 1954)
Magnificent Obsession (Universal, 1954)
Playgirl (Universal, 1954)
Taza, Son of Cochise (Universal, 1954)
To Hell and Back (Universal, 1955)
The Creature Walks Among Us (Universal, 1956)
Hilda Crane (20th Century–Fox, 1956)
Footsteps in the Night (Allied Artists, 1957)
Revolt at Fort Laramie (United Artists, 1957)
From Hell It Came (Allied Artists, 1957)
Zombies of Mora Tau (Columbia, 1957)
The Female Animal (Universal, 1958)
Thundering Jets (20th Century–Fox, 1958)
The Sad Horse (20th Century–Fox, 1959)
The Rebel Set (Allied Artists, 1959)
Five Guns to Tombstone (United Artists, 1961)
Gun Fight (United Artists, 1961)
The Cat Burglar (United Artists, 1961)
Most Dangerous Man Alive (Columbia, 1961)
The Comancheros (20th Century–Fox, 1961)
The Absent-Minded Professor (Buena Vista, 1961)
Forty Pounds of Trouble (Universal, 1962)
The Prize (MGM, 1963)
Advance to the Rear (MGM, 1964)
The Quick Gun (Columbia, 1964)
Shenandoah (Universal, 1965)
The Rare Breed (Universal, 1966)
If He Hollers, Let Him Go! (Cinerama Releasing, 1968)
The Undefeated (20th Century–Fox, 1969)
The McKenzie Break (United Artists, 1970)
Chisum (Warners, 1970)
Rio Lobo (National General, 1970)
Big Jake (National General, 1971)
La Vita, A Volte E Molto Dura, Vero Providenza? (Italian-French-West German, 1972)

Ci Risiamo Vero Providenza (Italian-Spanish, 197?)
The Shootist (Paramount, 1976)
Hot Lead and Cold Feet (Buena Vista, 1978)
The Man with Bogart's Face (Sam Marlow, Private Eye) (20th Century-Fox, 1980)
Scream (The Outing) (Cal-Com, 1985)

*I just loved good roles: I would love to have done
great big roles in great big A pictures, roles that had
meat in them.... It never quite happened for me in that way,
but I had some wonderfully satisfying experiences, I learned a
tremendous lot, I had a marvelous teacher, and who knows
what'll happen at this point? I don't necessarily
know that I've finished with acting.*

Mala Powers

TALENT AND BEAUTY go a long way toward helping a young actress up the ladder of stardom, but the elusive element of luck also plays a large part in the process. "Discovered" by Ida Lupino, Mala Powers co-starred in several prestigious films at the beginning of her career, including *Cyrano de Bergerac* (1950) with Oscar-winner Jose Ferrer, but after an illness interrupted her career momentum she fell into the clutches of the B science fiction and Western moviemakers. The mainstream's loss was fandom's gain, however, as brown-haired, gray-eyed Mala Powers has brought poise and charm to such genre productions as *The Unknown Terror, The Colossus of New York, Flight of the Lost Balloon, Doomsday Machine* and *Daddy's Gone A-Hunting*.

Do you remember how you became involved on The Unknown Terror?
I'm sure that it was simply a question of my agent calling me and telling me that they wanted me to do it. I do remember that I was pregnant then and that I didn't want anybody to know it at that point. I was eager to do as much work as I could, before I *couldn't [laughs]*! If memory serves, we shot *The Unknown Terror* at the old Producers Studio in Hollywood.

Did you consider a low-budget monster movie like The Unknown Terror *a comedown?*
You may read a script and say to yourself, "I wonder why this is being made at all." But if you need to work, if you need to stay in front of the public, if you need the money—whatever your reason is—and you say yes, at that point it is incumbent upon you to fall in love with the script and fall in love with your part. At that point you put on blinders that enable you to permit your love for your profession to shine a radiance over everything. This allows you to put all of yourself into it. I remember that our shooting title for *The Unknown Terror* was *Beyond Terror*, which I think might have been a better title.

Were you on hand for the scenes where the fungus is cascading down the cave walls?
Yeah, I was there. They used a lot of soap suds and some other stuff that was kind of like a plastic goo. It was a real conglomeration, and to find out exactly how it was done you'd have to go to Merlin the Magician *[laughs]*! The prop man was very inventive, and it was quite effective. It's quite different now that they have these special effects laboratories—it's much more sophisticated today. The effects in *The Unknown Terror* were just done by very good, inventive prop men.

Do you remember the fungus-men in the film?
Yes, they were made up by a makeup man. A lot of that makeup was just

Previous page: **Mala Powers and Ed Wolff,** *The Colossus of New York.*

Stalked by one of the fungus men in *The Unknown Terror,* Powers wonders why the script was filmed at all.

cotton, put on with liquid adhesive or spirit gum. Then they gave it a little glitter, to make it look more *[laughs]* ... fungus-y! I don't know how it came out in the picture, but I do remember that at the time I wasn't really impressed with that aspect. When I "fell in love" with my part and so on, I guess I just ignored it!

Really, what I remember about *The Unknown Terror* is that I liked working with Paul Richards—he was a good actor—and I also liked John Howard [q.v.] very much. I thought the three of us worked well together. The director, Charles Marquis Warren, was pretty permissive, and he let us do whatever we wanted to do. It was just a very congenial set: John and Paul and I got along fine, and as far as I can remember, we all got along with Warren.

Was The Colossus of New York *the first film you made at Paramount?*

Yes, it was. But, you know, we shot a lot of that picture on location, in a house. It was a house not far from the studio—maybe 20 minutes away. We'd go to Paramount and get made-up there, get in the car and go to the location. Perhaps somebody thought it would seem more real if we did it in an actual house.

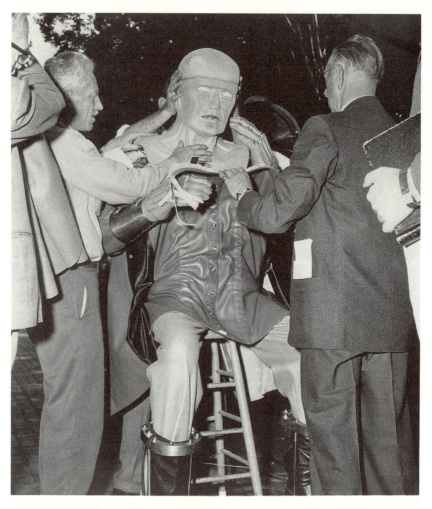

Eight-foot circus giant Ed Wolff is helped into (out of?) his robot suit backstage on *The Colossus of New York.*

Did you enjoy working with the director, Eugene Lourie?

I remember that I got along well with him, but really not too much more than that. I do remember that I always liked the producer, William Alland. He's a very pleasant man, and as I recall, whenever he came on the set, he did what I believe a producer should do: He made everybody feel that everything was fine. That's very important on a picture. If a producer comes on and he has a gloomy look on his face, everybody vibrates with gloom—it reverberates all the way around! My advice to any producer is always, if you come on the set unhappy about something, put on your best actor's face until you can handle it, because your face very materially affects the set.

Any special memories of your co-stars from that film?

I do have some very special memories of Ross Martin, because I later went out with Ross for a long time — it was on *The Colossus of New York* that we first met. I was very impressed with him on that film, and with the way he worked. After the first scene or two, he was only the voice of the Colossus, but he was really very impressive and a very, very good actor. And although he certainly had a great success, I always felt that he should have had even greater success, because he had the talent, ability and the training for it. I also loved working with Otto Kruger, he was so full of fun. Quite often he would play a menacing type of character, but he had this tremendous sense of humor — he was always coming up with some joke or something that caught you off-guard. I really liked him so much. *The Colossus of New York* was fun in those respects, but all in all it's not one of my favorite pictures.

At one point in your career you made the statement, "There are pictures I've made which I'd just as soon blank out of my mind." Were you mostly talking about these horror and science fiction films?

No, there were other pictures as well, for one reason or another. I can recall a picture I did called *Fear No More* [1961] where I really liked the script, and then all of a sudden in the last scene of the picture it falls apart so badly that the audience laughed at it. And the producers didn't have money enough to go back and change the ending. Up until the last scene it was a good picture, so that was a painful experience. There are various reasons why certain pictures weren't so pleasant to do, and others were great fun even if they weren't tremendous pictures!

How did you become interested in being an actress?

It started the summer my family and I moved down here to L.A. from San Francisco, where my father was an executive with United Press. This was in 1940, and it was the first summer that I had not been up at our summer home, on the Russian River near Guerneville. And for me it was pretty grim because I didn't know anybody. There was a drama school a few blocks away, the Max Reinhardt Junior Workshop, and my mother thought that it would be a good place for me to go for the summer, 'til school started, where I would meet other children. Also, she had always loved drama, and had done a lot of it when she was in college. So I went there for the summer, and while I was studying drama I did a play. And with the first play that I ever did in front of a live audience, that was it — I had the fever.

It still didn't occur to me that I was going to be an actress, I was just a kid, and I just went on being in amateur plays. At one point my parents were planning to send me to a private school, and my mother said to me, "We'll have to stop your dramatic lessons until next summer, because I can't afford to keep up with your lessons *and* send you to this school." And I said, "Then I don't want to go to that school!" And I got my way: We all talked about it and we found another school that was nearby, not so expensive, and that my parents felt was a good school, so I continued my drama lessons.

How did you break into pictures?

I guess close to a year later I was doing a play and an agent came back after the performance and asked my mother if he could submit me for a part in a movie. I'll never forget that night, because that was the first time it had ever occurred to me that I was going to be an actress — up until then, acting was just something that I loved doing. My mother said to me, "Well, what do you want to do?" and I said, "I want to *go*!" So I went out on the audition. It was a part in a Dead End Kids picture called *Tough as They Come* [1942] at Universal Studio. They wanted someone slightly older for the part that the agent had taken me out for, but they liked me and decided to write in the part of this giggly little girl at a party, and they gave me that part. And then they actually wrote it in for a second day, so I worked two days on it.

People talk about the smell of the greasepaint and the roar of the crowd; for me, it was the smell of the sound stage. It was just wonderful. And I knew that this was what I wanted to do.

Did you have any other roles as a child?

No, as a matter of fact, because very soon after that I started working with Max Reinhardt's wife, Helene Thimig, who was a great Austrian actress, and she more or less persuaded us to wait until I was at least in my teens, rather than to start out on the whole circuit of being a child actress. She felt that I should study and really prepare myself, and delay working professionally until a bit later.

When I was 16 I decided to try to break into radio, which I was fortunate enough to be able to do. I worked quite extensively for a couple of years, and was kind of making my mark in radio. I did everything that was out here in Hollywood: *Cisco Kid* and *Red Ryder*, *This Is Your F.B.I.*, *Lux Radio Theater*, *Rocky Jordan*, that kind of show. During that process I did a *Screen Guild on the Air* where I met Ida Lupino, and she asked me to come in and read for her for a part in *Outrage* [1950], which she was directing and producing. When I read for her, she jumped up and said, "You're it, you're it! Read me another scene!"

Howard Hughes [then head of RKO] had to okay whoever it was that was signed to do the lead in the picture. So after Ida Lupino decided that she wanted me, she had me come in the next day and they took me into the portrait gallery, and I posed for portraits. They were shown to Hughes, and he asked to meet me. So my mother and my agent and I all went over to the Beverly Hills Hotel and had a meeting with Howard Hughes, in January 1950, in the outside court of the Polo Lounge. The chairs were all turned over and it was cold *[laughs]* — a very unlikely place to have a meeting, but that's where we had it! Hughes turned over the chairs and wiped them off with his handkerchief, and we all sat out there in the cold for about an hour and ten minutes, and he talked to me about the part. And I then did three pictures—*Outrage, Edge of Doom* and *Cyrano de Bergerac*—all within a span of four months in 1950.

Wasn't it soon after that when you became dangerously sick?

I was entertaining troops in Korea and I came down with a virus of some kind, and they gave me a drug called chloromycetin when I got back home. But I was allergic to chloromycetin, it destroyed a great part of the bone marrow, and I sort of stopped producing blood. I had a great many transfusions, and the doctors really didn't hold out a lot of hope for me as far as living was concerned. During that time I had a very wonderful spiritual experience in which I was told that I would recover, but what I had to do in order to recover. And that's really what I did. It took about nine months, but I did, obviously, get better.

But you were out of work all that time, of course.

Right. When I came back from Korea I was taking this medicine and I went to work on a film called *City Beneath the Sea* [1953] with Robert Ryan and Anthony Quinn and Suzan Ball. We were doing a lot of underwater scenes and earthquakes, and it was a fairly strenuous picture. I started to feel ill again and I called the doctor and asked for another prescription, which they sent to me. And while I was on the medicine I started to bleed under the skin and so on. The makeup man called the doctor, and I was taken off the picture and put into the hospital. I had finished all but one scene in *City Beneath the Sea,* and they wrote me out of that scene. Later the sound crew came to my house and recorded a telephone conversation which explained my absence from that scene. So from that point on, of course, I didn't work.

And do you blame your illness for your career losing its momentum?

Yes, unquestionably. I had two problems: One, there were a couple of good parts which came around a little bit later, and they wouldn't hire me because they were afraid I couldn't get insurance. That was ridiculous, because I could have gotten insurance—I mean, when I was well, I was well! But there were some problems like that. And then there was a whole kind of aura around me that persisted; instead of being known as "the actress," I was "the girl who was so sick." In fact, there came a point when I didn't want to talk about my illness and recovery any more for a number of years. But, you're right, I had a momentum going for me which somehow got slowed at that point.

You co-starred with Marshall Thompson in Flight of the Lost Balloon, *a film with some mild fantastic elements and a kind of Jules Verne flavor.*

I remember a lot about that picture. I loved the script, and so did Marshall Thompson. We knew it was Jules Verne and we knew it was tongue-in-cheek. But when we went to shoot it, we found out that we were the only people who

Powers and Marshall Thompson trooped down to the site of an old Puerto Rican leper colony for the Jules Verne-ish cheapie *Flight of the Lost Balloon*.

did know it! Marshall and I, and James Lanphier, who played the villain, were really the only people who knew that it was supposed to be done in that style, and it wasn't directed in that style. We also found out right away that the menacing elements in the picture weren't going to work out. They had men in gorilla suits, and also this poor giant who could hardly move because he was so big! To try to make him menacing was just ridiculous. The menacing elements should have been menacing, and of course they just weren't, so it became a neither-this-nor-that type of picture.

But you sound as though you still have a slightly soft spot for it.

I have a soft spot for the script, not for the way the picture came out. But I loved my character — she was just so great, and I still like the moment at the end of the picture when she took this huge diamond from out of her mouth, where she had hidden it. And of course I had a wonderful time making the film because we went to Puerto Rico and we worked at some very interesting locations. We worked at the old Isla de Cabras — the Isle of the Goats — which used to be a leper colony! We shot a good deal of it there, and we shot in the castle in the bay in Puerto Rico, and then also in a jungle-type of location. I remember the picture so well because the whole atmosphere of it was just fun and it was enjoyable to make. But I also found myself getting internally very angry because things weren't going right. Not angry *at* anyone, just angry because I felt like it had the potential to be a really fun, spoof kind of picture with some elements of menace and drama. But the menace just disappeared, and the sophisticated elements of the spoof were not capitalized upon.

Did you try to convey this to the director, Nathan Juran?

No, I didn't. What can you say when you get there in the morning and you see a man in a gorilla suit? Or what can you do when you sit down to watch the dailies and you see it's coming out just as you suspected it would? You can make your comments, but what are the producers going to do at that point? It was a low-budget picture — are they going to fly all the way back to the United States and prepare to start over? They're not.

A lot of stuff was getting shot, and as long as it was passable, they'd print it. That's not too unusual, but it was getting to me. And I remember saying at one point *[firmly]*, "No, I want to do it again." Nathan Juran said, "It doesn't make any difference," and I said, "It *does* make a difference. This is going to be on film a lot longer than I'm going to be alive, and I want to do it again." It was a scene on the edge of a cliff, with the ocean behind me, and it had really been a terrible take. And I just wasn't going to let it go that way.

What do you remember about the scene where you're chased by the angry tribe?

[Laughs.] That was great fun. They were all Spanish-speaking, and there were relatively few extras that spoke English. It was a very hot day — it was terrible! — and very, very humid. And there was also a fire in that scene, and that didn't help! I remember that the hairspray that they put on me would collect water, and my hair would get to be stringy and very difficult. And of course we were also perspiring, and it was impossible to keep the makeup on. Then there was bug spray *[laughs]* — the bugs would have eaten us alive in there without it! I remember the makeup people trying to keep me dry with powder going on over bug spray — it sounds like a horror film!

Did you ever actually go up in the hot-air balloon seen in the film?

We were in the basket of the balloon, of course, but it was just swung over a cliff by a big crane. So, no, we didn't actually go up. The background scenery in the flight scenes was simply rear-projection.

You worked again with Ida Lupino on TV's Thriller *and in an episode of* The Wild Wild West. *You've kept in touch with her through the years?*

Oh, yes, definitely, and we're still friends to this day. I loved working with her because I always knew that as a director she protected her people. In other words, you could dare to do things because you knew if it didn't come out right, she would not print it. I think that's one of the worst fears of actors today, and it was true then, too. Many shows are done so quickly that as long as you get the words out right, they print it! That means that you don't dare to be very original: Sometimes, when you create, it doesn't turn out right! If you've got a director that you trust, then you can be much more creative, but if you've got one that's going to print it no matter what, you tend to play it safe. And whenever you play it safe, it's not your best work.

Every time I worked with Ida Lupino, the crew loved her—she really made chums out of the crew. She used to call them "chum," and a lot of people called her "mum"! I just loved working with her because, first of all, I felt that she knew what was going on in me all the time, almost before I did. And I knew that she would protect me, and that she gave me confidence.

Any memories at all regarding those Thriller *and* Wild Wild West *guest shots?*

The *Thriller* episode was called "The Bride Who Died Twice," and I do remember that because any time that an actor lies in a coffin, they remember *[laughs]*! It was an interesting experience because I was interested in observing my own reaction to lying in the coffin. And working on *The Wild Wild West* ["The Night of the Big Blast"] was a ball because I did that with Ross Martin, and I was going with him at that point. We just had such a good time and so many laughs; it was so campy and so wonderful. And it was like old home week having Ida on the set as well; we didn't have a scene together in it but we were in the same episode, so of course we visited with each other on the set and so on. It was a very fun, very festive experience all the way around—it was funtime, a playground. That to me was not work, it was sheer play, and I had a very good time.

How did Robert Conrad and Ross Martin get along together? Stories go around that they sometimes battled back and forth.

Well, you must remember that they worked together day in and day out, day in and day out. I know that basically Ross thought that Bob was a lot of fun, but I imagine that they had their tiffs occasionally. It wasn't an all-the-time fight: They had a whopper every once in a while, then they forgot about it and got along fine, and then something else would come up. But I never got the feeling that they were enemies.

What prompted you to accept a minor role in Daddy's Gone A-Hunting?

Mark Robson, who had directed me in *Edge of Doom*—I was still friendly with him. I was just about to get married when I went visiting at the Hal Roach Studio, and I saw an office door that said *Mark Robson*. I went in just to say hello, and he asked me if I was interested in being in this picture! It wasn't a real big part, he told me, but would I want to do it? And so I agreed that I would.

Not long after this I went on a trip to Europe. We were not scheduled to start shooting on *Daddy's Gone A-Hunting* for another ten days and I was just

Semi-retired from acting, Powers (seen here in a recent shot) has forged a new career as a writer of children's books.

arriving in London—my first trip there. And when I got there, there was a telephone message for me to call the studio immediately. I called, and they said I had to be in San Francisco in three days, that the schedule had all been changed! So I was in London exactly 24 hours, and got a plane direct from London to San Francisco and went to work. After that I didn't work on the picture again for another three or four weeks, and then I did a scene in Los Angeles. I went back to Europe in the meantime.

You enjoyed working with Robson?

I thought he was very creative, very warm, and that he had a very positive approach to things. He was firm, he knew what he was doing, but you could talk to him—he was not authoritarian. He came up with wonderful suggestions, and I really enjoyed working with Mark. I thought he was a first-rate director. *Daddy's Gone A-Hunting* was a good picture with a lot of suspense, and I enjoyed it.

In between your many film and TV appearances, you've done a lot of stage work. Do you prefer the stage to the screen?
I think they're two separate, very different things, and I love them both. I personally don't really like eight performances a week, month after month after month, so my preference would be limited runs as far as the stage is concerned. But I really do love working for a live audience; it's much more challenging in some ways. On the screen you can do short scenes and you can feel "that it was a little piece of art"—that's my teacher's, Michael Chekhov's, phrase. It has a beginning, a middle and an end, and you receive satisfaction from that, like a craftsman does. But the sustained experience of starting at the beginning of a play and moving all the way through it is also a very satisfying experience and quite different. And you get so much from a live audience which you have to work much harder to get on a sound stage. There are advantages to everything.

How do good actors get mixed up with the kind of filmmakers who'd make something like Doomsday Machine?
Doomsday Machine is a subject about which I could still scream. Once again, it had a certain premise that was okay. Then they ran out of money, twice. We had a director who was taken off the picture in the middle, and another director, Lee Sholem, was put on. The thing was not going well, and it was never finished because they ran out of money like two days before the end of the picture. One of the reasons I'm sure they were never able to raise the money to finish the picture was because of the really shoddy interior of that spaceship. The special effects hadn't been done yet, they couldn't sell it and they couldn't raise enough money to finish it.

Now is the point where I get really angry: A number of years later they had the audacity to sell that picture to someone who put doubles into spacesuits, and finished the picture with an ending that was never part of the script. I didn't even know about it until long after it had been shown on television, when somebody finally told me about it. They put somebody in a spacesuit—this was supposed to be me—and allowed them to speak without the Russian accent that I had used all the way through the picture! I just wanted to scream! I wanted to go to the Guild and start an action and see if anything could be legally done about it, but at that point I was simply too busy. I don't know that anything could be done, but that was my impulse. When I saw that on television, I was infuriated.

It's an unbearable movie to watch.

Absolutely. I don't think the whole thing was unbearable, but the special effects were . . . *so* . . . *bad*! They were added to the picture by the people who bought *Doomsday Machine* and decided to make money with it. But even the suits, the props and everything else that was in the picture while we were doing it were so junior-high-school, it was unbelievable. But we did have a good cast — Bobby Van was lots of fun; Denny Miller; Ruta Lee and I became real good friends; Grant Williams; Henry Wilcoxon I loved. We just had a good time.

Your last film to date is the Argentine-made fantasy Six Tickets to Hell *[1975], which has never been released.*

That was originally entitled *Temple of the Ravens,* and it was a co-production between Argentina and a group up here in the United States. It started out with a plane crash in the Andes; six people survive and trek across the mountains, and finally we find this abandoned monastery where one strange thing happens after another. I'm attacked by some kind of an invisible "thing"; you can't see anything but literally it's an attempted rape. Everybody has some sort of experience, 'cause we're kind of dealing with ghosts and so on. It becomes so frightening there that finally we leave, and we get to a city where no one can see us; we walk around and try to talk to people, but no one sees us! What finally happens is that we're captured by a strange group of people and end up in a kind of court where we are to be judged for our sins. The link between all of us is that all six of us had been responsible in various ways for the death of a human being; in my character's case, it was through my own selfishness and greed that someone committed suicide. John Russell plays a character that was actually supposed to be the Devil, and he wants to condemn us all, but because one of the other characters was found not guilty and because we had decided to be judged as a group, we were all exonerated. And the last shot in the film is of the plane wreckage, and now you see all six bodies there. So it really turns out to have been a purgatory story.

The whole film was shot in English, but nevertheless they still dubbed everything — none of the soundtrack was any good. So all of the scenes had to be dubbed, and we dubbed them in Argentina where there were no really professional facilities available to us. It was an impossible task.

What did you think of the film when you saw it?

I saw parts of it and it was so phony, so awful that I was glad that it was not released. It was a very interesting script, and photographically it was well done; the problem with it was that most of the actors were Spanish-speaking and they had to speak English phonetically. Which was very clever, except that the tempo of it was so different and so slow; when it was then dubbed into English, although their lips were making the proper shapes, it was so slow that it was ghastly! So it was one of those things where I enjoyed making it tremendously, and I thought it was an interesting story, but when I saw a rough cut of it I thought I would die. Everything was ruined by the dubbing, and again I admit that I was always glad that it was not released here.

Why didn't it get a U.S. release?

What happened with it was quite a story in itself, although I don't know all the details. At one point the group that had made the investments up here was indicted for having collected money for, like, 25 movies and only made 17, and pocketed the rest of the money. So all of the pictures were impounded, and as far as I know they have never been shown in this country; *Six Tickets to Hell* was shown in Argentina. The producer was a man by the name of Enrique Torres, who did a number of rather imaginative horror genre films, and the director was Fernando Ciro, who is a very well-known actor-director in Argentina.

How do you keep yourself active nowadays?

Right now I am in the midst of writing a play. I don't get very much time to work on it, so it's going to take me a while to finish it, but I'm enjoying myself. And I've been teaching the Michael Chekhov acting technique. I have a group that meets once a week, and I am really enjoying teaching, I'm really grabbed by it.

Which of your films are your favorites?

For various reasons—not necessarily because it was the best film—*Outrage*. I loved the part, and I think probably that has more to do with it than the quality of the film. Of course I think *Cyrano de Bergerac* is still an excellent movie, so from that standpoint it would definitely have to be called a favorite. The film I had the most fun on was *City Beneath the Sea* with Robert Ryan and Tony Quinn, and a crazy director—crazy-wonderful—by the name of Budd Boetticher. It was really fun making that movie, even though I became very ill during the filming.

Looking back over your film career, are there any major regrets or are you pleased with your Hollywood career?

That's a tough question. No, I'm not pleased with my career; yes, I am pleased with my *life*.

I just loved good roles; I would love to have done great big roles in great big A pictures, roles that had meat in them. Would any actress *not* like to play Scarlett O'Hara in *Gone With the Wind*? From a career standpoint, of course that's what I would like to have done. It never quite happened for me in that way, but I had some wonderfully satisfying experiences, I learned a tremendous lot, I had a marvelous teacher, and who knows what'll happen at this point? I don't necessarily know that I've finished with acting.

MALA POWERS FILMOGRAPHY

Tough as They Come (Universal, 1942)
Outrage (RKO, 1950)
Edge of Doom (RKO, 1950)
Cyrano de Bergerac (United Artists, 1950)
Rose of Cimarron (20th Century-Fox, 1952)
City Beneath the Sea (Universal, 1953)
City That Never Sleeps (Republic, 1953)
Geraldine (Republic, 1953)
The Yellow Mountain (Universal, 1954)
Rage at Dawn (RKO, 1955)
Bengazi (RKO, 1955)
Tammy and the Bachelor (Universal, 1957)
The Storm Rider (20th Century-Fox, 1957)
Death in Small Doses (Allied Artists, 1957)
The Unknown Terror (20th Century-Fox, 1957)
Man on the Prowl (United Artists, 1957)
Sierra Baron (20th Century-Fox, 1958)
The Colossus of New York (Paramount, 1958)
Fear No More (Sutton Pictures, 1961)
Flight of the Lost Balloon (Woolner Bros., 1961)
Doomsday Machine (Filmways/First Leisure, 1967)
Rogue's Gallery (Paramount, 1968)
Daddy's Gone A-Hunting (National General, 1969)
Six Tickets to Hell (Temple of the Ravens) (U.S./Argentine, 1975)

Most of us thought that Superman *was just a job. Even though it lasted season after season and I knew it was popular, I never had any idea that its popularity would last and that twenty-five years later we'd be going to conventions where people would mob us!*

Robert Shayne

BORN IN turn-of-the-century Yonkers, New York, Robert Shayne (born Robert Shaen Dawe) worked at a variety of jobs before his interests ultimately turned toward acting. He appeared in a long succession of legitimate theater productions throughout the '30s and even got a false start in motion pictures, appearing in two 1934 features and a 1937 New York–made comedy short. In 1942 Shayne signed up with Warner Bros. and trekked to Hollywood, where he became a contract player at their Culver City studios. "I remember my arrival in California, walking through the Burbank Airport and out the front door," Shayne reminisces. "The sun was shining, it was warm, it was beautiful and I said to myself, 'Oh, my—this is for *me*!' And I've been out here ever since!"

Warners starred the newly arrived stage actor in a series of two-reel Westerns before graduating him to supporting roles in A features. Shayne appeared opposite many of the top WB stars of the day in pictures like *Shine on, Harvest Moon, Mr. Skeffington* (1944), *Christmas in Connecticut, Rhapsody in Blue* (1945) and many more. In 1946 he left the studio to freelance and several years later became involved in the infant medium of television, where he would win his best-remembered role as Inspector Bill Henderson in the syndicated TV series *Adventures of Superman.*

Do you recall how you landed the part of Inspector Henderson on Adventures of Superman?

My agent, Sam Armstrong, called me on the phone and said, "I've got a job for you at RKO-Pathe. Meet me on the lot at such-and-such a time." When we got there, we walked into the office of the producer, Robert Maxwell, and Sam said to Bob, "Here's the man I want you to have to play the Inspector." Bob took one look at me and asked, "How long have you been in the picture business?" and I told him I'd been in it about seven or eight years at the time. He asked if I minded graying my hair, to look older than George Reeves, and I said, "No, of course not, I'd be glad to." And Bob said, "Okay, you're it." That's how it happened.

What can you tell me about working with George Reeves [Superman]?

I found him a wonderful fellow to work with. George was an awfully nice guy. He was very sensitive and very friendly—he always gave me a birthday cake if my birthday came around when I was on the set. He was always thinking about other people.

What about some of the other regulars?

The one I got to know most was Phyllis Coates [Lois Lane, q.v.], although she was only with us for the first season. Later on, after *Superman,* we did a play down in Palm Springs, a comedy called *Never Too Late,* in which she played the wife and I played the husband. She comes down and visits every once in a while, and stays at my daughter's house—my daughter was in that same play. Phyllis is a good, professional actress.

Previous page: George Reeves and Robert Shayne in a posed shot from the classic 1950s TV series *Adventures of Superman.*

She lost interest in the show after that first season.
　We were on layoff after the first 26 episodes, Phyllis had an offer to do another series, and she wouldn't give that up to come back to *Superman*. They had to get somebody to replace her, and they got Noel Neill, who was in the two original Kirk Alyn *Superman* serials at Columbia. Phyllis Coates was a much better Lois Lane than Noel Neill. Phyllis was believable whereas Noel Neill was never believable to me as a newspaperwoman. I didn't get to know either Noel or Jack Larson [Jimmy Olsen] very well, only professionally, from working with them on the lot. John Hamilton [Perry White] was a heavy drinker. He made the Brown Derby his club—he was at the bar always. But now let me quickly add that John never drank on the set, never drank before work or during work.

How did working in early TV compare to working in films?
　Television was much more hectic. Sometimes in an A movie you would do one scene a day, shooting from various angles, close-ups and so forth, making sure the lighting was just right and so on. In TV, it's "To hell with the lighting, let's get in the can!" However, I don't think that this was quite the case with the *Superman* directors. It seems to me that every time I see a *Superman* episode, it's pretty well done.

What can you recall about some of the behind-the-scenes people on the series?
　There's nothing much I can tell you about Bob Maxwell; he was my employer, I liked him and he liked me, but I didn't know anything about him personally. Whitney Ellsworth, who took over from Maxwell, I got to know fairly well because we were together much longer—Maxwell was only on the first 26 episodes. I remember that at one point Kellogg's wanted to drop me from the show, but Whitney stood up for me. This was during the blacklist period, and I was blacklisted. "He's done nothing wrong, I'm not going to fire him," Whitney told Kellogg's, and they backed down. I was out of the series for two or three episodes, then was back. That was a despicable era in Hollywood and in the United States, a despicable era.
　It was so unfair. Being a Communist was not a crime, it was a legal political party in the United States then and it is now. All this hullabaloo about Communist influence in Hollywood was originally started by Bob Montgomery. He said he didn't want to be president of a union where, every time the union's name was mentioned, somebody would say, "Oh, that *Communist* union." Bob Montgomery was the one who really pushed the inquiry out here, and if you were subpoenaed, you were blacklisted, regardless of whether you were guilty of anything or not. This same thing would have happened again, in my opinion, if Reagan had had his way, 'cause he sees a Communist under every rug.

So what exactly had you done, to make them turn the heat on you?

Shayne (seen here in a publicity shot from *The Face of Marble*) was blacklisted in Hollywood after a run-in with the Joe McCarthy crowd, but he has still managed to rack up a long list of film and TV credits.

I hadn't done anything! The investigator told me and my wife, after everything had quieted down, "We had no reason to call you, I don't know why we ever did."

Did you maybe work for an organization that was linked with the Communist party?

Not to my knowledge. I was part of a group in Actors Equity [in New York] that fought for pay for rehearsals, minimum wages and better working conditions—and we got them. I was a rabid union man and I still believe in unions, although I'm not rabid anymore *[laughs]*! Maybe that was part of it. I was never active out here at all except when I was on the Board of Directors of the Screen Actors Guild for a while, and incurred the enmity of Bob Montgomery and Leon Ames and a few others because I was always trying to get something better for the actors.

Do you have a favorite among your many Superman *episodes?*

I have two favorites. One of them was about my son getting in trouble ["The Talking Clue," 1954], and in the other one I played a *Fr-r-rench* Inspec*teur* ["Peril in Paris," 1956].

Being that Adventures of Superman *was an action show, can you recall any injuries or near-misses?*

Not to my recollection — we were always too careful. The nearest I ever came to an accident was when I was making two-reel Westerns for Warner Bros. We were doing a scene in a barroom where I was lying on the floor, pulling a gun and shooting up at a heavy on a balcony. The director, "Breezy" Eason, came over and said, "Bob, you're not doing this quite right. I want you to do it *this* way." I had never used a gun on the stage, this was perhaps my first time. After he showed me, I pulled the gun out and inadvertently I squeezed the trigger, and the blank shot out and just went by Eason's face! I've never forgotten that.

Have you seen the four new Superman *movies with Christopher Reeve?*

No, I've never seen them. They didn't ask me to be in any, and I haven't gone to see them *[laughs]*! I understand that all those movies, especially the third and fourth, are predominantly special effects shows, with no storyline.

What are your fondest memories of working on Superman?

That's hard to say. I just enjoyed going to work, because everyone in the company was compatible. George and I worked so well together. We would come in every morning, he'd ask me, "Bob, do you know your lines?" I'd say, "No, not too well," and he'd say, "Well, neither do I! Come on, let's go into my dressing room and we'll run 'em." We'd sit in the dressing room and go over the lines two or three times, and then we'd be ready. That was the kind of relationship that I had with George — you don't have that with other actors or actresses as a rule. I never had it with any of the ladies I worked with. George was an easygoing, lovable guy.

Do you really believe that he committed suicide?

I don't believe he committed suicide, but I don't know who would have killed him, or anything else about it. There was some talk a few months ago that the case was going to be reopened, but not too long ago an interviewer told me that he had checked with the police department and that there was no intention of reopening the investigation.

What leads you to believe that he did not kill himself?
There was a man I met not so long ago who was a plasterer, and he told me that he went into George's house to plaster up the bullet holes. There was more than one bullet hole—they were all over the bedroom! Now, how could a man commit suicide and have bullet holes all over the room?

People say that Reeves was disgruntled over being over-identified with the Superman role.
No, no—George was making good money on that job and we had just signed up for another 26 episodes, practically all of them written. He was not wanting for work and he was not wanting for money. And if he was over-exposed as Superman, then I was over-exposed as a police inspector—but I got plenty of work after the show ended. So I don't think it holds up.

Fans of science fiction and horror films also remember you from many of those, beginning with The Face of Marble *in 1946.*
The Face of Marble was the first freelance picture I made after leaving Warner Bros. After we had finished it, I went to see a preview of it over in South Los Angeles somewhere, with my wife and another couple. We were near the back of the house, and as this picture went along I hung my head, I was so embarrassed by it! Finally, when the thing was over, I got out into the lobby before anybody else did, and I was standing against a wall with my wife and this other couple. Two young ladies came out and stood against an opposite wall, and they did a double-take when they saw who I was. And one of them came over to me and said *[wagging his finger]*, "Mr. Shayne, you ought to be ashamed to be in a picture like that!"

Did you enjoy working with star John Carradine?
That's a story in itself. We broke for lunch one day, and I came back early, onto the semi-darkened stage. John Carradine was on the dark stage spouting the dialogue of some character from Shakespeare, I forget which one, and I started to laugh, and poked fun at him. I said, "What the hell are you doing? Are you spouting Shakespeare?" He didn't like that, he didn't like my kidding him, and he got mad as hell *[laughs]*!

Your one starring sci-fi role was in 1953's The Neanderthal Man. *How did you land that part?*
The same way I got the job as Inspector Henderson on *Superman*. Sam Armstrong called me and said that the producers, Aubrey Wisberg and Jack Pollexfen, wanted to see me about a picture they were doing. I went in to see them with Sam, and I was hired. In those days, if you were a well-established actor, all the casting people and the producers knew of you and knew about your work, and you were hired on the basis of your name and reputation. You didn't have to go and audition, like they do today. The little secretaries sitting

Shayne's first freelance job after leaving prestigious Warner Bros. was a scientist role in Monogram's lowly *The Face of Marble* with John Carradine.

at the casting desks don't know a damn thing about pictures or the actors. When I'm called for an interview like that, I go in and the girl asks me, "What have you done lately?" and I say, "What have *you* done lately?" *[Laughs.]* But it's insulting, really — the people in the business should know who the actors are, and should know something about what they've done. It's professional.

Pictures aren't anything like what they were when I came out here, when the big studios were in existence and dominated the industry. Today the conglomerates own the business and they don't give a damn, so long as it makes money.

Did you play the monster in The Neanderthal Man, *or is that a double?*

No, they had a double for me. However, I did have to wear the makeup for the transition scenes. The transition scenes, me changing into the monster and vice versa, were all made on a Sunday. It was just me and the makeup man, Harry Thomas, and a camera crew. They were laborious shots: they'd put the monster makeup on me, shoot just a few frames, cut, and then the makeup man would step in and make me look worse. We were there all day long.

What was your opinion of the finished film?

Is it Shayne or a stuntman beneath the *Neanderthal Man* makeup? Only makeup man Harry Thomas knows for sure.

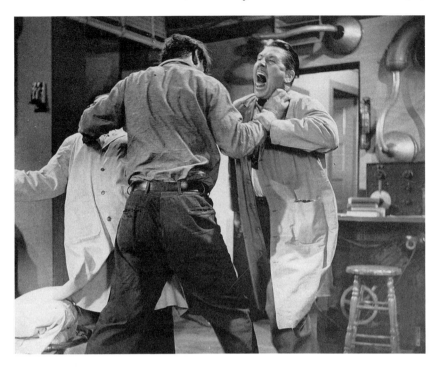

There's usually a price to be paid when medical science goes too far in a sci-fi film, as Joe Flynn and Shayne find out from *Indestructible Man* Lon Chaney.

If *The Neanderthal Man* had had good production, it would have been a good picture. But that was very cheaply done.

Many of the roles you played in science fiction films of the '50s were smallish or sometimes even bit parts — Invaders from Mars, Tobor the Great, Kronos, The Lost Missile *and others.*

Being a professional actor, it didn't matter much to me whether I was starred or if I played a much smaller part. I was interested in *work* — I had a wife and two young children to support at the time. I never had the ego that some of these so-called "name" stars have. But consequently I have a short memory on some of these science fiction things — after all, it's a long time ago.

One director you worked with on three occasions was Roger Corman.

Roger Corman was a driver. He made pictures on low budgets and made them fast, and I don't think he cared too much about the quality of the performances or the photography or anything else. He was more concerned with getting the film in the can, getting it out and getting the money! He may have changed — I have not worked with him since he's become a big-shot producer.

Shayne at home in 1987.

Certainly your most unusual role in a Corman film was as one of the Keepers of the Gifts in Teenage Caveman.

My son Bob, Jr., and daughter Stephanie wanted to be in that movie. I made a deal with Corman to put them in, and I would do a small part if I were disguised. Therefore, the heavy wig, beard, etc. No one knew it was me. It was a crappy little part.

You had a good-sized part in Sam Katzman's The Giant Claw.

I didn't see *The Giant Claw* when it was first released, I saw it somewhere later. And when I saw this giant bird, I said, "Oh, God!" to myself! They ruined that picture with cheap special effects. That was a classic piece of junk.

Did you ever get to meet Sam Katzman?

I got to know him fairly well. I remember that on one picture, I think it was *State Penitentiary* [1950], we were in Virginia City and the whole crew was gambling. I didn't gamble at all, so I came away with my salary, but most of 'em came away from that picture in debt to Sam because they borrowed not only their salaries, but money besides!

You've done stage, films, radio, TV—is there anything you haven't done?

I never shit on the captain's floor *[laughs]*!

Do you have a favorite part?

Among the A pictures that I was in, my favorite part was in *Christmas in Connecticut* with Barbara Stanwyck. So far as TV is concerned, I think my favorite part was on *Superman,* as Inspector Henderson—he was duck soup for me!

While working on the Superman *series, did you have any inkling that its popularity would be so long-lasting?*

Not the slightest. Most of us thought that *Superman* was just a job. Even though it lasted season after season and I knew it was popular, I never had any idea that its popularity would last and that 25 years later we'd be going to conventions where people would mob us!

ROBERT SHAYNE FILMOGRAPHY

Keep 'Em Rolling (RKO, 1934)
Wednesday's Child (RKO, 1934)
Off the Horses (Educational short, 1937)
Oklahoma Outlaws (Warners short, 1943)
Wagon Wheels West (Warners short, 1943)
Mission to Moscow (Warners, 1943)
Gun to Gun (Warners short, 1944)
Trial by Trigger (Warners short, 1944)
Roaring Guns (Warners short, 1944)
Hollywood Canteen (Warners, 1944)
Shine on, Harvest Moon (Warners, 1944)
Make Your Own Bed (Warners, 1944)
Mr. Skeffington (Warners, 1944)
Frontier Days (Warners short, 1945)
Law of the Badlands (Warners short, 1945)
Rhapsody in Blue (Warners, 1945)
Christmas in Connecticut (Warners, 1945)
San Antonio (Warners, 1945)
My Reputation (Warners, 1946)
Three Strangers (Warners, 1946)
Nobody Lives Forever (Warners, 1946)
The Face of Marble (Monogram, 1946)
Behind the Mask (Monogram, 1946)
Wife Wanted (Monogram, 1946)
I Ring Doorbells (PRC, 1946)
The Spirit of West Point (Film Classics, 1947)
The Swordsman (Columbia, 1947)
Backlash (20th Century–Fox, 1947)
I Cover Big Town (I Cover the Underworld) (Paramount, 1947)
Smash-Up, the Story of a Woman (Universal, 1947)
Welcome Stranger (Paramount, 1947)
Shaggy (Paramount, 1948)
The Strange Mrs. Crane (Eagle-Lion, 1948)
Let's Live a Little (Eagle-Lion, 1948)

Best Man Wins (Columbia, 1948)
The Inside Story (Republic, 1948)
Loaded Pistols (Columbia, 1948)
The Threat (RKO, 1949)
The Law of the Barbary Coast (Columbia, 1949)
Forgotten Women (Monogram, 1949)
Experiment Alcatraz (RKO, 1950)
Dynamite Pass (RKO, 1950)
Rider from Tucson (RKO, 1950)
Federal Man (Eagle-Lion, 1950)
Big Timber (Monogram, 1950)
When You're Smiling (Columbia, 1950)
State Penitentiary (Columbia, 1950)
Customs Agent (Columbia, 1950)
Missing Women (Republic, 1951)
The Dakota Kid (Republic, 1951)
Criminal Lawyer (Columbia, 1951)
Indian Uprising (Columbia, 1952)
Without Warning (United Artists, 1952)
Mr. Walkie Talkie (Lippert, 1952)
The Neanderthal Man (United Artists, 1953)
The Blue Gardenia (Warners, 1953)
Prince of Pirates (Columbia, 1953)
Flight Nurse (Republic, 1953)
The Lady Wants Mink (Republic, 1953)
Eyes of the Jungle (Lippert, 1953)
Marshal of Cedar Rock (Republic, 1953)
Invaders from Mars (20th Century-Fox, 1953)
Trader Tom of the China Seas (Republic serial, 1954)
The Desperado (Allied Artists, 1954)
Tobor the Great (Republic, 1954)
Double Jeopardy (Republic, 1955)
Murder Is My Beat (Allied Artists, 1955)
King of the Carnival (Republic serial, 1955)
The Eternal Sea (Republic, 1955)
Accused of Murder (Republic, 1956)
Indestructible Man (Allied Artists, 1956)
Dance with Me, Henry (United Artists, 1956)
Rumble on the Docks (Columbia, 1956)
Hot Shots (Allied Artists, 1956)
Spook Chasers (Allied Artists, 1957)
Kronos (20th Century-Fox, 1957)
Footsteps in the Night (Allied Artists, 1957)
The Giant Claw (Columbia, 1957)
Death in Small Doses (Allied Artists, 1957)
The Lost Missile (United Artists, 1958)
War of the Satellites (Allied Artists, 1958)
How to Make a Monster (AIP, 1958)
Teenage Caveman (AIP, 1958)
I, Mobster (20th Century-Fox, 1958)
Battle Flame (Allied Artists, 1959)
North by Northwest (MGM, 1959)

The Rebel Set (Allied Artists, 1959)
From the Terrace (20th Century–Fox, 1960)
Why Must I Die? (AIP, 1960)
Cage of Evil (United Artists, 1960)
Valley of the Redwoods (20th Century–Fox, 1960)
20,000 Eyes (20th Century–Fox, 1961)
Son of Flubber (Buena Vista, 1963)
A Tiger Walks (Buena Vista, 1964)
Runaway Girl (United Screen Arts, 1966)
The Arrangement (Warners-7 Arts, 1969)
Winning (Universal, 1969)
Tora! Tora! Tora! (20th Century–Fox, 1970)
The Million Dollar Duck (Buena Vista, 1971)
The Barefoot Executive (Buena Vista, 1971)
Cool Breeze (MGM, 1972)

*Of course, a lot of women believed I was really
like the roles I played. It was so funny — they would
practically rush with their husbands to the other side of the room
when they saw me! I thought to myself, "I didn't mean to be
that convincing!" I didn't know it was going to make
a social outcast out of me!*

Yvette Vickers

HAILING FROM Kansas City, Missouri, blue-eyed blond Yvette Vickers was the daugher of jazz musicians Charles and Iola Vedder. Vickers hit the road with her folks at an early age, but her career plans did not include show biz until she took an acting class at U.C.L.A. She subsequently began appearing in little theater productions and in revues as well as acting in TV and in commercials (as the dancing White Rain Girl).

Yvette was "introduced" into motion pictures via *Short Cut to Hell*, a 1957 crime drama directed by former movie gangster James Cagney, and some small film parts (*Reform School Girl, The Saga of Hemp Brown*, the Cormans' *I, Mobster*) quickly followed. Leading roles in *Attack of the 50 Foot Woman* and *Attack of the Giant Leeches* brought Vickers to the attention of science fiction fans, who later caught fleeting glimpses of their favorite pinup gal in pictures like *What's the Matter with Helen?* and TV's *The Dead Don't Die*.

How did you first become interested in being an actress?

I wanted to be a writer, and I was taking classes at U.C.L.A. to become a journalist. I needed an extra course, just to fill in, for three more units, and I took an acting class for that reason. I began taking the class, and I got very interested in the theater — there was something about it that seemed so natural. In Catholic school I had done a couple of plays and gotten a very good reaction, which is unusual because most of the time they don't suggest that you go into that field. The priest who gave the valedictory speech at my graduation actually encouraged me to go into the theater, and I thought that was really amazing. But I didn't do it at that time; I wanted to be a writer. Later, though, as a result of that one class at U.C.L.A., I got bit by the acting bug. I kept doing plays at school, and then outside of school — in the summer sessions I would do little theater at the Players Ring, and then professionally I would do revues. One thing led to another, I got on a roll and I just kept going with it. In fact, I didn't go back to school because I started really enjoying performing. I just kept working, and the next thing I knew I got a job as the White Rain Girl.

People ask me now how to get started, and I always say to them, "Go out and work in little theater, and perform in front of an audience." Now, I did have training in between all that — I was going to acting classes with Ben-Ari, I did a workshop with Anthony Quinn and so on. A lot of very, very good people were in my environment. I was very fortunate that way — I was always surrounded by top people. In fact, my first film, *Short Cut to Hell*, was directed by James Cagney — I mean, what more could a novice want? I didn't realize what a big thing it was at the time but, looking back, I'm amazed at my good fortune.

Was Cagney a good director?

Previous page: It isn't often that dramatic acting skill comes wrapped in a 34-20-34 package, but in the late 1950s actress Yvette Vickers embodied this piquant combination.

Yvette Vickers, '50s sex kitten *par excellence*.

He was just magnificent. But, as you know, the film just didn't turn out too well. I guess you've heard this fairly often, and it's really true: You can have the best ingredients, the greatest actors, the best director, a good story — and it can fall apart! And nobody ever knows why. While we were working on *Short Cut to Hell* we learned a lot from Cagney — he was so giving, he cared about actors so much. He was very serious about performing and about actors being respected and treated with dignity. Everything about him was wonderful. He encouraged me, and did a lot of press with me. Everyone who dropped by the set was curious to see *him* — he was really the star of the show — but he would always guide them over to the newcomers, especially myself and Robert Ivers, and say, "Now, *these* are the ones that are coming up." He was just generous that way. And, again, as far as the work itself was concerned, you couldn't have anybody that was more stimulating or more inspiring.

What about the press you got for being a beatnik during that era?

[Laughs.] There's a little bit of truth to that. I went to a lot of beatnik hangouts, and I used to go around with Mort Sahl — we'd go to bookshops and we'd go to coffee houses and listen to the music. I really liked that era, although I had a lot more fun in the late '60s and '70s as far as going out to clubs and so on. I was really working most of the time during that earlier era, and I didn't get to play very much. But I remember that beatnik era well, and I did enjoy those clubs — I went to Cosmo Alley, Chez Paulette, all of them.

You played your patented "bad girl" for the first time in AIP's Reform School Girl *[1957].*

One of the things I remember best about *Reform School Girl* was that I was scared of a snake that we used in one scene *[laughs]*, and that I told them I didn't think I could pick it up! But if something's required by a part, I can usually get up the courage to do it. I've played a deep sea diver, and I don't even *swim* — I've done a lot of things that I'm afraid to do!

I met Edd Byrnes on *Reform School Girl* and we became friends, and the same with Sally Kellerman — it was a good experience. There were a lot of people in *Reform School Girl* that were enduring in my life, and I thought that the show itself went very well. We were all very serious. I was reading *My Life in Art* by Stanislavsky at the time, and I remember one day on the set, while waiting for "action" to be called, whispering to Luana Anders, "Did you know that *My Life in Art* is out in paperback?" Acting, to me, was a serious business.

How did you become involved on Attack of the 50 Foot Woman?

I had started working a lot in television, and most of the time I did not have to go on interviews for work anymore. I'd been sort of established — I was a known quantity. They called my agency and asked for me, and we accepted. Of course I loved the idea of playing this vamp *[laughs]* — this *tramp*, this shameless hussy — and I still do! I think those are the fun parts. You get to do everything that you're afraid to do in life when you play those types, and I just had a ball doing it. I let out all the stops.

What do you remember about stars Allison Hayes and William Hudson?

Allison Hayes helped me a lot, because it was my first really large role. I'd been doing large roles on TV and on stage, but in film I'd never had a leading role. So I was a little insecure, and I used to go to her for advice. She gave me tips on how to behave on the set, that sort of thing. She was very, very helpful.

She came to a tragic end many years later.

Somehow Allison and I lost track of one another. We had been with the same agent, and of course that had a lot to do with my being cast in *50 Foot Woman*, too—they had already settled on her, and then since I was with that same office they made a sort of a package deal. I didn't know about her death until only a few years ago, and I was just shocked to hear about it.

And William Hudson?

He was fun. I think he's probably the only one that knew that *50 Foot Woman* was camp. Most of us were just playing it straight, but he had a little bit of a tongue-in-cheek attitude. I think he was a little wiser than the rest of us *[laughs]*, and seemed to know a little more what it was all about. He tried to guide me in that, too—I think he was tickled by how innocent I was. Here I was, playing this wild woman, and it was all pure acting.

Of course, a lot of women believed that I was really like the roles I played. It was so funny—they would practically rush with their husbands to the other side of the room when they saw me! Really, they'd just grab 'em and run! I thought to myself, "I didn't mean to be *that* convincing!" I didn't know it was going to make a social outcast out of me! And to this day I still have a little trouble with that—women see me as the husband-snatcher. Oddly enough, I've never knowingly dated a married man.

Knowingly.

[Laughs.] Twice I got fooled, but I claim the Fifth on that!

Do you remember working with the giant prop hand in 50 Foot Woman?

I was on the set just one day when they were using that. I don't know what it was made of—in the movie it looks like papier mache or something. And I don't know how they got it to move or anything. To be honest, I wasn't that interested in special effects at that time; my curiosity all tended to go into, "What is this scene about?", "What am *I* about?" and all that. I was pretty introspective about the parts that I played, and I was never that curious about the technical aspects.

Do you remember if you were around when Hudson was picked up by the hand?

No, I didn't see that. Of course I was there when *I* got killed, and that scene scared me to death. When the 50 foot woman started wrecking the cafe, I ran and hid under a table. All the people were screaming, lumber was falling into the room and so on. As soon as the scene was over, one of the prop men came up to me and said, "Don't . . . move." I looked around slowly, and there was a board with a nail through it, right at my ear! So from then on, when I had to do scenes like that, I'd go to the director and ask, "Are you *sure* everything's going to be all right?" *[Laughs.]*

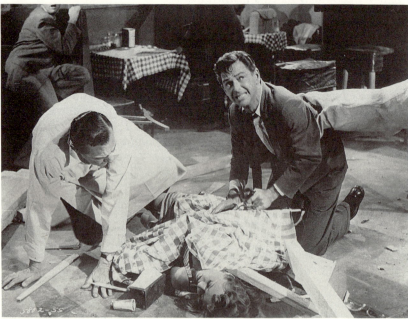

Scenes from *Attack of the 50 Foot Woman*. *Top:* William Hudson, Vickers and Frank Chase watch as the giant prop hand is swung through the door by offscreen stage hands. *Bottom:* Hudson is in the grip of the hand as Mike Ross checks over victim Vickers.

You can't believe what's happening in 50 Foot Woman *for a second, but the acting is really convincing while the story is not.*

People seem to get such a kick out of that, young people particularly. I've seen them watch the show at the Nuart Theater here in Los Angeles, and they respond to it. It's such a contradiction in a way: They watch this nutty movie and laugh at the special effects and so on, and yet they like the actors—Allison, Bill Hudson and myself. They come up to me afterwards and say, "I think you're a great actress," or, "I love your work." That's the response I'm getting, and I think they're really sincere when they say they like the actors. Maybe that's why *50 Foot Woman* has survived—maybe that's why the inadequacies of the special effects didn't really hang the picture up that much. Because the meat of the picture—the acting scenes—seemed to work.

Where was 50 Foot Woman *shot?*

We shot a lot of it over at a studio off of Cahuenga Boulevard. The bar scenes and my bedroom scenes were done there in that one building—it was almost like a TV setup. I'm sure right now it's probably a graphics studio. They did the location stuff at an old mansion in the Hollywood Hills. I was only up there for the driving-in and -out scene.

Was 50 Foot Woman *filmed quickly?*

Oh, yes—in eight days. A full, jam-packed eight days! But I kind of liked that—getting on with it, finishing and going on to the next thing. I think that's why the film had the momentum it did: We were just moving constantly and there weren't all those long waits you usually get. When I went to work on *Hud* [1963] at Paramount, I was just flabbergasted by all the waiting and waiting and *waiting* between setups. So that's why I liked *50 Foot Woman:* We shot fast and it was very intense, and that raised our energy level.

What do you recall about the director, Nathan Juran?

Very little, which I think means he's a terrific director. Everything was falling into place, and he let things happen. If there was help needed, he gave it, but he let work in progress be just that—he let it be. I think that was wisely done, and it turned out pretty well. Also, I thought his lighting was very good; it gave the picture some tone and style. I didn't know this at the time, but he had won an Academy Award for art direction for *How Green Was My Valley* [1941].

The producer, Jacques Marquette, told me that Juran was a producer's nightmare, that he was trying to make too much out of the picture.

As an actress I always want to make the most out of each part, so if he was doing that, too, I applaud him! I always want a picture to be the best that it can be; I don't ever think in terms of whether it's a low-budget film or a big-budget film. Whether it's TV or film, or whatever it is, I think if you're going

Vickers struts her stuff.

to work on that celluloid, you better do the best you can, because you never know who's going to see it or how long it'll last. I never dreamt that *Attack of the 50 Foot Woman* would come back the way it has.

Did you see 50 Foot Woman *when it was first released?*
No, I didn't, because I went to New York to do a Broadway play with Melvyn Douglas called *The Gang's All Here*. Oddly enough, I did see *Attack of the Giant Leeches* in New York — it was playing on 42nd Street. And, can you imagine, I actually got Melvyn Douglas and three or four other people from the cast to go over there with me, at midnight, to watch that movie! I told them, "I've got a movie playing over on 42nd Street," and they went, "Oh, my God!" But they came along: Melvyn Douglas, E.G. Marshall, Arthur Hill, Victor Kilian, maybe more. And they had a great time — they thought *Giant Leeches* was a lot of fun.

Some of those fellows used to be shocked that I would dare to do some of the things I did. I went up to the owner of that 42nd Street theater and told him, "You know, there *are* better pictures of me you could be displaying out there in front." But I was very young, and I would go up to anybody and say whatever I wanted. I'm trying to get back into that state of mind *[laughs]* — it's such a wonderful way to be!

Who hired you for Giant Leeches?
Again, I think that was a call to the agency — probably somebody who had seen my other work or heard about me. It might have been the director, Bernie Kowalski; I think he had seen me in something, and knew that he wanted me to play the part. I didn't have to go on an interview for it, I was just cast. That's my favorite way, because I'm not very good on interviews at all — in fact, I'm very bad! Bernie was just one of the best people I ever worked with; we really had a rapport, and got along very well. *Everybody* in that film did. It was one of the most cooperative groups of people I've ever seen.

What about the producer, Gene Corman?
Poor Gene almost died when we were doing the scenes over at the Pasadena Arboretum. We were there late one night, in the water, and he got violently ill — he caught pneumonia. Gene was such a nice person. I thought he was so helpful, so supportive, so *caring* about the actors. You *feel* that. I remember being on TV shows where "the New York people" would come on the set, and everybody would start shaking in their boots. It was time to shape up, shoulders back, chin up, like we were in the army. And I thought, "What are we, a bunch of trained animals or something?" We *are* human beings, and when a producer treats you like a human being they get a lot more out of you. I liked Gene Corman very much.

Interiors on Giant Leeches *were shot at the old Chaplin Studios.*

Right, over on Highland and Sunset. We did a lot of interiors there, including the scenes in the cave—which caved in! The tank that the water was in collapsed, the water went crashing across the sound stage and I remember seeing a camera whirling around really fast—luckily the cameraman jumped off in time. The water just carried everything to the back of the sound stage. Fortunately, one of the electricians pulled the main plug, which was smart because people could have very easily been electrocuted. I was up on a ledge in the cave set so I wasn't swept away, but it was really scary. The underwater shots of the dead bodies floating up toward the surface were filmed in somebody's swimming pool—it would have been pretty hard to get those shots out in the muddy waters of the Arboretum. Of course when my body surfaced and the guys pulled me up into the rowboat, we were shooting at the Arboretum. I remember that everybody was watching over me then, because I couldn't swim and I was afraid of the water.

Were your swamp scenes shot at night, or was that day-for-night?
A lot of it was shot at night, unintentionally. We started out shooting day-for-night but we went over, and we literally ended up shooting a couple of scenes by the light of flashlights and headlights from a car. Gene kept saying, "We gotta finish these scenes today, we gotta move!" So we kept going into the night, with whatever light we could find.

What were your first impressions of the leech costumes?
[*Laughs.*] Well, I guess the same as everybody else's: They looked like guys in plastic bags! Of course I'd seen the divers who played the leeches in their black scuba suits, so I knew who they were and I wasn't afraid of them—but I must admit that, in the cave scenes, when they crawled up to us and began to suck our blood, that I really was affected by that. A lot of people have told me that they saw *Giant Leeches* when they were ten or twelve years old, and that they were really scared by those cave scenes. And I can understand that—*The Blob,* that's my nightmare! But, again, when I first saw the leech actors on the set, I just thought they were not very well made. And those guys did have a little trouble in the water—they had to knock themselves out trying to make it look believable.

I understand that there was an effort made later to put together some better costumes, better special effects and so on, but for some reason the production end decided not to do it. They were actually offered the money to do better by those special effects scenes, because the show otherwise had turned out so well, but that never came to pass.

Were those swamp scenes any fun at all, or was it just hard, icky work?
It *was* hard work. That Arboretum does have a very swampy, jungle-like atmosphere—you felt like this was the real thing. So, yes, there were some uncomfortable moments, especially when Bruno Ve Sota forced us to wade

Spattered with swamp mud, Vickers strikes a glamorous pose behind the scenes on *Attack of the Giant Leeches*.

backwards into the swamp. I know I look scared in that scene, and I probably really was *[laughs]*! But I have to give Gene Corman credit again: He was waiting with the crew there on the sidelines, with army blankets and brandy, to keep us warm and to try and keep us healthy.

Bernard Kowalski told me he could tell you were unhappy about going into the swamp, but that you were a trouper.

[Laughs.] Bless his heart, that's very sweet of him. As I mentioned before, I know that I can overcome almost anything. There are times when you want to be sure that everybody's protecting you, and I think it's good to be up-front

about things that you're a little frightened of. But in general I'll do whatever the part requires.

You were especially good in the scene where you explain why you're married to Bruno Ve Sota.
They *had* to explain that—I'm sure everybody was wondering why my character was married to this big fat guy. And then when you hear the reason it's very believable—things like that do happen, where somebody treats you with kindness and you cannot see them as being an ugly or unattractive person. I liked that scene a lot. I was recently on a local TV show where they showed a filmclip from *Giant Leeches,* and an artist friend of mine saw it and thought it was a Kazan movie *[laughs]*—*Baby Doll* or some real important film! And he said, "Gee, I didn't know you worked in those Tennessee Williams movies!" Some of the scenes that we did came across as being real thoroughbred scenes.

Did you like working with Ve Sota?
Oh, yes—we got along very well, and he was a fine actor. I loved working with him, and we respected each other a lot. I was just heartbroken when he passed away; [actor] Barry Brown told me he had died, and I attended his funeral. I was really sad, because I felt that he was one of the very good character actors of this town and should have had more credit. All of our scenes in *Giant Leeches* had a lot of heart and a lot of meat to them.

Your other co-star, Michael Emmet, really seems to have dropped from sight.
I don't know what's become of him, either. As you know, it takes a lot of determination to stick with the business. A lot of people get into it and do a few jobs, but if it doesn't take off they go into something else. I'm a diehard career person; I never really wanted to do anything else once I got started. But Michael was great—he was another Bill Hudson in that he was tickled by the whole thing. He thought it was amusing, and I think this comes through a little bit in his performance. I was playing it very seriously, but he had a little more sophistication and, like Bill Hudson, I think he knew a little better than some of the rest of us.

Early on you got typecast as schemy seductresses. What other kinds of parts did you want to play?
Of course I would have loved to do musicals and comedies—I think it would have been helpful to lighten up my image. I was up for quite a few things that I didn't get, TV series especially: I was up for *Gidget,* which Sally Field got, and I was up for a part in the movie *This Earth Is Mine* [1959] with Rock Hudson. That would have been pivotal; that would have represented a big step toward getting up to the next level. A girl named Cindy Robbins got the part—she was a friend of Rock Hudson's, and I think he felt more comfortable doing a love scene with her. Even though the producer and the director

really wanted me, he just felt ill at ease since he had to do scenes that were romantic, and he wanted to be with somebody he knew. That was something I really was sorry to miss. Then Edward Dmytryk was very interested in me for a part in *The Carpetbaggers* [1964], and Martha Hyer ended up with *that* — there were quite a few. So, yes, I did want to play other kinds of parts and to go on into bigger pictures, but these things just eluded me — they slipped right through my fingers. Sometimes it was hard to accept, but I kept going.

In the early '60s you co-starred in an interesting-sounding play called Grand Guignol.

I was the leading lady opposite two real fine actors, Tom Troupe and Charles Macaulay. There were two one-act plays, and I played the lead in both of them. In the first one I was this Southern woman who was real trashy and down-dirty and all that, who henpecked her husband [Troupe], drove him crazy 'til he killed her with a drill in her neck. Then he cut her up — you see all this, through a scrim. Oh, it was grotesque, it was all the way *[laughs]*! Then in the end you see my head in this potbelly stove — actually it was the Shelley Winters head from *The Night of the Hunter* [1955]. It was a great head, and it looked enough like me that we could get away with it. The second one was a Hollywood story, very much a '20s or '30s period piece, where I played a Louella Parsons type. I found this old guy, this Phantom of the Opera type [Macaulay] — he's playing Bach on the organ when I come in to interview him — and it ended up with him trying to get a gorilla to kill me. They were fun, and I'm so sorry that we weren't able to keep it going. It did run several months, but we were thinking in terms of establishing a real institution, like it is in Paris: getting a Grand Guignol theater to survive in Hollywood. That was a good experience, it worked, but it didn't run.

You had a small part in the 1971 horror film What's the Matter with Helen?

The director, Curtis Harrington, knew me and knew my work, and wanted me to do that part. I did go on an interview for it, with Curtis and George Edwards, the producer, and the major part of that interview was, would I actually dye my hair henna red for the part? I told them I would, but I stipulated in my contract that they had to restore my hair afterwards to its blond color. They were so meticulous about getting everything right in that picture: They wanted to marcel and comb our hair into this certain '30s hairdo, they didn't want us to wear wigs, and in my case they definitely wanted the red hair. But I had fun being a redhead for a while — people were so amazed, I looked so different.

Everything went very well on *What's the Matter with Helen?* Debbie Reynolds was nice, it was a wonderful experience, and I enjoyed doing it.

Why aren't you mentioning Shelley Winters?

I never got to know her. Curtis had some problems with her — he had to

She was the July 1959 Playmate of the Month; today, Yvette Vickers is working to make a comeback as a singer.

go and bring her to the set a few times, she didn't want to come. She thought she was photographing too heavy, and—

No kidding!

[Laughs.] She was playing it as a character, with a character's attitude, but she didn't want to *look* like that! I found that hard to understand, because she is such a fine actress and she had done character parts before. At the wrap party I started to talk to her and she turned away from me, so I didn't pursue it. I never intrude on somebody if they don't look like they're open.

What about the TV movie The Dead Don't Die?

I did that as a favor to Curtis Harrington. I played a marathon dancer, and my scene was with Ray Milland, asking for work. He was very gracious—I love working with old troupers.

Recently you've been on the comeback trail again.

I've had about four comebacks *[laughs]*, and this one, I hope, will be the one that works. All those times in the '70s that I tried to get started again, I'd do a couple of jobs, but it just did not take off. I couldn't figure out what was happening, and I would get very depressed and unhappy about that. So right now I'm working on a cabaret act, since I do sing and dance. It'll be a kind of a reprise of the great Hollywood blondes—imitating and singing in the style of Mae West, Jean Harlow, Marilyn Monroe and so on. And of course I'm also looking to work more in movies and TV — that's a very good possibility as well. Lately there's been a lot of attention and a lot of interest in the appearances I have been making, so the time is right and it's up to me now to do my best and to find my place in the "new" Hollywood.

You just did a new horror film called Evil Spirits.

My part is quite nice for a "re-entry." I play Karen Black's snoopy neighbor and I stumble onto the fact that she is disposing of her tenants. The story is based on the Social Security check murders in Sacramento. I have a juicy scene with Karen during a party plus some fun scream stuff in her basement. We had a good time, lunched together and enjoyed working together.

Are you pleased with your cult actress status today?

Yes. I think it's very flattering, *remarkable* to be remembered for pictures that I did that long ago. I like people to know that I've been a little more active — a lot of people think that *50 Foot Woman* and *Giant Leeches* are all I ever did. I have done a lot of theater work, especially since then. But I'm just amazed and delighted and totally happy about the reaction I'm getting, and the fact that young people are so complimentary and so supportive and encouraging about my idea of working again now. It's very surprising and wonderful.

YVETTE VICKERS FILMOGRAPHY

As Yvette Vedder:

Sunset Boulevard (Paramount, 1950)

As Yvette Vickers:

Short Cut to Hell (Paramount, 1957)
Reform School Girl (AIP, 1957)
The Sad Sack (Paramount, 1957)
Juvenile Jungle (Republic, 1957)
Attack of the 50 Foot Woman (Allied Artists, 1958)
The Saga of Hemp Brown (Universal, 1958)
I, Mobster (20th Century-Fox, 1958)
Attack of the Giant Leeches (AIP, 1959)
Pressure Point (United Artists, 1962)
Hud (Paramount, 1963)
Beach Party (AIP, 1963)
What's the Matter with Helen? (United Artists, 1971)
Vigilante Force (United Artists, 1976)
It Came from Hollywood (Paramount, 1982) Clips from *Attack of the 50 Foot Woman*
Evil Spirits (Grand Am, 1990)

*Many times I'd say to Jerry Warren,
"For God's sake, Jerry, let's do something
good for a change," and he'd say, "Why? People
aren't interested in anything good, they don't know
and they don't care. Just give them garbage!"
That was his philosophy.*

Katherine Victor

WHAT BAD THINGS can be said about the films of Jerry Warren that haven't been said already? Everything that could be wrong with a motion picture afflicted the films of Hollywood's most notoriously underskilled auteur. His casts did the best they could under the circumstances, but they were defeated every time by the dirt-poor production values, lousy scripts and Warren's own "who-cares?" attitude. Warren (who died in 1988) more than lived up to his self-stated credo, "I have never seriously wanted to be a director, or to do great things"; yet even today, more than a quarter-century after Warren was in the heyday of his ill-contrived career, the films continue to turn up on TV, on pre-recorded tape and in the conversation of horror film buffs.

Among the cast members wading through the dullness of these films, Warren's most frequent star, Katherine (now Kathrin) Victor, gave color to stereotypic roles and turned in performances better than the production in flicks like *Teenage Zombies, The Wild World of Batwoman, Frankenstein Island* and the non-Warren *The Cape Canaveral Monsters*. Born Katena Ktenavea in the Hell's Kitchen district of Manhattan, the future TV and movie actress grew up in L.A. and began her acting career on the stage and on radio in the late '40s. She made her film debut in the dashed-off sci-fi adventure *Mesa of Lost Women* in 1952, and in 1957 she starred as the imperious Dr. Myra in Jerry Warren's *Teenage Zombies*, which led to a series of roles in Warren's impoverished productions. Always busy outside of acting (in modeling, real estate or, more recently, in various jobs in the animated cartoon business), she feels that the stigma of being a Warren regular has stymied her mainstream acting career, but is working to turn things around in her acting future.

Do you remember how you got your small part in Mesa of Lost Women?

In those days actors could stop by and visit producers and ask if there would be any work coming up. I just dropped in at Sam Goldwyn Studios, where Howco Productions had their office, and I met Ron Ormond, who was producing *Mesa of Lost Women.* He told me that it was coming up and I'd be right for it. Actually *Mesa of Lost Women* was a patch job: It had already been done, but it was unsalable because it was a mixed-up story. So Ron deleted a certain amount and put in new stuff to make it more cohesive—that opening part with me, that was new. My scene, which was set in the desert, had me driving up to a certain point in my car and then stepping out; we had to do it several times because I wasn't stopping right on the mark. A weed, that was my mark *[laughs]*! I had to stop on the mark and climb out of the car, and I didn't have time to put on the brakes or anything! I pulled the hand brake fast but it didn't hold, the car started to slip back and the door caught me. Ron said, "Obviously this is the first time that you've driven a car in a movie." (It was one of those great big old Cadillacs.) "You just have to pull the hand brake, fast, and jump out." The next time I did it I pulled it real hard and junped out, and it worked. Something always happens on a picture, so that was par for the course!

Previous page: **Notorious even among fans of** *bad* **movies, the awful** *Wild World of Batwoman* **continues to embarrass its star, Katherine Victor, to the present day.**

I also remember driving home from that location. We had done that scene in the Mojave Desert, at Red Rock Canyon, and it was hot, hot, hot. I was wearing velvet pants and a wool top, and it was very hot — I got sun-blindness from the reflectors and all of that sort of thing! There were other girls in the film — spider-women who wore skimpy undergarments *[laughs]* — and it was such a terribly hot day that on the ride home I wore one of the girls' costumes. Ron Ormond said, "If I had known you had such great legs, I would have put you on as one of the girls!"

How exactly did you come in contact with Jerry Warren for the first time?
I had just come back from New York, where I had been working in various phases of show biz — acting, modeling, singing in night clubs and dancing, keeping busy and making a living. Anyway, I came back and an old friend said, "I have some friends whose home is being used to shoot a picture, and the producer is looking for a leading lady." Now, when you hear that a fellow is ready to shoot a picture and doesn't have a leading lady, it strikes you as a little farfetched *[laughs]*, but that's the way it was! So I went up to the house, which was on a five-acre estate in Mandeville Canyon, and that's where I met Jerry Warren. I told him my credits and showed him some pictures and he said, "You've got the part." That's how I ended up in *Teenage Zombies*. And then after that, over the years, he used me in a lot of different pictures.

The people I've talked to tell me that Warren disliked actors.
Jerry misused actors, he yelled at them ... well, a lot of directors do. Jerry was one of those, and it was his style to yell at the actors. But he would not be very clear, and he'd yell repeatedly in order to make the actor nervous. I've worked with a lot of real professionals and big-name directors that do that, but I guess when they get to be big names and so forth it's their prerogative! George Cukor did that, and Paul Wendkos, that's just their style. But you'd think that since Jerry was using people on a low budget, that maybe he should be a little bit more compassionate!

When you say yell, do you mean yell instructions or belittle them?
He belittled them — belittled them to the point that it would make them very, very nervous. Now, he didn't do it to me, he told me that he respected me and that I was different from other actors because I earned a living in another field and I didn't "use" people. The average actor, in order to pursue his career, needs sponsorship and plugs away at it; I always kept a job going and didn't have to mooch off of people. Also, if an actor rubbed him the wrong way, Jerry wrote them out of the script or really reduced their part. In *The Wild World of Batwoman* the pretty brunette that was kidnaped at the beginning of the picture was supposed to be the lead girl, but for some reason Jerry thought she was getting too big for her britches and he gave all her lines to the

Victor, as the calculating Dr. Myra, in Jerry Warren's infamous rock-bottom *Teenage Zombies.*

girl in the leopard tights. Then on *Frankenstein Island,* Steve Brodie was drinking an awful lot and so Jerry had him killed off! Jerry used me because I was very reliable—he could give me hunks of dialogue and I could do my lines in one take. I wish now that things hadn't worked out that way, but they did!

Anyway, that's how I met him—it was a strange way to get a part, but I thought, "Gee, I've just come back from New York and isn't this great?" I was sure there were going to be better things coming because of the way this had worked out. And I wouldn't have to go through the casting couch bit and all that sort of thing!

Warren wasn't a casting couch producer?

He was strictly business and he never approached me in that way. He liked me and we were good friends, but he never made a pass.

How old was Warren at the time? He wanted me to believe he was in his early twenties then, but that's not possible.

We did *Teenage Zombies* in 1957 and he had to be in his early to mid-thirties, something like that. In talking to you he took off at least ten years.

Did the cast of Teenage Zombies *get together to rehearse?*
No, we met for the first time on the set. The first time we ever did the scenes it was right in front of the cameras, which were rolling! A lot of the actors that he used had been doing little theater and so forth, and they were good actors—Jerry always got competent actors. If he had had bad actors that couldn't remember their lines, he would have been in a world of trouble *[laughs]*! Most of the time it was one take, but occasionally he took a few. Jerry shot master shots, he would shoot a scene continuously for ten minutes and he didn't shoot closeups. In *Teenage Zombies* I think I had one closeup and the rest was master shots. That saved him money and saved time in editing.

Warren doesn't even allow you an entrance in the film. The first we really see of your femme fatale character is when you open that old screen door like a housewife.
Here I was, supposed to be the villainess, and he didn't introduce me at all; it was just terrible, me opening that screen door! In Jerry's last picture, *Frankenstein Island,* he tried to give me an entrance but he really wasn't very creative: First he showed the wine bottle I was holding, then he tilted up to the cleavage, and then up to my face. So he tried on that *[laughs]*! But, you're right, in *Teenage Zombies* he didn't dramatize it at all and I had a terrible entrance, really awful. Now, the funny part is that that house had a gorgeous front entrance—which they used for the sheriff's office—and they gave me the back screen door *[laughs]*!

Was making Teenage Zombies *a hectic experience?*
Yes, it was—very. There was a lot of dialogue and Jerry just wanted it done. There was no finesse, no chance to develop any characterization. As I said, I had one closeup in the whole thing and the rest was mostly master shots. Also, the sound was very, very bad; my voice came across very tinny because the recording equipment was bad. We didn't do scenes with an eye toward perfecting them, we just did 'em to get through 'em and to get it done fast. So, yes, it was frustrating; all of his shows were frustrating, because his manner was just yelling and intimidating everybody, from the crew to the actors.

What can you tell me about some of your co-stars?
Don Sullivan, who played the hero, was a very nice person, good to work with. He was a very handsome boy and I thought he had charisma and that he would do well. He made two or three movies afterwards but then I guess he just gave it up. I saw him on a talk show a couple of years ago and he was pushing his own Don Sullivan beauty products. His hair had a touch of silver

and he was a very handsome, distinguished-looking man. Don Morrison, who owned the house where we shot, played one of the enemy agents, the one with the glasses; he's passed away since. And Ivan the zombie was played by Chuck Niles; he's a disc jockey at KKGO here and he's been very prominent for years, a household name in L.A.

Warren's wife, Bri Murphy, was also in the cast.
She is now a very well-known cinematographer—in fact, the only woman cinematographer in Hollywood. Jerry was married to her and she was assisting him with this picture, and then they divorced right after *Teenage Zombies* and she went on to bigger and better things. She was a great gal. After Jerry, she married this fellow Ralph Brooke, who was also a filmmaker of sorts—he's since passed away. I remember I ran into them at one point and we got to talking, and Ralph asked if I would do one of his pictures. And Bri piped up, "No, Katherine doesn't do *that* type!"—it must have been a porno or something! Bri and (I think) Ralph did do a picture called *House of the Black Death* and it wasn't cohesive. So Jerry took it over and I think he made it *less* cohesive *[laughs]*! He put me into some added scenes.

How much were you paid on Teenage Zombies?
At that time I was paid a flat $300, which was a little bit over the Screen Actors Guild minimum at the time. S.A.G. at the time called for $285 a week. That's why I didn't hesitate to work for him, because it was in line with what S.A.G. called for. If he had offered to pay me like $200, I wouldn't have done it! (Jerry's were non-union pictures.) On February 1, 1958, the pay went up to $300 a week, and it was a two-year contract. And every two years it went up in $15 increments until 1970, and then it started going up $100 each time.

What sort of roles did you hope Teenage Zombies *would lead to?*
I was always the villainess; I had to be the Continental siren or "vamp." I looked very haughty and very aloof, that's the bearing I always had, and I was usually cast that way; my first TV show was a femme fatale role in *Lights, Camera, Action* way back in 1950. So I was hoping that *Teenage Zombies* would lead to some "other woman"-type roles.

Were you happy with your performance in Teenage Zombies?
No, I wasn't, I wasn't at all. As I said, it was just a matter of getting through the words, not giving it any nuance or characterization. I think the reason that *Teenage Zombies* has become a cult picture (if that's what you want to call it!) is because it did have an atmosphere that the kids liked. I saw *Teenage Zombies* for the first time at a grand opening in Long Beach; I went there, and I was invited to sign autographs. I didn't realize that I should look like I did in the picture; I dressed up in a white evening gown and put my hair up, wore a tiara and a lot of rhinestones—and nobody recognized me *[laughs]*!

Even though "Jacques Lecotier" gets screen credit for writing some of these Warren movies, weren't they written by Warren himself?

As far as I know, Jerry wrote the movies; he used two or three pseudonyms. He also did the music, and used pseudonyms there, too; on *Teenage Zombies* he used the name Erich Bromberg. Jerry was talented on the piano.

Bri Murphy divorced Jerry after *Teenage Zombies;* he found a girlfriend, Gloria, and she then became his wife. I liked her. She was a very naive girl but very sweet and nice; she thought Jerry was the greatest *[laughs]*, but that is the way it should be. Gloria was very, very good to Jerry, because he needed certain diets. Jerry had a problem with his health, I don't know exactly what it was, but during the time of the lawsuit on *The Wild World of Batwoman* he went to the Philippines, to one of those witch doctors who waves chickens over you *[laughs]*! Jerry was into spiritualism or metaphysics or something, and at one point, right after *Teenage Zombies,* he wrote a script, set in the Himalayas, in which he wanted me to play a high priestess. I read the script and I thought it was great. The whole cast got together and we had costumes made and were going to shoot up in Stockton. Then all of a sudden Jerry called it off, because he said he was really not ready to go into this sort of thing.

Do you remember how you got hired to do The Cape Canaveral Monsters?

Yes, I do. *Cape Canaveral Monsters* is in my opinion the best picture in my whole lot — but I looked the worst. Billy Greene, who was one of the actors on *Cape Canaveral Monsters,* told me that [director] Phil Tucker was going to be doing a picture and that he was looking for a leading woman. I went over to see him and he liked me. He told me that I looked beautiful, but of course when I got into making the picture I had to wear all that scar makeup and I was anything *but* beautiful!

On the first day of shooting *Teenage Zombies,* my dear Siamese cat died — I'd had that cat for years — and I was just crying and crying. That was the first day of *Teenage Zombies.* Then, the first day of shooting *Cape Canaveral Monsters,* I got word that my first cousin passed away, of cancer. And I began thinking, jeepers, every time I start something, a loved one dies, and I just maybe better not make any more pictures *[laughs]*!

Did you like working with Tucker?

It was a pleasure working with Phil and working on that picture. He had control of everything and he kept a firm hand, but he knew what he wanted. A group of dentists or doctors were putting up the money for *Cape Canaveral Monsters;* it was going to be in color and there was a nice budget. But then, just the day before shooting started, they cut the budget in half. The first thing that went, of course, was the color, and then other things had to go as well. But I think that in spite of everything Phil was very creative; it's just too bad that he didn't get the opportunity to do more, because he was good. He did the

Director of photography W. Merle Connell prepares to give Victor a closeup in *The Cape Canaveral Monsters.*

best he could under the circumstances. We shot the interiors at a small independent studio on Western Avenue in Hollywood. The cave scenes were shot in Bronson Canyon and the beach scenes at Malibu. I remember it was December and it was freezing!

The "look" they gave you in Cape Canaveral *certainly wasn't very flattering.*

No, it wasn't. I wanted to wear something that might be flattering, maybe something tight-fitting, but, no, they told me I had to wear the costume that I did, which were like men's coveralls. If I had had my wits about me, I would have looked better—at least had eye makeup or something—but I just went along with what they wanted. They had a fellow, a monster makeup man, do the scar makeup on me a few times, and then when we ran out of money I did it myself.

Any other Cape Canaveral *recollections?*

No, other than to mention again that Phil was very nice and so was

When the film's paltry budget could no longer support a makeup man, Katherine Victor applied her own scar makeup for *The Cape Canaveral Monsters*.

Richard Greer, who produced and did the editing. It was a very pleasant group, and it was sad that we ran out of money and had to cut back and make all those compromises. S.A.G. was up to $300 a week and Phil paid me $420 or $450, so I did a little bit better than I did with *Teenage Zombies*. Phil was broke about that time, and he came with me to the bank after he gave me the check and borrowed back half of it *[laughs]*! The poor guy, he was really flat broke.

You next turned up in added footage in Warren's Americanized versions of the south-of-the-border films Curse of the Stone Hand *and* Creature of the Walking Dead.

Those were just patch jobs. I remember *Curse of the Stone Hand* because we did that with John Carradine. We shot that in a beautiful home in the Los Feliz area; these people were friends of Jerry's. I remember talking to John Carradine and I asked him, "Why do you *do* pictures like this?" and he said, "The color of the money's the same!" For *Creature of the Walking Dead* we shot our scenes in a little studio on Fairfax Avenue. I really don't remember too much about that, again it was a hectic thing and just a matter of getting the words out. I worked with Bruno Ve Sota on that one, and Bruno was a great fellow, easy to work with. He was a very talented person and a natural actor.

What can you remember about The Wild World of Batwoman?
This was when the TV show *Batman* with Adam West was very, very popular. Jerry called me up and said that he wanted to do a Batwoman movie and asked me if I would play Batwoman. He said, "Look, we've got a great budget and we're gonna do it in color. You're gonna have your own Batmobile, you're gonna have your own Batboat, it's just gonna be great." And I thought, "Boy, this is terrific!" Then, as we got into it, little by little it all dropped away; I don't know whether his backers let him down, but I think he eventually put up all the money for it himself. Maybe when he was telling me about the color and the Bat-props and everything, that was just a story to get me to do it; I had told him I wouldn't be doing anything else for him unless we did a Class A movie.

Of course, if it was going to be first-rate, he would have hired a costume designer. But he asked me to bring what I thought would be good as a costume *[laughs]*! So I brought some things and also two or three different capes — he picked the one that he thought would be right, but on the rest of the costume he just went by my suggestions. I did everything. I wore a wig which I attached to the top of my head, and then I had red feathers that I just pinned into my hair. I wanted something that would look a little bit different, and *[laughs]* I guess I got it! I even designed the bat insignia on my chest; I made a cardboard form in the shape of a bat, I outlined it on my chest with a drawing pencil and then filled it in with black eyeliner.

Didn't Warren know he was heading for trouble, infringing on Batman's *copyrights like that?*
We kept telling him that DC Comics would bring a lawsuit because he was infringing, but Jerry kept saying everything would be okay and not to worry about it. I guess he thought he could finagle it — somehow or other, he thought, he could bluff it through. He was going to four-wall the picture in Philadelphia, to open in 30 theaters there, and I had a nice new velvet cape tailor-made for me because I was ready to go and make a weekend appearance in Philadelphia. But just a couple of days before this was all supposed to happen, Jerry called me and said everything was off — it was in litigation. I don't know who it was, whether it was 20th Century–Fox or [*Batman* executive

producer] William Dozier or *who*, but they put a stop on the prints at the lab and that was it, period. But it had gotten that far—I had even seen coming attractions on TV, that it was going to open!

Jerry had to go back to New York, and he told me he went up in this skyscraper with all these huge offices and he said it was like getting the third degree. He said that was the worst experience he'd ever had in his life, because he went in this giant conference room and all of these V.I.P.s were hammering at him. At one point they even asked him if *I* was behind it—they asked, "This Katherine Victor, was *she* behind this? Did *she* do this for the publicity?" And Jerry said that, no, I had nothing to do with it. Which was very nice of him *[laughs]*, especially since I *didn't* have anything to do with it! They offered him a settlement of $330,000 to just stop the picture, because they didn't want any further publicity, and he thought, "Well, if they're offering me $330,000, maybe I can get a million!" So he turned it down and he asked for a million. It was a bad mistake. I don't know what he did settle for, but I know that he said that he should have taken the $330,000, because when the settlement finally came out, it was much less than that. I'm not sure what the final amount was, but it was something like $50,000, a small amount in comparison.

When did you see the film for the first time?

Jerry had a showing in some screening room in Hollywood, and

Victor designed her own costume for *The Wild World of Batwoman*.

there was a group of us that saw it. After the lights came up I remember there was this one fellow, I don't know if he was a backer or a distributor or what, but he was in a daze, absolutely dumbfounded — he was probably expecting something like the TV show. And Jerry said to him, "After all, this *is* a low-budget picture!" *[Laughs.]*

The film's a real stinker, just about the worst thing Warren ever did.
The production values were absolutely nil, really embarrassing. And I was horrified by the indoor sets. Of course Jerry is famous for that, for sets that are absolutely awful. And he doesn't know how to photograph them! You can photograph anything and make it look terrific if you know how, but when he moves the camera back and takes a master shot, it's terrible. He just didn't have the creativity to do anything like that.

I don't think it was a case of not being creative, it was a case of just not caring.
You're right, absolutely right. Many times I'd say to him, "For God's sake, Jerry, let's do something *good* for a change," and he'd say, "Why? People aren't interested in anything good, they don't know and they don't care. Just give them garbage!" That was his philosophy.

Bruno Ve Sota called him the only person in Hollywood that ever set out to make a bad picture.
That's it exactly. But unfortunately he would con the actors into thinking that he had changed and that each new film would be different. I kept coming back thinking that, but it never worked out that way. As a matter of fact, it was because of *The Wild World of Batwoman* that I took the two *es* out of my first name, and ever since that time I've been going around as K-a-t-h-r-i-n Victor. I wanted to have a new start, I didn't want to be associated with that film in any way! But now it's out on video cassette and it's back to haunt me, so it just goes to prove that you can't hide anything in your life. *The Wild World of Batwoman* has always been the skeleton in my closet.

You had other skeletons in your closet early in your life that also restricted your career, didn't you?
I was first-generation here and my mother was mentally ill and my father was a compulsive gambler. He left us and Mother was trying to raise us. I was the one in the family who had the talent — I was an artist, a musician and an actress, and acting was dearest to my heart. But my mother had paranoia and she had a possessiveness, and she wouldn't allow me to go out with people — she kept us tied down. My father started me on the violin when I was young and I got to be very good; I was asked to join a children's orchestra but my mother wouldn't allow me to do it. So I had to go out through a bathroom window and my sister had to cover for me! I had to do things like that because of my mother, and it was very difficult growing up. Also, there was no money,

Although she nearly torpedoed her own film career by becoming too closely associated with rock-bottom horror pictures, Katherine (now Kathrin) Victor is working on an acting comeback.

because my father had gambled everything away *[laughs]*! Finally we had to commit my mother, and not until we did that was I able to do something with my talent. But sometimes I wonder what would have happened if I'd had a decent family life and the support of my parents — I had to fight the family besides fighting the world. I always had continuous obstacles.

You seemed to drop out of films not long after Batwoman.

What happened was that I got married and my husband was very possessive — that worked out badly. I had never wanted to get married, but he chased me for about a year and a half, telling me that we'd be traveling all the time, and finally it began to sound pretty good. But then he said, "No more acting, because I don't want you running off with somebody else." The only thing I did do during the 13 years I was married, besides being a nursemaid to him (it turned out he was ill), a housewife and a mother to his three kids, was practice my piano. During that period I studied with Vladimir Horowitz's teacher, Sergei Tarnowsky, who was a tremendous inspiration. I put all my artistic effort into my piano.

Jerry Warren retired from pictures after that Batwoman *debacle.*

After the *Batwoman* experience he said that was it. That was a pretty harrowing experience and it really took a lot out of him. So he bought an avocado ranch down in San Diego. I'd go down about once a year and visit him, and then after I married, my husband and I would go down. We started to get after Jerry, to tell him that things had changed, and why didn't he try and do another picture? My husband was once a computer man, and he promised Jerry that he would handle all the computer stuff and special effects and it would really be authentic. Jerry began to get fired up and started to write a screenplay. Then when he actually called me to ask me to be in the picture [*Frankenstein Island*], my husband said, "You're not going to *do* it, are you?" I said, "Yes!" and that's when things started going wrong with me and my husband. He was a great talker but when it came down to the nitty-gritty he backed out, and he was very unhappy about my being in it!

I was surprised to find that Frankenstein Island *was a semi-remake of* Teenage Zombies.

It was worse, because *Teenage Zombies* at least had a little bit of a story. *Frankenstein Island* is *Teenage Zombies* in color, but worse because Jerry tried to squeeze too much into it.

Where was Frankenstein Island *shot?*

Jerry had 20 acres down in Escondido, and he built the native village there. We shot some interiors in Jerry's house and the lab interiors at a studio on Seward Street in Hollywood. I shot about 10 days, and the four fellows who were the heroes, Robert Clarke and Robert Christopher and the two young actors [Tain Bodkin and Patrick O'Neil], shot about 20. Those fellows had it rough; they went to New Mexico and as I understand it they had a tough time there. They also did a scene where they were in a rubber raft, it was a one- or two-man raft and the four of them were crowded into it, and the thing nearly sank under them! Jerry ended up cutting all those scenes out and having the characters *talk* about what happened to them.

Actually, Jerry had a not-bad cast in that one: Cameron Mitchell, Andrew Duggan, Steve Brodie, John Carradine, Bob Clarke and Bob Christopher. Bob Christopher was the co-producer and he put up a lot of money, about

$85,000. Jerry also got a lot of young actors out of San Diego, little theater people, and they were all very competent. The dancing girls he got at a night club.

Bob Clarke never got paid for doing Frankenstein Island.
Bob *and* I did not get paid; we were the only two that didn't. Jerry kept telling us we were his best friends *[laughs]*, because both of us had worked with him several times before, but we're still waiting for our money!

He probably figured you were the two he could take advantage of.
Exactly. Which is kind of sad. Bob Christopher and Jerry's wife are still hoping to get some money out of the picture (the thing is in litigation right now) but I don't think anything'll come of that either. And Bob Clarke and I were shocked, because Jerry always did pay us in the past. I was supposed to get a thousand and Bob was supposed to get two thousand, but we didn't get anything. Bob I feel especially bad for, because as I said he went through a lot of hardships making those scenes that got cut out.

You also didn't get any sort of decent billing in the picture.
Everybody was very unhappy about that and said it wasn't fair. I confronted Jerry with that when we had the cast party at my home in Woodland Hills. I guess I had a little bit to drink and I said, "Jerry, you had me listed in the credits as a 'with'—I haven't been a 'with' for a long time." And he said, "I had too many stars." I pressed him and then he turned on me: "Who do you think you are anyway? Just because you got the star billing in *Batwoman*—." I said, "Jerry, what are you talking about? Who's ever going to see *Batwoman*?" It was crazy, but he threw *that* at me *[laughs]*! I just couldn't believe that Jerry would do that to me, but I guess some people do things like that to their friends, figuring they can get away with it. That's the only time we ever really argued.

Bob Clarke told me that when Warren found out he had lung cancer he didn't tell anyone except Robert Christopher.
And of course he told his wife, Gloria. Gloria told me that all the symptoms were there but that they didn't realize it; right in front of her eyes she saw him gradually disintegrate. Jerry used to have a terrific physique and a lot of muscle, and he would play tennis in his tennis shorts; she noticed that the muscles in his legs were disappearing and that he lost his backhand. She was with him when he died; in his last few days he couldn't even get out of bed. It was a Sunday afternoon. He could hardly talk but he told her to leave the room. She left and then she heard this awful sound, like a *whoosh*, and she went back and there he was, just slumped over in bed. It was very sad.

How happy are you with the way your career has gone?

I thought my career was off to a good start but it just went nowhere *[laughs]*! But then fans like Barry Brown, who interviewed me for the book *Scream Queens,* made me aware that people were interested and that I did have a lot of fans. That opened my eyes. I have started back in and I've done some stageplays and some dinner theater murder mysteries, but I still don't have an agent; they're looking for drop-dead-beautiful gals and gorgeous hunk guys 18-to-25. But I'm like an old firehorse and I'm still hoping that, the more exposure I have, maybe somebody will see me and there might be a part for me. I'm not going to break my heart over it *[laughs]*, I'm too old for that, but I do love acting and I would love to earn my living in acting and do something worthwhile and be remembered. Right now it's on account of the sci-fi pictures I did that I'm remembered, and I think that's nice. If I were to die tomorrow at least I've made my mark in the annals of horror and science fiction *[laughs]* — however dubious!

KATHERINE VICTOR FILMOGRAPHY

Mesa of Lost Women (Howco, 1953)
Sabrina (Paramount, 1954)
The Eddy Duchin Story (Columbia, 1956)
Teenage Zombies (Governor Films, 1960)
The Cape Canaveral Monsters (C.C.M. Productions, 1960)
Creature of the Walking Dead (Associated Distributors Pictures, 1965)
Curse of the Stone Hand (Associated Distributors Pictures, 1965)
House of the Black Death (Medallion, 1965)
The Wild World of Batwoman (She Was a Hippy Vampire) (Associated Distributors Pictures, 1966)
Justine (20th Century–Fox, 1969)
Frankenstein Island (Chriswar Productions, 1981)

Universal went into [The Land Unknown] *planning to make it the biggest science fiction picture of its time. But then the effects department and the makeup department spent all their money! Universal spent so much on the monsters, they didn't have any money left to make the picture. They didn't know they couldn't make the biggest show of all time without spending money!*

Virgil W. Vogel

Now a respected and well-known TV director, Virgil W. Vogel cut his directorial teeth on science fiction films at Universal-International in the mid-1950s. His initial assignment, *The Mole People*, pitted archaeologists against the denizens of an underground civilization, while *The Land Unknown* found polar explorers battling prehistoric animals in a lost world beneath the Antarctic ice. These titles, together with the Swedish-made *Invasion of the Animal People*, have made Virgil Vogel's a highly recognizable name among science fiction fans.

Vogel began his career at Universal in 1940, as an assistant editor. He worked as an editor for many years, although by the mid-'50s he began to tire of the job and pressed Universal executive Ed Muhl for a shot at directing. Because he was known as a "special effects kind of fellow," Universal handed Vogel *The Mole People* with John Agar, and his capable handling of that film led to other assignments at the studio. Still highly active on the Hollywood scene, Vogel fondly remembers his early directing days of sci-fi/horror.

Were you pleased when Universal assigned you to The Mole People, *or would you have preferred a more conventional film for openers?*

It really didn't matter to me, I just wanted to get out of the job I had and get into directing. *The Mole People* seemed like a real challenge to me because of all the special effects. Of course Universal never had a lot of money—it was always a very inexpensive company, and I always prided myself on knowing all the tricks and short cuts. For instance, for the mountain-climbing scenes I took some footage of Sir Edmund Hillary climbing Everest, made a lot of plates and such out of that, and *my* actors did all their climbing on the stage. And I was real proud of the review I got out of *Variety,* which said that somebody deserved a great kudo for the way the film was put together. We were able to put *The Mole People* together on a 17-day schedule.

Did you work with screenwriter Laszlo Gorog on the script, or make any script changes?

No, the script was given to me—Laszlo had written it under [producer] Bill Alland's supervision. If I had known then what I know now, I would have demanded some script changes, but at that time I thought the script was pretty good. You've got to remember that I was a young man then, and I didn't know too much what I was doing!

The scenes with the mole-monsters were the highlights of that film.

I can tell you a funny story about them. We went into a meeting, prior to production, where they were cutting down the costs. They were trying to cut the costs on the costumes for the monsters. Jack Kevan, the fellow who was making them, detailed his expenses, and he mentioned that it was going to cost X-number of dollars to make the rubber humps on their backs. Bill Alland

Previous page: Virgil Vogel and the hydraulically controlled lake monster from Universal's *The Land Unknown.* (Photo courtesy Robert Skotak.)

Vogel *(right)* and director of photography Ellis Carter pose with the monster masks from *The Mole People*. (Photo courtesy Robert Skotak.)

immediately said, "Well, take that money out." Kevan asked him, "You want to forget about the humps?" and Alland said, "No, no—we'll just put newspapers in there!" So instead of making rubber humps, they stuffed the backs of the monsters' shirts with newspapers.

Now here's the funny part I mentioned. There's a scene at the end of the picture where the mosnters revolt, and there's a giant fight between them and the palace guards. Even though I had never directed before, they had me directing this, the biggest scene in the picture, on my first or second day *[laughs]*—in Hollywood, that's normal procedure! Anyway, I'm up on a crane and the stuntmen start battling, and they put on a really good fight. When it was over I yelled, "Great! Cut! Print it!" That's when my asistant director Ronnie Rondell said to me, "But—look over on the stage!" There were newspapers all over the place *[laughs]*! The newspapers had fallen out of all their shirts during the fight, and we had to do the whole thing over!

What was your budget on The Mole People?
   It must have been less than $200,000.

And was it a hectic 17 days of shooting?
   Let's just say that I wasn't smart enough then to know how hectic it was!

What more can you tell me about producer William Alland?

Bill Alland was a brilliant young man, but to me he was an enigma. He had great ideas, and if he had had a little more push and just a touch more suavity about him, he probably could have been one of the top men in Hollywood. I liked Bill, but he thought a little bit too small. He did not know how to fight the studio hierarchy and he did not know how to take people on — he was always interested in making pictures within their budgets. Sometimes you just have to stop and say the hell with it, and fight for something better.

How did you get along with stars John Agar and Cynthia Patrick?

I liked working with John, he was a lovely man. But Cynthia Patrick, being quite inexperienced at the time, was a bit of a trial. You'll remember that in the picture the mole-monsters pull their victims down into the ground? What we did was, we had very stiff rubber across the top of an empty swimming pool — in fact, it was the same pool we later used as the lake in *The Land Unknown!* We slit the rubber and covered it with ground cork. That way, when the monsters pulled a body down through the slit, the rubber was so thick and stiff that it split just wide enough for the body — the cork couldn't all run through. There's a scene where Cynthia Patrick runs into the area where the monsters are working, and one of them grabs her and pulls her under the ground. As we were getting ready to shoot that, she came up to me and said, "I'm not going down through that hole." And I said *[sweetly]*, "Well, of course not, darling, a stuntwoman will do that. All I need you to do is run across there." She said she would do it. So I went to Al, the stuntman playing the monster, and I said, "Al, when she hits that god-damned hole you grab her legs and *pull!*" So he did it *[laughs]* — she screamed and yelled as she went down, but it was probably the best acting she did in the picture!

John Agar told me that he felt The Mole People *was just too far-out, and in fact he quit Universal right after it was made because he was fed up with sci-fi roles. Would you agree with his complaint?*

No, I wouldn't. I will admit, though, that when I saw the film at the preview I thought it was piss-poor. I was a little disappointed with my own dealing with people in those days — I thought actors could act, I didn't know that some of them take a lot of direction *[laughs]*! Now it's turned into kind of a cult picture and I'm proud of it, but 30 years ago I was ashamed of *The Mole People*. But it did do exceedingly well at the box office.

Let me tell you a story about the preview. The very first day of shooting, we had done the scene where the explorers climb down the vertical shaft, from the mountaintop to the land of the Mole People. One member of the expedition had fallen in there, and the other men climb down to see if they can help him. They find the body, roll it over and someone says, "He's dead." Universal gave me three 18-foot rocks, on rollers, and a lot of black velvet — that

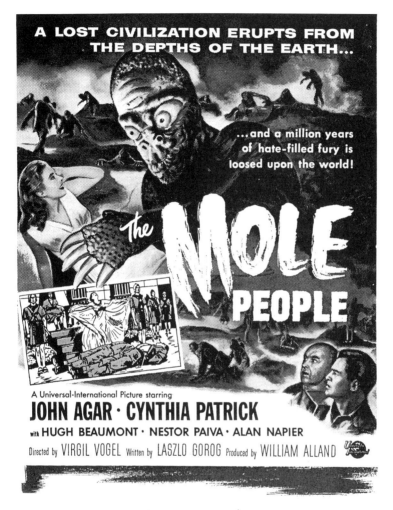

Ad for *The Mole People*.

was my set. All I had to do this first day was shoot this one climb-down scene. But we worked so fast and so well that I actually finished everything I wanted by noon, so we spent the rest of the day shooting inserts—hands climbing, feet slipping, all that kind of stuff.

When the show was finished, we found that it ran five or six minutes short. So they told me, "That climb-down scene was so great, put some more of that in." And we did. Then, in the editing stage, we started cutting some stuff that was really bad—and every time we cut something out, we put some more climb-down in. Eventually we put in every bit of climb-down that I had shot—and *then* they said, "Well, now let's duplicate some of it, it's great!" So we put more and more in, and pulled some other crap out of the picture.

Now we're at the preview, and the climb-down scene is running. The suspense is terrific—you could just feel the tension in the audience, it really was good. The climbers went down deeper and deeper, into the very bowels of the Earth—it seemed like about five miles. They get down to the bottom, they turn the body over—and someone says, "He's dead." *Dead?* He should have been a *greasespot [laughs]*! There were about 1,500 people in this theater, and they all burst into incredible laughter! The assistant head of the studio, Jim Pratt, tapped my shoulder and said, "We've got a car waiting out back with the engine running, just for directors at times like this!"

How did you land your second science fiction assignment, The Land Unknown?

Jack Arnold was originally assigned to direct *The Land Unknown*, and I was helping him storyboard the picture. It was supposed to be in color, have an all-star cast—it was really going to be a big picture. In fact, one of the guys they talked about for the lead was Cary Grant, although I don't think they ever approached him on it. Universal sent me to New York, to the Astoria Studios, where I spent three or four weeks going through footage of the Byrd Expedition looking for stock footage we could use in *The Land Unknown*.

So what happened to the "epic" The Land Unknown?

Universal went into this planning to make it the biggest science fiction picture of its time. But then the effects department and the makeup department spent all their money! Universal spent so much on the monsters, they didn't have any money left to make the picture. They didn't know that they couldn't make the biggest show of all time without spending money! Jack Arnold found out that Universal was pulling all the money from *Land Unknown*—they took color away, they took the cast away—and Jack kind of lost interest in it. It was no longer going to be an epic, it was going to be a typical, cheap Universal picture. So Jack said, "I don't wanna do it, let Virgil do it!" I was preparing another show then which I wanted to do, a small musical, but being the lowest man on the 12-man directorial team at Universal at that time, they pointed a finger at me and said, "You have to do it because you're familiar with it." So that's the way I was assigned to *The Land Unknown*. They paid me a minimum salary, they cast it with their own stock company, who were paid minimum, too, and they went into it.

Was your lost world entirely an interior set?

All interior. Originally, when Jack Arnold was to do it, they were going to shoot it on the backlot. They had a big place called Fall's Lake, which was surrounded by big rock cliffs—they were going to use that in the picture. But when Universal decided they were going to pull the plug on the money it all went onto the process stage, which was the biggest stage they had. When we were on that big stage, we had a big cyclorama all the way around. That's a big

The Land Unknown. Top: Vogel (*in water, on right*) prepares for a low angle shot of the lake monster. (Photo courtesy Robert Skotak.) *Bottom:* The monster menaces Shawn Smith and Jock Mahoney.

piece of canvas, about 75 feet tall and about 300 feet long. It had the scenery painted on it and it hung all around the edge of the stage, like a backdrop in a theater. We also had that big pool in there, much bigger than an Olympic pool—it was 300 feet long and 100 feet wide. It's still there at Universal. To create the fog we had baby bottle warmers under each tree and put dry ice in them, and then we also had guys with fog guns running around in the background. And it was a tremendous task to get one shot—after we made a shot, we had to stop and clear all the fog out for an hour and a half, two hours, and then we'd get ready for the next shot. I'd get four shots a day.

And what was your schedule this time?
It was a 90-day shooting schedule—30 days first unit and 60 days second unit.

You had a number of impressive prehistoric monsters in The Land Unknown, *especially the Tyrannosaurus Rex.*
That was about 12 feet high. There was a man in the suit, but all he did was make it walk—it was a *heavy* piece of equipment. Everything was hydraulic—the eyelids, the mouth and so on. Small rubber hoses came from the end of the tail, six or eight of 'em wrapped together, and they were hooked up to a hydraulic console where a man would sit and operate the different things. They spent a lot of money on that elasmosaurus [the monster in the lake]—that was one that they spent a fortune on. That thing was on railroad tracks on the bottom of the pool, and it must have been 15 feet across, from wingtip to wingtip, and about six or eight feet high when it rose up out of the water. Again, that was all hydraulic—the mouth and the wings and everything were worked by a man on the shore. It was a magnificent monster. The miniature helicopter was about 15 feet long, a great-looking piece of machinery. All of these things were built for the "epic" *Land Unknown.* The pterodactyl was one of the cheapest things we had—it was a prop on a fishpole!

What about the actual lizards seen in a few scenes?
Those were real monitor lizards, about eight or nine feet long. They were handled by a guy by the name of Jimmy Dannaldson, who was probably one of the best animal trainers alive at that time. He was a friend of mine. He brought these things in and, boy, he could handle them like crazy. Those lizards are worse than alligators, but he would walk out on that miniature set and pick 'em up by the tail—these things would be snapping at him—and just throw 'em on top of each other. It scared me to watch him.

Did the requirements of CinemaScope present any problems?
No. In fact, I was happy they gave it to me, because it added "bigness" to

the picture. I told them, "Look, you've taken the name cast and everything else away from me, I've got to have *something* to sell this show!"

Jock Mahoney's "hero" comes across as a pedantic and unromantic character.
You've got to remember that Jock Mahoney was probably one of the best stuntmen in Hollywood. Universal made him into a leading man. He was not a leading man, he was a stuntman. For a scene at the end of the picture where Henry Brandon is floating unconscious in the pool, they hired a stuntman [Saul Gorss] to take his place. But they had hired a stuntman who couldn't *swim!* We also had the two monitor lizards in the pool; that was kind of dangerous but I didn't care because I knew a good swimmer could get away from them. Also, we had a wire mesh 18 inches under the water, to keep the lizards from coming up on shore and taking legs off the crew. Anyway, this stuntman who can't swim starts screaming for help and so forth, and Jock, who was standing there alongside the camera, does a shallow dive into this foot-and-a-half of water, swam out there and pulled the guy to safety in nothin' flat. Jock could do any damn thing.

Were you happier with the results on Land Unknown *than you were with* Mole People?
Much happier. I thought that *The Land Unknown* had a lot of good special effects, which I was partially responsible for, and it was a great premise. I wish I could do it now, with what I know today.

How did you become involved on Terror in the Midnight Sun [Invasion of the Animal People]?
Gustav Unger, a Swedish newspaper columnist here in town who had been connected with the picture business for years, decided to make a science fiction picture in Sweden. He contacted a fellow in the Universal publicity department and asked him who was a good director. I had been very heavily connected with all the Universal sci-fi things, so this fellow recommended me. Universal had just gone broke, and just as they were closing up, this publicity fellow told me to call Unger, that he was looking for a director. So I did, and I went. We stayed in Riksgränsen in Northern Sweden, above the rail center in Abisko. It's a very interesting place up there — but colder than shit! We were up there in the wintertime, and it was 60 degrees below zero. I was very young then, but I don't think I've ever been so cold.
Gustav and his brother Bertil [the co-producer] are identical twins, and to this day they dress alike and they wear monocles. One wears the monocle in the right eye, one wears it in the left eye — they *are* characters.

What kind of money went into this film?
The American investment in that film was something like $20,000 — that was supposed to have been half of it — and the Swedes put up the other

Top: The camera crew gets a worm's-eye view of the space monster in *Invasion of the Animal People* (a.k.a. *Terror in the Midnight Sun*). *Bottom:* Vogel and friend take five.

$20,000. But of course working above the Arctic Circle, work slowed down to a halt at times, and everything took longer than we'd anticipated. We went out one day and we did some aerial photography—really, we got some beautiful footage that day. When the picture ran out of money, they ran this footage for the lab, and the lab came up with some money for us because they thought it looked so good.

I could not ski, and there was no other method of transportation up there; if you didn't go on skis, you went by helicopter. One morning they put the cameraman and myself and two Arriflexes with tripods and batteries and film in the helicopter to fly us down to the location. As we were flying down we flew over the site of an accident: There had been an avalanche which had descended on an ore train, and it scattered the cars like matchboxes all over the white snow. The engines were all smoking, making lots of steam, and a few guys were running around. We flew over there and looked at it, and the cameraman pointed out to me how it happened and so on. Then we went down to Abisko and shot our scene. Later I realized how dumb I was—here I was, doing this story about a monster attacking the Northland, and all we'd have had to do was put the helicopter down and we could have made a whole sequence out of it. But we looked at it like a couple of tourists, and then went on about our business!

There's a lot wrong with Terror in the Midnight Sun, *but many fans like its strange, arty atmosphere.*
I had just worked with Orson Welles on *Touch of Evil* [1958, as film editor], and my heart was full of Orson *[laughs]*, so I did all I could. But then of course Jerry Warren, who released the picture in the United States, took as much of that out of the picture as he could! You should have seen it before he got ahold of it—it was a great piece of artistic work.

What do you remember about the man who played the monster?
He was a newspaperman, and he came in and did it as a lark. I think he also put some of the Swedish money in it. He just had the ball of his life.

Were you pleased with the other members of your Swedish cast?
The acting in *Terror in the Midnight Sun* was horrendous, but that's because we were dealing with Swedish actors, most of whom couldn't speak English and I couldn't speak Swedish. We had this great Swedish comedian, Bengt Blomgren, who did this one major role, and he had his English-language lines written phonetically in Swedish on *everything*—he had them hidden every place he was going to work. He would have a piece of paper with the phonetic lines wrapped around the barrel of his pipe! It was really tough on everyone. I hid the performances with production values—there was some really great, beautiful stuff I shot. We brought it home and I got my agent to look at the film, and he said, "The story's not worth a shit, the performances

aren't any good, but visually it's a beautiful film. You've got a lot to be proud of here." It was released in Europe and did quite well, so Gustav and the guys in Sweden got their money out of it right away.

But there was a delay before it was released over here.

There was a delay, yes. Why, I don't know, it was not my job to sell it. A lot of people who saw it thought it was a very, very artistic piece of work. As I mentioned before, some of the Swedish people who were speaking English were not the best performers because a lot of times they didn't comprehend what they were saying, but the effects were very good and the scenery was gorgeous. It had all the values; maybe part of the delay was the fact that it had no recognizable names in it except Robert Burton, and he was not what you'd call a major star by any manner or means. Finally Jerry Warren gave them $20,000 for the rights in the United States. He took the film and put John Carradine in it — Carradine sat around and just *talked* for half the show — and he cut out all this great stuff I had shot. Great skiing stuff and really fabulous scenery. He cut that all out and had people sit and talk. He also changed the title, to *Invasion of the Animal People*. The original show was a hell of a lot better.

Would you have any objections to tackling science fiction projects again in the future?

I wouldn't mind it, if we had enough money. In 1986 I did a movie-of-the-week called *Condor* — it was made as a pilot, but it didn't really fly — but they ran out of money. It was a story about a futuristic cop whose partner was killed, and who gets a woman android as a partner.

Sounds a little like RoboCop.

RoboCop was copied from it; they were both made by Orion. Ray Wise was the star — a fine actor — and he was also in *RoboCop,* by the way, in a minor role. I thought the first hour of *Condor* was really fabulous — I was really proud of it, I did some very innovative special effects in the first half of it. If you can get ahold of it I recommend it highly. Just turn it off in the last 15 minutes!

Whenever you killed Vincent Price in a movie, he was always so dramatic about it — he'd writhe around and scream and holler and carry on. I remember I told Vincent, when he got shot in House on Haunted Hill, *"When someone gets hit with a .45 caliber bullet, they fall backwards. You always* fall forwards *when you get hit." And Vincent said, "My boy, no actor falls* away *from the camera!"*

Robb White

OF THE SMALL GROUP of Hollywood filmmakers who made the ghost and horror film genre their specialty during the 1950s, the late producer/director William Castle was the most unusual. His name overwhelms the nostalgic film fan with vivid memories: a luminous skeleton sailing from the screen into the audience (*House on Haunted Hill*); the guarantee of a free burial, insured by Lloyds of London, should a patron expire from fright (*Macabre*); and, most remarkably, audiences being swept into a film's action by small vibrating motors affixed to the bottoms of theater seats (*The Tingler*). These were but a few of the unorthodox ploys engineered by Castle to lure thousands away from their TV sets and back into the faltering theaters of the era.

Too often overlooked by fans of the films of William Castle, writer Robb White was partnered with Castle during this most popular and productive period. Born in the Philippine Islands in 1909, White was a preacher's son who held a wide variety of odd jobs before landing in the Navy during World War II. White initially collaborated with Castle on the short-lived television series *Men of Annapolis*, then joined forces with the enterprising producer/director on the horror thrillers *Macabre, House on Haunted Hill, The Tingler, Homicidal* and the kiddie-oriented "chiller" *13 Ghosts*. A self-described "ol' country boy from the South" (he still has the Dixie accent to prove it), White has fond memories of this classic quintet as well as some *not*-so-fond remembrances of Hollywood's Abominable Showman.

How did you first come in contact with William Castle?

After seven years in the Navy I went back home to Thomasville, Georgia, back to my wife and children that I didn't know. One day a guy called up from Hollywood and asked me if I wanted to write for television. I told him no because I didn't think they'd pay me enough money; I was making a pretty good living then as a freelancer. My book *Our Virgin Island* was a best-seller for 18 weeks; I also got $186,000 for it from *Reader's Digest*, which was a lot of money in those days. So I told this guy, no, I didn't want to write for TV. Then he wrote and said he'd pay me $4,000 for a script for this series he was going to do. His problem was his series was called *Men of Annapolis*, and he didn't know anybody from Annapolis who knew anything about writing a TV script! So I went up to Annapolis to meet this fellow, William Castle. The first time I met him he was squeezing two tennis balls *[laughs]*, and I thought, "What the hell is this?" Turns out he wanted to stop smoking, and that was the way he was gonna do it. He showed me a script, and it was idiotic! I went back to my hotel room, and by morning I had a script for him which was the first one that the Navy would approve.

I remember that after I had written about six or seven scripts for *Men of Annapolis*, I was talking to Bill one day when he happened to mention the Writers Guild and I said, "What's that?" You can't write for television without

Previous page: **Robb White** *(right)* confers with Vincent Price behind the scenes on *House on Haunted Hill.* Price's inscription on the photo reads, "Dear Robb, You wrote a great script. I hope we do it justice. Ever, Vincent."

White's partner, the self-proclaimed King of the Take One, was horror movie entrepreneur William Castle.

belonging to the Writers Guild, but how was *I* supposed to know that? He turned white as a sheet and went into a panic *[laughs]*!

One of the directors on Men of Annapolis *was Herbert Strock, and he told me that Castle didn't seem to know some of the most basic things about directing.*
 Bill was a cut-and-print director. He'd say to the actors, "Do such-and-such a thing," and he'd never take another shot because it was too expensive! He liked to call himself the King of Take One. I wrote 28 episodes of *Men of Annapolis,* made a whole lot more money. And after that series was over I went out to Hollywood to talk to him because we agreed to go into business making horror movies. He said we'd go into it fifty-fifty—"finkty-finkty" was his term.
 Bill was absolutely the coldest, most ruthless con man I've ever known. All he knew was promotion, he really could sell anything. The first movie we made was *Macabre,* based on a book called *The Marble Forest.* Bill got his old

friend Howard W. Koch to agree to help us out on the picture, and I put up the money. Bill said he was gonna put up 50 percent and I was gonna put up 50 percent, but somehow he couldn't quite make it. So I put up the money, $86,000 cash, which is what the picture cost.

Who had picked The Marble Forest?

Bill had—he gave me the book and said, "Write a movie about this." *The Marble Forest* had been written by 12 mystery writers—each one of them had written a chapter—and so it was just a mishmash. I read the thing and I didn't like it, I didn't understand it and I couldn't see any point in trying to make a movie of it. So in writing my screenplay I just ignored it. I wrote a screenplay that had nothing to do with the book, and Bill never said anything about it! My screenplay did have the essence of the little girl supposedly being buried alive in the ground, but that was all I took out of it. And then these 12 mystery writers all got mad and said, why did I change this, that and the other thing? We paid them $2500, I think.

Were you on the set of Macabre?

Yeah. It only took six days, I think *[laughs]*—we did it in a hurry! As soon as production started I learned what Bill meant when he called himself the Earl of Deferral. We deferred everything, even the cost of the film! We didn't pay anybody, we deferred all the salaries, including the actors. Even [star] William Prince—I don't know why we got him. He came all the way from New York, I couldn't see that, but Castle wanted him.

I didn't know anything about making a movie, and I made myself unpopular right away. I remember one day I was talking to this old guy and I asked him, "Which one is the best boy, and what does he do?" And the guy said, "*I'm* the best boy!" He must have been at least 65 *[laughs]*! Then there was the script girl who claimed to be 35 and would never see 50 again. I asked Bill, "What the hell do we need with an art director?" 'cause I knew we weren't gonna be putting up any paintings! I didn't know a damn thing about the movies, but I learned.

Where was Macabre *shot?*

Most of the outside stuff was in Chino, California, the rest in the Ziv Studio on Santa Monica Boulevard. The fancy house where the blind girl [Christine White] lived was a wealthy playboy's mansion up in Beverly Hills. He had a swimming pool that went from inside to outside, he had five Ferraris in the garage—it really was an elegant place. Howard Koch got us that place for next to nothing—I think for $75. Later we got sued for messing up the carpet or something *[laughs]*, but they dropped it when they found out we didn't have any money!

There was lots of great atmosphere in the graveyard scenes.

Sudden shocks were the hallmarks of the William Castle thrillers. Here, Jacqueline Scott unexpectedly trains her flashlight on the propped-up corpse of Howard Hoffman in *Macabre*.

The graveyard was very simple. We went over to MGM and rented 12 tombstones that you could move around and make a huge graveyard out of 'em. The open grave was a box on the set, that you could shoot from above and below and stuff like that. Then we smoked up everything and shot the scenes, inside the studio at Ziv.

Where were you and Castle headquartered at this point?
In the Ziv building, upstairs, in a room where they had old files. We had a desk and two chairs.

Didn't Koch and his partners [Aubrey Schenck and Edwin Zabel] have money in the movie?
No. They had little pieces of it, they had a percentage, but they hadn't put any money in. Zabel was supposed to give us all the western theaters, because he was a big theater owner; Schenck just stood around and rubbed his

stomach. I guess they did something for us, but it wasn't visible to me. Koch came out to Chino as we were shooting the thing, and he got a lot of things done that Bill didn't know how to do, and I couldn't. He was a buddy of ours; he also found us a good editor for the picture, that sort of thing, and gave us good advice. Howard was the only guy I remember liking down in that town.

Part of the problem with Macabre *is the ho-hum cast.*
Yeah, and the fact that it was so sloppily, cheaply done. That cast was the best we could afford, because Bill didn't put up anything! The reason we were able to make *Macabre* so cheap was, I went around with a Volkswagen and khaki pants and a Southern accent, and people just didn't want to charge me the money that they'd charge a production crew from Columbia or Paramount or somewhere. As I said, we got that fancy house for $65, $75—they didn't know that we were going to tear it up, though!

One actor who did do a good job in Macabre *was Jim Backus.*
Yeah. He was a good, solid man, and he hated both of us! Bill promised him a big salary, which he didn't get, and that kind of thing. Originally Bill didn't want him because people might think he was Mr. Magoo. I liked Jim Backus, I insisted on him, so we had an argument about that.

Do you appear in any of these Castle films?
Yes, in *Macabre*. We had shot the scenes in the graveyard and we had forgotten to take a shot that we needed of somebody's feet walking on some gravel. So *I* walked on the gravel—my feet are in the movie *[laughs]*! But that was the only time I appeared in one of these films. I didn't want to have to join any more guilds!

One interesting touch in Macabre *is the way you cut back and forth between the action and the clock, to underline the passage of time.*
That was my idea. As a book writer, I know that you have to have a cliffhanger every now and then—you have to stop and start another whole thing, and let the last part sink in. That's what the movie needed, something to pace it. So we got the clock.

Did Castle have any trouble setting up the Lloyds of London insurance policy gimmick?
That I don't know; he was doing that while I was writing the screenplay down in Thomasville. He told me he had it all sewed up before I started, but you never could tell what was true with Bill. I do know that Bill was very pissed off that nobody died watching that picture *[laughs]*!

How did Castle treat his actors?
He was nice. The only time I saw him get mad at an actor was with the

girl [Jo Morrow] in *13 Ghosts*. She was supposed to be playing a teenage girl, but she wouldn't wear a bra—she came flopping in there all the time. This pissed off Bill 'cause it made her look like the grown-up she really was—she was supposed to be playing a sweet little girl, not a working whore. And she was a method actress. I remember in one shot, she came in, stopped and said, "I don't know who I'm supposed to be." And Bill said, "All you're supposed to do is get your ass up here and put your feet on the mark!" *[Laughs.]*

Once you turned in a script, would Castle insist on changes?
   No, very seldom. I do remember that I put one line in *Macabre* that didn't sit too well with him, though. One character's name was Polly, somebody asked her if she wanted something to eat and she said, "Yes, we haven't had a cracker all day." Well *[laughs]*, Bill didn't like that, and I don't blame him—it took away the "spellbinding" mood of the movie! But I thought it was funny.
   When *Macabre* was finished, we invited Howard Koch and Schenck and Zabel to look at it, in a screening room on the Ziv lot. After we got through the end of the movie, Koch took me by the elbow and he said, "Come on out." We stood out on a balcony and looked at Los Angeles for a while and he said, "That is the worst movie I have ever seen in my whole life. I just advise you to forget the $86,000 it cost you, and take up another line of work." The problem with that suggestion was the choice of paying the deferrals or going to jail. So Bill and I trudged around Hollywood with our cans of film until at last Allied Artists agreed to handle it, putting up $5000 ad money and taking 30 percent off the top, leaving us 70 percent to pay the deferrals. The only thing the picture had going for it was Castle's Lloyds of London policy, but *Macabre* just took off and we made a lot of money. Bill told *The Saturday Evening Post* we made $6,000,000 on *Macabre*. The I.R.S. came roaring down to my house and said, "You didn't show that on your return!" Well *[laughs]*, they determined what the figure really was, and I didn't go to jail.

Once the money did start rolling in, did you and Castle split "finkty-finkty"?
   No, it turned out that I didn't get my 50 percent, he got 75 to my 25 somehow or other. When it came to money, Bill could be very . . . careless.

If you disliked Castle, how were you able to get along with him as long as you did?
   I didn't have to see him too often. One time I went to a party at his house; I never went there again. I really didn't want to see him socially.

About a year elapsed between Macabre *and* House on Haunted Hill. *Did you and he go your separate ways in the meantime?*
   After *Macabre* was finished I went back to Thomasville; at first I didn't think *Macabre* was going to make any money. Then, when the money began to come in, Bill called up and asked me if I wanted to do another one.

By that time I was getting ready to get a divorce anyway — my marriage had gone to hell in a handbasket. So I went out to California again and rented an apartment in Malibu, where I did the script. This time we got some high-class people: We got Vincent Price, Carol Ohmart, Alan Marshal and Elisha Cook, Jr., and we made *House on Haunted Hill*.

Who came up with the basic idea for House on Haunted Hill?
I came up with the whole story on that one. Bill and I discussed the ancient plot of having somebody trapped in a house, couldn't get out — that was just so basic that I'd written short stories about that for several years *[laughs]*!

It also used the plot device of the errant wife, which seems to be a favorite of yours. A wife that's no good at all.
Well, I've had two of 'em *[laughs]*!

Where did you shoot this time?
House on Haunted Hill was shot mostly at Allied Artists. The exteriors were shot at Frank Lloyd Wright's Ennis House on Los Feliz, built during his Egyptian period. We were not allowed to shoot in there, but the guy who owned it let us look inside. And it was a weird house — the ceilings were 22 feet high! In one room there was a closet door that was 22 feet high and two feet wide with nothing in the closet to hold up clothes or anything else. The man who owned the house had furnished only one of the many rooms with a bed, a chair, a nightstand and, in the kitchen, a card table. He complained that the famous glass walls, which joined each other at the corner with only edges of the glass panes meeting, leaked when it rained and made a weird screaming noise when the wind blew. And there was nothing you could do about it! The swimming pool was about three feet deep; ten feet wide; a hundred feet long; and in the middle there was the statue of a horse! It was just god-damned ridiculous!

House on Haunted Hill *really is the* Citizen Kane *of low-budget haunted house movies. You did a great job on that picture.*
I liked the whole thing, liked it right from the beginning. I liked Carol Ohmart, I was the one that insisted on having her. Vincent Price, we could have had him for $12,000, but Bill said, "No, we'll give him a piece of the movie." He got a tremendous amount of money out of it. I went to a party at his house after the movie was out, and he had just bought another painting for about $200,000. I said, "I'm glad we could afford it!" *[Laughs.]* Yeah, I loved Vincent Price, and I still do. Elisha Cook was also a great guy, just wonderful; he came down in a trailer, from up in Bishop or somewhere. I still

Opposite: White and producer-director William Castle collaborated on the *crème de la crème* of low-budget haunted house pictures, *House on Haunted Hill*.

write to him a lot. I remember that I objected to hiring the guy who played the hero, Richard Long, because he had a scar on his mouth which made him look like he was smiling all the time, even in the grimmest parts. But he turned out to be a good actor and I liked him very much.

How did Vincent Price get along with Castle?
Vincent was a professional get-along-wither. He knew his lines, he knew what to do, he didn't need much direction and he gave nobody any trouble.

The gimmick for House on Haunted Hill *was "Emergo" — the skeleton which seemed to appear right out of the movie screen.*
That thing operated from a fishing reel up in the projection booth — the projectionist's job was to pull the skeleton over from the stage, over the heads of the audience. We got the thing made and everything, rigged it all up, rented an empty theater and got in about 22 big producers — I mean, John Huston and people like that. We sat them down and ran the picture, and then this skeleton came out floating over them. Well, they thought that was great, until the line snapped and the skeleton fell straight down on top of them *[laughs]*! They all got up and walked out!

The government specified how much our skeleton could weigh and made us guarantee that they couldn't hurt anybody if they fell on them. We finally got it figured out so they worked all right, and then the kids shot them down — they'd come in with everything short of bazookas, and kill our skeletons! They cost us more than the movie!

How did you get interested in becoming a writer?
Damned if I know *[laughs]*! I just couldn't see anything that seemed more appealing — I liked it because it promised some freedom. I was a preacher's son and I didn't have the aptitude that people should have; I didn't see any use in going to work, that kind of thing. I started writing when I was 13. There was no money to go to college, so I went to the Naval Academy at Annapolis, Maryland, and I wrote all the time I was there. People thought I was crazy. When I graduated from the Naval Academy, I realized that writing and being a naval officer were not compatible; the Navy doesn't hire you nine to five, they own you all day long and all night, too. So I quit, and everybody got very mad at me for quitting — 1931 was not the year to quit a cushy job as an officer in the Navy. But I did.

I went to Cleveland for some reason and found out that $700 doesn't last very long, so I had to get a job. I lived with a guy named Tex Wheeler, a sculptor, very nice guy. He drank a lot of corn whiskey and he had a funny habit: He got up in the morning, he'd put on his cowboy hat and his boots, he took a big shot of that whiskey and that's all he'd put on for the rest of the day! A lot of the rich Cleveland ladies liked to have him sculpt their horses, that was his specialty. One lady was sitting there one day watching him sculpt, she asked me what I did and I told her I was looking for a job. She said, "Well, go see so-and-so down at the Dupont plant." So I went down there and got a job as a draftsman, and I drafted a thing called a space ore roaster. I didn't know what the hell the thing was. Then the boss came in one day and said, "We're going to send you down to New Castle, Pennsylvania to put up this thing you been drafting!" *[Laughs.]* I struggled down there in New Castle for a long time, about a year and a half, and we got this thing built—turns out it made sulfuric acid.

Were you still writing and sending out manuscripts all this time?

Yes, I was. I worked for Dupont from eight to six, then from eight at night 'til two in the morning I did the writing, in a little boarding house. One day there was a letter addressed to me from a magazine: They had bought a story for a hundred dollars. That would be about 1933. So I went right up to Cleveland, to the head of Dupont, and I told him, "I quit!" Because I was a writer!

Anyway, the next job I got was on a schooner, up in Boston—a 72 foot schooner where we were gonna teach kids school. We were gonna take 12 kids as passengers, and this skipper and his wife and I were gonna run the boat. I was also gonna teach English. All the mothers came down with their kids, took one look at this boat, which was then 35 years old, and they said, "No way!" The only one that was left was this six-foot, 16-year-old kid that looked like something from outer space. So we

Vincent Price emceed a night of horror in the White-scripted *House on Haunted Hill.*

Skin and bones: Carolyn Craig and friend in a cheesecake shot from *House on Haunted Hill.*

took him, because we needed the money. The only trouble was, the skipper would not go out of sight of land *[laughs]*! I had a sextant and a chronometer and knew how to use 'em, but he wouldn't do it. So between Plymouth and Morehead City, North Carolina, we scraped bottom 108 times, because the thing had a ten-foot draft on it. It was a bastard to sail—a square-rigged schooner, 1,100 feet in the mainsail. This kid didn't do anything, and the wife just went around moaning all the time. We ran into a big storm that took all the masts out and things like that, and they decided that somebody had to swim ashore and get the Coast Guard. The wife couldn't go and the kid *wouldn't* go and the captain couldn't leave his ship, so I had to do it. I put a rope around me and wrapped the end around a cleat, and said, "If it's too cold, I'm coming back." So I swam a ways and it *was* too cold, so I pulled on the rope and all the rope came over 'cause he had untied the other end *[laughs]*! That was lovely. So I swam in, five miles, in the night.

After that I hitchhiked down to the West Indies, to Dominica, where I got a job with a British preacher who wasn't there but he had a plantation where he grew oranges and coconuts. I was the manager there but he never paid me anything, so I finally had to come back home. I got married in Thomasville, Georgia, and we went to the British Virgin Islands and rented a miserable place on Tortola—we paid $10 a month for this crappy little house. We started looking around for some better place to live down there, sailed around every day, went to different islands, and one day we ended up on this little island called Marina Cay. She went around one way and I went around the other, and we met on the other side—it was a little island, about six or seven acres. So we bought it, for $60. There was no water, no phone, no electricity—no nothing. We moved in and slept in a shed that we had put up and built a concrete house on the top of it, which is still there*. I kept on writing, I won a prize—one book called *Smuggler's Sloop* won for Best Juvenile Book—and I kept writing for magazines, any kind of magazines. I wrote for the Jewish Saturday magazines and the Catholic Sunday *[laughs]*; I wrote for *American Boy, Boys' Life;* I wrote as a woman in *True Stories*, and got raped in a hayloft about once a month! Things got to going pretty good, we lived there about four years, then the War started and I was back in the Navy.

The British government just took that island away from me; they said they didn't like something I wrote, but they never told me why. I just heard that the island sold again for $6,000,000, but *[laughs]* I didn't get any! They took everything I had.

Were you a fan of horror or science fiction films?

No, I hated 'em. And for years I didn't see some of these movies that I made with Bill Castle. I mean, they're so dumb—God! There's not a worm in your backbone when you get scared!

You're talking about The Tingler *now.*

Right. The only thing I didn't like about *House on Haunted Hill* was that it made enough noise around town to attract Columbia Pictures, who, when I didn't want to be bought, swallowed us like a shark.

Then why did you and Castle allow yourselves to be swallowed?

Columbia offered us fabulous things. Bill was very impressed with Columbia: We had a corner office, we had a bar, we had two secretaries, and it

---

*White's adventure on Marina Cay formed the basis for two of his books, *Our Virgin Island* and *Two on the Isle*. *Our Virgin Island* was made into the movie *Virgin Island* (1959).

cost us a fortune! But it upgraded Bill, it gave him character. Years before, he had been fired from Columbia for some sort of dereliction of morals or something — he never talked to me about it.

For some unexplained and mysterious reason Bill either couldn't, or wouldn't, or was not allowed to drive a car. This resulted in his late afternoon dance routine in every studio he worked. During the last half hour Bill would roam around trying to con somebody into driving him home to his house in the Holmby Hills. During this dance period everybody with a car ran around trying to either hide or disappear entirely. I had a Volkswagen — which Bill hated — but I was available to carry him around on his many errands. And he wanted me to put a phone in the Volkswagen! I wouldn't do that, so he bought — or ripped loose — a phone handset, which had just enough cord left on it to dangle down inside the VW. And as we'd drive along through Beverly Hills Bill would be talking into this handset *[laughs]*! He was a phony son of a bitch!

So moving over to Columbia didn't sit well with you.

No, but — I was sort of "unconscious" by that time. I was having a lot of fun down in Malibu, and I had more money than I knew what to do with. But the shenanigans that went on at Columbia were sometimes more than I could deal with. I remember we had a woman, a real high-class broad, assigned to us; Bill didn't know what she was supposed to do, and I certainly didn't. But at least she got us into trouble with the Executive Dining Room. You had to be in the Executive Dining Room on time, but at five minutes before the fixed time for lunch the woman would disappear into the ladies' room, asking us to wait for her, and then would not come out for 45 minutes. I sent my secretary in to find out what the hell she did in there, and she came out and said, "She strips to the waist, takes off her bra, washes her tits, then dries herself off and gets dressed again!" I never found out what that woman's job was, and I've never heard of her since.

How did you think up the idea for The Tingler?

The makeup guy that we had on *House on Haunted Hill,* Jack Dusick, had made a rubber worm. He showed me this worm one day, a horrible looking thing, about a foot long. In those days we didn't have the violent makeup and special effects they have today, but this worm, it haunted you — it scared you! I began thinking about that, and I told Bill, "Let's find out where fear comes from and we'll use this worm!" It was a lot of fun writing the script, but I didn't like the movie.

In one scene we wanted to have Vincent Price drop the worm, and we figured the best way was to have a cat leap up on the operating table, snarling and clawing, and startle him. The cat's fee was $1500, the trainer got $1000, the S.P.C.A. man cost $500, Columbia got a fee for having a cat on stage and the contract stipulated that if anybody stepped on that cat's tail the fine was $2000. Well, in one take that cat began screaming bloody murder, as though Vincent

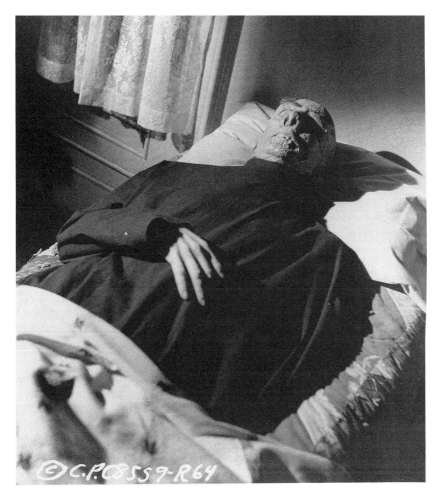

Philip Coolidge (or, more likely, a stand-in) in the ghoul-man get-up from White's *The Tingler*.

Price had stepped on its tail. The rushes made a liar out of the cat, but by that time our $2000 was long gone. The punchline to this story is, I'm in a bar one night someplace and I could hear this guy talking about his cat — it was the guy who owned the cat we used. And he said that this cat was trained to walk by somebody and scream and holler and writhe around. If I was a belligerent man, I would have gone over there and —!

The Tingler is also the movie where Vincent Price goes on the LSD trip.

I wanted something different from the typical shot or pill that you see in movie "trips." Aldous Huxley told me about a doctor at U.C.L.A. who was running an experiment on lysurgic acid [LSD]. So I went up there to see this man, Dr. Cohen, and he gave me some of it. He took me into a nice little room with a cot and a radio and he got something out of his refrigerator and gave me a shot. It was all legal then. I watched the grain in the wood writhing around and listened to the music. It was very pleasant, although I didn't ever want to do it again. I went back and told Vincent about it, what the real reaction would be — I just wondered if it wasn't something that Vincent could be dramatic about without falling around and all that stuff. He said, "Forget it." And when he took the shot in the movie, he jumped around and did the same god-damned thing he always did *[laughs]*!

Whenever you killed Vincent Price in a movie, he was always so dramatic about it — he'd writhe around and scream and holler and carry on. I remember I told Vincent, when he got shot in *House on Haunted Hill*, "When someone gets hit with a .45 caliber bullet, they fall backwards. You always fall *forwards* when you get hit." And Vincent said, "My boy, no actor falls *away* from the camera!" *[Laughs.]*

The gimmick this time was Percepto, with small motors on the bottoms of theater seats giving audience members a "tingle."

Bill's idea was to take the motors out of thousands of vibrators and screw them under the seats, then rig the wiring so that at crucial moments in the film the audience would suddenly begin vibrating in waves, six rows at a time. We didn't want to buy thousands of vibrators without knowing whether they would really work out, so we scouted around until we found a theater in the Valley that was running *The Nun's Story* [1959] — *The Nun's Story* was going to close on a Sunday night and *The Tingler* was going to open on Monday. We got in a huge crew of people to spend the day attaching the vibrators to the seats. But that night, just at the most tragic moment of *The Nun's Story*, somebody touched the master switch and the seats began vibrating in wave after wave. There was absolute pandemonium!

The other problem was the kids. They came and unscrewed the motors — broke them off and stole them. And they cost a lot of money. So that didn't work very long.

Did your films' budgets go up considerably now that you were at a major studio?

Yeah, Columbia charged us a lot, like $25,000 just to be there. Bill didn't tell me that at the beginning. And once we were at Columbia we never made the kind of money we did with *Macabre* and *House on Haunted Hill*. I also didn't hang around as much now that we were at Columbia.

13 Ghosts really was a departure, a very tame ghost movie which seemed like it was written for small kids.

[Laughs.] I didn't give a shit about that thing; I'd say it was my least favorite of the five films I made with Bill. *13 Ghosts* was his idea and I couldn't see any point in it at all. I don't think it made any sense and I've forgotten all

Neither the gimmicky "Ghost Viewer" nor a baker's dozen phantoms relieved the tedium of the disappointing *13 Ghosts*.

about it. Really, the only thing I remember about *13 Ghosts* was the lion that's in the picture. I had expected the King of Beasts, but what we got was an ancient, slightly mangy female. So we're shooting one of the lion scenes, when this old lion starts to pee! Lions don't pee in the same direction we do, they pee out the back, and it has a great deal more velocity and volume. As the stream kept coming, the lion made a slow, and I believe deliberate, turn through 360 degrees. She wet down everybody but the cameraman, who yanked a sheet of plywood out of the floor and used it as a shield. All hands took it very well except Jo Morrow, who declared she was gonna sue the entire state of California, starting with me!

The music in these films does wonders for them, really helps them to work. Did you get to meet any of these composures?

Yeah, I met Von Dexter *[House on Haunted Hill, The Tingler, 13 Ghosts]* and I thought he was a good guy. I saw him several times after that; he was a real estate agent last time I heard from him. He wasn't making it in the business and he didn't like it, either, and I'll bet he's making a lot more money now than he was then. Les Baxter, who wrote the music for *Macabre,* he was a pain in the ass. He wanted $10,000, he saw the movie and the only comment he made was, "Put a loud trumpet in there." I didn't like him and I didn't like his music, but this wasn't any of my business.

Homicidal *and* Psycho *have a lot in common but you claimed in a previous interview that you had no knowledge of* Psycho *going into* Homicidal.

Bill gave me the idea for *Homicidal,* and when I started to work on that screenplay he worked on it more than I did—more than he had on any other script that I did for him. It just felt very funny to me, that he was helping out so much, and that he wanted it exactly this way and that way and so on. One day after working at the studio I was on my way home when I saw that *Psycho* was playing somewhere in Santa Monica. I'd heard about the picture, I went in there and, Jesus Christ, I was afraid I was going to get arrested before I could get out! I was so embarrassed—he stole everything! And *Homicidal* was already in production by that time. But apparently nobody gave a shit that he had stolen it from Hitchcock.

You picked out some of the locations on Homicidal, *didn't you?*

Yeah, out in Solvang, California, a funny little place, totally Swedish. Somebody had told me there was a great old "haunted"-looking house there, so I went up to Solvang and located it. The script also called for a plant nursery, I found one up there and told them we were making a picture called *The Marble Forest.* We didn't want them to know it was really a horror movie. We tore up that nursery—God, we just ruined it! Solvang wanted to sue me and everybody else. I've never been back there, I'll tell you that *[laughs]*!

What do you think of the job "Jean Arless" [Joan Marshall] does in the film?

For years I tried to figure out, was that a girl or a guy? Now that I know it was an actress, I think she did a wonderful job.

Did you ever think about giving directing a shot?

No. I'm basically a book writer.

Homicidal *was your last film for Castle. Did you and he have some kind of tiff, or did you just drift apart?*

I just said I didn't want to work for him anymore. I didn't like working for Bill. Just as soon as I wasn't putting my own money into these pictures anymore, he got very bossy. Also, there had been the business about the

Homicidal script, the way he ripped off *Psycho* — when I found that out, I told Bill I would never work for him again. There was also a contract changed on me, on *Homicidal*. He said he'd give me 12 percent of it, he sent the contract down to me in Malibu and it said 12 percent and I signed it. But later, when it came back, there was a period between the one and the two — that was put in afterward! I wanted to talk it over with Bill, but he got "very sick" — he couldn't discuss it, he was "too sick." So I settled for my 1.2 percent, I didn't want to fight about it, but eventually I started getting awful tired of that bullshit. I figured, if I was going to work for a salary, I'd rather work with someone other than Bill. I never saw Bill again after *Homicidal*.

What did you do after leaving Castle?
The first thing I did was to finish a book that I had promised Doubleday. Then I met the producer of *Perry Mason*, a fellow by the name of Art Seid. He lived down in Malibu, and I said, "Let me write one of those things." I wrote one script and they bought it, and then I kept on writing for them.

After you left Castle he floundered for a few years with lousy pictures like Zotz! *and* The Old Dark House, *then got back on track by hiring Robert Bloch.*
Bloch talked to me about Bill one time, and he had the same opinion I did. That Castle was just impossible.

Did you follow Castle's career at all in later years?
No. I did happen to see *Rosemary's Baby* and I asked Howard Koch what that was all about, and he said that nobody else wanted it.

In his autobiography Castle makes it sound as though every producer in Hollywood wanted it.
Nobody wanted it, according to Koch. Bill didn't really do anything on that picture, he just filled a space. He didn't direct or put up any money or anything like that.

Looking back over the Castle years, was it an enjoyable time, or was there too much aggravation involved?
No, I liked that experience. I had never done anything except some TV — *Men of Annapolis* and another series called *Silent Service* — and it was a relief to be able to whomp out all that stuff and then let the camera do the hard work. Writing a book is a hell of a lot different from writing a screenplay, a lot more work. Between movies I wrote three or four books while I was in Hollywood; I didn't socialize very much. I had a series of affairs that were nice — not serious. I didn't go to town if I didn't have to. I had a beautiful house in Malibu that kept sliding into the sea, and I spent a lot of time repairing that.

You ever think about writing another horror film?
  [Laughs.] Never!

Author's note: Robb White died at age 81 in November, 1990, as this book was in the final stages of production.

Index

Every movie title is followed by year of release. Television series, stageplays, etc., are identified as such in parentheses. The titles of novels, short stories, magazines, etc., appear in quotation marks. Page numbers in bold indicate photographs.

A

The A-Team (TV) 93
Abbott, Bud 33
Abe Lincoln in Illinois (1940) 166
The Abominable Dr. Phibes (1971) 156, 175, 178–82, **180, 181**
Acquanetta 1–17, **1, 4, 6, 7, 13**
Act of Violence (1948) 276
Adams, Beverly 238
Adams, Richard 153
Adler, Buddy 110
Adventures of Superman (TV) 20, 21, 22–31, **23,** 33, 34, 36, 356–60, **355,** 365
Agar, John x, 228, 328, 402, 404
Aherne, Brian 268
Alberghetti, Anna Maria 231
Albert, Eddie 139
Aldrich, Robert 268
The Alfred Hitchcock Hour (TV) 142–3
Alfred Hitchcock Presents (TV) 46, 47, 142–3
Alienator (1989) x
Alland, William 342, 402–3, 404
The Alligator People (1959) ix
Alperson, Edward 87–8
Altman, Robert 130
Alves, Joe 318
Alyn, Kirk 26, 27, 357
The Amazing Colossal Man (1957) 104
Amazing Grace and Chuck (1987) 286
Amazzini, Bill xi
Amazzini, Roberta xi
"The American Weekly" 15

Ames, Ed 139
Ames, Leon 359
Anders, Luana 372
Anders, Merry xi
Anderson, Judith 231
Anderson, Richard xi
Andrews, Dana 125
Angel, Heather 197
The Angry Red Planet (1960) 113
Ankers, Evelyn 8
Ankrum, Morris 328, 332–3
Annapolis Farewell (1935) 187
Anne of the Thousand Days (1969) 149
Apache (1954) 110
Arabian Nights (1942) 3–4, 5
Argento, Dario 222
Arkoff, Samuel Z. 49, 73–4, 144, 148–9, 156, 158–9, 160–1, 166, **167,** 168, 170, 174, 179, 183, 184, 293, 294, 297, 300, 301, 304–5, **309,** 310, 315
Arlen, Richard 233
Arless, Jean *see* Marshall, Joan
Armstrong, Todd **245,** 246
Arnall, Julia **227**
Arnold, Jack ix, 291, 292, 293, 406
Around the World in 80 Days (1956) 293
Arrighi, Nike 314
Asher, Jane 50
Ashley, Joel 329
Ashley, John x
Asquith, Anthony 42
Assignment: Underwater (TV) 117
Assola, Henri 125
The Astounding She-Monster (1958) x
Attack of the Crab Monsters (1957) 57

Attack of the 50 Foot Woman (1958) 370, 372–7, **374**, 383
Attack of the Giant Leeches (1959) 370, 377–80, **379**, 383
Attack of the Puppet People (1958) 104
Away All Boats (1956) 293
Ayash, Mon xi
"Ayesha" 154
Aykroyd, Dan 319

B

Backus, Jim 418
Badiyi, Reza 130, 134
Balcon, Michael 42
Ball, Suzan 345
Balsam, Martin 222
Bandit xi
Bankhead, Tallulah 312, 313, 314
Barbeau, Adrienne **287**
Barclay, Jerry **63**
Barker, Clive x
The Baron of Arizona (1950) 116
Barry, Joan 114
Barry, John 107
Barrymore, Ethel 28
Barrymore, John 192–4
Baschuk, Luciano 15
Batman (TV) 248, 394
Batman (1989) ix
Battle, John Tucker 87
Battle for the Planet of the Apes (1973) 220
Battle of Blood Island (1961) 65–6
Battle of the Bulge (1965) 110
Bava, Mario 163, 164, 165
Baxt, George 305
Baxter, Les 148, **300**, 310, 430
Beal, John 89, **90**
The Beat Generation (1959) 290
Beat the Clock (TV) 244
The Beatles 50
Beaumont, Charles 305
Becker, Joe 114, 116
Bedlam (1946) 254, 264–7, **266**
Beery, Noah, Jr. **102**
"Being" 311
Ben (1972) 284
Benchley, Robert 261
Beneath the Planet of the Apes (1970) **216**, 220
Benét, Stephen Vincent 191
Bengell, Norma 164, **164**
Bennett, Charles 161, 254
Benny, Jack 261

Berger, Sidney 130, **139**
Bergman, Ingmar 137
Bergman, Ingrid 208, 260
Bergner, Elisabeth 148, 174
Berkeley, Busby 323
Berle, Milton 156
Bernay, Lynn **58**, 59
Bernds, Edward 110, 111, 112, 113, 114, 115, **116**, 117, 126
Bernhard, Harvey 50
Best, Edna 261
Beswick, Martine xi
Betrayed see *When Strangers Marry*
Bewitched (TV) 248
Bickman, Stan 65
"Bid Time Return" 317
The Big Bluff (1955) 226
Big Jake (1971) 322, **333**, 334
The Big Red One (1980) 80
The Big Valley (TV) 82
Bikini Paradise (1967) 122
"The Bishop's Wife" 254
Bissell, Whit 34, **34**, 70
Black, Karen x, 142, 383
Blair, George 25, 29
Blair, Janet 305
Blees, Robert 182, 183
The Blob (1958) xi
The Blob (1988) xi
Bloch, Robert 143, 146, 431
Blomgren, Bengt 411
Blood of Dracula (1957) 61–2
Blues Busters (1950) 20
Bodkin, Tain 398
The Body Snatcher (1945) 319
Boetticher, Budd 352
Bogdanovich, Peter 267
Bogeaus, Benedict 332, 333
Bond, Ward 263
Boone, Richard 334
"Born of Man and Woman" 290
Boston, George 276
Boyce, William 233
Boyer, Charles 9
Brahm, John 197
Brainard, Karl **58**
Brando, Marlon **211**
Brandon, Henry 409
Brauner, Arthur 170–171
Brent, Bill xi
Bridges, James 27
Bridges, Lloyd **102**
Bright Lights, Big City (1988) 27
Broccoli, Albert R. 235
Brodie, Steve 388, 398

Broidy, Steve 121, 122
Bronson, Charles 65, 299
Bronston, Samuel 120
Brooke, Ralph 390
Brooke, Rupert 257
Brooks, Albert 319
Brooks, Richard 15
Brown, Arthur William 2
Brown, Barry 380, 400
Brown, David 110
Brown, Peter 301
Brown, Robert **93**
Browning, Ricou 327
Brunas, John xii, **201**
Brunas, Michael xii, **201**
Buchanan, Larry 31, 36
Bunky *see* Runser, Mary
Burn, Witch, Burn (1962) 305, 315
Burton, Richard 149
Burton, Robert 233, 412
Byrnes, Edd 372
Byron, Jean **231**
Byron, Kathleen **210**

C

Cabot, Susan x, **xi**, 59, 63
Cagney, James 370–2
Cahn, Edward L. 328, 329
Calthrop, Donald 259
The Camels Are Coming (1934) 256, 257
A Canterbury Tale (1949) 212
Cantinflas 293
The Cape Canaveral Monsters (1960) 386, 391–3, **392, 393**
Capp, Al 323
Capra, Frank 107, 186, 187, 188, 190
Captive Wild Woman (1943) 1, 2, 5–9, **6, 7,** 10
Carbone, Antony 65
Carnival (1946) 46
Carnival of Souls (1962) ix, 127–39, **127, 131, 133, 139,** 140
Carpenter, John 276, 286, **287**
The Carpetbaggers (1964) 381
Carr, Tommy 25, 29
Carradine, John **6,** 8, 35, 301, 360, **361,** 394, 398, 412
Carreras, James 42, 43, 176
Carreras, Michael 42, 43, 314
Carroll, Earl 20
Carson, Jack 33
Carter, Ellis **403**
Caruso, Anthony 332

Casanova's Big Night (1954) 238
Castle, Peggie **104**
Castle, William 96, 208, 414, 415–6, **415,** 417, 418–9, 421, 422, 425–6, 428, 430–1
Cat People (1942) 88, 265, 311
Cellier, Frank 259
Chaffey, Don 240
Chamberlain, Richard 259
Chambers, John 214, 217
Champagne Charlie (1944) 42
Champion (1949) 266
Chandler, Jeff 228, 324, 326
Chaney, Lon, Jr. 9, 136, **363**
Chase, Frank **374**
Chase, Stanley 316
Chekhov, Michael 350, 352
China Smith (TV) 74, 75, 77–8
Chinatown (1974) 65
Chisum (1970) 322
Christmas in Connecticut (1945) 356, 365
Christopher, Robert 398–9
Chudnow, David 99
CinderFella (1960) 230–1
Ciro, Fernando 352
Citizen Kane (1941) 226
City Beneath the Sea (1953) 345, 352
Clarke, Alyce 35
Clarke, Mae 267
Clarke, Robert x, 35, **266,** 267, 398, 399
Clifford, John 128, 129, 133, 137, **139**
Clive, Henry 15
Coates, Phyllis 19–37, **19, 21, 23, 31, 34,** 356–7
Cocchi, John xi
Cohen, Herman 70, 71, 73, 74, 75, 76
Cohn, Harry 187–8, 246, 248
Colman, Ronald 186, 187, 188, 189, **189,** 190
Colossus: The Forbin Project (1970) 316
The Colossus of New York (1958) 227–8, **339,** 340, 341–3, **342**
The Comedy of Terrors (1964) 301, 307, 310–2
Condon, Richard 283
Condor (1986 TV movie) 412
"Conjure Wife" 305
Connell, W. Merle **392**
Conover, Harry 2
Conqueror Worm (1968) 156, 166–9, **167,** 178
Conquest of the Planet of the Apes (1972) 220
Conrad, Robert 348

Conried, Hans 84
Conway, Gary **34**
Cook, Elisha, Jr. 421–2
Coote, Robert **210**
Corby, Ellen 266–7
Corey, Jeff 22, 28
Corey, Wendell 86
Corman, Gene 117, 377, 378, 379
Corman, Roger ix, 48, 49, 54–5, 56, 57, 59, 60, 62, 64, 65, 66, 67, 70, 96, 105, 110, 142, 151, 170, 294–5, 297–8, **302**, 303, 310, 313, 363, 364
Corri, Adrienne 40
Corrigan, Ray "Crash" **1**
Costello, Lou 33
Cotten, Joseph 180–1
Coulouris, George 226, **227**
Court, Hazel 39–51, **39**, **41**, **44**, **45**, **47**
Crack in the World (1965) 110, 123–5, **124**, 126
Craig, Carolyn **424**
Craven, James **23**
Crawford, Broderick 235
Crawford, Joan 238–9, 268, 269
Creature of the Walking Dead (1965) 393–4
The Creature Walks Among Us (1956) 326–8, **327**
The Creeping Unknown (1956) ix
The Crimson Cult (1970) 156, 159, 172–3, **173**
Cronenberg, David x
Crosby, Floyd 310
Cry for Happy (1961) 244
Cry of the Banshee (1970) 142, 144, 146–9, 174–5, 238
Cukor, George 387
Cummings, Robert 33
Curse of Dracula see *The Return of Dracula*
The Curse of Frankenstein (1957) 40, 43–4, **44**, 45
Curse of the Stone Hand (1965) 393–4
Curtis, Dan 307
Curtis, Jamie Lee 276, 283, 286, **287**
Curtis, Tony 276, 277, 278, **278**, 279, 326
Cushing, Peter 40, 43, 44, 48, 146, **147**, 176, **177**, 312
Cutting, Richard 57
The Cyclops (1957) 104
Cyrano de Bergerac (1950) 198, 340, 345, 352

D

Daddy's Gone A-Hunting (1969) 340, 348–50
Dalton, Abby **58**, 59
Damien—Omen II (1978) 50
Damon, Mark 298
Dannaldson, Jim 408
Dante, Joe 318, 319
Danton, Ray 301
Danziger, Edward J. 41
Danziger, Harry Lee 41
Darin, Bobby 230
The Dark at the Top of the Stairs (1960) 87
Dark August (1976) 221
Darkness at Noon (play) 212–3
Darrow, Barbara **86**
The Dave Garroway Show (TV) 244
David, Saul 270
Davies, Marion 3, 15
Davis, Bette 142, 181, 230, 239, 268
Davis, "Killer" Karl **321**
Day, Robert xi, 248–9
"The Day of the Triffids" 121
The Day of the Triffids (1963) 110, 117–22, **118**, **120**, 123, 126
The Dead Don't Die (1975 TV movie) 370, 382
Dead Man's Eyes (1944) 2, 9–10
Dead of Night (1946) 238
Death Valley Days (TV) 329
de Carlo, Yvonne 5
de Kova, Frank 57
Del Ruth, Roy 75
Del Vecchio, Carl xi
Del Vecchio, Debbie xi
Denning, Richard xi
De Sade (1969) 144, 169–72, 178, 182, 313
Destination Inner Space (1966) 186, 201
Destination Moon (1950) 100
Destination Tokyo (1943) 226
The Destructors (1968) 201
The Detectives Starring Robert Taylor (TV) 82
Devil Girl from Mars (1955) 40–2, **41**
"The Devil Rides Out" 305, 314
The Devil's Bride (1968) 305, 314
The Devil's Messenger (1962) 136, 137
Devon, Richard 53–68, **53**, **56**, **58**, **61**, **63**, **64**
Dexter, Von 430
Diabolique (1955) 315
Diary of a Madman (1963) 246–7, **247**

Dick and the Duchess (TV) 42, 46
The Dick Clark Show (TV) 156, 175
Die! Die! My Darling! (1965) 305, 313-4
Dietrich, Marlene 257, 261
Diffring, Anton 45, **45**, 46
"Discover" 195
The Disenchanted (play) 246
"The Disoriented Man" 146
Disputed Passage (1939) 192
Dmytryk, Edward 7, 8, 10, 381
Doctor Blood's Coffin (1961) 40, 46, **47**
Dr. Goldfoot and the Bikini Machine (1965) 157-8, 165-6
Dr. Goldfoot and the Girl Bombs (1966) 165, 166
Dr. Hudson's Secret Journal (TV) 198
Dr. Phibes Rises Again (1972) 156, 179, 182-3
Dominick and Eugene (1988) 286
Donlevy, Brian 126
Doomsday Machine (1967) 340, 350-1
Douglas, John 125
Douglas, Melvyn 377
Dozier, William 395
"Dracula" 89
Dracula (1931) 228, 284, 307
Dracula (1973 TV movie) 318
"A Dreadful Man" 268
Drew, Ellen 192
Driving Miss Daisy (1989) 222
Dru, Joanne 272
Duel (1971 TV movie) 318, 319
Duggan, Andrew 398
Dullea, Keir 171
Dunas, Ronald S. 178, 179-80
Duncan, David 83
Duncan, Pamela 56-7
Dunninger 276, 278
Duryea, Dan 75, 78
Dusick, Jack 426
Duvivier, Julien 263
Dwan, Allan 331-2, 333
Dwyer, Hilary 168
Dying Room Only (1973 TV movie) 318

E

Eason, B. Reeves 359
Eason, Jim 27
Eastwood, Clint 324
Eatwell, Brian 179
Ebb Tide (1932) 256
Edge of Doom (1950) 345, 348
Edward VIII 228

Edwards, George 381
Eisley, Anthony x
Ekberg, Anita 166, 324
Ellison, James **139**, 196-7
Ellsworth, Whitney 22, 24, 30, 357
Embassy (1972) 152
Emery, John **102**
Emmet, Michael 380
Endfield, Cy 144, 170, 171, 313
Epstein, Allen 318
The Ernie Kovacs Show (TV) 156, 175
Escape from Red Rock (1958) 126
Escape from the Planet of the Apes (1971) 215, 216, **219**, 220
Evans, Maurice 218, 219
Evil Spirits (1990) x-xi, 383
The Exorcist (1973) 317

F

The Face of Marble (1946) **358**, 360, **361**
Fahey, Myrna **296**
"The Fall of the House of Usher" 295
Family Plot (1976) 143
"Fanatic" 313
Fanatic see *Die! Die! My Darling!*
"Fangoria" xi, xii
The Fantastic Little Girl (unmade) 292, 293
The Fast and the Furious (1954) 110
"Father Goose" 75
Faye, Janina 122
The Faye Emerson Show (TV) 157
Fear No More (1961) 343
Felton, Earl 299
Ferrante, Tim xi
Ferrer, Jose 340
Field, Sally 380
Fielder, Pat 81-93
"Filmfax" xii
The Final Conflict (1981) 50
Fine, Larry **111**
Fisher, Terence 43
Fitzgerald, F. Scott 261
Fitzgerald, Michael xi
The Flame Barrier (1958) 83, 92, **93**
Flaming Star (1960) 79
Fleming, Ian 236
Flesh and Fantasy (1943) 9, 254, 263-4, **264**
Flight of the Lost Balloon (1961) 340, 345-7, **346**
"The Fly" 115
The Fly (1958) 115

Flying Tigers (1942) 267
Flynn, Errol 230
Flynn, Joe **363**
The Fog (1980) 276, 286, **287**
Fogarty, Elsie 256
The Forbin Project see *Colossus: The Forbin Project*
Forbstein, Leo 97, 98
Ford, John 254, 261, 262, 263, 264, 272, 301
"The Forgotten Ones" 65
Fort Apache (1948) 254
Foster, John xi
The Four Feathers (1939) 299
The Four Skulls of Jonathan Drake (1959) ix
Fowler, Gene, Jr. 69–80, **69**
Fowler, Gene, Sr. 70, 75
Francis, Freddie **118**, 121–2, 236–7, 238, 239, 240
Francis, Kevin 239, 240
Francis Goes to West Point (1952) 324–6
Frankenheimer, John 276, 284
Frankenstein (1931) 43, 228, 284
Frankenstein Island (1981) 386, 388, 398–9
Frankham, David **300**
Frankie and Johnny (1966) 244
Franklin, Pamela 315
Frankovich, Mike 251
Franz, Arthur **93**
Fraser, Richard 266
Fried, Gerald 106
Friml, Rudolf 96
Frogs (1972) 284
From Hell It Came (1957) 329–31, **330**, **331**
"From Here to Eternity" 284
Fuest, Robert 179, 182
Fuller, Sam 79–80, 105
Furie, Sidney J. 46
Furness, Lady Thelma 228

G

Gable, Clark 82, 261
Gabor, Zsa Zsa 234, 270
Gage, Erford **207**
Gang War (1958) 75
The Gang's All Here (play) 377
Garbo, Greta 258
Gardner, Arthur 81–93, **81**
Garland, Richard 56–7
The Garry Moore Show (TV) 156, 175

Garson, Greer 262
Gavin, John **280**, 281, 282
General Hospital (TV) 254, 272
George VI 210
Georgy Girl (1966) 313
Geronimo (1962) 82
Ghost (1990) xi
The Ghost and Mrs. Muir (1947) 254, 267
The Ghost in the Invisible Bikini (1966) 157, **158**, 159–60
The Ghost Ship (1953) 40
The Giant Claw (1957) 364
Giant from the Unknown (1958) 106
Gidding, Nelson 154
Gidget (TV) 380
Gielgud, John 256
Gilbert, W.S. 238
Gittens, George 76
The Glass Sphinx (1967) 166, 171
Glasser, Albert 95–107, **95**, **101**
Glasser, Bernard 109–26, **109**, **111**, **116**, **118**
Gleason, Jackie 244, 246
Gohdé, Katie iv
Gold Raiders (1951) 110, **111**
Golden, Michael **227**
The Golden Voyage of Sinbad (1974) 142, 151–2, **153**
Goldman, Martin 221
Goldsmith, Jerry 107
Goldstein, Bruce xi
Goldstein, William 178, 183
Gone with the Wind (1939) 206, 261, 265
Good Night, Sweet Marilyn (1987) 31–3, 36
Gordon, Alex xi
Gordon, Bernard 120, 121, 123
Gordon, Bert I. 96, 103, 104, 105
Gordon, Richard xi
Gorgo (1961) 124
Goring, Marius **210**
Gorog, Laszlo 402
Gorss, Saul 409
Gothard, Michael 176
Gough, Michael 237, **237**
Grand Guignol (play) 381
Granet, Bert 311
Granger, Stewart 259
Grant, Cary 406
Gray, Coleen **90**, 314
The Great Sioux Massacre (1965) 244
Green, Johnny 98
Greene, Billy 391

Greene, Leon 314
Greene, Richard 187
Greenstreet, Sydney 308
Greer, Jane 264
Greer, Richard 393
Griffith, Charles B. 298
Griffith, Hugh 180, 181–2, 183
Grofe, Ferde 96, 100, 101
Guber, Peter 152
Gulliver's Travels (unmade) 293
Gunsmoke (TV) 198, 327

H

Hadley, Reed 106
Haggard, H. Rider 154
Halevy, Julian 123
Haller, Dan 160, 161, 310
Halloween (1978) 286
Hamilton, John 26, 27, 357
Hanawalt, Chuck 58
Hansen, Donald 235
Harrington, Curtis 183, 381–2
Harris, Jack H. xi
Harrison, Joan 142
Harrison, Linda 219
Harryhausen, Ray 142, 151, 152, 244
Hart, John 331
Hart, Susan 157, 158, 160, 232–3
Harvey, Herk 127–39, **127**, **133**, **136**, **138**, **139**
Harvey, Laurence 47
Hasso, Signe 270
The Haunting (1963) 154, 315
Haunting Fear (1990) x
Hayers, Sidney 305
Hayes, Allison 328, 372–3, 375
Hayward, Leland 198
Hayward, Susan 228
Hayworth, Rita 186, 246
Head, Edith 277
Hearst, William Randolph 3
"Hell House" 315, 317
Henie, Sonja 15
Henry, Mike 249–50, **250**
Henry V (1945) 299
Hepburn, Katharine 186, 263
Here Come the Jets (1959) 75–6
Herrmann, Bernard 106–7
Herron, Robert **232**, 234
Herts, Kenneth 136, 137, 138, 139
Hessler, Gordon 141–54, **141**, **147**, 173, 174, 175, 176, 177, 178, 183
Heston, Charlton 218
Heyward, Louis M. 142, 144, 146, 148,
155–84, **155**, **167**
Hill, Arthur 377
Hill Street Blues (TV) 93
Hillary, Sir Edmund 402
Hilligoss, Candace 128, 129, 130–2, 133, **133**, 134, **139**
Hilton, James 186, 187
Hinds, Anthony 306, 313
Hitchcock, Alfred 46, 47, 76, 89, 142, 143, 146, 174, 208, 263, 276, 279–80, **280**, 282, 283, 430
Hitchcock, Pat 47
Hobart, Rose xi
Hoffman, Dustin 317
Hoffman, Howard **417**
Hogarth, William 265
Holbrook, Victor 267
Holden, William 82
Hollywood Canteen (1944) 226
Holt, Tim 83
Homicidal (1961) 414, 430, 431
Hoos, Allan xi
Hoover, J. Edgar 3
Hope, Donna xi
Horowitz, Vladimir 398
Horror Hotel (1963) ix
Horror House (1970) 172
Houdini (1953) 276–9, **278**
Houdini, Bess 277, 278, 279
Houdini, Harry 277, 278, 279
House, Billy 266
House of a Thousand Dolls (1967) 166
House of the Black Death (1965) 390
House of Usher (1960) 293–8, **296**, 303
House on Haunted Hill (1959) 413, 414, 419–22, **420**, **423**, **424**, 425, 426, 428
How Green Was My Valley (1941) 254, 261–3, **262**, 264, 375
Howard, John 185–203, **185**, **188**, **189**, **201**, 341
Howard, Moe **111**, 112–3
Howard, Shemp **111**
Howard, Trevor 239
Hud (1963) 375
Hudson, Rock 324, 326, 380–1
Hudson, William 372, 373, **374**, 375, 380
Hughes, Howard 267, 344, 345
Huk (1956) 103, 106
Hulbert, Jack 257
Hull, Henry 300
Hunter, Ian 46
Hunter, Kim 205–23, **205**, **207**, **210**, **211**, **214**, **216**, **219**
Hunter, Ross 191

Index

Huntington, Lawrence 236
Hush . . . Hush, Sweet Charlotte (1965) 314
Hussein (ibn Talal) x
Huston, John 171, 313, 422
Hutton, Robert 225–42, **225**, **227**, **231**, **237**
Huxley, Aldous 427
Hyer, Martha 381

I

I Am Curious – Yellow (1968) 174
"I Am Legend" 291, 302, 306, 307, 314
I Married a Monster from Outer Space (1958) 70, 74, 76–9, **78**
I, Mobster (1958) 370
I Shot Jesse James (1949) 100, 105–6
I Want to Live! (1958) 154
I Was a Teenage Frankenstein (1957) 26, 34, **34**, 35
I Was a Teenage Werewolf (1957) 70–4, **72**, 76
If Winter Comes (1947) 276
"Implosion" 312
In Like Flint (1967) 254, 270–2
In Old New Mexico (1945) 99
The Incredible Petrified World (1960) 34–5
The Incredible Shrinking Man (1957) 290–3, **292**, **294**, 304
The Incredible Shrinking Woman (1981) 293
Indestructible Man (1956) **363**
Inge, William 87
The Innocents (1961) 305
Intermezzo (1936) 260
Intermezzo (1939) 260
"Interviews with B Science Fiction and Horror Movie Makers" ix
Invaders from Mars (1953) 87–8, 363
Invasion of the Animal People (1962) 402, 209–12, **410**
Invasion U.S.A. (1952) 103, **104**
Invisible Invaders (1959) **225**, 226, 228, **229**, **231**, 237
The Invisible Man (1933) 228
The Invisible Woman (1940) **185**, 186, 192–5
It Happened One Night (1934) 186
Ivers, Robert 371

J

Jack the Giant Killer (1962) 254, 269–70
Jackson, Brad **58**
Jackson, Jesse 26
Jacobs, Arthur P. 215, 217
Jacques, Della 35
Jagged Edge (1985) 153
Jagger, Dean 208
Jameson, Joyce 308
Jane Eyre (1944) 106
Jason and the Argonauts (1963) **243**, 244–6, **245**
Jaws (1975) 315
Jaws 2 (1978) 318
Jaws 3-D (1983) 318
Jayne, Jennifer **237**
Jeffries, Lionel 183
Jenkins, Allen 33
Jochsberger, Steve xi
Johnson, Arte xi
Johnson, Nunnally 75, 79
Johnson, Tom xi
Jones, Christopher x
Jones, Marshall **147**
Jones-Moreland, Betsy 59
Joseph, Wilfred 148
The Jungle Captive (1945) 12
Jungle Drums of Africa (1953 serial) 33
Jungle Girl (1941 serial) 33
Jungle Woman (1944) 2, 10–2, **11**
Juran, Nathan 347, 375

K

Kandel, Aben 73
Karloff, Boris 40, 43, 48, 49, 157, 159, 172–3, 180, **253**, 254, 258, 259, 265, **266**, 267, 308, 309, 310, 312
Karloff, Evelyn 267
Katzman, Leonard 328
Katzman, Sam 92, 328, 364
Kaufman, Robert 165, 166
Keaton, Buster 157
Keel, Howard 121, 122
Keitel, Harvey 222
Kellerman, Sally 372
Kelly, Dan 3, 5, 12, 13
Kemp, Valli 179
Kennedy, John F. 283
Kerr, Deborah 259
Kevan, Jack 402, 403
Kid Galahad (1962) 65
Kidder, Margot 26

Index 441

Kilian, Victor 377
Kincaid, Aron **158**
The Kindred (1987) 221–2
King, Frank 208
King, Maurice 208
King Solomon's Mines (1937) 254, 259, 260
King Solomon's Mines (1950) 259
King Solomon's Mines (1985) 259
King, Stephen 302
Kingsley, Sidney 212
Knowles, Patric 263
Koch, Howard W. xi, 416, 417, 418, 419, 431
Korngold, Erich Wolfgang 96, 98, 105
Kovack, Nancy 243–51, **243**, **245**, **247**, **249**, **250**
Kovacs, Ernie 156, 178, 179
Kowalski, Bernard 377, 379
Kramer, Stanley 79
Kraushaar, Raoul 106
Kronos (1957) 363
Kruger, Otto 227, 343

L

LaBarre, James xi
Laffan, Patricia 40, **41**
Lahr, Bert 33
Lamarr, Hedy 265, 270
Lamont, Jack O. 235, 236
Lamparski, Richard xi
Lancaster, Burt 110, 234
The Land Unknown (1957) **401**, 402, 404, 406–9, **407**
Landis, John 318
Landon, Michael 70, 71, **72**, 73
Landres, Paul 81–93
Lane, Vicky 12
Lang, Fritz 74, 79, 80, 306
Lang, Matheson 255
Langelaan, George 115
Lanphier, James 346
Lansbury, Angela 228, 272
Larson, Jack 22, 23, 27, 28, 30, 357
LaShelle, Joseph 71, 72
Lassie (TV) 24
The Last Man on Earth (1964) 306, **306**, 307
Last Woman on Earth (1960) 65
Laughton, Charles 230
Laurie, Piper 324
Laven, Arnold 81–93, **81**
Law, John Phillip 152, **153**

The Lawman (TV) 301
Lawrence, Jock 210–1
Lawrence, Sheldon **227**
Lawson, Sarah 314
Leachman, Cloris 318
LeBorg, Reginald ix–x, 7, 9–10, 247
Lederer, Francis 89, **90**, **91**
Lee, Anna 253–74, **253**, **255**, **262**, **264**, **266**, **271**
Lee, Bernard 256
Lee, Christopher 40, 43, **44**, 145, 146, 172, 176, 312, 314
Lee, Ruta 351
The Legend of Hell House (1973) 315–7, **316**
Lehman, Ernest 143
Leiber, Fritz 305
Leigh, Janet 275–88, **275**, **278**, **280**, **285**, **287**
Leigh, Vivien **211**, 265
Let's Do It Again (1953) 290
Levitt, Stan **139**
Levy, Jules V. **81**, 82, 83, 84, 86, 87, 89, 92
Lewis, Jerry 230–1
Lewton, Val 88, 206–7, 208, 222, 254, 264, 265, 295, 311, 319
"Life" 100
Lights, Camera, Action (TV) 390
"Li'l Abner" 323
Link, John 112
Lippert, Robert 75, 76, 100, 110–1, 112, 115, 116, 117, 306
Lithgow, John 319
Little Women (1949) 276
Livesey, Roger 210, **210**
Lloyd, Norman 142
Loder, John 259, 260
Loeffler, Louis 76
Lohman, Augie 85
Lom, Herbert **150**, 151, 177
Lombard, Carole 261
London, Steve **78**
The Lone Ranger (TV) 331
Long, Richard 422
"Long Rider Jones" 110
Lorre, Peter 40, 48, 49, 307–8, 309, **309**, 312
Lost Continent (1951) 2, **14**, 15
"Lost Horizon" 186, 187
Lost Horizon (1937) 186–91, **188**, **189**, 201–2
Lost Horizon (1973) 191
The Lost Missile (1958) 363
Lotito, Leo 215, 216

442 Index

Lourie, Eugene 123–5, 227, 342
Lovecraft, H.P. 302
Lubin, Arthur 324, 325
Lucas, George 85
Luce, Greg xi
Lucisano, Fulvio 165, 166, 168
Lugones, Alex xi
Lupino, Ida 36, 340, 344, 347, 348

M

Macabre (1958) 414, 415–9, **417**, 428, 430
McCarthy, Joseph 22, 28, 212
McCartney, Paul 50
Macaulay, Charles 381
McDermott, Hugh 40
MacDonald, David 41
McDonnell, Dave xi
McDowall, Roddy 214, 215, 216, 217, 218, **219**, 220, 262, 263, 315
McGee, Mark xi
Machine-Gun Kelly (1958) 54, 64–5
Mackenzie, Jack 88
The McKenzie Break (1970) 82
McLaglen, Victor 263
MacLaine, Shirley 279
McNeil, Allen 74–5
The Mad Doctor (1941) 186, 192, **193**
Madron (1970) 125–6
"The Magazine of Fantasy and Science Fiction" 290
Magginetti, Bill 111, 112, 115
The Magnificent Ambersons (1942) 84
Magnificent Obsession (1954) 182
Mahoney, Jock **407**, 409
Mainwaring, Dan 112
Malden, Karl **211**
The Man from U.N.C.L.E. (TV) 248
The Man in Half Moon Street (1944) 46
A Man in Love (1987) 286
The Man on the Eiffel Tower (1949) 230
The Man Who Changed His Mind see *The Man Who Lived Again*
The Man Who Could Cheat Death (1959) 43, 45–6, **45**
The Man Who Lived Again (1936) 253, 254, 258–9, 260
The Man Who Shot Liberty Valance (1962) 263
The Man Who Turned to Stone (1957) 329
Man with a Camera (TV) 65
The Man Without a Body (1959) 226–7, **227**

"The Manchurian Candidate" 283–4
The Manchurian Candidate (1962) 276, 283–4
Mank, Greg xi
Manley, Walter 139
Mannix, Eddie 20
Mannix, Toni 20–1, 30
Mannix (TV) 244
"The Marble Forest" 415, 416
Margo 186, **188**, **189**, 190
Mark of the Vampire (1957) see *The Vampire*
Marooned (1969) 244, 251
Marquette, Jacques 65, 66, 375
Marrazzo, Kevin xi
Marshal, Alan 421
Marshall, E.G. 377
Marshall, Herbert 261
Marshall, Joan 430
Martin, Dean 230, 248
Martin, Ross 343, 348
Marton, Andrew 125
Martucci, Mark xi
Marvin, Lee 86, 263
Mary Poppins (1964) 160
The Masque of the Red Death (1964) **39**, 40, 42, 49–50
Massen, Osa **102**
Massey, Raymond 210, **210**
"Master of the World" 299
Master of the World (1961) 295, 299–301, **300**
Matheson, Richard 169, 172, **289**–320, **289**
Matheson, Richard Christian 291, 307
A Matter of Life and Death see *Stairway to Heaven*
Maude, Joan **210**
Maurer, Norman 112–3, 114
Maurey, Nicole 122
Maxwell, Jessica 25, 29
Maxwell, Lois 315
Maxwell, Robert 20, 24, 25, 28, 29, 356, 357
Mayo, Virginia x
A Medal for Benny (1945) 12
Megowan, Don 326, 327
Mehta, Zubin 244, 251
Melchior, Ib J. 165
Men of Annapolis (TV) 414, 415, 431
Mercer, Ray 112
Meredith, Burgess 230
Merrill, B.D. 268
Merritt, Abraham E. 305
Mesa of Lost Women (1953) 386–7

Mike Hammer (TV) 93
Mildred Pierce (1945) 239
Miles, Bob **232**
Miles, Vera **280**, 281
Milland, Ray 48, 290, 382
Miller, Arthur 71
Miller, Denny 351
Miller, Dick xi–xii, **64**
Miller, George 319
Milner, Dan 329
Milner, Jack 329
Mineo, Sal 215
Miracle Mile (1989) x
Mr. Skeffington (1944) 356
Mitchell, Cameron xii, 398
Mitchum, Robert 208
Mohr, Gerald **104**
The Mole People (1956) 402–6, **403**, **405**, 409
Monroe, Marilyn 31, 323
Monster from the Ocean Floor (1954) 55
The Monster Maker (1944) 98–9, **99**
The Monster That Challenged the World (1957) 82, 83–7, **86**, 88, 92, 93
Montez, Maria 3–4, 5
Montgomery, Elizabeth 248
Montgomery, Robert 357, 359
Moore, Clayton 331
Moore, Gene 135
Moore, Kieron 46, **118**, 125
Morgan, Ralph **99**
Morison, Patricia **101**
The Morning After (1974 TV movies) 318, 320
Morrison, Don 390
Morrow, Jeff 326
Morrow, Jo 419, 429
Most Dangerous Man Alive (1961) 331–3
Mower, Patrick 314
Muhl, Edward 402
The Mummy's Ghost (1944) 9
Munro, Caroline **153**
"Murders in the Rue Morgue" 149
Murders in the Rue Morgue (1971) 142, 144, 149–51, **150**, 176
Murphy, Audie 324, 326
Murphy, Bri 390, 391
Murray, Ken 20
"My Life in Art" 372
My Life with Caroline (1941) 261, 262–3

N

Naish, J. Carrol 10–1, **99**

The Naked Spur (1953) 276
Napier, Alan 48
Narizzano, Silvio 313
Nathan, Robert 254, 272
Neame, Ronald 257
The Neanderthal Man (1953) 360–3, **362**
Neill, Noel 22, 26–7, 29, 357
Nelson, Ed xii
Nelson, Lori 324
Nesbitt, Cathleen 257–8
Neumann, Kurt 101
Newman, Paul 85, 87
Ney, Richard 48
Nicholson, Jack 49, 170
Nicholson, James H. 49, 73–4, 148–9, 150, 156, 157–8, 159, 160, 161, 169, 170, 172, 175, 178, 183, 233, 294, 297, 300, 301, 305, **309**, 310, 311, 312, 313, 315, 316
Night of the Eagle see *Burn, Witch, Burn*
The Night of the Hunter (1955) 381
Night of the Lepus (1972) 276, 284–6, **285**
Night of the Living Dead (1968) 307
The Night Stalker (1971 TV movie) 318
The Night Strangler (1972 TV movie) 318
Nightbreed (1990) x
Niles, Chuck 390
Niven, David 187, **210**, 293
Non-Stop New York (1937) 259, 260
North by Northwest (1959) 143
The Nun's Story (1959) 428

O

The Oblong Box (1969) 142, 144–5, **145**, 148, 156, 173–4
O'Brian, Hugh **102**
O'Brien, Edmond 86
O'Brien, George **111**
O'Connor, Donald 324
Ogilvy, Ian 168
O'Hara, Maureen 263
Ohmart, Carol 421
The Old Dark House (1932) 284
The Old Dark House (1963) 431
Olivier, Laurence 255, 256
The Omega Man (1971) 307
The Omen (1976) 50
"Omni" 195
One Hour Late (1934) 186
O'Neal, Patrick 42
O'Neil, Patrick 398

Index

The Oregon Trail (1959) 75, 76
Ormond, Ron 386, 387
"Our Virgin Island" 414, 425
The Outing see *Scream*
The Outlaws Is Coming (1965) 248
Outlaws of Texas (1950) 20
Outrage (1950) 344, 345, 352

P

Paige, Marvin 270
Pajama Party (1964) 156, 157, 160
Pal, George 100, 276-7
Palance, Jack 212-3
Palmer, Gregg 321-37, **321, 325, 330, 333, 334**
Palmer, Lilli 151, 176
Panther Girl of the Kongo (1955 serial) 31, **32,** 33-4
Park Row (1952) 79
Parker, Cecil 259
Parker, Jean 197
Parks, Larry 230
Parla, Donna xi
Parla, Paul xi
Parry, Harvey 312
Pascal, Jorge 12
The Passing of the Third Floor Back (1936) 254, 257-8
Pate, Michael xii
Patrick, Cynthia 404
Peck, Gregory 318-9
Peckinpah, Sam 76
Penitentiary (1938) 197
Perkins, Anthony 282, 283
Perry Mason (TV) 431
Persecution (1974) 239-40
Persson, Essy 174-5
The Philadelphia Story (1940) 186
Picture Mommy Dead (1966) 254, 270
Pidgeon, Walter 86
Pierce, Maggie 308
Pink, Sidney 113
Pit and the Pendulum (1961) 301-5, **302**
Pitcher, George 117, 119
Pitt, Ingrid **177**
Planet of the Apes (1968) 206, 213-20, **214**
Planet of the Apes (TV) 220
Planet of the Vampires (1965) 163-5, **164**
Playboy 115
Poe, Edgar Allan 48, 88, 142, 149, 151, 156, 157, 161, 174, 222, 294, 295, 298, 301, 302, 304, 308, 310

Polanski, Roman 307
Pollexfen, Jack 102-3, 360
Porter, Jean 10
"Portrait of Jennie" 254
Powell, Michael 208, 209, 210, 212
Powers, John 2
Powers, Mala 198, 199, 200, 339-53, **339, 341, 346, 349**
Powers, Stefanie 305, 313
Prather, Maurice 129-30
Pratt, Jim 406
Pray for Death (1985) 152-3
"The Premature Burial" x
The Premature Burial (1962) 42, 47, 48, 50
Preminger, Otto 76
Presley, Elvis 79
Pressburger, Emeric 208, 209, 212
Price, Vincent xii, 40, 48, 49, 50, 116, 142, 145, 146, **147,** 149, 157, 163, 166, **167,** 168, 174, 176, 178, 179, **180, 181,** 183, 238, 246, **247,** 267, 295, **296,** 297, 298, 299, **300,** 302, 304, **304,** 306, **306,** 307, 308, **309,** 310, 312, 413, 421, 422, **423,** 426-7, 428
Prince, William 416
The Prodigal (1955) 54
"Psycho" 143, 146, 279, 281
Psycho (1960) 143, 146, **275,** 276, 279-83, **280,** 284, 286-7, 294, 430, 431
Psycho II (1983) 283
Psycho III (1986) 283
Psycho Sisters see *So Evil, My Sister*

Q

Quarry, Robert xi, 182-3
Quinn, Anthony 345, 352, 370

R

The Rack (1956) 85-6, 87
Rains, Claude 212, 213
Randolph, John 220
Rapp, Joel 65
Rathbone, Basil 157, 159, 192, 310, 311, 312
Rathbone, Ouida 311
"The Raven" 308
The Raven (1963) 40, 42, 43, 47, 49, 50, 308-10, **309**
Rawhide (TV) 198
Ray, Aldo 290

Index

Ray, Fred Olen x, xii
Reagan, Ronald 82, 357
Reason, Rex 326
Rebel Without a Cause (1955) 86
Redgrave, Michael 238
Reed, Rex 240
Reeve, Christopher 26, 317, 359
Reeves, George 20–1, 22–3, **23**, 24, 25–6, 27, 28, 29, 30, 34, **355**, 356, 359–60
Reeves, Michael 144, 168–9, 170, 173
Reform School Girl (1957) 370, 372
Reinhardt, Max 344
Remarque, Erich Maria 261
Requiem for a Heavyweight (TV) 213, 218
The Return of Dracula (1958) ix, 82, 83, 88, 89, **90, 91**, 92
Return of the Fly (1959) 110, 114, 115–6, **116**, 126
The Return of Wildfire (1948) 100, **101**
Revill, Clive 315
"The Revolt of the Triffids" see "The Day of the Triffids"
Reynolds, Debbie 381
Rhapsody in Blue (1945) 356
Richards, Frank 23–4
Richards, Paul 199, 200, 341
Richardson, Ralph 183, 256
The Rifleman (TV) 82
Riggs, Rita **280**
Rio Lobo (1970) 322
Riskin, Robert 187
Robards, Jason, Jr. 151, 176–177, 246
Robards, Jason, Sr. 266
Robbins, Cindy 380
Robertson, Joseph F. 231, 233, 234, 235
Robinson, Edward G. 218, 263–4, **264**
RoboCop (1987) 412
Robson, Mark 208, 264, 265–6, 267, 348, 349–50
"Robur the Conqueror" 299
Rocketship X-M (1950) 96, 100–2, **102**
Roeg, Nicolas 50
Rolling in Money (1934) 256
Roman, Timothy Cabot v, vi
The Romance of Rosy Ridge (1947) 276
Romero, George 222, 307
Rondell, Ronnie 403
Rooney, Mickey 218
Roosevelt, Franklin Delano 2, 12
Rosemary's Baby (1968) 295, 307, 314 431
Rosenberg, Max xii, 146, 175–6
Ross, Jack 15
Ross, Mike **374**

Rozsa, Miklos 101, 107
Run of the Arrow (1957) 79–80
Runser, Mary xii
Russell, John 301, 351
Rutherford, Ann 230
Ryan, Robert 345, 352

S

Saboteur (1942) 142
Sade, Marquis de 169
The Saga of Hemp Brown (1958) 370
The Saga of the Viking Women and Their Voyage to the Waters of the Great Sea Serpent (1957) 54, 57–60, **58, 61**, 105
Sahara (1943) 12
Sahl, Mort 372
Salkow, Sidney 36, 306
Sanders, George 267, 268
Sangster, Jimmy 183
Sansom, Lester **118**, 121, 125
Sarafian, Richard 301
Sarecky, Barney 25
Saunders, Charles 227
Saxon, Peter 146
Sayer, Jay **58**
Schaffner, Franklin J. 217
Scheider, Roy 315, 318
Schenck, Aubrey 417–8, 419
Schenck, Joseph M. 12
Schermer, Jules 301
Schneer, Charles H. 151–2, 244, 245
Scott, Jacqueline **417**
Scott, Janette **118**, 125
Scott, Lizabeth 209
Scream (1985) 334–5
Scream and Scream Again (1970) 142, 144, 146, **147**, 173, 175–6
Scream, Pretty Peggy (1973 TV movie) 142
"Scream Queens" 400
The Secret Door (1964) 235
Seid, Art 431
Sekely, Steve 119, 121, 122
Selznick, David O. 206, 208, 260, 261, 266
Sennett, Mack 75
Sergeant Deadhead (1965) 156, 157
Serling, Rod 86, 218
Seven Women (1966) 254–5
The Seventh Sign (1988) 67
The Seventh Victim (1943) 206–8, **207**, 222

Index

Sewell, Vernon 40, 172
Seyler, Athene 259
Seymour, Jane 317
Shadow of a Doubt (1943) 89
Shatner, William 248
Shayne, Robert 27–8, 355–67, **355**, **358**, **361**, **363**, **364**
She Was a Hippy Vampire see *The Wild World of Batwoman*
Shearer, Norma 276
Shields, Arthur 263
Shine on, Harvest Moon (1944) 356
Sholem, Lee 21, 24, 25, 29, 350
The Shootist (1976) 322
Short Cut to Hell (1957) 370–2
Showdown at Boot Hill (1958) 75
"The Shrinking Man" 290, 291, 293
The Silencers (1966) 248, **249**
Silent Service (TV) 431
Simmons, Richard Alan 291
Simon, Simone 15
Sinatra, Frank 284
Sinatra, Nancy **158**
Siodmak, Curt 194
Six Tickets to Hell (1975) 351–2
Skillen, Hugh 119
Skillin, John xii
Skotak, Robert xi
Skouras, Spyros 76
The Slime People (1963) 226, 231–5, **232**
Smith, Shawn **407**
Sneegas, Larry **139**
So Evil, My Sister (1972) 201
Sobol, Louis 2
Sofaer, Abraham **210**
Something Is Out There (TV) x
Somewhere in Time (1980) 317–8
Space Master X-7 (1958) 110, 111–5, **113**
Space Patrol (TV) 54
Spalding, Harry 111, 112, 115, 117
Spellbound (1945) 101, 208
Spielberg, Steven 85, 301, 318, 319
Stader, Paul 85
Stairway to Heaven (1946) 208–12, **210**
Stanislavsky, Konstantin 372
Stanwyck, Barbara 9, 16, 365
Star Trek (TV) 248
"Starlog" xi, xii
State Penitentiary (1950) 364
Steele, Barbara 172, 303
Stefano, Joseph 143, 146
Steiger, Rod 221, 222
Stein, Michael xii
Stein, Ronald 106
Steiner, Max 96, 98, 105

"Step Right Up! I'm Gonna Scare the Pants Off America" 431
Stern, Stewart 86
Stevens, Leith 106
Stevenson, Robert 254, 257, 260, 261
Stevenson, Venetia xii, 260
Stockman, Paul **47**
Stoker, Bram 89
Stone, Milburn 8
The Storm Rider (1957) 110
The Strange Possession of Mrs. Oliver (1977 TV movie) 142
Strangers When We Meet (1960) 244
A Streetcar Named Desire (1951) 206, **211**, 213
A Streetcar Named Desire (play) 206
Strock, Herbert L. xii, 61, 71, 137, 415
Stromsoe, Fred 234
Stuart, Randy 293
Subotsky, Milton 146, 175
Sullivan, Barry 165
Sullivan, Don 389–90
Sullivan, Francis L. 259
Superman (1978) 317
Superman and the Mole-Men (1951) 20–2, 27
Svehla, Gary xii
Sweet, John 212
Sweethearts and Horrors (unmade) 312, 313
Sylvia (1965) 244

T

Take the High Ground (1953) 15
Talbott, Gloria 77
Tales from the Crypt (1972) 238
Tales of Terror (1962) 295, 303, **304**, 307, 308, 311
Tamiroff, Akim 235, 236
Tarantula (1955) ix
Tarnowsky, Sergei 398
Tarzan and the Great River (1967) 250
Tarzan and the Leopard Woman (1946) 2, 13–5, **13**
Tarzan and the Valley of Gold (1966) 248–50, **250**
Taurog, Norman 165–6
Taylor, Don 46, 50
Taylor, Robert 166
Teenage Caveman (1958) 57, 364
Teenage Zombies (1960) 386, 387, 388–91, **388**, 393, 398
Temple of the Ravens see *Six Tickets to Hell*

Index

Tenser, Tony 168, 169, 172
Terror in the Midnight Sun see *Invasion of the Animal People*
Tester, Desmond 259
Thalberg, Irving 184
Thanks a Million (1935) 75
Them! (1954) 84, 295
"There Really Was a Hollywood" 276, 281
They Came from Beyond Space (1967) 236-8, **237**
Thimig, Helene 344
The Thin Red Line (1964) 122, 123
13 Ghosts (1960) 414, 419, 428-9, **429**, 430
This Earth Is Mine (1959) 380-1
This Is Alice (TV) 33, 36
Thomas, Harry 361, **362**
Thomas, Leslie 72
Thompson, Marshall 345, 346, **346**
Thompson's Ghost (TV) 33
Thorndike, Sybil 255-6
The Three Stooges 110, **111**, 248
Thriller (TV) 347, 348
Tierney, Gene 267
Tilly, Meg 283
"Time" 49
A Time for Killing (1967) 55
Timpone, Tony xi
The Tingler (1959) 425-8, **427**, 430
Tiomkin, Dimitri 98, 100, 103-4, 107
To Hell and Back (1955) 293
Tobor the Great (1954) 363
The Today Show (TV) 244
Todd (1967) 125
Toland, Gregg 71
Tomasini, George 76
Tomlinson, David 160
Tone, Franchot 230
Tonge, Philip **231**
Torres, Enrique 352
Torture Garden (1968) 238
Touch of Evil (1958) 411
Tough as They Come (1942) 344
Tourneur, Jacques 161, 206, 311, 312
Towers, Harry Alan 166
Towne, Robert 65
The Treasure of the Sierra Madre (1948) 84
Tremayne, Les 233
The Trip (1967) 170-1
Trog (1970) 238-9
Troupe, Tom 381
Tryon, Tom 77
Tucker, Phil 391-2
Turner, Lana 54, 239, 240

Twelve O'Clock High (1949) 319
20,000 Leagues Under the Sea (1954) 299
The Twilight Zone (TV) 301, 303, 311, 319
Twilight Zone – The Movie (1983) 318-9
Two Evil Eyes (1990) 222
"Two on the Isle" 425

U

Ulmer, Edgar G. ix
The Undead (1957) 54-7, **56**
The Undefeated (1969) 322
The Undying Monster (1942) 186, 195-7, **196**
Unger, Bertil 409
Unger, Gustav 409, 412
The Unknown Terror (1957) 186, 198-200, **199**, 340-1, **341**
The Untouchables (TV) 30, 36
Up Front (1951) 324

V

The Vampire (1957) 82, 83, 88, 89, **90**, 92, 93
The Vampire Lovers (1970) 176, **177**
Van, Bobby 351
Van Dyke, Dick 318
Vanderbilt, Gloria, Sr. 228
Vaughn, Robert 57
Veevers, Wally 119
Verne, Jules 161, 299
Ve Sota, Bruno 378, 380, 394, 396
Veidt, Conrad 257, 258
Verne, Jules 345
Vice Squad (1953) 82
Vickers, Martha 226
Vickers, Yvette xi, 369-83, **369, 371, 374, 376, 379, 382**
Victor, Katherine 385-400, **385, 388, 392, 393, 395, 397**
Viertel, Berthold 258
Viertel, Salka 258
"Virgin Island" (1959) 425
Vittes, Louis 75, 76
Vogel, Virgil W. 401-12, **401, 403, 407, 410**
The Vulture (1967) 235-6

W

Wait Until Dark (1967) 319–20
Walsh, Dermot 40
Wanger, Walter 3, 8
War-Gods of the Deep (1965) 160–3, **162**
War of the Colossal Beast (1958) 104
War of the Satellites (1958) 54, 62–3, **63, 64**
Warner, Jack 87
Warren, Charles Marquis 198, 200, 341
Warren, Jerry x, 35, 386, 387–9, 390, 391, 393, 394, 395, 396, 398, 399, 411, 412
"Watership Down" 153
Watson, David 216
Watz, Ed xii
Wayne, Ethan 334
Wayne, John 263, 322, 335
Weaver, Jon xii
Webster, Mary **300**
Weird Woman (1944) 305
Weissmuller, Johnny 13–5
Welborn, Charles 84–5
Weldon, Alex 124
Welles, Mel 56
Welles, Orson 226, 278, 411
Wendkos, Paul 387
Werewolf (TV) x
West, Adam 248, 394
West Side Story (1961) 311
Westmore, Bud 326
What Ever Happened to Baby Jane? (1962) 239, 268–9
What's the Matter with Helen? (1971) 370, 381–2
Wheatley, Dennis 305, 314
Whelan, Tim 192
When Strangers Marry (1944) 208
White, Christine 416
White, Jon Manchip 123
White, Robb 413–31, **413**
Whiton, James 178, 183
Who Slew Auntie Roo? (1971) 183
Wicking, Christopher 43, 142, 144, 146, 148, 175, 176, 178
Wilcoxon, Henry 351
The Wild Angels (1966) 170
The Wild Bunch (1969) 76
The Wild Wild West (TV) 347, 348
The Wild World of Batwoman (1966) **385**, 386, 387–8, 391, 394–6, **395,** 397, 398, 399
Wilder, Billy 226
Wilder, Thornton 89
Wilder, W. Lee 226
Willard (1971) 284
Williams, Grant **292**, 293, **294,** 351
Williams, John 107
Wills, Chill 326
Winchell, Walter 2
Winters, Shelley 183, 381–2
Wisberg, Aubrey 102–3, 360
Wise, Ray 412
Witchfinder General see *Conqueror Worm*
Witney, William 300
Wolfe, Ian 266
Wolff, Ed 116, **116, 339, 342**
Wolper, David 320
The Woman Who Wouldn't Die (1965) 142
Wooley, John xii
Wright, Frank Lloyd 421
Wuthering Heights (1970) 184
Wyatt, Jane 186, 201
Wyler, William 261–2
Wyman, Jane 290
Wyndham, John 121
Wyngarde, Peter 305
Wynn, Ed 213, 231

Y

Yancy Derringer (TV) 60–1
Yates, George Worthing 112
Yordan, Philip 117, 119, 120, 121, 122, 123
You Came Along (1945) 209
You Only Live Twice (1967) 236
Young Man's Fancy (1939) 258

Z

Zabel, Edwin 417, 419
Zanuck, Richard 219
Zombies of Mora Tau (1957) **321, 325,** 328–9
Zotz! (1962) 431
Zugsmith, Albert 103, 290–1, 292, 293
Zulu (1964) 170, 313